D1741811

Henry James

Henry James OM (15 April 1843 – 28 February 1916) was an American-British author regarded as a key transitional figure between literary realism and literary modernism, and is considered by many to be among the greatest novelists in the English language. He was the son of Henry James Sr. and the brother of renowned philosopher and psychologist William James and diarist Alice James.

He is best known for a number of novels dealing with the social and marital interplay between émigré Americans, English people, and continental Europeans. Examples of such novels include The Portrait of a Lady, The Ambassadors, and The Wings of the Dove. His later works were increasingly experimental. In describing the internal states of mind and social dynamics of his characters, James often made use of a style in which ambiguous or contradictory motives and impressions were overlaid or juxtaposed in the discussion of a character's psyche.(Source: Wikipedia)

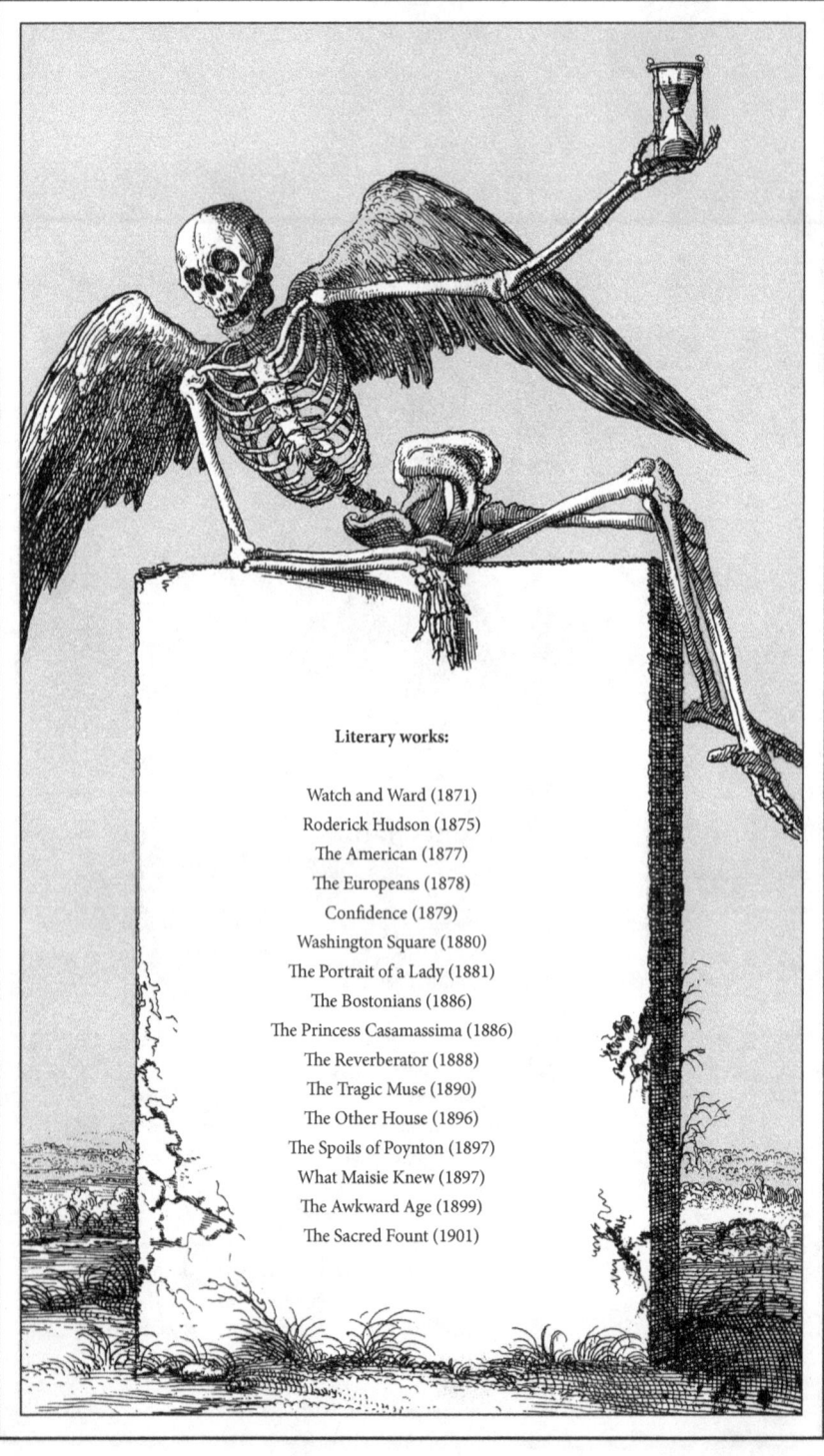

Literary works:

Watch and Ward (1871)

Roderick Hudson (1875)

The American (1877)

The Europeans (1878)

Confidence (1879)

Washington Square (1880)

The Portrait of a Lady (1881)

The Bostonians (1886)

The Princess Casamassima (1886)

The Reverberator (1888)

The Tragic Muse (1890)

The Other House (1896)

The Spoils of Poynton (1897)

What Maisie Knew (1897)

The Awkward Age (1899)

The Sacred Fount (1901)

BOOKLAND
CLASSICS

THE COLLECTED WORKS
OF
HENRY JAMES
VOL. 35 (OF 36)

THE TWO MAGICS
THE WINGS OF THE DOVE

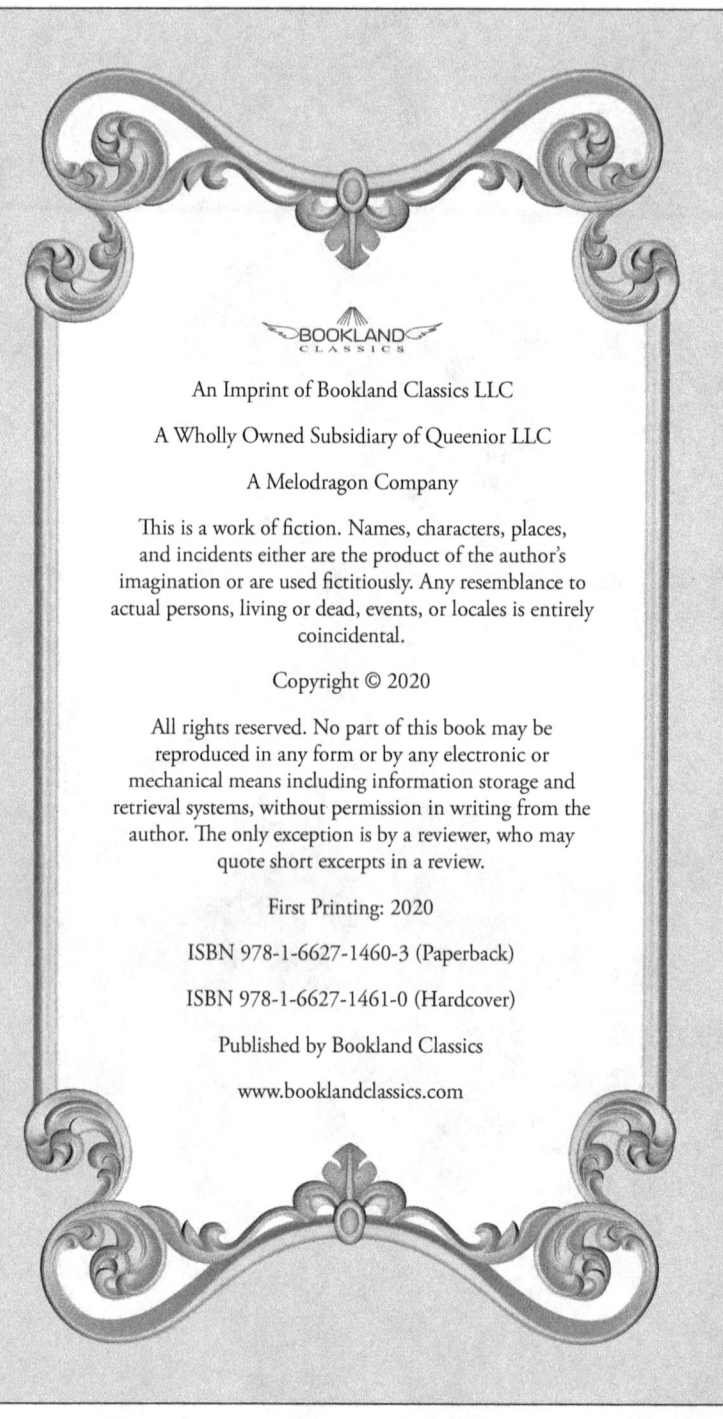

An Imprint of Bookland Classics LLC

A Wholly Owned Subsidiary of Queenior LLC

A Melodragon Company

This is a work of fiction. Names, characters, places, and incidents either are the product of the author's imagination or are used fictitiously. Any resemblance to actual persons, living or dead, events, or locales is entirely coincidental.

Copyright © 2020

All rights reserved. No part of this book may be reproduced in any form or by any electronic or mechanical means including information storage and retrieval systems, without permission in writing from the author. The only exception is by a reviewer, who may quote short excerpts in a review.

First Printing: 2020

ISBN 978-1-6627-1460-3 (Paperback)

ISBN 978-1-6627-1461-0 (Hardcover)

Published by Bookland Classics

www.booklandclassics.com

Contents

THE COLLECTED WORKS

OF

HENRY JAMES

VOL. 35 (OF 36)

THE TWO MAGICS

THE TURN OF THE SCREW

THE story had held us, round the fire, sufficiently breathless, but except the obvious remark that it was gruesome, as, on Christmas eve in an old house, a strange tale should essentially be, I remember no comment uttered till somebody happened to say that it was the only case he had met in which such a visitation had fallen on a child. The case, I may mention, was that of an apparition in just such an old house as had gathered us for the occasion—an appearance, of a dreadful kind, to a little boy sleeping in the room with his mother and waking her up in the terror of it; waking her not to dissipate his dread and soothe him to sleep again, but to encounter also, herself, before she had succeeded in doing so, the same sight that had shaken him. It was this observation that drew from Douglas—not immediately, but later in the evening—a reply that had the interesting consequence to which I call attention. Someone else told a story not particularly effective, which I saw he was not following. This I took for a sign that he had himself something to produce and that we should only have to wait. We waited in fact till two nights later; but that same evening, before we scattered, he brought out what was in his mind.

"I quite agree—in regard to Griffin's ghost, or whatever it was—that its appearing first to the little boy, at so tender an age, adds a particular touch. But it's not the first occurrence of its charming kind that I know to have involved a child. If the child gives the effect another turn of the screw, what do you say to *two* children——?"

"We say, of course," somebody exclaimed, "that they give two turns! Also that we want to hear about them."

I can see Douglas there before the fire, to which he had got up to present his back, looking down at his interlocutor with his hands in his pockets. "Nobody but me, till now, has ever heard. It's quite too horrible." This, naturally, was declared by several voices to give the thing the utmost price, and our friend, with quiet art, prepared his triumph by turning his eyes over the rest of us and going on: "It's beyond everything. Nothing at all that I know touches it."

"For sheer terror?" I remember asking.

He seemed to say it was not so simple as that; to be really at a loss how to qualify it. He passed his hand over his eyes, made a little wincing grimace. "For dreadful—dreadfulness!"

"Oh, how delicious!" cried one of the women.

He took no notice of her; he looked at me, but as if, instead of me, he saw what he spoke of. "For general uncanny ugliness and horror and pain."

"Well then," I said, "just sit right down and begin."

He turned round to the fire, gave a kick to a log, watched it an instant. Then as he faced us again: "I can't begin. I shall have to send to town." There was a unanimous groan at this, and much reproach; after which, in his preoccupied way, he explained. "The story's written. It's in a locked drawer— it has not been out for years. I could write to my man and enclose the key; he could send down the packet as he finds it." It was to me in particular that he appeared to propound this—appeared almost to appeal for aid not to hesitate. He had broken a thickness of ice, the formation of many a winter; had had his reasons for a long silence. The others resented postponement, but it was just his scruples that charmed me. I adjured him to write by the first post and to agree with us for an early hearing; then I asked him if the experience in question had been his own. To this his answer was prompt. "Oh, thank God, no!"

"And is the record yours? You took the thing down?"

"Nothing but the impression. I took that *here*"—he tapped his heart. "I've never lost it."

"Then your manuscript——?"

"Is in old, faded ink, and in the most beautiful hand." He hung fire again. "A woman's. She has been dead these twenty years. She sent me the pages in question before she died." They were all listening now, and of course there was somebody to be arch, or at any rate to draw the inference. But if he put the inference by without a smile it was also without irritation. "She was a most charming person, but she was ten years older than I. She was my sister's governess," he quietly said. "She was the most agreeable woman I've ever known in her position; she would have been worthy of any whatever. It was long ago, and this episode was long before. I was at Trinity, and I found her at home on my coming down the second summer. I was much there that year—it was a beautiful one; and we had, in her off-hours, some strolls and talks in the garden—talks in which she struck me as awfully clever and nice. Oh yes; don't grin: I liked her extremely and am glad to this day to think she liked me too. If she hadn't she wouldn't have told me. She had never told anyone. It wasn't simply that she said so, but that I knew she hadn't. I was sure; I could see. You'll easily judge why when you hear."

"Because the thing had been such a scare?"

He continued to fix me. "You'll easily judge," he repeated: "*you* will."

I fixed him too. "I see. She was in love."

He laughed for the first time. "You *are* acute. Yes, she was in love. That is, she had been. That came out—she couldn't tell her story without its coming out. I saw it, and she saw I saw it; but neither of us spoke of it. I remember the time and the place—the corner of the lawn, the shade of the great beeches and the long, hot summer afternoon. It wasn't a scene for a shudder; but oh——!" He quitted the fire and dropped back into his chair.

"You'll receive the packet Thursday morning?" I inquired.

"Probably not till the second post."

"Well then; after dinner——"

"You'll all meet me here?" He looked us round again. "Isn't anybody going?" It was almost the tone of hope.

"Everybody will stay!"

"*I* will—and *I* will!" cried the ladies whose departure had been fixed. Mrs. Griffin, however, expressed the need for a little more light. "Who was it she was in love with?"

"The story will tell," I took upon myself to reply.

"Oh, I can't wait for the story!"

"The story *won't* tell," said Douglas; "not in any literal, vulgar way."

"More's the pity, then. That's the only way I ever understand."

"Won't *you* tell, Douglas?" somebody else inquired.

He sprang to his feet again. "Yes—tomorrow. Now I must go to bed. Good-night." And quickly catching up a candlestick, he left us slightly bewildered. From our end of the great brown hall we heard his step on the stair; whereupon Mrs. Griffin spoke. "Well, if I don't know who she was in love with, I know who *he* was."

"She was ten years older," said her husband.

"*Raison de plus*—at that age! But it's rather nice, his long reticence."

"Forty years!" Griffin put in.

"With this outbreak at last."

"The outbreak," I returned, "will make a tremendous occasion of Thursday night;" and everyone so agreed with me that, in the light of it, we lost all attention for everything else. The last story, however incomplete and like the mere opening of a serial, had been told; we handshook and "candlestuck," as somebody said, and went to bed.

I knew the next day that a letter containing the key had, by the first post, gone off to his London apartments; but in spite of—or perhaps just on account of—the eventual diffusion of this knowledge we quite let him alone till after dinner, till such an hour of the evening, in fact, as might best accord with the kind of emotion on which our hopes were fixed. Then he became as communicative as we could desire and indeed gave us his best reason for being so. We had it from him again before the fire in the hall, as we had had our mild wonders of the previous night. It appeared that the narrative he had promised to read us really required for a proper intelligence a few words of prologue. Let me say here distinctly, to have done with it, that this narrative, from an exact transcript of my own made much later, is what I shall presently give. Poor Douglas, before his death—when it was in sight—committed to me the manuscript that reached him on the third of these days and that, on the same spot, with immense effect, he began to read to our hushed little circle on the night of the fourth. The departing ladies who had said they would stay didn't, of course, thank heaven, stay: they departed, in consequence of arrangements made, in a rage of curiosity, as they professed, produced by the touches with which he had already worked us up. But that only made his little final auditory more compact and select, kept it, round the hearth, subject to a common thrill.

The first of these touches conveyed that the written statement took up the tale at a point after it had, in a manner, begun. The fact to be in possession of was therefore that his old friend, the youngest of several daughters of a poor country parson, had, at the age of twenty, on taking service for the first time in the schoolroom, come up to London, in trepidation, to answer in person an advertisement that had already placed her in brief correspondence with the advertiser. This person proved, on her presenting herself, for judgment, at a house in Harley Street, that impressed her as vast and imposing—this prospective patron proved a gentleman, a bachelor in the prime of life, such a figure as had never risen, save in a dream or an old novel, before a fluttered, anxious girl out of a Hampshire vicarage. One could easily fix his type; it never, happily, dies out. He was handsome and bold and pleasant, off-hand and gay and kind. He struck her, inevitably, as gallant and splendid, but what took her most of all and gave her the courage she afterwards showed was that he put the whole thing to her as a kind of favour, an obligation he should gratefully incur. She conceived him as rich, but as fearfully extravagant—saw him all in a glow of high fashion, of good looks, of expensive habits, of charming ways with women. He had for his own town residence a big house filled with the spoils of travel and the trophies of the chase; but it was to his country home, an old family place in Essex, that he wished her immediately to proceed.

He had been left, by the death of their parents in India, guardian to a small nephew and a small niece, children of a younger, a military brother, whom he had lost two years before. These children were, by the strangest of chances for a man in his position,—a lone man without the right sort of experience or a grain of patience,—very heavily on his hands. It had all been a great worry and, on his own part doubtless, a series of blunders, but he immensely pitied the poor chicks and had done all he could; had in particular sent them down to his other house, the proper place for them being of course the country, and kept them there, from the first, with the best people he could find to look after them, parting even with his own servants to wait on them and going down himself, whenever he might, to see how they were doing. The awkward thing was that they had practically no other relations and that his own affairs took up all his time. He had put them in possession of Bly, which was healthy and secure, and had placed at the head of their little establishment—but below stairs only—an excellent woman, Mrs. Grose, whom he was sure his visitor would like and who had formerly been maid to his mother. She was now housekeeper and was also acting for the time as superintendent to the little girl, of whom, without children of her own, she was, by good luck, extremely fond. There were plenty of people to help, but of course the young lady who should go down as governess would be in supreme authority. She would also have, in holidays, to look after the small boy, who had been for a term at school—young as he was to be sent, but what else could be done?—and who, as the holidays were about to begin, would be back from one day to the other. There had been for the two children at first a young lady whom they had had the misfortune to lose. She had done for them quite beautifully—she was a most respectable person—till her death, the great awkwardness of which had, precisely, left no alternative but the school for little Miles. Mrs. Grose, since then, in the way of manners and things, had done as she could for Flora; and there were, further, a cook, a housemaid, a dairywoman, an old pony, an old groom, and an old gardener, all likewise thoroughly respectable.

So far had Douglas presented his picture when someone put a question. "And what did the former governess die of?—of so much respectability?"

Our friend's answer was prompt. "That will come out. I don't anticipate."

"Excuse me—I thought that was just what you *are* doing."

"In her successor's place," I suggested, "I should have wished to learn if the office brought with it——"

"Necessary danger to life?" Douglas completed my thought. "She did wish to learn, and she did learn. You shall hear tomorrow what she learnt. Meanwhile, of course, the prospect struck her as slightly grim. She was young, untried, nervous: it was a vision of serious duties and little company, of really great loneliness. She hesitated—took a couple of days to consult and consider. But the salary offered much exceeded her modest measure, and on a second interview she faced the music, she engaged." And Douglas, with this, made a pause that, for the benefit of the company, moved me to throw in—

"The moral of which was of course the seduction exercised by the splendid young man. She succumbed to it."

He got up and, as he had done the night before, went to the fire, gave a stir to a log with his foot, then stood a moment with his back to us. "She saw him only twice."

"Yes, but that's just the beauty of her passion."

A little to my surprise, on this, Douglas turned round to me. "It *was* the beauty of it. There were others," he went on, "who hadn't succumbed. He told her frankly all his difficulty—that for several applicants the conditions had been prohibitive. They were, somehow, simply afraid. It sounded dull—it sounded strange; and all the more so because of his main condition."

"Which was——?"

"That she should never trouble him—but never, never: neither appeal nor complain nor write about anything; only meet all questions herself, receive all moneys from his solicitor, take the whole thing over and let him alone. She promised to do this, and she mentioned to me that when, for a moment, disburdened, delighted, he held her hand, thanking her for the sacrifice, she already felt rewarded."

21

"But was that all her reward?" one of the ladies asked.

"She never saw him again."

"Oh!" said the lady; which, as our friend immediately left us again, was the only other word of importance contributed to the subject till, the next night, by the corner of the hearth, in the best chair, he opened the faded red cover of a thin old-fashioned gilt-edged album. The whole thing took indeed more nights than one, but on the first occasion the same lady put another question. "What is your title?"

"I haven't one."

"Oh, *I* have!" I said. But Douglas, without heeding me, had begun to read with a fine clearness that was like a rendering to the ear of the beauty of his author's hand.

I

I REMEMBER the whole beginning as a succession of flights and drops, a little see-saw of the right throbs and the wrong. After rising, in town, to meet his appeal, I had at all events a couple of very bad days—found myself doubtful again, felt indeed sure I had made a mistake. In this state of mind I spent the long hours of bumping, swinging coach that carried me to the stopping-place at which I was to be met by a vehicle from the house. This convenience, I was told, had been ordered, and I found, toward the close of the June afternoon, a commodious fly in waiting for me. Driving at that hour, on a lovely day, through a country to which the summer sweetness seemed to offer me a friendly welcome, my fortitude mounted afresh and, as we turned into the avenue, encountered a reprieve that was probably but a proof of the point to which it had sunk. I suppose I had expected, or had dreaded, something so melancholy that what greeted me was a good surprise. I remember as a most pleasant impression the broad, clear front, its open windows and fresh curtains and the pair of maids looking out; I remember the lawn and the bright flowers and the crunch of my wheels on the gravel and the clustered treetops over which the rooks circled and cawed in the golden sky. The scene had a greatness that made it a different affair from my own scant home, and there immediately appeared at the door, with a little girl in her hand, a civil person who dropped me as decent a curtsey as if I had been the mistress or a distinguished visitor. I had received in Harley Street a narrower notion of the place, and that, as I recalled it, made me think the proprietor still more of a gentleman, suggested that what I was to enjoy might be something beyond his promise.

I had no drop again till the next day, for I was carried triumphantly through the following hours by my introduction to the younger of my pupils. The little girl who accompanied Mrs. Grose appeared to me on the spot a creature so charming as to make it a great fortune to have to do with her. She was the most beautiful child I had ever seen, and I afterwards wondered that my employer had not told me more of her. I slept little that night—I was too much excited; and this astonished me too, I recollect, remained with me, adding to my sense of the liberality with which I was treated. The large, impressive room, one of the best in the house, the great state bed, as I almost felt it, the full, figured draperies, the long glasses in which, for the first time, I could see myself from head to foot, all struck me—like the extraordinary charm of my small charge—as so many things thrown in. It was thrown in as well, from the first moment, that I should get on with Mrs. Grose in a relation over which, on my way, in the coach, I fear I had rather brooded. The only thing indeed that in this early outlook might have made me shrink again was the clear circumstance of her being so glad to see me. I perceived within half an hour that she was so glad—stout, simple, plain, clean, wholesome woman—as to be positively on her guard against showing it too much. I wondered even then a little why she should wish not to show it, and that, with reflection, with suspicion, might of course have made me uneasy.

But it was a comfort that there could be no uneasiness in a connection with anything so beatific as the radiant image of my little girl, the vision of whose angelic beauty had probably more than anything else to do with the restlessness that, before morning, made me several times rise and wander about my room to take in the whole picture and prospect; to watch, from my open window, the faint summer dawn, to look at such portions of the rest of the house as I could catch, and to listen, while, in the fading dusk, the first birds began to twitter, for the possible recurrence of a sound or two, less natural and not without, but within, that I had fancied I heard. There had been a moment when I believed I recognised, faint and far, the cry of a child; there had been another when I found myself just consciously starting as at the passage, before my door, of a light footstep. But these fancies were not marked enough not to be thrown off, and it is only in the light, or the gloom, I should rather say, of other and subsequent matters that they now come back to me. To watch, teach, "form" little Flora would too evidently be the making of a happy and useful life. It had been agreed between us downstairs that after this first occasion I should have her as a matter of course at night, her small white bed being already arranged, to that end, in my room. What I had undertaken was the whole care of her, and she had remained, just this last time, with Mrs. Grose only as an effect of our consideration for my inevitable strangeness and her natural timidity. In spite of this timidity—which the child herself, in the oddest way in the world, had been perfectly frank and brave about, allowing it, without a sign of uncomfortable consciousness, with the deep, sweet serenity indeed of one of Raphael's holy infants, to be discussed, to be imputed to her and to determine us—I felt quite sure she would presently like me. It was part of what I already liked Mrs. Grose herself for, the pleasure I could see her feel in my admiration and wonder as I sat at supper with four tall candles and with my pupil, in a high chair and a bib, brightly facing me, between them, over bread and milk. There were naturally things that in Flora's presence could pass between us only as prodigious and gratified looks, obscure and roundabout allusions.

"And the little boy—does he look like her? Is he too so very remarkable?"

One wouldn't flatter a child. "Oh, Miss, *most* remarkable. If you think well of this one!"—and she stood there with a plate in her hand, beaming at our companion, who looked from one of us to the other with placid heavenly eyes that contained nothing to check us.

"Yes; if I do——?"

"You *will* be carried away by the little gentleman!"

"Well, that, I think, is what I came for—to be carried away. I'm afraid, however," I remember feeling the impulse to add, "I'm rather easily carried away. I was carried away in London!"

I can still see Mrs. Grose's broad face as she took this in. "In Harley Street?"

"In Harley Street."

"Well, Miss, you're not the first—and you won't be the last."

"Oh, I've no pretension," I could laugh, "to being the only one. My other pupil, at any rate, as I understand, comes back tomorrow?"

"Not tomorrow—Friday, Miss. He arrives, as you did, by the coach, under care of the guard, and is to be met by the same carriage."

I forthwith expressed that the proper as well as the pleasant and friendly thing would be therefore that on the arrival of the public conveyance I should be in waiting for him with his little sister; an idea in which Mrs. Grose concurred so heartily that I somehow took her manner as a kind of comforting pledge—never falsified, thank heaven!—that we should on every question be quite at one. Oh, she was glad I was there!

What I felt the next day was, I suppose, nothing that could be fairly called a reaction from the cheer of my arrival; it was probably at the most only a slight oppression produced by a fuller measure of the scale, as I walked round them, gazed up at them, took them in, of my new circumstances. They had, as it were, an extent and mass for which I had not been prepared and in the presence of which I found myself, freshly, a little scared as well as a little proud. Lessons, in this agitation, certainly suffered some delay; I reflected that my first duty was, by the gentlest arts I could contrive, to win the child into the sense of knowing me. I spent the day with her out of doors; I arranged with her, to her great satisfaction, that it should be she, she only, who might show me the place. She showed it step by step and room by room and secret by secret, with droll, delightful, childish talk about it and with the result, in half an hour, of our becoming immense friends. Young as she was, I was struck, throughout our little tour, with her confidence and courage with the way, in empty chambers and dull corridors, on crooked staircases that made me pause and even on the summit of an old machicolated square tower that made me dizzy, her morning music, her disposition to tell me so many more things than she asked, rang out and led me on. I have not seen Bly since the day I left it, and I dare say that to my older and more informed eyes it would now appear sufficiently contracted. But as my little conductress, with her hair of gold and her frock of blue, danced before me round corners and pattered down passages, I had the view of a castle of romance inhabited by a rosy sprite, such a place as would somehow, for diversion of the young idea, take all colour out of storybooks and fairy-tales. Wasn't it just a storybook over which I had fallen a-doze and a-dream? No; it was a big, ugly, antique, but convenient house, embodying a few features of a building still older, half replaced and half utilised, in which I had the fancy of our being almost as lost as a handful of passengers in a great drifting ship. Well, I was, strangely, at the helm!

II

THIS came home to me when, two days later, I drove over with Flora to meet, as Mrs. Grose said, the little gentleman; and all the more for an incident that, presenting itself the second evening, had deeply disconcerted me. The first day had been, on the whole, as I have expressed, reassuring; but I was to see it wind up in keen apprehension. The postbag, that evening,—it came late,—contained a letter for me, which, however, in the hand of my employer, I found to be composed but of a few words enclosing another, addressed to himself, with a seal still unbroken. "This, I recognise, is from the head-master, and the head-master's an awful bore. Read him, please; deal with him; but mind you don't report. Not a word. I'm off!" I broke the seal with a great effort—so great a one that I was a long time coming to it; took the unopened missive at last up to my room and only attacked it just before going to bed. I had better have let it wait till morning, for it gave me a second sleepless night. With no counsel to take, the next day, I was full of distress; and it finally got so the better of me that I determined to open myself at least to Mrs. Grose.

"What does it mean? The child's dismissed his school."

She gave me a look that I remarked at the moment; then, visibly, with a quick blankness, seemed to try to take it back. "But aren't they all——?"

"Sent home—yes. But only for the holidays. Miles may never go back at all."

Consciously, under my attention, she reddened. "They won't take him?"

"They absolutely decline."

At this she raised her eyes, which she had turned from me; I saw them fill with good tears. "What has he done?"

I hesitated; then I judged best simply to hand her my letter—which, however, had the effect of making her, without taking it, simply put her hands behind her. She shook her head sadly. "Such things are not for me, Miss."

My counsellor couldn't read! I winced at my mistake, which I attenuated as I could, and opened my letter again to repeat it to her; then, faltering in the act and folding it up once more, I put it back in my pocket. "Is he really *bad*?"

The tears were still in her eyes. "Do the gentlemen say so?"

"They go into no particulars. They simply express their regret that it should be impossible to keep him. That can have only one meaning." Mrs. Grose listened with dumb emotion; she forbore to ask me what this meaning might be; so that, presently, to put the thing with some coherence and with the mere aid of her presence to my own mind, I went on: "That he's an injury to the others."

At this, with one of the quick turns of simple folk, she suddenly flamed up. "Master Miles! *him* an injury?"

27

There was such a flood of good faith in it that, though I had not yet seen the child, my very fears made me jump to the absurdity of the idea. I found myself, to meet my friend the better, offering it, on the spot, sarcastically. "To his poor little innocent mates!"

"It's too dreadful," cried Mrs. Grose, "to say such cruel things! Why, he's scarce ten years old."

"Yes, yes; it would be incredible."

She was evidently grateful for such a profession. "See him, Miss, first. *Then* believe it!" I felt forthwith a new impatience to see him; it was the beginning of a curiosity that, for all the next hours, was to deepen almost to pain. Mrs. Grose was aware, I could judge, of what she had produced in me, and she followed it up with assurance. "You might as well believe it of the little lady. Bless her," she added the next moment—"*look* at her!"

I turned and saw that Flora, whom, ten minutes before, I had established in the schoolroom with a sheet of white paper, a pencil, and a copy of nice "round O's," now presented herself to view at the open door. She expressed in her little way an extraordinary detachment from disagreeable duties, looking to me, however, with a great childish light that seemed to offer it as a mere result of the affection she had conceived for my person, which had rendered necessary that she should follow me. I needed nothing more than this to feel the full force of Mrs. Grose's comparison, and, catching my pupil in my arms, covered her with kisses in which there was a sob of atonement.

None the less, the rest of the day, I watched for further occasion to approach my colleague, especially as, toward evening, I began to fancy she rather sought to avoid me. I overtook her, I remember, on the staircase; we went down together, and at the bottom I detained her, holding her there with a hand on her arm. "I take what you said to me at noon as a declaration that *you've* never known him to be bad."

She threw back her head; she had clearly, by this time, and very honestly, adopted an attitude. "Oh, never known him—I don't pretend *that*!"

I was upset again. "Then you *have* known him——?"

"Yes indeed, Miss, thank God!"

On reflection I accepted this. "You mean that a boy who never is——?"

"Is no boy for *me*!"

I held her tighter. "You like them with the spirit to be naughty?" Then, keeping pace with her answer, "So do I!" I eagerly brought out. "But not to the degree to contaminate——"

"To contaminate?"—my big word left her at a loss. I explained it. "To corrupt."

She stared, taking my meaning in; but it produced in her an odd laugh. "Are you afraid he'll corrupt *you*?" She put the question with such a fine bold humour that, with a laugh, a little silly doubtless, to match her own, I gave way for the time to the apprehension of ridicule.

But the next day, as the hour for my drive approached, I cropped up in another place. "What was the lady who was here before?"

"The last governess? She was also young and pretty—almost as young and almost as pretty, Miss, even as you."

"Ah, then, I hope her youth and her beauty helped her!" I recollect throwing off. "He seems to like us young and pretty!"

"Oh, he *did*," Mrs. Grose assented: "it was the way he liked everyone!" She had no sooner spoken indeed than she caught herself up. "I mean that's *his* way—the master's."

I was struck. "But of whom did you speak first?"

She looked blank, but she coloured. "Why, of *him*."

"Of the master?"

"Of who else?"

There was so obviously no one else that the next moment I had lost my impression of her having accidentally said more than she meant; and I merely asked what I wanted to know. "Did *she* see anything in the boy——?"

"That wasn't right? She never told me."

I had a scruple, but I overcame it. "Was she careful—particular?"

Mrs. Grose appeared to try to be conscientious. "About some things—yes."

"But not about all?"

Again she considered. "Well, Miss—she's gone. I won't tell tales."

"I quite understand your feeling," I hastened to reply; but I thought it, after an instant, not opposed to this concession to pursue: "Did she die here?"

"No—she went off."

I don't know what there was in this brevity of Mrs. Grose's that struck me as ambiguous. "Went off to die?" Mrs. Grose looked straight out of the window, but I felt that, hypothetically, I had a right to know what young persons engaged for Bly were expected to do. "She was taken ill, you mean, and went home?"

"She was not taken ill, so far as appeared, in this house. She left it, at the end of the year, to go home, as she said, for a short holiday, to which the time she had put in had certainly given her a right. We had then a young woman—a nursemaid who had stayed on and who was a good girl and clever; and *she* took the children altogether for the interval. But our young lady never came back, and at the very moment I was expecting her I heard from the master that she was dead."

I turned this over. "But of what?"

"He never told me! But please, Miss," said Mrs. Grose, "I must get to my work."

III

HER thus turning her back on me was fortunately not, for my just preoccupations, a snub that could check the growth of our mutual esteem. We met, after I had brought home little Miles, more intimately than ever on the ground of my stupefaction, my general emotion: so monstrous was I then ready to pronounce it that such a child as had now been revealed to me should be under an interdict. I was a little late on the scene, and I felt, as he stood wistfully looking out for me before the door of the inn at which the coach had put him down, that I had seen him, on the instant, without and within, in the great glow of freshness, the same positive fragrance of purity, in which I had, from the first moment, seen his little sister. He was incredibly beautiful, and Mrs. Grose had put her finger on it: everything but a sort of passion of tenderness for him was swept away by his presence. What I then and there took him to my heart for was something divine that I have never found to the same degree in any child—his indescribable little air of knowing nothing in the world but love. It would have been impossible to carry a bad name with a greater sweetness of innocence, and by the time I had got back to Bly with him I remained merely bewildered—so far, that is, as I was not outraged—by the sense of the horrible letter locked up in my room, in a drawer. As soon as I could compass a private word with Mrs. Grose I declared to her that it was grotesque.

She promptly understood me. "You mean the cruel charge——?"

"It doesn't live an instant. My dear woman, *look* at him!"

She smiled at my pretension to have discovered his charm. "I assure you, Miss, I do nothing else! What will you say, then?" she immediately added.

"In answer to the letter?" I had made up my mind. "Nothing."

"And to his uncle?"

I was incisive. "Nothing."

"And to the boy himself?"

I was wonderful. "Nothing."

She gave with her apron a great wipe to her mouth. "Then I'll stand by you. We'll see it out."

"We'll see it out!" I ardently echoed, giving her my hand to make it a vow.

She held me there a moment, then whisked up her apron again with her detached hand. "Would you mind, Miss, if I used the freedom——"

"To kiss me? No!" I took the good creature in my arms and, after we had embraced like sisters, felt still more fortified and indignant.

This, at all events, was for the time: a time so full that, as I recall the way it went, it reminds me of all the art I now need to make it a little distinct. What I look back at with amazement is the situation I accepted. I had undertaken, with my companion, to see it out, and I was under a charm, apparently, that could smooth away the extent and the far and difficult connections of such an effort. I was lifted aloft on a great wave of infatuation and pity. I found it simple, in my ignorance, my confusion, and perhaps my conceit, to assume that I could deal with a boy whose education for the world was all on the point of beginning. I am unable even to remember at this day what proposal I framed for the end of his holidays and the resumption of his studies. Lessons with me, indeed, that charming summer, we all had a theory that he was to have; but I now feel that, for weeks, the lessons must have been rather my own. I learnt something—at first certainly—that had not been one of the teachings of my small, smothered life; learnt to be amused, and even amusing, and not to think for the morrow. It was the first time, in a manner, that I had known space and air and freedom, all the music of summer and all the mystery of nature. And then there was consideration—and consideration was sweet. Oh, it was a trap—not designed, but deep—to my imagination, to my delicacy, perhaps to my vanity; to whatever, in me, was most excitable. The best way to picture it all is to say that I was off my guard. They gave me so little trouble—they were of a gentleness so extraordinary. I used to speculate—but even this with a dim disconnectedness—as to how the rough future (for all futures are rough!) would handle them and might bruise them. They had the bloom of health and happiness; and yet, as if I had been in charge of a pair of little grandees, of princes of the blood, for whom everything, to be right, would have to be enclosed and protected, the only form that, in my fancy, the after-years could take for them was that of a romantic, a really royal extension of the garden and the park. It may be, of course, above all, that what suddenly broke into this gives the previous time a charm of stillness—that hush in which something gathers or crouches. The change was actually like the spring of a beast.

In the first weeks the days were long; they often, at their finest, gave me what I used to call my own hour, the hour when, for my pupils, tea-time and bed-time having come and gone, I had, before my final retirement, a small interval alone. Much as I liked my companions, this hour was the thing in the day I liked most; and I liked it best of all when, as the light faded—or rather, I should say, the day lingered and the last calls of the last birds sounded, in a flushed sky, from the old trees—I could take a turn into the grounds and enjoy, almost with a sense of property that amused and flattered me, the beauty and dignity of the place. It was a pleasure at these moments to feel myself tranquil and justified; doubtless, perhaps, also to reflect that by my discretion, my quiet good sense and general high propriety, I was giving pleasure—if he ever thought of it!—to the person to whose pressure I had responded. What I was doing was what he had earnestly hoped and directly asked of me, and that I *could*, after all, do it proved even a greater joy than I had expected. I dare say I fancied myself, in short, a remarkable young woman and took comfort in the faith that this would more publicly appear. Well, I needed to be remarkable to offer a front to the remarkable things that presently gave their first sign.

It was plump, one afternoon, in the middle of my very hour: the children were tucked away and I had come out for my stroll. One of the thoughts that, as I don't in the least shrink now from noting, used to be with me in these wanderings was that it would be as charming as a charming story suddenly to meet someone. Someone would appear there at the turn of a path and would stand before me and smile and approve. I didn't ask more than that—I only asked that he should *know*; and the only way to be sure he knew would be to see it, and the kind light of it, in his handsome face. That was exactly present to me—by which I mean the face was—when, on the first of these occasions, at the end of a long June day, I stopped short on emerging from one of the plantations and coming into view of the house. What arrested me on the spot—and with a shock much greater than any vision had allowed for—was the sense that my imagination had, in a flash, turned real. He did stand there!—but high up, beyond the lawn and at the very top of the tower to which, on that first morning, little Flora had conducted me. This tower was one of a pair—square, incongruous, crenelated structures—that were distinguished, for some reason, though I could see little difference, as the new and the old. They flanked opposite ends of the house and were probably architectural absurdities, redeemed in a measure indeed by not being wholly disengaged nor of a height too pretentious, dating, in their gingerbread antiquity, from a romantic revival that was already a respectable past. I admired them, had fancies about them, for we could all profit in a degree, especially when they loomed through the dusk, by the grandeur of their actual battlements; yet it was not at such an elevation that the figure I had so often invoked seemed most in place.

It produced in me, this figure, in the clear twilight, I remember, two distinct gasps of emotion, which were, sharply, the shock of my first and that of my second surprise. My second was a violent perception of the mistake of my first: the man who met my eyes was not the person I had precipitately supposed. There came to me thus a bewilderment of vision of which, after these years, there is no living view that I can hope to give. An unknown man in a lonely place is a permitted object of fear to a young woman privately bred; and the figure that faced me was—a few more seconds assured me—as little anyone else I knew as it was the image that had been in my mind. I had not seen it in Harley Street—I had not seen it anywhere. The place, moreover, in the strangest way in the world, had, on the instant, and by the very fact of its appearance, become a solitude. To me at least, making my statement here with a deliberation with which I have never made it, the whole feeling of the moment returns. It was as if, while I took in—what I did take in—all the rest of the scene had been stricken with death. I can hear again, as I write, the intense hush in which the sounds of evening dropped. The rooks stopped cawing in the golden sky and the friendly hour lost, for the minute, all its voice. But there was no other change in nature, unless indeed it were a change that I saw with a stranger sharpness. The gold was still in the sky, the clearness in the air, and the man who looked at me over the battlements was as definite as a picture in a frame. That's how I thought, with extraordinary quickness, of each person that he might have been and that he was not. We were confronted across our distance quite long enough for me to ask myself with intensity who then he was and to feel, as an effect of my inability to say, a wonder that in a few instants more became intense.

The great question, or one of these, is, afterwards, I know, with regard to certain matters, the question of how long they have lasted. Well, this matter of mine, think what you will of it, lasted while I caught at a dozen possibilities, none of which made a difference for the better, that I could see, in there having been in the house—and for how long, above all?—a person of whom I was in ignorance. It lasted while I just bridled a little with the sense that my office demanded that there should be no such ignorance and no such person. It lasted while this visitant, at all events,—and there was a touch of the strange freedom, as I remember, in the sign of familiarity of his wearing no hat,—seemed to fix me, from his position, with just the question, just the scrutiny through the fading light, that his own presence provoked. We were too far apart to call to each other, but there was a moment at which, at shorter range, some challenge between us, breaking the hush, would have been the right result of our straight mutual stare. He was in one of the angles, the one away from the house, very erect, as it struck me, and with both hands on the ledge. So I saw him as I see the letters I form on this page; then, exactly, after a minute, as if to add to the spectacle, he slowly changed his place—passed, looking at me hard all the while, to the opposite corner of the platform. Yes, I had the sharpest sense that during this transit he never took his eyes from me, and I can see at this moment the way his hand, as he went, passed from one of the crenelations to the next. He stopped at the other corner, but less long, and even as he turned away still markedly fixed me. He turned away; that was all I knew.

IV

IT was not that I didn't wait, on this occasion, for more, for I was rooted as deeply as I was shaken. Was there a "secret" at Bly—a mystery of Udolpho or an insane, an unmentionable relative kept in unsuspected confinement? I can't say how long I turned it over, or how long, in a confusion of curiosity and dread, I remained where I had had my collision; I only recall that when I re-entered the house darkness had quite closed in. Agitation, in the interval, certainly had held me and driven me, for I must, in circling about the place, have walked three miles; but I was to be, later on, so much more overwhelmed that this mere dawn of alarm was a comparatively human chill. The most singular part of it in fact—singular as the rest had been—was the part I became, in the hall, aware of in meeting Mrs. Grose. This picture comes back to me in the general train—the impression, as I received it on my return, of the wide white panelled space, bright in the lamplight and with its portraits and red carpet, and of the good surprised look of my friend, which immediately told me she had missed me. It came to me straightway, under her contact, that, with plain heartiness, mere relieved anxiety at my appearance, she knew nothing whatever that could bear upon the incident I had there ready for her. I had not suspected in advance that her comfortable face would pull me up, and I somehow measured the importance of what I had seen by my thus finding myself hesitate to mention it. Scarce anything in the whole history seems to me so odd as this fact that my real beginning of fear was one, as I may say, with the instinct of sparing my companion. On the spot, accordingly, in the pleasant hall and with her eyes on me, I, for a reason that I couldn't then have phrased, achieved an inward revolution—offered a vague pretext for my lateness and, with the plea of the beauty of the night and of the heavy dew and wet feet, went as soon as possible to my room.

Here it was another affair; here, for many days after, it was a queer affair enough. There were hours, from day to day,—or at least there were moments, snatched even from clear duties,—when I had to shut myself up to think. It was not so much yet that I was more nervous than I could bear to be as that

I was remarkably afraid of becoming so; for the truth I had now to turn over was, simply and clearly, the truth that I could arrive at no account whatever of the visitor with whom I had been so inexplicably and yet, as it seemed to me, so intimately concerned. It took little time to see that I could sound without forms of inquiry and without exciting remark any domestic complication. The shock I had suffered must have sharpened all my senses; I felt sure, at the end of three days and as the result of mere closer attention, that I had not been practised upon by the servants nor made the object of any "game." Of whatever it was that I knew nothing was known around me. There was but one sane inference: someone had taken a liberty rather gross. That was what, repeatedly, I dipped into my room and locked the door to say to myself. We had been, collectively, subject to an intrusion; some unscrupulous traveller, curious in old houses, had made his way in unobserved, enjoyed the prospect from the best point of view, and then stolen out as he came. If he had given me such a bold hard stare, that was but a part of his indiscretion. The good thing, after all, was that we should surely see no more of him.

This was not so good a thing, I admit, as not to leave me to judge that what, essentially, made nothing else much signify was simply my charming work. My charming work was just my life with Miles and Flora, and through nothing could I so like it as through feeling that I could throw myself into it in trouble. The attraction of my small charges was a constant joy, leading me to wonder afresh at the vanity of my original fears, the distaste I had begun by entertaining for the probable grey prose of my office. There was to be no grey prose, it appeared, and no long grind; so how could work not be charming that presented itself as daily beauty? It was all the romance of the nursery and the poetry of the schoolroom. I don't mean by this, of course, that we studied only fiction and verse; I mean I can express no otherwise the sort of interest my companions inspired. How can I describe that except by saying that instead of growing used to them—and it's a marvel for a governess: I call the sisterhood to witness!—I made constant fresh discoveries. There was one direction, assuredly, in which these discoveries stopped: deep obscurity continued to cover the region of the boy's conduct at school. It had been promptly given me, I have noted, to face that mystery without a pang. Perhaps even it would be nearer the truth to say that—without a word—he himself had cleared it up. He had made the whole charge absurd. My conclusion bloomed there with the real rose-flush of his innocence: he was only too fine and fair for the little horrid, unclean school-world, and he had paid a price for it. I reflected acutely that the sense of such differences, such superiorities of quality, always, on the part of the majority—which could include even stupid, sordid head-masters—turns infallibly to the vindictive.

Both the children had a gentleness (it was their only fault, and it never made Miles a muff) that kept them—how shall I express it?—almost impersonal and certainly quite unpunishable. They were like the cherubs of the anecdote, who had—morally, at any rate—nothing to whack! I remember feeling with Miles in especial as if he had had, as it were, no history. We expect of a small child a scant one, but there was in this beautiful little boy something extraordinarily sensitive, yet extraordinarily happy, that, more than in any creature of his age I have seen, struck me as beginning anew each day. He had never for a second suffered. I took this as a direct disproof of his having really been chastised. If he had been wicked he would have "caught" it, and I should have caught it by the rebound—I should have found the trace. I found nothing at all, and he was therefore an angel. He never spoke of his school, never mentioned a comrade or a master; and I, for my part, was quite too much disgusted to allude to them. Of course I was under the spell, and the wonderful part is that, even at the time, I perfectly knew I was. But I gave myself up to it; it was an antidote to any pain, and I had more pains than one. I was in receipt in these days of disturbing letters from home, where things were not going well. But with my children, what things in the world mattered? That was the question I used to put to my scrappy retirements. I was dazzled by their loveliness.

There was a Sunday—to get on—when it rained with such force and for so many hours that there could be no procession to church; in consequence of which, as the day declined, I had arranged with Mrs. Grose that, should the evening show improvement, we would attend together the late service. The rain happily stopped, and I prepared for our walk, which, through the park and by the good road to the village, would be a matter of twenty minutes. Coming downstairs to meet my colleague in the hall, I remembered a pair of gloves that had required three stitches and that had received them—with a publicity perhaps not edifying—while I sat with the children at their tea, served on Sundays, by exception, in that cold, clean temple of mahogany and brass, the "grown-up" dining-room. The gloves had been dropped there, and I turned in to recover them. The day was grey enough, but the afternoon light still lingered, and it enabled me, on crossing the threshold, not only to recognise, on a chair near the wide window, then closed, the articles I wanted, but to become aware of a person on the other side of the window and looking straight in. One step into the room had sufficed; my vision was instantaneous; it was all there. The person looking straight in was the person who had already appeared to me. He appeared thus again with I won't say greater distinctness, for that was impossible, but with a nearness that represented a forward stride in our intercourse and made me, as I met him, catch my breath and turn cold. He was the same—he was the same, and seen, this time, as he had been seen before, from the waist up, the window, though the dining-room was on the ground-floor, not going down to the terrace on which he stood. His face was close to the glass, yet the effect of this better view was, strangely, only to show me how intense the former had been. He remained but a few seconds— long enough to convince me he also saw and recognised; but it was as if I had been looking at him for years and had known him always. Something, however, happened this time that had not happened before; his stare into my face, through the glass and across the room, was as deep and hard as then, but it quitted me for a moment during which I could still watch it, see it fix successively several other things. On the spot there came to me the added shock of a certitude that it was not for me he had come there. He had come for someone else.

The flash of this knowledge—for it was knowledge in the midst of dread—produced in me the most extraordinary effect, started, as I stood there, a sudden vibration of duty and courage. I say courage because I was beyond all doubt already far gone. I bounded straight out of the door again, reached that of the house, got, in an instant, upon the drive, and, passing along the terrace as fast as I could rush, turned a corner and came full in sight. But it was in sight of nothing now—my visitor had vanished. I stopped, I almost dropped, with the real relief of this; but I took in the whole scene—I gave him time to reappear. I call it time, but how long was it? I can't speak to the purpose today of the duration of these things. That kind of measure must have left me: they couldn't have lasted as they actually appeared to me to last. The terrace and the whole place, the lawn and the garden beyond it, all I could see of the park, were empty with a great emptiness. There were shrubberies and big trees, but I remember the clear assurance I felt that none of them concealed him. He was there or was not there: not there if I didn't see him. I got hold of this; then, instinctively, instead of returning as I had come, went to the window. It was confusedly present to me that I ought to place myself where he had stood. I did so; I applied my face to the pane and looked, as he had looked, into the room. As if, at this moment, to show me exactly what his range had been, Mrs. Grose, as I had done for himself just before, came in from the hall. With this I had the full image of a repetition of what had already occurred. She saw me as I had seen my own visitant; she pulled up short as I had done; I gave her something of the shock that I had received. She turned white, and this made me ask myself if I had blanched as much. She stared, in short, and retreated on just *my* lines, and I knew she had then passed out and come round to me and that I should presently meet her. I remained where I was, and while I waited I thought of more things than one. But there's only one I take space to mention. I wondered why *she* should be scared.

V

Oh, she let me know as soon as, round the corner of the house, she loomed again into view. "What in the name of goodness is the matter——?" She was now flushed and out of breath.

I said nothing till she came quite near. "With me?" I must have made a wonderful face. "Do I show it?"

"You're as white as a sheet. You look awful."

I considered; I could meet on this, without scruple, any innocence. My need to respect the bloom of Mrs. Grose's had dropped, without a rustle, from my shoulders, and if I wavered for the instant it was not with what I kept back. I put out my hand to her and she took it; I held her hard a little, liking to feel her close to me. There was a kind of support in the shy heave of her surprise. "You came for me for church, of course, but I can't go."

"Has anything happened?"

"Yes. You must know now. Did I look very queer?"

"Through this window? Dreadful!"

"Well," I said, "I've been frightened." Mrs. Grose's eyes expressed plainly that *she* had no wish to be, yet also that she knew too well her place not to be ready to share with me any marked inconvenience. Oh, it was quite settled that she *must* share! "Just what you saw from the dining-room a minute ago was the effect of that. What *I* saw—just before—was much worse."

Her hand tightened. "What was it?"

"An extraordinary man. Looking in."

"What extraordinary man?"

"I haven't the least idea."

Mrs. Grose gazed round us in vain. "Then where is he gone?"

"I know still less."

"Have you seen him before?"

"Yes—once. On the old tower."

She could only look at me harder. "Do you mean he's a stranger?"

"Oh, very much!"

"Yet you didn't tell me?"

"No—for reasons. But now that you've guessed——"

41

Mrs. Grose's round eyes encountered this charge. "Ah, I haven't guessed!" she said very simply. "How can I if *you* don't imagine?"

"I don't in the very least."

"You've seen him nowhere but on the tower?"

"And on this spot just now."

Mrs. Grose looked round again. "What was he doing on the tower?"

"Only standing there and looking down at me."

She thought a minute. "Was he a gentleman?"

I found I had no need to think. "No." She gazed in deeper wonder. "No."

"Then nobody about the place? Nobody from the village?"

"Nobody—nobody. I didn't tell you, but I made sure."

She breathed a vague relief: this was, oddly, so much to the good. It only went indeed a little way. "But if he isn't a gentleman——"

"What *is* he? He's a horror."

"A horror?"

"He's—God help me if I know *what* he is!"

Mrs. Grose looked round once more; she fixed her eyes on the duskier distance, then, pulling herself together, turned to me with abrupt inconsequence. "It's time we should be at church."

"Oh, I'm not fit for church!"

"Won't it do you good?"

"It won't do *them*——!" I nodded at the house.

"The children?"

"I can't leave them now."

"You're afraid——?"

I spoke boldly. "I'm afraid of *him*."

Mrs. Grose's large face showed me, at this, for the first time, the far-away faint glimmer of a consciousness more acute: I somehow made out in it the delayed dawn of an idea I myself had not given her and that was as yet quite obscure to me. It comes back to me that I thought instantly of this as something I could get from her; and I felt it to be connected with the desire she presently showed to know more. "When was it—on the tower?"

"About the middle of the month. At this same hour."

"Almost at dark," said Mrs. Grose.

"Oh no, not nearly. I saw him as I see you."

"Then how did he get in?"

"And how did he get out?" I laughed. "I had no opportunity to ask him! This evening, you see," I pursued, "he has not been able to get in."

"He only peeps?"

"I hope it will be confined to that!" She had now let go my hand; she turned away a little. I waited an instant; then I brought out: "Go to church. Good-bye. I must watch."

Slowly she faced me again. "Do you fear for them?"

We met in another long look. "Don't *you*?" Instead of answering she came nearer to the window and, for a minute, applied her face to the glass. "You see how he could see," I meanwhile went on.

She didn't move. "How long was he here?"

"Till I came out. I came to meet him."

Mrs. Grose at last turned round, and there was still more in her face. "*I* couldn't have come out."

"Neither could I!" I laughed again. "But I did come. I have my duty."

"So have I mine," she replied; after which she added: "What is he like?"

"I've been dying to tell you. But he's like nobody."

"Nobody?" she echoed.

"He has no hat." Then seeing in her face that she already, in this, with a deeper dismay, found a touch of picture, I quickly added stroke to stroke. "He has red hair, very red, close-curling, and a pale face, long in shape, with straight, good features and little, rather queer whiskers that are as red as his hair. His eyebrows are, somehow, darker; they look particularly arched and as if they might move a good deal. His eyes are sharp, strange—awfully; but I only know clearly that they're rather small and very fixed. His mouth's wide, and his lips are thin, and except for his little whiskers he's quite clean-shaven. He gives me a sort of sense of looking like an actor."

"An actor!" It was impossible to resemble one less, at least, than Mrs. Grose at that moment.

"I've never seen one, but so I suppose them. He's tall, active, erect," I continued, "but never—no, never!—a gentleman."

My companion's face had blanched as I went on; her round eyes started and her mild mouth gaped. "A gentleman?" she gasped, confounded, stupefied: "a gentleman *he?*"

"You know him then?"

She visibly tried to hold herself. "But he *is* handsome?"

I saw the way to help her. "Remarkably!"

"And dressed——?"

"In somebody's clothes. They're smart, but they're not his own."

She broke into a breathless affirmative groan. "They're the master's!"

I caught it up. "You *do* know him?"

She faltered but a second. "Quint!" she cried.

"Quint?"

"Peter Quint—his own man, his valet, when he was here!"

"When the master was?"

Gaping still, but meeting me, she pieced it all together. "He never wore his hat, but he did wear—well, there were waistcoats missed! They were both here—last year. Then the master went, and Quint was alone."

I followed, but halting a little. "Alone?"

"Alone with *us*." Then, as from a deeper depth, "In charge," she added.

"And what became of him?"

She hung fire so long that I was still more mystified. "He went too," she brought out at last.

"Went where?"

Her expression, at this, became extraordinary. "God knows where! He died."

"Died?" I almost shrieked.

She seemed fairly to square herself, plant herself more firmly to utter the wonder of it. "Yes. Mr. Quint is dead."

VI

It took of course more than that particular passage to place us together in presence of what we had now to live with as we could—my dreadful liability to impressions of the order so vividly exemplified, and my companion's knowledge, henceforth,—a knowledge half consternation and half compassion,—of that liability. There had been, this evening, after the revelation that left me, for an hour, so prostrate—there had been, for either of us, no attendance on any service but a little service of tears and vows, of prayers and promises, a climax to the series of mutual challenges and pledges that had straightway ensued on our retreating together to the schoolroom and shutting ourselves up there to have everything out. The result of our having everything out was simply to reduce our situation to the last rigour of its elements. She herself had seen nothing, not the shadow of a shadow, and nobody in the house but the governess was in the governess's plight; yet she accepted without directly impugning my sanity the truth as I gave it to her, and ended by showing me, on this ground, an awe-stricken tenderness, an expression of the sense of my more than questionable privilege, of which the very breath has remained with me as that of the sweetest of human charities.

What was settled between us, accordingly, that night, was that we thought we might bear things together; and I was not even sure that, in spite of her exemption, it was she who had the best of the burden. I knew at this hour, I think, as well as I knew later what I was capable of meeting to shelter my pupils; but it took me some time to be wholly sure of what my honest ally was prepared for to keep terms with so compromising a contract. I was queer company enough—quite as queer as the company I received; but as I trace over what we went through I see how much common ground we must have found in the one idea that, by good fortune, *could* steady us. It was the idea, the second movement, that led me straight out, as I may say, of the inner chamber of my dread. I could take the air in the court, at least, and there Mrs. Grose could join me. Perfectly can I recall now the particular way strength came to me before we separated for the night. We had gone over and over every feature of what I had seen.

"He was looking for someone else, you say—someone who was not you?"

"He was looking for little Miles." A portentous clearness now possessed me. "*That's* whom he was looking for."

46

"But how do you know?"

"I know, I know, I know!" My exaltation grew. "And *you* know, my dear!"

She didn't deny this, but I required, I felt, not even so much telling as that. She resumed in a moment, at any rate: "What if *he* should see him?"

"Little Miles? That's what he wants!"

She looked immensely scared again. "The child?"

"Heaven forbid! The man. He wants to appear to *them*." That he might was an awful conception, and yet, somehow, I could keep it at bay; which, moreover, as we lingered there, was what I succeeded in practically proving. I had an absolute certainty that I should see again what I had already seen, but something within me said that by offering myself bravely as the sole subject of such experience, by accepting, by inviting, by surmounting it all, I should serve as an expiatory victim and guard the tranquillity of my companions. The children, in especial, I should thus fence about and absolutely save. I recall one of the last things I said that night to Mrs. Grose.

"It does strike me that my pupils have never mentioned——"

She looked at me hard as I musingly pulled up. "His having been here and the time they were with him?"

"The time they were with him, and his name, his presence, his history, in any way."

"Oh, the little lady doesn't remember. She never heard or knew."

"The circumstances of his death?" I thought with some intensity. "Perhaps not. But Miles would remember—Miles would know."

"Ah, don't try him!" broke from Mrs. Grose.

I returned her the look she had given me. "Don't be afraid." I continued to think. "It is rather odd."

"That he has never spoken of him?"

"Never by the least allusion. And you tell me they were 'great friends'?"

"Oh, it wasn't *him*!" Mrs. Grose with emphasis declared. "It was Quint's own fancy. To play with him, I mean—to spoil him." She paused a moment; then she added: "Quint was much too free."

This gave me, straight from my vision of his face—*such* a face!—a sudden sickness of disgust. "Too free with *my* boy?"

"Too free with everyone!"

I forbore, for the moment, to analyse this description further than by the reflection that a part of it applied to several of the members of the household, of the half-dozen maids and men who were still of our small colony. But there was everything, for our apprehension, in the lucky fact that no discomfortable legend, no perturbation of scullions, had ever, within anyone's memory, attached to the kind old place. It had neither bad name nor ill fame, and Mrs. Grose, most apparently, only desired to cling to me and to quake in silence. I even put her, the very last thing of all, to the test. It was when, at midnight, she had her hand on the schoolroom door to take leave. "I have it from you then—for it's of great importance—that he was definitely and admittedly bad?"

"Oh, not admittedly. *I* knew it—but the master didn't."

"And you never told him?"

"Well, he didn't like tale-bearing—he hated complaints. He was terribly short with anything of that kind, and if people were all right to *him*——"

"He wouldn't be bothered with more?" This squared well enough with my impression of him: he was not a trouble-loving gentleman, nor so very particular perhaps about some of the company *he* kept. All the same, I pressed my interlocutress. "I promise you *I* would have told!"

She felt my discrimination. "I dare say I was wrong. But, really, I was afraid."

"Afraid of what?"

"Of things that man could do. Quint was so clever—he was so deep."

I took this in still more than, probably, I showed. "You weren't afraid of anything else? Not of his effect——?"

"His effect?" she repeated with a face of anguish and waiting while I faltered.

"On innocent little precious lives. They were in your charge."

"No, they were not in mine!" she roundly and distressfully returned. "The master believed in him and placed him here because he was supposed not to be well and the country air so good for him. So he had everything to say. Yes"—she let me have it—"even about *them*."

"Them—that creature?" I had to smother a kind of howl. "And you could bear it!"

"No. I couldn't—and I can't now!" And the poor woman burst into tears.

A rigid control, from the next day, was, as I have said, to follow them; yet how often and how passionately, for a week, we came back together to the subject! Much as we had discussed it that Sunday night, I was, in the immediate later hours in especial—for it may be imagined whether I slept—still haunted with the shadow of something she had not told me. I myself had kept back nothing, but there was a word Mrs. Grose had kept back. I was sure, moreover, by morning, that this was not from a failure of frankness, but because on every side there were fears. It seems to me indeed, in retrospect, that by the time the morrow's sun was high I had restlessly read into the facts before us almost all the meaning they were to receive from subsequent and more cruel occurrences. What they gave me above all was just the sinister figure of the living man—the dead one would keep awhile!—and of the months he had continuously passed at Bly, which, added up, made a formidable stretch. The limit of this evil time had arrived only when, on the dawn of a winter's morning, Peter Quint was found, by a labourer going to early work, stone dead on the road from the village: a catastrophe explained—superficially at least—by a visible wound to his head; such a wound as might have been produced—and as, on the final evidence, *had* been—by a fatal slip, in the dark and after leaving the public house, on the steepish icy slope, a wrong path altogether, at the bottom of which he lay. The icy slope, the turn mistaken at night and in liquor, accounted for much—practically, in the end and after the inquest and boundless chatter, for everything; but there had been matters in his life—strange passages and perils, secret disorders, vices more than suspected—that would have accounted for a good deal more.

I scarce know how to put my story into words that shall be a credible picture of my state of mind; but I was in these days literally able to find a joy in the extraordinary flight of heroism the occasion demanded of me. I now saw that I had been asked for a service admirable and difficult; and there would be a greatness in letting it be seen—oh, in the right quarter!—that I could succeed where many another girl might have failed. It was an immense help to me—I confess I rather applaud myself as I look back!—that I saw my service so strongly and so simply. I was there to protect and defend the little creatures in the world the most bereaved and the most loveable, the appeal of whose helplessness had suddenly become only too explicit, a deep, constant ache of one's own committed heart. We were cut off, really, together; we were united in our danger. They had nothing but me, and I—well, I had *them*. It was in short a magnificent chance. This chance presented itself to me in an image richly material. I was a screen—I was to stand before them. The more I saw, the less they would. I began to watch them in a stifled suspense, a disguised excitement that might well, had it continued too long, have turned to something like madness. What saved me, as I now see, was that it turned to something else altogether. It didn't last as suspense—it was superseded by horrible proofs. Proofs, I say, yes—from the moment I really took hold.

This moment dated from an afternoon hour that I happened to spend in the grounds with the younger of my pupils alone. We had left Miles indoors, on the red cushion of a deep window-seat; he had wished to finish a book, and I had been glad to encourage a purpose so laudable in a young man whose only defect was an occasional excess of the restless. His sister, on the contrary, had been alert to come out, and I strolled with her half an hour, seeking the shade, for the sun was still high and the day exceptionally warm. I was aware afresh, with her, as we went, of how, like her brother, she contrived—it was the charming thing in both children—to let me alone without appearing to drop me and to accompany me without appearing to surround. They were never importunate and yet never listless. My attention to them all really went to seeing them amuse themselves immensely without me: this was a spectacle they seemed actively to prepare and that engaged me as an active admirer. I walked in a world of their invention—they had no occasion whatever to draw upon mine; so that my time was taken only with being, for them, some remarkable person or thing that the game of the moment required and that was merely, thanks to my superior, my exalted stamp, a happy and highly distinguished sinecure. I forget what I was on the present occasion; I only remember that I was something very important and very quiet and that Flora was playing very hard. We were on the edge of the lake, and, as we had lately begun geography, the lake was the Sea of Azof.

Suddenly, in these circumstances, I became aware that, on the other side of the Sea of Azof, we had an interested spectator. The way this knowledge gathered in me was the strangest thing in the world—the strangest, that is, except the very much stranger in which it quickly merged itself. I had sat down with a piece of work—for I was something or other that could sit—on the old stone bench which overlooked the pond; and in this position I began to take in with certitude, and yet without direct vision, the presence, at a distance, of a third person. The old trees, the thick shrubbery, made a great and pleasant shade, but it was all suffused with the brightness of the hot, still hour. There was no ambiguity in anything; none whatever, at least, in the conviction I from one moment to another found myself forming as to what I should see straight before me and across the lake as a consequence of raising my eyes. They were attached at this juncture to the stitching in which I was engaged, and I can feel once more the spasm of my effort not to move them till I should so have steadied myself as to be able to make up my mind what to do. There was an alien object in view—a figure whose right of presence I instantly, passionately questioned. I recollect counting over perfectly the possibilities, reminding myself that nothing was more natural, for instance, than the appearance of one of the men about the place, or even of a messenger, a postman or a tradesman's boy, from the village. That reminder had as little effect on my practical certitude as I was conscious—still even without looking—of its having upon the character and attitude of our visitor. Nothing was more natural than that these things should be the other things that they absolutely were not.

Of the positive identity of the apparition I would assure myself as soon as the small clock of my courage should have ticked out the right second; meanwhile, with an effort that was already sharp enough, I transferred my eyes straight to little Flora, who, at the moment, was about ten yards away. My heart had stood still for an instant with the wonder and terror of the question whether she too would see; and I held my breath while I waited for what a cry from her, what some sudden innocent sign either of interest or of alarm, would tell me. I waited, but nothing came; then, in the first place— and there is something more dire in this, I feel, than in anything I have to relate—I was determined by a sense that, within a minute, all sounds from her had previously dropped; and, in the second, by the circumstance that, also within the minute, she had, in her play, turned her back to the water. This was her attitude when I at last looked at her—looked with the confirmed conviction that we were still, together, under direct personal notice. She had picked up a small flat piece of wood, which happened to have in it a little hole that had evidently suggested to her the idea of sticking in another fragment that might figure as a mast and make the thing a boat. This second morsel, as I watched her, she was very markedly and intently attempting to tighten in its place. My apprehension of what she was doing sustained me so that after some seconds I felt I was ready for more. Then I again shifted my eyes—I faced what I had to face.

VII

I GOT hold of Mrs. Grose as soon after this as I could; and I can give no intelligible account of how I fought out the interval. Yet I still hear myself cry

52

as I fairly threw myself into her arms: "They *know*—it's too monstrous: they know, they know!"

"And what on earth——?" I felt her incredulity as she held me.

"Why, all that *we* know—and heaven knows what else besides!" Then, as she released me, I made it out to her, made it out perhaps only now with full coherency even to myself. "Two hours ago, in the garden"—I could scarce articulate—"Flora *saw*!"

Mrs. Grose took it as she might have taken a blow in the stomach. "She has told you?" she panted.

"Not a word—that's the horror. She kept it to herself! The child of eight, *that* child!" Unutterable still, for me, was the stupefaction of it.

Mrs. Grose, of course, could only gape the wider. "Then how do you know?"

"I was there—I saw with my eyes: saw that she was perfectly aware."

"Do you mean aware of *him*?"

"No—of *her*." I was conscious as I spoke that I looked prodigious things, for I got the slow reflection of them in my companion's face. "Another person—this time; but a figure of quite as unmistakeable horror and evil: a woman in black, pale and dreadful—with such an air also, and such a face!—on the other side of the lake. I was there with the child—quiet for the hour; and in the midst of it she came."

"Came how—from where?"

"From where they come from! She just appeared and stood there—but not so near."

"And without coming nearer?"

"Oh, for the effect and the feeling, she might have been as close as you!"

My friend, with an odd impulse, fell back a step. "Was she someone you've never seen?"

"Yes. But someone the child has. Someone *you* have." Then, to show how I had thought it all out: "My predecessor—the one who died."

"Miss Jessel?"

"Miss Jessel. You don't believe me?" I pressed.

She turned right and left in her distress. "How can you be sure?"

This drew from me, in the state of my nerves, a flash of impatience. "Then ask Flora—*she's* sure!" But I had no sooner spoken than I caught myself up. "No, for God's sake, *don't*! She'll say she isn't—she'll lie!"

Mrs. Grose was not too bewildered instinctively to protest. "Ah, how *can* you?"

"Because I'm clear. Flora doesn't want me to know."

"It's only then to spare you."

"No, no—there are depths, depths! The more I go over it, the more I see in it, and the more I see in it the more I fear. I don't know what I *don't* see— what I *don't* fear!"

Mrs. Grose tried to keep up with me. "You mean you're afraid of seeing her again?"

"Oh, no; that's nothing—now!" Then I explained. "It's of *not* seeing her."

But my companion only looked wan. "I don't understand you."

"Why, it's that the child may keep it up—and that the child assuredly *will*—without my knowing it."

At the image of this possibility Mrs. Grose for a moment collapsed, yet presently to pull herself together again, as if from the positive force of the sense of what, should we yield an inch, there would really be to give way to. "Dear, dear—we must keep our heads! And after all, if she doesn't mind it——!" She even tried a grim joke. "Perhaps she likes it!"

"Likes *such* things—a scrap of an infant!"

"Isn't it just a proof of her blessed innocence?" my friend bravely inquired.

She brought me, for the instant, almost round. "Oh, we must clutch at *that*—we must cling to it! If it isn't a proof of what you say, it's a proof of—God knows what! For the woman's a horror of horrors."

Mrs. Grose, at this, fixed her eyes a minute on the ground; then at last raising them, "Tell me how you know," she said.

"Then you admit it's what she was?" I cried.

"Tell me how you know," my friend simply repeated.

"Know? By seeing her! By the way she looked."

"At you, do you mean—so wickedly?"

"Dear me, no—I could have borne that. She gave me never a glance. She only fixed the child."

Mrs. Grose tried to see it. "Fixed her?"

"Ah, with such awful eyes!"

She stared at mine as if they might really have resembled them. "Do you mean of dislike?"

"God help us, no. Of something much worse."

"Worse than dislike?"—this left her indeed at a loss.

"With a determination—indescribable. With a kind of fury of intention."

I made her turn pale. "Intention?"

"To get hold of her." Mrs. Grose—her eyes just lingering on mine—gave a shudder and walked to the window; and while she stood there looking out I completed my statement. "*That's* what Flora knows."

After a little she turned round. "The person was in black, you say?"

"In mourning—rather poor, almost shabby. But—yes—with extraordinary beauty." I now recognised to what I had at last, stroke by stroke, brought the victim of my confidence, for she quite visibly weighed this. "Oh, handsome—very, very," I insisted; "wonderfully handsome. But infamous."

She slowly came back to me. "Miss Jessel—*was* infamous." She once more took my hand in both her own, holding it as tight as if to fortify me against the increase of alarm I might draw from this disclosure. "They were both infamous," she finally said.

So, for a little, we faced it once more together; and I found absolutely a degree of help in seeing it now so straight. "I appreciate," I said, "the great decency of your not having hitherto spoken; but the time has certainly come to give me the whole thing." She appeared to assent to this, but still only in silence; seeing which I went on: "I must have it now. Of what did she die? Come, there was something between them."

"There was everything."

"In spite of the difference——?"

"Oh, of their rank, their condition"—she brought it woefully out. "*She* was a lady."

I turned it over; I again saw. "Yes—she was a lady."

"And he so dreadfully below," said Mrs. Grose.

I felt that I doubtless needn't press too hard, in such company, on the place of a servant in the scale; but there was nothing to prevent an acceptance of my companion's own measure of my predecessor's abasement. There was a way to deal with that, and I dealt; the more readily for my full vision—on the evidence—of our employer's late clever, good-looking "own" man; impudent, assured, spoiled, depraved. "The fellow was a hound."

Mrs. Grose considered as if it were perhaps a little a case for a sense of shades. "I've never seen one like him. He did what he wished."

"With *her*?"

"With them all."

It was as if now in my friend's own eyes Miss Jessel had again appeared. I seemed at any rate, for an instant, to see their evocation of her as distinctly as I had seen her by the pond; and I brought out with decision: "It must have been also what *she* wished!"

Mrs. Grose's face signified that it had been indeed, but she said at the same time: "Poor woman—she paid for it!"

"Then you do know what she died of?" I asked.

"No—I know nothing. I wanted not to know; I was glad enough I didn't; and I thanked heaven she was well out of this!"

"Yet you had, then, your idea——"

"Of her real reason for leaving? Oh, yes—as to that. She couldn't have stayed. Fancy it here—for a governess! And afterwards I imagined—and I still imagine. And what I imagine is dreadful."

"Not so dreadful as what *I* do," I replied; on which I must have shown her—as I was indeed but too conscious—a front of miserable defeat. It brought out again all her compassion for me, and at the renewed touch of her kindness my power to resist broke down. I burst, as I had, the other time, made her burst, into tears; she took me to her motherly breast, and my lamentation overflowed. "I don't do it!" I sobbed in despair; "I don't save or shield them! It's far worse than I dreamed—they're lost!"

VIII

WHAT I had said to Mrs. Grose was true enough: there were in the matter I had put before her depths and possibilities that I lacked resolution to sound; so that when we met once more in the wonder of it we were of a common mind about the duty of resistance to extravagant fancies. We were to keep our heads if we should keep nothing else—difficult indeed as that might be in the face of what, in our prodigious experience, was least to be questioned. Late that night, while the house slept, we had another talk in my room, when she went all the way with me as to its being beyond doubt that I had seen exactly what I had seen. To hold her perfectly in the pinch of that, I found I had only to ask her how, if I had "made it up," I came to be able to give, of each of the persons appearing to me, a picture disclosing, to the last detail, their special marks—a portrait on the exhibition of which she had instantly recognised and named them. She wished, of course,—small blame to her!—to sink the whole subject; and I was quick to assure her that my own interest in it had now violently taken the form of a search for the way to escape from it. I encountered her on the ground of a probability that with recurrence—for recurrence we took for granted—I should get used to my danger, distinctly professing that my personal exposure had suddenly become the least of my discomforts. It was my new suspicion that was intolerable; and yet even to this complication the later hours of the day had brought a little ease.

On leaving her, after my first outbreak, I had of course returned to my pupils, associating the right remedy for my dismay with that sense of their charm which I had already found to be a thing I could positively cultivate and which had never failed me yet. I had simply, in other words, plunged afresh into Flora's special society and there become aware—it was almost a luxury!— that she could put her little conscious hand straight upon the spot that ached. She had looked at me in sweet speculation and then had accused me to my face of having "cried." I had supposed I had brushed away the ugly signs: but I could literally—for the time, at all events—rejoice, under this fathomless charity, that they had not entirely disappeared. To gaze into the depths of blue of the child's eyes and pronounce their loveliness a trick of premature cunning was to be guilty of a cynicism in preference to which I naturally preferred to abjure my judgment and, so far as might be, my agitation. I couldn't abjure for merely wanting to, but I could repeat to Mrs. Grose—as I did there, over and over, in the small hours—that with their voices in the air, their pressure on one's heart and their fragrant faces against one's cheek, everything fell to the ground but their incapacity and their beauty. It was a pity that, somehow, to settle this once for all, I had equally to re-enumerate the signs of subtlety that, in the afternoon, by the lake, had made a miracle of my show of self-possession. It was a pity to be obliged to re-investigate the certitude of the moment itself and repeat how it had come to me as a revelation that the inconceivable communion I then surprised was a matter, for either party, of habit. It was a pity that I should have had to quaver out again the reasons for my not having, in my delusion, so much as questioned that the little girl saw our visitant even as I actually saw Mrs. Grose herself, and that she wanted, by just so much as she did thus see, to make me suppose she didn't, and at the same time, without showing anything, arrive at a guess as to whether I myself did! It was a pity that I needed once more to describe the portentous little activity by which she sought to divert my attention—the perceptible increase of movement, the greater intensity of play, the singing, the gabbling of nonsense, and the invitation to romp.

Yet if I had not indulged, to prove there was nothing in it, in this review, I should have missed the two or three dim elements of comfort that still remained to me. I should not for instance have been able to asseverate to my friend that I was certain—which was so much to the good—that *I* at least had not betrayed myself. I should not have been prompted, by stress of need, by desperation of mind,—I scarce know what to call it,—to invoke such further aid to intelligence as might spring from pushing my colleague fairly to the wall. She had told me, bit by bit, under pressure, a great deal; but a small shifty spot on the wrong side of it all still sometimes brushed my brow like the wing of a bat; and I remember how on this occasion—for the sleeping house and the concentration alike of our danger and our watch seemed to help—I felt the importance of giving the last jerk to the curtain. "I don't believe anything so horrible," I recollect saying; "no, let us put it definitely, my dear, that I don't. But if I did, you know, there's a thing I should require now, just without sparing you the least bit more—oh, not a scrap, come!—to get out of you. What was it you had in mind when, in our distress, before Miles came back, over the letter from his school, you said, under my insistence, that you didn't pretend for him that he had not literally *ever* been 'bad'? He has *not* literally 'ever,' in these weeks that I myself have lived with him and so closely watched him; he has been an imperturbable little prodigy of delightful, loveable goodness. Therefore you might perfectly have made the claim for him if you had not, as it happened, seen an exception to take. What was your exception, and to what passage in your personal observation of him did you refer?"

It was a dreadfully austere inquiry, but levity was not our note, and, at any rate, before the grey dawn admonished us to separate I had got my answer. What my friend had had in mind proved to be immensely to the purpose. It was neither more nor less than the circumstance that for a period of several months Quint and the boy had been perpetually together. It was in fact the very appropriate truth that she had ventured to criticise the propriety, to hint at the incongruity, of so close an alliance, and even to go so far on the subject as a frank overture to Miss Jessel. Miss Jessel had, with a most strange manner, requested her to mind her business, and the good woman had, on this, directly approached little Miles. What she had said to him, since I pressed, was that *she* liked to see young gentlemen not forget their station.

I pressed again, of course, at this. "You reminded him that Quint was only a base menial?"

"As you might say! And it was his answer, for one thing, that was bad."

"And for another thing?" I waited. "He repeated your words to Quint?"

"No, not that. It's just what he *wouldn't*!" she could still impress upon me. "I was sure, at any rate," she added, "that he didn't. But he denied certain occasions."

"What occasions?"

"When they had been about together quite as if Quint were his tutor— and a very grand one—and Miss Jessel only for the little lady. When he had gone off with the fellow, I mean, and spent hours with him."

"He then prevaricated about it—he said he hadn't?" Her assent was clear enough to cause me to add in a moment: "I see. He lied."

"Oh!" Mrs. Grose mumbled. This was a suggestion that it didn't matter; which indeed she backed up by a further remark. "You see, after all, Miss Jessel didn't mind. She didn't forbid him."

I considered. "Did he put that to you as a justification?"

At this she dropped again. "No, he never spoke of it."

"Never mentioned her in connection with Quint?"

She saw, visibly flushing, where I was coming out. "Well, he didn't show anything. He denied," she repeated; "he denied."

Lord, how I pressed her now! "So that you could see he knew what was between the two wretches?"

"I don't know—I don't know!" the poor woman groaned.

"You do know, you dear thing," I replied; "only you haven't my dreadful boldness of mind, and you keep back, out of timidity and modesty and delicacy, even the impression that, in the past, when you had, without my aid, to flounder about in silence, most of all made you miserable. But I shall get it out of you yet! There was something in the boy that suggested to you," I continued, "that he covered and concealed their relation."

"Oh, he couldn't prevent——"

"Your learning the truth? I dare say! But, heavens," I fell, with vehemence, a-thinking, "what it shows that they must, to that extent, have succeeded in making of him!"

"Ah, nothing that's not nice *now*!" Mrs. Grose lugubriously pleaded.

"I don't wonder you looked queer," I persisted, "when I mentioned to you the letter from his school!"

"I doubt if I looked as queer as you!" she retorted with homely force. "And if he was so bad then as that comes to, how is he such an angel now?"

"Yes, indeed—and if he was a fiend at school! How, how, how? Well," I said in my torment, "you must put it to me again, but I shall not be able to tell you for some days. Only, put it to me again!" I cried in a way that made my friend stare. "There are directions in which I must not for the present let myself go." Meanwhile I returned to her first example—the one to which she had just previously referred—of the boy's happy capacity for an occasional slip. "If Quint—on your remonstrance at the time you speak of—was a base menial, one of the things Miles said to you, I find myself guessing, was that you were another." Again her admission was so adequate that I continued: "And you forgave him that?"

"Wouldn't *you*?"

"Oh, yes!" And we exchanged there, in the stillness, a sound of the oddest amusement. Then I went on: "At all events, while he was with the man——"

"Miss Flora was with the woman. It suited them all!"

It suited me too, I felt, only too well; by which I mean that it suited exactly the particularly deadly view I was in the very act of forbidding myself to entertain. But I so far succeeded in checking the expression of this view that I will throw, just here, no further light on it than may be offered by the mention of my final observation to Mrs. Grose. "His having lied and been impudent are, I confess, less engaging specimens than I had hoped to have from you of the outbreak in him of the little natural man. Still," I mused, "they must do, for they make me feel more than ever that I must watch."

It made me blush, the next minute, to see in my friend's face how much more unreservedly she had forgiven him than her anecdote struck me as presenting to my own tenderness an occasion for doing. This came out when, at the schoolroom door, she quitted me. "Surely you don't accuse *him*——"

"Of carrying on an intercourse that he conceals from me? Ah, remember that, until further evidence, I now accuse nobody." Then, before shutting her out to go, by another passage, to her own place, "I must just wait," I wound up.

IX

I WAITED and waited, and the days, as they elapsed, took something from my consternation. A very few of them, in fact, passing, in constant sight of my pupils, without a fresh incident, sufficed to give to grievous fancies and even to odious memories a kind of brush of the sponge. I have spoken of the surrender to their extraordinary childish grace as a thing I could actively cultivate, and it may be imagined if I neglected now to address myself to this source for whatever it would yield. Stranger than I can express, certainly, was the effort to struggle against my new lights; it would doubtless have been, however, a greater tension still had it not been so frequently successful. I used to wonder how my little charges could help guessing that I thought strange things about them; and the circumstance that these things only made them more interesting was not by itself a direct aid to keeping them in the dark. I trembled lest they should see that they *were* so immensely more interesting. Putting things at the worst, at all events, as in meditation I so often did, any clouding of their innocence could only be—blameless and foredoomed as they were—a reason the more for taking risks. There were moments when, by an irresistible impulse, I found myself catching them up and pressing them to my heart. As soon as I had done so I used to say to myself: "What will they think of that? Doesn't it betray too much?" It would have been easy to get into a sad, wild tangle about how much I might betray; but the real account, I feel, of the hours of peace that I could still enjoy was that the immediate charm of my companions was a beguilement still effective even under the shadow of the possibility that it was studied. For if it occurred to me that I might occasionally excite suspicion by the little outbreaks of my sharper passion for them, so too I remember wondering if I mightn't see a queerness in the traceable increase of their own demonstrations.

They were at this period extravagantly and preternaturally fond of me; which, after all, I could reflect, was no more than a graceful response in children perpetually bowed over and hugged. The homage of which they were so lavish succeeded, in truth, for my nerves, quite as well as if I never appeared to myself, as I may say, literally to catch them at a purpose in it. They had never, I think, wanted to do so many things for their poor protectress; I mean—though they got their lessons better and better, which was naturally what would please her most—in the way of diverting, entertaining, surprising her; reading her passages, telling her stories, acting her charades, pouncing out at her, in disguises, as animals and historical characters, and above all astonishing her by the "pieces" they had secretly got by heart and could interminably recite. I should never get to the bottom—were I to let myself go even now—of the prodigious private commentary, all under still more private correction, with which, in these days, I overscored their full hours. They had shown me from the first a facility for everything, a general faculty which, taking a fresh start, achieved remarkable flights. They got their little tasks as if they loved them, and indulged, from the mere exuberance of the gift, in the most unimposed little miracles of memory. They not only popped out at me as tigers and as Romans, but as Shakespeareans, astronomers, and navigators. This was so singularly the case that it had presumably much to do with the fact as to which, at the present day, I am at a loss for a different explanation: I allude to my unnatural composure on the subject of another school for Miles. What I remember is that I was content not, for the time, to open the question, and that contentment must have sprung from the sense of his perpetually striking show of cleverness. He was too clever for a bad governess, for a parson's daughter, to spoil; and the strangest if not the brightest thread in the pensive embroidery I just spoke of was the impression I might have got, if I had dared to work it out, that he was under some influence operating in his small intellectual life as a tremendous incitement.

If it was easy to reflect, however, that such a boy could postpone school, it was at least as marked that for such a boy to have been "kicked out" by a school-master was a mystification without end. Let me add that in their company now—and I was careful almost never to be out of it—I could follow no scent very far. We lived in a cloud of music and love and success and private theatricals. The musical sense in each of the children was of the quickest, but the elder in especial had a marvellous knack of catching and repeating. The schoolroom piano broke into all gruesome fancies; and when that failed there were confabulations in corners, with a sequel of one of them going out in the highest spirits in order to "come in" as something new. I had had brothers myself, and it was no revelation to me that little girls could be slavish idolaters of little boys. What surpassed everything was that there was a little boy in the world who could have for the inferior age, sex, and intelligence so fine a consideration. They were extraordinarily at one, and to say that they never either quarrelled or complained is to make the note of praise coarse for their quality of sweetness. Sometimes, indeed, when I dropped into coarseness, I perhaps came across traces of little understandings between them by which one of them should keep me occupied while the other slipped away. There is a *naïf* side, I suppose, in all diplomacy; but if my pupils practised upon me, it was surely with the minimum of grossness. It was all in the other quarter that, after a lull, the grossness broke out.

I find that I really hang back; but I must take my plunge. In going on with the record of what was hideous at Bly, I not only challenge the most liberal faith—for which I little care; but—and this is another matter—I renew what I myself suffered, I again push my way through it to the end. There came suddenly an hour after which, as I look back, the affair seems to me to have been all pure suffering; but I have at least reached the heart of it, and the straightest road out is doubtless to advance. One evening—with nothing to lead up or to prepare it—I felt the cold touch of the impression that had breathed on me the night of my arrival and which, much lighter then, as I have mentioned, I should probably have made little of in memory had my subsequent sojourn been less agitated. I had not gone to bed; I sat reading by a couple of candles. There was a roomful of old books at Bly—last-century fiction, some of it, which, to the extent of a distinctly deprecated renown, but never to so much as that of a stray specimen, had reached the sequestered home and appealed to the unavowed curiosity of my youth. I remember that the book I had in my hand was Fielding's *Amelia*; also that I was wholly awake. I recall further both a general conviction that it was horribly late and a particular objection to looking at my watch. I figure, finally, that the white curtain draping, in the fashion of those days, the head of Flora's little bed, shrouded, as I had assured myself long before, the perfection of childish rest. I recollect in short that, though I was deeply interested in my author, I found myself, at the turn of a page and with his spell all scattered, looking straight up from him and hard at the door of my room. There was a moment during which I listened, reminded of the faint sense I had had, the first night, of there being something undefineably astir in the house, and noted the soft breath of the open casement just move the half-drawn blind. Then, with all the marks of a deliberation that must have seemed magnificent had there been anyone to admire it, I laid down my book, rose to my feet, and, taking a candle, went straight out of the room and, from the passage, on which my light made little impression, noiselessly closed and locked the door.

I can say now neither what determined nor what guided me, but I went straight along the lobby, holding my candle high, till I came within sight of the tall window that presided over the great turn of the staircase. At this point I precipitately found myself aware of three things. They were practically simultaneous, yet they had flashes of succession. My candle, under a bold flourish, went out, and I perceived, by the uncovered window, that the yielding dusk of earliest morning rendered it unnecessary. Without it, the next instant, I saw that there was someone on the stair. I speak of sequences, but I required no lapse of seconds to stiffen myself for a third encounter with Quint. The apparition had reached the landing half-way up and was therefore on the spot nearest the window, where at sight of me, it stopped short and fixed me exactly as it had fixed me from the tower and from the garden. He knew me as well as I knew him; and so, in the cold, faint twilight, with a glimmer in the high glass and another on the polish of the oak stair below, we faced each other in our common intensity. He was absolutely, on this occasion, a living, detestable, dangerous presence. But that was not the wonder of wonders; I reserve this distinction for quite another circumstance: the circumstance that dread had unmistakeably quitted me and that there was nothing in me there that didn't meet and measure him.

I had plenty of anguish after that extraordinary moment, but I had, thank God, no terror. And he knew I had not—I found myself at the end of an instant magnificently aware of this. I felt, in a fierce rigour of confidence, that if I stood my ground a minute I should cease—for the time, at least—to have him to reckon with; and during the minute, accordingly, the thing was as human and hideous as a real interview: hideous just because it *was* human, as human as to have met alone, in the small hours, in a sleeping house, some enemy, some adventurer, some criminal. It was the dead silence of our long gaze at such close quarters that gave the whole horror, huge as it was, its only note of the unnatural. If I had met a murderer in such a place and at such an hour, we still at least would have spoken. Something would have passed, in life, between us; if nothing had passed one of us would have moved. The moment was so prolonged that it would have taken but little more to make me doubt if even *I* were in life. I can't express what followed it save by saying that the silence itself—which was indeed in a manner an attestation of my strength—became the element into which I saw the figure disappear; in which I definitely saw it turn as I might have seen the low wretch to which it had once belonged turn on receipt of an order, and pass, with my eyes on the villainous back that no hunch could have more disfigured, straight down the staircase and into the darkness in which the next bend was lost.

X

I REMAINED awhile at the top of the stair, but with the effect presently of understanding that when my visitor had gone, he had gone: then I returned to my room. The foremost thing I saw there by the light of the candle I had left burning was that Flora's little bed was empty; and on this I caught my breath with all the terror that, five minutes before, I had been able to resist. I dashed at the place in which I had left her lying and over which (for the small silk counterpane and the sheets were disarranged) the white curtains had been deceivingly pulled forward; then my step, to my unutterable relief, produced an answering sound: I perceived an agitation of the window-blind, and the child, ducking down, emerged rosily from the other side of it. She stood there in so much of her candour and so little of her nightgown, with her pink bare feet and the golden glow of her curls. She looked intensely grave, and I had never had such a sense of losing an advantage acquired (the thrill of which had just been so prodigious) as on my consciousness that she addressed me with a reproach. "You naughty: where *have* you been?"—instead of challenging her own irregularity I found myself arraigned and explaining.

She herself explained, for that matter, with the loveliest, eagerest simplicity. She had known suddenly, as she lay there, that I was out of the room, and had jumped up to see what had become of me. I had dropped, with the joy of her reappearance, back into my chair—feeling then, and then only, a little faint; and she had pattered straight over to me, thrown herself upon my knee, given herself to be held with the flame of the candle full in the wonderful little face that was still flushed with sleep. I remember closing my eyes an instant, yieldingly, consciously, as before the excess of something beautiful that shone out of the blue of her own. "You were looking for me out of the window?" I said. "You thought I might be walking in the grounds?"

"Well, you know, I thought someone was"—she never blanched as she smiled out that at me.

Oh, how I looked at her now! "And did you see anyone?"

"Ah, *no!*" she returned, almost with the full privilege of childish inconsequence, resentfully, though with a long sweetness in her little drawl of the negative.

At that moment, in the state of my nerves, I absolutely believed she lied; and if I once more closed my eyes it was before the dazzle of the three or four possible ways in which I might take this up. One of these, for a moment, tempted me with such singular intensity that, to withstand it, I must have gripped my little girl with a spasm that, wonderfully, she submitted to without a cry or a sign of fright. Why not break out at her on the spot and have it all over?—give it to her straight in her lovely little lighted face? "You see, you see, you *know* that you do and that you already quite suspect I believe it; therefore why not frankly confess it to me, so that we may at least live with it together and learn perhaps, in the strangeness of our fate, where we are and what it means?" This solicitation dropped, alas, as it came: if I could immediately have succumbed to it I might have spared myself——well you'll see what. Instead of succumbing I sprang again to my feet, looked at her bed, and took a helpless middle way. "Why did you pull the curtain over the place to make me think you were still there?"

Flora luminously considered; after which, with her little divine smile: "Because I don't like to frighten you!"

"But if I had, by your idea, gone out——?"

She absolutely declined to be puzzled; she turned her eyes to the flame of the candle as if the question were as irrelevant, or at any rate as impersonal, as Mrs. Marcet or nine-times-nine. "Oh, but you know," she quite adequately answered, "that you might come back, you dear, and that you *have*!" And after a little, when she had got into bed, I had, for a long time, by almost sitting on her to hold her hand, to prove that I recognised the pertinence of my return.

You may imagine the general complexion, from that moment, of my nights. I repeatedly sat up till I didn't know when; I selected moments when my room-mate unmistakeably slept, and, stealing out, took noiseless turns in the passage and even pushed as far as to where I had last met Quint. But I never met him there again; and I may as well say at once that I on no other occasion saw him in the house. I just missed, on the staircase, on the other hand, a different adventure. Looking down it from the top I once recognised the presence of a woman seated on one of the lower steps with her back presented to me, her body half bowed and her head, in an attitude of woe, in her hands. I had been there but an instant, however, when she vanished without looking round at me. I knew, none the less, exactly what dreadful face she had to show; and I wondered whether, if instead of being above I had been below, I should have had, for going up, the same nerve I had lately shown Quint. Well, there continued to be plenty of chance for nerve. On the eleventh night after my latest encounter with that gentleman—they were all numbered now—I had an alarm that perilously skirted it and that indeed, from the particular quality of its unexpectedness, proved quite my sharpest shock. It was precisely the first night during this series that, weary with watching, I had felt that I might again without laxity lay myself down at my old hour. I slept immediately and, as I afterwards knew, till about one o'clock; but when I woke it was to sit straight up, as completely roused as if a hand had shook me. I had left a light burning, but it was now out, and I felt an instant certainty that Flora had extinguished it. This brought me to my feet and straight, in the darkness, to her bed, which I found she had left. A glance at the window enlightened me further, and the striking of a match completed the picture.

The child had again got up—this time blowing out the taper, and had again, for some purpose of observation or response, squeezed in behind the blind and was peering out into the night. That she now saw—as she had not, I had satisfied myself, the previous time—was proved to me by the fact that she was disturbed neither by my re-illumination nor by the haste I made to get into slippers and into a wrap. Hidden, protected, absorbed, she evidently rested on the sill—the casement opened forward—and gave herself up. There was a great still moon to help her, and this fact had counted in my quick decision. She was face to face with the apparition we had met at the lake, and could now communicate with it as she had not then been able to do. What I, on my side, had to care for was, without disturbing her, to reach, from the corridor, some other window in the same quarter. I got to the door without her hearing me; I got out of it, closed it and listened, from the other side, for some sound from her. While I stood in the passage I had my eyes on her brother's door, which was but ten steps off and which, indescribably, produced in me a renewal of the strange impulse that I lately spoke of as my temptation. What if I should go straight in and march to *his* window?—what if, by risking to his boyish bewilderment a revelation of my motive, I should throw across the rest of the mystery the long halter of my boldness?

This thought held me sufficiently to make me cross to his threshold and pause again. I preternaturally listened; I figured to myself what might portentously be; I wondered if his bed were also empty and he too were secretly at watch. It was a deep, soundless minute, at the end of which my impulse failed. He was quiet; he might be innocent; the risk was hideous; I turned away. There was a figure in the grounds—a figure prowling for a sight, the visitor with whom Flora was engaged; but it was not the visitor most concerned with my boy. I hesitated afresh, but on other grounds and only a few seconds; then I had made my choice. There were empty rooms at Bly, and it was only a question of choosing the right one. The right one suddenly presented itself to me as the lower one—though high above the gardens—in the solid corner of the house that I have spoken of as the old tower. This was a large, square chamber, arranged with some state as a bedroom, the extravagant size of which made it so inconvenient that it had not for years, though kept by Mrs. Grose in exemplary order, been occupied. I had often admired it and I knew my way about in it; I had only, after just faltering at the first chill gloom of its disuse, to pass across it and unbolt as quietly as I could one of the shutters. Achieving this transit, I uncovered the glass without a sound and, applying my face to the pane, was able, the darkness without being much less than within, to see that I commanded the right direction. Then I saw something more. The moon made the night extraordinarily penetrable and showed me on the lawn a person, diminished by distance, who stood there motionless and as if fascinated, looking up to where I had appeared—looking, that is, not so much straight at me as at something that was apparently above me. There was clearly another person above me—there was a person on the tower; but the presence on the lawn was not in the least what I had conceived and had confidently hurried to meet. The presence on the lawn—I felt sick as I made it out—was poor little Miles himself.

XI

It was not till late next day that I spoke to Mrs. Grose; the rigour with which I kept my pupils in sight making it often difficult to meet her privately, and the more as we each felt the importance of not provoking—on the part of the servants quite as much as on that of the children—any suspicion of a secret flurry or of a discussion of mysteries. I drew a great security in this particular from her mere smooth aspect. There was nothing in her fresh face to pass on to others my horrible confidences. She believed me, I was sure, absolutely: if she hadn't I don't know what would have become of me, for I couldn't have borne the business alone. But she was a magnificent monument to the blessing of a want of imagination, and if she could see in our little charges nothing but their beauty and amiability, their happiness and cleverness, she had no direct communication with the sources of my trouble. If they had been at all visibly blighted or battered, she would doubtless have grown, on tracing it back, haggard enough to match them; as matters stood, however, I could feel her, when she surveyed them, with her large white arms folded and the habit of serenity in all her look, thank the Lord's mercy that if they were ruined the pieces would still serve. Flights of fancy gave place, in her mind, to a steady fireside glow, and I had already begun to perceive how, with the development of the conviction that—as time went on without a public accident—our young things could, after all, look out for themselves, she addressed her greatest solicitude to the sad case presented by their instructress. That, for myself, was a sound simplification: I could engage that, to the world, my face should tell no tales, but it would have been, in the conditions, an immense added strain to find myself anxious about hers.

At the hour I now speak of she had joined me, under pressure, on the terrace, where, with the lapse of the season, the afternoon sun was now agreeable; and we sat there together while, before us, at a distance, but within call if we wished, the children strolled to and fro in one of their most manageable moods. They moved slowly, in unison, below us, over the lawn, the boy, as they went, reading aloud from a storybook and passing his arm round his sister to keep her quite in touch. Mrs. Grose watched them with positive placidity; then I caught the suppressed intellectual creak with which she conscientiously turned to take from me a view of the back of the tapestry. I had made her a receptacle of lurid things, but there was an odd recognition of my superiority—my accomplishments and my function—in her patience under my pain. She offered her mind to my disclosures as, had I wished to mix a witch's broth and proposed it with assurance, she would have held out a large clean saucepan. This had become thoroughly her attitude by the time that, in my recital of the events of the night, I reached the point of what Miles had said to me when, after seeing him, at such a monstrous hour, almost on the very spot where he happened now to be, I had gone down to bring him in; choosing then, at the window, with a concentrated need of not alarming the house, rather that method than a signal more resonant. I had left her meanwhile in little doubt of my small hope of representing with success even to her actual sympathy my sense of the real splendour of the little inspiration with which, after I had got him into the house, the boy met my final articulate challenge. As soon as I appeared in the moonlight on the terrace, he had come to me as straight as possible; on which I had taken his hand without a word and led him, through the dark spaces, up the staircase where Quint had so hungrily hovered for him, along the lobby where I had listened and trembled, and so to his forsaken room.

Not a sound, on the way, had passed between us, and I had wondered—oh, *how* I had wondered!—if he were groping about in his little mind for something plausible and not too grotesque. It would tax his invention, certainly, and I felt, this time, over his real embarrassment, a curious thrill of triumph. It was a sharp trap for the inscrutable! He couldn't play any longer at innocence; so how the deuce would he get out of it? There beat in me indeed, with the passionate throb of this question, an equal dumb appeal as to how the deuce *I* should. I was confronted at last, as never yet, with all the risk attached even now to sounding my own horrid note. I remember in fact that as we pushed into his little chamber, where the bed had not been slept in at all and the window, uncovered to the moonlight, made the place so clear that there was no need of striking a match—I remember how I suddenly dropped, sank upon the edge of the bed from the force of the idea that he must know how he really, as they say, "had" me. He could do what he liked, with all his cleverness to help him, so long as I should continue to defer to the old tradition of the criminality of those caretakers of the young who minister to superstitions and fears. He "had" me indeed, and in a cleft stick; for who would ever absolve me, who would consent that I should go unhung, if, by the faintest tremor of an overture, I were the first to introduce into our perfect intercourse an element so dire? No, no: it was useless to attempt to convey to Mrs. Grose, just as it is scarcely less so to attempt to suggest here, how, in our short, stiff brush in the dark, he fairly shook me with admiration. I was of course thoroughly kind and merciful; never, never yet had I placed on his little shoulders hands of such tenderness as those with which, while I rested against the bed, I held him there well under fire. I had no alternative but, in form at least, to put it to him.

"You must tell me now—and all the truth. What did you go out for? What were you doing there?"

I can still see his wonderful smile, the whites of his beautiful eyes, and the uncovering of his little teeth shine to me in the dusk. "If I tell you why, will you understand?" My heart, at this, leaped into my mouth. *Would* he tell me why? I found no sound on my lips to press it, and I was aware of replying only with a vague, repeated, grimacing nod. He was gentleness itself, and while I wagged my head at him he stood there more than ever a little fairy prince. It was his brightness indeed that gave me a respite. Would it be so great if he were really going to tell me? "Well," he said at last, "just exactly in order that you should do this."

"Do what?"

"Think me—for a change—*bad!*" I shall never forget the sweetness and gaiety with which he brought out the word, nor how, on top of it, he bent forward and kissed me. It was practically the end of everything. I met his kiss and I had to make, while I folded him for a minute in my arms, the most stupendous effort not to cry. He had given exactly the account of himself that permitted least of my going behind it, and it was only with the effect of confirming my acceptance of it that, as I presently glanced about the room, I could say—

"Then you didn't undress at all?"

He fairly glittered in the gloom. "Not at all. I sat up and read."

"And when did you go down?"

"At midnight. When I'm bad I *am* bad!"

"I see, I see—it's charming. But how could you be sure I would know it?"

"Oh, I arranged that with Flora." His answers rang out with a readiness! "She was to get up and look out."

"Which is what she did do." It was I who fell into the trap!

"So she disturbed you, and, to see what she was looking at, you also looked—you saw."

"While you," I concurred, "caught your death in the night air!"

He literally bloomed so from this exploit that he could afford radiantly to assent. "How otherwise should I have been bad enough?" he asked. Then, after another embrace, the incident and our interview closed on my recognition of all the reserves of goodness that, for his joke, he had been able to draw upon.

XII

THE particular impression I had received proved in the morning light, I repeat, not quite successfully presentable to Mrs. Grose, though I reinforced it with the mention of still another remark that he had made before we separated. "It all lies in half-a-dozen words," I said to her, "words that really settle the matter. 'Think, you know, what I *might* do!' He threw that off to show me how good he is. He knows down to the ground what he 'might' do. That's what he gave them a taste of at school."

"Lord, you do change!" cried my friend.

"I don't change—I simply make it out. The four, depend upon it, perpetually meet. If on either of these last nights you had been with either child, you would clearly have understood. The more I've watched and waited the more I've felt that if there were nothing else to make it sure it would be made so by the systematic silence of each. *Never*, by a slip of the tongue, have they so much as alluded to either of their old friends, any more than Miles has alluded to his expulsion. Oh yes, we may sit here and look at them, and they may show off to us there to their fill; but even while they pretend to be lost in their fairy-tale they're steeped in their vision of the dead restored. He's not reading to her," I declared; "they're talking of *them*—they're talking horrors! I go on, I know, as if I were crazy; and it's a wonder I'm not. What I've seen would have made *you* so; but it has only made me more lucid, made me get hold of still other things."

My lucidity must have seemed awful, but the charming creatures who were victims of it, passing and repassing in their interlocked sweetness, gave my colleague something to hold on by; and I felt how tight she held as, without stirring in the breath of my passion, she covered them still with her eyes. "Of what other things have you got hold?"

"Why, of the very things that have delighted, fascinated, and yet, at bottom, as I now so strangely see, mystified and troubled me. Their more than earthly beauty, their absolutely unnatural goodness. It's a game," I went on; "it's a policy and a fraud!"

"On the part of little darlings——?"

"As yet mere lovely babies? Yes, mad as that seems!" The very act of bringing it out really helped me to trace it—follow it all up and piece it all together. "They haven't been good—they've only been absent. It has been easy to live with them, because they're simply leading a life of their own. They're not mine—they're not ours. They're his and they're hers!"

"Quint's and that woman's?"

"Quint's and that woman's. They want to get to them."

Oh, how, at this, poor Mrs. Grose appeared to study them! "But for what?"

"For the love of all the evil that, in those dreadful days, the pair put into them. And to ply them with that evil still, to keep up the work of demons, is what brings the others back."

"Laws!" said my friend under her breath. The exclamation was homely, but it revealed a real acceptance of my further proof of what, in the bad time—for there had been a worse even than this!—must have occurred. There could have been no such justification for me as the plain assent of her experience to whatever depth of depravity I found credible in our brace of scoundrels. It was in obvious submission of memory that she brought out after a moment: "They *were* rascals! But what can they now do?" she pursued.

"Do?" I echoed so loud that Miles and Flora, as they passed at their distance, paused an instant in their walk and looked at us. "Don't they do enough?" I demanded in a lower tone, while the children, having smiled and nodded and kissed hands to us, resumed their exhibition. We were held by it a minute; then I answered: "They can destroy them!" At this my companion did turn, but the inquiry she launched was a silent one, the effect of which was to make me more explicit. "They don't know, as yet, quite how—but they're trying hard. They're seen only across, as it were, and beyond—in strange places and on high places, the top of towers, the roof of houses, the outside of windows, the further edge of pools; but there's a deep design, on either side, to shorten the distance and overcome the obstacle; and the success of the tempters is only a question of time. They've only to keep to their suggestions of danger."

"For the children to come?"

"And perish in the attempt!" Mrs. Grose slowly got up, and I scrupulously added: "Unless, of course, we can prevent!"

Standing there before me while I kept my seat, she visibly turned things over. "Their uncle must do the preventing. He must take them away."

"And who's to make him?"

She had been scanning the distance, but she now dropped on me a foolish face. "You, Miss."

"By writing to him that his house is poisoned and his little nephew and niece mad?"

"But if they *are*, Miss?"

"And if I am myself, you mean? That's charming news to be sent him by a governess whose prime undertaking was to give him no worry."

Mrs. Grose considered, following the children again. "Yes, he do hate worry. That was the great reason——"

77

"Why those fiends took him in so long? No doubt, though his indifference must have been awful. As I'm not a fiend, at any rate, I shouldn't take him in."

My companion, after an instant and for all answer, sat down again and grasped my arm. "Make him at any rate come to you."

I stared. "To *me*?" I had a sudden fear of what she might do. "'Him'?"

"He ought to *be* here—he ought to help."

I quickly rose, and I think I must have shown her a queerer face than ever yet. "You see me asking him for a visit?" No, with her eyes on my face she evidently couldn't. Instead of it even—as a woman reads another—she could see what I myself saw: his derision, his amusement, his contempt for the break-down of my resignation at being left alone and for the fine machinery I had set in motion to attract his attention to my slighted charms. She didn't know—no one knew—how proud I had been to serve him and to stick to our terms; yet she none the less took the measure, I think, of the warning I now gave her. "If you should so lose your head as to appeal to him for me——"

She was really frightened. "Yes, Miss?"

"I would leave, on the spot, both him and you."

XIII

IT was all very well to join them, but speaking to them proved quite as much as ever an effort beyond my strength—offered, in close quarters, difficulties as insurmountable as before. This situation continued a month, and with new aggravations and particular notes, the note above all, sharper and sharper, of the small ironic consciousness on the part of my pupils. It was not, I am as sure today as I was sure then, my mere infernal imagination: it was absolutely traceable that they were aware of my predicament and that this strange relation made, in a manner, for a long time, the air in which we moved. I don't mean that they had their tongues in their cheeks or did anything vulgar, for that was not one of their dangers: I do mean, on the other hand, that the element of the unnamed and untouched became, between us, greater than any other, and that so much avoidance could not have been so successfully effected without a great deal of tacit arrangement. It was as if, at moments, we were perpetually coming into sight of subjects before which we must stop short, turning suddenly out of alleys that we perceived to be blind, closing with a little bang that made us look at each other—for, like all bangs, it was something louder than we had intended—the doors we had indiscreetly opened. All roads lead to Rome, and there were times when it might have struck us that almost every branch of study or subject of conversation skirted forbidden ground. Forbidden ground was the question of the return of the dead in general and of whatever, in especial, might survive, in memory, of the friends little children had lost. There were days when I could have sworn that one of them had, with a small invisible nudge, said to the other: "She thinks she'll do it this time—but she *won't*!" To "do it" would have been to indulge for instance—and for once in a way—in some direct reference to the lady who had prepared them for my discipline. They had a delightful endless appetite for passages in my own history, to which I had again and again treated them; they were in possession of everything that had ever happened to me, had had, with every circumstance the story of my smallest adventures and of those of my brothers and sisters and of the cat and the dog at home, as well as many particulars of the eccentric nature of my father, of the furniture and arrangement of our house, and of the conversation of the old women of our village. There were things enough, taking one with another, to chatter about, if one went very fast and knew by instinct when to go round. They pulled with an art of their own the strings of my invention and my memory; and nothing else perhaps, when I thought of such occasions afterwards, gave me so the suspicion of being watched from under cover. It was in any case over *my* life, *my* past, and *my* friends alone that we could take anything like our ease—a state of affairs that led them sometimes without the least pertinence to break out into sociable reminders. I was invited—with no visible connection—to repeat afresh Goody Gosling's celebrated *mot* or to confirm the details already supplied as to the cleverness of the vicarage pony.

It was partly at such junctures as these and partly at quite different ones that, with the turn my matters had now taken, my predicament, as I have called it, grew most sensible. The fact that the days passed for me without another encounter ought, it would have appeared, to have done something toward soothing my nerves. Since the light brush, that second night on the upper landing, of the presence of a woman at the foot of the stair, I had seen nothing, whether in or out of the house, that one had better not have seen. There was many a corner round which I expected to come upon Quint, and many a situation that, in a merely sinister way, would have favoured the appearance of Miss Jessel. The summer had turned, the summer had gone; the autumn had dropped upon Bly and had blown out half our lights. The place, with its grey sky and withered garlands, its bared spaces and scattered dead leaves, was like a theatre after the performance—all strewn with crumpled playbills. There were exactly states of the air, conditions of sound and of stillness, unspeakable impressions of the *kind* of ministering moment, that brought back to me, long enough to catch it, the feeling of the medium in which, that June evening out-of-doors, I had had my first sight of Quint, and in which, too, at those other instants, I had, after seeing him through the window, looked for him in vain in the circle of shrubbery. I recognised the signs, the portents—I recognised the moment, the spot. But they remained unaccompanied and empty, and I continued unmolested; if unmolested one could call a young woman whose sensibility had, in the most extraordinary fashion, not declined but deepened. I had said in my talk with Mrs. Grose on that horrid scene of Flora's by the lake—and had perplexed her by so saying—that it would from that moment distress me much more to lose my power than to keep it. I had then expressed what was vividly in my mind: the truth that, whether the children really saw or not—since, that is, it was not yet definitely proved—I greatly preferred, as a safeguard, the fulness of my own exposure. I was ready to know the very worst that was to be known. What I had then had an ugly glimpse of was that my eyes might be sealed just while theirs were most opened. Well, my eyes *were* sealed, it appeared, at present—a consummation for which it seemed blasphemous not to thank God. There was, alas, a difficulty about that: I would have thanked him with all my soul had I not had in a proportionate measure this conviction of the secret of my pupils.

How can I retrace today the strange steps of my obsession? There were times of our being together when I would have been ready to swear that, literally, in my presence, but with my direct sense of it closed, they had visitors who were known and were welcome. Then it was that, had I not been deterred by the very chance that such an injury might prove greater than the injury to be averted, my exultation would have broken out. "They're here, they're here, you little wretches," I would have cried, "and you can't deny it now!" The little wretches denied it with all the added volume of their sociability and their tenderness, in just the crystal depths of which—like the flash of a fish in a stream—the mockery of their advantage peeped up. The shock, in truth, had sunk into me still deeper than I knew on the night when, looking out to see either Quint or Miss Jessel under the stars, I had beheld the boy over whose rest I watched and who had immediately brought in with him—had straightway, there, turned it on me—the lovely upward look with which, from the battlements above me, the hideous apparition of Quint had played. If it was a question of a scare, my discovery on this occasion had scared me more than any other, and it was in the condition of nerves produced by it that I made my actual inductions. They harassed me so that sometimes, at odd moments, I shut myself up audibly to rehearse—it was at once a fantastic relief and a renewed despair—the manner in which I might come to the point. I approached it from one side and the other while, in my room, I flung myself about, but I always broke down in the monstrous utterance of names. As they died away on my lips, I said to myself that I should indeed help them to represent something infamous if, by pronouncing them, I should violate as rare a little case of instinctive delicacy as any schoolroom, probably, had ever known. When I said to myself: "*They* have the manners to be silent, and you, trusted as you are, the baseness to speak!" I felt myself crimson and I covered my face with my hands. After these secret scenes I chattered more than ever, going on volubly enough till one of our prodigious, palpable hushes occurred—I can call them nothing else—the strange, dizzy lift or swim (I try for terms!) into a stillness, a pause of all life, that had nothing to do with the more or less noise that at the moment we might be engaged in making and that I could hear through any deepened exhilaration or quickened recitation or louder strum of the piano. Then it was that the others, the outsiders, were there. Though they were not angels, they "passed," as the French, say, causing me, while they stayed, to tremble with the fear of their addressing to their younger victims some yet more infernal message or more vivid image than they had thought good enough for myself.

What it was most impossible to get rid of was the cruel idea that, whatever I had seen, Miles and Flora saw *more*—things terrible and unguessable and that sprang from dreadful passages of intercourse in the past. Such things naturally left on the surface, for the time, a chill which we vociferously denied that we felt; and we had, all three, with repetition, got into such splendid training that we went, each time, almost automatically, to mark the close of the incident, through the very same movements. It was striking of the children, at all events, to kiss me inveterately with a kind of wild irrelevance and never to fail—one or the other—of the precious question that had helped us through many a peril. "When do you think he *will* come? Don't you think we *ought* to write?"—there was nothing like that inquiry, we found by experience, for carrying off an awkwardness. "He" of course was their uncle in Harley Street; and we lived in much profusion of theory that he might at any moment arrive to mingle in our circle. It was impossible to have given less encouragement than he had done to such a doctrine, but if we had not had the doctrine to fall back upon we should have deprived each other of some of our finest exhibitions. He never wrote to them—that may have been selfish, but it was a part of the flattery of his trust of me; for the way in which a man pays his highest tribute to a woman is apt to be but by the more festal celebration of one of the sacred laws of his comfort; and I held that I carried out the spirit of the pledge given not to appeal to him when I let my charges understand that their own letters were but charming literary exercises. They were too beautiful to be posted; I kept them myself; I have them all to this hour. This was a rule indeed which only added to the satiric effect of my being plied with the supposition that he might at any moment be among us. It was exactly as if my charges knew how almost more awkward than anything else that might be for me. There appears to me, moreover, as I look back, no note in all this more extraordinary than the mere fact that, in spite of my tension and of their triumph, I never lost patience with them. Adorable they must in truth have been, I now reflect, that I didn't in these days hate them! Would exasperation, however, if relief had longer been postponed, finally have betrayed me? It little matters, for relief arrived. I call it relief, though it was only the relief that a snap brings to a strain or the burst of a thunderstorm to a day of suffocation. It was at least change, and it came with a rush.

XIV

Walking to church a certain Sunday morning, I had little Miles at my side and his sister, in advance of us and at Mrs. Grose's, well in sight. It was a crisp, clear day, the first of its order for some time; the night had brought a touch of frost, and the autumn air, bright and sharp, made the church-bells almost gay. It was an odd accident of thought that I should have happened at such a moment to be particularly and very gratefully struck with the obedience of my little charges. Why did they never resent my inexorable, my perpetual society? Something or other had brought nearer home to me that I had all but pinned the boy to my shawl and that, in the way our companions were marshalled before me, I might have appeared to provide against some danger of rebellion. I was like a gaoler with an eye to possible surprises and escapes. But all this belonged—I mean their magnificent little surrender—just to the special array of the facts that were most abysmal. Turned out for Sunday by his uncle's tailor, who had had a free hand and a notion of pretty waistcoats and of his grand little air, Miles's whole title to independence, the rights of his sex and situation, were so stamped upon him that if he had suddenly struck for freedom I should have had nothing to say. I was by the strangest of chances wondering how I should meet him when the revolution unmistakeably occurred. I call it a revolution because I now see how, with the word he spoke, the curtain rose on the last act of my dreadful drama and the catastrophe was precipitated. "Look here, my dear, you know," he charmingly said, "when in the world, please, am I going back to school?"

Transcribed here the speech sounds harmless enough, particularly as uttered in the sweet, high, casual pipe with which, at all interlocutors, but above all at his eternal governess, he threw off intonations as if he were tossing roses. There was something in them that always made one "catch" and I caught, at any rate, now so effectually that I stopped as short as if one of the trees of the park had fallen across the road. There was something new, on the spot, between us, and he was perfectly aware that I recognised it, though, to enable me to do so, he had no need to look a whit less candid and charming than usual. I could feel in him how he already, from my at first finding nothing to reply, perceived the advantage he had gained. I was so slow to find anything that he had plenty of time, after a minute, to continue with his suggestive but inconclusive smile: "You know, my dear, that for a fellow to be with a lady *always*——!" His "my dear" was constantly on his lips for me, and nothing could have expressed more the exact shade of the sentiment with which I desired to inspire my pupils than its fond familiarity. It was so respectfully easy.

But, oh, how I felt that at present I must pick my own phrases! I remember that, to gain time, I tried to laugh, and I seemed to see in the beautiful face with which he watched me how ugly and queer I looked. "And always with the same lady?" I returned.

He neither blenched nor winked. The whole thing was virtually out between us. "Ah, of course, she's a jolly, 'perfect' lady; but, after all, I'm a fellow, don't you see? that's—well, getting on."

I lingered there with him an instant ever so kindly. "Yes, you're getting on." Oh, but I felt helpless!

I have kept to this day the heartbreaking little idea of how he seemed to know that and to play with it. "And you can't say I've not been awfully good, can you?"

I laid my hand on his shoulder, for, though I felt how much better it would have been to walk on, I was not yet quite able. "No, I can't say that, Miles."

"Except just that one night, you know——!"

"That one night?" I couldn't look as straight as he.

"Why, when I went down—went out of the house."

"Oh, yes. But I forget what you did it for."

"You forget?"—he spoke with the sweet extravagance of childish reproach. "Why, it was to show you I could!"

"Oh, yes, you could."

"And I can again."

I felt that I might, perhaps, after all, succeed in keeping my wits about me. "Certainly. But you won't."

"No, not *that* again. It was nothing."

"It was nothing," I said. "But we must go on."

He resumed our walk with me, passing his hand into my arm. "Then when *am* I going back?"

I wore, in turning it over, my most responsible air. "Were you very happy at school?"

He just considered. "Oh, I'm happy enough anywhere!"

"Well, then," I quavered, "if you're just as happy here——!"

"Ah, but that isn't everything! Of course *you* know a lot——"

"But you hint that you know almost as much?" I risked as he paused.

"Not half I want to!" Miles honestly professed. "But it isn't so much that."

"What is it, then?"

"Well—I want to see more life."

"I see; I see." We had arrived within sight of the church and of various persons, including several of the household of Bly, on their way to it and clustered about the door to see us go in. I quickened our step; I wanted to get there before the question between us opened up much further; I reflected hungrily that, for more than an hour, he would have to be silent; and I thought with envy of the comparative dusk of the pew and of the almost spiritual help of the hassock on which I might bend my knees. I seemed literally to be running a race with some confusion to which he was about to reduce me, but I felt that he had got in first when, before we had even entered the churchyard, he threw out—

"I want my own sort!"

It literally made me bound forward. "There are not many of your own sort, Miles!" I laughed. "Unless perhaps dear little Flora!"

"You really compare me to a baby girl?"

This found me singularly weak. "Don't you, then, *love* our sweet Flora?"

"If I didn't—and you too; if I didn't——!" he repeated as if retreating for a jump, yet leaving his thought so unfinished that, after we had come into the gate, another stop, which he imposed on me by the pressure of his arm, had become inevitable. Mrs. Grose and Flora had passed into the church, the other worshippers had followed, and we were, for the minute, alone among the old, thick graves. We had paused, on the path from the gate, by a low, oblong, tablelike tomb.

"Yes, if you didn't——?"

He looked, while I waited, about at the graves. "Well, you know what!" But he didn't move, and he presently produced something that made me drop straight down on the stone slab, as if suddenly to rest. "Does my uncle think what *you* think?"

I markedly rested. "How do you know what I think?"

"Ah, well, of course I don't; for it strikes me you never tell me. But I mean does *he* know?"

"Know what, Miles?"

"Why, the way I'm going on."

I perceived quickly enough that I could make, to this inquiry, no answer that would not involve something of a sacrifice of my employer. Yet it appeared to me that we were all, at Bly, sufficiently sacrificed to make that venial. "I don't think your uncle much cares."

Miles, on this, stood looking at me. "Then don't you think he can be made to?"

"In what way?"

"Why, by his coming down."

"But who'll get him to come down?"

"*I* will!" the boy said with extraordinary brightness and emphasis. He gave me another look charged with that expression and then marched off alone into church.

XV

THE business was practically settled from the moment I never followed him. It was a pitiful surrender to agitation, but my being aware of this had somehow no power to restore me. I only sat there on my tomb and read into what my little friend had said to me the fulness of its meaning; by the time I had grasped the whole of which I had also embraced, for absence, the pretext that I was ashamed to offer my pupils and the rest of the congregation such an example of delay. What I said to myself above all was that Miles had got something out of me and that the proof of it, for him, would be just this awkward collapse. He had got out of me that there was something I was much afraid of and that he should probably be able to make use of my fear to gain, for his own purpose, more freedom. My fear was of having to deal with the intolerable question of the grounds of his dismissal from school, for that was really but the question of the horrors gathered behind. That his uncle should arrive to treat with me of these things was a solution that, strictly speaking, I ought now to have desired to bring on; but I could so little face the ugliness and the pain of it that I simply procrastinated and lived from hand to mouth. The boy, to my deep discomposure, was immensely in the right, was in a position to say to me: "Either you clear up with my guardian the mystery of this interruption of my studies, or you cease to expect me to lead with you a life that's so unnatural for a boy." What was so unnatural for the particular boy I was concerned with was this sudden revelation of a consciousness and a plan.

That was what really overcame me, what prevented my going in. I walked round the church, hesitating, hovering; I reflected that I had already, with him, hurt myself beyond repair. Therefore I could patch up nothing, and it was too extreme an effort to squeeze beside him into the pew: he would be so much more sure than ever to pass his arm into mine and make me sit there for an hour in close, silent contact with his commentary on our talk. For the first minute since his arrival I wanted to get away from him. As I paused beneath the high east window and listened to the sounds of worship, I was taken with an impulse that might master me, I felt, completely should I give it the least encouragement. I might easily put an end to my predicament by getting away altogether. Here was my chance; there was no one to stop me; I could give the whole thing up—turn my back and retreat. It was only a question of hurrying again, for a few preparations, to the house which the attendance at church of so many of the servants would practically have left unoccupied. No one, in short, could blame me if I should just drive desperately off. What was it to get away if I got away only till dinner? That would be in a couple of hours, at the end of which—I had the acute prevision—my little pupils would play at innocent wonder about my non-appearance in their train.

"What *did* you do, you naughty, bad thing? Why in the world, to worry us so—and take our thoughts off too, don't you know?—did you desert us at the very door?" I couldn't meet such questions nor, as they asked them, their false little lovely eyes; yet it was all so exactly what I should have to meet that, as the prospect grew sharp to me, I at last let myself go.

I got, so far as the immediate moment was concerned, away; I came straight out of the churchyard and, thinking hard, retraced my steps through the park. It seemed to me that by the time I reached the house I had made up my mind I would fly. The Sunday stillness both of the approaches and of the interior, in which I met no one, fairly excited me with a sense of opportunity. Were I to get off quickly, this way, I should get off without a scene, without a word. My quickness would have to be remarkable, however, and the question of a conveyance was the great one to settle. Tormented, in the hall, with difficulties and obstacles, I remember sinking down at the foot of the staircase—suddenly collapsing there on the lowest step and then, with a revulsion, recalling that it was exactly where more than a month before, in the darkness of night and just so bowed with evil things, I had seen the spectre of the most horrible of women. At this I was able to straighten myself; I went the rest of the way up; I made, in my bewilderment, for the schoolroom, where there were objects belonging to me that I should have to take. But I opened the door to find again, in a flash, my eyes unsealed. In the presence of what I saw I reeled straight back upon my resistance.

Seated at my own table in clear noonday light I saw a person whom, without my previous experience, I should have taken at the first blush for some housemaid who might have stayed at home to look after the place and who, availing herself of rare relief from observation and of the schoolroom table and my pens, ink, and paper, had applied herself to the considerable effort of a letter to her sweetheart. There was an effort in the way that, while her arms rested on the table, her hands with evident weariness supported her head; but at the moment I took this in I had already become aware that, in spite of my entrance, her attitude strangely persisted. Then it was—with the very act of its announcing itself—that her identity flared up in a change of posture. She rose, not as if she had heard me, but with an indescribable grand melancholy of indifference and detachment, and, within a dozen feet of me, stood there as my vile predecessor. Dishonoured and tragic, she was all before me; but even as I fixed and, for memory, secured it, the awful image passed away. Dark as midnight in her black dress, her haggard beauty and her unutterable woe, she had looked at me long enough to appear to say that her right to sit at my table was as good as mine to sit at hers. While these instants lasted indeed I had the extraordinary chill of a feeling that it was I who was

the intruder. It was as a wild protest against it that, actually addressing her—
"You terrible, miserable woman!"—I heard myself break into a sound that,
by the open door, rang through the long passage and the empty house. She
looked at me as if she heard me, but I had recovered myself and cleared the
air. There was nothing in the room the next minute but the sunshine and a
sense that I must stay.

XVI

I HAD so perfectly expected that the return of my pupils would be marked
by a demonstration that I was freshly upset at having to take into account
that they were dumb about my absence. Instead of gaily denouncing and
caressing me, they made no allusion to my having failed them, and I was left,
for the time, on perceiving that she too said nothing, to study Mrs. Grose's
odd face. I did this to such purpose that I made sure they had in some way
bribed her to silence; a silence that, however, I would engage to break down
on the first private opportunity. This opportunity came before tea: I secured
five minutes with her in the housekeeper's room, where, in the twilight, amid
a smell of lately-baked bread, but with the place all swept and garnished, I
found her sitting in pained placidity before the fire. So I see her still, so I see
her best: facing the flame from her straight chair in the dusky, shining room,
a large clean image of the "put away"—of drawers closed and locked and rest
without a remedy.

"Oh, yes, they asked me to say nothing; and to please them—so long
as they were there—of course I promised. But what had happened to you?"

"I only went with you for the walk," I said. "I had then to come back to
meet a friend."

She showed her surprise. "A friend—*you?*"

"Oh, yes, I have a couple!" I laughed. "But did the children give you a
reason?"

"For not alluding to your leaving us? Yes; they said you would like it better. Do you like it better?"

My face had made her rueful. "No, I like it worse!" But after an instant I added: "Did they say why I should like it better?"

"No; Master Miles only said, 'We must do nothing but what she likes!'"

"I wish indeed he would! And what did Flora say?"

"Miss Flora was too sweet. She said, 'Oh, of course, of course!'—and I said the same."

I thought a moment. "You were too sweet too—I can hear you all. But none the less, between Miles and me, it's now all out."

"All out?" My companion stared. "But what, Miss?"

"Everything. It doesn't matter. I've made up my mind. I came home, my dear," I went on, "for a talk with Miss Jessel."

I had by this time formed the habit of having Mrs. Grose literally well in hand in advance of my sounding that note; so that even now, as she bravely blinked under the signal of my word, I could keep her comparatively firm. "A talk! Do you mean she spoke?"

"It came to that. I found her, on my return, in the schoolroom."

"And what did she say?" I can hear the good woman still, and the candour of her stupefaction.

"That she suffers the torments——!"

It was this, of a truth, that made her, as she filled out my picture, gape. "Do you mean," she faltered, "—of the lost?"

"Of the lost. Of the damned. And that's why, to share them——" I faltered myself with the horror of it.

But my companion, with less imagination, kept me up. "To share them——?"

"She wants Flora." Mrs. Grose might, as I gave it to her, fairly have fallen away from me had I not been prepared. I still held her there, to show I was. "As I've told you, however, it doesn't matter."

"Because you've made up your mind? But to what?"

"To everything."

"And what do you call 'everything'?"

"Why, sending for their uncle."

"Oh, Miss, in pity do," my friend broke out.

"Ah, but I will, I *will!* I see it's the only way. What's 'out,' as I told you, with Miles is that if he thinks I'm afraid to—and has ideas of what he gains by that—he shall see he's mistaken. Yes, yes; his uncle shall have it here from me on the spot (and before the boy himself if necessary) that if I'm to be reproached with having done nothing again about more school——"

"Yes, Miss——" my companion pressed me.

"Well, there's that awful reason."

There were now clearly so many of these for my poor colleague that she was excusable for being vague. "But—a—which?"

"Why, the letter from his old place."

"You'll show it to the master?"

"I ought to have done so on the instant."

"Oh, no!" said Mrs. Grose with decision.

"I'll put it before him," I went on inexorably, "that I can't undertake to work the question on behalf of a child who has been expelled——"

"For we've never in the least known what!" Mrs. Grose declared.

"For wickedness. For what else—when he's so clever and beautiful and perfect? Is he stupid? Is he untidy? Is he infirm? Is he ill-natured? He's exquisite—so it can be only *that*; and that would open up the whole thing. After all," I said, "it's their uncle's fault. If he left here such people——!"

"He didn't really in the least know them. The fault's mine." She had turned quite pale.

"Well, you shan't suffer," I answered.

"The children shan't!" she emphatically returned.

I was silent awhile; we looked at each other. "Then what am I to tell him?"

"You needn't tell him anything. *I'll* tell him."

I measured this. "Do you mean you'll write——?" Remembering she couldn't, I caught myself up. "How do you communicate?"

"I tell the bailiff. *He* writes."

"And should you like him to write our story?"

My question had a sarcastic force that I had not fully intended, and it made her, after a moment, inconsequently break down. The tears were again in her eyes. "Ah, Miss, *you* write!"

"Well—tonight," I at last answered; and on this we separated.

XVII

I WENT so far, in the evening, as to make a beginning. The weather had changed back, a great wind was abroad, and beneath the lamp, in my room, with Flora at peace beside me, I sat for a long time before a blank sheet of paper and listened to the lash of the rain and the batter of the gusts. Finally I went out, taking a candle; I crossed the passage and listened a minute at Miles's door. What, under my endless obsession, I had been impelled to listen for was some betrayal of his not being at rest, and I presently caught one, but not in the form I had expected. His voice tinkled out. "I say, you there—come in." It was a gaiety in the gloom!

I went in with my light and found him, in bed, very wide awake, but very much at his ease. "Well, what are *you* up to?" he asked with a grace of sociability in which it occurred to me that Mrs. Grose, had she been present, might have looked in vain for proof that anything was "out."

I stood over him with my candle. "How did you know I was there?"

"Why, of course I heard you. Did you fancy you made no noise? You're like a troop of cavalry!" he beautifully laughed.

"Then you weren't asleep?"

"Not much! I lie awake and think."

I had put my candle, designedly, a short way off, and then, as he held out his friendly old hand to me, had sat down on the edge of his bed. "What is it," I asked, "that you think of?"

"What in the world, my dear, but *you?*"

"Ah, the pride I take in your appreciation doesn't insist on that! I had so far rather you slept."

"Well, I think also, you know, of this queer business of ours."

I marked the coolness of his firm little hand. "Of what queer business, Miles?"

"Why, the way you bring me up. And all the rest!"

I fairly held my breath a minute, and even from my glimmering taper there was light enough to show how he smiled up at me from his pillow. "What do you mean by all the rest?"

"Oh, you know, you know!"

I could say nothing for a minute, though I felt, as I held his hand and our eyes continued to meet, that my silence had all the air of admitting his charge and that nothing in the whole world of reality was perhaps at that moment so fabulous as our actual relation. "Certainly you shall go back to school," I said, "if it be that that troubles you. But not to the old place—we must find another, a better. How could I know it did trouble you, this question, when you never told me so, never spoke of it at all?" His clear, listening face, framed in its smooth whiteness, made him for the minute as appealing as some wistful patient in a children's hospital; and I would have given, as the resemblance came to me, all I possessed on earth really to be the nurse or the sister of charity who might have helped to cure him. Well, even as it was, I perhaps might help! "Do you know you've never said a word to me about your school—I mean the old one; never mentioned it in any way?"

He seemed to wonder; he smiled with the same loveliness. But he clearly gained time; he waited, he called for guidance. "Haven't I?" It wasn't for *me* to help him—it was for the thing I had met!

Something in his tone and the expression of his face, as I got this from him, set my heart aching with such a pang as it had never yet known; so unutterably touching was it to see his little brain puzzled and his little resources taxed to play, under the spell laid on him, a part of innocence and consistency. "No, never—from the hour you came back. You've never mentioned to me one of your masters, one of your comrades, nor the least little thing that ever happened to you at school. Never, little Miles—no, never—have you given me an inkling of anything that *may* have happened there. Therefore you can fancy how much I'm in the dark. Until you came out, that way, this morning, you had, since the first hour I saw you, scarce even made a reference to anything in your previous life. You seemed so perfectly to accept the present." It was extraordinary how my absolute conviction of his secret precocity (or whatever I might call the poison of an influence that I dared but half to phrase) made him, in spite of the faint breath of his inward trouble, appear as accessible as an older person—imposed him almost as an intellectual equal. "I thought you wanted to go on as you are."

It struck me that at this he just faintly coloured. He gave, at any rate, like a convalescent slightly fatigued, a languid shake of his head. "I don't—I don't. I want to get away."

"You're tired of Bly?"

95

"Oh, no, I like Bly."

"Well, then——?"

"Oh, *you* know what a boy wants!"

I felt that I didn't know so well as Miles, and I took temporary refuge. "You want to go to your uncle?"

Again, at this, with his sweet ironic face, he made a movement on the pillow. "Ah, you can't get off with that!"

I was silent a little, and it was I, now, I think, who changed colour. "My dear, I don't want to get off!"

"You can't, even if you do. You can't, you can't!"—he lay beautifully staring. "My uncle must come down, and you must completely settle things."

"If we do," I returned with some spirit, "you may be sure it will be to take you quite away."

"Well, don't you understand that that's exactly what I'm working for? You'll have to tell him—about the way you've let it all drop: you'll have to tell him a tremendous lot!"

The exultation with which he uttered this helped me somehow, for the instant, to meet him rather more. "And how much will *you*, Miles, have to tell him? There are things he'll ask you!"

He turned it over. "Very likely. But what things?"

"The things you've never told me. To make up his mind what to do with you. He can't send you back——"

"Oh, I don't want to go back!" he broke in. "I want a new field."

He said it with admirable serenity, with positive unimpeachable gaiety; and doubtless it was that very note that most evoked for me the poignancy, the unnatural childish tragedy, of his probable reappearance at the end of three months with all this bravado and still more dishonour. It overwhelmed me now that I should never be able to bear that, and it made me let myself go. I threw myself upon him and in the tenderness of my pity I embraced him. "Dear little Miles, dear little Miles——!"

My face was close to his, and he let me kiss him, simply taking it with indulgent good-humour. "Well, old lady?"

"Is there nothing—nothing at all that you want to tell me?"

He turned off a little, facing round toward the wall and holding up his hand to look at as one had seen sick children look. "I've told you—I told you this morning."

Oh, I was sorry for him! "That you just want me not to worry you?"

He looked round at me now, as if in recognition of my understanding him; then ever so gently, "To let me alone," he replied.

There was even a singular little dignity in it, something that made me release him, yet, when I had slowly risen, linger beside him. God knows I never wished to harass him, but I felt that merely, at this, to turn my back on him was to abandon or, to put it more truly, to lose him. "I've just begun a letter to your uncle," I said.

"Well, then, finish it!"

I waited a minute. "What happened before?"

He gazed up at me again. "Before what?"

"Before you came back. And before you went away."

For some time he was silent, but he continued to meet my eyes. "What happened?"

It made me, the sound of the words, in which it seemed to me that I caught for the very first time a small faint quaver of consenting consciousness—it made me drop on my knees beside the bed and seize once more the chance of possessing him. "Dear little Miles, dear little Miles, if you *knew* how I want to help you! It's only that, it's nothing but that, and I'd rather die than give you a pain or do you a wrong—I'd rather die than hurt a hair of you. Dear little Miles"—oh, I brought it out now even if I *should* go too far—"I just want you to help me to save you!" But I knew in a moment after this that I had gone too far. The answer to my appeal was instantaneous, but it came in the form of an extraordinary blast and chill, a gust of frozen air and a shake of the room as great as if, in the wild wind, the casement had crashed in. The boy gave a loud, high shriek, which, lost in the rest of the shock of sound, might have seemed, indistinctly, though I was so close to him, a note either of jubilation or of terror. I jumped to my feet again and was conscious of darkness. So for a moment we remained, while I stared about me and saw that the drawn curtains were unstirred and the window tight. "Why, the candle's out!" I then cried.

"It was I who blew it, dear!" said Miles.

XVIII

THE next day, after lessons, Mrs. Grose found a moment to say to me quietly: "Have you written, Miss?"

"Yes—I've written." But I didn't add—for the hour—that my letter, sealed and directed, was still in my pocket. There would be time enough to send it before the messenger should go to the village. Meanwhile there had been, on the part of my pupils, no more brilliant, more exemplary morning. It was exactly as if they had both had at heart to gloss over any recent little friction. They performed the dizziest feats of arithmetic, soaring quite out of *my* feeble range, and perpetrated, in higher spirits than ever, geographical and historical jokes. It was conspicuous of course in Miles in particular that he appeared to wish to show how easily he could let me down. This child, to my memory, really lives in a setting of beauty and misery that no words can translate; there was a distinction all his own in every impulse he revealed; never was a small natural creature, to the uninitiated eye all frankness and freedom, a more ingenious, a more extraordinary little gentleman. I had perpetually to guard against the wonder of contemplation into which my initiated view betrayed me; to check the irrelevant gaze and discouraged sigh in which I constantly both attacked and renounced the enigma of what such a little gentleman could have done that deserved a penalty. Say that, by the dark prodigy I knew, the imagination of all evil *had* been opened up to him: all the justice within me ached for the proof that it could ever have flowered into an act.

He had never, at any rate, been such a little gentleman as when, after our early dinner on this dreadful day, he came round to me and asked if I shouldn't like him, for half an hour, to play to me. David playing to Saul could never have shown a finer sense of the occasion. It was literally a charming exhibition of tact, of magnanimity, and quite tantamount to his saying outright: "The true knights we love to read about never push an advantage too far. I know what you mean now: you mean that—to be let alone yourself and not followed up—you'll cease to worry and spy upon me, won't keep me so close to you, will let me go and come. Well, I 'come,' you see—but I don't go! There'll be plenty of time for that. I do really delight in your society, and I only want to show you that I contended for a principle." It may be imagined whether I resisted this appeal or failed to accompany him again, hand in hand, to the schoolroom. He sat down at the old piano and played as he had never played, and if there are those who think he had better have been kicking a football I can only say that I wholly agree with them. For at the end of a time that under his influence I had quite ceased to measure I started up with a strange sense of having literally slept at my post. It was after luncheon, and by the schoolroom fire, and yet I hadn't really, in the least, slept: I had only done something much worse—I had forgotten. Where, all this time, was Flora? When I put the question to Miles he played on a minute before answering, and then could only say: "Why, my dear, how do *I* know?"—breaking moreover into a happy laugh which, immediately after, as if it were a vocal accompaniment, he prolonged into incoherent, extravagant song.

I went straight to my room, but his sister was not there; then, before going downstairs, I looked into several others. As she was nowhere about she would surely be with Mrs. Grose, whom, in the comfort of that theory, I accordingly proceeded in quest of. I found her where I had found her the evening before, but she met my quick challenge with blank, scared ignorance. She had only supposed that, after the repast, I had carried off both the children; as to which she was quite in her right, for it was the very first time I had allowed the little girl out of my sight without some special provision. Of course now indeed she might be with the maids, so that the immediate thing was to look for her without an air of alarm. This we promptly arranged between us; but when, ten minutes later and in pursuance of our arrangement, we met in the hall, it was only to report on either side that after guarded inquiries we had altogether failed to trace her. For a minute there, apart from observation, we exchanged mute alarms, and I could feel with what high interest my friend returned me all those I had from the first given her.

"She'll be above," she presently said—"in one of the rooms you haven't searched."

"No; she's at a distance." I had made up my mind. "She has gone out."

Mrs. Grose stared. "Without a hat?"

I naturally also looked volumes. "Isn't that woman always without one?"

"She's with *her*?"

"She's with *her*!" I declared. "We must find them."

My hand was on my friend's arm, but she failed for the moment, confronted with such an account of the matter, to respond to my pressure. She communed, on the contrary, on the spot, with her uneasiness. "And where's Master Miles?"

"Oh, *he's* with Quint. They're in the schoolroom."

"Lord, Miss!" My view, I was myself aware—and therefore I suppose my tone—had never yet reached so calm an assurance.

"The trick's played," I went on; "they've successfully worked their plan. He found the most divine little way to keep me quiet while she went off."

"'Divine'?" Mrs. Grose bewilderedly echoed.

"Infernal, then!" I almost cheerfully rejoined. "He has provided for himself as well. But come!"

She had helplessly gloomed at the upper regions. "You leave him——?"

"So long with Quint? Yes—I don't mind that now."

She always ended, at these moments, by getting possession of my hand, and in this manner she could at present still stay me. But after gasping an instant at my sudden resignation, "Because of your letter?" she eagerly brought out.

I quickly, by way of answer, felt for my letter, drew it forth, held it up, and then, freeing myself, went and laid it on the great hall-table. "Luke will take it," I said as I came back. I reached the house-door and opened it; I was already on the steps.

My companion still demurred: the storm of the night and the early morning had dropped, but the afternoon was damp and grey. I came down to the drive while she stood in the doorway. "You go with nothing on?"

"What do I care when the child has nothing? I can't wait to dress," I cried, "and if you must do so, I leave you. Try meanwhile, yourself, upstairs."

"With *them*?" Oh, on this, the poor woman promptly joined me!

XIX

WE went straight to the lake, as it was called at Bly, and I dare say rightly called, though I reflect that it may in fact have been a sheet of water less remarkable than it appeared to my untravelled eyes. My acquaintance with sheets of water was small, and the pool of Bly, at all events on the few occasions of my consenting, under the protection of my pupils, to affront its surface in the old flat-bottomed boat moored there for our use, had impressed me both with its extent and its agitation. The usual place of embarkation was half a mile from the house, but I had an intimate conviction that, wherever

Flora might be, she was not near home. She had not given me the slip for any small adventure, and, since the day of the very great one that I had shared with her by the pond, I had been aware, in our walks, of the quarter to which she most inclined. This was why I had now given to Mrs. Grose's steps so marked a direction—a direction that made her, when she perceived it, oppose a resistance that showed me she was freshly mystified. "You're going to the water, Miss?—you think she's *in*——?"

"She may be, though the depth is, I believe, nowhere very great. But what I judge most likely is that she's on the spot from which, the other day, we saw together what I told you."

"When she pretended not to see——?"

"With that astounding self-possession! I've always been sure she wanted to go back alone. And now her brother has managed it for her."

Mrs. Grose still stood where she had stopped. "You suppose they really *talk* of them?"

I could meet this with a confidence! "They say things that, if we heard them, would simply appal us."

"And if she *is* there——?"

"Yes?"

"Then Miss Jessel is?"

"Beyond a doubt. You shall see."

"Oh, thank you!" my friend cried, planted so firm that, taking it in, I went straight on without her. By the time I reached the pool, however, she was close behind me, and I knew that, whatever, to her apprehension, might befall me, the exposure of my society struck her as her least danger. She exhaled a moan of relief as we at last came in sight of the greater part of the water without a sight of the child. There was no trace of Flora on that nearer side of the bank where my observation of her had been most startling, and none on the opposite edge, where, save for a margin of some twenty yards, a thick copse came down to the water. The pond, oblong in shape, had a width so scant compared to its length that, with its ends out of view, it might have been taken for a scant river. We looked at the empty expanse, and then I felt the suggestion of my friend's eyes. I knew what she meant and I replied with a negative headshake.

"No, no; wait! She has taken the boat."

My companion stared at the vacant mooring-place and then again across the lake. "Then where is it?"

"Our not seeing it is the strongest of proofs. She has used it to go over, and then has managed to hide it."

"All alone—that child?"

"She's not alone, and at such times she's not a child: she's an old, old woman." I scanned all the visible shore while Mrs. Grose took again, into the queer element I offered her, one of her plunges of submission; then I pointed out that the boat might perfectly be in a small refuge formed by one of the recesses of the pool, an indentation masked, for the hither side, by a projection of the bank and by a clump of trees growing close to the water.

"But if the boat's there, where on earth's *she*?" my colleague anxiously asked.

"That's exactly what we must learn." And I started to walk further.

"By going all the way round?"

"Certainly, far as it is. It will take us but ten minutes, but it's far enough to have made the child prefer not to walk. She went straight over."

"Laws!" cried my friend again; the chain of my logic was ever too much for her. It dragged her at my heels even now, and when we had got half-way round—a devious, tiresome process, on ground much broken and by a path choked with overgrowth—I paused to give her breath. I sustained her with a grateful arm, assuring her that she might hugely help me; and this started us afresh, so that in the course of but few minutes more we reached a point from which we found the boat to be where I had supposed it. It had been intentionally left as much as possible out of sight and was tied to one of the stakes of a fence that came, just there, down to the brink and that had been an assistance to disembarking. I recognised, as I looked at the pair of short, thick oars, quite safely drawn up, the prodigious character of the feat for a little girl; but I had lived, by this time, too long among wonders and had panted to too many livelier measures. There was a gate in the fence, through which we passed, and that brought us, after a trifling interval, more into the open. Then, "There she is!" we both exclaimed at once.

Flora, a short way off, stood before us on the grass and smiled as if her performance was now complete. The next thing she did, however, was to stoop straight down and pluck—quite as if it were all she was there for—a big, ugly spray of withered fern. I instantly became sure she had just come out of the copse. She waited for us, not herself taking a step, and I was conscious of the rare solemnity with which we presently approached her. She smiled and smiled, and we met; but it was all done in a silence by this time flagrantly ominous. Mrs. Grose was the first to break the spell: she threw herself on her knees and, drawing the child to her breast, clasped in a long embrace the little tender, yielding body. While this dumb convulsion lasted I could only watch it—which I did the more intently when I saw Flora's face peep at me over our companion's shoulder. It was serious now—the flicker had left it; but it strengthened the pang with which I at that moment envied Mrs. Grose the simplicity of *her* relation. Still, all this while, nothing more passed between us save that Flora had let her foolish fern again drop to the ground. What she and I had virtually said to each other was that pretexts were useless now. When Mrs. Grose finally got up she kept the child's hand, so that the two were still before me; and the singular reticence of our communion was even more marked in the frank look she launched me. "I'll be hanged," it said, "if *I'll* speak!"

It was Flora who, gazing all over me in candid wonder, was the first. She was struck with our bareheaded aspect. "Why, where are your things?"

"Where yours are, my dear!" I promptly returned.

Henry James

She had already got back her gaiety, and appeared to take this as an answer quite sufficient. "And where's Miles?" she went on.

There was something in the small valour of it that quite finished me: these three words from her were, in a flash like the glitter of a drawn blade, the jostle of the cup that my hand, for weeks and weeks, had held high and full to the brim and that now, even before speaking, I felt overflow in a deluge. "I'll tell you if you'll tell *me*——" I heard myself say, then heard the tremor in which it broke.

"Well, what?"

Mrs. Grose's suspense blazed at me, but it was too late now, and I brought the thing out handsomely. "Where, my pet, is Miss Jessel?"

XX

JUST as in the churchyard with Miles, the whole thing was upon us. Much as I had made of the fact that this name had never once, between us, been sounded, the quick, smitten glare with which the child's face now received it fairly likened my breach of the silence to the smash of a pane of glass. It added to the interposing cry, as if to stay the blow, that Mrs. Grose, at the same instant, uttered over my violence—the shriek of a creature scared, or rather wounded, which, in turn, within a few seconds, was completed by a gasp of my own. I seized my colleague's arm. "She's there, she's there!"

Miss Jessel stood before us on the opposite bank exactly as she had stood the other time, and I remember, strangely, as the first feeling now produced in me, my thrill of joy at having brought on a proof. She was there, and I was justified; she was there, and I was neither cruel nor mad. She was there for poor scared Mrs. Grose, but she was there most for Flora; and no moment of my monstrous time was perhaps so extraordinary as that in which I consciously threw out to her—with the sense that, pale and ravenous demon as she was, she would catch and understand it—an inarticulate message of gratitude. She rose erect on the spot my friend and I had lately quitted, and there was not,

105

in all the long reach of her desire, an inch of her evil that fell short. This first vividness of vision and emotion were things of a few seconds, during which Mrs. Grose's dazed blink across to where I pointed struck me as a sovereign sign that she too at last saw, just as it carried my own eyes precipitately to the child. The revelation then of the manner in which Flora was affected startled me, in truth, far more than it would have done to find her also merely agitated, for direct dismay was of course not what I had expected. Prepared and on her guard as our pursuit had actually made her, she would repress every betrayal; and I was therefore shaken, on the spot, by my first glimpse of the particular one for which I had not allowed. To see her, without a convulsion of her small pink face, not even feign to glance in the direction of the prodigy I announced, but only, instead of that, turn at *me* an expression of hard, still gravity, an expression absolutely new and unprecedented and that appeared to read and accuse and judge me—this was a stroke that somehow converted the little girl herself into the very presence that could make me quail. I quailed even though my certitude that she thoroughly saw was never greater than at that instant, and in the immediate need to defend myself I called it passionately to witness. "She's there, you little unhappy thing— there, there, *there*, and you see her as well as you see me!" I had said shortly before to Mrs. Grose that she was not at these times a child, but an old, old woman, and that description of her could not have been more strikingly confirmed than in the way in which, for all answer to this, she simply showed me, without a concession, an admission, of her eyes, a countenance of deeper and deeper, of indeed suddenly quite fixed, reprobation. I was by this time— if I can put the whole thing at all together—more appalled at what I may properly call her manner than at anything else, though it was simultaneously with this that I became aware of having Mrs. Grose also, and very formidably, to reckon with. My elder companion, the next moment, at any rate, blotted out everything but her own flushed face and her loud, shocked protest, a burst of high disapproval. "What a dreadful turn, to be sure, Miss! Where on earth do you see anything?"

I could only grasp her more quickly yet, for even while she spoke the hideous plain presence stood undimmed and undaunted. It had already lasted a minute, and it lasted while I continued, seizing my colleague, quite thrusting her at it and presenting her to it, to insist with my pointing hand. "You don't see her exactly as *we* see?—you mean to say you don't now—*now*? She's as big as a blazing fire! Only look, dearest woman, *look*——!" She looked, even as I did, and gave me, with her deep groan of negation, repulsion, compassion— the mixture with her pity of her relief at her exemption—a sense, touching to me even then, that she would have backed me up if she could. I might well have needed that, for with this hard blow of the proof that her eyes were hopelessly sealed I felt my own situation horribly crumble, I felt—I saw—my livid predecessor press, from her position, on my defeat, and I was conscious, more than all, of what I should have from this instant to deal with in the astounding little attitude of Flora. Into this attitude Mrs. Grose immediately and violently entered, breaking, even while there pierced through my sense of ruin a prodigious private triumph, into breathless reassurance.

"She isn't there, little lady, and nobody's there—and you never see nothing, my sweet! How can poor Miss Jessel—when poor Miss Jessel's dead and buried? *We* know, don't we, love?"—and she appealed, blundering in, to the child. "It's all a mere mistake and a worry and a joke—and we'll go home as fast as we can!"

Our companion, on this, had responded with a strange, quick primness of propriety, and they were again, with Mrs. Grose on her feet, united, as it were, in pained opposition to me. Flora continued to fix me with her small mask of reprobation, and even at that minute I prayed God to forgive me for seeming to see that, as she stood there holding tight to our friend's dress, her incomparable childish beauty had suddenly failed, had quite vanished. I've said it already—she was literally, she was hideously, hard; she had turned common and almost ugly. "I don't know what you mean. I see nobody. I see nothing. I never *have*. I think you're cruel. I don't like you!" Then, after this deliverance, which might have been that of a vulgarly pert little girl in the street, she hugged Mrs. Grose more closely and buried in her skirts the dreadful little face. In this position she produced an almost furious wail. "Take me away, take me away—oh, take me away from *her*!"

"From *me*?" I panted.

"From you—from you!" she cried.

Even Mrs. Grose looked across at me dismayed, while I had nothing to do but communicate again with the figure that, on the opposite bank, without a movement, as rigidly still as if catching, beyond the interval, our voices, was as vividly there for my disaster as it was not there for my service. The wretched child had spoken exactly as if she had got from some outside source each of her stabbing little words, and I could therefore, in the full despair of all I had to accept, but sadly shake my head at her. "If I had ever doubted, all my doubt would at present have gone. I've been living with the miserable truth, and now it has only too much closed round me. Of course I've lost you: I've interfered, and you've seen—under *her* dictation"—with which I faced, over the pool again, our infernal witness—"the easy and perfect way to meet it. I've done my best, but I've lost you. Good-bye." For Mrs. Grose I had an imperative, an almost frantic "Go, go!" before which, in infinite distress, but mutely possessed of the little girl and clearly convinced, in spite of her blindness, that something awful had occurred and some collapse engulfed us, she retreated, by the way we had come, as fast as she could move.

Of what first happened when I was left alone I had no subsequent memory. I only knew that at the end of, I suppose, a quarter of an hour, an odorous dampness and roughness, chilling and piercing my trouble, had made me understand that I must have thrown myself, on my face, on the ground and given way to a wildness of grief. I must have lain there long and cried and sobbed, for when I raised my head the day was almost done. I got up and looked a moment, through the twilight, at the grey pool and its blank, haunted edge, and then I took, back to the house, my dreary and difficult course. When I reached the gate in the fence the boat, to my surprise, was gone, so that I had a fresh reflection to make on Flora's extraordinary command of the situation. She passed that night, by the most tacit, and I should add, were not the word so grotesque a false note, the happiest of arrangements, with Mrs. Grose. I saw neither of them on my return, but, on the other hand, as by an ambiguous compensation, I saw a great deal of Miles. I saw—I can use no other phrase—so much of him that it was as if it were more than it had ever been. No evening I had passed at Bly had the portentous quality of this one; in spite of which—and in spite also of the deeper depths of consternation that had opened beneath my feet— there was literally, in the ebbing actual, an extraordinarily sweet sadness. On reaching the house I had never so much as looked for the boy; I had simply gone straight to my room to change what I was wearing and to take in, at a glance, much material testimony to Flora's rupture. Her little belongings had all been removed. When later, by the schoolroom fire, I was served with tea by the usual maid, I indulged, on the article of my other pupil, in no inquiry whatever. He had his freedom now—he might have it to the end! Well, he did have it; and it consisted—in part at least—of his coming in at about eight o'clock and sitting down with me in silence. On the removal of the tea-things I had blown out the candles and drawn my chair closer: I was conscious of a mortal coldness and felt as if I should never again be warm. So, when he appeared, I was sitting in the glow with my thoughts. He paused a moment by the door as if to look at me; then—as if to share them—came to the other side of the hearth and sank into a chair. We sat there in absolute stillness; yet he wanted, I felt, to be with me.

XXI

BEFORE a new day, in my room, had fully broken, my eyes opened to Mrs. Grose, who had come to my bedside with worse news. Flora was so markedly feverish that an illness was perhaps at hand; she had passed a night of extreme unrest, a night agitated above all by fears that had for their subject not in the least her former, but wholly her present, governess. It was not against the possible re-entrance of Miss Jessel on the scene that she protested—it was conspicuously and passionately against mine. I was promptly on my feet of course, and with an immense deal to ask; the more that my friend had discernibly now girded her loins to meet me once more. This I felt as soon as I had put to her the question of her sense of the child's sincerity as against my own. "She persists in denying to you that she saw, or has ever seen, anything?"

My visitor's trouble, truly, was great. "Ah, Miss, it isn't a matter on which I can push her! Yet it isn't either, I must say, as if I much needed to. It has made her, every inch of her, quite old."

"Oh, I see her perfectly from here. She resents, for all the world like some high little personage, the imputation on her truthfulness and, as it were, her respectability. 'Miss Jessel indeed—*she*!' Ah, she's 'respectable,' the chit! The impression she gave me there yesterday was, I assure you, the very strangest of all; it was quite beyond any of the others. I *did* put my foot in it! She'll never speak to me again."

Hideous and obscure as it all was, it held Mrs. Grose briefly silent; then she granted my point with a frankness which, I made sure, had more behind it. "I think indeed, Miss, she never will. She do have a grand manner about it!"

"And that manner"—I summed it up—"is practically what's the matter with her now!"

Oh, that manner, I could see in my visitor's face, and not a little else besides! "She asks me every three minutes if I think you're coming in."

"I see—I see." I too, on my side, had so much more than worked it out. "Has she said to you since yesterday—except to repudiate her familiarity with anything so dreadful—a single other word about Miss Jessel?"

"Not one, Miss. And of course you know," my friend added, "I took it from her, by the lake, that, just then and there at least, there *was* nobody."

"Rather! And, naturally, you take it from her still."

"I don't contradict her. What else can I do?"

"Nothing in the world! You've the cleverest little person to deal with. They've made them—their two friends, I mean—still cleverer even than nature did; for it was wondrous material to play on! Flora has now her grievance, and she'll work it to the end."

"Yes, Miss; but to *what* end?"

"Why, that of dealing with me to her uncle. She'll make me out to him the lowest creature——!"

I winced at the fair show of the scene in Mrs. Grose's face; she looked for a minute as if she sharply saw them together. "And him who thinks so well of you!"

"He has an odd way—it comes over me now," I laughed, "—of proving it! But that doesn't matter. What Flora wants, of course, is to get rid of me."

My companion bravely concurred. "Never again to so much as look at you."

"So that what you've come to me now for," I asked, "is to speed me on my way?" Before she had time to reply, however, I had her in check. "I've a better idea—the result of my reflections. My going *would* seem the right thing, and on Sunday I was terribly near it. Yet that won't do. It's *you* who must go. You must take Flora."

My visitor, at this, did speculate. "But where in the world——?"

"Away from here. Away from *them*. Away, even most of all, now, from me. Straight to her uncle."

"Only to tell on you——?"

"No, not 'only'! To leave me, in addition, with my remedy."

She was still vague. "And what *is* your remedy?"

"Your loyalty, to begin with. And then Miles's."

She looked at me hard. "Do you think he——?"

"Won't if he has the chance, turn on me? Yes, I venture still to think it. At all events, I want to try. Get off with his sister as soon as possible and leave me with him alone." I was amazed, myself, at the spirit I had still in reserve, and therefore perhaps a trifle the more disconcerted at the way in which, in spite of this fine example of it, she hesitated. "There's one thing, of course," I went on: "they mustn't, before she goes, see each other for three seconds."

Then it came over me that, in spite of Flora's presumable sequestration from the instant of her return from the pool, it might already be too late. "Do you mean," I anxiously asked, "that they *have* met?"

At this she quite flushed. "Ah, Miss, I'm not such a fool as that! If I've been obliged to leave her three or four times, it has been each time with one of the maids, and at present, though she's alone, she's locked in safe. And yet—and yet!" There were too many things.

"And yet what?"

"Well, are you so sure of the little gentleman?"

"I'm not sure of anything but *you*. But I have, since last evening, a new hope. I think he wants to give me an opening. I do believe that—poor little exquisite wretch!—he wants to speak. Last evening, in the firelight and the silence, he sat with me for two hours as if it were just coming."

Mrs. Grose looked hard, through the window, at the grey, gathering day. "And did it come?"

"No, though I waited and waited, I confess it didn't, and it was without a breach of the silence or so much as a faint allusion to his sister's condition and absence that we at last kissed for good-night. All the same," I continued, "I can't, if her uncle sees her, consent to his seeing her brother without my having given the boy—and most of all because things have got so bad—a little more time."

My friend appeared on this ground more reluctant than I could quite understand. "What do you mean by more time?"

"Well, a day or two—really to bring it out. He'll then be on *my* side—of which you see the importance. If nothing comes, I shall only fail, and you will, at the worst, have helped me by doing, on your arrival in town, whatever you may have found possible." So I put it before her, but she continued for a little so inscrutably embarrassed that I came again to her aid. "Unless, indeed," I wound up, "you really want *not* to go."

I could see it, in her face, at last clear itself; she put out her hand to me as a pledge. "I'll go—I'll go. I'll go this morning."

I wanted to be very just. "If you *should* wish still to wait, I would engage she shouldn't see me."

"No, no: it's the place itself. She must leave it." She held me a moment with heavy eyes, then brought out the rest. "Your idea's the right one. I myself, Miss——"

"Well?"

"I can't stay."

The look she gave me with it made me jump at possibilities. "You mean that, since yesterday, you *have* seen——?"

She shook her head with dignity. "I've *heard*——!"

"Heard?"

"From that child—horrors! There!" she sighed with tragic relief. "On my honour, Miss, she says things——!" But at this evocation she broke down; she dropped, with a sudden sob, upon my sofa and, as I had seen her do before, gave way to all the grief of it.

It was quite in another manner that I, for my part, let myself go. "Oh, thank God!"

She sprang up again at this, drying her eyes with a groan. "'Thank God'?"

"It so justifies me!"

"It does that, Miss!"

I couldn't have desired more emphasis, but I just hesitated. "She's so horrible?"

I saw my colleague scarce knew how to put it. "Really shocking."

"And about me?"

113

"About you, Miss—since you must have it. It's beyond everything, for a young lady; and I can't think wherever she must have picked up——"

"The appalling language she applied to me? I can, then!" I broke in with a laugh that was doubtless significant enough.

It only, in truth, left my friend still more grave. "Well, perhaps I ought to also—since I've heard some of it before! Yet I can't bear it," the poor woman went on while, with the same movement, she glanced, on my dressing-table, at the face of my watch. "But I must go back."

I kept her, however. "Ah, if you can't bear it——!"

"How can I stop with her, you mean? Why, just *for* that: to get her away. Far from this," she pursued, "far from *them*——"

"She may be different? she may be free?" I seized her almost with joy. "Then, in spite of yesterday, you *believe*——"

"In such doings?" Her simple description of them required, in the light of her expression, to be carried no further, and she gave me the whole thing as she had never done. "I believe."

Yes, it was a joy, and we were still shoulder to shoulder: if I might continue sure of that I should care but little what else happened. My support in the presence of disaster would be the same as it had been in my early need of confidence, and if my friend would answer for my honesty, I would answer for all the rest. On the point of taking leave of her, none the less, I was to some extent embarrassed. "There's one thing of course—it occurs to me—to remember. My letter, giving the alarm, will have reached town before you."

I now perceived still more how she had been beating about the bush and how weary at last it had made her. "Your letter won't have got there. Your letter never went."

"What then became of it?"

"Goodness knows! Master Miles——"

114

"Do you mean *he* took it?" I gasped.

She hung fire, but she overcame her reluctance. "I mean that I saw yesterday, when I came back with Miss Flora, that it wasn't where you had put it. Later in the evening I had the chance to question Luke, and he declared that he had neither noticed nor touched it." We could only exchange, on this, one of our deeper mutual soundings, and it was Mrs. Grose who first brought up the plumb with an almost elate "You see!"

"Yes, I see that if Miles took it instead he probably will have read it and destroyed it."

"And don't you see anything else?"

I faced her a moment with a sad smile. "It strikes me that by this time your eyes are open even wider than mine."

They proved to be so indeed, but she could still blush, almost, to show it. "I make out now what he must have done at school." And she gave, in her simple sharpness, an almost droll disillusioned nod. "He stole!"

I turned it over—I tried to be more judicial. "Well—perhaps."

She looked as if she found me unexpectedly calm. "He stole *letters!*"

She couldn't know my reasons for a calmness after all pretty shallow; so I showed them off as I might. "I hope then it was to more purpose than in this case! The note, at any rate, that I put on the table yesterday," I pursued, "will have given him so scant an advantage—for it contained only the bare demand for an interview—that he is already much ashamed of having gone so far for so little, and that what he had on his mind last evening was precisely the need of confession." I seemed to myself, for the instant, to have mastered it, to see it all. "Leave us, leave us"—I was already, at the door, hurrying her off. "I'll get it out of him. He'll meet me—he'll confess. If he confesses, he's saved. And if he's saved——"

"Then *you* are?" The dear woman kissed me on this, and I took her farewell. "I'll save you without him!" she cried as she went.

XXII

YET it was when she had got off—and I missed her on the spot—that the great pinch really came. If I had counted on what it would give me to find myself alone with Miles, I speedily perceived, at least, that it would give me a measure. No hour of my stay in fact was so assailed with apprehensions as that of my coming down to learn that the carriage containing Mrs. Grose and my younger pupil had already rolled out of the gates. Now I *was*, I said to myself, face to face with the elements, and for much of the rest of the day, while I fought my weakness, I could consider that I had been supremely rash. It was a tighter place still than I had yet turned round in; all the more that, for the first time, I could see in the aspect of others a confused reflection of the crisis. What had happened naturally caused them all to stare; there was too little of the explained, throw out whatever we might, in the suddenness of my colleague's act. The maids and the men looked blank; the effect of which on my nerves was an aggravation until I saw the necessity of making it a positive aid. It was precisely, in short, by just clutching the helm that I avoided total wreck; and I dare say that, to bear up at all, I became, that morning, very grand and very dry. I welcomed the consciousness that I was charged with much to do, and I caused it to be known as well that, left thus to myself, I was quite remarkably firm. I wandered with that manner, for the next hour or two, all over the place and looked, I have no doubt, as if I were ready for any onset. So, for the benefit of whom it might concern, I paraded with a sick heart.

The person it appeared least to concern proved to be, till dinner, little Miles himself. My perambulations had given me, meanwhile, no glimpse of him, but they had tended to make more public the change taking place in our relation as a consequence of his having at the piano, the day before, kept me, in Flora's interest, so beguiled and befooled. The stamp of publicity had of course been fully given by her confinement and departure, and the change itself was now ushered in by our non-observance of the regular custom of the schoolroom. He had already disappeared when, on my way down, I pushed open his door, and I learned below that he had breakfasted—in the presence of a couple of the maids—with Mrs. Grose and his sister. He had then gone out, as he said, for a stroll; than which nothing, I reflected, could better have expressed his frank view of the abrupt transformation of my office. What he would now permit this office to consist of was yet to be settled: there was a queer relief, at all events—I mean for myself in especial—in the renouncement of one pretension. If so much had sprung to the surface, I scarce put it too strongly in saying that what had perhaps sprung highest was the absurdity of our prolonging the fiction that I had anything more to teach him. It sufficiently stuck out that, by tacit little tricks in which even more than myself he carried out the care for my dignity, I had had to appeal to him to let me off straining to meet him on the ground of his true capacity. He had at any rate his freedom now; I was never to touch it again; as I had amply shown, moreover, when, on his joining me in the schoolroom the previous night, I had uttered, on the subject of the interval just concluded, neither challenge nor hint. I had too much, from this moment, my other ideas. Yet when he at last arrived the difficulty of applying them, the accumulations of my problem, were brought straight home to me by the beautiful little presence on which what had occurred had as yet, for the eye, dropped neither stain nor shadow.

To mark, for the house, the high state I cultivated I decreed that my meals with the boy should be served, as we called it, downstairs; so that I had been awaiting him in the ponderous pomp of the room outside of the window of which I had had from Mrs. Grose, that first scared Sunday, my flash of something it would scarce have done to call light. Here at present I felt afresh—for I had felt it again and again—how my equilibrium depended on the success of my rigid will, the will to shut my eyes as tight as possible to the truth that what I had to deal with was, revoltingly, against nature. I could only get on at all by taking "nature" into my confidence and my account, by treating my monstrous ordeal as a push in a direction unusual, of course, and unpleasant, but demanding, after all, for a fair front, only another turn of the screw of ordinary human virtue. No attempt, none the less, could well require more tact than just this attempt to supply, one's self, *all* the nature. How could I put even a little of that article into a suppression of reference to what had occurred? How, on the other hand, could I make a reference without a new plunge into the hideous obscure? Well, a sort of answer, after a time, had come to me, and it was so far confirmed as that I was met, incontestably, by the quickened vision of what was rare in my little companion. It was indeed as if he had found even now—as he had so often found at lessons—still some other delicate way to ease me off. Wasn't there light in the fact which, as we shared our solitude, broke out with a specious glitter it had never yet quite worn?—the fact that (opportunity aiding, precious opportunity which had now come) it would be preposterous, with a child so endowed, to forgo the help one might wrest from absolute intelligence? What had his intelligence been given him for but to save him? Mightn't one, to reach his mind, risk the stretch of an angular arm over his character? It was as if, when we were face to face in the dining-room, he had literally shown me the way. The roast mutton was on the table, and I had dispensed with attendance. Miles, before he sat down, stood a moment with his hands in his pockets and looked at the joint, on which he seemed on the point of passing some humorous judgment. But what he presently produced was: "I say, my dear, is she really very awfully ill?"

"Little Flora? Not so bad but that she'll presently be better. London will set her up. Bly had ceased to agree with her. Come here and take your mutton."

He alertly obeyed me, carried the plate carefully to his seat, and, when he was established, went on. "Did Bly disagree with her so terribly suddenly?"

"Not so suddenly as you might think. One had seen it coming on."

"Then why didn't you get her off before?"

"Before what?"

"Before she became too ill to travel."

I found myself prompt. "She's *not* too ill to travel: she only might have become so if she had stayed. This was just the moment to seize. The journey will dissipate the influence"—oh, I was grand!—"and carry it off."

"I see, I see"—Miles, for that matter, was grand too. He settled to his repast with the charming little "table manner" that, from the day of his arrival, had relieved me of all grossness of admonition. Whatever he had been driven from school for, it was not for ugly feeding. He was irreproachable, as always, today; but he was unmistakeably more conscious. He was discernibly trying to take for granted more things than he found, without assistance, quite easy; and he dropped into peaceful silence while he felt his situation. Our meal was of the briefest—mine a vain pretence, and I had the things immediately removed. While this was done Miles stood again with his hands in his little pockets and his back to me—stood and looked out of the wide window through which, that other day, I had seen what pulled me up. We continued silent while the maid was with us—as silent, it whimsically occurred to me, as some young couple who, on their wedding-journey, at the inn, feel shy in the presence of the waiter. He turned round only when the waiter had left us. "Well—so we're alone!"

XXIII

"Oh, more or less." I fancy my smile was pale. "Not absolutely. We shouldn't like that!" I went on.

"No—I suppose we shouldn't. Of course we have the others."

"We have the others—we have indeed the others," I concurred.

"Yet even though we have them," he returned, still with his hands in his pockets and planted there in front of me, "they don't much count, do they?"

I made the best of it, but I felt wan. "It depends on what you call 'much'!"

"Yes"—with all accommodation—"everything depends!" On this, however, he faced to the window again and presently reached it with his vague, restless, cogitating step. He remained there awhile, with his forehead against the glass, in contemplation of the stupid shrubs I knew and the dull things of November. I had always my hypocrisy of "work," behind which, now, I gained the sofa. Steadying myself with it there as I had repeatedly done at those moments of torment that I have described as the moments of my knowing the children to be given to something from which I was barred, I sufficiently obeyed my habit of being prepared for the worst. But an extraordinary impression dropped on me as I extracted a meaning from the boy's embarrassed back—none other than the impression that I was not barred now. This inference grew in a few minutes to sharp intensity and seemed bound up with the direct perception that it was positively *he* who was. The frames and squares of the great window were a kind of image, for him, of a kind of failure. I felt that I saw him, at any rate, shut in or shut out. He was admirable, but not comfortable: I took it in with a throb of hope. Wasn't he looking, through the haunted pane, for something he couldn't see?—and wasn't it the first time in the whole business that he had known such a lapse? The first, the very first: I found it a splendid portent. It made him anxious, though he watched himself; he had been anxious all day and, even while in his usual sweet little manner he sat at table, had needed all his small strange genius to give it a gloss. When he at last turned round to meet me, it was almost as if this genius had succumbed. "Well, I think I'm glad Bly agrees with *me*!"

"You would certainly seem to have seen, these twenty-four hours, a good deal more of it than for some time before. I hope," I went on bravely, "that you've been enjoying yourself."

"Oh, yes, I've been ever so far; all round about—miles and miles away. I've never been so free."

He had really a manner of his own, and I could only try to keep up with him. "Well, do you like it?"

He stood there smiling; then at last he put into two words—"Do *you*?"—more discrimination than I had ever heard two words contain. Before I had time to deal with that, however, he continued as if with the sense that this was an impertinence to be softened. "Nothing could be more charming than the way you take it, for of course if we're alone together now it's you that are alone most. But I hope," he threw in, "you don't particularly mind!"

"Having to do with you?" I asked. "My dear child, how can I help minding? Though I've renounced all claim to your company,—you're so beyond me,—I at least greatly enjoy it. What else should I stay on for?"

He looked at me more directly, and the expression of his face, graver now, struck me as the most beautiful I had ever found in it. "You stay on just for *that*?"

"Certainly. I stay on as your friend and from the tremendous interest I take in you till something can be done for you that may be more worth your while. That needn't surprise you." My voice trembled so that I felt it impossible to suppress the shake. "Don't you remember how I told you, when I came and sat on your bed the night of the storm, that there was nothing in the world I wouldn't do for you?"

"Yes, yes!" He, on his side, more and more visibly nervous, had a tone to master; but he was so much more successful than I that, laughing out through his gravity, he could pretend we were pleasantly jesting. "Only that, I think, was to get me to do something for *you*!"

"It was partly to get you to do something," I conceded. "But, you know, you didn't do it."

"Oh, yes," he said with the brightest superficial eagerness, "you wanted me to tell you something."

"That's it. Out, straight out. What you have on your mind, you know."

"Ah, then, is *that* what you've stayed over for?"

He spoke with a gaiety through which I could still catch the finest little quiver of resentful passion; but I can't begin to express the effect upon me of an implication of surrender even so faint. It was as if what I had yearned for had come at last only to astonish me. "Well, yes—I may as well make a clean breast of it. It was precisely for that."

He waited so long that I supposed it for the purpose of repudiating the assumption on which my action had been founded; but what he finally said was: "Do you mean now—here?"

"There couldn't be a better place or time." He looked round him uneasily, and I had the rare—oh, the queer!—impression of the very first symptom I had seen in him of the approach of immediate fear. It was as if he were suddenly afraid of me—which struck me indeed as perhaps the best thing to make him. Yet in the very pang of the effort I felt it vain to try sternness, and I heard myself the next instant so gentle as to be almost grotesque. "You want so to go out again?"

"Awfully!" He smiled at me heroically, and the touching little bravery of it was enhanced by his actually flushing with pain. He had picked up his hat, which he had brought in, and stood twirling it in a way that gave me, even as I was just nearly reaching port, a perverse horror of what I was doing. To do it in *any* way was an act of violence, for what did it consist of but the obtrusion of the idea of grossness and guilt on a small helpless creature who had been for me a revelation of the possibilities of beautiful intercourse? Wasn't it base to create for a being so exquisite a mere alien awkwardness? I suppose I now read into our situation a clearness it couldn't have had at the time, for I seem to see our poor eyes already lighted with some spark of a prevision of the anguish that was to come. So we circled about, with terrors and scruples, like fighters not daring to close. But it was for each other we feared! That kept us a little longer suspended and unbruised. "I'll tell you everything," Miles said—"I mean I'll tell you anything you like. You'll stay on with me, and we shall both be all right and I *will* tell you—I *will*. But not now."

"Why not now?"

My insistence turned him from me and kept him once more at his window in a silence during which, between us, you might have heard a pin drop. Then he was before me again with the air of a person for whom, outside, someone who had frankly to be reckoned with was waiting. "I have to see Luke."

I had not yet reduced him to quite so vulgar a lie, and I felt proportionately ashamed. But, horrible as it was, his lies made up my truth. I achieved thoughtfully a few loops of my knitting. "Well, then, go to Luke, and I'll wait for what you promise. Only, in return for that, satisfy, before you leave me, one very much smaller request."

He looked as if he felt he had succeeded enough to be able still a little to bargain. "Very much smaller——?"

"Yes, a mere fraction of the whole. Tell me"—oh, my work preoccupied me, and I was off-hand!—"if, yesterday afternoon, from the table in the hall, you took, you know, my letter."

XXIV

My sense of how he received this suffered for a minute from something that I can describe only as a fierce split of my attention—a stroke that at first, as I sprang straight up, reduced me to the mere blind movement of getting hold of him, drawing him close, and, while I just fell for support against the nearest piece of furniture, instinctively keeping him with his back to the window. The appearance was full upon us that I had already had to deal with here: Peter Quint had come into view like a sentinel before a prison. The next thing I saw was that, from outside, he had reached the window, and then I knew that, close to the glass and glaring in through it, he offered once more to the room his white face of damnation. It represents but grossly what took place within me at the sight to say that on the second my decision was made; yet I believe that no woman so overwhelmed ever in so short a time recovered her grasp of the *act*. It came to me in the very horror of the immediate presence that the act would be, seeing and facing what I saw and faced, to keep the boy himself unaware. The inspiration—I can call it by no other name—was that I felt how voluntarily, how transcendently, I *might*. It was like fighting with a demon for a human soul, and when I had fairly so appraised it I saw how the human soul—held out, in the tremor of my hands, at arm's length—had a perfect dew of sweat on a lovely childish forehead. The face that was close to mine was as white as the face against the glass, and out of it presently came a sound, not low nor weak, but as if from much further away, that I drank like a waft of fragrance.

"Yes—I took it."

At this, with a moan of joy, I enfolded, I drew him close; and while I held him to my breast, where I could feel in the sudden fever of his little body the tremendous pulse of his little heart, I kept my eyes on the thing at the window and saw it move and shift its posture. I have likened it to a sentinel, but its slow wheel, for a moment, was rather the prowl of a baffled beast. My present quickened courage, however, was such that, not too much to let it through, I had to shade, as it were, my flame. Meanwhile the glare of the face was again at the window, the scoundrel fixed as if to watch and wait. It was the very confidence that I might now defy him, as well as the positive certitude, by this time, of the child's unconsciousness, that made me go on. "What did you take it for?"

"To see what you said about me."

"You opened the letter?"

"I opened it."

My eyes were now, as I held him off a little again, on Miles's own face, in which the collapse of mockery showed me how complete was the ravage of uneasiness. What was prodigious was that at last, by my success, his sense was sealed and his communication stopped: he knew that he was in presence, but knew not of what, and knew still less that I also was and that I did know. And what did this strain of trouble matter when my eyes went back to the window only to see that the air was clear again and—by my personal triumph—the influence quenched? There was nothing there. I felt that the cause was mine and that I should surely get *all*. "And you found nothing!"—I let my elation out.

He gave the most mournful, thoughtful little headshake. "Nothing."

"Nothing, nothing!" I almost shouted in my joy.

"Nothing, nothing," he sadly repeated.

I kissed his forehead; it was drenched. "So what have you done with it?"

"I've burnt it."

"Burnt it?" It was now or never. "Is that what you did at school?"

Oh, what this brought up! "At school?"

"Did you take letters?—or other things?"

"Other things?" He appeared now to be thinking of something far off and that reached him only through the pressure of his anxiety. Yet it did reach him. "Did I *steal*?"

I felt myself redden to the roots of my hair as well as wonder if it were more strange to put to a gentleman such a question or to see him take it with allowances that gave the very distance of his fall in the world. "Was it for that you mightn't go back?"

The only thing he felt was rather a dreary little surprise. "Did you know I mightn't go back?"

"I know everything."

He gave me at this the longest and strangest look. "Everything?"

"Everything. Therefore *did* you——?" But I couldn't say it again.

Miles could, very simply. "No. I didn't steal."

My face must have shown him I believed him utterly; yet my hands— but it was for pure tenderness—shook him as if to ask him why, if it was all for nothing, he had condemned me to months of torment. "What then did you do?"

He looked in vague pain all round the top of the room and drew his breath, two or three times over, as if with difficulty. He might have been standing at the bottom of the sea and raising his eyes to some faint green twilight. "Well—I said things."

"Only that?"

"They thought it was enough!"

"To turn you out for?"

125

Never, truly, had a person "turned out" shown so little to explain it as this little person! He appeared to weigh my question, but in a manner quite detached and almost helpless. "Well, I suppose I oughtn't."

"But to whom did you say them?"

He evidently tried to remember, but it dropped—he had lost it. "I don't know!"

He almost smiled at me in the desolation of his surrender, which was indeed practically, by this time, so complete that I ought to have left it there. But I was infatuated—I was blind with victory, though even then the very effect that was to have brought him so much nearer was already that of added separation. "Was it to everyone?" I asked.

"No; it was only to——" But he gave a sick little headshake. "I don't remember their names."

"Were they then so many?"

"No—only a few. Those I liked."

Those he liked? I seemed to float not into clearness, but into a darker obscure, and within a minute there had come to me out of my very pity the appalling alarm of his being perhaps innocent. It was for the instant confounding and bottomless, for if he *were* innocent, what then on earth was *I*? Paralysed, while it lasted, by the mere brush of the question, I let him go a little, so that, with a deep-drawn sigh, he turned away from me again; which, as he faced toward the clear window, I suffered, feeling that I had nothing now there to keep him from. "And did they repeat what you said?" I went on after a moment.

He was soon at some distance from me, still breathing hard and again with the air, though now without anger for it, of being confined against his will. Once more, as he had done before, he looked up at the dim day as if, of what had hitherto sustained him, nothing was left but an unspeakable anxiety. "Oh, yes," he nevertheless replied—"they must have repeated them. To those *they* liked," he added.

There was, somehow, less of it than I had expected; but I turned it over. "And these things came round——?"

"To the masters? Oh, yes!" he answered very simply. "But I didn't know they'd tell."

"The masters? They didn't—they've never told. That's why I ask you."

He turned to me again his little beautiful fevered face. "Yes, it was too bad."

"Too bad?"

"What I suppose I sometimes said. To write home."

I can't name the exquisite pathos of the contradiction given to such a speech by such a speaker; I only know that the next instant I heard myself throw off with homely force: "Stuff and nonsense!" But the next after that I must have sounded stern enough. "What *were* these things?"

My sternness was all for his judge, his executioner; yet it made him avert himself again, and that movement made *me*, with a single bound and an irrepressible cry, spring straight upon him. For there again, against the glass, as if to blight his confession and stay his answer, was the hideous author of our woe—the white face of damnation. I felt a sick swim at the drop of my victory and all the return of my battle, so that the wildness of my veritable leap only served as a great betrayal. I saw him, from the midst of my act, meet it with a divination, and on the perception that even now he only guessed, and that the window was still to his own eyes free, I let the impulse flame up to convert the climax of his dismay into the very proof of his liberation. "No more, no more, no more!" I shrieked, as I tried to press him against me, to my visitant.

"Is she *here*?" Miles panted as he caught with his sealed eyes the direction of my words. Then as his strange "she" staggered me and, with a gasp, I echoed it, "Miss Jessel, Miss Jessel!" he with a sudden fury gave me back.

I seized, stupefied, his supposition—some sequel to what we had done to Flora, but this made me only want to show him that it was better still than that. "It's not Miss Jessel! But it's at the window—straight before us. It's *there*—the coward horror, there for the last time!"

At this, after a second in which his head made the movement of a baffled dog's on a scent and then gave a frantic little shake for air and light, he was at me in a white rage, bewildered, glaring vainly over the place and missing wholly, though it now, to my sense, filled the room like the taste of poison, the wide, overwhelming presence. "It's *he*?"

I was so determined to have all my proof that I flashed into ice to challenge him. "Whom do you mean by 'he'?"

"Peter Quint—you devil!" His face gave again, round the room, its convulsed supplication. "*Where?*"

They are in my ears still, his supreme surrender of the name and his tribute to my devotion. "What does he matter now, my own?—what will he *ever* matter? *I* have you," I launched at the beast, "but he has lost you for ever!" Then, for the demonstration of my work, "There, *there*!" I said to Miles.

But he had already jerked straight round, stared, glared again, and seen but the quiet day. With the stroke of the loss I was so proud of he uttered the cry of a creature hurled over an abyss, and the grasp with which I recovered him might have been that of catching him in his fall. I caught him, yes, I held him—it may be imagined with what a passion; but at the end of a minute I began to feel what it truly was that I held. We were alone with the quiet day, and his little heart, dispossessed, had stopped.

COVERING END

I

At the foot of the staircase he waited and listened, thinking he had heard her call to him from the gallery, high aloft but out of view, to which he had allowed her independent access and whence indeed, on her first going up, the sound of her appreciation had reached him in rapid movements, evident rushes and dashes, and in droll, charming cries that echoed through the place. He had afterwards, expectant and restless, been, for another look, to the house-door, and then had fidgeted back into the hall, where her voice again caught him. It was many a day since such a voice had sounded in those empty chambers, and never perhaps, in all the years, for poor Chivers, had any voice at all launched a note so friendly and so free.

"Oh, no, mum, there ain't no one whatever come yet. It's quite all right, mum,—you can please yourself!" If he left her to range, all his pensive little economy seemed to say, wasn't it just his poor pickings? He quitted the stairs, but stopped again, with his hand to his ear, as he heard her once more appeal to him. "Lots of lovely——? Lovely *what*, mum? Little ups and downs?" he quavered aloft. "Oh, as you say, mum: as many as in a poor man's life!" She was clearly disposed, as she roamed in delight from point to point, to continue to talk, and, with his better ear and his scooped hand, he continued to listen hard. "'Dear little crooked steps'? Yes, mum; please mind 'em, mum: they be cruel in the dark corners!" She appeared to take another of her light scampers, the sign of a fresh discovery and a fresh response; at which he felt his heart warm with the success of a trust of her that might after all have been rash. Once more her voice reached him and once more he gossiped back. "Coming up too? Not if you'll kindly indulge me, mum—I must be where I can watch the bell. It takes watching as well as hearing!"—he dropped, as he resumed his round, to a murmur of great patience. This was taken up the next moment by the husky plaint of the signal itself, which seemed to confess equally to short wind and creaking joints. It moved, however, distinguishably, and its motion made him start much more as if he had been guilty of sleeping at his post than as if he had waited half the day. "Mercy, if I *didn't* watch——!" He shuffled across the wide stone-paved hall and, losing himself beneath the great arch of the short passage to the entrance-front, hastened to admit his new visitor. He gives us thereby the use of his momentary absence for a look at the place he has left.

This is the central hall, high and square, brown and grey, flagged beneath and timbered above, of an old English country-house; an apartment in which a single survey is a perception of long and lucky continuities. It would have been difficult to find elsewhere anything at once so old and so actual, anything that had plainly come so far, far down without, at any moment of the endless journey, losing its way. To stand there and look round was to wonder a good deal—yet without arriving at an answer—whether it had been most neglected or most cherished; there was such resignation in its long survival and yet such bravery in its high polish. If it had never been spoiled, this was partly, no doubt, because it had been, for a century, given up; but what it had been given up to was, after all, homely and familiar use. It had in it at the present moment indeed much of the chill of fallen fortunes; but there was no concession in its humility and no hypocrisy in its welcome. It was magnificent and shabby, and the eyes of the dozen dark old portraits seemed, in their eternal attention, to count the cracks in the pavement, the rents in the seats of the chairs, and the missing tones in the Flemish tapestry. Above the tapestry, which, in its turn, was above the high oak wainscot, most of these stiff images—on the side on which it principally reigned—were placed; and they held up their heads to assure all comers that a tone or two was all that *was* missing, and that they had never waked up in winter dawns to any glimmer of bereavement, in the long night, of any relic or any feature. Such as it was, the company was all there; every inch of old oak, every yard of old arras, every object of ornament or of use to which these surfaces formed so rare a background. If the watchers on the walls had ever found a gap in their own rank, the ancient roof, of a certainty, would have been shaken by their collective gasp. As a matter of fact it was rich and firm—it had almost the dignity of the vault of a church. On this Saturday afternoon in August, a hot, still day, such of the casements as freely worked in the discoloured glass of the windows stood open in one quarter to a terrace that overlooked a park and in another to a wonderful old empty court that communicated with a wonderful old empty garden. The staircase, wide and straight, mounted, full in sight, to a landing that was half-way up; and on the right, as you faced this staircase, a door opened out of the brown panelling into a glimpse of a little morning-room, where, in a slanted, gilded light, there was brownness too, mixed with notes of old yellow. On the left, toward court and garden, another door stood open to the warm air. Still as you faced the staircase you had at your right, between that monument and the morning-room, the arch through which Chivers had disappeared.

His reappearance interrupts and yet in a manner, after all, quickens our intense impression; Chivers on the spot, and in this severe but spacious setting, was so perfect an image of immemorial domesticity. It would have been impossible perhaps, however, either to tell his age or to name his use: he was of the age of all the history that lurked in all the corners and of any use whatever you might be so good as still to find for him. Considerably shrunken and completely silvered, he had perpetual agreement in the droop of his kind white head and perpetual inquiry in the jerk of the idle old hands now almost covered by the sleeves of the black dress-coat which, twenty years before, must have been by a century or two the newest thing in the house and into which his years appeared to have declined very much as a shrunken family moves into a part of its habitation. This attire was completed by a white necktie that, in honour of the day, he himself had this morning done up. The humility he betrayed and the oddity he concealed were alike brought out by his juxtaposition with the gentleman he had admitted.

To admit Mr. Prodmore was anywhere and at any time, as you would immediately have recognised, an immense admission. He was a personage of great presence and weight, with a large smooth face in which a small sharp meaning was planted like a single pin in the tight red toilet-cushion of a guest-chamber. He wore a blue frock-coat and a stiff white waistcoat and a high white hat that he kept on his head with a kind of protesting cock, while in his buttonhole nestled a bold prize plant on which he occasionally lowered a proprietary eye that seemed to remind it of its being born to a public career. Mr. Prodmore's appearance had evidently been thought out, but it might have struck you that the old portraits took it in with a sterner stare, with a fixedness indeed in which a visitor more sensitive would have read a consciousness of his remaining, in their presence, so jauntily, so vulgarly covered. He had never a glance for them, and it would have been easy after a minute to see that this was an old story between them. Their manner, as it were, sensibly increased the coolness. This coolness became a high rigour as Mr. Prodmore encountered, from the very threshold, a disappointment.

"No one here?" he indignantly demanded.

"I'm sorry to say no one has come, sir," Chivers replied; "but I've had a telegram from Captain Yule."

Mr. Prodmore's apprehension flared out. "Not to say he ain't coming?"

"He was to take the 2.20 from Paddington; he certainly *should* be here!" The old man spoke as if his non-arrival were the most unaccountable thing in the world, especially for a poor person ever respectful of the mystery of causes.

"He should have been here this hour or more. And so should my fly-away daughter!"

Chivers surrounded this description of Miss Prodmore with the deep discretion of silence, and then, after a moment, evidently reflected that silence, in a world bestrewn with traps to irreverence, might be as rash as speech. "Were they coming—a—together, sir?"

He had scarcely mended the matter, for his visitor gave an inconsequent stare. "Together?—for what do you take Miss Prodmore?" This young lady's parent glared about him again as if to alight on something else that was out of place; but the good intentions expressed in the attitude of every object might presently have been presumed to soothe his irritation. It had at any rate the effect of bridging, for poor Chivers, some of his gaps. "It *is* in a sense true that their 'coming together,' as you call it, is exactly what I've made my plans for today: my calculation was that we should all punctually converge on this spot. Attended by her trusty maid, Miss Prodmore, who happens to be on a week's visit to her grandmother at Bellborough, was to take the 1.40 from that place. I was to drive over—ten miles—from the most convenient of my seats. Captain Yule"—the speaker wound up his statement as with the mention of the last touch in a masterpiece of his own sketching—"was finally to shake off for a few hours the peculiar occupations that engage him."

The old man listened with his head askance to favour his good ear, but his visible attention all on a sad spot in one of the half-dozen worn rugs. "They *must* be peculiar, sir, when a gentleman comes into a property like this and goes three months without so much as a nat'ral curiosity——! I don't speak of anything but what *is* nat'ral, sir; but there have *been* people here——"

"There have repeatedly been people here!" Mr. Prodmore complacently interrupted.

"As you say, sir—to be shown over. With the master himself never shown!" Chivers dismally commented.

"He *shall* be, so that nobody can miss him!" Mr. Prodmore, for his own reassurance as well, hastened to retort.

His companion risked a tiny explanation. "It will be a mercy indeed to look on him; but I meant that he has not been taken round."

"That's what I meant too. *I'll* take him—round and round: it's exactly what I've come for!" Mr. Prodmore rang out; and his eyes made the lower circuit again, looking as pleased as such a pair of eyes could look with nobody as yet quite good enough either to terrify or to tickle. "He can't fail to be affected, though he *has* been up to his neck in such a different class of thing."

Chivers clearly wondered awhile what class of thing it could be. Then he expressed a timid hope. "In nothing, I dare say, but what's right, sir——?"

"In everything," Mr. Prodmore distinctly informed him, "that's wrong! But here he is!" that gentleman added with elation as the doorbell again sounded. Chivers, under the double agitation of the appeal and the disclosure, proceeded to the front as fast as circumstances allowed; while Mr. Prodmore, left alone, would have been observed—had not his solitude been so bleak—to recover a degree of cheerfulness. Cheerfulness in solitude at Covering End was certainly not irresistible, but particular feelings and reasons had pitched, for their campaign, the starched, if now somewhat ruffled, tent of his large white waistcoat. If they had issued audibly from that pavilion, they would have represented to us his consciousness of the reinforcement he might bring up for attack should Captain Yule really resist the house. The sound he next heard from the front caused him none the less, for that matter, to articulate a certain drop. "Only Cora?—Well," he added in a tone somewhat at variance with his "only," "he shan't, at any rate, resist *her!*" This announcement would have quickened a spectator's interest in the young lady whom Chivers now introduced and followed, a young lady who straightway found herself the subject of traditionary discipline. "I've waited. What do you mean?"

Cora Prodmore, who had a great deal of colour in her cheeks and a great deal more—a bold variety of kinds—in the extremely high pitch of her new, smart clothes, meant, on the whole, it was easy to see, very little, and met this challenge with still less show of support either from the sources I have mentioned or from any others. A dull, fresh, honest, overdressed damsel of two-and-twenty, she was too much out of breath, too much flurried and frightened, to do more than stammer: "Waited, papa? Oh, I'm sorry!"

Her regret appeared to strike her father still more as an impertinence than as a vanity. "Would you then, if I had not had patience for you, have wished not to find me? Why the dickens are you so late?"

Agitated, embarrassed, the girl was at a loss. "I'll tell you, papa!" But she followed up her pledge with an air of vacuity and then, dropping into the nearest seat, simply closed her eyes to her danger. If she desired relief, she had caught at the one way to get it. "I feel rather faint. Could I have some tea?"

Mr. Prodmore considered both the idea and his daughter's substantial form. "Well, as I shall expect you to put forth *all* your powers—yes!" He turned to Chivers. "Some tea."

The old man's eyes had attached themselves to Miss Prodmore's symptoms with more solicitude than those of her parent. "I did think it might be required!" Then as he gained the door of the morning-room: "I'll lay it out here."

The young lady, on his withdrawal, recovered herself sufficiently to rise again. "It was my train, papa—so very awfully behind. I walked up, you know, also, from the station—there's such a lovely footpath across the park."

"You've been roaming the country then alone?" Mr. Prodmore inquired.

The girl protested with instant eagerness against any such picture. "Oh, dear no, not *alone*!" She spoke, absurdly, as if she had had a train of attendants; but it was an instant before she could complete the assurance. "There were ever so many people about."

"Nothing is more possible than that there should be *too* many!" said her father, speaking as for his personal convenience, but presenting that as enough. "But where, among them all," he demanded, "is your trusty maid?"

Cora's reply made up in promptitude what it lacked in felicity. "I didn't bring her." She looked at the old portraits as if to appeal to them to help her to remember why. Apparently indeed they gave a sign, for she presently went on: "She was so extremely unwell."

Mr. Prodmore met this with reprobation. "Wasn't she to understand from the first that we don't permit——"

"Anything of that sort?"—the girl recalled it at least as a familiar law. "Oh, yes, papa—I *thought* she did."

"But she doesn't?"—Mr. Prodmore pressed the point. Poor Cora, at a loss again, appeared to wonder if the point had better be a failure of brain or of propriety, but her companion continued to press. "What on earth's the matter with her?"

She again communed with their silent witnesses. "I really don't quite know, but I think that at Granny's she eats too much."

"I'll soon put an end to *that*!" Mr. Prodmore returned with decision. "You expect then to pursue your adventures quite into the night—to return to Bellborough as you came?"

The girl had by this time begun a little to find her feet. "Exactly as I came, papa dear,—under the protection of a new friend I've just made, a lady whom I met in the train and who is also going back by the 6.19. She was, like myself, on her way to this place, and I expected to find her here."

Mr. Prodmore chilled on the spot any such expectations. "What does she want at this place?"

Cora was clearly stronger for her new friend than for herself. "She wants to see it."

Mr. Prodmore reflected on this complication. "Today?" It was practically presumptuous. "Today won't do."

"So I suggested," the girl declared. "But do you know what she said?"

"How should I know," he coldly demanded, "what a nobody says?"

But on this, as if with the returning taste of a new strength, his daughter could categorically meet him. "She's not a nobody. She's an American."

Mr. Prodmore, for a moment, was struck: he embraced the place, instinctively, in a flash of calculation. "An American?"

"Yes, and she's wild——"

He knew all about that. "Americans mostly *are*!"

"I mean," said Cora, "to see this place. 'Wild' was what she herself called it—and I think she also said she was 'mad.'"

"She gave"—Mr. Prodmore reviewed the affair—"a fine account of herself! But she won't do."

The effect of her new acquaintance on his companion had been such that she could, after an instant, react against this sentence. "Well, when I told her that this particular day perhaps wouldn't, she said it would just *have* to."

"Have to do?" Mr. Prodmore showed again, through a chink, his speculative eye. "For *what*, then, with such grand airs?"

"Why, I suppose, for what Americans want."

He measured the quantity. "They want everything."

"Then I wonder," said Cora, "that she hasn't arrived."

"When she does arrive," he answered, "I'll tackle her; and I shall thank you, in future, not to take up, in trains, with indelicate women of whom you know nothing."

"Oh, I did know something," his daughter pleaded; "for I saw her yesterday at Bellborough."

Mr. Prodmore contested even this freedom. "And what was she doing at Bellborough?"

"Staying at the Blue Dragon, to see the old abbey. She says she just loves old abbeys. It seems to be the same feeling," the girl went on, "that brought her over, today, to see this old house."

"She 'just loves' old houses? Then why the deuce didn't she accompany you properly, since she is so pushing, to the door?"

"Because she went off in a fly," Cora explained, "to see, first, the old hospital. She just loves old hospitals. She asked me if this isn't a show-house. I told her"—the girl was anxious to disclaim responsibility—"that I hadn't the least idea."

"It *is*!" Mr. Prodmore cried almost with ferocity. "I wonder, on such a speech, what she thought of *you*!"

Miss Prodmore meditated with distinct humbleness. "I know. She told me."

He had looked her up and down. "That you're really a hopeless frump?"

Cora, oddly enough, seemed almost to court this description. "That I'm not, as she rather funnily called it, a show-girl."

"Think of your having to be reminded—by the very strangers you pick up," Mr. Prodmore groaned, "of what my daughter should pre-eminently be! Your friend, all the same," he bethought himself, "is evidently loud."

"Well, when she comes," the girl again so far agreed as to reply, "you'll certainly hear her. But don't judge her, papa, till you do. She's tremendously clever," she risked—"there seems to be nothing she doesn't know."

"And there seems to be nothing you do! You're *not* tremendously clever," Mr. Prodmore pursued; "so you'll permit me to demand of you a slight effort of intelligence." Then, as for the benefit of the listening walls themselves, he struck the high note. "I'm expecting Captain Yule."

Cora's consciousness blinked. "The owner of this property?"

Her father's tone showed his reserves. "That's what it depends on you to make him!"

"On me?" the girl gasped.

"He came into it three months ago by the death of his great-uncle, who had lived to ninety-three, but who, having quarrelled mortally with his father, had always refused to receive either sire or son."

Our young lady bent her eyes on this page of family history, then raised them but dimly lighted. "But now, at least, doesn't he live here?"

"So little," her companion replied, "that he comes here today for the very first time. I've some business to discuss with him that can best be discussed on this spot; and it's a vital part of that business that you too should take pains to make him welcome."

Miss Prodmore failed to ignite. "In his own house?"

"That it's *not* his own house is just the point I seek to make! The way I look at it is that it's *my* house! The way I look at it even, my dear"—in his demonstration of his ways of looking Mr. Prodmore literally expanded—"is that it's *our* house. The whole thing is mortgaged, as it stands, for every penny of its value; and I'm in the pleasant position—do you follow me?" he trumpeted.

Cora jumped. "Of holding the mortgages?"

He caught her with a smile of approval and indeed of surprise. "You keep up with me better than I hoped. I hold every scrap of paper, and it's a precious collection."

She smothered, perceptibly, a vague female sigh, glancing over the place more attentively than she had yet done. "Do you mean that you can come down on him?"

"I don't need to 'come,' my dear—I *am* 'down.' *This* is down!"—and the iron point of Mr. Prodmore's stick fairly struck, as he rapped it, a spark from the cold pavement. "I came many weeks ago—commercially speaking—and haven't since budged from the place."

The girl moved a little about the hall, then turned with a spasm of courage. "Are you going to be very hard?"

If she read the eyes with which he met her she found in them, in spite of a certain accompanying show of pleasantry, her answer. "Hard with *you*?"

"No—that doesn't matter. Hard with the Captain."

Mr. Prodmore thought an instant. "'Hard' is a stupid, shuffling term. What do you mean by it?"

"Well, I don't understand business," Cora said; "but I think I understand *you*, papa, enough to gather that you've got, as usual, a striking advantage."

"As usual, I *have* scored; but my advantage won't be striking perhaps till I have sent the blow home. What I appeal to you, as a father, at present to do"—he continued broadly to demonstrate—"is to nerve my arm. I look to you to see me through."

"Through what, then?"

"Through this most important transaction. Through the speculation of which you've been the barely dissimulated subject. I've brought you here to receive an impression, and I've brought you, even more, to make one."

The girl turned honestly flat. "But on whom?"

"On me, to begin with—by not being a fool. And then, Miss, on *him*."

Erect, but as if paralysed, she had the air of facing the worst. "On Captain Yule?"

"By bringing him to the point."

"But, father," she asked in evident anguish—"to *what* point?"

"The point where a gentleman *has* to."

Miss Prodmore faltered. "Go down on his knees?"

Her father considered. "No—they don't do that now."

"What *do* they do?"

Mr. Prodmore carried his eyes with a certain sustained majesty to a remote point. "He will know himself."

"Oh, no, indeed, he won't," the girl cried; "they don't *ever!*"

"Then the sooner they learn—whoever teaches 'em!—the better: the better I mean in particular," Mr. Prodmore added with an intention discernibly vicious, "for the master of this house. I'll guarantee that he shall understand that," he concluded, "for I shall do my part."

She looked at him as if his part were really to be hated. "But how on earth, sir, can I ever do mine? To begin with, you know, I've never even seen him."

Mr. Prodmore took out his watch; then, having consulted it, put it back with a gesture that seemed to dispose at the same time and in the same manner of the objection. "You'll see him *now*—from one moment to the other. He's remarkably handsome, remarkably young, remarkably ambitious, and remarkably clever. He has one of the best and oldest names in this part of the country—a name that, far and wide here, one could do so much with that I'm simply indignant to see him do so little. I propose, my dear, to do with it all he hasn't, and I further propose, to that end, first to get hold of it. It's you, Miss Prodmore, who shall take it out of the fire."

"The fire?"—he had terrible figures.

"Out of the mud, if you prefer. You must pick it up, do you see? My plan is, in short," Mr. Prodmore pursued, "that when we've brushed it off and rubbed it down a bit, blown away the dust and touched up the rust, my daughter shall gracefully bear it."

She could only oppose, now, a stiff, thick transparency that yielded a view of the course in her own veins, after all, however, mingled with a feebler fluid, of the passionate blood of the Prodmores. "And pray is it also Captain Yule's plan?"

Her father's face warned her off the ground of irony, but he replied without violence. "His plans have not yet quite matured. But nothing is more natural," he added with an ominous smile, "than that they shall do so on the sunny south wall of Miss Prodmore's best manner."

Miss Prodmore's spirit was visibly rising, and a note that might have meant warning for warning sounded in the laugh produced by this sally. "You speak of them, papa, as if they were sour little plums! You exaggerate, I think, the warmth of Miss Prodmore's nature. It has always been thought remarkably cold."

"Then you'll be so good, my dear, as to confound—it mightn't be amiss even a little to scandalise—that opinion. I've spent twenty years in giving you what your poor mother used to call advantages, and they've cost me hundreds and hundreds of pounds. It's now time that, both as a parent and as a man of business, I should get my money back. I couldn't help your temper," Mr. Prodmore conceded, "nor your taste, nor even your unfortunate resemblance to the estimable, but far from ornamental, woman who brought you forth; but I paid out a small fortune that you should have, damn you, don't you know? a good manner. You never show it to me, certainly; but do you mean to tell me that, at this time of day—for other persons—you *haven't* got one?"

This pulled our young lady perceptibly up; there was a directness in the argument that was like the ache of old pinches. "If you mean by 'other persons' persons who are particularly civil—well, Captain Yule may not see his way to be one of them. He may not *think*—don't you see?—that I've a good manner."

"Do your duty, Miss, and never mind what he thinks!" Her father's conception of her duty momentarily sharpened. "Don't look at him like a sick turkey, and he'll be sure to think right."

The colour that sprang into Cora's face at this rude comparison was such, unfortunately, as perhaps a little to justify it. Yet she retained, in spite of her emotion, some remnant of presence of mind. "I remember your saying once, some time ago, that that was just what he would be sure *not* to do: I mean when he began to go in for his dreadful ideas——"

Mr. Prodmore took her boldly up. "About the 'radical programme,' the 'social revolution,' the spoliation of everyone, and the destruction of everything? Why, you stupid thing, I've worked round to a complete agreement with him. The taking from those who have by those who haven't——"

"Well?" said the girl, with some impatience, as he sought the right way of expressing his notion.

"What is it but to receive, from consenting hands, the principal treasure of the rich? If I'm rich, my daughter is my largest property, and I freely make her over. I shall, in other words, forgive my young friend his low opinions if he renounces them for *you*."

Cora, at this, started as with a glimpse of delight. "He won't renounce them! He *shan't*!"

Her father appeared still to enjoy the ingenious way he had put it, so that he had good humour to spare. "If you suggest that you're in political sympathy with him, you mean then that you'll take him as he *is*?"

"I won't take him at all!" she protested with her head very high; but she had no sooner uttered the words than the sound of the approach of wheels caused her dignity to drop. "A fly?—it must be *he*!" She turned right and left, for a retreat or an escape, but her father had already caught her by the wrist. "Surely," she pitifully panted, "you don't want me to bounce on him *thus*?"

Mr. Prodmore, as he held her, estimated the effect. "Your frock won't do—with what it cost me?"

"It's not my frock, papa,—it's his thinking I've come here for him to see me!"

He let her go and, as she moved away, had another look for the social value of the view of her stout back. It appeared to determine him, for, with a touch of mercy, he passed his word. "He doesn't think it, and he shan't know it."

The girl had made for the door of the morning-room, before reaching which she flirted breathlessly round. "But he knows you want me to hook him!"

Mr. Prodmore was already in the parliamentary attitude the occasion had suggested to him for the reception of his visitor. "The way to 'hook' him will be not to be hopelessly vulgar. He doesn't know that you know anything." The house-bell clinked, and he waved his companion away. "Await us there with tea, and mind you toe the mark!"

Chivers, at this moment, summoned by the bell, reappeared in the morning-room doorway, and Cora's dismay brushed him as he sidled past her and off into the passage to the front. Then, from the threshold of her refuge, she launched a last appeal. "Don't *kill* me, father: give me time!" With which she dashed into the room, closing the door with a bang.

II

Mr. Prodmore, in Chivers's absence, remained staring as if at a sudden image of something rather fine. His child had left with him the sense of a quick irradiation, and he failed to see why, at the worst, such lightnings as she was thus able to dart shouldn't strike somewhere. If he had spoken to her of her best manner perhaps *that* was her best manner. He heard steps and voices, however, and immediately invited to his aid his own, which was simply magnificent. Chivers, returning, announced solemnly "Captain Yule!" and ushered in a tall young man in a darkish tweed suit and a red necktie, attached in a sailor's knot, who, as he entered, removed a soft brown hat. Mr. Prodmore, at this, immediately saluted him by uncovering. "Delighted at last to see you here!"

It was the young man who first, in his comparative simplicity, put out a hand. "If I've not come before, Mr. Prodmore, it was—very frankly speaking—from the dread of seeing *you*!" His speech contradicted, to some extent, his gesture, but Clement Yule's was an aspect in which contradictions were rather remarkably at home. Erect and slender, but as strong as he was straight, he was set up, as the phrase is, like a soldier, and yet finished, in certain details—matters of expression and suggestion only indeed—like a man in whom sensibility had been recklessly cultivated. He was hard and fine, just as he was sharp and gentle, just as he was frank and shy, just as he was serious and young, just as he looked, though you could never have imitated it, distinctly "kept up" and yet considerably reduced. His features were thoroughly regular, but his complete shaving might have been designed to show that they were, after all, not absurd. The face Mr. Prodmore offered him fairly glowed, on this new showing, with instant pride of possession, and there was that in Captain Yule's whole air which justified such a sentiment without consciously rewarding it.

"Ah, surely," said the elder man, "my presence is not without a motive!"

"It's just the motive," Captain Yule returned, "that makes me wince at it! Certainly I've no illusions," he added, "about the ground of our meeting. Your thorough knowledge of what you're about has placed me at your mercy—you hold me in the hollow of your hand."

It was vivid in every inch that Mr. Prodmore's was a nature to expand in the warmth, or even in the chill, of any tribute to his financial subtlety. "Well, I won't, on my side, deny that when, in general, I go in deep I don't go in for nothing. I make it pay double!" he smiled.

"You make it pay so well—'double' surely doesn't do you justice!—that, if I've understood you, you can do quite as you like with this preposterous place. Haven't you brought me down exactly that I may *see* you do it?"

"I've certainly brought you down that you may open your eyes!" This, apparently, however, was not what Mr. Prodmore himself had arrived to do with his own. These fine points of expression literally contracted with intensity. "Of course, you know, you can always clear the property. You can pay off the mortgages."

Captain Yule, by this time, had, as he had not done at first, looked up and down, round about and well over the scene, taking in, though at a mere glance, it might have seemed, more particularly, the row, high up, of strenuous ancestors. But Mr. Prodmore's last words rang none the less on his ear, and he met them with mild amusement. "Pay off——? What can I pay off with?"

"You can always raise money."

"What can I raise it on?"

Mr. Prodmore looked massively gay. "On your great political future."

"Oh, I've not taken—for the short run at least—the lucrative line," the young man said, "and I know what you think of *that*."

Mr. Prodmore's blandness confessed, by its instant increase, to this impeachment. There was always the glory of intimacy in Yule's knowing what he thought. "I hold that you keep, in public, very dangerous company; but I also hold that you're extravagant mainly because you've nothing at stake. A man has the right opinions," he developed with pleasant confidence, "as soon as he has something to lose by having the wrong. Haven't I already hinted to you how to set your political house in order? You drop into the lower regions because you keep the best rooms empty. You're a firebrand, in other words my dear Captain, simply because you're a bachelor. That's one of the early complaints we all pass through, but it's soon over, and the treatment for it quite simple. I have your remedy."

145

The young man's eyes, wandering again about the house, might have been those of an auditor of the fiddling before the rise of the curtain. "A remedy worse than the disease?"

"There's nothing worse, that I've ever heard of," Mr. Prodmore sharply replied, "than your particular fix. Least of all a heap of gold——"

"A heap of gold?" His visitor idly settled, as if the curtain were going up.

Mr. Prodmore raised it bravely. "In the lap of a fine fresh lass! Give pledges to fortune, as somebody says—*then* we'll talk. You want money—that's what you want. Well, marry it!"

Clement Yule, for a little, never stirred, save that his eyes yet again strayed vaguely. At last they stopped with a smile. "Of course I could do that in a moment!"

"It's even just my own danger from you," his companion returned. "I perfectly recognise that any woman would now jump——"

"I don't like jumping women," Captain Yule threw in; "but that perhaps is a detail. It's more to the point that I've yet to see the woman whom, by an advance of my own——"

"You'd care to keep in the really attractive position——?"

"Which can never, of course, be anything"—Yule took his friend up again—"but that of waiting quietly."

"Never, never anything!" Mr. Prodmore, most assentingly, banished all other thought. "But I haven't asked you, you know, to make an advance."

"You've only asked me to receive one?"

Mr. Prodmore waited a little. "Well, I've asked you—I asked you a month ago—to think it all over."

"I *have* thought it all over," Clement Yule said; "and the strange sequel seems to be that my eyes have got accustomed to my darkness. I seem to make out, in the gloom of my meditations, that, at the worst, I can let the whole thing slide."

"The property?"—Mr. Prodmore jerked back as if it were about to start.

"Isn't it the property," his visitor inquired, "that positively throws me up? If I can afford neither to live on it nor to disencumber it, I can at least let it save its own bacon and pay its own debts. I can say to you simply: 'Take it, my dear sir, and the devil take *you!*'"

Mr. Prodmore gave a quick, strained smile. "You wouldn't be so shockingly rude!"

"Why not—if I'm a firebrand and a keeper of low company and a general nuisance? Sacrifice for sacrifice, that might very well be the least!"

This was put with such emphasis that Mr. Prodmore was for a moment arrested. He could stop very short, however, and yet talk as still going. "How do you know, if you haven't compared them? It's just to make the comparison—in all the proper circumstances—that you're here at this hour." He took, with a large, though vague, exhibitory gesture, a few turns about. "Now that you stretch yourself—for an hour's relaxation and rocked, as it were, by my friendly hand—in the ancient cradle of your race, can you seriously entertain the idea of parting with such a venerable family relic?"

It was evident that, as he decorously embraced the scene, the young man, in spite of this dissuasive tone, was entertaining ideas. It might have appeared at the moment to a spectator in whom fancy was at all alert that the place, becoming in a manner conscious of the question, felt itself on its honour, and that its honour could make no compromise. It met Clement Yule with no grimace of invitation, with no attenuation of its rich old sadness. It was as if the two hard spirits, the grim *genius loci* and the quick modern conscience, stood an instant confronted. "The cradle of my race bears, for me, Mr. Prodmore, a striking resemblance to its tomb." The sigh that dropped from him, however, was not quite void of tenderness. It might, for that matter, have been a long, sad creak, portending collapse, of some immemorial support of the Yules. "Heavens, how melancholy——!"

Mr. Prodmore, somewhat ambiguously, took up the sound. "Melancholy?"—he just balanced. That well might be, even a little *should* be—yet agreement might depreciate.

"Musty, mouldy;" then with a poke of his stick at a gap in the stuff with which an old chair was covered, "mangy!" Captain Yule responded. "Is this the character throughout?"

Mr. Prodmore fixed a minute the tell-tale tatter. "You must judge for yourself—you must go over the house." He hesitated again; then his indecision vanished—the right line was clear. "It does look a bit run down, but I'll tell you what I'll do. I'll do it up for you—neatly: I'll throw *that* in!"

His young friend turned on him an eye that, though markedly enlivened by his offer, was somehow only the more inscrutable. "Will you put in the electric light?"

Mr. Prodmore's own twinkle—at this touch of a spring he had not expected to work—was, on the other hand, temporarily veiled. "Well, if you'll meet me half-way! We're dealing here"—he backed up his gravity—"with fancy-values. Don't you feel," he appealed, "as you take it all in, a kind of a something-or-other down your back?"

Clement Yule gazed awhile at one of the pompous quarterings in the faded old glass that, in tones as of late autumn, crowned with armorial figures the top of the great hall-window; then with abruptness he turned away. "Perhaps I *don't* take it all in; but what I do feel is—since you mention it—a sort of stiffening of the spine! The whole thing is too queer—too cold—too cruel."

"Cruel?"—Mr. Prodmore's demur was virtuous.

"Like the face of some stuck-up distant relation who won't speak first. I see in the stare of the old dragon, I taste in his very breath, all the helpless mortality he has tucked away!"

"Lord, sir—you *have* fancies!" Mr. Prodmore was almost scandalised.

But the young man's fancies only multiplied as he moved, not at all critical, but altogether nervous, from object to object. "I don't know what's the matter—but there *is* more here than meets the eye." He tried as for his amusement or his relief to figure it out. "I miss the old presences. I feel the old absences. I hear the old voices. I see the old ghosts."

This last was a profession that offered some common ground. "The old ghosts, Captain Yule," his companion promptly replied, "are worth so much a dozen, and with no reduction, I must remind you—with the price indeed rather raised—for the quantity taken!" Feeling then apparently that he had cleared the air a little by this sally, Mr. Prodmore proceeded to pat his interlocutor on a back that he by no means wished to cause to be put to the wall. "Look about you, at any rate, a little more." He crossed with his toes well out the line that divides encouragement from patronage. "Do make yourself at home."

"Thank you very much, Mr. Prodmore. May I light a cigarette?" his visitor asked.

"In your own house, Captain?"

"That's just the question: it seems so much less my own house than before I had come into it!" The Captain offered Mr. Prodmore a cigarette which that gentleman, also taking a light from him, accepted; then he lit his own and began to smoke. "As I understand you," he went on, "you *lump* your two conditions? I mean I must accept both or neither?"

Mr. Prodmore threw back his shoulders with a high recognition of the long stride represented by this question. "You *will* accept both, for, by doing so, you'll clear the property at a stroke. The way I put it is—see?—that if you'll stand for Gossage, you'll get returned for Gossage."

"And if I get returned for Gossage, I shall marry your daughter. Accordingly," the young man pursued, "if I marry your daughter——"

"I'll burn up, before your eyes," said this young lady's proprietor, "every scratch of your pen. It will be a bonfire of signatures. There won't be a penny to pay—there'll only be a position to take. You'll take it with peculiar grace."

"Peculiar, Mr. Prodmore—very!"

The young man had assented more than he desired, but he was not deterred by it from completing the picture. "You'll settle down here in comfort and honour."

Clement Yule took several steps; the effect of his host was the reverse of soothing; yet the latter watched his irritation as if it were the working of a charm. "Are you very sure of the 'honour' if I turn my political coat?"

"You'll only be turning it back again to the way it was always worn. Gossage will receive you with open arms and press you to a heaving Tory bosom. That bosom"—Mr. Prodmore followed himself up—"has never heaved but to sound Conservative principles. The cradle, as I've called it,—or at least the rich, warm coverlet,—of your race, Gossage was the political property, so to speak, of generations of your family. Stand therefore in the good old interest and you'll stand like a lion."

"I'm afraid you mean," Captain Yule laughed, "that I must first roar like one."

"Oh, *I'll* do the roaring!"—and Mr. Prodmore shook his mane. "Leave that to me."

"Then why the deuce don't you stand yourself?"

Mr. Prodmore knew so familiarly why! "Because I'm not a remarkably handsome young man with the grand old home and the right old name. Because I'm a different sort of matter altogether. But if I haven't these advantages," he went on, "you'll do justice to my natural desire that my daughter at least shall have them."

Clement Yule watched himself smoke a minute. "Doing justice to natural desires is just what, of late, I've tried to make a study of. But I confess I don't quite grasp the deep attraction you appear to discover in so large a surrender of your interests."

"My surrenders are my own affair," Mr. Prodmore rang out, "and as for my interests, as I never, on principle, give anything for nothing, I dare say I may be trusted to know them when I see them. You come high—I don't for a moment deny it; but when I look at you, in this pleasant, intimate way, my dear boy—if you'll allow me so to describe things—I recognise one of those cases, unmistakeable when really met, in which one must put down one's money. There's not an article in the whole shop, if you don't mind the comparison, that strikes me as better value. I intend you shall be, Captain," Mr. Prodmore wound up in a frank, bold burst, "the true comfort of my life!"

The young man was as hushed for a little as if an organ-tone were still in the air. "May I inquire," he at last returned, "if Miss Prodmore's ideas of comfort are as well defined—and in her case, I may add, as touchingly modest—as her father's? Is she a responsible party of this ingenious arrangement?"

Mr. Prodmore rendered homage—his appreciation was marked—to the elevated character of his young friend's scruple. "Miss Prodmore, Captain Yule, may be perhaps best described as a large smooth sheet of blank, though gilt-edged, paper. No image of any tie but the true and perfect filial has yet, I can answer for it, formed itself on the considerable expanse. But for that image to be projected——"

"I've only, in person, to appear?" Yule asked with an embarrassment that he tried to laugh off.

"And, naturally, in person," Mr. Prodmore intelligently assented, "do yourself, as well as the young lady, justice. Do you remember what you said when I first, in London, laid the matter before you?"

Clement Yule did remember, but his amusement increased. "I think I said it struck me I should first take a look at—what do you call it?—the *corpus delicti.*"

"You should first see for yourself what you had really come into? I was not only eager for that," said Mr. Prodmore, "but I'm willing to go further: I'm quite ready to hear you say that you think you should also first see the young lady."

Captain Yule continued to laugh. "There is something in that then, since you mention it!"

"I think you'll find that there's everything." Mr. Prodmore again looked at his watch. "Which will you take first?"

"First?"

"The young lady or the house?"

His companion, at this, unmistakeably started. "Do you mean your daughter's *here*?"

Mr. Prodmore glowed with consciousness. "In the morning-room."

"Waiting for me?"

The tone showed a consternation that Mr. Prodmore's was alert to soothe. "Ah, as long, you know, as you like!"

Yule's alarm, however, was not assuaged; it appeared to grow as he stared, much discomposed, yet sharply thinking, at the door to which his friend had pointed. "Oh, longer than *this*, please!" Then as he turned away: "Do you mean she knows——?"

"That she's here on view?" Mr. Prodmore hung fire a moment, but was equal to the occasion. "She knows nothing whatever. She's as unconscious as the rose on its stem!"

His companion was visibly relieved. "That's right—let her remain so! I'll first take the house," said Clement Yule.

"Shall I go round *with* you?" Mr. Prodmore asked.

The young man's reflection was brief. "Thank you. I'd rather, on the whole, go round alone."

The old servant who had admitted the gentlemen came back at this crisis from the morning-room, looking from under a bent brow and with much limpid earnestness from one of them to the other. The one he first addressed had evidently, though quite unaware of it, inspired him with a sympathy from which he now took a hint. "There's tea on, sir!" he persuasively jerked as he passed the younger man.

The elder answered. "Then I'll join my daughter." He gained the morning-room door, whence he repeated with an appropriate gesture—that of offering proudly, with light, firm fingers, a flower of his own celebrated raising—his happy formula of Miss Prodmore's state. "The rose on its stem!" Scattering petals, diffusing fragrance, he thus passed out.

Chivers, meanwhile, had rather pointlessly settled once more in its place some small object that had not strayed; to whom Clement Yule, absently watching him, abruptly broke out. "I say, my friend, what colour is the rose?"

The old man looked up with a dimness that presently glimmered. "The rose, sir?" He turned to the open door and the shining day. "Rather a brilliant———"

"A brilliant———?" Yule was interested.

"Kind of old-fashioned red." Chivers smiled with the pride of being thus able to testify, but the next instant his smile went out. "It's the only one left—on the old west wall."

His visitor's mirth, at this, quickly enough revived. "My dear fellow, I'm not alluding to the sole ornament of the garden, but to the young lady at present in the morning-room. Do you happen to have noticed if she's pretty?"

Chivers stood queerly rueful. "Laws, sir—it's a matter I mostly notice; but isn't it, at the same time, sir, a matter—like—of taste?"

"Pre-eminently. That's just why I appeal with such confidence to yours."

The old man acknowledged with a flush of real embarrassment a responsibility he had so little invited. "Well, sir,—mine was always a sort of fancy for something more merry-like."

"She isn't merry-like then, poor Miss Prodmore?" Captain Yule's attention, however, dropped before the answer came, and he turned off the subject with an "Ah, if you come to that, neither am I! But it doesn't signify," he went on. "What are *you*?" he more sociably demanded.

Chivers clearly had to think a bit. "Well, sir, I'm not quite *that*. Whatever has there been to make me, sir?" he asked in dim extenuation.

153

"How in the world do *I* know? I mean to whom do you belong?"

Chivers seemed to scan impartially the whole field. "If you could just only *tell* me, sir! I quite seem to waste away—for someone to take an order of."

Clement Yule, by this time, had become aware he was amusing. "Who pays your wages?"

"No one at all, sir," said the old man very simply.

His friend, fumbling an instant in a waistcoat pocket, produced something that his hand, in obedience to a little peremptory gesture and by a trick of which he had unlearned, through scant custom, the neatness, though the propriety was instinctive, placed itself in a shy practical relation to. "Then there's a sovereign. And I haven't many!" the young man, turning away resignedly, threw after it.

Chivers, for an instant, intensely studied him. "Ah, then, shouldn't it stay in the family?"

Clement Yule wheeled round, first struck, then, at the sight of the figure made by his companion in this offer, visibly touched. "I think it does, old boy."

Chivers kept his eyes on him now. "I've served your house, sir."

"How long?"

"All my life."

So, for a time, they faced each other, and something in Chivers made Yule at last speak. "Then I won't give *you* up!"

"Indeed, sir, I hope you won't give up anything."

The Captain took up his hat. "It remains to be seen." He looked over the place again; his eyes wandered to the open door. "Is that the garden?"

"It *was!*"—and the old man's sigh was like the creak of the wheel of time. "Shall I show you how it used to be?"

"It's just as it *is*, alas, that I happen to require it!" Captain Yule reached the door and stood looking beyond. "Don't come," he then said; "I want to think." With which he walked out.

Chivers, left alone, appeared to wonder at it, and his wonder, like that of most old people, lay near his lips. "What does he want, poor dear, to think about?" This speculation, however, was immediately checked by a high, clear voice that preceded the appearance on the stairs, before she had reached the middlemost landing, of the wonderful figure of a lady, a lady who, with the almost trumpeted cheer of her peremptory but friendly call—"Housekeeper, Butler, old Family Servant!"—fairly waked the sleeping echoes. Chivers gazed up at her in quick remembrance, half dismayed, half dazzled, of a duty neglected. She appeared now; she shone at him out of the upper dusk; reaching the middle, she had begun to descend, with beautiful laughter and rustling garments; and though she was alone she gave him the sense of coming in a crowd and with music. "Oh, I should have told him of *her*!"

III

SHE was indeed an apparition, a presence requiring announcement and explanation just in the degree in which it seemed to show itself in a relation quite of its own to all social preliminaries. It evidently either assumed them to be already over or wished to forestall them altogether; what was clear at any rate was that it allowed them scant existence. She was young, tall, radiant, lovely, and dressed in a manner determined at once, obviously, by the fact and by the humour of her journey—it might have proclaimed her so a pilgrim or so set her up as a priestess. Most journeys, for this lady, at all events, were clearly a brush of Paris. "Did you think I had got snapped down in an old box like that poor girl—what's her name? the one who was poking round too—in the celebrated poem? You dear, delightful man, why didn't you tell me?"

"Tell you, mum——?"

155

"Well, that you're so perfectly—perfect! You're ever so much better than anyone has ever said. Why, in the name of common sense, has nobody ever said *anything*? You're everything in the world you ought to be, and not the shade of a shade of anything you oughtn't!"

It was a higher character to be turned out with than poor Chivers had ever dreamed. "Well, mum, I try!" he gaped.

"Oh, no, you don't—that's just your charm! *I* try," cried his friend, "but you do nothing: here you simply *are*—you can't help it!"

He stood overwhelmed. "Me, mum?"

She took him in at the eyes—she could take everything at once. "Yes, you too, you positive old picture! I've seen the old masters—but you're the old master!"

"The master—I?" He fairly fell back.

"'The good and faithful servant'—Rembrandt van Rhyn: with three stars. *That's* what you are!" Nothing would have been more droll to a spectator than her manner of meeting his humbleness, or more charming indeed than the practical sweetness of her want of imagination of it. "The house is a vision of beauty, and you're simply worthy of the house. I can't say more for you!"

"I find it a bit of a strain, mum," Chivers candidly replied, "to keep up—fairly to call it—with what you *do* say."

"That's just what everyone finds it!"—she broke into the happiest laugh. "Yet I haven't come here to suffer in silence, you know—to suffer, I mean, from envy and despair." She was in constant movement, from side to side, observing, comparing, returning, taking notes while she gossiped and gossiping, too, for remembrance. The intention of remembrance even had in it, however, some prevision of failure or some alloy of irritation. "You're so fatally right and so deadly complete, all the same, that I can really scarcely bear it: with every fascinating feature that I had already heard of and thought I was prepared for, and ever so many others that, strange to say, I hadn't and wasn't, and that you just spring right *at* me like a series of things going off. What do you call it," she asked—"a royal salute, a hundred guns?"

Her enthusiasm had a bewildering form, but it had by this time warmed the air, and the old man rubbed his hands as over a fire to which the bellows had been applied. "I saw as soon as you arrived, mum, that you were looking for more things than ever *I* heard tell of!"

"Oh, I had got you by heart," she returned, "from books and drawings and photos; I had you in my pocket when I came: so, you see, as soon as you were so good as to give me my head and let me loose, I knew my way about. It's all here, every inch of it," she competently continued, "and now at last I can do what I want!"

A light of consternation, at this, just glimmered in Chivers's face. "And pray, mum, what might that be?"

"Why, take you right back with me—to Missoura Top."

This answer seemed to fix his bewilderment, but he was there for the general convenience.

"Do I understand you, mum, that you require to take *me*?"

Her particular convenience, on the spot, embraced him, so new and delightful a sense had he suddenly read into her words. "Do you mean to say you'd come—as the old Family Servant? Then *do*, you nice real thing: it's just what I'm dying for—an old Family Servant! You're somebody's else, yes—but everything, over here, is somebody's else, and I want, too, a first-rate second-hand one, all ready made, as you are, but not too much done up. You're the best I've seen yet, and I wish I could have you packed—put up in paper and bran—as I shall have my old pot there." She whisked about, remembering, recovering, eager: "Don't let me *forget* my precious pot!" Excited, with quick transitions, she quite sociably appealed to her companion, who shuffled sympathetically to where, out of harm, the object had been placed on a table. "Don't you just love old crockery? That's awfully sweet old Chelsea."

He took up the piece with tenderness, though, in his general agitation, not perhaps with all the caution with which, for daily service, he handled ancient frailties. He at any rate turned on this fresh subject an interested,

157

puzzled eye. "Where is it I've known this very bit—though not to say, as *you* do, by name?" Suddenly it came to him. "In the pew-opener's front parlour!"

"No," his interlocutress cried, "in the pew-opener's best bedroom: on the old chest of drawers, you know—with those ducks of brass handles. I've got the handles too—I mean the whole thing; and the brass fender and fire-irons, and the chair her grandmother died in. Not in the fly," she added—"it was such a bore that they have to be sent."

Chivers, with the pot still in his hands, fairly rocked in the high wind of so much confidence and such great transactions. He had nothing for these, however, but approval. "You did right to take this out, mum, when the fly went to the stables. Them flymen do be cruel rash with anything that's delicate." Of the delicacy of the vessel it now rested with him to deposit safely again he was by this time so appreciatively aware that in returning with it to its safe niche he stumbled into some obscure trap literally laid for him by his nervousness. It was the matter of a few seconds, of a false movement, a knock of the elbow, a gasp, a shriek, a complete little crash. There was the pot on the pavement, in several pieces, and the clumsy cup-bearer blue with fear. "Mercy *on* us, mum,—I've brought shame on my old grey hairs!"

The little shriek of his companion had smothered itself in the utterance, and the next minute, with the ruin between them, they were contrastedly face to face. The charming woman, who had already found more voices in the air than anyone had found before, could, in the happy play of this power, find a poetry in her accident. "Oh, but the way you *take* it!" she laughed—"you're too quaint to live!" She looked at him as if he alone had suffered—as if his suffering indeed positively added to his charm. "The way you said that now—it's just the very 'type'! That's all I want of you now—to *be* the very type. It's what you are, you poor dear thing—for you *can't* help it; and it's what everything and everyone else is, over here; so that you had just better all make up your minds to it and not try to shirk it. There was a type in the train with me—the 'awfully nice girl' of all the English novels, the 'simple maiden in her flower' of—who is it?—your great poet. *She* couldn't help it either—in fact I wouldn't have *let* her!" With this, while Chivers picked up his fragments, his lady had a happy recall. His face, as he stood there with the shapeless elements of his humiliation fairly rattling again in his hands, was a reflection of her extraordinary manner of enlarging the subject, or rather, more beneficently perhaps, the space that contained it. "By the way, the girl was coming right here. Has she come?"

Chivers crept solemnly away, as if to bury his dead, which he consigned, with dumb rites, to a situation of honourable publicity; then, as he came back, he replied without elation: "Miss Prodmore is here, mum. She's having her tea."

This, for his friend, was a confirmatory touch to be fitted with eagerness into the picture. "Yes, that's exactly it—they're always having their tea!"

"With Mr. Prodmore—in the morning-room," the old man supplemented. "Captain Yule's in the garden."

"Captain Yule?"

"The new master. He's also just arrived."

The wonderful lady gave an immediate "Oh!" to the effect of which her silence for another moment seemed to add. "She didn't tell me about *him*."

"Well, mum," said Chivers, "it do be a strange thing to tell. He had never—like, mum—so much as seen the place."

"Before today—his very own?" This too, for the visitor, was an impression among impressions, and, like most of her others, it ended after an instant as a laugh. "Well, I hope he likes it!"

"I haven't seen many, mum," Chivers boldly declared, "that like it as much as *you*."

She made with her handsome head a motion that appeared to signify still deeper things than he had caught. Her beautiful wondering eyes played high and low, like the flight of an imprisoned swallow, then, as she sank upon a seat, dropped at last as if the creature were bruised with its limits. "I should like it still better if it were *my* very own!"

"Well, mum," Chivers sighed, "if it wasn't against my duty I could wish indeed it were! But the Captain, mum," he conscientiously added, "is the lawful heir."

It was a wonder what she found in whatever he said; he touched with every word the spring of her friendly joy. "That's another of your lovely old things—I adore your lawful heirs!" She appeared to have, about everything that came up, a general lucid vision that almost glorified the particular case. "He has come to take possession?"

Chivers accepted, for the credit of the house, this sustaining suggestion. "He's a-taking of it now."

This evoked, for his companion, an instantaneous show. "What does he do and how does he do it? Can't I *see?*" She was all impatience, but she dropped to disappointment as her guide looked blank. "There's no grand fuss——?"

"I scarce think him, mum," Chivers with propriety hastened to respond, "the gentleman to make any about anything."

She had to resign herself, but she smiled as she thought. "Well, perhaps I like them better when they don't!" She had clearly a great range of taste, and it all came out in the wistfulness with which, before the notice apparently served on her, she prepared to make way. "I also"—she lingered and sighed— "have taken possession!"

Poor Chivers really rose to her. "It was you, mum," he smiled, "took it first!"

She sadly shook her head. "Ah, but for a poor little hour! *He's* for life."

The old man gave up, after a little, with equal depression, the pretence of dealing with such realities. "For mine, mum, I do at least hope."

She made again the circuit of the great place, picking up without interest the jacket she had on her previous entrance laid down. "I shall think of you, you know, here together." She vaguely looked about her as for anything else to take; then abruptly, with her eyes again on Chivers: "Do you suppose he'll be kind to you?"

His hand, in his trousers-pocket, seemed to turn the matter over. "He has already been, mum."

"Then be sure to be so to *him*!" she replied with some emphasis. The house-bell sounded as she spoke, giving her quickly another thought. "Is that his bell?"

Chivers was hardly less struck. "I must see whose!"—and hurrying, on this, to the front, he presently again vanished.

His companion, left alone, stood a minute with an air in which happy possession was oddly and charmingly mingled with desperate surrender; so much as to have left you in doubt if the next of her lively motions were curiosity or disgust. Impressed, in her divided state, with a small framed plaque of enamel, she impulsively detached it from the wall and examined it with hungry tenderness. Her hovering thought was so vivid that you might almost have traced it in sound. "Why, bless me if it isn't Limoges! I wish awfully I were a *bad* woman: then, I do devoutly hope, I'd just quietly take it!" It testified to the force of this temptation that on hearing a sound behind her she started like a guilty thing; recovering herself, however, and—just, of course, not to appear at fault—keeping the object familiarly in her hand as she jumped to a recognition of the gentleman who, coming in from the garden, had stopped in the open doorway. She gathered indeed from his being there a positive advantage, the full confidence of which was already in her charming tone. "Oh, Captain Yule, I'm delighted to meet you! It's such a comfort to ask you if I *may*!"

His surprise kept him an instant dumb, but the effort not too closely to betray it appeared in his persuasive inflection. "If you 'may,' madam——?"

"Why, just *be* here, don't you know? and poke round!" She presented such a course as almost vulgarly natural. "Don't tell me I can't now, because I already *have*: I've been upstairs and downstairs and in my lady's chamber—I won't answer for it even perhaps that I've not been in my lord's! I got round your lovely servant—if you don't look out I'll grab him. If you don't look out, you know, I'll grab everything." She gave fair notice and went on with amazing serenity; she gathered positive gaiety from his frank stupefaction. "That's what I came over for—just to lay your country waste. Your house is a wild old dream; and besides"—she dropped, oddly and quaintly, into real responsible judgment—"you've got some quite good things. Oh, yes, you *have*—several: don't coyly pretend you haven't!" Her familiarity took these flying leaps, and she alighted, as her victim must have phrased it to himself, without turning a hair. "Don't you *know* you have? Just look at that!" She thrust her enamel before him, but he took it and held it so blankly, with an attention so absorbed in the mere woman, that at the sight of his manner her zeal for his interest and her pity for his detachment again flashed out. "Don't you know *anything*? Why, it's Limoges!"

Clement Yule simply broke into a laugh—though his laugh indeed was comprehensive. "It seems absurd, but I'm not in the least acquainted with my house. I've never happened to see it."

She seized his arm. "Then do let me show it to you!"

"I shall be delighted." His laughter had redoubled in a way that spoke of his previous tension; yet his tone, as he saw Chivers return breathless from the front, showed that he had responded sincerely enough to desire a clear field. "Who in the world's there?"

The old man was full of it. "A party!"

"A party?"

Chivers confessed to the worst. "Over from Gossage—to see the house."

The worst, however, clearly, was quite good enough for their companion, who embraced the incident with sudden enthusiasm. "Oh, let *me* show it!" But before either of the men could reply she had, addressing herself to Chivers, one of those droll drops that betrayed the quickness of her wit and the freedom of her fancy. "Dear me, I forgot—*you* get the tips! But, you dear old creature," she went on, "I'll get them, too, and I'll simply make them

162

over to you." She again pressed Yule—pressed him into this service. "Perhaps they'll be bigger—for me!"

He continued to be highly amused. "I should think they'd be enormous—for you! But I *should* like," he added with more concentration—"I should like extremely, you know, to go over with you alone."

She was held a moment. "Just you and me?"

"Just you and me—as you kindly proposed."

She stood reminded; but, throwing it off, she had her first inconsequence. "That must be for after——!"

"Ah, but not too late." He looked at his watch. "I go back tonight."

"Laws, sir!" Chivers irrepressibly groaned.

"You want to keep him?" the stranger asked. Captain Yule turned away at the question, but her look went after him, and she found herself, somehow, instantly answered. "Then I'll help you," she said to Chivers; "and the oftener we go over the better."

Something further, on this, quite immaterial, but quite adequate, passed, while the young man's back was turned, between the two others; in consequence of which Chivers again appealed to his master. "Shall I show them straight in, sir?"

His master, still detached, replied without looking at him. "By all means—if there's money in it!" This was jocose, but there would have been, for an observer, an increase of hope in the old man's departing step. The lady had exerted an influence.

She continued, for that matter, with a start of genial remembrance, to exert one in his absence. "Oh, and I promised to show it to Miss Prodmore!" Her conscience, with a kind smile for the young person she named, put the question to Clement Yule. "Won't you call her?"

The coldness of his quick response made it practically none. "'Call' her? Dear lady, I don't *know* her!"

"You must, then—she's wonderful." The face with which he met this drew from the dear lady a sharper look; but, for the aid of her good-nature, Cora Prodmore, at the moment she spoke, presented herself in the doorway of the morning-room. "See? She's charming!" The girl, with a glare of recognition, dashed across the open as if under heavy fire; but heavy fire, alas—the extremity of exposure—was promptly embodied in her friend's public embrace. "Miss Prodmore," said this terrible friend, "let me present Captain Yule." Never had so great a gulf been bridged in so free a span. "Captain Yule, Miss Prodmore. Miss Prodmore, Captain Yule."

There was stiffness, the cold mask of terror, in such notice as either party took of this demonstration, the convenience of which was not enhanced for the divided pair by the perception that Mr. Prodmore had now followed his daughter. Cora threw herself confusedly into it indeed, as with a vain rebound into the open. "Papa, let me 'present' you to Mrs. Gracedew. Mrs. Gracedew, Mr. Prodmore. Mr. Prodmore, Mrs. Gracedew."

Mrs. Gracedew, with a free salute and a distinct repetition, took in Mr. Prodmore as she had taken everything else. "Mr. Prodmore"—oh, she pronounced him, spared him nothing of himself. "So happy to meet your daughter's father. Your daughter's so perfect a specimen."

Mr. Prodmore, for the first moment, had simply looked large and at sea; then, like a practical man and without more question, had quickly seized the long perch held out to him in this statement. "So perfect a specimen, yes!"—he seemed to pass it on to his young friend.

Mrs. Gracedew, if she observed his emphasis, drew from it no deterrence; she only continued to cover Cora with a gaze that kept her well in the middle. "So fresh, so quaint, so droll!"

It was apparently a result of what had passed in the morning-room that Mr. Prodmore had grasped afresh the need for effective action, which he clearly felt he did something to meet in clutching precipitately the helping hand popped so suddenly out of space, yet so beautifully gloved and so pressingly and gracefully brandished. "So fresh, so quaint, so droll!"—he again gave Captain Yule the advantage of the stranger's impression.

To what further appreciation this might have prompted the lady herself was not, however, just then manifest; for the return of Chivers had been almost simultaneous with the advance of the Prodmores, and it had taken place with forms that made it something of a circumstance. There was positive pomp in the way he preceded several persons of both sexes, not tourists at large, but simple sightseers of the half-holiday order, plain provincial folk already, on the spot, rather awestruck. The old man, with suppressed pulls and prayers, had drawn them up in a broken line, and the habit of more peopled years, the dull drone of the dead lesson, sounded out in his prompt beginning. The party stood close, in this manner, on one side of the apartment, while the master of the house and his little circle were grouped on the other. But as Chivers, guiding his squad, reached the centre of the space, Mrs. Gracedew, markedly moved, quite unreservedly engaged, came slowly forward to meet him. "This, ladies and gentlemen," he mechanically quavered, "is perhaps the most important feature—the grand old feudal, baronial 'all. Being, from all accounts, the most ancient portion of the edifice, it was erected in the very earliest ages." He paused a moment, to mark his effect, then gave a little cough which had become, obviously, in these great reaches of time, an essential part of the trick. "Some do say," he dispassionately remarked, "in the course of the fifteenth century."

Mrs. Gracedew, who had visibly thrown herself into the working of the charm, following him with vivid sympathy and hanging on his lips, took the liberty, at this, of quite affectionately pouncing on him. "*I* say in the fourteenth, my dear—you're robbing us of a hundred years!"

Her victim yielded without a struggle. "I do seem, in them dark old centuries, sometimes to trip a little." Yet the interruption of his ancient order distinctly discomposed him, all the more that his audience, gaping with a sense of the importance of the fine point, moved in its mass a little nearer. Thus put upon his honour, he endeavoured to address the group with a dignity

165

undiminished. "The Gothic roof is much admired, but the west gallery is a modern addition."

His discriminations had the note of culture, but his candour, all too promptly, struck Mrs. Gracedew as excessive. "What in the name of Methuselah do you call 'modern'? It was here at the visit of James the First, in 1611, and is supposed to have served, in the charming detail of its ornament, as a model for several that were constructed in his reign. The great fireplace," she handsomely conceded, "*is* Jacobean."

She had taken him up with such wondrous benignant authority—as if, for her life, if they *were* to have it, she couldn't help taking care that they had it out; she had interposed with an assurance that so converted her—as by the wave of a great wand, the motion of one of her own free arms—from mere passive alien to domesticated dragon, that poor Chivers could only assent with grateful obeisances. She so plunged into the old book that he had quite lost his place. The two gentlemen and the young lady, moreover, were held there by the magic of her manner. His own, as he turned again to his cluster of sightseers, took refuge in its last refinement. "The tapestry on the left Italian—the elegant wood-work Flemish."

Mrs. Gracedew was upon him again. "Excuse me if I just deprecate a misconception. The elegant wood-work Italian—the tapestry on the left Flemish." Suddenly she put it to him before them all, pleading as familiarly and gaily as she had done when alone with him, and looking now at the others, all round, gentry and poor folk alike, for sympathy and support. She had an idea that made her dance. "Do you really mind if *I* just do it? Oh, I know how: I can do quite beautifully the housekeeper last week at Castle Gaunt." She fraternised with the company as if it were a game they must play with her, though this first stage sufficiently hushed them. "How do you do? Ain't it thrilling?" Then with a laugh as free as if, for a disguise, she had thrown her handkerchief over her head or made an apron of her tucked-up skirt, she passed to the grand manner. "Keep well together, please—we're not doing puss-in-the-corner. I've my duty to all parties—I can't be partial to one!"

The contingent from Gossage had, after all, like most contingents, its spokesman—a very erect little personage in a very new suit and a very green necktie, with a very long face and upstanding hair. It was on an evident sense of having been practically selected for encouragement that he, in turn, made choice of a question which drew all eyes. "How many parties, now, can you manage?"

Mrs. Gracedew was superbly definite. "Two. The party up and the party down." Chivers gasped at the way she dealt with this liberty, and his impression was conspicuously deepened as she pointed to one of the escutcheons in the high hall-window. "Observe in the centre compartment the family arms." She did take his breath away, for before he knew it she had crossed with the lightest but surest of gestures to the black old portrait, on the opposite wall, of a long-limbed gentleman in white trunk-hose. "And observe the family legs!" Her method was wholly her own, irregular and broad; she flew, familiarly, from the pavement to the roof and then dropped from the roof to the pavement as if the whole air of the place were an element in which she floated. "Observe the suit of armour worn at Tewkesbury—observe the tattered banner carried at Blenheim." They bobbed their heads wherever she pointed, but it would have come home to any spectator that they saw her alone. This was the case quite as much with the opposite trio—the case especially with Clement Yule, who indeed made no pretence of keeping up with her signs. It was the signs themselves he looked at—not at the subjects indicated. But he never took his eyes from her, and it was as if, at last, she had been peculiarly affected by a glimpse of his attention. All her own, for a moment, frankly went back to him and was immediately determined by it. "Observe, above all, that you're in one of the most interesting old houses, of its type, in England; for which the ages have been tender and the generations wise: letting it change so slowly that there's always more left than taken—living their lives in it, but letting it shape their lives!"

Though this pretty speech had been unmistakeably addressed to the younger of the temporary occupants of Covering End, it was the elder who, on the spot, took it up. "A most striking and appropriate tribute to a real historical monument!" Mr. Prodmore had a natural ease that could deal handsomely with compliments, and he manifestly, moreover, like a clever man, saw even more in such an explosion of them than fully met the ear. "You do, madam, bring the whole thing out!"

The visitor who had already with such impunity ventured had, on this, a loud renewal of boldness, but for the benefit of a near neighbour. "Doesn't she indeed, Jane, bring it out?"

Mrs. Gracedew, with a friendly laugh, caught the words in their passage. "But who in the world wants to keep it *in*? It isn't a secret—it isn't a strange cat or a political party!" The housekeeper, as she talked, had already dropped from her; her sense of the place was too fresh for control, though instead of half an hour it might have taken six months to become so fond. She soared again, at random, to the noble spring of the roof. "Just look at those lovely lines!" They all looked, all but Clement Yule, and several of the larger company, subdued, overwhelmed, nudged each other with strange sounds. Wherever she turned Mrs. Gracedew appeared to find a pretext for breaking out. "Just look at the tone of that glass, and the gilding of that leather, and the cutting of that oak, and the dear old flags of the very floor." It came back, came back easily, her impulse to appeal to the lawful heir, and she seemed, with her smile of universal intelligence, just to demand the charity of another moment for it. "To look, in this place, is to love!"

A voice from the party she had in hand took it up with an artless guffaw that resounded more than had doubtless been meant and that, at any rate, was evidently the accompaniment of some private pinch applied to one of the ladies. "I *say*—to love!"

It was one of the ladies who very properly replied. "It depends on who you look at!"

Mr. Prodmore, in the geniality of the hour, made his profit of the simple joke. "Do you hear *that*, Captain? You must look at the right person!"

Mrs. Gracedew certainly had not been looking at the wrong one. "I don't think Captain Yule cares. He doesn't do justice——!"

Though her face was still gay, she had faltered, which seemed to strike the young man even more than if she had gone on. "To what, madam?"

Well, on the chance she let him have it. "To the value of your house."

He took it beautifully. "I like to hear *you* express it!"

"I *can't* express it!" She once more looked all round, and so much more gravely than she had yet done that she might have appeared in trouble. She tried but, with a sigh, broke down. "It's too inexpressible!"

This was a view of the case to which Mr. Prodmore, for his own reasons, was not prepared to assent. Expression and formulation were what he naturally most desired, and he had just encountered a fountain of these things that he couldn't prematurely suffer to fail him. "Do what you can for it, madam. It would bring it quite home."

Thus excited, she gave with sudden sombre clearness another try. "Well—the value's a fancy value!"

Mr. Prodmore, receiving it as more than he could have hoped, turned triumphant to his young friend. "Exactly what I told you!"

Mrs. Gracedew explained indeed as if Mr. Prodmore's triumph was not perhaps exactly what she had argued for. Still, the truth was too great. "When a thing's unique, it's unique!"

That was every bit Mr. Prodmore required. "It's unique!"

This met, moreover, the perception of the gentleman in the green necktie. "It's unique!" They all, in fact, demonstratively—almost vociferously now—caught the point.

Mrs. Gracedew, finding herself so sustained, and still with her eyes on the lawful heirs, put it yet more strongly. "It's worth anything you like."

What was this but precisely what Mr. Prodmore had always striven to prove? "Anything you like!" he richly reverberated.

The pleasant discussion and the general interest seemed to bring them all together. "Twenty thousand now?" one of the gentlemen from Gossage archly inquired—a very young gentleman with an almost coaxing voice, who blushed immensely as soon as he had spoken.

He blushed still more at the way Mrs. Gracedew faced him. "I wouldn't *look* at twenty thousand!"

Mr. Prodmore, on the other hand, was proportionately uplifted. "She wouldn't look at twenty thousand!" he announced with intensity to the Captain.

The visitor who had been the first to speak gave a shrewder guess. "Thirty, then, as it stands?"

Mrs. Gracedew looked more and more responsible; she communed afresh with the place; but she too evidently had her conscience. "It would be giving it away!"

Mr. Prodmore, at this, could scarcely contain himself. "It would be giving it away!"

The second speaker had meanwhile conceived the design of showing that, though still crimson, he was not ashamed. "You'd hold out for forty——?"

Mrs. Gracedew required a minute to answer—a very marked minute during which the whole place, pale old portraits and lurking old echoes and all, might have made you feel how much depended on her; to the degree that the consciousness in her face became finally a reason for her not turning it to Gossage. "Fifty thousand, Captain Yule, is what I think I should propose."

If the place had seemed to listen it might have been the place that, in admiring accents from the gentleman with the green tie, took up the prodigious figure. "Fifty thousand pound!"

It was echoed in a high note from the lady he had previously addressed. "Fifty thousand!"

Yet it was Mr. Prodmore who caught it up loudest and appeared to make it go furthest. "Fifty thousand—fifty thousand!" Mrs. Gracedew had put him in such spirits that he found on the spot, indicating to her his young friend, both the proper humour and the proper rigour for any question of what anyone might "propose." "He'll never part with the dear old home!"

Mrs. Gracedew could match at least the confidence. "Then I'll go over it again while I have the chance." Her own humour enjoined that she should drop into the housekeeper, in the perfect tone of which character she addressed herself once more to the party. "We now pass to the grand staircase." She gathered her band with a brave gesture, but before she had fairly impelled them to the ascent she heard herself rather sharply challenged by Captain Yule, who, during the previous scene, had uttered no sound, yet had remained as attentive as he was impenetrable. "Please let them pass without you!"

She was taken by surprise. "And stay here with *you*?"

"If you'll be so good. I want to speak to you." Turning then to Chivers and frowning on the party, he delivered himself for the first time as a person in a position. "For God's sake, remove them!"

The old man, at this blast of impatience, instantly fluttered forward. "We now pass to the grand staircase."

They all passed, Chivers covering their scattered ascent as a shepherd scales a hillside with his flock; but it became evident during the manœuvre that Cora Prodmore was quite out of tune. She had been standing beyond and rather behind Captain Yule; but she now moved quickly round and reached her new friend's right. "Mrs. Gracedew, may *I* speak to you?"

Her father, before the reply could come, had taken up the place. "*After* Captain Yule, my dear." He was in a state of positively polished lucidity. "You must make the most—don't you see?—of the opportunity of the others!"

He waved her to the staircase as one who knew what he was about, but, while the young man, turning his back, moved consciously and nervously away, the girl renewed her effort to provoke Mrs. Gracedew to detain her. It happened, to her sorrow, that this lady appeared for the moment, to the detriment of any free attention, to be absorbed in Captain Yule's manner; so that Cora could scarce disengage her without some air of invidious reference to it. Recognising as much, she could only for two seconds, but with great yearning, parry her own antagonist. "She'll *help* me, I think, papa!"

"That's exactly what strikes me, love!" he cheerfully replied. "But *I'll* help you too!" He gave her, toward the stairs, a push proportioned both to his authority and to her weight; and while she reluctantly climbed in the wake of the visitors, he laid on Mrs. Gracedew's arm, with a portentous glance at Captain Yule, a hand of commanding significance. "Just pile it on!"

Her attention came back—she seemed to see. "He doesn't like it?"

"Not half enough. Bring him round."

Her eyes rested again on their companion, who had fidgeted further away and who now, with his hands in his pockets and unaware of this private passage, stood again in the open doorway and gazed into the grey court. Something in the sight determined her. "I'll bring him round."

But at this moment Cora, pausing half-way up, sent down another entreaty. "Mrs. Gracedew, will you see *me*?"

The charming woman looked at her watch. "In ten minutes," she smiled back.

Mr. Prodmore, bland and assured, looked at his own. "You could put him through in five—but I'll allow you twenty. There!" he decisively cried to his daughter, whom he quickly rejoined and hustled on her course. Mrs. Gracedew kissed after her a hand of vague comfort.

IV

THE silence that reigned between the pair might have been registered as embarrassing had it lasted a trifle longer. Yule had continued to turn his back, but he faced about, though he was distinctly grave, in time to avert an awkwardness. "How do you come to know so much about my house?"

She was as distinctly not grave. "How do *you* come to know so little?"

"It's not my fault," he said very gently. "A particular combination of misfortunes has forbidden me, till this hour, to come within a mile of it."

These words evidently struck her as so exactly the right ones to proceed from the lawful heir that such a felicity of misery could only quicken her interest. He was plainly as good in his way as the old butler—the particular combination of misfortunes corresponded to the lifelong service. Her interest, none the less, in its turn, could only quicken her pity, and all her emotions, we have already seen, found prompt enough expression. What could any expression do indeed now but mark the romantic reality? "Why, you poor thing!"—she came toward him on the weary road. "Now that you've got here I hope at least you'll stay." Their intercourse must pitch itself—so far as she was concerned—in some key that would make up for things. "Do make yourself comfortable. Don't mind me."

Yule looked a shade less serious. "That's exactly what I wanted to say to *you*!"

She was struck with the way it came in. "Well, if you *had* been haughty, I shouldn't have been quite crushed, should I?"

The young man's gravity, at this, completely yielded. "I'm never haughty—oh, no!"

She seemed even more amused. "Fortunately then, as *I'm* never crushed. I don't think," she added, "that I'm really as crushable as you."

The smile with which he received this failed to conceal completely that it was something of a home thrust. "Aren't we really *all* crushable—by the right thing?"

She considered a little. "Don't you mean rather by the wrong?"

He had got, clearly, a trifle more accustomed to her being extraordinary. "Are you sure we always know them apart?"

173

She weighed the responsibility. "I always do. Don't you?"

"Not quite every time!"

"Oh," she replied, "I don't think, thank goodness, we have positively 'every time' to distinguish."

"Yet we must always act," he objected.

She turned this over; then with her wonderful living look, "I'm glad to hear it," she exclaimed, "because, I fear, I always *do*! You'll certainly think," she added with more gravity, "that I've taken a line today!"

"Do you mean that of mistress of the house? Yes—you do seem in possession!"

"*You* don't!" she honestly answered; after which, as to attenuate a little the rigour of the charge: "You don't comfortably look it, I mean. You don't look"—she was very serious—"as I want you to."

It was when she was most serious that she was funniest. "How do you 'want' me to look?"

She endeavoured, while he watched her, to make up her mind, but seemed only, after an instant, to recognise a difficulty. "When you look at *me*, you're all right!" she sighed. It was an obstacle to her lesson, and she cast her eyes about. "Look at that chimneypiece."

"Well——?" he inquired as his eyes came back from it.

"You mean to say it isn't lovely?"

He returned to it without passion—gave a vivid sign of mere disability. "I'm sure I don't know. I don't mean to say anything. I'm a rank outsider."

It had an instant effect on her—she almost pounced upon him. "Then you must let me put you up!"

"Up to what?"

"Up to everything!"—his levity added to her earnestness. "You were smoking when you came in," she said as she glanced about. "Where's your cigarette?"

The young man appreciatively produced another. "I thought perhaps I mightn't—here."

"You may everywhere."

He bent his head to the information. "Everywhere."

She laughed at his docility, yet could only wish to presume upon it. "It's a rule of the house!"

He took in the place with greater pleasure. "What delightful rules!"

"How could such a house have any others?"—she was already launched again in her brave relation to it. "I *may* go up just once more—mayn't I—to the long gallery?"

How could he tell? "The long gallery?"

With an added glow she remembered. "I forgot you've never seen it. Why, it's the leading thing about you!" She was full, on the spot, of the pride of showing it. "Come right up!"

Clement Yule, half seated on a table from which his long left leg nervously swung, only looked at her and smiled and smoked. "There's a party up."

She remembered afresh. "So *we* must be the party down? Well, you must give me a chance. That long gallery's the principal thing I came over for."

She was strangest of all when she explained. "Where in heaven's name did you come over from?"

"Missoura Top, where I'm building—just in this style. I came for plans and ideas," Mrs. Gracedew serenely pursued. "I felt I must look right *at* you."

"But what did you know about us?"

She kept it a moment as if it were too good to give him all at once. "Everything!"

He seemed indeed almost afraid to touch it. "At 'Missoura Top'?"

"Why not? It's a growing place—forty thousand the last census." She hesitated; then as if her warrant should be slightly more personal: "My husband left it to me."

The young man presently changed his posture. "You're a widow?"

Nothing was wanting to the simplicity of her quiet assent. "A very lone woman." Her face, for a moment, had the vision of a long distance. "My loneliness is great enough to want something big to hold it—and my taste good enough to want something beautiful. You see, I had your picture."

Yule's innocence made a movement. "Mine?"

Her smile reassured him; she nodded toward the main entrance. "A water colour I chanced on in Boston."

"In Boston?"

She stared. "Haven't you heard of Boston either?"

"Yes—but what has Boston heard of *me*?"

"It wasn't 'you,' unfortunately—it was your divine south front. The drawing struck me so that I got you up—in the books."

He appeared, however, rather comically, but half to make it out, or to gather at any rate that there was even more of it than he feared. "Are we in the books?"

"Did you never discover it?" Before his blankness, the dim apprehension in his fine amused and troubled face of how much there was of it, her frank, gay concern for him sprang again to the front. "Where in heaven's name, Captain Yule, have *you* come over from?"

He looked at her very kindly, but as if scarce expecting her to follow. "The East End of London."

She had followed perfectly, he saw the next instant, but she had by no means equally accepted. "What were you doing there?"

He could only put it, though a little over-consciously, very simply. "Working, you see. When I left the army—it was much too slow, unless one was personally a whirlwind of war—I began to make out that, for a fighting man——"

"There's always," she took him up, "somebody or other to go for?"

He considered her, while he smoked, with more confidence; as if she might after all understand. "The enemy, yes—everywhere in force. I went for *him*: misery and ignorance and vice—injustice and privilege and wrong. Such as you see me——"

"You're a rabid reformer?"—she understood beautifully. "I wish we had you at Missoura Top!"

He literally, for a moment, in the light of her beauty and familiarity, appeared to measure his possible use there; then, looking round him again, announced with a sigh that, predicament for predicament, his own would do. "I fear my work is nearer home. I hope," he continued, "since you're so good as to seem to care, to perform a part of that work in the next House of Commons. My electors have wanted me——"

"And you've wanted *them*," she lucidly put in, "and that has been why you couldn't come down."

"Yes, for all this last time. And before that, from my childhood up, there was another reason." He took a few steps away and brought it out as rather a shabby one. "A family feud."

She proved to be quite delighted with it. "Oh, I'm so glad—I *hoped* I'd strike a 'feud'! That rounds it off, and spices it up, and, for the heartbreak with which I take leave of you, just neatly completes the fracture!" Her reference to her going seemed suddenly, on this, to bring her back to a sense of proportion and propriety, and she glanced about once more for some wrap or reticule. This, in turn, however, was another recall. "Must I really wait—to go up?"

He had watched her movement, had changed colour, had shifted his place, had tossed away, plainly unwitting, a cigarette but half smoked; and now he stood in her path to the staircase as if, still unsatisfied, he abruptly sought a way to turn the tables. "Only till you tell me this: if you absolutely meant, awhile ago, that this old thing is so precious."

She met his doubt with amazement and his density with compassion. "Do you literally need I should *say* it? Can you stand here and not feel it?" If he had the misfortune of bandaged eyes, she could at least rejoice in her own vision, which grew intenser with her having to speak for it. She spoke as with a new rush of her impression. "It's a place to love——" Yet to say the whole thing was not easy.

"To love——?" he impatiently insisted.

"Well, as you'd love a person!" If that was saying the whole thing, saying the whole thing could only be to go. A sound from the "party up" came down at that moment, and she took it so clearly as a call that, for a sign of separation, she passed straight to the stairs. "Good-bye!"

The young man let her reach the foot, but then, though the greatest width of the hall now divided them, spoke, anxiously and nervously, as if the point she had just made brought them still more together. "I think I 'feel' it, you know; but it's simply you—your presence, as I may say, and the remarkable way you put it—that make me. I'm afraid that in your absence——" He struck a match to smoke again.

It gave her time apparently to make out something to pause for. "In my absence?"

He lit his cigarette. "I may come back——"

"Come back?" she took him almost sharply up. "I should like to see you *not*!"

He smoked a moment. "I mean to my old idea——"

She had quite turned round on him now. "Your old idea——?"

He faced her over the width still between them. "Well—that one *could* give it up."

Her stare, at this, fairly filled the space. "Give up Covering? How in the world—or why?"

"Because I can't afford to keep it."

It brought her straight back, but only half-way: she pulled up short as at a flash. "Can't you let it?"

Again he smoked before answering. "Let it to *you*?"

She gave a laugh, and her laugh brought her nearer. "I'd take it in a minute!"

Clement Yule remained grave. "I shouldn't have the face to charge you a rent that would make it worth one's while, and I think even you, dear lady"— his voice just trembled as he risked that address—"wouldn't have the face to offer me one." He paused, but something in his aspect and manner checked in her now any impulse to read his meaning too soon. "My lovely inheritance is Dead Sea fruit. It's mortgaged for all it's worth and I haven't the means to pay the interest. If by a miracle I could scrape the money together, it would leave me without a penny to live on." He puffed his cigarette profusely. "So if I find the old home at last—I lose it by the same luck!"

Mrs. Gracedew had hung upon his words, and she seemed still to wait, in visible horror, for something that would improve on them. But when she had to take them for his last, "I never heard of anything so awful!" she broke out. "Do you mean to say you can't arrange——?"

"Oh, yes," he promptly replied, "an arrangement—if that be the name to give it—has been definitely proposed to me."

"What's the matter, then?"—she had dropped into relief. "For heaven's sake, you poor thing, definitely accept it!"

He laughed, though with little joy, at her sweet simplifications. "I've made up my mind in the last quarter of an hour that I can't. It's such a peculiar case."

179

Mrs. Gracedew frankly wondered; her bias was clearly sceptical. "*How* peculiar——?"

He found the measure difficult to give. "Well—more peculiar than most cases."

Still she was not satisfied. "More peculiar than mine?"

"Than yours?"—Clement Yule knew nothing about that.

Something, at this, in his tone, his face—it might have been his "British" density—seemed to pull her up. "I forgot—you don't know mine. No matter. What *is* yours?"

He took a few steps in thought. "Well, the fact that I'm asked to change."

"To change what?"

He wondered how he could put it; then at last, on his own side, simplified. "My attitude."

"Is that all?"—she was relieved again. "Well, you're not a statue."

"No, I'm not a statue; but on the other hand, don't you see? I'm not a windmill." There was good-humour, none the less, in his rigour. "The mortgages I speak of have all found their way, like gregarious silly sheep, into the hands of one person—a devouring wolf, a very rich, a very sharp man of money. He holds me in this manner at his mercy. He consents to make things comfortable for me, but he requires that, in return, I shall do something for him that—don't you know?—rather sticks in my crop."

It appeared on this light showing to stick for a moment even in Mrs. Gracedew's. "Do you mean something wrong?"

He had not a moment's hesitation. "Exceedingly so!"

She turned it over as if pricing a Greek Aldus. "Anything immoral?"

"Yes—I may literally call it immoral."

She courted, however, frankly enough, the strict truth. "Too bad to tell?"

He indulged in another pensive fidget, then left her to judge. "He wants me to give up——" Yet again he faltered.

"To give up what?" What could it be, she appeared to ask, that was barely nameable?

He quite blushed to her indeed as he came to the point. "My fundamental views."

She was disappointed—she had waited for more. "Nothing but *them*?"

He met her with astonishment. "Surely they're quite enough, when one has unfortunately"—he rather ruefully smiled—"so very many!"

She laughed aloud; this was frankly so odd a plea. "Well, *I've* a neat collection too, but I'd 'swap,' as they say in the West, the whole set——!" She looked about the hall for something of equivalent price; after which she pointed, as it caught her eye, to the great cave of the fireplace. "I'd take *that* set!"

The young man scarcely followed. "The fire-irons?"

"For the whole fundamental lot!" She gazed with real yearning at the antique group. "*They're* three hundred years old. Do you mean to tell me your wretched 'views'——?"

"Have anything like that age? No, thank God," Clement Yule laughed, "my views—wretched as you please!—are quite in their prime! They're a hungry little family that has got to be fed. They keep me awake at night."

"Then you must make up your sleep!" Her impatience grew with her interest. "Listen to *me*!"

"That would scarce be the way!" he returned. But he added more sincerely: "You must surely see a fellow can't chuck his politics."

"'Chuck' them——?"

"Well—sacrifice them."

181

"I'd sacrifice mine," she cried, "for that old fire-back with your arms!" He glanced at the object in question, but with such a want of intelligence that she visibly resented it. "See how it has stood!"

"See how *I've* stood!" he answered with spirit. "I've glowed with a hotter fire than anything in any chimney, and the warmth and light I diffuse have attracted no little attention. How can I consent to reduce them to the state of that desolate hearth?"

His companion, freshly struck with the fine details of the desolation, had walked over to the chimney-corner, where, lost in her deeper impression, she lingered and observed. At last she turned away with her impatience controlled. "It's magnificent!"

"The fire-back?"

"Everything—everywhere. I don't understand your haggling."

He hesitated. "That's because you're ignorant." Then seeing in the light of her eye that he had applied to her the word in the language she least liked, he hastened to attenuate. "I mean of what's behind my reserves."

She was silent in a way that made their talk more of a discussion than if she had spoken. "What *is* behind them?" she presently asked.

"Why, my whole political history. Everything I've said, everything I've done. My scorching addresses and letters, reproduced in all the papers. I needn't go into details, but I'm a pure, passionate, pledged Radical."

Mrs. Gracedew looked him full in the face. "Well, what if you *are*?"

He broke into mirth at her tone. "Simply this—that I can't therefore, from one day to the other, pop up at Gossage in the purple pomp of the opposite camp. There's a want of transition. It may be timid of me—it may be abject. But I can't."

If she was not yet prepared to contest she was still less prepared to surrender it, and she confined herself for the instant to smoothing down with her foot the corner of an old rug. "Have you thought very much about it?"

He was vague. "About what?"

"About what Mr. Prodmore wants you to do."

He flushed up. "Oh, then, you know it's *he*?"

"I'm not," she said, still gravely enough, "of an intelligence absolutely infantile."

"You're the cleverest Tory I've ever met!" he laughed. "I didn't mean to mention my friend's name, but since *you've* done so——!" He gave up with a shrug his scruple.

Oh, she had already cleared the ground of it! "It's he who's the devouring wolf? It's he who holds your mortgages?"

The very lucidity of her interest just checked his assent. "He holds plenty of others, and he treats me very handsomely."

She showed of a sudden an inconsequent face. "Do you call *that* handsome—such a condition?"

He shed surprise. "Why, I thought it was just the condition you could meet."

She measured her inconsistency, but was not abashed. "We're not talking of what *I* can meet." Yet she found also a relief in dropping the point. "Why doesn't he stand himself?"

"Well, like other devouring wolves, he's not personally adored."

"Not even," she asked, "when he offers such liberal terms?"

Clement Yule had to explain. "I dare say he doesn't offer them to everyone."

"Only to you?"—at this she quite sprang. "You *are* personally adored; you will be still more if you stand; and that, you poor lamb, is why he wants you!"

The young man, obviously pleased to find her after all more at one with him, accepted gracefully enough the burden her sympathy imposed. "I'm the bearer of my name, I'm the representative of my family; and to my family and my name—since you've led me to it—this countryside has been for generations indulgently attached."

She listened to him with a sentiment in her face that showed how now, at last, she felt herself deal with the lawful heir. She seemed to perceive it with a kind of passion. "You do of course what you will with the countryside!"

"Yes"—he went with her—"if we do it as genuine Yules. I'm obliged of course to grant you that your genuine Yule's a Tory of Tories. It's Mr. Prodmore's belief that I should carry Gossage in that character, but in that character only. They won't look at me in any other."

It might have taxed a spectator to say in what character Mrs. Gracedew, on this, for a little, considered him. "Don't be too sure of people's not looking at you!"

He blushed again, but he laughed. "We must leave out my personal beauty."

"We can't!" she replied with decision. "Don't we take in Mr. Prodmore's?"

Captain Yule was not prepared. "You call him beautiful?"

"Hideous." She settled it; then pursued her investigation. "What's the extraordinary interest that he attaches——?"

"To the return of a Tory?" Here the young man *was* prepared. "Oh, his desire is born of his fear—his terror on behalf of Property, which he sees, somehow, with an intensely Personal, with a quite colossal 'P.' He has a great deal of that article, and very little of anything else."

Mrs. Gracedew, accepting provisionally his demonstration, had one of her friendly recalls. "Do you call that nice daughter 'very little'?"

The young man looked quite at a loss. "Is she very big? I really didn't notice her—and moreover she's just a part of the Property. He thinks things are going too far."

She sat straight down on a stiff chair; on which, with high distinctness: "Well, they *are!*"

He stood before her in the discomposure of her again thus appearing to fail him. "Aren't you then a lover of justice?"

"A passionate one!" She sat there as upright as if she held the scales. "Where's the justice of your losing this house?" Generous as well as strenuous, all her fairness thrown out by her dark old high-backed seat, she put it to him as from the judicial bench. "To keep Covering, you must carry Gossage!"

The odd face he made at it might have betrayed a man dazzled. "As a renegade?"

"As a genuine Yule. What business have you to be anything else?" She had already arranged it all. "You must close with Mr. Prodmore—you must stand in the Tory interest." She hung fire a moment; then as she got up: "If you will, I'll conduct your canvass!"

He stared at the distracting picture. "That puts the temptation high!"

But she brushed the mere picture away. "Ah, don't look at me as if *I* were the temptation! Look at this sweet old human home, and feel all its gathered memories. Do you want to know what they do to me?" She took the survey herself again, as if to be really sure. "They speak to me for Mr. Prodmore."

He followed with a systematic docility the direction of her eyes, but as if with the result only of its again coming home to him that there was no accounting for what things might do. "Well, there are others than these, you know," he good-naturedly pleaded—"things for which I've spoken, repeatedly and loudly, to others than you." The very manner of his speaking on such occasions appeared, for that matter, now to come back to him. "One's 'human home' is all very well, but the rest of one's humanity is better!" She gave, at this, a droll soft wail; she turned impatiently away. "I see you're disgusted with me, and I'm sorry; but one must take one's self as circumstances and experience have made one, and it's not my fault, don't you know? if they've made me a very modern man. I see something else in the world than the beauty of old show-houses and the glory of old show-families. There are thousands of people in England who can show no houses at all, and I don't feel it utterly shameful to share their poor fate!"

She had moved away with impatience, and it was the advantage of this for her that the back she turned prevented him from seeing how intently she listened. She seemed to continue to listen even after he had stopped; but if that gave him a sense of success, he might have been checked by the way she at last turned round with a sad and beautiful headshake. "We share the poor fate of humanity whatever we do, and we do something to help and console when we've something precious to show. What on earth is more precious than what the ages have slowly wrought? They've trusted us, in such a case, to keep it—to do something, in our turn, for *them*." She shone out at him as if her contention had the evidence of the noonday sun, and yet in her generosity she superabounded and explained. "It's such a virtue, in anything, to have lasted; it's such an honour, for anything, to have been spared. To all strugglers from the wreck of time hold out a pitying hand!"

Yule, on this argument,—of a strain which even a good experience of debate could scarce have prepared him to meet,—had not a congruous rejoinder absolutely pat, and his hesitation unfortunately gave him time to see how soon his companion made out that what had touched him most in it was her particular air in presenting it. She would manifestly have preferred he should have been floored by her mere moral reach; yet he was aware that his own made no great show as he took refuge in general pleasantry. "What a plea for looking backward, dear lady, to come from Missoura Top!"

"We're making a Past at Missoura Top as fast as ever we can, and I should like to see you lay your hand on an hour of the one we've made! It's a tight fit, as yet, I grant," she said, "and that's just why I like, in yours, to find room, don't you see? to turn round. You're *in* it, over here, and you can't get out; so just make the best of that and treat the thing as part of the fun!"

"The whole of the fun, to me," the young man replied, "is in hearing you defend it! It's like your defending hereditary gout or chronic rheumatism and sore throat—the things I feel aching in every old bone of these walls and groaning in every old draught that, I'm sure, has for centuries blown through them."

Mrs. Gracedew looked as if no woman could be shaken who was so prepared to be just all round. "If there be aches—there may be—you're here to soothe them, and if there be draughts—there *must* be!—you're here to stop them up. And do you know what *I'm* here for? If I've come so far and so straight, I've almost wondered myself. I've felt with a kind of passion—but now I see *why* I've felt." She moved about the hall with the excitement of this perception, and, separated from him at last by a distance across which he followed her discovery with a visible suspense, she brought out the news. "I'm here for an act of salvation—I'm here to avert a sacrifice!"

So they stood a little, with more, for the minute, passing between them than either really could say. She might have flung down a glove that he decided on the whole, passing his hand over his head as the seat of some confusion, not to pick up. Again, but flushed as well as smiling, he sought the easiest cover. "You're here, I think, madam, to be a memory for all my future!"

Well, she was willing, she showed as she came nearer, to take it, at the worst, for that. "You'll be one for mine, if I can see you by that hearth. Why do you make such a fuss about changing your politics? If you'd come to Missoura Top, you'd change them quick enough!" Then, as she saw further and struck harder, her eyes grew deep, her face even seemed to pale, and she paused, splendid and serious, with the force of her plea. "What do politics amount to, compared with religions? Parties and programmes come and go, but a duty like this abides. There's nothing you can break with"—she pressed him closer, ringing out—"that would be like breaking *here*. The very words are violent and ugly—as much a sacrilege as if you had been trusted with the key of the temple. This *is* the temple—don't profane it! Keep up the old altar kindly—you can't set up a new one as good. You *must* have beauty in your life, don't you see?—that's the only way to make sure of it for the lives of others. Keep leaving it to *them*, to all the poor others," she went on with her bright irony, "and heaven only knows what will become of it! Does it take one of *us* to feel that?—to preach you the truth? Then it's good, Captain Yule, we come right over—just to see, you know, what you may happen to be about. We know," she went on while her sense of proportion seemed to play into her sense of humour, "what we haven't got, worse luck; so that if you've happily got it you've got it also for *us*. You've got it in trust, you see, and oh! we have an eye on you. You've had it so for me, all these dear days that I've been drinking it in, that, to be grateful, I've wanted regularly to *do* something." With which, as if in the rich confidence of having convinced him, she came so near as almost to touch him. "Tell me now I shall have done it—I shall have kept you at your post!"

If he moved, on this, immediately further, it was with the oddest air of seeking rather to study her remarks at his ease than to express an independence of them. He kept, to this end, his face averted—he was so completely now in intelligent possession of her own. The sacrifice in question carried him even to the door of the court, where he once more stood so long engaged that the persistent presentation of his back might at last have suggested either a confession or a request.

Mrs. Gracedew, meanwhile, a little spent with her sincerity, seated herself again in the great chair, and if she sought, visibly enough, to read a meaning into his movement, she had as little triumph for one possible view of it as she had resentment for the other. The possibility that he yielded left her after all as vague in respect to a next step as the possibility that he merely wished to get rid of her. The moments elapsed without her abdicating; and indeed when he finally turned round his expression was an equal check to any power to feel she might have won. "You have," he queerly smiled at her, "a standpoint quite your own and a style of eloquence that the few scraps of parliamentary training I've picked up don't seem at all to fit me to deal with. Of course I don't pretend, you know, that I don't *care* for Covering."

That, at all events, she could be glad to hear, if only perhaps for the tone in it that was so almost comically ingenuous. But her relief was reasonable and her exultation temperate. "You haven't even seen it yet." She risked, however, a laugh. "Aren't you a bit afraid?"

He took a minute to reply, then replied—as if to make it up—with a grand collapse. "Yes; awfully. But if I am," he hastened in decency to add, "it isn't only Covering that makes me."

This left his friend apparently at a loss. "What else is it?"

"Everything. But it doesn't in the least matter," he loosely pursued. "You may be quite correct. When we talk of the house your voice comes to me somehow as the wind in its old chimneys."

Her amusement distinctly revived. "I hope you don't mean I roar!"

He blushed again; there was no doubt he was confused. "No—nor yet perhaps that you whistle! I don't believe the wind does either, here. It only whispers," he sought gracefully to explain; "and it sighs——"

"And I hope," she broke in, "that it sometimes laughs!"

The sound she gave only made him, as he looked at her, more serious. "Whatever it does, it's all right."

"All right?"—they were sufficiently together again for her to lay her hand straight on his arm. "Then you promise?"

"Promise what?"

He had turned as pale as if she hurt him, and she took her hand away. "To meet Mr. Prodmore."

"Oh, dear, no; not yet!"—he quite recovered himself. "I must wait—I must think."

She looked disappointed, and there was a momentary silence. "When have you to answer him?"

"Oh, he gives me time!" Clement Yule spoke very much as he might have said, "Oh, in two minutes!"

"*I* wouldn't give you time," Mrs. Gracedew cried with force—"I'd give you a shaking! For God's sake, at any rate"—and she really tried to push him off—"go upstairs!"

"And literally *find* the dreadful man?" This was so little his personal idea that, distinctly dodging her pressure, he had already reached the safe quarter.

But it befell that at the same moment she saw Cora reappear on the upper landing—a circumstance that promised her a still better conclusion. "He's coming down!"

Cora, in spite of this announcement, came down boldly enough without him and made directly for Mrs. Gracedew, to whom her eyes had attached themselves with an undeviating glare. Her plain purpose of treating this lady as an isolated presence allowed their companion perfect freedom to consider her arrival with sharp alarm. His disconcerted stare seemed for a moment to balance; it wandered, gave a wild glance at the open door, then searched the ascent of the staircase, in which, apparently, it now found a coercion. "I'll go up!" he gasped; and he took three steps at a time.

V

THE girl threw herself, in her flushed eagerness, straight upon the wonderful lady. "I've come back to you—I want to speak to you!" The need had been a rapid growth, but it was clearly immense. "May I confide in you?"

Her instant overflow left Mrs. Gracedew both astonished and amused. "You too?" she laughed. "Why it *is* good we come over!"

"It is, indeed!" Cora gratefully echoed. "You were so very kind to me and seemed to think me so curious."

The mirth of her friend redoubled. "Well, I loved you for it, and it was nothing moreover to what you thought *me*!"

Miss Prodmore found, for this, no denial—she only presented her frank high colour. "I loved *you*. But I'm the worst!" she generously added. "And I'm solitary."

"Ah, so am I!" Mrs. Gracedew declared with gaiety, but with emphasis. "A *very* queer thing always *is* solitary! But, since we have that link, by all means confide."

"Well, I was met here by tremendous news." Cora produced it with a purple glow. "He wants me to marry him!"

Mrs. Gracedew looked amiably receptive, but as if she failed as yet to follow. "'He' wants you?"

"Papa, of course. He has settled it!"

Mrs. Gracedew was still vague. "Settled what?"

"Why, the whole question. That I must take him."

Mrs. Gracedew seemed to frown at her own scattered wits. "But, my dear, take *whom*?"

The girl looked surprised at this lapse of her powers. "Why, Captain Yule, who just went up."

"Oh!" said Mrs. Gracedew with a full stare. "Oh!" she repeated, looking straight away.

"I thought you would know," Cora gently explained.

Her friend's eyes, with a kinder light now, came back to her. "I didn't know." Mrs. Gracedew looked, in truth, as if that had been sufficiently odd, and seemed also to wonder at two or three things more. It all, however, broke quickly into a question. "Has Captain Yule asked you?"

"No, but he *will*"—Cora was clear as a bell. "He'll do it to keep the house. It's mortgaged to papa, and Captain Yule buys it back."

Her friend had an illumination that was rapid for the way it spread. "By marrying you?" she quavered.

Cora, under further parental instruction, had plainly mastered the subject. "By giving me his name and his position. They're awfully great, and

191

they're the price, don't you see?" she modestly mentioned. "*My* price. Papa's price. Papa wants them."

Mrs. Gracedew had caught hold; yet there were places where her grasp was weak, and she had, strikingly, begun again to reflect. "But his name and his position, great as they may be, are his dreadful politics!"

Cora threw herself with energy into this advance. "You *know* about his dreadful politics? He's to change them," she recited, "to get *me*. And if he gets me——"

"He keeps the house?"—Mrs. Gracedew snatched it up.

Cora continued to show her schooling. "I go *with* it—he's to have us both. But only," she admonishingly added, "if he changes. The question is—*will* he change?"

Mrs. Gracedew appeared profoundly to entertain it. "I see. *Will* he change?"

Cora's consideration of it went even further. "*Has* he changed?"

It went—and the effect was odd—a little too far for her companion, in whom, just discernibly, it had touched the spring of impatience. "My dear child, how in the world should *I* know?"

But Cora knew exactly how anyone would know. "He hasn't seemed to care enough for the house. *Does* he care?"

Mrs. Gracedew moved away, passed over to the fireplace, and stood a moment looking at the old armorial fire-back she had praised to its master—yet not, it must be added, as if she particularly saw it. Then as she faced about: "You had better ask him!"

They stood thus confronted, with the fine old interval between them, and the girl's air was for a moment that of considering such a course. "If he does care," she said at last, "he'll propose."

Mrs. Gracedew, from where she stood in relation to the stairs, saw at this point the subject of their colloquy restored to view: Captain Yule was just upon them—he had turned the upper landing. The sight of him forced from her in a flash an ejaculation that she tried, however, to keep private—"He does care!" She passed swiftly, before he reached them, back to the girl and, in a quick whisper, but with full conviction, let her have it: "He'll propose!"

Her movement had made her friend aware, and the young man, hurrying down, was now in the hall. Cora, at his hurry, looked dismay—"Then I fly!" With which, casting about for a direction, she reached the door to the court.

Captain Yule, however, at this result of his return, expressed instant regret. "I drive Miss Prodmore away!"

Mrs. Gracedew, more quickly still, eased off the situation. "It's all right!" She had embraced both parties with a smile, but it was most liberal now for Cora. "Do you mind, one moment?"—it conveyed, unmistakeably, a full intelligence and a fine explanation. "I've something to say to Captain Yule."

Cora stood in the doorway, robust against the garden-light, and looking from one to the other. "Yes—but I've also something more to say to *you*."

"Do you mean now?" the young man asked.

It was the first time he had spoken to her, and her hesitation might have signified a maidenly flutter. "No—but before she goes."

Mrs. Gracedew took it amiably up. "Come back, then; I'm not going." And there was both dismissal and encouragement in the way that, as on the occasion of the girl's former retreat, she blew her a familiar kiss. Cora, still with her face to them, waited just enough to show that she took it without a response; then, with a quick turn, dashed out, while Mrs. Gracedew looked at their visitor in vague surprise. "What's the matter with her?"

She had turned away as soon as she spoke, moving as far from him as she had moved a few moments before from Cora. The silence that, as he watched her, followed her question would have been seen by a spectator to be a hard one for either to break. "I don't know what's the matter with her," he said at last; "I'm afraid I only know what's the matter with *me*. It will doubtless give you pleasure to learn," he added, "that I've closed with Mr. Prodmore."

It was a speech that, strangely enough, seemed but half to dissipate the hush. Mrs. Gracedew reached the great chimney again; again she stood there with her face averted; and when she finally replied it was in other words than he might have supposed himself naturally to inspire. "I thought you said he gave you time."

"Yes; but you produced just now so deep an effect on me that I thought best not to take any." He appeared to listen to a sound from above, and, for a moment, under this impulse, his eyes travelled about almost as if he were alone. Then he completed, with deliberation, his statement. "I came upon him right there, and I burnt my ships."

Mrs. Gracedew continued not to meet his face. "You do what he requires?"

The young man was markedly, consciously caught. "I do what he requires. I felt the tremendous force of all you said to me."

She turned round on him now, as if perhaps with a slight sharpness, the face of responsibility—even, it might be, of reproach. "So did I—or I shouldn't have said it!"

It was doubtless this element of justification in her tone that drew from him a laugh a tiny trifle dry. "You're perhaps not aware that you wield an influence of which it's not too much to say——"

But he paused at the important point so long that she took him up. "To say what?"

"Well, that it's practically irresistible!"

It sounded a little as if it had not been what he first meant; but it made her, none the less, still graver and just faintly ironical. "You've given me the most flattering proof of my influence that I've ever enjoyed in my life!"

He fixed her very hard, now distinctly so mystified that he could only wonder what different recall of her previous attitude she would have looked for. "This was inevitable, dear madam, from the moment you had converted me—and in about three minutes too!—into the absolute echo of your raptures."

Nothing was, indeed, more extraordinary than her air of having suddenly forgotten them. "My 'raptures'?"

He was amazed. "Why, about my home."

He might look her through and through, but she had no eyes for himself, though she had now quitted the fireplace and finally recognised this allusion. "Oh, yes—your home!" From where had she come back to it? "It's a nice tattered, battered old thing." This account of it was the more shrunken that her observation, even as she spoke, freshly went the rounds. "It has defects of course"—with this renewed attention they appeared suddenly to strike her. They had popped out, conspicuous, and for a little it might have been a matter of conscience. However, her conscience dropped. "But it's no use mentioning them now!"

They had half an hour earlier been vividly present to himself, but to see her thus oddly pulled up by them was to forget on the spot the ground he had taken. "I'm particularly sorry," he returned with some spirit, "that you didn't mention them before!"

At this imputation of inconsequence, of a levity not, after all, without its excuse, Mrs. Gracedew was reduced, in keeping her resentment down, to an effort not quite successfully disguised. It was in a tone, nevertheless, all the more mild in intention that she reminded him of where he had equally failed. "If you had really gone over the house, as I almost went on my knees to you to do, you might have discovered some of them yourself!"

"How can you say that," the young man asked with heat, "when I was precisely in the very act of it? It was just *because* I was that the first person I met above was Mr. Prodmore; on which, feeling that I must come to it sooner or later, I simply gave in to him on the spot—yielded him, to have it well over, the whole of his point."

195

She listened to this account of the matter as she might have gazed, from afar, at some queer object that was scarce distinguishable. It left her a moment in the deepest thought, but she presently recovered her tone. "Let me then congratulate you on at last knowing what you want!"

But there were, after all, he instantly showed, no such great reasons for that. "I only know it so far as *you* know it! I struck while the iron was hot—or at any rate while the hammer was."

"Of course I recognise"—she adopted his image with her restored gaiety—"that it can rarely have been exposed to such a fire. I blazed up, and I know that when I burn——"

She had pulled up with the foolish sense of this. "When you burn?"

"Well, I do it as Chicago does."

He also could laugh out now. "Isn't that usually down to the ground?"

Meeting his laugh, she threw up her light arms. "As high as the sky!" Then she came back, as with a scruple, to the real question. "I suppose you've still formalities to go through."

"With Mr. Prodmore?" Well, he would suppose it too if she liked. "Oh, endless, tiresome ones, no doubt!"

This sketch of them made her wonder. "You mean they'll take so very, very long?"

He seemed after all to know perfectly what he meant. "Every hour, every month, that I can possibly make them last!"

She was with him here, however, but to a certain point. "You mustn't drag them out *too* much—must you? Won't he think in that case you may want to retract?"

Yule apparently tried to focus Mr. Prodmore under this delusion, and with a success that had a quick, odd result. "I shouldn't be so terribly upset by his mistake, you know, even if he did!"

His manner, with its slight bravado, left her proportionately shocked. "Oh, it would never do to give him any colour whatever for supposing you to have any doubt that, as one may say, you've pledged your honour."

He devoted to this proposition more thought than its simplicity would have seemed to demand; but after a minute, at all events, his intelligence triumphed. "Of course not—not when I *haven't* any doubt!"

Though his intelligence had triumphed, she still wished to show she was there to support it. "How can you *possibly* have any—any more than you can possibly have that one's honour is everything in life?" And her charming eyes expressed to him her need to feel that he was quite at one with her on *that* point.

He could give her every assurance. "Oh, yes—everything in life!"

It did her much good, brought back the rest of her brightness. "Wasn't it just of the question of the honour of things that we talked awhile ago—and of the difficulty of sometimes keeping our sense of it clear? There's no more to be said therefore," she went on with the faintest soft sigh about it, "except that I leave you to your ancient glory as I leave you to your strict duty." She had these things there before her; they might have been a well-spread board from which she turned away fasting. "I hope you'll do justice to dear old Covering in spite of its weak points, and I hope above all you'll not be incommoded——"

As she hesitated here he was too intent. "Incommoded——?"

She saw it better than she could express it. "Well, by such a rage——!"

He challenged this description with a strange gleam. "You suppose it will be a rage?"

She laughed out at his look. "Are you afraid of the love that kills?"

He grew singularly grave. "*Will* it kill——?"

"Great passions *have*!"—she was highly amused.

197

But he could only stare. "Is it a great passion?"

"Surely—when so many feel it!"

He was fairly bewildered. "But how many——?"

She reckoned them up. "Let's see. If you count them all——"

"'All'?" Clement Yule gasped.

She looked at him, in turn, slightly mystified. "I see. You knock off some. About half?"

It was too obscure—he broke down. "Whom on earth are you talking about?"

"Why, the electors——"

"Of Gossage?"—he leaped at it. "Oh!"

"I got the whole thing up—there are six thousand. It's such a fine figure!" said Mrs. Gracedew.

He had sharply passed from her, to cover his mistake, and it carried him half round the hall. Then, as if aware that this pause itself compromised him, he came back confusedly and with her last words in his ear. "*Has* she a fine figure?"

But her own thoughts were off. "'She'?"

He blushed and recovered himself. "Aren't we talking——"

"Of Gossage? Oh, yes—she has every charm! Good-bye," said Mrs. Gracedew.

He pulled, at this, the longest face, but was kept dumb a moment by the very decision with which she again began to gather herself. It held him helpless, and there was finally real despair in his retarded protest. "You don't mean to say you're going?"

"You don't mean to say you're surprised at it? Haven't I done," she luminously asked, "what I told you I had been so mystically moved to come for?" She recalled to him by her renewed supreme survey the limited character of this errand, which she then in a brisk familiar word expressed to the house itself. "You dear old thing—you're saved!"

Clement Yule might on the other hand, by his simultaneous action, have given himself out for lost. "For God's sake," he cried as he circled earnestly round her, "don't go till I can come back to thank you!" He pulled out his watch. "I promised to return immediately to Prodmore."

This completely settled his visitor. "Then don't let me, for a moment more, keep you away from him. You must have such lots"—it went almost without saying—"to talk comfortably over."

The young man's embrace of that was, in his restless movement, to roam to the end of the hall furthest from the stairs. But here his assent was entire. "I certainly feel, you know, that I must see him again." He rambled even to the open door and looked with incoherence into the court. "Yes, decidedly, I *must*!"

"Is he out there?" Mrs. Gracedew lightly asked.

He turned short round. "No—I left him in the long gallery."

"You *saw* that, then?"—she flashed back into eagerness. "Isn't it lovely?"

Clement Yule rather wondered. "I didn't notice it. How *could* I?"

His face was so woeful that she broke into a laugh. "How *couldn't* you? Notice it now, then. Go up to him!"

He crossed at last to the staircase, but at the foot he stopped again. "Will you wait for me?"

He had such an air of proposing a bargain, of making the wait a condition, that she had to look it well in the face. The result of her doing so, however, was apparently a strong sense that she could give him no pledge. Her silence, after a moment, expressed that; but, for a further emphasis, moving away, she sank suddenly into the chair she had already occupied and in which, serious again and very upright, she continued to withhold her promise. "Go up to him!" she simply repeated. He obeyed, with an abrupt turn, mounting briskly enough several steps, but pausing midway and looking back at her as if he were after all irresolute. He was in fact so much so that, at the sight of her still in her chair and alone by his cold hearth, he descended a few steps again and seemed, with too much decidedly on his mind, on the point of breaking out. She had sat a minute in such thought, figuring him clearly as gone, that at the sound of his return she sprang up with a protest. This checked him afresh, and he remained where he had paused, still on the ascent and exchanging with her a look to which neither party was inspired, oddly enough, to contribute a word. It struck him, without words, at all events, as enough, and he now took his upward course at such a pace that he presently disappeared. She listened awhile to his retreating tread; then her own, on the old flags of the hall, became rapid, though, it may perhaps be added, directed to no visible end. It conveyed her, in the great space, from point to point, but she now for the first time moved there without attention and without joy, her course determined by a series of such inward throbs as might have been the suppressed beats of a speech. A real observer, had such a monster been present, would have followed this tacit evolution from sign to sign and from shade to shade. "Why didn't he tell me *all?*—But it was none of my business!—What does he mean to do?—What should he do but what he *has* done?—And what *can* he do, when he's so deeply committed, when he's practically engaged, when he's just the same as married—and buried?—The thing for *me* to 'do' is just to pull up short and bundle out: to remove from the scene they encumber the numerous fragments—well, of what?"

Her thought was plainly arrested by the sight of Cora Prodmore, who, returning from the garden, reappeared first in the court and then in the open doorway. Mrs. Gracedew's was a thought, however, that, even when desperate, was never quite vanquished, and it found a presentable public solution in the pieces of the vase smashed by Chivers and just then, on the table where he had laid them, catching her eye. "Of my old Chelsea pot!" Her gay, sad headshake as she took one of them up pronounced for Cora's benefit its funeral oration. She laid the morsel thoughtfully down, while her visitor seemed with simple dismay to read the story.

VI

"Has he been *breaking*——?" the girl asked in horror.

Mrs. Gracedew laughingly tapped her heart. "Yes, we've had a scene! He went up again to your father."

Cora was disconcerted. "Papa's not there. He just came down to me by the other way."

"Then he can join you here," said Mrs. Gracedew with instant resignation. "I'm going."

"Just when I've come back to you—at the risk," Cora made bold to throw off, "of again interrupting, though I really hoped he had gone, your conversation with Captain Yule?"

But Mrs. Gracedew let the ball quite drop. "I've nothing to say to Captain Yule."

Cora picked it up for another toss. "You had a good deal to say a few minutes ago!"

"Well, I've said it, and it's over. I've nothing more to say at all," Mrs. Gracedew insisted. But her announcement of departure left her on this occasion, as each of its predecessors had done, with a last, with indeed a fresh, solicitude. "What has become of my delightful 'party'?"

"They've been dismissed, through the grounds, by the other door. But they mentioned," the girl pursued, "the probable arrival of a fresh lot."

Mrs. Gracedew showed on this such a revival of interest as fairly amounted to yearning. "Why, what times you have! *You*," she nevertheless promptly decreed, "must take the fresh lot—since the house is now practically yours!"

Poor Cora looked blank. "Mine?"

201

Her companion matched her stare. "Why, if you're going to marry Captain Yule."

Cora coloured, in a flash, to the eyes. "I'm *not* going to marry Captain Yule!"

Her friend as quickly paled again. "Why on earth then did you tell me only ten minutes ago that you were?"

Cora could only look bewildered at the charge. "I told you nothing of the sort. I only told you"—she was almost indignantly positive—"that he had been ordered me!"

It sent Mrs. Gracedew off; she moved away to indulge an emotion that presently put on the form of extravagant mirth. "Like a dose of medicine or a course of baths?"

The girl's gravity and lucidity sustained themselves. "As a remedy for the single life." Oh, she had mastered the matter now! "But I won't take him!"

"Ah, then, why didn't you let me know?" Mrs. Gracedew panted.

"I was on the very point of it when he came in and interrupted us." Cora clearly felt she might be wicked, but was at least not stupid. "It's just to let you know that I'm here now."

Ah, the difference it made! This difference, for Mrs. Gracedew, suddenly shimmered in all the place, and her companion's fixed eyes caught in her face the reflection of it. "Excuse me—I misunderstood. I somehow took for granted——!" She stopped, a trifle awkwardly—suddenly tender, for Cora, as to the way she had inevitably seen it.

"You took for granted I'd jump at him? Well, you can take it for granted I won't!"

Mrs. Gracedew, fairly admiring her, put it sympathetically. "You prefer the single life?"

"No—but I don't prefer *him*!" Cora was crystal-bright.

Her light, indeed, for her friend, was at first almost blinding; it took Mrs. Gracedew a moment to distinguish—which she then did, however, with immense eagerness. "You prefer someone else?" Cora's promptitude dropped at this, and, starting to hear it, as you might well have seen, for the first time publicly phrased, she abruptly moved away. A minute's sense of her scruple was enough for Mrs. Gracedew: this was proved by the tone of soft remonstrance and high benevolence with which that lady went on. She had looked very hard, first, at one of the old warriors hung on the old wall, and almost spoke as if he represented their host. "He seems remarkably clever."

Cora, at something in the sound, quite jumped about. "Then why don't you marry him yourself?"

Mrs. Gracedew gave a sort of happy sigh. "Well, I've got fifty reasons! I rather think one of them must be that he hasn't happened to ask me."

It was a speech, however, that her visitor could easily better. "I haven't got fifty reasons, but I *have* got one."

Mrs. Gracedew smiled as if it were indeed a stroke of wit. "You mean your case is one of those in which safety is *not* in numbers?" And then on Cora's visibly not understanding: "It *is* when reasons are bad that one needs so many!"

The proposition was too general for the girl to embrace, but the simplicity of her answer was far from spoiling it. "My reason is awfully good."

Mrs. Gracedew did it complete justice. "I see. An older friend."

Cora listened as at a warning sound; yet she had by this time practically let herself go, and it took but Mrs. Gracedew's extended encouraging hand, which she quickly seized, to bring the whole thing out. "I've been trying this hour, in my terrible need of advice, to tell you about him!" It came in a small clear torrent, a soft tumble-out of sincerity. "After we parted—you and I—at the station, he suddenly turned up there, and I took a little quiet walk with him which gave you time to get here before me and of which my father is in a state of ignorance that I don't know whether to regard as desirable or dreadful."

Mrs. Gracedew, attentive and wise, might have been, for her face, the old family solicitor. "You want me then to *inform* your father?" It was a wonderful intonation.

Poor Cora, for that matter too, might suddenly have become under this touch the prodigal with a list of debts. She seemed an instant to look out of a blurred office window-pane at a grey London sky; then she broke away. "I really don't know *what* I want. I think," she honestly admitted, "I just want kindness."

Mrs. Gracedew's expression might have hinted—but not for too long— that Bedford Row was an odd place to apply for it; she appeared for an instant to make the revolving office-chair creak. "What do you mean by kindness?"

Cora was a model client—she perfectly knew. "I mean help."

Mrs. Gracedew closed an inkstand with a clap and locked a couple of drawers. "What do you mean by help?"

The client's inevitable answer seemed to perch on the girl's lips: "A thousand pounds." But it came out in another, in a much more charming form. "I mean that I love him."

The family solicitor got up: it was a high figure. "And does he love *you*?"

Cora hesitated. "Ask *him*."

Mrs. Gracedew weighed the necessity. "Where is he?"

"Waiting." And the girl's glance, removed from her companion and wandering aloft and through space, gave the scale of his patience.

Her adviser, however, required the detail. "But *where*?"

Cora briefly demurred again. "In that funny old grotto."

Mrs. Gracedew thought. "Funny?"

"Half-way from the park gate. It's very *nice*!" Cora more eagerly added.

Mrs. Gracedew continued to reflect. "Oh, I know it!" She spoke as if she had known it most of her life.

Her tone encouraged her client. "Then will you see him?"

"No." This time it was almost dry.

"No?"

"No. If you want help——" Mrs. Gracedew, still musing, explained.

"Yes?"

"Well—you want a great deal."

"Oh, so much!"—Cora but too woefully took it in. "I want," she quavered, "all there is!"

"Well—you shall have it."

"All there is?"—she convulsively held her to it.

Mrs. Gracedew had finally mastered it. "I'll see your father."

"You dear, delicious lady!" Her young friend had again encompassed her; but, passive and preoccupied, she showed some of the chill of apprehension. It was indeed as if to meet this that Cora went earnestly on: "He's intensely sympathetic!"

"Your father?" Mrs. Gracedew had her reserves.

"Oh, no—the other person. I so believe in him!" Cora cried.

Mrs. Gracedew looked at her a moment. "Then so do I—and I like him for believing in *you*."

"Oh, he does that," the girl hurried on, "far more than Captain Yule—I could see just with one glance that *he* doesn't at all. Papa has of course seen the young man I mean, but we've been so sure papa would hate it that we've had to be awfully careful. He's the son of the richest man at Bellborough, he's Granny's godson, and he'll inherit his father's business, which is simply immense. Oh, from the point of view of the things he's *in*"—and Cora found herself sharp on this—"he's quite as good as papa himself. He has been away for three days, and if he met me at the station, where, on his way back, he has to change, it was by the merest chance in the world. I wouldn't love him," she brilliantly wound up, "if he wasn't nice."

"A man's always nice if you *will* love him!" Mrs. Gracedew laughed.

Her young friend more than met it. "He's nicer still if he 'will' love *you*!"

But Mrs. Gracedew kept her head. "Nicer of course than if he won't! But are you sure this gentleman *does* love you?"

"As sure as that the other one doesn't."

"Ah, but the other one doesn't know you."

"Yes, thank goodness—and never shall!"

Mrs. Gracedew watched her a little, but on the girl's meeting her eyes turned away with a quick laugh. "You mean of course till it's too late."

"Altogether!" Cora spoke as with quite the measure of the time.

Mrs. Gracedew, revolving a moment in silence, appeared to accept her showing. "Then what's the matter?" she impatiently asked.

"The matter?"

"Your father's objection to the gentleman in the grotto."

Cora now for the first time faltered. "His name."

This for a moment pulled up her friend, in whom, however, relief seemed to contend with alarm. "Only his name?"

"Yes, but——" Cora's eyes rolled.

Her companion invitingly laughed. "But it's enough?"

Her roll confessingly fixed itself. "*Not* enough—that's just the trouble!"

Mrs. Gracedew looked kindly curious. "What then *is* it?"

Cora faced the music. "Pegg."

Mrs. Gracedew stared. "Nothing else?"

"Nothing to speak of." The girl was quite candid now. "Hall."

"Nothing before——?"

"Not a letter."

"Hall Pegg?" Mrs. Gracedew had winced, but she quickly recovered herself, and, for a further articulation, appeared, from delicacy, to form the sound only with her mind. The sound she formed with her lips was, after an instant, simply "Oh!"

It was to the combination of the spoken and the unspoken that Cora desperately replied. "It sounds like a hat-rack!"

"'Hall Pegg'? 'Hall Pegg'?" Mrs. Gracedew now made it, like a questionable coin, ring upon the counter. But it lay there as lead and without, for a moment, her taking it up again. "How many has your father?" she inquired instead.

"How many names?" Miss Prodmore seemed dimly to see that there was no hope in that. "He somehow makes out five."

"Oh, that's *too* many!" Mrs. Gracedew jeeringly declared.

"Papa unfortunately doesn't think so, when Captain Yule, I believe, has six."

"Six?" Mrs. Gracedew, alert, looked as if that might be different.

"Papa, in the morning-room, told me them all."

Mrs. Gracedew visibly considered, then for a moment dropped Mr. Pegg. "And what *are* they!"

"Oh, all sorts. 'Marmaduke Clement——'" Cora tried to recall.

Mrs. Gracedew, however, had already checked her. "I see—'Marmaduke Clement' will do." She appeared for a minute intent, but, as with an energetic stoop, she picked up Mr. Pegg. "But so will yours," she said, with decision.

"Mine?—you mean *his*!"

207

"The same thing—what you'll *be*."

"Mrs. Hall Pegg!"—Cora tried it, with resolution, loudly.

It fell a little flat in the noble space, but Mrs. Gracedew's manner quickly covered it. "It won't make you a bit less charming."

Cora wondered—she hoped. "Only for papa."

And what was *he*? Mrs. Gracedew by this time seemed assentingly to ask. "Never for *me*!" she soothingly declared.

Cora took this in with deep thanks that gripped and patted her companion's hand. "You accept it more than gracefully. But if you could only make *him*——!"

Mrs. Gracedew was all concentration. "'Him'? Mr. Pegg?"

"No—he naturally *has* to accept it. But papa."

She looked harder still at this greater feat, then seemed to see light. "Well, it will be difficult—but I will."

Doubt paled before it. "Oh, you heavenly thing!"

Mrs. Gracedew after an instant, sustained by this appreciation, went a step further. "And I'll make him *say* he does!"

Cora closed her eyes with the dream of it. "Oh, if I could only hear him!"

Her benefactress had at last run it to earth. "It will be enough if *I* do."

Cora quickly considered; then, with prompt accommodation, gave the comfortable measure of her faith. "Yes—I think it will." She was quite ready to retire. "I'll give you time."

"Thank you," said Mrs. Gracedew; "but before you give me time give me something better."

This pulled the girl up a little, as if in parting with her secret she had parted with her all. "Something better?"

"If I help you, you know," Mrs. Gracedew explained, "you must help me."

"But how?"

"By a clear assurance." The charming woman's fine face now gave the real example of clearness. "That if Captain Yule should propose to you, you would unconditionally refuse him."

Cora flushed with the surprise of its being only that. "With my dying breath!"

Mrs. Gracedew scanned her robust vitality. "Will you make it even a promise?"

The girl looked about her in solid certainty. "Do you want me to sign——?"

Mrs. Gracedew was quick. "No, don't sign!"

Yet Cora was so ready to oblige. "Then what shall I do?"

Mrs. Gracedew turned away, but after a few vague steps faced her again. "Kiss me."

Cora flew to her arms, and the compact had scarce been sealed before the younger of the parties was already at the passage to the front. "We meet of course at the station."

Mrs. Gracedew thought. "If all goes well. But where shall you be meanwhile?"

Her confederate had no need to think. "Can't you guess?"

The bang of the house-door, the next minute, so helped the answer to the riddle as fairly to force it, when she found herself alone, from her lips. "At that funny old grotto? Well," she sighed, "I *like* funny old grottos!" She found herself alone, however, only for a minute; Mr. Prodmore's formidable presence had darkened the door from the court.

VII

"My daughter's not here?" he demanded from the threshold.

"Your daughter's not here." She had rapidly got under arms. "But it's a convenience to me, Mr. Prodmore, that *you* are, for I've something very particular to ask you."

Her interlocutor crossed straight to the morning-room. "I shall be delighted to answer your question, but I must first put my hand on Miss Prodmore." This hand the next instant stayed itself on the latch, and he appealed to the amiable visitor. "Unless indeed she's occupied in there with Captain Yule?"

The amiable visitor met the appeal. "I don't think she's occupied—anywhere—with Captain Yule."

Mr. Prodmore came straight away from the door. "Then where the deuce *is* Captain Yule?"

The amiable visitor turned a trifle less direct. "His absence, for which I'm responsible, is just what renders the inquiry I speak of to you possible." She had already assumed a most inquiring air, yet it was soon clear that she needed every advantage her manner could give her. "What will you take——? what will you take——?"

It had the sound, as she faltered, of a general question, and Mr. Prodmore raised his eyebrows. "Take? Nothing, thank you—I've just had a cup of tea." Then suddenly, as if on the broad hint: "Won't *you* have one?"

"Yes, with pleasure—but not yet." She looked about her again; she was now at close quarters and, concentrated, anxious, pressed her hand a moment to her brow.

This struck her companion. "Don't you think you'd be better for it immediately?"

"No." She was positive. "No." Her eyes consciously wandered. "I want to know how you'd value——"

He took her, as his own followed them, more quickly up, expanding in the presence of such a tribute from a real connoisseur. "One of these charming old things that take your fancy?"

She looked at him straight now. "They *all* take my fancy!"

"All?" He enjoyed it as the joke of a rich person—the kind of joke he sometimes made himself.

"Every single one!" said Mrs. Gracedew. Then with still a finer shade of the familiar: "Should you be willing to treat, Mr. Prodmore, for your interest in this property?"

He threw back his head: she had scattered over the word "interest" such a friendly, faded colour. She was either *not* joking or was rich indeed; and there was a place always kept in his conversation for the arrival of money, as there is always a box in a well-appointed theatre for that of royalty. "Am I to take it from you then that you *know* about my interest——?"

"Everything!" said Mrs. Gracedew with a world of wit.

"Excuse me, madam!"—he himself was now more reserved. "You don't know everything if you don't know that my interest—considerable as it might well have struck you—has just ceased to exist. I've given it up"—Mr. Prodmore softened the blow—"for a handsome equivalent."

The blow fell indeed light enough. "You mean for a handsome son-in-law?"

"It will be by some such description as the term you use that I shall doubtless, in the future, permit myself, in the common course, to allude to Captain Yule. Unless indeed I call him——" But Mr. Prodmore dropped the bolder thought. "It will depend on what he calls *me*."

Mrs. Gracedew covered him a moment with the largeness of her charity. "Won't it depend a little on what your daughter herself calls him?"

211

Mr. Prodmore seriously considered. "No. That," he declared with delicacy, "will be between the happy pair."

"Am I to take it from you then—I adopt your excellent phrase," Mrs. Gracedew said—"that Miss Prodmore has already accepted him?"

Her companion, with his head still in the air, seemed to signify that he simply put it down on the table and that she could take it or not as she liked. "Her character—formed by my assiduous care—enables me to locate her, I may say even to *time* her, from moment to moment." His massive watch, as he opened it, further sustained him in this process. "It's my assured conviction that she's accepting him while we stand here."

Mrs. Gracedew was so affected by his assured conviction that, with an odd, inarticulate sound, she forbore to stand longer—she rapidly moved away, taking one of the brief excursions of step and sense that had been for her, from the first, under the noble roof, so many dumb but decisive communions. But it was soon over, and she floated back on a wave that showed her to be, since she had let herself go, by this time quite in the swing and describing a considerable curve. "Dear Mr. Prodmore, why are you so imprudent as to make your daughter afraid of you? You should have taught her to confide in you. She has clearly shown me," she almost soothingly pursued, "that she *can* confide."

Mr. Prodmore, however, suddenly starting, looked far from soothed. "She confides in *you*?"

"You may take it from me!" Mrs. Gracedew laughed. "Let me suggest that, as fortune has thrown us together a minute, you follow her good example." She put out a reassuring hand—she could perfectly show him the way. "Tell me, for instance, the ground of your objection to poor Mr. Pegg. I mean Mr. Pegg of Bellborough, Mr. Hall Pegg, the godson of your daughter's grandmother and the associate of his father in their flourishing house; to whom (as *he* is to *it* and to *her*) Miss Prodmore's devotedly attached."

Mr. Prodmore had in the course of this speech availed himself of the support of the nearest chair, where, in spite of his subsidence, he appeared in his amazement twice his natural size. "It has gone so far as *that*?"

She rose before him as if in triumph. "It has gone so far that you had better let it go the rest of the way!"

He had lost breath, but he had positively gained dignity. "It's too monstrous, to have plotted to keep me in the dark!"

"Why, it's only when you're kept in the dark that your daughter's kept in the light!" She argued it with a candour that might have served for brilliancy. "It's at her own earnest request that I plead to you for her liberty of choice. She's an honest girl—perhaps even a peculiar girl; and she's not a baby. You over-do, I think, the nursing. She has a perfect right to her preference."

Poor Mr. Prodmore couldn't help taking it from her, and, this being the case, he still took it in the most convenient way. "And pray haven't I a perfect right to mine?" he asked from his chair.

She fairly seemed to serve it up to him—to put down the dish with a flourish. "Not at her expense. You expect her to give up too much."

"And what has she," he appealed, "expected *me* to give up? What but the desire of my heart and the dream of my life? Captain Yule announced to me but a few minutes since his intention to offer her his hand."

She faced him on it as over the table. "Well, if he does, I think he'll simply find——"

"Find what?" They looked at each other hard.

"Why, that she won't have it."

Oh, Mr. Prodmore now sprang up. "She *will!*"

"She won't!" Mrs. Gracedew more distinctly repeated.

"She *shall!*" returned her adversary, making for the staircase with the evident sense of where reinforcement might be most required.

Mrs. Gracedew, however, with a spring, was well before him. "She shan't!" She spoke with positive passion and practically so barred the way that he stood arrested and bewildered, and they faced each other, for a flash, like enemies. But it all went out, on her part, in a flash too—in a sudden wonderful smile. "Now tell me how much!"

Mr. Prodmore continued to glare—the sweat was on his brow. But while he slowly wiped it with a pocket-handkerchief of splendid scarlet silk, he remained so silent that he would have had for a spectator the effect of meeting in a manner her question. More formally to answer it he had at last to turn away. "How can I tell you anything so preposterous?"

She was all ready to inform him. "Simply by computing the total amount to which, for your benefit, this unhappy estate is burdened." He listened with his back presented, but that appeared to strike her, as she fixed this expanse, as an encouragement to proceed. "If I've troubled you by showing you that your speculation is built on the sand, let me atone for it by my eagerness to take off your hands an investment from which you derive so little profit."

He at last gave her his attention, but quite as if there were nothing in it. "And pray what profit will *you* derive——?"

"Ah, that's my own secret!" She would show him as well no glimpse of it—her laugh but rattled the box. "I want this house!"

"So do I, damn me!" he roundly returned; "and that's why I've practically paid for it!" He stuffed away his pocket-handkerchief.

There was nevertheless something in her that could hold him, and it came out, after an instant, quietly and reasonably enough. "I'll practically pay for it, Mr. Prodmore—if you'll only tell me your figure."

"My figure?"

"Your figure."

Mr. Prodmore waited—then removed his eyes from her face. He appeared to have waited on purpose to let her hope of a soft answer fall from a greater height. "My figure would be quite my own!"

"Then it will match, in that respect," Mrs. Gracedew laughed, "this overture, which is quite *my* own! As soon as you've let me know it I cable to Missoura Top to have the money sent right out to you."

Mr. Prodmore surveyed in a superior manner this artless picture of a stroke of business. "You imagine that having the money sent right out to me will make you owner of this place?"

She herself, with her head on one side, studied her sketch and seemed to twirl her pencil. "No—not quite. But I'll settle the rest with Captain Yule."

Her companion looked, over his white waistcoat, at his large tense shoes, the patent-leather shine of which so flashed propriety back at him that he became, the next moment, doubly erect on it. "Captain Yule has nothing to sell."

She received the remark with surprise. "Then what have you been trying to buy?"

She had touched in himself even a sharper spring. "Do you mean to say," he cried, "you want to buy *that*?" She stared at his queer emphasis, which was intensified by a queer grimace; then she turned from him with a change of colour and an ejaculation that led to nothing more, after a few seconds, than a somewhat conscious silence—a silence of which Mr. Prodmore made use to follow up his unanswered question with another. "Is your proposal that I should transfer my investment to you for the mere net amount of it your conception of a fair bargain?"

This second inquiry, however, she could, as she slowly came round, substantially meet. "Pray, then, what is yours?"

"Mine would be, not that I should simply get my money back, but that I should get the effective value of the house."

Mrs. Gracedew considered it. "But isn't the effective value of the house just what your money expresses?"

The lid of his hard left eye, the harder of the two, just dipped with the effect of a wink. "No, madam. It's just what *yours* does. It's moreover just what your lips have already expressed so distinctly!"

She clearly did her best to follow him. "To those people—when I showed the place off?"

215

Mr. Prodmore laughed. "You seemed to be *taking* bids then!"

She was candid, but earnest. "Taking them?"

"Oh, like an auctioneer! You ran it up high!" And Mr. Prodmore laughed again.

She turned a little pale, but it added to her brightness. "I certainly did, if saying it was charming——"

"Charming?" Mr. Prodmore broke in. "You said it was magnificent. You said it was unique. That was your very word. You said it was the *perfect* specimen of its class in England." He was more than accusatory, he was really crushing. "Oh, you got in deep!"

It was indeed an indictment, and her smile was perhaps now rather set. "Possibly. But taunting me with my absurd high spirits and the dreadful liberties I took doesn't in the least tell me how deep *you're* in!"

"For you, Mrs. Gracedew?" He took a few steps, looking at his shoes again and as if to give her time to plead—since he wished to be quite fair—that it was *not* for her. "I'm in to the tune of fifty thousand."

She was silent, on this announcement, so long that he once more faced her; but if what he showed her in doing so at last made her speak, it also took the life from her tone. "That's a great deal of money, Mr. Prodmore."

The tone didn't matter, but only the truth it expressed, which he so thoroughly liked to hear. "So I've often had occasion to say to myself!"

"If it's a large sum for you, then," said Mrs. Gracedew, "it's a still larger one for me." She sank into a chair with a vague melancholy; such a mass loomed huge, and she sat down before it as a solitary herald, resigning himself with a sigh to wait, might have leaned against a tree before a besieged city. "We women"—she wished to conciliate—"have more modest ideas."

But Mr. Prodmore would scarce condescend to parley. "Is it as a 'modest idea' that you describe your extraordinary intrusion——?"

His question scarce reached her; she was so lost for the moment in the sense of innocent community with her sex. "I mean I think we measure things often rather more exactly."

There would have been no doubt of Mr. Prodmore's very different community as he rudely replied: "Then you measured *this* thing exactly half an hour ago!"

It was a long way to go back, but Mrs. Gracedew, in her seat, musingly made the journey, from which she then suddenly returned with a harmless, indeed quite a happy, memento. "Was I *very* grotesque?"

He demurred. "Grotesque?"

"I mean—*did* I go on about it?"

Mr. Prodmore would have no general descriptions; he was specific, he was vivid. "You banged the desk. You raved. You shrieked."

This was a note she appeared indulgently, almost tenderly, to recognise. "We *do* shriek at Missoura Top!"

"I don't know what you do at Missoura Top, but I know what you did at Covering End!"

She warmed at last to his tone. "So do *I* then! I surprised you. You weren't at all prepared——"

He took her briskly up. "No—and I'm not prepared yet!"

Mrs. Gracedew could quite see it. "Yes, you're too astonished."

"My astonishment's my own affair," he retorted—"not less so than my memory!"

"Oh, I yield to your memory," said the charming woman, "and I confess my extravagance. But quite, you know, *as* extravagance."

"I don't at all know,"—Mr. Prodmore shook it off,—"nor what you *call* extravagance."

"Why, banging the desk. Raving. Shrieking. I over-did it," she exclaimed; "I wanted to please you!"

She had too happy a beauty, as she sat in her high-backed chair, to have been condemned to say that to any man without a certain effect. The effect on Mr. Prodmore was striking. "So you said," he sternly inquired, "what you didn't believe?"

She flushed with the avowal. "Yes—for you."

He looked at her hard. "For *me*?"

Under his eye—for her flush continued—she slowly got up. "And for those good people."

"Oh!"—he sounded most sarcastic. "Should you like me to call them back?"

"No." She was still gay enough, but very decided. "I took them in."

"And now you want to take *me*?"

"Oh, Mr. Prodmore!" she almost pitifully, but not quite adequately, moaned.

He appeared to feel he had gone a little far. "Well, if we're not what you say——"

"Yes?"—she looked up askance at the stroke.

"Why the devil do you want us?" The question rang out and was truly for the poor lady, as the quick suffusion of her eyes showed, a challenge it would take more time than he left her properly to pick up. He left her in fact no time at all before he went on: "Why the devil did you say you'd offer fifty?"

She looked quite wan and seemed to wonder. "*Did* I say that?" She could only let his challenge lie. "It was a figure of speech!"

"Then that's the kind of figure we're talking about!" Mr. Prodmore's sharpness would have struck an auditor as the more effective that, on the heels of this thrust, seeing the ancient butler reappear, he dropped the victim of it as comparatively unimportant and directed his fierceness instantly to Chivers, who mildly gaped at him from the threshold of the court. "Have you seen Miss Prodmore? If you haven't, find her!"

Mrs. Gracedew addressed their visitor in a very different tone, though with the full authority of her benevolence. "You won't, my dear man." To Mr. Prodmore also she continued bland. "I happen to know she has gone for a walk."

"A walk—alone?" Mr. Prodmore gasped.

"No—not alone." Mrs. Gracedew looked at Chivers with a vague smile of appeal for help, but he could only give her, from under his bent old brow, the blank decency of his wonder. It seemed to make her feel afresh that she was, after all, alone—so that in her loneliness, which had also its fine sad charm, she risked another brush with their formidable friend. "Cora has gone with Mr. Pegg."

"Pegg has *been* here?"

It was like a splash in a full basin, but she launched the whole craft. "He walked with her from the station."

"When she arrived?" Mr. Prodmore rose like outraged Neptune. "That's why she was so late?"

Mrs. Gracedew assented. "Why I got here first. I get everywhere first!" she bravely laughed.

Mr. Prodmore looked round him in purple dismay—it was so clearly a question for him where *he* should get, and what! "In which direction did they go?" he imperiously asked.

His rudeness was too evident to be more than lightly recognised. "I think I must let you ascertain for yourself!"

All he could do then was to shout it to Chivers. "Call my carriage, you ass!" After which, as the old man melted into the vestibule, he dashed about blindly for his hat, pounced upon it and seemed, furious but helpless, on the point of hurling it at his contradictress as a gage of battle. "So you abetted and protected this wicked, low intrigue?"

She had something in her face now that was indifferent to any violence. "You're too disappointed to see your real interest: oughtn't I therefore in common charity to point it out to you?"

He faced her question so far as to treat it as one. "What do *you* know of my disappointment?"

There was something in his very harshness that even helped her, for it added at this moment to her sense of making out in his narrowed glare a couple of tears of rage. "I know everything."

"What do you know of my real interest?" he went on as if he had not heard her.

"I know enough for my purpose—which is to offer you a handsome condition. I think it's not I who have protected the happy understanding that you call by so ugly a name; it's the happy understanding that has put me"—she gained confidence—"well, in a position. Do drive after them, if you like—but catch up with them only to forgive them. If you'll do that, I'll pay your price."

The particular air with which, a minute after Mrs. Gracedew had spoken these words, Mr. Prodmore achieved a transfer of his attention to the inside of his hat—this special shade of majesty would have taxed the descriptive resources of the most accomplished reporter. It is none the less certain that he appeared for some time absorbed in that receptacle—appeared at last to breathe into it hard. "What do you call my price?"

"Why, the sum you just mentioned—fifty thousand!" Mrs. Gracedew feverishly quavered.

He looked at her as if stupefied. "*That's* not my price—and it never for a moment was!" If derision can be dry, Mr. Prodmore's was of the driest. "Besides," he rang out, "my price is up!"

She caught it with a long wail. "Up?"

Oh, he let her have it now! "Seventy thousand."

She turned away overwhelmed, but still with voice for her despair. "Oh, deary me!"

Mr. Prodmore was already at the door, from which he launched his ultimatum. "It's to take or to leave!"

She would have had to leave it, perhaps, had not something happened at this moment to nerve her for the effort of staying him with a quick motion. Captain Yule had come into sight on the staircase and, after just faltering at what he himself saw, had marched resolutely enough down. She watched him arrive—watched him with an attention that visibly and responsively excited his own; after which she passed nearer to their companion. "Seventy thousand, then!"—it gleamed between them, in her muffled hiss, as if she had planted a dagger.

Mr. Prodmore, to do him justice, took his wound in front. "Seventy thousand—done!" And, without another look at Yule, he was presently heard to bang the outer door after him for a sign.

VIII

The young man, meanwhile, had approached in surprise. "He's gone? I've been looking for him!"

Mrs. Gracedew was out of breath; there was a disturbed whiteness of bosom in her which needed time to subside and which she might have appeared to retreat before him on purpose to veil. "I don't think, you know, that you need him—now."

Clement Yule was mystified. "Now?"

She recovered herself enough to explain—made an effort at least to be plausible. "I mean that—if you don't mind—you must deal with *me*. I've arranged with Mr. Prodmore to take it over."

221

Oh, he gave her no help! "Take what over?"

She looked all about as if not quite thinking what it could be called; at last, however, she offered with a smile a sort of substitute for a name. "Why, your debt."

But he was only the more bewildered. "*Can* you—without arranging with *me?*"

She turned it round, but as if merely to oblige him. "That's precisely what I want to do." Then, more brightly, as she thought further: "That is, I mean, I want you to arrange with *me*. Surely you will," she said encouragingly.

His own processes, in spite of a marked earnestness, were much less rapid. "But if I arrange with anybody——"

"Yes?" She cheerfully waited.

"How do I perform my engagement?"

"The one to Mr. Prodmore?"

He looked surprised at her speaking as if he had half-a-dozen. "Yes—that's the worst."

"Certainly—the worst!" And she gave a happy laugh that made him stare.

He broke into quite a different one. "You speak as if its being the worst made it the best!"

"It does—for me. You don't," said Mrs. Gracedew, "perform any engagement."

He required a moment to take it in; then something extraordinary leaped into his face. "He lets me off?"

Ah, she could ring out now! "He lets you off."

It lifted him high, but only to drop him with an audible thud. "Oh, I see—I lose my house!"

"Dear, no—*that* doesn't follow!" She spoke as if the absurdity he indicated were the last conceivable, but there was a certain want of sharpness of edge in her expression of the alternative. "You arrange with *me* to keep it."

There was quite a corresponding want, clearly, in the image presented to the Captain—of which, for a moment, he seemed with difficulty to follow the contour. "How do I arrange?"

"Well, we must think," said Mrs. Gracedew; "we must wait." She spoke as if this were a detail for which she had not yet had much attention; only bringing out, however, the next instant in an encouraging cry and as if it were by itself almost a solution: "We must find some way!" She might have been talking to a reasonable child.

But even reasonable children ask too many questions. "Yes—and what way *can* we find?" Clement Yule, glancing about him, was so struck with the absence of ways that he appeared to remember with something of regret how different it had been before. "With Prodmore it was simple enough. You see I could marry his daughter."

Mrs. Gracedew was silent just long enough for her soft ironic smile to fill the cup of the pause. "*Could* you?"

It was as if he had tasted in the words the wine at the brim; for he gave, under the effect of them, a sudden headshake and an awkward laugh. "Well, never perhaps *that* exactly—when it came to the point. But I had to, you see——" It was difficult to say just what.

She took advantage of it, looking hard, but not seeing at all. "You had to——?"

"Well," he repeated ruefully, "think a lot about it. You didn't suspect that?"

Oh, if he came to suspicions she could only break off! "Don't ask me too many questions."

223

He looked an instant as if he wondered why. "But isn't this just the moment for them?" He fronted her, with a quickness he tried to dissimulate, from the other side. "What *did* you suppose?"

She looked everywhere but into his face. "Why, I supposed you were in distress."

He was very grave. "About his terms?"

"About his terms of course!" she laughed. "Not about his religious opinions."

His gratitude was too great for gaiety. "You really, in your beautiful sympathy, *guessed* my fix?"

But she declined to be too solemn. "Dear Captain Yule, it all quite stuck out of you!"

"You mean I floundered like a drowning man——?"

Well, she consented to have meant that. "Till I plunged in!"

He appeared there for a few seconds, to see her again take the jump and to listen again to the splash; then, with an odd, sharp impulse, he turned his back. "You saved me."

She wouldn't deny it—on the contrary. "What a pity, now, *I* haven't a daughter!"

On this he slowly came round again. "What should I do with her?"

"You'd treat her, I hope, better than you've treated Miss Prodmore."

The young man positively coloured. "But I haven't been bad——?"

The sight of this effect of her small joke produced on Mrs. Gracedew's part an emotion less controllable than any she had yet felt. "Oh, you delightful goose!" she irrepressibly dropped.

She made his blush deepen, but the aggravation was a relief. "Of course—I'm all right, and there's only one pity in the matter. I've nothing—

nothing whatever, not a scrap of service nor a thing you'd care for—to offer you in compensation."

She looked at him ever so kindly. "I'm not, as they say, 'on the make.'" Never had he been put right with a lighter hand. "I didn't do it for payment."

"Then what did you do it for?"

For something, it might have seemed, as her eyes dropped and strayed, that had got brushed into a crevice of the old pavement. "Because I hated Mr. Prodmore."

He conscientiously demurred. "So much as all that?"

"Oh, well," she replied impatiently, "of course you also know how much I like the house. My hates and my likes," she subtly explained, "can never live together. I get one of them out. The one this time was that man."

He showed a candour of interest. "Yes—you got him out. Yes—I saw him go." And his inner vision appeared to attend for some moments Mr. Prodmore's departure. "But how did you do it?"

"Oh, I don't know. Women———!" Mrs. Gracedew but vaguely sketched it.

A touch or two, however, for that subject, could of course almost always suffice. "Precisely—women. May I smoke again?" Clement Yule abruptly asked.

"Certainly. But I managed Mr. Prodmore," she laughed as he re-lighted, "without cigarettes."

Her companion puffed. "*I* couldn't manage him."

"So I saw!"

"*I* couldn't get him out."

"So *he* saw!"

Captain Yule, for a little, lost himself in his smoke. "Where is he gone?"

"I haven't the least idea. But I meet him again," she hastened to add—"very soon."

"And when do you meet *me*?"

"Why, whenever you'll come to see me." For the twentieth time she gathered herself as if the words she had just spoken were quite her last hand. "At present, you see, I *have* a train to catch."

Absorbed in the trivial act that engaged him, he gave her no help. "A train?"

"Surely. I didn't walk."

"No; but even trains——!" His eyes clung to her now. "You fly?"

"I try to. Good-bye."

He had got between her and the door of departure quite as, on her attempt to quit him half an hour before, he had anticipated her approach to the stairs; and in this position he took no notice of her farewell. "I said just now that I had nothing to offer you. But of course I've the house itself."

"The house?" She stared. "Why, I've *got* it?"

"Got it?"

"All in my head, I mean. That's all I want." She had not yet, save to Mr. Prodmore, made quite so light of it.

This had its action in his markedly longer face. "Why, I thought you loved it so!"

Ah, she was perfectly consistent. "I love it far too much to deprive *you* of it."

Yet Clement Yule could in a fashion meet her. "Oh, it wouldn't be depriving——!"

She altogether protested. "Not to turn you out——?"

226

"Dear lady, I've never been *in*!"

Oh, she was none the less downright. "You're in *now*—I've put you, and you must stay." He looked round so woefully, however, that she presently attenuated. "I don't mean *all* the while, but long enough——!"

"Long enough for what?"

"For me to feel you're here."

"And how long will that take?"

"Well, you think me very fast—but sometimes I'm slow. I told you just now, at any rate," she went on, "that I had arranged you should lose nothing. Is the very next thing I do, then, to make you lose everything?"

"It isn't a question of what I lose," the young man anxiously cried; "it's a question of what I *do*! What *have* I done to find it all so plain?" Fate was really—fate reversed, improved, and unnatural—too much for him, and his heated young face showed honest stupefaction. "I haven't lifted a finger. It's you who have done all."

"Yes, but if you're just where you were before, how in the world are you saved?" She put it to him with still superior lucidity.

"By my life's being my own again—to do what I want."

"What you 'want'"—Mrs. Gracedew's handsome uplifted head had it all there, every inch of it—"is to keep your house."

"Ah, but only," he perfectly assented, "if, as you said, you find a way!"

"I *have* found a way—and there the way is: for *me* just simply not to touch the place. What you 'want,'" she argued more closely, "is what made you give in to Prodmore. What you 'want' is these walls and these acres. What you 'want' is to take the way I first showed you."

Her companion's eyes, quitting for the purpose her face, looked to the quarter marked by her last words as at an horizon now remote. "Why, the way you first showed me was to marry Cora!"

227

She had to admit it, but as little as possible. "Practically—yes."

"Well, it's just 'practically' that I can't!"

"I didn't know that then," said Mrs. Gracedew. "You didn't tell me."

He passed, with an approach to a grimace, his hand over the back of his head. "I felt a delicacy!"

"I didn't even know *that*." She spoke it almost sadly.

"It didn't strike you that I might?"

She thought a moment. "No." She thought again. "No. But don't quarrel with me about it *now*!"

"Quarrel with you?" he looked amazement.

She laughed, but she had changed colour. "Cora, at any rate, felt no delicacy. Cora told me."

Clement Yule fairly gaped. "Then she did know——?"

"She knew all; and if her father said she didn't, he simply told you what was not." She frankly gave him this, but the next minute, as if she had startled him more than she meant, she jumped to reassurance. "It was quite right of her. She would have refused you."

The young man stared. "Oh!" He was quick, however, to show—by an amusement perhaps a trifle over-done—that he felt no personal wound. "Do you call that quite right?"

Mrs. Gracedew looked at it again. "For *her*—yes; and for Prodmore."

"Oh, for Prodmore"—his laugh grew more grim—"with all my heart!"

This, then,—her kind eyes seemed to drop it upon him,—was all she meant. "To stay at your post—*that* was the way I showed you."

He had come round to it now, as mechanically, in intenser thought, he smoothed down the thick hair he had rubbed up; but his face soon enough gave out, in wonder and pain, that his freedom was somehow only a new predicament. "How can I take any way at all, dear lady——?"

"If I only stick here in your path?" She had taken him straight up, and with spirit; and the same spirit bore her to the end. "I won't stick a moment more! Haven't I been trying this age to leave you?"

Clement Yule, for all answer, caught her sharply, in her passage, by the arm. "You surrender your rights?" He was for an instant almost terrible.

She quite turned pale with it. "Weren't you ready to surrender *yours?*"

"I hadn't any, so it was deuced easy. I hadn't paid for them."

Oh that, she let him see,—even though with his continued grasp he might hurt her,—had nothing in it! "Your ancestors had paid: it's the same thing." Erect there in the brightness of her triumph and the force of her logic, she must yet, to anticipate his return, take a stride—like a sudden dip into a gully and the scramble up on the other bank—that put her dignity to the test. "You're just, in a manner, my tenant."

"But how can I treat that as such a mere detail? I'm your tenant on what terms?"

"Oh, *any* terms—choose them for yourself!" She made an attempt to free her arm—gave it a small vain shake. Then, as if to bribe him to let her go: "You can write me about them."

He appeared to consider it. "To Missoura Top?"

She fully assented. "I go right back." As if it had put him off his guard she broke away. "Farewell!"

She broke away, but he broke faster, and once more, nearer the door, he had barred her escape. "Just one little moment, please. If you won't tell me your own terms, you must at least tell me Prodmore's."

Ah, the fiend—she could never squeeze past *that*! All she could do, for the instant, was to reverberate foolishly "Prodmore's?"

But there was nothing foolish, at last, about *him*. "How you did it—how you managed him." His feet were firm while he waited, though he had to wait some time. "You bought him out?"

She made less of it than, clearly, he had ever heard made of a stroke of business; it might have been a case of his owing her ninepence. "I bought him out."

He wanted at least the exact sum. "For how much?" Her silence seemed to say that she had made no note of it, but his pressure only increased. "I really must know."

She continued to try to treat it as if she had merely paid for his cab—she put even what she could of that suggestion into a tender, helpless, obstinate headshake. "You shall never know!"

The only thing his own manner met was the obstinacy. "I'll get it from *him*!"

She repeated her headshake, but with a world of sadness added, "Get it if you can!"

He looked into her eyes now as if it was the sadness that struck him most. "He won't say, because he *did* you?"

They showed each other, on this, the least separated faces yet. "He'll never, never say."

The confidence in it was so tender that it sounded almost like pity, and the young man took it up with all the flush of the sense that pity could be but for *him*. This sense broke full in her face. "The scoundrel!"

"Not a bit!" she returned, with equal passion—"I was only too clever for him!" The thought of it was again an exaltation in which she pushed her friend aside. "So let me go!"

The push was like a jar that made the vessel overflow, and he was before her now as if he stretched across the hall. "With the heroic view of your power and the barren beauty of your sacrifice? You pour out money, you move a mountain, and to let you 'go,' to close the door fast behind you, is all I can figure out to do for you?" His emotion trembled out of him with the stammer of a new language, but it was as if in a minute or two he had thrown over all consciousness. "You're the most generous—you're the noblest of women! The wonderful chance that brought you here——!"

His own arm was grasped now—she knew better than he about the wonderful chance. "It brought *you* at the same happy hour! I've done what I liked," she went on very simply; "and the only way to thank me is to believe it."

"You've done it for a proud, poor man"—his answer was quite as direct. "He has nothing—in the light of such a magic as yours—either to give or to hope; but you've made him, in a little miraculous hour, think of you——"

He stumbled with the rush of things, and if silence can, in its way, be active, there was a collapse too, for an instant, on her closed lips. These lips, however, she at last opened. "How have I made him think of me?"

"As he has thought of no other woman!" He had personal possession of her now, and it broke, as he pressed her, as he pleaded, the helpless fall of his eloquence. "Mrs. Gracedew—don't leave me." He jerked his head passionately at the whole place and the yellow afternoon. "If you made me care——"

"It was surely that you had made *me* first!" She laughed, and her laugh disengaged her, so that before he could reply she had again put space between them.

He accepted the space now—he appeared so sure of his point. "Then let me go on caring. When I asked you awhile back for some possible adjustment to my new source of credit, you simply put off the question—told me I must trust to time for it. Well," said Clement Yule, "I've trusted to time so effectually that ten little minutes have made me find it. I've found it because I've so quickly found *you*. May I, Mrs. Gracedew, keep *all* that I've found? I offer you in return the only thing I have to give—I offer you my hand and my life."

She held him off, across the hall, for a time almost out of proportion to the previous wait he had just made so little of. Then at last also, when she answered, it might have passed for a plea for further postponement, even for a plea for mercy. "Ah, Captain Yule———!" But she turned suddenly off: the flower had been nipped in the bud by the re-entrance of Chivers, at whom his master veritably glowered.

"What the devil is it?"

The old man showed the shock, but he had his duty. "Another party."

Mrs. Gracedew, at this, wheeled round. "The 'party up'!" It brought back her voice—indeed, all her gaiety. And her gaiety was always determinant. "Show them in."

Clement Yule's face fell while Chivers proceeded to obey. "You'll *have* them?" he wailed across the hall.

"Ah! mayn't I be proud of my house?" she tossed back at him.

At this, radiant, he had rushed at her. "Then you accept———?"

Her raised hand checked him. "Hush!"

He fell back—the party was there. Chivers ushered it as he had ushered the other, making the most, this time, of more scanty material—four persons so spectacled, satchelled, shawled, and handbooked that they testified on the spot to a particular foreign origin and presented themselves indeed very much as tourists who, at an hotel, casting up the promise of comfort or the portent of cost, take possession, while they wait for their keys, with expert looks and free sounds. Clement Yule, who had receded, effacing himself, to the quarter opposed to that of his companion, addressed to their visitors a covert but dismayed stare and then, edging round, in his agitation, to the rear, instinctively sought relief by escape through the open passage. One of the invaders meanwhile—a broad-faced gentleman with long hair tucked behind his ears and a ring on each forefinger—had lost no time in showing he knew where to begin. He began at the top—the proper place, and took in the dark pictures ranged above the tapestry. "Olt vamily bortraits?"—he appealed to Chivers and spoke very loud.

Chivers rose to the occasion and, gracefully pawing the air, began also at the beginning. "Dame Dorothy Yule—who lived to a hundred and one."

"A hundred and one—ach *so!*" broke, with a resigned absence of criticism, from each of the interested group; another member of which, however, indicated with a somewhat fatigued skip the central figure of the series, the personage with the long white legs that Mrs. Gracedew had invited the previous inquirers to remark. "Who's dis?" the present inquirer asked.

The question affected the lovely lady over by the fireplace as the trumpet of battle affects a generous steed. She flashed on the instant into the middle of the hall and into the friendliest and most familiar relation with everyone and with everything. "John Anthony Yule, sir,—who passed away, poor duck, in his flower!"

They met her with low salutations, a sweep of ugly shawls, and a brush of queer German hats: she had issued, to their glazed convergence, from the dusk of the Middle Ages and the shade of high pieces, and now stood there, beautiful and human and happy, in a light that, whatever it was for themselves, the very breadth of their attention, the expression of their serious faces, converted straightway for her into a new, and oh! into the right, one. To a detached observer of the whole it would have been promptly clear that she found herself striking these good people very much as the lawful heir had, half an hour before, struck another stranger—that she produced in them, in her setting of assured antiquity, quite the romantic vibration that she had responded to in the presence of that personage. They read her as she read *him*, and a bright and deepening cheer, reflected dimly in their thick thoroughness, went out from her as she accepted their reading. An impression was exchanged, for the minute, from side to side—their grave admiration of the finest feature of the curious house and the deep free radiance of her silent, grateful "Why not?" It made a passage of some intensity and some duration, of which the effect, indeed, the next minute, was to cause the only lady of the party—a matron of rich Jewish type, with small nippers on a huge nose and a face out of proportion to her little Freischütz hat—to break the spell by an uneasy turn and a stray glance at one of the other pictures. "Who's *dat?*"

"That?" The picture chanced to be a portrait over the wide arch, and something happened, at the very moment, to arrest Mrs. Gracedew's eyes rather above than below. What took place, in a word, was that Clement Yule, already fidgeting in his impatience back from the front, just occupied the arch, completed her thought, and filled her vision. "Oh, that's my future husband!" He caught the words, but answered them only by a long look at her as he moved, with a checked wildness of which she alone, of all the spectators, had a sense, straight across the hall again and to the other opening. He paused there as he had done before, then with a last dumb appeal to her dropped into the court and passed into the garden. Mrs. Gracedew, already so wonderful to their visitors, was, before she followed him, wonderful with a greater wonder to poor Chivers. "You dear old thing—I give it all back to you!"

THE WINGS OF THE DOVE

VOL. I

BOOK FIRST

I

She waited, Kate Croy, for her father to come in, but he kept her unconscionably, and there were moments at which she showed herself, in the glass over the mantel, a face positively pale with the irritation that had brought her to the point of going away without sight of him. It was at this point, however, that she remained; changing her place, moving from the shabby sofa to the armchair upholstered in a glazed cloth that gave at once—she had tried it—the sense of the slippery and of the sticky. She had looked at the sallow prints on the walls and at the lonely magazine, a year old, that combined, with a small lamp in coloured glass and a knitted white centre-piece wanting in freshness, to enhance the effect of the purplish cloth on the principal table; she had above all, from time to time, taken a brief stand on the small balcony to which the pair of long windows gave access. The vulgar little street, in this view, offered scant relief from the vulgar little room; its main office was to suggest to her that the narrow black house-fronts, adjusted to a standard that would have been low even for backs, constituted quite the publicity implied by such privacies. One felt them in the room exactly as one felt the room—the hundred like it or worse—in the street. Each time she turned in again, each time, in her impatience, she gave him up, it was to sound to a deeper depth, while she tasted the faint, flat emanation of things, the failure of fortune and of honour. If she continued to wait it was really, in a manner, that she might not add the shame of fear, of individual, personal collapse, to all the other shames. To feel the street, to feel the room, to feel the table-cloth and the centre-piece and the lamp, gave her a small, salutary sense, at least, of neither shirking nor lying. This whole vision was the worst thing yet—as including, in particular, the interview for which she had prepared herself; and for what had she come but for the worst? She tried to be sad, so as not to be angry; but it made her angry that she couldn't be sad. And yet where was misery, misery too beaten for blame and chalk-marked by fate like a "lot" at a common auction, if not in these merciless signs of mere mean, stale feelings?

Her father's life, her sister's, her own, that of her two lost brothers—the whole history of their house had the effect of some fine florid, voluminous phrase, say even a musical, that dropped first into words, into notes, without sense, and then, hanging unfinished, into no words, no notes at all. Why should a set of people have been put in motion, on such a scale and with such an air of being equipped for a profitable journey, only to break down without an accident, to stretch themselves in the wayside dust without a reason? The answer to these questions was not in Chirk Street, but the questions themselves bristled there, and the girl's repeated pause before the mirror and the chimney-place might have represented her nearest approach to an escape from them. Was it not in fact the partial escape from this "worst" in which she was steeped to be able to make herself out again as agreeable to see? She stared into the tarnished glass too hard indeed to be staring at her beauty alone. She readjusted the poise of her black, closely-feathered hat; retouched, beneath it, the thick fall of her dusky hair; kept her eyes, aslant, no less on her beautiful averted than on her beautiful presented oval. She was dressed altogether in black, which gave an even tone, by contrast, to her clear face and made her hair more harmoniously dark. Outside, on the balcony, her eyes showed as blue; within, at the mirror, they showed almost as black. She was handsome, but the degree of it was not sustained by items and aids; a circumstance moreover playing its part at almost any time in the impression she produced. The impression was one that remained, but as regards the sources of it no sum in addition would have made up the total. She had stature without height, grace without motion, presence without mass. Slender and simple, frequently soundless, she was somehow always in the line of the eye—she counted singularly for its pleasure. More "dressed," often, with fewer accessories, than other women, or less dressed, should occasion require, with more, she probably could not have given the key to these felicities. They were mysteries of which her friends were conscious—those friends whose general explanation was to say that she was clever, whether or no it were taken by the world as the cause or as the effect of her charm. If she saw more things than her fine face in the dull glass of her father's lodgings, she might have seen that, after all, she was not herself a fact in the collapse. She didn't judge herself cheap, she didn't make for misery. Personally, at least, she was not chalk-marked for the auction. She hadn't given up yet, and the broken sentence, if she was the last word, would end with a sort of meaning. There was a minute during which, though her eyes were fixed, she quite visibly lost herself in the thought of the way she might still pull things round had she only been a man. It was the name, above all, she would take in hand—the precious name she so liked and that, in spite of the harm her wretched father had done it, was not yet past praying for. She loved it in fact the more tenderly for that bleeding wound. But what could a penniless girl do with it but let it go?

When her father at last appeared she became, as usual, instantly aware of the futility of any effort to hold him to anything. He had written her that he was ill, too ill to leave his room, and that he must see her without delay; and if this had been, as was probable, the sketch of a design, he was indifferent even to the moderate finish required for deception. He had clearly wanted, for perversities that he called reasons, to see her, just as she herself had sharpened for a talk; but she now again felt, in the inevitability of the freedom he used with her, all the old ache, her poor mother's very own, that he couldn't touch you ever so lightly without setting up. No relation with him could be so short or so superficial as not to be somehow to your hurt; and this, in the strangest way in the world, not because he desired it to be—feeling often, as he surely must, the profit for him of its not being—but because there was never a mistake for you that he could leave unmade or a conviction of his impossibility in you that he could approach you without strengthening. He might have awaited her on the sofa in his sitting-room, or might have stayed in bed and received her in that situation. She was glad to be spared the sight of such *penetralia,* but it would have reminded her a little less that there was no truth in him. This was the weariness of every fresh meeting; he dealt out lies as he might the cards from the greasy old pack for the game of diplomacy to which you were to sit down with him. The inconvenience—as always happens in such cases—was not that you minded what was false, but that you missed what was true. He might be ill, and it might suit you to know it, but no contact with him, for this, could ever be straight enough. Just so he even might die, but Kate fairly wondered on what evidence of his own she would some day have to believe it.

He had not at present come down from his room, which she knew to be above the one they were in: he had already been out of the house, though he would either, should she challenge him, deny it or present it as a proof of his extremity. She had, however, by this time, quite ceased to challenge him; not only, face to face with him, vain irritation dropped, but he breathed upon the tragic consciousness in such a way that after a moment nothing of it was left. The difficulty was not less that he breathed in the same way upon the comic: she almost believed that with this latter she might still have found a foothold for clinging to him. He had ceased to be amusing—he was really too inhuman. His perfect look, which had floated him so long, was practically perfect still; but one had long since for every occasion taken it for granted. Nothing could have better shown than the actual how right one had been. He looked exactly as much as usual—all pink and silver as to skin and hair, all straitness and starch as to figure and dress—the man in the world least connected with anything unpleasant. He was so particularly the English gentleman and the fortunate, settled, normal person. Seen at a foreign *table d'hôte,* he suggested but one thing: "In what perfection England produces them!" He had kind, safe eyes, and a voice which, for all its clean fulness, told, in a manner, the happy history of its having never had once to raise itself. Life had met him so, half-way, and had turned round so to walk with him, placing a hand in his arm and fondly leaving him to choose the pace. Those who knew him a little said, "How he does dress!"—those who knew him better said, "How *does* he?" The one stray gleam of comedy just now in his daughter's eyes was the funny feeling he momentarily made her have of being herself "looked up" by him in sordid lodgings. For a minute after he came in it was as if the place were her own and he the visitor with susceptibilities. He gave you funny feelings, he had indescribable arts, that quite turned the tables: that had been always how he came to see her mother so long as her mother would see him. He came from places they had often not known about, but he patronised Lexham Gardens. Kate's only actual expression of impatience, however, was "I'm glad you're so much better!"

"I'm not so much better, my dear—I'm exceedingly unwell; the proof of which is, precisely, that I've been out to the chemist's—that beastly fellow at the corner." So Mr. Croy showed he could qualify the humble hand that assuaged him. "I'm taking something he has made up for me. It's just why I've sent for you—that you may see me as I really am."

"Oh papa, it's long since I've ceased to see you otherwise than as you really are! I think we've all arrived by this time at the right word for that: 'You're beautiful—*n'en parlons plus.*' You're as beautiful as ever—you look lovely." He judged meanwhile her own appearance, as she knew she could always trust him to do; recognising, estimating, sometimes disapproving, what she wore, showing her the interest he continued to take in her. He might really take none at all, yet she virtually knew herself the creature in the world to whom he was least indifferent. She had often enough wondered what on earth, at the pass he had reached, could give him pleasure, and she had come back, on these occasions, to that. It gave him pleasure that she was handsome, that she was, in her way, a sensible value. It was at least as marked, nevertheless, that he derived none from similar conditions, so far as they *were* similar, in his other child. Poor Marian might be handsome, but he certainly didn't care. The hitch here, of course, was that, with whatever beauty, her sister, widowed and almost in want, with four bouncing children, was not a sensible value. She asked him, the next thing, how long he had been in his actual quarters, though aware of how little it mattered, how little any answer he might make would probably have in common with the truth. She failed in fact to notice his answer, truthful or not, already occupied as she was with what she had on her own side to say to him. This was really what had made her wait—what superseded the small remainder of her resentment at his constant practical impertinence; the result of all of which was that, within a minute, she had brought it out. "Yes—even now I'm willing to go with you. I don't know what you may have wished to say to me, and even if you hadn't written you would within a day or two have heard from me. Things have happened, and I've only waited, for seeing you, till I should be quite sure. I *am* quite sure. I'll go with you."

It produced an effect. "Go with me where?"

"Anywhere. I'll stay with you. Even here." She had taken off her gloves and, as if she had arrived with her plan, she sat down.

Lionel Croy hung about in his disengaged way—hovered there as if, in consequence of her words, looking for a pretext to back out easily: on which she immediately saw she had discounted, as it might be called, what he had himself been preparing. He wished her not to come to him, still less to settle with him, and had sent for her to give her up with some style and state; a part of the beauty of which, however, was to have been his sacrifice to her own detachment. There was no style, no state, unless she wished to forsake him. His idea had accordingly been to surrender her to her wish with all nobleness; it had by no means been to have positively to keep her off. She cared, however, not a straw for his embarrassment—feeling how little, on her own part, she was moved by charity. She had seen him, first and last, in so many attitudes that she could now deprive him quite without compunction of the luxury of a new one. Yet she felt the disconcerted gasp in his tone as he said: "Oh my child, I can never consent to that!"

"What then are you going to do?"

"I'm turning it over," said Lionel Croy. "You may imagine if I'm not thinking."

"Haven't you thought then," his daughter asked, "of what I speak of? I mean of my being ready."

Standing before her with his hands behind him and his legs a little apart, he swayed slightly to and fro, inclined toward her as if rising on his toes. It had an effect of conscientious deliberation. "No. I haven't. I couldn't. I wouldn't." It was so respectable, a show that she felt afresh, and with the memory of their old despair, the despair at home, how little his appearance ever by any chance told about him. His plausibility had been the heaviest of her mother's crosses; inevitably so much more present to the world than whatever it was that was horrid—thank God they didn't really know!—that he had done. He had positively been, in his way, by the force of his particular type, a terrible husband not to live with; his type reflecting so invidiously on the woman who had found him distasteful. Had this thereby not kept directly present to Kate herself that it might, on some sides, prove no light thing for her to leave uncompanioned a parent with such a face and such a manner? Yet if there was much she neither knew nor dreamed of, it passed between them at this very moment that he was quite familiar with himself as the subject of such quandaries. If he recognised his younger daughter's happy aspect as a sensible value, he had from the first still more exactly appraised his own. The great wonder was not that in spite of everything his own had helped him; the great wonder was that it hadn't helped him more. However, it was, to its old, eternal, recurrent tune, helping him all the while; her drop into patience with him showed how it was helping him at this moment. She saw the next instant precisely the line he would take. "Do you really ask me to believe you've been making up your mind to that?"

She had to consider her own line. "I don't think I care, papa, what you believe. I never, for that matter, think of you as believing anything; hardly more," she permitted herself to add, "than I ever think of you as yourself believed. I don't know you, father, you see."

"And it's your idea that you may make that up?"

"Oh dear, no; not at all. That's no part of the question. If I haven't understood you by this time, I never shall, and it doesn't matter. It has seemed to me that you may be lived with, but not that you may be understood. Of course I've not the least idea how you get on."

"I don't get on," Mr. Croy almost gaily replied.

His daughter took in the place again, and it might well have seemed odd that in so little to meet the eye there should be so much to show. What showed was the ugliness—so positive and palpable that it was somehow sustaining. It was a medium, a setting, and to that extent, after all, a dreadful sign of life; so that it fairly put a point into her answer. "Oh, I beg your pardon. You flourish."

"Do you throw it up at me again," he pleasantly inquired, "that I've not made away with myself?"

She treated the question as needing no reply; she sat there for real things. "You know how all our anxieties, under mamma's will, have come out. She had still less to leave than she feared. We don't know how we lived. It all makes up about two hundred a year for Marian, and two for me, but I give up a hundred to Marian."

"Oh, you weak thing!" her father kindly sighed.

"For you and me together," she went on, "the other hundred would do something."

"And what would do the rest?"

"Can you yourself do nothing?" He gave her a look; then, slipping his hands into his pockets and turning away, stood for a little at the window she had left open. She said nothing more—she had placed him there with that question, and the silence lasted a minute, broken by the call of an appealing costermonger, which came in with the mild March air, with the shabby sunshine, fearfully unbecoming to the room, and with the small homely hum of Chirk Street. Presently he moved nearer, but as if her question had quite dropped. "I don't see what has so suddenly wound you up."

"I should have thought you might perhaps guess. Let me at any rate tell you. Aunt Maud has made me a proposal. But she has also made me a condition. She wants to keep me."

"And what in the world else *could* she possibly want?"

246

"Oh, I don't know—many things. I'm not so precious a capture," the girl a little dryly explained. "No one has ever wanted to keep me before."

Looking always what was proper, her father looked now still more surprised than interested. "You've not had proposals?" He spoke as if that were incredible of Lionel Croy's daughter; as if indeed such an admission scarce consorted, even in filial intimacy, with her high spirit and general form.

"Not from rich relations. She's extremely kind to me, but it's time, she says, that we should understand each other."

Mr. Croy fully assented. "Of course it is—high time; and I can quite imagine what she means by it."

"Are you very sure?"

"Oh, perfectly. She means that she'll 'do' for you handsomely if you'll break off all relations with me. You speak of her condition. Her condition's of course that."

"Well then," said Kate, "it's what has wound me up. Here I am."

He showed with a gesture how thoroughly he had taken it in; after which, within a few seconds, he had, quite congruously, turned the situation about. "Do you really suppose me in a position to justify your throwing yourself upon me?"

She waited a little, but when she spoke it was clear. "Yes."

"Well then, you're a bigger fool than I should have ventured to suppose you."

"Why so? You live. You flourish. You bloom."

"Ah, how you've all always hated me!" he murmured with a pensive gaze again at the window.

"No one could be less of a mere cherished memory," she declared as if she had not heard him. "You're an actual person, if there ever was one. We agreed just now that you're beautiful. You strike me, you know, as—in your own way—much more firm on your feet than I am. Don't put it to me therefore as monstrous that the fact that we are, after all, parent and child should at present in some manner count for us. My idea has been that it should have some effect for each of us. I don't at all, as I told you just now," she pursued, "make out your life; but whatever it is I hereby offer you to accept it. And, on my side, I'll do everything I can for you."

"I see," said Lionel Croy. Then, with the sound of extreme relevance, "And what *can* you?" She only, at this, hesitated, and he took up her silence. "You can describe yourself—*to* yourself—as, in a fine flight, giving up your aunt for me; but what good, I should like to know, would your fine flight do me?" As she still said nothing he developed a little. "We're not possessed of so much, at this charming pass, please to remember, as that we can afford not to take hold of any perch held out to us. I like the way you talk, my dear, about 'giving up!' One doesn't give up the use of a spoon because one's reduced to living on broth. And your spoon, that is your aunt, please consider, is partly mine as well." She rose now, as if in sight of the term of her effort, in sight of the futility and the weariness of many things, and moved back to the poor little glass with which she had communed before. She retouched here again the poise of her hat, and this brought to her father's lips another remark in which impatience, however, had already been replaced by a funny flare of appreciation. "Oh, you're all right! Don't muddle yourself up with *me!*"

His daughter turned round to him. "The condition Aunt Maud makes is that I shall have absolutely nothing to do with you; never see you, nor speak, nor write to you, never go near you nor make you a sign, nor hold any sort of communication with you. What she requires is that you shall simply cease to exist for me."

He had always seemed—it was one of the marks of what they called the "unspeakable" in him—to walk a little more on his toes, as if for jauntiness, in the presence of offence. Nothing, however, was more wonderful than what he sometimes would take for offence, unless it might be what he sometimes wouldn't. He walked at any rate on his toes now. "A very proper requirement of your Aunt Maud, my dear—I don't hesitate to say it!" Yet as this, much as she had seen, left her silent at first from what might have been a sense of sickness, he had time to go on: "That's her condition then. But what are her promises? Just what does she engage to do? You must work it, you know."

"You mean make her feel," Kate asked after a moment, "how much I'm attached to you?"

"Well, what a cruel, invidious treaty it is for you to sign. I'm a poor old dad to make a stand about giving up—I quite agree. But I'm not, after all, quite the old dad not to get something *for* giving up."

"Oh, I think her idea," said Kate almost gaily now, "is that I shall get a great deal."

He met her with his inimitable amenity. "But does she give you the items?"

The girl went through the show. "More or less, I think. But many of them are things I dare say I may take for granted—things women can do for each other and that you wouldn't understand."

"There's nothing I understand so well, always, as the things I needn't! But what I want to do, you see," he went on, "is to put it to your conscience that you've an admirable opportunity; and that it's moreover one for which, after all, damn you, you've really to thank *me.*"

"I confess I don't see," Kate observed, "what my 'conscience' has to do with it."

"Then, my dear girl, you ought simply to be ashamed of yourself. Do you know what you're a proof of, all you hard, hollow people together?" He put the question with a charming air of sudden spiritual heat. "Of the deplorably superficial morality of the age. The family sentiment, in our vulgarised, brutalised life, has gone utterly to pot. There was a day when a man like me—by which I mean a parent like me—would have been for a daughter like you a quite distinct value; what's called in the business world, I believe, an 'asset.'" He continued sociably to make it out. "I'm not talking only of what you might, with the right feeling do *for* me, but of what you might—it's what I call your opportunity—do *with* me. Unless indeed," he the next moment imperturbably threw off, "they come a good deal to the same thing. Your duty as well as your chance, if you're capable of seeing it, is to use me. Show family feeling by seeing what I'm good for. If you had it as *I* have it you'd see I'm still good—well, for a lot of things. There's in fact, my dear," Mr. Croy wound up, "a coach-and-four to be got out of me." His drop, or rather his climax, failed a little of effect, indeed, through an undue precipitation of memory. Something his daughter had said came back to him. "You've settled to give away half your little inheritance?"

Her hesitation broke into laughter. "No—I haven't 'settled' anything."

"But you mean, practically, to let Marian collar it?" They stood there face to face, but she so denied herself to his challenge that he could only go on. "You've a view of three hundred a year for her in addition to what her husband left her with? Is *that,*" the remote progenitor of such wantonness audibly wondered, "your morality?"

Kate found her answer without trouble. "Is it your idea that I should give you everything?"

The "everything" clearly struck him—to the point even of determining the tone of his reply. "Far from it. How can you ask that when I refuse what you tell me you came to offer? Make of my idea what you can; I think I've sufficiently expressed it, and it's at any rate to take or to leave. It's the only one, I may nevertheless add; it's the basket with all my eggs. It's my conception, in short, of your duty."

The girl's tired smile watched the word as if it had taken on a small grotesque visibility. "You're wonderful on such subjects! I think I should leave you in no doubt," she pursued, "that if I were to sign my aunt's agreement I should carry it out, in honour, to the letter."

"Rather, my own love! It's just your honour that I appeal to. The only way to play the game *is* to play it. There's no limit to what your aunt can do for you."

"Do you mean in the way of marrying me?"

"What else should I mean? Marry properly——"

"And then?" Kate asked as he hung fire.

"And then—well, I *will* talk with you. I'll resume relations."

She looked about her and picked up her parasol. "Because you're not so afraid of any one else in the world as you are of *her?* My husband, if I should marry, would be, at the worst, less of a terror? If that's what you mean, there may be something in it. But doesn't it depend a little also on what you mean by my getting a proper one? However," Kate added as she picked out the frill of her little umbrella, "I don't suppose your idea of him is *quite* that he should persuade you to live with us."

"Dear no—not a bit." He spoke as not resenting either the fear or the hope she imputed; met both imputations, in fact, with a sort of intellectual relief. "I place the case for you wholly in your aunt's hands. I take her view, with my eyes shut; I accept in all confidence any man she selects. If he's good enough for *her*—elephantine snob as she is—he's good enough for me; and quite in spite of the fact that she'll be sure to select one who can be trusted to be nasty to me. My only interest is in your doing what she wants. You shan't be so beastly poor, my darling," Mr. Croy declared, "if I can help it."

"Well then, good-bye, papa," the girl said after a reflection on this that had perceptibly ended for her in a renunciation of further debate. "Of course you understand that it may be for long."

Her companion, hereupon, had one of his finest inspirations. "Why not, frankly, for ever? You must do me the justice to see that I don't do things, that I've never done them, by halves—that if I offer you to efface myself, it's for the final, fatal sponge that I ask, well saturated and well applied."

She turned her handsome, quiet face upon him at such length that it might well have been for the last time. "I don't know what you're like."

"No more do I, my dear. I've spent my life in trying, in vain, to discover. Like nothing—more's the pity. If there had been many of us, and we could have found each other out, there's no knowing what we mightn't have done. But it doesn't matter now. Good-bye, love." He looked even not sure of what she would wish him to suppose on the subject of a kiss, yet also not embarrassed by his uncertainty.

She forbore in fact for a moment longer to clear it up. "I wish there were some one here who might serve—for any contingency—as a witness that I *have* put it to you that I'm ready to come."

"Would you like me," her father asked, "to call the landlady?"

"You may not believe me," she pursued, "but I came really hoping you might have found some way. I'm very sorry, at all events, to leave you unwell." He turned away from her, on this, and, as he had done before, took refuge, by the window, in a stare at the street. "Let me put it—unfortunately without a witness," she added after a moment, "that there's only one word you really need speak."

When he took this up it was still with his back to her. "If I don't strike you as having already spoken it, our time has been singularly wasted."

"I'll engage with you in respect to my aunt exactly to what she wants of me in respect to you. She wants me to choose. Very well, I *will* choose. I'll wash my hands of her for you to just that tune."

He at last brought himself round. "Do you know, dear, you make me sick? I've tried to be clear, and it isn't fair."

But she passed this over; she was too visibly sincere. "Father!"

"I don't quite see what's the matter with you," he said, "and if you can't pull yourself together I'll—upon my honour—take you in hand. Put you into a cab and deliver you again safe at Lancaster Gate."

She was really absent, distant. "Father."

It was too much, and he met it sharply. "Well?"

Henry James

"Strange as it may be to you to hear me say it, there's a good you can do me and a help you can render."

"Isn't it then exactly what I've been trying to make you feel?"

"Yes," she answered patiently, "but so in the wrong way. I'm perfectly honest in what I say, and I know what I'm talking about. It isn't that I'll pretend I could have believed a month ago in anything to call aid or support from you. The case is changed—that's what has happened; my difficulty's a new one. But even now it's not a question of anything I should ask you in a way to 'do.' It's simply a question of your not turning me away—taking yourself out of my life. It's simply a question of your saying: 'Yes then, since you will, we'll stand together. We won't worry in advance about how or where; we'll have a faith and find a way.' That's all—*that* would be the good you'd do me. I should *have* you, and it would be for my benefit. Do you see?"

If he didn't it was not for want of looking at her hard. "The matter with you is that you're in love, and that your aunt knows and—for reasons, I'm sure, perfect—hates and opposes it. Well she may! It's a matter in which I trust her with my eyes shut. Go, please." Though he spoke not in anger—rather in infinite sadness—he fairly turned her out. Before she took it up he had, as the fullest expression of what he felt, opened the door of the room. He had fairly, in his deep disapproval, a generous compassion to spare. "I'm sorry for her, deluded woman, if she builds on you."

Kate stood a moment in the draught. "She's not the person *I* pity most, for, deluded in many ways though she may be, she's not the person who's most so. I mean," she explained, "if it's a question of what you call building on me."

He took it as if what she meant might be other than her description of it. "You're deceiving *two* persons then, Mrs. Lowder and somebody else?"

She shook her head with detachment. "I've no intention of that sort with respect to any one now—to Mrs. Lowder least of all. If you fail me"—she seemed to make it out for herself—"that has the merit at least that it simplifies. I shall go my way—as I see my way."

"Your way, you mean then, will be to marry some blackguard without a penny?"

"You ask a great deal of satisfaction," she observed, "for the little you give."

It brought him up again before her as with a sense that she was not to be hustled; and, though he glared at her a little, this had long been the practical limit to his general power of objection. "If you're base enough to incur your aunt's disgust, you're base enough for my argument. What, if you're not thinking of an utterly improper person, do your speeches to me signify? Who *is* the beggarly sneak?" he demanded as her response failed. Her response, when it came, was cold but distinct. "He has every disposition to make the best of you. He only wants in fact to be kind to you."

"Then he *must* be an ass! And how in the world can you consider it to improve him for me," her father pursued, "that he's also destitute and impossible? There are asses and asses, even—the right and the wrong— and you appear to have carefully picked out one of the wrong. Your aunt knows *them,* by good fortune; I perfectly trust, as I tell you, her judgment for them; and you may take it from me once for all that I won't hear of any one of whom *she* won't." Which led up to his last word. "If you should really defy us both——!"

"Well, papa?"

"Well, my sweet child, I think that—reduced to insignificance as you may fondly believe me—I should still not be quite without some way of making you regret it."

She had a pause, a grave one, but not, as appeared, that she might measure this danger. "If I shouldn't do it, you know, it wouldn't be because I'm afraid of you."

"Oh, if you don't do it," he retorted, "you may be as bold as you like!"

"Then you can do nothing at all for me?"

He showed her, this time unmistakably—it was before her there on the landing, at the top of the tortuous stairs and in the midst of the strange smell that seemed to cling to them—how vain her appeal remained. "I've never pretended to do more than my duty; I've given you the best and the clearest advice." And then came up the spring that moved him. "If it only displeases you, you can go to Marian to be consoled." What he couldn't forgive was her dividing with Marian her scant share of the provision their mother had been able to leave them. She should have divided it with *him*.

II

She had gone to Mrs. Lowder on her mother's death—gone with an effort the strain and pain of which made her at present, as she recalled them, reflect on the long way she had travelled since then. There had been nothing else to do—not a penny in the other house, nothing but unpaid bills that had gathered thick while its mistress lay mortally ill, and the admonition that there was nothing she must attempt to raise money on, since everything belonged to the "estate." How the estate would turn out at best presented itself as a mystery altogether gruesome; it had proved, in fact, since then a residuum a trifle less scant than, with Marian, she had for some weeks feared; but the girl had had at the beginning rather a wounded sense of its being watched on behalf of Marian and her children. What on earth was it supposed that *she* wanted to do to it? She wanted in truth only to give up—to abandon her own interest, which she, no doubt, would already have done had not the point been subject to Aunt Maud's sharp intervention. Aunt Maud's intervention was all sharp now, and the other point, the great one, was that it was to be, in this light, either all put up with or all declined. Yet at the winter's end, nevertheless, she could scarce have said what stand she conceived she had taken. It wouldn't be the first time she had seen herself obliged to accept with smothered irony other people's interpretation of her conduct. She often ended by giving up to them—it seemed really the way to live—the version that met their convenience.

The tall, rich, heavy house at Lancaster Gate, on the other side of the Park and the long South Kensington stretches, had figured to her, through childhood, through girlhood, as the remotest limit of her vague young world. It was further off and more occasional than anything else in the comparatively compact circle in which she revolved, and seemed, by a rigour early marked, to be reached through long, straight, discouraging vistas, which kept lengthening and straightening, whereas almost everything else in life was either, at the worst, round about Cromwell Road, or, at the furthest, in the nearer parts of Kensington Gardens. Mrs. Lowder was her only "real" aunt, not the wife of an uncle, and had been thereby, both in ancient days and when the greater trouble came, the person, of all persons, properly to make some sign; in accord with which our young woman's feeling was founded on the impression, quite cherished for years, that the signs made across the interval just mentioned had never been really in the note of the situation. The main office of this relative, for the young Croys—apart from giving them their fixed measure of social greatness—had struck them as being to form them to a conception of what they were not to expect. When Kate came to think matters over with the aid of knowledge, she failed quite to see how Aunt Maud could have been different—she had rather perceived by this time how many other things might have been; yet she also made out that if they had all consciously lived under a liability to the chill breath of *ultima Thule* they couldn't, either, on the facts, very well have done less. What in the event appeared established was that if Mrs. Lowder had disliked them she had yet not disliked them so much as they supposed. It had at any rate been for the purpose of showing how she struggled with her aversion that she sometimes came to see them, that she at regular periods invited them to her house, and in short, as it now looked, kept them along on the terms that would best give her sister the perennial luxury of a grievance. This sister, poor Mrs. Croy, the girl knew, had always judged her resentfully, and had brought them up, Marian, the boys and herself, to the idea of a particular attitude, for signs of the practice of which they watched each other with awe. The attitude was to make plain to Aunt Maud, with the same regularity as her invitations, that they sufficed—thanks awfully—to themselves. But the ground of it, Kate lived to discern, was that this was only because *she* didn't suffice to them. The little she offered was to be accepted under protest, yet not, really, because it was excessive. It wounded them—there was the rub!—because it fell short.

The number of new things our young lady looked out on from the high south window that hung over the Park—this number was so great (though some of the things were only old ones altered and, as the phrase was of other matters, done up), that life at present turned to her view from week to week more and more the face of a striking and distinguished stranger. She had reached a great age—for it quite seemed to her that at twenty-five it was late to reconsider; and her most general sense was a shade of regret that she had not known earlier. The world was different—whether for worse or for better—from her rudimentary readings, and it gave her the feeling of a wasted past. If she had only known sooner she might have arranged herself more to meet it. She made, at all events, discoveries every day, some of which were about herself and others about other persons. Two of these—one under each head—more particularly engaged, in alternation, her anxiety. She saw as she had never seen before how material things spoke to her. She saw, and she blushed to see, that if, in contrast with some of its old aspects, life now affected her as a dress successfully "done up," this was exactly by reason of the trimmings and lace, was a matter of ribbons and silk and velvet. She had a dire accessibility to pleasure from such sources. She liked the charming quarters her aunt had assigned her—liked them literally more than she had in all her other days liked anything; and nothing could have been more uneasy than her suspicion of her relative's view of this truth. Her relative was prodigious— she had never done her relative justice. These larger conditions all tasted of her, from morning till night; but she was a person in respect to whom the growth of acquaintance could only—strange as it might seem—keep your heart in your mouth.

The girl's second great discovery was that, so far from having been for Mrs. Lowder a subject of superficial consideration, the blighted home in Lexham Gardens had haunted her nights and her days. Kate had spent, all winter, hours of observation that were not less pointed for being spent alone; recent events, which her mourning explained, assured her a measure of isolation, and it was in the isolation above all that her neighbour's influence worked. Sitting far downstairs Aunt Maud was yet a presence from which a sensitive niece could feel herself extremely under pressure. She knew herself now, the sensitive niece, as having been marked from far back. She knew more than she could have told you, by the upstairs fire, in a whole dark December afternoon. She knew so much that her knowledge was what fairly kept her there, making her at times more endlessly between the small silk-covered sofa that stood for her in the firelight and the great grey map of Middlesex spread beneath her lookout. To go down, to forsake her refuge, was to meet some of her discoveries half-way, to have to face them or fly before them; whereas they were at such a height only like the rumble of a far-off siege heard in the provisioned citadel. She had almost liked, in these weeks, what had created her suspense and her stress: the loss of her mother, the submersion of her father, the discomfort of her sister, the confirmation of their shrunken prospects, the certainty, in especial, of her having to recognise that, should she behave, as she called it, decently—that is still do something for others—she would be herself wholly without supplies. She held that she had a right to sadness and stillness; she nursed them for their postponing power. What they mainly postponed was the question of a surrender—though she could not yet have said exactly of what: a general surrender of everything—that was at moments the way it presented itself—to Aunt Maud's looming "personality." It was by her personality that Aunt Maud was prodigious, and the great mass of it loomed because, in the thick, the foglike air of her arranged existence, there were parts doubtless magnified and parts certainly vague. They represented at all events alike, the dim and the distinct, a strong will and a high hand. It was perfectly present to Kate that she might be devoured, and she likened herself to a trembling kid, kept apart a day or two till her turn should come, but sure sooner or later to be introduced into the cage of the lioness.

The cage was Aunt Maud's own room, her office, her counting-house, her battlefield, her especial scene, in fine, of action, situated on the ground-floor, opening from the main hall and figuring rather to our young woman on exit and entrance as a guard house or a toll-gate. The lioness waited—the kid had at least that consciousness; was aware of the neighbourhood of a morsel she had reason to suppose tender. She would have been meanwhile a wonderful lioness for a show, an extraordinary figure in a cage or anywhere; majestic, magnificent, high-coloured, all brilliant gloss, perpetual satin, twinkling bugles and flashing gems, with a lustre of agate eyes, a sheen of raven hair, a polish of complexion that was like that of well-kept china and that—as if the skin were too tight—told especially at curves and corners. Her niece had a quiet name for her—she kept it quiet; thinking of her, with a free fancy, as somehow typically insular, she talked to herself of Britannia of the Market Place—Britannia unmistakable, but with a pen in her ear, and felt she should not be happy till she might on some occasion add to the rest of the panoply a helmet, a shield, a trident and a ledger. It was not in truth, however, that the forces with which, as Kate felt, she would have to deal were those most suggested by an image simple and broad; she was learning, after all, each day, to know her companion, and what she had already most perceived was the mistake of trusting to easy analogies. There was a whole side of Britannia, the side of her florid philistinism, her plumes and her train, her fantastic furniture and heaving bosom, the false gods of her taste and false notes of her talk, the sole contemplation of which would be dangerously misleading. She was a complex and subtle Britannia, as passionate as she was practical, with a reticule for her prejudices as deep as that other pocket, the pocket full of coins stamped in her image, that the world best knew her by. She carried on, in short, behind her aggressive and defensive front, operations determined by her wisdom. It was in fact, we have hinted, as a besieger that our young lady, in the provisioned citadel, had for the present most to think of her, and what made her formidable in this character was that she was unscrupulous and immoral. So, at all events, in silent sessions and a youthful off-hand way, Kate conveniently pictured her: what this sufficiently represented being that her weight was in the scale of certain dangers—those dangers that, by our showing, made the younger woman linger and lurk above, while the elder, below, both militant and diplomatic, covered as much of the ground as possible. Yet what were the dangers, after all, but just the dangers of life and of London? Mrs. Lowder *was* London, *was* life—the roar of the siege and the thick of the fray. There were some things, after all, of which Britannia was afraid; but Aunt Maud was afraid of nothing—not even, it would appear, of arduous thought. These impressions, none the less, Kate kept so much to herself that she scarce shared them with poor Marian, the ostensible purpose of her frequent visits to whom yet continued to be to talk over everything. One of her reasons for holding off from the last concession to Aunt Maud was that she might be the more free to commit herself to this so much nearer and so much less fortunate relative, with whom Aunt Maud would have, directly, almost nothing to do. The sharpest pinch of her state, meanwhile, was exactly that all intercourse with her sister had the effect of casting down her courage and tying her hands, adding daily to her sense of the part, not always either uplifting or sweetening, that the bond of blood might play in one's life. She was face to face with it now, with the bond of blood; the consciousness of it was what she seemed most clearly to have "come into" by the death of her mother, much of that consciousness as her mother had absorbed and carried away. Her haunting, harrassing father, her menacing, uncompromising aunt, her portionless little nephews and nieces, were figures that caused the chord of natural piety superabundantly to vibrate. Her manner of putting it to herself—but more especially in respect to Marian—was that she saw what you might be brought to by the cultivation of consanguinity. She had taken, in the old days, as she supposed, the measure of this liability; those being the days when, as the second-born, she had thought no one in the world so pretty as Marian, no one so charming, so clever, so assured, in advance, of happiness and success. The view was different now, but her attitude had been obliged, for many reasons, to show as the same. The subject of this estimate was no longer pretty, as the reason for thinking her clever was no longer plain; yet, bereaved, disappointed, demoralised, querulous, she was all the more sharply and insistently Kate's elder and Kate's own. Kate's most constant feeling about her was that she would make her, Kate, do things; and always, in comfortless Chelsea, at the door of the small house the small rent of which she couldn't help having on her mind, she fatalistically asked herself, before going in, which thing it would probably be this time. She noticed with profundity that disappointment made people selfish; she marvelled at the serenity—it was the poor woman's only one—of what Marian took for granted: her own state of abasement as the second-born, her life reduced to mere inexhaustible sisterhood. She existed, in that view, wholly for the small house in Chelsea; the moral of which moreover, of course, was that the more one gave oneself the less of one was left. There were always people to snatch at one, and it would never occur to *them* that they were eating one up. They did that without tasting.

There was no such misfortune, or at any rate no such discomfort, she further reasoned, as to be formed at once for being and for seeing. You always saw, in this case, something else than what you were, and you got, in consequence, none of the peace of your condition. However, as she never really let Marian see what she was, Marian might well not have been aware that she herself saw. Kate was accordingly, to her own vision, not a hypocrite of virtue, for she gave herself up; but she was a hypocrite of stupidity, for she kept to herself everything that was not herself. What she most kept was the particular sentiment with which she watched her sister instinctively neglect nothing that would make for her submission to their aunt; a state of the spirit that perhaps marked most sharply how poor you might become when you minded so much the absence of wealth. It was through Kate that Aunt Maud should be worked, and nothing mattered less than what might become of Kate in the process. Kate was to burn her ships, in short, so that Marian should profit; and Marian's desire to profit was quite oblivious of a dignity that had, after all, its reasons—if it had only cared for them—for keeping itself a little stiff. Kate, to be properly stiff for both of them, would therefore have had to be selfish, have had to prefer an ideal of behaviour—than which nothing, ever, was more selfish—to the possibility of stray crumbs for the four small creatures. The tale of Mrs. Lowder's disgust at her elder niece's marriage to Mr. Condrip had lost little of its point; the incredibly fatuous behaviour of Mr. Condrip, the parson of a dull suburban parish, with a saintly profile which was always in evidence, being so distinctly on record to keep criticism consistent. He had presented his profile on system, having, goodness knew, nothing else to present—nothing at all to full-face the world with, no imagination of the propriety of living and minding his business. Criticism had remained on Aunt Maud's part consistent enough; she was not a person to regard such proceedings as less of a mistake for having acquired more of the privilege of pathos. She had not been forgiving, and the only approach she made to overlooking them was by overlooking—with the surviving delinquent—the solid little phalanx that now represented them. Of the two sinister ceremonies that she lumped together, the marriage and the interment, she had been present at the former, just as she had sent Marian, before it, a liberal cheque; but this had not been for her more than the shadow of an admitted link with Mrs. Condrip's course. She disapproved of clamorous children for whom there was no prospect; she disapproved of weeping widows who couldn't make their errors good; and she had thus put within Marian's reach one of the few luxuries left when so much else had gone, an easy pretext for a constant grievance. Kate Croy remembered well what their mother, in a different quarter, had made of it; and it was Marian's marked failure to pluck the fruit of resentment that committed them, as sisters, to an almost equal fellowship in abjection. If the theory was that, yes, alas, one of the pair had ceased to be noticed, but that the other was noticed enough to make up for it, who would fail to see that Kate couldn't separate herself without a cruel pride? That lesson became sharp for our young lady the day after her interview with her father.

"I can't imagine," Marian on this occasion said to her, "how you can think of anything else in the world but the horrid way we're situated."

"And, pray, how do you know," Kate inquired in reply, "anything about my thoughts? It seems to me I give you sufficient proof of how much I think of *you*. I don't, really, my dear, know what else you've to do with!"

Marian's retort, on this, was a stroke as to which she had supplied herself with several kinds of preparation, but there was, none the less, something of an unexpected note in its promptitude. She had foreseen her sister's general fear; but here, ominously, was the special one. "Well, your own business is of course your own business, and you may say there's no one less in a position than I to preach to you. But, all the same, if you wash your hands of me for ever for it, I won't, for this once, keep back that I don't consider you've a right, as we all stand, to throw yourself away."

It was after the children's dinner, which was also their mother's, but which their aunt mostly contrived to keep from ever becoming her own luncheon; and the two young women were still in the presence of the crumpled table-cloth, the dispersed pinafores, the scraped dishes, the lingering odour of boiled food. Kate had asked, with ceremony, if she might put up a window a little, and Mrs. Condrip had replied without it that she might do as she liked. She often received such inquiries as if they reflected in a manner on the pure essence of her little ones. The four had retired, with much movement and noise, under imperfect control of the small Irish governess whom their aunt had hunted out for them and whose brooding resolve not to prolong so uncrowned a martyrdom she already more than suspected. Their mother had become for Kate—who took it just for the effect of being their mother— quite a different thing from the mild Marian of the past: Mr. Condrip's widow expansively obscured that image. She was little more than a ragged relic, a plain, prosaic result of him, as if she had somehow been pulled through him as through an obstinate funnel, only to be left crumpled and useless and with nothing in her but what he accounted for. She had grown red and almost fat, which were not happy signs of mourning; less and less like any Croy, particularly a Croy in trouble, and sensibly like her husband's two unmarried sisters, who came to see her, in Kate's view, much too often and stayed too long, with the consequence of inroads upon the tea and bread-and-butter— matters as to which Kate, not unconcerned with the tradesmen's books, had feelings. About them, moreover, Marian *was* touchy, and her nearer relative, who observed and weighed things, noted as an oddity that she would have taken any reflection on them as a reflection on herself. If that was what marriage necessarily did to you, Kate Croy would have questioned marriage. It was a grave example, at any rate, of what a man—and such a man!—might make of a woman. She could see how the Condrip pair pressed their brother's widow on the subject of Aunt Maud—who wasn't, after all, *their* aunt; made her, over their interminable cups, chatter and even swagger about Lancaster Gate, made her more vulgar than it had seemed written that any Croy could possibly become on such a subject. They laid it down, they rubbed it in, that Lancaster Gate was to be kept in sight, and that she, Kate, was to keep it; so that, curiously, or at all events sadly, our young woman was sure of being, in her own person, more permitted to them as an object of comment than they would in turn ever be permitted to herself. The beauty of which, too, was that Marian didn't love them. But they were Condrips—they had grown near

263

the rose; they were almost like Bertie and Maudie, like Kitty and Guy. They talked of the dead to her, which Kate never did; it being a relation in which Kate could but mutely listen. She couldn't indeed too often say to herself that if that was what marriage did to you——! It may easily be guessed, therefore, that the ironic light of such reserves fell straight across the field of Marian's warning. "I don't quite see," she answered, "where, in particular, it strikes you that my danger lies. I'm not conscious, I assure you, of the least 'disposition' to throw myself anywhere. I feel as if, for the present, I have been quite sufficiently thrown."

"You don't feel"—Marian brought it all out—"as if you would like to marry Merton Densher?"

Kate took a moment to meet this inquiry. "Is it your idea that if I should feel so I would be bound to give you notice, so that you might step in and head me off? Is that your idea?" the girl asked. Then, as her sister also had a pause, "I don't know what makes you talk of Mr. Densher," she observed.

"I talk of him just because you don't. That you never do, in spite of what I know—that's what makes me think of him. Or rather perhaps it's what makes me think of *you*. If you don't know by this time what I hope for you, what I dream of—my attachment being what it is—it's no use my attempting to tell you." But Marian had in fact warmed to her work, and Kate was sure she had discussed Mr. Densher with the Miss Condrips. "If I name that person I suppose it's because I'm so afraid of him. If you want really to know, he fills me with terror. If you want really to know, in fact, I dislike him as much as I dread him."

"And yet don't think it dangerous to abuse him to me?"

"Yes," Mrs. Condrip confessed, "I do think it dangerous; but how can I speak of him otherwise? I dare say, I admit, that I shouldn't speak of him at all. Only I do want you for once, as I said just now, to know."

"To know what, my dear?"

"That I should regard it," Marian promptly returned, "as far and away the worst thing that has happened to us yet."

"Do you mean because he hasn't money?"

"Yes, for one thing. And because I don't believe in him."

Kate was civil, but perfunctory. "What do you mean by not believing in him?"

"Well, being sure he'll never get it. And you *must* have it. You *shall* have it."

"To give it to you?"

Marian met her with a readiness that was practically pert. "To *have* it, first. Not, at any rate, to go on not having it. Then we should see."

"We should indeed!" said Kate Croy. It was talk of a kind she loathed, but if Marian chose to be vulgar what was one to do? It made her think of the Miss Condrips with renewed aversion. "I like the way you arrange things—I like what you take for granted. If it's so easy for us to marry men who want us to scatter gold, I wonder we any of us do anything else. I don't see so many of them about, nor what interest I might ever have for them. You live, my dear," she presently added, "in a world of vain thoughts."

"Not so much as you, Kate; for I see what I see, and you can't turn it off that way." The elder sister paused long enough for the younger's face to show, in spite of superiority, an apprehension. "I'm not talking of any man but Aunt Maud's man, nor of any money, even, if you like, but Aunt Maud's money. I'm not talking of anything but your doing what *she* wants. You're wrong if you speak of anything that I want of you; I want nothing but what she does. That's good enough for me!"—and Marian's tone struck her companion as dreadful. "If I don't believe in Merton Densher, I do at least in Mrs. Lowder."

"Your ideas are the more striking," Kate returned, "that they're the same as papa's. I had them from him, you may be interested to know—and with all the brilliancy you may imagine—yesterday."

265

Marian clearly was interested to know. "He has been to see you?"

"No, I went to him."

"Really?" Marian wondered. "For what purpose?"

"To tell him I'm ready to go to him."

Marian stared. "To leave Aunt Maud——?"

"For my father, yes."

She had fairly flushed, poor Mrs. Condrip, with horror. "You're ready——?"

"So I told him. I couldn't tell him less."

"And, pray, could you tell him more?" Marian gasped in her distress. "What in the world is he *to* us? You bring out such a thing as that this way?"

They faced each other—the tears were in Marian's eyes. Kate watched them there a moment and then said: "I had thought it well over—over and over. But you needn't feel injured. I'm not going. He won't have me."

Her companion still panted—it took time to subside. "Well, *I* wouldn't have you—wouldn't receive you at all, I can assure you—if he had made you any other answer. I do feel injured—at your having been willing. If you were to go to papa, my dear, you would have to stop coming to me." Marian put it thus, indefinably, as a picture of privation from which her companion might shrink. Such were the threats she could complacently make, could think herself masterful for making. "But if he won't take you," she continued, "he shows at least his sharpness."

Marian had always her views of sharpness; she was, as her sister privately commented, great on it. But Kate had her refuge from irritation. "He won't take me," she simply repeated. "But he believes, like you, in Aunt Maud. He threatens me with his curse if I leave her."

"So you *won't?*" As the girl at first said nothing her companion caught at it. "You won't, of course? I see you won't. But I don't see why, nevertheless, I

266

shouldn't insist to you once for all on the plain truth of the whole matter. The truth, my dear, of your duty. Do you ever think about *that?* It's the greatest duty of all."

"There you are again," Kate laughed. "Papa's also immense on my duty."

"Oh, I don't pretend to be immense, but I pretend to know more than you do of life; more even perhaps than papa." Marian seemed to see that personage at this moment, nevertheless, in the light of a kinder irony. "Poor old papa!"

She sighed it with as many condonations as her sister's ear had more than once caught in her "Dear old Aunt Maud!" These were things that made Kate, for the time, turn sharply away, and she gathered herself now to go. They were the note again of the abject; it was hard to say which of the persons in question had most shown how little they liked her. The younger woman proposed, at any rate, to let discussion rest, and she believed that, for herself, she had done so during the ten minutes that, thanks to her wish not to break off short, elapsed before she could gracefully withdraw. It then appeared, however, that Marian had been discussing still, and there was something that, at the last, Kate had to take up. "Whom do you mean by Aunt Maud's young man?"

"Whom should I mean but Lord Mark?"

"And where do you pick up such vulgar twaddle?" Kate demanded with her clear face. "How does such stuff, in this hole, get to you?"

She had no sooner spoken than she asked herself what had become of the grace to which she had sacrificed. Marian certainly did little to save it, and nothing indeed was so inconsequent as her ground of complaint. She desired her to "work" Lancaster Gate as she believed that scene of abundance could be worked; but she now didn't see why advantage should be taken of the bloated connection to put an affront on her own poor home. She appeared in fact for the moment to take the position that Kate kept her in her "hole" and then heartlessly reflected on her being in it. Yet she didn't explain how she had picked up the report on which her sister had challenged her—so that it was thus left to her sister to see in it, once more, a sign of the creeping curiosity of the Miss Condrips. They lived in a deeper hole than Marian, but they kept their ear to the ground, they spent their days in prowling, whereas Marian, in garments and shoes that seemed steadily to grow looser and larger, never prowled. There were times when Kate wondered if the Miss Condrips were offered her by fate as a warning for her own future—to be taken as showing her what she herself might become at forty if she let things too recklessly go. What was expected of her by others—and by so many of them—could, all the same, on occasion, present itself as beyond a joke; and this was just now the aspect it particularly wore. She was not only to quarrel with Merton Densher to oblige her five spectators—with the Miss Condrips there were five; she was to set forth in pursuit of Lord Mark on some preposterous theory of the premium attached to success. Mrs. Lowder's hand had attached it, and it figured at the end of the course as a bell that would ring, break out into public clamour, as soon as touched. Kate reflected sharply enough on the weak points of this fond fiction, with the result at last of a certain chill for her sister's confidence; though Mrs. Condrip still took refuge in the plea—which was after all the great point—that their aunt would be munificent when their aunt should be pleased. The exact identity of her candidate was a detail; what was of the essence was her conception of the kind of match it was open to her niece to make with her aid. Marian always spoke of marriages as "matches," but that was again a detail. Mrs. Lowder's "aid" meanwhile awaited them— if not to light the way to Lord Mark, then to somebody better. Marian would put up, in fine, with somebody better; she only wouldn't put up with somebody so much worse. Kate had, once more, to go through all this before a graceful issue was reached. It was reached by her paying with the sacrifice of Mr. Densher for her reduction of Lord Mark to the absurd. So they separated softly enough. She was to be let off hearing about Lord Mark so long as she made it good that she wasn't underhand about anybody else. She had denied everything and every one, she reflected as she went away—and that was a relief; but it also made rather a clean sweep of the future. The prospect put on a bareness that already gave her something in common with the Miss Condrips.

BOOK SECOND

III

Merton Densher, who passed the best hours of each night at the office of his newspaper, had at times, during the day, to make up for it, a sense, or at least an appearance, of leisure, in accordance with which he was not infrequently to be met, in different parts of the town, at moments when men of business are hidden from the public eye. More than once, during the present winter's end, he had deviated, toward three o'clock, or toward four, into Kensington Gardens, where he might for a while, on each occasion, have been observed to demean himself as a person with nothing to do. He made his way indeed, for the most part, with a certain directness, over to the north side; but once that ground was reached his behaviour was noticeably wanting in point. He moved seemingly at random from alley to alley; he stopped for no reason and remained idly agaze; he sat down in a chair and then changed to a bench; after which he walked about again, only again to repeat both the vagueness and the vivacity. Distinctly, he was a man either with nothing at all to do or with ever so much to think about; and it was not to be denied that the impression he might often thus easily make had the effect of causing the burden of proof, in certain directions, to rest on him. It was a little the fault of his aspect, his personal marks, which made it almost impossible to name his profession.

He was a longish, leanish, fairish young Englishman, not unamenable, on certain sides, to classification—as for instance by being a gentleman, by being rather specifically one of the educated, one of the generally sound and generally pleasant; yet, though to that degree neither extraordinary nor abnormal, he would have failed to play straight into an observer's hands. He was young for the House of Commons, he was loose for the army. He was refined, as might have been said, for the city, and, quite apart from the cut of his cloth, he was sceptical, it might have been felt, for the church. On the other hand he was credulous for diplomacy, or perhaps even for science, while he was perhaps at the same time too much in his mere senses for poetry, and yet too little in them for art. You would have got fairly near him by making out in his eyes the potential recognition of ideas; but you would have quite fallen away again on the question of the ideas themselves. The difficulty with Densher was that he looked vague without looking weak—idle without looking empty. It was the accident, possibly, of his long legs, which were apt to stretch themselves; of his straight hair and his well-shaped head, never, the latter, neatly smooth, and apt, into the bargain, at the time of quite other calls upon it, to throw itself suddenly back and, supported behind by his uplifted arms and interlocked hands, place him for unconscionable periods in communion with the ceiling, the tree-tops, the sky. He was in short visibly absent-minded, irregularly clever, liable to drop what was near and to take up what was far; he was more a respecter, in general, than a follower of custom. He suggested above all, however, that wondrous state of youth in which the elements, the metals more or less precious, are so in fusion and fermentation that the question of the final stamp, the pressure that fixes the value, must wait for comparative coolness. And it was a mark of his interesting mixture that if he was irritable it was by a law of considerable subtlety—a law that, in intercourse with him, it might be of profit, though not easy, to master. One of the effects of it was that he had for you surprises of tolerance as well as of temper.

He loitered, on the best of the relenting days, the several occasions we speak of, along the part of the Gardens nearest to Lancaster Gate, and when, always, in due time, Kate Croy came out of her aunt's house, crossed the road and arrived by the nearest entrance, there was a general publicity in the proceeding which made it slightly anomalous. If their meeting was to be bold and free it might have taken place within doors; if it was to be shy or secret it might have taken place almost anywhere better than under Mrs. Lowder's windows. They failed indeed to remain attached to that spot; they wandered and strolled, taking in the course of more than one of these interviews a considerable walk, or else picked out a couple of chairs under one of the great trees and sat as much apart—apart from every one else—as possible. But Kate had, each time, at first, the air of wishing to expose herself to pursuit and capture if those things were in question. She made the point that she was not underhand, any more than she was vulgar; that the Gardens were charming in themselves and this use of them a matter of taste; and that, if her aunt chose to glare at her from the drawing-room or to cause her to be tracked and overtaken, she could at least make it convenient that this should be easily done. The fact was that the relation between these young persons abounded in such oddities as were not inaptly symbolised by assignations that had a good deal more appearance than motive. Of the strength of the tie that held them we shall sufficiently take the measure; but it was meanwhile almost obvious that if the great possibility had come up for them it had done so, to an exceptional degree, under the protection of the famous law of contraries. Any deep harmony that might eventually govern them would not be the result of their having much in common—having anything, in fact, but their affection; and would really find its explanation in some sense, on the part of each, of being poor where the other was rich. It is nothing new indeed that generous young persons often admire most what nature hasn't given them— from which it would appear, after all, that our friends were both generous.

Merton Densher had repeatedly said to himself—and from far back— that he should be a fool not to marry a woman whose value would be in her differences; and Kate Croy, though without having quite so philosophised, had quickly recognised in the young man a precious unlikeness. He represented what her life had never given her and certainly, without some such aid as his, never would give her; all the high, dim things she lumped together as of the mind. It was on the side of the mind that Densher was rich for her, and mysterious and strong; and he had rendered her in especial the sovereign service of making that element real. She had had, all her days, to take it terribly on trust; no creature she had ever encountered having been able in any degree to testify for it directly. Vague rumours of its existence had made their precarious way to her; but nothing had, on the whole, struck her as more likely than that she should live and die without the chance to verify them. The chance had come—it was an extraordinary one—on the day she first met Densher; and it was to the girl's lasting honour that she knew on the spot what she was in the presence of. That occasion indeed, for everything that straightway flowered in it, would be worthy of high commemoration; Densher's perception went out to meet the young woman's and quite kept pace with her own recognition. Having so often concluded on the fact of his weakness, as he called it, for life—his strength merely for thought—life, he logically opined, was what he must somehow arrange to annex and possess. This was so much a necessity that thought by itself only went on in the void; it was from the immediate air of life that it must draw its breath. So the young man, ingenious but large, critical but ardent too, made out both his case and Kate Croy's. They had originally met before her mother's death—an occasion marked for her as the last pleasure permitted by the approach of that event; after which the dark months had interposed a screen and, for all Kate knew, made the end one with the beginning.

The beginning—to which she often went back—had been a scene, for our young woman, of supreme brilliancy; a party given at a "gallery" hired by a hostess who fished with big nets. A Spanish dancer, understood to be at that moment the delight of the town, an American reciter, the joy of a kindred people, an Hungarian fiddler, the wonder of the world at large—in the name of these and other attractions the company in which, by a rare privilege, Kate found herself had been freely convoked. She lived under her mother's roof, as she considered, obscurely, and was acquainted with few persons who entertained on that scale; but she had had dealings with two or three connected, as appeared, with such—two or three through whom the stream of hospitality, filtered or diffused, could thus now and then spread to outlying receptacles. A good-natured lady in fine, a friend of her mother and a relative of the lady of the gallery, had offered to take her to the party in question and had there fortified her, further, with two or three of those introductions that, at large parties, lead to other things—that had at any rate, on this occasion, culminated for her in conversation with a tall, fair, slightly unbrushed and rather awkward, but on the whole not dreary, young man. The young man had affected her as detached, as—it was indeed what he called himself—awfully at sea, as much more distinct from what surrounded them than any one else appeared to be, and even as probably quite disposed to be making his escape when pulled up to be placed in relation with her. He gave her his word for it indeed, that same evening, that only their meeting had prevented his flight, but that now he saw how sorry he should have been to miss it. This point they had reached by midnight, and though in respect to such remarks everything was in the tone, the tone was by midnight there too. She had had originally her full apprehension of his coerced, certainly of his vague, condition—full apprehensions often being with her immediate; then she had had her equal consciousness that, within five minutes, something between them had—well, she couldn't call it anything but *come*. It was nothing, but it was somehow everything—it was that something for each of them had happened.

They had found themselves looking at each other straight, and for a longer time on end than was usual even at parties in galleries; but that, after all, would have been a small affair, if there hadn't been something else with it. It wasn't, in a word, simply that their eyes had met; other conscious organs, faculties, feelers had met as well, and when Kate afterwards imaged to herself the sharp, deep fact she saw it, in the oddest way, as a particular performance. She had observed a ladder against a garden wall, and had trusted herself so to climb it as to be able to see over into the probable garden on the other side. On reaching the top she had found herself face to face with a gentleman engaged in a like calculation at the same moment, and the two inquirers had remained confronted on their ladders. The great point was that for the rest of that evening they had been perched—they had not climbed down; and indeed, during the time that followed, Kate at least had had the perched feeling—it was as if she were there aloft without a retreat. A simpler expression of all this is doubtless but that they had taken each other in with interest; and without a happy hazard six months later the incident would have closed in that account of it. The accident, meanwhile, had been as natural as anything in London ever is: Kate had one afternoon found herself opposite Mr. Densher on the Underground Railway. She had entered the train at Sloane Square to go to Queen's Road, and the carriage in which she had found a place was all but full. Densher was already in it—on the other bench and at the furthest angle; she was sure of him before they had again started. The day and the hour were darkness, there were six other persons, and she had been busy placing herself; but her consciousness had gone to him as straight as if they had come together in some bright level of the desert. They had on neither part a second's hesitation; they looked across the choked compartment exactly as if she had known he would be there and he had expected her to come in; so that, though in the conditions they could only exchange the greeting of movements, smiles, silence, it would have been quite in the key of these passages that they should have alighted for ease at the very next station. Kate was in fact sure that the very next station was the young man's true goal— which made it clear that he was going on only from the wish to speak to her. He had to go on, for this purpose, to High Street, Kensington, as it was not till then that the exit of a passenger gave him his chance.

His chance put him, however, in quick possession of the seat facing her, the alertness of his capture of which seemed to show her his impatience. It helped them, moreover, with strangers on either side, little to talk; though this very restriction perhaps made such a mark for them as nothing else could have done. If the fact that their opportunity had again come round for them could be so intensely expressed between them without a word, they might very well feel on the spot that it had not come round for nothing. The extraordinary part of the matter was that they were not in the least meeting where they had left off, but ever so much further on, and that these added links added still another between High Street and Notting Hill Gate, and then between the latter station and Queen's Road an extension really inordinate. At Notting Hill Gate, Kate's right-hand neighbour descended, whereupon Densher popped straight into that seat; only there was not much gained when a lady, the next instant, popped into Densher's. He could say almost nothing to her—she scarce knew, at least, what he said; she was so occupied with a certainty that one of the persons opposite, a youngish man with a single eyeglass, which he kept constantly in position, had made her out from the first as visibly, as strangely affected. If such a person made her out, what then did Densher do?—a question in truth sufficiently answered when, on their reaching her station, he instantly followed her out of the train. That had been the real beginning—the beginning of everything else; the other time, the time at the party, had been but the beginning of *that.* Never in life before had she so let herself go; for always before—so far as small adventures could have been in question for her—there had been, by the vulgar measure, more to go upon. He had walked with her to Lancaster Gate, and then she had walked with him away from it—for all the world, she said to herself, like the housemaid giggling to the baker.

This appearance, she was afterwards to feel, had been all in order for a relation that might precisely best be described in the terms of the baker and the housemaid. She could say to herself that from that hour they had kept company; that had come to represent, technically speaking, alike the range and the limit of their tie. He had on the spot, naturally, asked leave to call upon her—which, as a young person who wasn't really young, who didn't pretend to be a sheltered flower, she as rationally gave. That—she was promptly clear about it—was now her only possible basis; she was just the contemporary London female, highly modern, inevitably battered, honourably free. She had of course taken her aunt straight into her confidence—had gone through the form of asking her leave; and she subsequently remembered that though, on this occasion, she had left the history of her new alliance as scant as the facts themselves, Mrs. Lowder had struck her at the time surprisingly mild. It had been, in every way, the occasion, full of the reminder that her hostess was deep: it was definitely then that she had begun to ask herself what Aunt Maud was, in vulgar parlance, "up to." "You may receive, my dear, whom you like"— that was what Aunt Maud, who in general objected to people's doing as they liked, had replied; and it bore, this unexpectedness, a good deal of looking into. There were many explanations, and they were all amusing—amusing, that is, in the line of the sombre and brooding amusement, cultivated by Kate in her actual high retreat. Merton Densher came the very next Sunday; but Mrs. Lowder was so consistently magnanimous as to make it possible to her niece to see him alone. She saw him, however, on the Sunday following, in order to invite him to dinner; and when, after dining, he came again—which he did three times, she found means to treat his visit as preponderantly to herself. Kate's conviction that she didn't like him made that remarkable; it added to the evidence, by this time voluminous, that she was remarkable all round. If she had been, in the way of energy, merely usual, she would have kept her dislike direct; whereas it was now as if she were seeking to know him in order to see best where to "have" him. That was one of the reflections made in our young woman's high retreat; she smiled from her lookout, in the silence that was only the fact of hearing irrelevant sounds, as she caught the truth that you could easily accept people when you wanted them so to be delivered to you. When Aunt Maud wished them despatched, it was not to be done by deputy; it was clearly always a matter reserved for her own hand. But what made the girl wonder most was the implications of so much diplomacy in respect to her own value. What view might she take of her position in the light of this appearance that her companion feared so, as yet, to upset her? It was as if Densher were accepted partly under the dread that if he hadn't been she would act in resentment. Hadn't her aunt considered the danger that she would in that case have broken off, have seceded? The danger was exaggerated—she would have done nothing so gross; but that, it seemed, was the way Mrs. Lowder saw her and believed her to be reckoned with. What importance therefore did she really attach to her, what strange interest could she take on their keeping on terms? Her father and her sister had their answer to this—even without knowing how the question struck her; they saw the lady of Lancaster Gate as panting to make her fortune, and the explanation of that appetite was that, on the accident of a nearer view than she had before enjoyed, she had been charmed, been dazzled. They approved, they admired in her one of the belated fancies of rich, capricious, violent old women—the more marked, moreover, because the result of no plot; and they piled up the possible results for the person concerned. Kate knew what to think of her own power thus to carry by storm; she saw herself as handsome, no doubt, but as hard, and felt herself as clever but as cold; and as so much too imperfectly ambitious, furthermore, that it was a pity, for a quiet life, she couldn't settle to be either finely or stupidly indifferent. Her intelligence sometimes kept her still—too still—but her want of it was restless; so that she got the good, it seemed to her, of neither extreme. She saw herself at present, none the less, in a situation, and even her sad, disillusioned mother, dying, but with Aunt Maud interviewing the nurse on the stairs, had not failed to remind her that it was of the essence of situations to be, under Providence, worked. The dear woman had died in the belief that she was actually working the one then produced.

Kate took one of her walks with Densher just after her visit to Mr. Croy; but most of it went, as usual, to their sitting in talk. They had, under the trees, by the lake, the air of old friends—phases of apparent earnestness, in particular, in which they might have been settling every question in their vast young world; and periods of silence, side by side, perhaps even more, when "a long engagement!" would have been the final reading of the signs on the part of a passer struck with them, as it was so easy to be. They would have presented themselves thus as very old friends rather than as young persons who had met for the first time but a year before and had spent most of the interval without contact. It was indeed for each, already, as if they were older friends; and though the succession of their meetings might, between them, have been straightened out, they only had a confused sense of a good many, very much alike, and a confused intention of a good many more, as little different as possible. The desire to keep them just as they were had perhaps to do with the fact that in spite of the presumed diagnosis of the stranger there had been for them as yet no formal, no final understanding. Densher had at the very first pressed the question, but that, it had been easy to reply, was too soon; so that a singular thing had afterwards happened. They had accepted their acquaintance as too short for an engagement, but they had treated it as long enough for almost anything else, and marriage was somehow before them like a temple without an avenue. They belonged to the temple and they met in the grounds; they were in the stage at which grounds in general offered much scattered refreshment. But Kate had meanwhile had so few confidants that she wondered at the source of her father's suspicions. The diffusion of rumour was of course, in London, remarkable, and for Marian not less—as Aunt Maud touched neither directly—the mystery had worked. No doubt she had been seen. Of course she had been seen. She had taken no trouble not to be seen, and it was a thing, clearly, she was incapable of taking. But she had been seen how?—and *what* was there to see? She was in love—she knew that: but it was wholly her own business, and she had the sense of having conducted herself, of still so doing, with almost violent conformity.

"I've an idea—in fact I feel sure—that Aunt Maud means to write to you; and I think you had better know it." So much as this she said to him as soon as they met, but immediately adding to it: "So as to make up your mind how to take her. I know pretty well what she'll say to you."

"Then will you kindly tell me?"

She thought a little. "I can't do that. I should spoil it. She'll do the best for her own idea."

"Her idea, you mean, that I'm a sort of a scoundrel; or, at the best, not good enough for you?"

They were side by side again in their penny chairs, and Kate had another pause. "Not good enough for *her.*"

"Oh, I see. And that's necessary."

He put it as a truth rather more than as a question; but there had been plenty of truths between them that each had contradicted. Kate, however, let this one sufficiently pass, only saying the next moment: "She has behaved extraordinarily."

"And so have we," Densher declared. "I think, you know, we've been awfully decent."

"For ourselves, for each other, for people in general, yes. But not for *her.* For her," said Kate, "we've been monstrous. She has been giving us rope. So if she does send for you," the girl repeated, "you must know where you are."

"That I always know. It's where *you* are that concerns me."

"Well," said Kate after an instant, "her idea of that is what you'll have from her." He gave her a long look, and whatever else people who wouldn't let her alone might have wished, for her advancement, his long looks were the thing in the world she could never have enough of. What she felt was that, whatever might happen, she must keep them, must make them most completely her possession; and it was already strange enough that she reasoned, or at all events began to act, as if she might work them in with other and alien things, privately cherish them, and yet, as regards the rigour of it, pay no price. She looked it well in the face, she took it intensely home, that they were lovers; she rejoiced to herself and, frankly, to him, in their wearing of the name; but, distinguished creature that, in her way, she was, she took a view of this character that scarce squared with the conventional. The character itself she insisted on as their right, taking that so for granted that it didn't seem even bold; but Densher, though he agreed with her, found himself moved to wonder at her simplifications, her values. Life might prove difficult—was evidently going to; but meanwhile they had each other, and that was everything. This was her reasoning, but meanwhile, for *him,* each other was what they didn't have, and it was just the point. Repeatedly, however, it was a point that, in the face of strange and special things, he judged it rather awkwardly gross to urge. It was impossible to keep Mrs. Lowder out of their scheme. She stood there too close to it and too solidly; it had to open a gate, at a given point, do what they would to take her in. And she came in, always, while they sat together rather helplessly watching her, as in a coach-in-four; she drove round their prospect as the principal lady at the circus drives round the ring, and she stopped the coach in the middle to alight with majesty. It was our young man's sense that she was magnificently vulgar, but yet, quite, that this wasn't all. It wasn't with her vulgarity that she felt his want of means, though that might have helped her richly to embroider it; nor was it with the same infirmity that she was strong, original, dangerous.

His want of means—of means sufficient for anyone but himself—was really the great ugliness, and was, moreover, at no time more ugly for him than when it rose there, as it did seem to rise, shameless, face to face with the elements in Kate's life colloquially and conveniently classed by both of them as funny. He sometimes indeed, for that matter, asked himself if these elements were as funny as the innermost fact, so often vivid to him, of his own consciousness—his private inability to believe he should ever be rich. His conviction on this head was in truth quite positive and a thing by itself; he failed, after analysis, to understand it, though he had naturally more lights on it than any one else. He knew how it subsisted in spite of an equal consciousness of his being neither mentally nor physically quite helpless, neither a dunce nor a cripple; he knew it to be absolute, though secret, and also, strange to say, about common undertakings, not discouraging, not prohibitive. Only now was he having to think if it were prohibitive in respect to marriage; only now, for the first time, had he to weigh his case in scales. The scales, as he sat with Kate, often dangled in the line of his vision; he saw them, large and black, while he talked or listened, take, in the bright air, singular positions. Sometimes the right was down and sometimes the left; never a happy equipoise—one or the other always kicking the beam. Thus was kept before him the question of whether it were more ignoble to ask a woman to take her chance with you, or to accept it from one's conscience that her chance could be at the best but one of the degrees of privation; whether, too, otherwise, marrying for money mightn't after all be a smaller cause of shame than the mere dread of marrying without. Through these variations of mood and view, all the same, the mark on his forehead stood clear; he saw himself remain without whether he married or not. It was a line on which his fancy could be admirably active; the innumerable ways of making money were beautifully present to him; he could have handled them, for his newspaper, as easily as he handled everything. He was quite aware how he handled everything; it was another mark on his forehead; the pair of smudges from the thumb of fortune, the brand on the passive fleece, dated from the primal hour and kept each other company. He wrote, as for print, with deplorable ease; since there had been nothing to stop him even at the age of ten, so there was as little at twenty; it was part of his fate in the first place and part of the wretched public's in the second. The innumerable ways of making money were, no doubt, at all events, what his imagination often was busy with after he had tilted his chair and thrown back his head with his hands clasped behind it. What would most have prolonged that attitude, moreover, was the reflection that the ways were ways only for others. Within the minute, now—however this might be—he was aware of a nearer view than he had yet quite had of those circumstances on his companion's part that made least for simplicity of relation. He saw above all how she saw them herself, for she spoke of them at present with the last frankness, telling him of her visit to her father and giving him, in an account of her subsequent scene with her sister, an instance of how she was perpetually reduced to patching up, in one way or another, that unfortunate woman's hopes.

"The tune," she exclaimed, "to which we're a failure as a family!" With which he had it again all from her—and this time, as it seemed to him, more than all: the dishonour her father had brought them, his folly and cruelty and wickedness; the wounded state of her mother, abandoned, despoiled and helpless, yet, for the management of such a home as remained to them, dreadfully unreasonable too; the extinction of her two young brothers—one, at nineteen, the eldest of the house, by typhoid fever, contracted at a poisonous little place, as they had afterwards found out, that they had taken for a summer; the other, the flower of the flock, a middy on the *Britannia,* dreadfully drowned, and not even by an accident at sea, but by cramp, unrescued, while bathing, too late in the autumn, in a wretched little river during a holiday visit to the home of a shipmate. Then Marian's unnatural marriage, in itself a kind of spiritless turning of the other cheek to fortune: her actual wretchedness and plaintiveness, her greasy children, her impossible claims, her odious visitors—these things completed the proof of the heaviness, for them all, of the hand of fate. Kate confessedly described them with an excess of impatience; it was much of her charm for Densher that she gave in general that turn to her descriptions, partly as if to amuse him by free and humorous colour, partly—and that charm was the greatest—as if to work off, for her own relief, her constant perception of the incongruity of things. She had seen the general show too early and too sharply, and she was so intelligent that she knew it and allowed for that misfortune; therefore when, in talk with him, she was violent and almost unfeminine, it was almost as if they had settled, for intercourse, on the short cut of the fantastic and the happy language of exaggeration. It had come to be definite between them at a primary stage that, if they could have no other straight way, the realm of thought at least was open to them. They could think whatever they liked about whatever they would—or, in other words, they could say it. Saying it for each other, for each other alone, only of course added to the taste. The implication was thereby constant that what they said when not together had no taste for them at all, and nothing could have served more to launch them, at special hours, on their small floating island than such an assumption that they were only making believe everywhere else. Our young man, it must be added, was conscious enough that it was Kate who profited most by this particular play of the fact of intimacy. It always seemed to him that she had more life than he to react from, and when she recounted the dark disasters of her house and glanced at the hard, odd offset of her present exaltation— since as exaltation it was apparently to be considered—he felt his own grey domestic annals to make little show. It was naturally, in all such reference, the question of her father's character that engaged him most, but her picture of her adventure in Chirk Street gave him a sense of how little as yet that character was clear to him. What was it, to speak plainly, that Mr. Croy had originally done?

"I don't know—and I don't want to. I only know that years and years ago—when I was about fifteen—something or other happened that made him impossible. I mean impossible for the world at large first, and then, little by little, for mother. We of course didn't know it at the time," Kate explained, "but we knew it later; and it was, oddly enough, my sister who first made out that he had done something. I can hear her now—the way, one cold, black Sunday morning when, on account of an extraordinary fog, we had not gone to church, she broke it to me by the school-room fire. I was reading a history-book by the lamp—when we didn't go to church we had to read history-books—and I suddenly heard her say, out of the fog, which was in the room, and *apropos* of nothing: 'Papa has done something wicked.' And the curious thing was that I believed it on the spot and have believed it ever since, though she could tell me nothing more—neither what was the wickedness, nor how she knew, nor what would happen to him, nor anything else about it. We had our sense, always, that all sorts of things *had* happened, were all the while happening, to him; so that when Marian only said she was sure, tremendously sure, that she had made it out for herself, but that that was enough, I took her word for it—it seemed somehow so natural. We were not, however, to ask mother—which made it more natural still, and I said never a word. But mother, strangely enough, spoke of it to me, in time, of her own accord very much later on. He hadn't been with us for ever so long, but we were used to that. She must have had some fear, some conviction that I had an idea, some idea of her own that it was the best thing to do. She came out as abruptly as Marian had done: 'If you hear anything against your father—anything I mean, except that he's odious and vile—remember it's perfectly false.' That was the way I knew—it was true, though I recall that I said to her then that I of course knew it wasn't. She might have told me it was true, and yet have trusted me to contradict fiercely enough any accusation of him that I should meet—to contradict it much more fiercely and effectively, I think, than she would have done herself. As it happens, however," the girl went on, "I've never had occasion, and I've been conscious of it with a sort of surprise. It has made the world, at times, seem more decent. No one has so much as breathed to me. That has been a part of the silence, the silence that surrounds him, the silence that, for the world, has washed him out. He doesn't exist for people. And yet I'm as sure as ever. In fact, though I know no more than I did then, I'm more sure. And that," she wound up, "is what I sit here and tell you about my own father. If you don't call it a proof of confidence I don't know what will satisfy you."

"It satisfies me beautifully," Densher declared, "but it doesn't, my dear child, very greatly enlighten me. You don't, you know, really tell me anything. It's so vague that what am I to think but that you may very well be mistaken? What has he done, if no one can name it?"

"He has done everything."

"Oh—everything! Everything's nothing."

"Well then," said Kate, "he has done some particular thing. It's known—only, thank God, not to us. But it has been the end of him. You could doubtless find out with a little trouble. You can ask about."

Densher for a moment said nothing; but the next moment he made it up. "I wouldn't find out for the world, and I'd rather lose my tongue than put a question."

"And yet it's a part of me," said Kate.

"A part of you?"

"My father's dishonour." Then she sounded for him, but more deeply than ever yet, her note of proud, still pessimism. "How can such a thing as that not be the great thing in one's life?"

She had to take from him again, on this, one of his long looks, and she took it to its deepest, its headiest dregs. "I shall ask you, for the great thing in your life," he said, "to depend on *me* a little more." After which, just hesitating, "Doesn't he belong to some club?" he inquired.

She had a grave headshake. "He used to—to many."

"But he has dropped them?"

"They've dropped *him*. Of that I'm sure. It ought to do for you. I offered him," the girl immediately continued—"and it was for that I went to him— to come and be with him, make a home for him so far as is possible. But he won't hear of it."

Densher took this in with visible, but generous, wonder. "You offered him—'impossible' as you describe him to me—to live with him and share his disadvantages?" The young man saw for the moment but the high beauty of it. "You *are* gallant!"

"Because it strikes you as being brave for him?" She wouldn't in the least have this. "It wasn't courage—it was the opposite. I did it to save myself—to escape."

He had his air, so constant at this stage, as of her giving him finer things than any one to think about. "Escape from what?"

"From everything."

"Do you by any chance mean from me?"

"No; I spoke to him of you, told him—or what amounted to it—that I would bring you, if he would allow it, with me."

"But he won't allow it," said Densher.

"Won't hear of it on any terms. He won't help me, won't save me, won't hold out a finger to me," Kate went on; "he simply wriggles away, in his inimitable manner, and throws me back."

"Back then, after all, thank goodness," Densher concurred, "on me."

But she spoke again as with the sole vision of the whole scene she had evoked. "It's a pity, because you'd like him. He's wonderful—he's charming." Her companion gave one of the laughs that marked in him, again, his feeling in her tone, inveterately, something that banished the talk of other women, so far as he knew other women, to the dull desert of the conventional, and she had already continued. "He would make himself delightful to you."

"Even while objecting to me?"

"Well, he likes to please," the girl explained—"personally. He would appreciate you and be clever with you. It's to *me* he objects—that is as to my liking you."

"Heaven be praised then," Densher exclaimed, "that you like me enough for the objection!"

But she met it after an instant with some inconsequence. "I don't. I offered to give you up, if necessary, to go to him. But it made no difference, and that's what I mean," she pursued, "by his declining me on any terms. The point is, you see, that I don't escape."

Densher wondered. "But if you didn't wish to escape *me?*"

"I wished to escape Aunt Maud. But he insists that it's through her and through her only that I may help him; just as Marian insists that it's through her, and through her only, that I can help *her*. That's what I mean," she again explained, "by their turning me back."

The young man thought. "Your sister turns you back too?"

"Oh, with a push!"

"But have you offered to live with your sister?"

"I would in a moment if she'd have me. That's all my virtue—a narrow little family feeling. I've a small stupid piety—I don't know what to call it." Kate bravely sustained it; she made it out. "Sometimes, alone, I've to smother my shrieks when I think of my poor mother. She went through things—they pulled her down; I know what they were now—I didn't then, for I was a pig; and my position, compared with hers, is an insolence of success. That's what Marian keeps before me; that's what papa himself, as I say, so inimitably does. My position's a value, a great value, for them both"—she followed and followed. Lucid and ironic, she knew no merciful muddle. "It's *the* value—the only one they have."

Everything between our young couple moved today, in spite of their pauses, their margin, to a quicker measure—the quickness and anxiety playing lightning-like in the sultriness. Densher watched, decidedly, as he had never done before. "And the fact you speak of holds you!"

"Of course, it holds me. It's a perpetual sound in my ears. It makes me ask myself if I've any right to personal happiness, any right to anything but to be as rich and overflowing, as smart and shining, as I can be made."

Densher had a pause. "Oh, you might, with good luck, have the personal happiness too."

Her immediate answer to this was a silence like his own; after which she gave him straight in the face, but quite simply and quietly: "Darling!"

It took him another moment; then he was also quiet and simple. "Will you settle it by our being married to-morrow—as we can, with perfect ease, civilly?"

"Let us wait to arrange it," Kate presently replied, "till after you've seen her."

"Do you call that adoring me?" Densher demanded.

They were talking, for the time, with the strangest mixture of deliberation and directness, and nothing could have been more in the tone of it than the way she at last said: "You're afraid of her yourself."

He gave a smile a trifle glassy. "For young persons of a great distinction and a very high spirit, we're a caution!"

"Yes," she took it straight up; "we're hideously intelligent. But there's fun in it too. We must get our fun where we can. I think," she added, and for that matter, not without courage, "our relation's beautiful. It's not a bit vulgar. I cling to some saving romance in things."

It made him break into a laugh which had more freedom than his smile. "How you must be afraid you'll chuck me!"

"No, no, *that* would be vulgar. But, of course, I do see my danger," she admitted, "of doing something base."

"Then what can be so base as sacrificing me?"

"I *shan't* sacrifice you; don't cry out till you're hurt. I shall sacrifice nobody and nothing, and that's just my situation, that I want and that I shall try for everything. That," she wound up, "is how I see myself, and how I see you quite as much, acting for them."

"For 'them'?" and the young man strongly, extravagantly marked his coldness. "Thank you!"

"Don't you care for them?"

"Why should I? What are they to me but a serious nuisance?"

As soon as he had permitted himself this qualification of the unfortunate persons she so perversely cherished, he repented of his roughness—and partly because he expected a flash from her. But it was one of her finest sides that she sometimes flashed with a mere mild glow. "I don't see why you don't make out a little more that if we avoid stupidity we may do *all*. We may keep her."

He stared. "Make her pension us?"

"Well, wait at least till we have seen."

He thought. "Seen what can be got out of her?"

Kate for a moment said nothing. "After all I never asked her; never, when our troubles were at the worst, appealed to her nor went near her. She fixed upon me herself, settled on me with her wonderful gilded claws."

"You speak," Densher observed, "as if she were a vulture."

"Call it an eagle—with a gilded beak as well, and with wings for great flights. If she's a thing of the air, in short—say at once a balloon—I never myself got into her car. I was her choice."

It had really, her sketch of the affair, a high colour and a great style; at all of which he gazed a minute as at a picture by a master. "What she must see in you!"

"Wonders!" And, speaking it loud, she stood straight up. "Everything. There it is."

Yes, there it was, and as she remained before him he continued to face it. "So that what you mean is that I'm to do my part in somehow squaring her?"

"See her, see her," Kate said with impatience.

"And grovel to her?"

"Ah, do what you like!" And she walked in her impatience away.

IV

His eyes had followed her at this time quite long enough, before he overtook her, to make out more than ever, in the poise of her head, the pride of her step—he didn't know what best to call it—a part, at least, of Mrs. Lowder's reasons. He consciously winced while he figured his presenting himself as a reason opposed to these; though, at the same moment, with the source of Aunt Maud's inspiration thus before him, he was prepared to conform, by almost any abject attitude or profitable compromise, to his companion's easy injunction. He would do as *she* liked—his own liking might come off as it would. He would help her to the utmost of his power; for, all the rest of that day and the next, her easy injunction, tossed off that way as she turned her beautiful back, was like the crack of a great whip in the blue air, the high element in which Mrs. Lowder hung. He wouldn't grovel perhaps—he wasn't quite ready for that; but he would be patient, ridiculous, reasonable, unreasonable, and above all deeply diplomatic. He would be clever, with all his cleverness—which he now shook hard, as he sometimes shook his poor, dear, shabby, old watch, to start it up again. It wasn't, thank goodness, as if there weren't plenty of that, and with what they could muster between them it would be little to the credit of their star, however pale, that defeat and surrender—surrender so early, so immediate—should have to ensue. It was not indeed that he thought of that disaster as, at the worst, a direct sacrifice of their possibilities: he imaged—it which was enough as some proved vanity, some exposed fatuity, in the idea of bringing Mrs. Lowder round. When, shortly afterwards, in this lady's vast drawing-room—the apartments at Lancaster Gate had struck him from the first as of prodigious extent—he awaited her, at her request, conveyed in a "reply-paid" telegram, his theory was that of their still clinging to their idea, though with a sense of the difficulty of it really enlarged to the scale of the place.

He had the place for a long time—it seemed to him a quarter of an hour—to himself; and while Aunt Maud kept him and kept him, while observation and reflection crowded on him, he asked himself what was to be expected of a person who could treat one like that. The visit, the hour were of her own proposing, so that her delay, no doubt, was but part of a general plan of putting him to inconvenience. As he walked to and fro, however, taking in the message of her massive, florid furniture, the immense expression of her signs and symbols, he had as little doubt of the inconvenience he was prepared to suffer. He found himself even facing the thought that he had nothing to fall back on, and that that was as great a humiliation in a good cause as a proud man could desire. It had not yet been so distinct to him that he made no show—literally not the smallest; so complete a show seemed made there all about him; so almost abnormally affirmative, so aggressively erect, were the huge, heavy objects that syllabled his hostess story. "When all's said and done, you know, she's colossally vulgar"—he had once all but said that of Mrs. Lowder to her niece; only just keeping it back at the last, keeping it to himself with all its danger about it. It mattered because it bore so directly, and he at all events quite felt it a thing that Kate herself would some day bring out to him. It bore directly at present, and really all the more that somehow, strangely, it didn't in the least imply that Aunt Maud was dull or stale. She was vulgar with freshness, almost with beauty, since there was beauty, to a degree, in the play of so big and bold a temperament. She was in fine quite the largest possible quantity to deal with; and he was in the cage of the lioness without his whip—the whip, in a word, of a supply of proper retorts. He had no retort but that he loved the girl—which in such a house as that was painfully cheap. Kate had mentioned to him more than once that her aunt was Passionate, speaking of it as a kind of offset and uttering it as with a capital P, marking it as something that he might, that he in fact ought to, turn about in some way to their advantage. He wondered at this hour to what advantage he could turn it; but the case grew less simple the longer he waited. Decidedly there was something he hadn't enough of. He stood as one fast.

His slow march to and fro seemed to give him the very measure; as he paced and paced the distance it became the desert of his poverty; at the sight of which expanse moreover he could pretend to himself as little as before that the desert looked redeemable. Lancaster Gate looked rich—that was all the effect; which it was unthinkable that any state of his own should ever remotely resemble. He read more vividly, more critically, as has been hinted, the appearances about him; and they did nothing so much as make him wonder at his aesthetic reaction. He hadn't known—and in spite of Kate's repeated reference to her own rebellions of taste—that he should "mind" so much how an independent lady might decorate her house. It was the language of the house itself that spoke to him, writing out for him, with surpassing breadth and freedom, the associations and conceptions, the ideals and possibilities of the mistress. Never, he flattered himself, had he seen anything so gregariously ugly—operatively, ominously so cruel. He was glad to have found this last name for the whole character; "cruel" somehow played into the subject for an article—that his impression put straight into his mind.

He would write about the heavy horrors that could still flourish, that lifted their undiminished heads, in an age so proud of its short way with false gods; and it would be funny if what he should have got from Mrs. Lowder were to prove, after all, but a small amount of copy. Yet the great thing, really the dark thing, was that, even while he thought of the quick column he might add up, he felt it less easy to laugh at the heavy horrors than to quail before them. He couldn't describe and dismiss them collectively, call them either Mid-Victorian or Early; not being at all sure they were rangeable under one rubric. It was only manifest they were splendid and were furthermore conclusively British. They constituted an order and they abounded in rare material—precious woods, metals, stuffs, stones. He had never dreamed of anything so fringed and scalloped, so buttoned and corded, drawn everywhere so tight, and curled everywhere so thick. He had never dreamed of so much gilt and glass, so much satin and plush, so much rosewood and marble and malachite. But it was, above all, the solid forms, the wasted finish, the misguided cost, the general attestation of morality and money, a good conscience and a big balance. These things finally represented for him a portentous negation of his own world of thought—of which, for that matter, in the presence of them, he became as for the first time hopelessly aware. They revealed it to him by their merciless difference. His interview with Aunt Maud, none the less, took by no means the turn he had expected. Passionate though her nature, no doubt Mrs. Lowder, on this occasion, neither threatened nor appealed. Her arms of aggression, her weapons of defence, were presumably close at hand, but she left them untouched and unmentioned, and was in fact so bland that he properly perceived only afterwards how adroit she had been. He properly perceived something else as well, which complicated his case; he shouldn't have known what to call it if he hadn't called it her really imprudent good-nature. Her blandness, in other words, was not mere policy—he wasn't dangerous enough for policy; it was the result, he could see, of her fairly liking him a little. From the moment she did that she herself became more interesting; and who knew what might happen should he take to liking *her*? Well, it was a risk he naturally must face. She fought him, at any rate, but with one hand, with a few loose grains of stray powder. He recognised at the end of ten minutes, and even without her explaining it, that if she had made him wait it had not been to wound him; they had by that time almost directly met on the fact of her intention. She had wanted him to think for himself of what she proposed to say to him—not having otherwise announced it; wanted to let it come home to him on the spot, as she had shrewdly believed it would. Her first question, on appearing, had practically been as to whether he hadn't taken her hint, and this inquiry assumed so many things that it made discussion, immediately, frank and large. He knew, with the question put, that the hint was just what he *had* taken; knew that she had made him quickly forgive her the display of her power; knew that if he didn't take care he should understand her, and the strength of her purpose, to say nothing of that of her imagination, nothing of the length of her purse, only too well. Yet he pulled himself up with the thought, too, that he was not going to be afraid of understanding her; he was just going to understand and understand without detriment to the feeblest, even, of his passions. The play of one's mind let one in, at the best, dreadfully, in action, in the need of action, where simplicity was all; but when one couldn't prevent it the thing was to make it complete. There would never be mistakes but for the original fun of mistakes. What he must use his fatal intelligence for was to resist. Mrs. Lowder, meanwhile, might use it for whatever she liked.

It was after she had begun her statement of her own idea about Kate that he began, on his side, to reflect that—with her manner of offering it as really sufficient if he would take the trouble to embrace—it she couldn't half hate him. That was all, positively, she seemed to show herself for the time as attempting; clearly, if she did her intention justice, she would have nothing more disagreeable to do. "If I hadn't been ready to go very much further, you understand, I wouldn't have gone so far. I don't care what you repeat to her—the more you repeat to her, perhaps the better; and, at any rate, there's nothing she doesn't already know. I don't say it for her; I say it for you—when I want to reach my niece I know how to do it straight." So Aunt Maud delivered herself—as with homely benevolence, in the simplest, but the clearest terms; virtually conveying that, though a word to the wise was, doubtless, in spite of the advantage, *not* always enough, a word to the good could never fail to be. The sense our young man read into her words was that she liked him because he was good—was really, by her measure, good enough: good enough, that is, to give up her niece for her and go his way in peace. But *was* he good enough—by his own measure? He fairly wondered, while she more fully expressed herself, if it might be his doom to prove so. "She's the finest possible creature—of course you flatter yourself that you know it. But I know it, quite as well as you possibly can—by which I mean a good deal better yet; and the tune to which I'm ready to prove my faith compares favourably enough, I think, with anything *you* can do. I don't say it because she's my niece—that's nothing to me: I might have had fifty nieces, and I wouldn't have brought one of them to this place if I hadn't found her to my taste. I don't say I wouldn't have done something else, but I wouldn't have put up with her presence. Kate's presence, by good fortune, I marked early; Kate's presence—unluckily for *you*—is everything I could possibly wish; Kate's presence is, in short, as fine as you know, and I've been keeping it for the comfort of my declining years. I've watched it long; I've been saving it up and letting it, as you say of investments, appreciate, and you may judge whether, now it has begun to pay so, I'm likely to consent to treat for it with any but a high bidder. I can do the best with her, and I've my idea of the best."

"Oh, I quite conceive," said Densher, "that your idea of the best isn't me."

It was an oddity of Mrs. Lowder's that her face in speech was like a lighted window at night, but that silence immediately drew the curtain. The occasion for reply allowed by her silence was never easy to take; yet she was still less easy to interrupt. The great glaze of her surface, at all events, gave her visitor no present help. "I didn't ask you to come to hear what it isn't—I asked you to come to hear what it is."

"Of course," Densher laughed, "it's very great indeed."

His hostess went on as if his contribution to the subject were barely relevant. "I want to see her high, high up—high up and in the light."

"Ah, you naturally want to marry her to a duke, and are eager to smooth away any hitch."

She gave him so, on this, the mere effect of the drawn blind that it quite forced him, at first, into the sense, possibly just, of having affected her as flip pant, perhaps even as low. He had been looked at so, in blighted moments of presumptuous youth, by big cold public men, but never, so far as he could recall, by any private lady. More than anything yet it gave him the measure of his companion's subtlety, and thereby of Kate's possible career. "Don't be *too* impossible!"—he feared from his friend, for a moment, some such answer as that; and then felt, as she spoke otherwise, as if she were letting him off easily. "I want her to marry a great man." That was all; but, more and more, it was enough; and if it hadn't been her next words would have made it so. "And I think of her what I think. There you are."

They sat for a little face to face upon it, and he was conscious of something deeper still, of something she wished him to understand if he only would. To that extent she did appeal—appealed to the intelligence she desired to show she believed him to possess. He was meanwhile, at all events, not the man wholly to fail of comprehension. "Of course I'm aware how little I can answer to any fond, proud dream. You've a view—a magnificent one; into which I perfectly enter. I thoroughly understand what I'm not, and I'm much obliged to you for not reminding me of it in any rougher way." She said nothing—she kept that up; it might even have been to let him go further, if he was capable of it, in the way of poorness of spirit. It was one of those cases in which a man couldn't show, if he showed at all, save for poor; unless indeed he preferred to show for asinine. It was the plain truth: he *was*—on Mrs. Lowder's basis, the only one in question—a very small quantity, and he did know, damnably, what made quantities large. He desired to be perfectly simple; yet in the midst of that effort a deeper apprehension throbbed. Aunt Maud clearly conveyed it, though he couldn't later on have said how. "You don't really matter, I believe, so much as you think, and I'm not going to make you a martyr by banishing you. Your performances with Kate in the Park are ridiculous so far as they're meant as consideration for me; and I had much rather see you myself—since you're, in your way, my dear young man, delightful—and arrange with you, count with you, as I easily, as I perfectly should. Do you suppose me so stupid as to quarrel with you if it's not really necessary? It won't—it would be too absurd!—*be* necessary. I can bite your head off any day, any day I really open my mouth; and I'm dealing with you now, see—and successfully judge—without opening it. I do things handsomely all round—I place you in the presence of the plan with which, from the moment it's a case of taking you seriously, you're incompatible. Come then as near it as you like, walk all round it—don't be afraid you'll hurt it!—and live on with it before you."

He afterwards felt that if she hadn't absolutely phrased all this it was because she so soon made him out as going with her far enough. He was so pleasantly affected by her asking no promise of him, her not proposing he should pay for her indulgence by his word of honour not to interfere, that he gave her a kind of general assurance of esteem. Immediately afterwards, then, he spoke of these things to Kate, and what then came back to him first of all was the way he had said to her—he mentioned it to the girl—very much as one of a pair of lovers says in a rupture by mutual consent: "I hope immensely, of course, that you'll always regard me as a friend." This had perhaps been going far—he submitted it all to Kate; but really there had been so much in it that it was to be looked at, as they might say, wholly in its own light. Other things than those we have presented had come up before the close of his scene with Aunt Maud, but this matter of her not treating him as a peril of the first order easily predominated. There was moreover plenty to talk about on the occasion of his subsequent passage with our young woman, it having been put to him abruptly, the night before, that he might give himself a lift and do his newspaper a service—so flatteringly was the case expressed—by going, for fifteen or twenty weeks, to America. The idea of a series of letters from the United States from the strictly social point of view had for some time been nursed in the inner sanctuary at whose door he sat, and the moment was now deemed happy for letting it loose. The imprisoned thought had, in a word, on the opening of the door, flown straight out into Densher's face, or perched at least on his shoulder, making him look up in surprise from his mere inky office-table. His account of the matter to Kate was that he couldn't refuse—not being in a position, as yet, to refuse anything; but that his being chosen for such an errand confounded his sense of proportion. He was definite as to his scarce knowing how to measure the honour, which struck him as equivocal; he had not quite supposed himself the man for the class of job. This confused consciousness, he intimated, he had promptly enough betrayed to his manager; with the effect, however, of seeing the question surprisingly clear up. What it came to was that the sort of twaddle that was not in his chords was, unexpectedly, just what they happened this time not to want. They wanted his letters, for queer reasons, about as good as he could let them come; he was to play his own little tune and not be afraid; that was the whole point.

It would have been the whole, that is, had there not been a sharper one still in the circumstance that he was to start at once. His mission, as they called it at the office, would probably be over by the end of June, which was desirable; but to bring that about he must now not lose a week; his inquiries, he understood, were to cover the whole ground, and there were reasons of State—reasons operating at the seat of empire in Fleet Street—why the nail should be struck on the head. Densher made no secret to Kate of his having asked for a day to decide; and his account of that matter was that he felt he owed it to her to speak to her first. She assured him on this that nothing so much as that scruple had yet shown her how they were bound together; she was clearly proud of his letting a thing of such importance depend on her; but she was clearer still as to his instant duty. She rejoiced in his prospect and urged him to his task; she should miss him intensely—of course she should miss him; but she made so little of it that she spoke with jubilation of what he would see and would do. She made so much of this last quantity that he laughed at her innocence, though also with scarce the heart to give her the real size of his drop in the daily bucket. He was struck at the same time with her happy grasp of what had really occurred in Fleet Street—all the more that it was his own final reading. He was to pull the subject up—that was just what they wanted; and it would take more than all the United States together, visit them each as he might, to let *him* down. It was just because he didn't nose about and wasn't the usual gossipmonger that they had picked him out; it was a branch of their correspondence with which they evidently wished a new tone associated, such a tone as, from now on, it would have always to take from his example.

"How you ought indeed, when you understand so well, to be a journalist's wife!" Densher exclaimed in admiration, even while she struck him as fairly hurrying him off.

But she was almost impatient of the praise. "What do you expect one *not* to understand when one cares for you?"

"Ah then, I'll put it otherwise and say 'How much you care for me!'"

"Yes," she assented; "it fairly redeems my stupidity. I *shall,* with a chance to show it," she added, "have some imagination for you."

She spoke of the future this time as so little contingent, that he felt a queerness of conscience in making her the report that he presently arrived at on what had passed for him with the real arbiter of their destiny. The way for that had been blocked a little by his news from Fleet Street; but in the crucible of their happy discussion this element soon melted into the other, and in the mixture that ensued the parts were not to be distinguished. The young man moreover, before taking his leave, was to see why Kate had just spoken of the future as if they now really possessed it, and was to come to the vision by a devious way that deepened the final cheer. Their faces were turned to the illumined quarter as soon as he had answered her question in respect to the appearance of their being able to play a waiting game with success. It was for the possibility of that appearance that she had, a few days before, so earnestly pressed him to see her aunt; and if after his hour with that lady it had not struck Densher that he had seen her to the happiest purpose the poor facts flushed with a better meaning as Kate, one by one, took them up.

"If she consents to your coming, why isn't that everything?"

"It *is* everything; everything *she* thinks it. It's the probability—I mean as Mrs. Lowder measures probability—that I may be prevented from becoming a complication for her by some arrangement, *any* arrangement, through which you shall see me often and easily. She's sure of my want of money, and that gives her time. She believes in my having a certain amount of delicacy, in my wishing to better my state before I put the pistol to your head in respect to sharing it. The time that will take figures for her as the time that will help her if she doesn't spoil her chance by treating me badly. She doesn't at all wish moreover," Densher went on, "to treat me badly, for I believe, upon my honour, funny as it may sound to you, that she personally rather likes me, and that if you weren't in question I might almost become her pet young man. She doesn't disparage intellect and culture—quite the contrary; she wants them to adorn her board and be named in her programme; and I'm sure it has sometimes cost her a real pang that I should be so desirable, at once, and so impossible." He paused a moment, and his companion then saw that a strange smile was in his face—a smile as strange even as the adjunct, in her own, of this informing vision. "I quite suspect her of believing that, if the truth were known, she likes me literally better than—deep down—you yourself do: wherefore she does me the honour to think that I may be safely left to kill my own cause. There, as I say, comes in her margin. I'm not the sort of stuff of romance that wears, that washes, that survives use, that resists familiarity. Once in any degree admit that, and your pride and prejudice will take care of the rest! the pride fed full, meanwhile, by the system she means to practise with you, and the prejudice excited by the comparison she'll enable you to make, from which I shall come off badly. She likes me, but she'll never like me so much as when she succeeded a little better in making me look wretched. For then *you'll* like me less."

Kate showed for this evocation a due interest, but no alarm; and it was a little as if to pay his tender cynicism back in kind that she after an instant replied: "I see, I see; what an immense affair she must think me! One was aware, but you deepen the impression."

"I think you'll make no mistake," said Densher, "in letting it go as deep as it will."

He had given her indeed, she made no scruple of showing, plenty to consider. "Her facing the music, her making you boldly as welcome as you say—that's an awfully big theory, you know, and worthy of all the other big things that, in one's acquaintance with people, give her a place so apart."

"Oh, she's grand," the young man conceded; "she's on the scale, altogether, of the car of Juggernaut which was a kind of image that came to me yesterday while I waited for her at Lancaster Gate. The things in your drawing-room there were like the forms of the strange idols, the mystic excrescences, with which one may suppose the front of the car to bristle."

"Yes, aren't they?" the girl returned; and they had, over all that aspect of their wonderful lady, one of those deep and free interchanges that made everything but confidence a false note for them. There were complications, there were questions; but they were so much more together than they were anything else. Kate uttered for a while no word of refutation of Aunt Maud's "big" diplomacy, and they left it there, as they would have left any other fine product, for a monument to her powers. But, Densher related further, he had had in other respects too the car of Juggernaut to face; he omitted nothing from his account of his visit, least of all the way Aunt Maud had frankly at last—though indeed only under artful pressure—fallen foul of his very type, his want of the right marks, his foreign accidents, his queer antecedents. She had told him he was but half a Briton, which, he granted Kate, would have been dreadful if he hadn't so let himself in for it.

"I was really curious, you see," he explained, "to find out from her what sort of queer creature, what sort of social anomaly, in the light of such conventions as hers, such an education as mine makes one pass for."

Kate said nothing for a little; but then, "Why should you care?" she asked.

"Oh," he laughed, "I like her so much; and then, for a man of my trade, her views, her spirit, are essentially a thing to get hold of; they belong to the great public mind that we meet at every turn and that we must keep setting up 'codes' with. Besides," he added, "I want to please her personally."

"Ah, yes, we must please her personally!" his companion echoed; and the words may represent all their definite recognition, at the time, of Densher's politic gain. They had in fact between this and his start for New York many matters to handle, and the question he now touched upon came up for Kate above all. She looked at him as if he had really told her aunt more of his immediate personal story than he had ever told herself. That, if it were so, was an accident, and it put him, for half an hour, on as much of the picture of his early years abroad, his migratory parents, his Swiss schools, his German university, as she had easy attention for. A man, he intimated, a man of their world, would have spotted him straight as to many of these points; a man of their world, so far as they had a world, would have been through the English mill. But it was none the less charming to make his confession to a woman; women had, in fact, for such differences, so much more imagination. Kate showed at present all his case could require; when she had had it from beginning to end she declared that she now made out more than ever yet of what she loved him for. She had herself, as a child, lived with some continuity in the world across the Channel, coming home again still a child; and had participated after that, in her teens, in her mother's brief but repeated retreats to Dresden, to Florence, to Biarritz, weak and expensive attempts at economy from which there stuck to her—though in general coldly expressed, through the instinctive avoidance of cheap raptures—the religion of foreign things. When it was revealed to her how many more foreign things were in Merton Densher than he had hitherto taken the trouble to catalogue, she almost faced him as if he were a map of the continent or a handsome present of a delightful new "Murray." He hadn't meant to swagger, he had rather meant to plead, though with Mrs. Lowder he had meant also a little to explain. His father had been, in strange countries, in twenty settlements of the English, British chaplain, resident or occasional, and had had for years the unusual luck of never wanting a billet. His career abroad had therefore been unbroken, and, as his stipend had never been great, he had educated his children at the smallest cost, in the schools nearest; which was also a saving of railway fares. Densher's mother, it further appeared, had practised on her side a distinguished industry, to the success of which—so far as success ever crowned it—this period of exile had much contributed: she copied, patient lady, famous pictures in great museums, having begun with a happy natural gift and taking in betimes the scale of her opportunity. Copyists abroad of course swarmed, but Mrs. Densher had had a sense and a hand of her own, had arrived at a perfection that persuaded, that even deceived, and that made the disposal of her work blissfully usual. Her son, who had lost her, held her image sacred, and the effect of his telling Kate all about her, as well as about other matters until then mixed and dim, was to render his history rich, his sources full, his outline anything but common. He had come round, he had come back, he insisted abundantly, to being a Briton: his Cambridge years, his happy connection, as it had proved, with his father's college, amply certified to that, to say nothing of his subsequent plunge into London, which filled up the measure. But brave enough though his descent to English earth, he had passed, by the way, through zones of air that had left their ruffle on his wings, had been exposed to initiations ineffaceable. Something had happened to him that could never be undone.

When Kate Croy said to him as much he besought her not to insist, declaring that this indeed was what was too much the matter with him, that he had been but too probably spoiled for native, for insular use. On which, not unnaturally, she insisted the more, assuring him, without mitigation, that if he was complicated and brilliant she wouldn't for the world have had him any thing less; so that he was reduced in the end to accusing her of putting the dreadful truth to him in the hollow guise of flattery. She was making out how abnormal he was in order that she might eventually find him impossible; and, as she could fully make it out but with his aid, she had to bribe him by feigned delight to help her. If her last word for him, in the connection, was that the way he saw himself was just a precious proof the more of his having tasted of the tree and being thereby prepared to assist her to eat, this gives the happy tone of their whole talk, the measure of the flight of time in the near presence of his settled departure. Kate showed, however, that she was to be more literally taken when she spoke of the relief Aunt Maud would draw from the prospect of his absence.

"Yet one can scarcely see why," he replied, "when she fears me so little."

His friend weighed his objection. "Your idea is that she likes you so much that she'll even go so far as to regret losing you?"

Well, he saw it in their constant comprehensive way. "Since what she builds on is the gradual process of your alienation, she may take the view that the process constantly requires me. Mustn't I be there to keep it going? It's in my exile that it may languish."

He went on with that fantasy, but at this point Kate ceased to attend. He saw after a little that she had been following some thought of her own, and he had been feeling the growth of something determinant even through the extravagance of much of the pleasantry, the warm, transparent irony, into which their livelier intimacy kept plunging like a confident swimmer. Suddenly she said to him with extraordinary beauty: "I engage myself to you for ever."

The beauty was in everything, and he could have separated nothing—couldn't have thought of her face as distinct from the whole joy. Yet her face had a new light. "And I pledge you—I call God to witness!—every spark of my faith; I give you every drop of my life." That was all, for the moment, but it was enough, and it was almost as quiet as if it were nothing. They were in the open air, in an alley of the Gardens; the great space, which seemed to arch just then higher and spread wider for them, threw them back into deep concentration. They moved by a common instinct to a spot, within sight, that struck them as fairly sequestered, and there, before their time together was spent, they had extorted from concentration every advance it could make them. They had exchanged vows and tokens, sealed their rich compact, solemnized, so far as breathed words and murmured sounds and lighted eyes and clasped hands could do it, their agreement to belong only, and to belong tremendously, to each other. They were to leave the place accordingly an affianced couple; but before they left it other things still had passed. Densher had declared his horror of bringing to a premature end her happy relation with her aunt; and they had worked round together to a high level of wisdom and patience. Kate's free profession was that she wished not to deprive *him* of Mrs. Lowder's countenance, which, in the long run, she was convinced he would continue to enjoy; and as, by a blessed turn, Aunt Maud had demanded of him no promise that would tie his hands, they should be able to cultivate their destiny in their own way and yet remain loyal. One difficulty alone stood out, which Densher named.

"Of course it will never do—we must remember that—from the moment you allow her to found hopes of you for any one else in particular. So long as her view is content to remain as general as at present appears, I don't see that we deceive her. At a given moment, you see, she must be undeceived: the only thing therefore is to be ready for the moment and to face it. Only, after all, in that case," the young man observed, "one doesn't quite make out what we shall have got from her."

"What she'll have got from *us?*" Kate inquired with a smile. "What she'll have got from us," the girl went on, "is her own affair—it's for *her* to measure. I asked her for nothing," she added; "I never put myself upon her. She must take her risks, and she surely understands them. What we shall have got from her is what we've already spoken of," Kate further explained; "it's that we shall have gained time. And so, for that matter, will she."

Densher gazed a little at all this clearness; his gaze was not at the present hour into romantic obscurity. "Yes; no doubt, in our particular situation, time's everything. And then there's the joy of it."

She hesitated. "Of our secret?"

"Not so much perhaps of our secret in itself, but of what's represented and, as we must somehow feel, protected and made deeper and closer by it." And his fine face, relaxed into happiness, covered her with all his meaning. "Our being as we are."

It was as if for a moment she let the meaning sink into her. "So gone?"

"So gone. So extremely gone. However," he smiled, "we shall go a good deal further." Her answer to which was only the softness of her silence—a silence that looked out for them both at the far reach of their prospect. This was immense, and they thus took final possession of it. They were practically united and they were splendidly strong; but there were other things—things they were precisely strong enough to be able successfully to count with and safely to allow for; in consequence of which they would, for the present, subject to some better reason, keep their understanding to themselves. It was not indeed, however, till after one more observation of Densher's that they felt the question completely straightened out. "The only thing of course is that she may any day absolutely put it to you."

Kate considered. "Ask me where, on my honour, we are? She may, naturally; but I doubt if in fact she will. While you're away she'll make the most of it. She'll leave me alone."

"But there'll be my letters."

The girl faced his letters. "Very, very many?"

"Very, very, very many—more than ever; and you know what that is! And then," Densher added, "there'll be yours."

"Oh, I shan't leave mine on the hall-table. I shall post them myself."

He looked at her a moment. "Do you think then I had best address you elsewhere?" After which, before she could quite answer, he added with some emphasis: "I'd rather not, you know. It's straighter."

She might again have just waited. "Of course it's straighter. Don't be afraid I shan't be straight. Address me," she continued, "where you like. I shall be proud enough of its being known you write to me."

He turned it over for the last clearness. "Even at the risk of its really bringing down the inquisition?"

Well, the last clearness now filled her. "I'm not afraid of the inquisition. If she asks if there's anything definite between us, I know perfectly what I shall say."

"That I *am,* of course, 'gone' for you?"

"That I love you as I shall never in my life love any one else, and that she can make what she likes of that." She said it out so splendidly that it was like a new profession of faith, the fulness of a tide breaking through; and the effect of that, in turn, was to make her companion meet her with such eyes that she had time again before he could otherwise speak. "Besides, she's just as likely to ask *you.* "

"Not while I'm away."

"Then when you come back."

"Well then," said Densher, "we shall have had our particular joy. But what I feel is," he candidly added, "that, by an idea of her own, her superior policy, she *won't* ask me. She'll let me off. I shan't have to lie to her."

"It will be left all to me?" asked Kate.

"All to you!" he tenderly laughed.

But it was, oddly, the very next moment as if he had perhaps been a shade too candid. His discrimination seemed to mark a possible, a natural reality, a reality not wholly disallowed by the account the girl had just given of her own intention. There *was* a difference in the air—even if none other than the supposedly usual difference in truth between man and woman; and it was almost as if the sense of this provoked her. She seemed to cast about an instant, and then she went back a little resentfully to something she had suffered to pass a minute before. She appeared to take up rather more seriously than she need the joke about her freedom to deceive. Yet she did this too in a beautiful way. "Men are too stupid—even you. You didn't understand just now why, if I post my letters myself, it won't be for any thing so vulgar as to hide them."

"Oh, you said—for the pleasure."

"Yes; but you didn't, you don't understand what the pleasure may be. There are refinements——!" she more patiently dropped. "I mean of consciousness, of sensation, of appreciation," she went on. "No," she sadly insisted—"*men* don't know. They know, in such matters, almost nothing but what women show them."

This was one of the speeches, frequent in her, that, liberally, joyfully, intensely adopted and, in itself, as might be, embraced, drew him again as close to her, and held him as long, as their conditions permitted. "Then that's exactly why we've such an abysmal need of you!"

BOOK THIRD

V

The two ladies who, in advance of the Swiss season, had been warned that their design was unconsidered, that the passes would not be clear, nor the air mild, nor the inns open—the two ladies who, characteristically, had braved a good deal of possibly interested remonstrance were finding themselves, as their adventure turned out, wonderfully sustained. It was the judgment of the head-waiters and other functionaries on the Italian lakes that approved itself now as interested; they themselves had been conscious of impatiences, of bolder dreams—at least the younger had; so that one of the things they made out together—making out as they did an endless variety—was that in those operatic palaces of the Villa d'Este, of Cadenabbia, of Pallanza and Stresa, lone women, however reinforced by a travelling-library of instructive volumes, were apt to be beguiled and undone. Their flights of fancy moreover had been modest; they had for instance risked nothing vital in hoping to make their way by the Brünig. They were making it in fact happily enough as we meet them, and were only wishing that, for the wondrous beauty of the early high-climbing spring, it might have been longer and the places to pause and rest more numerous.

Such at least had been the intimated attitude of Mrs. Stringham, the elder of the companions, who had her own view of the impatiences of the younger, to which, however, she offered an opposition but of the most circuitous. She moved, the admirable Mrs. Stringham, in a fine cloud of observation and suspicion; she was in the position, as she believed, of knowing much more about Milly Theale than Milly herself knew, and yet of having to darken her knowledge as well as make it active. The woman in the world least formed by nature, as she was quite aware, for duplicities and labyrinths, she found herself dedicated to personal subtlety by a new set of circumstances, above all by a new personal relation; had now in fact to recognise that an education in the occult—she could scarce say what to call it—had begun for her the day she left New York with Mildred. She had come on from Boston for that purpose; had seen little of the girl—or rather had seen her but briefly, for Mrs. Stringham, when she saw anything at all, saw much, saw everything—before accepting her proposal; and had accordingly placed herself, by her act, in a boat that she more and more estimated as, humanly speaking, of the biggest, though likewise, no doubt, in many ways, by reason of its size, of the safest. In Boston, the winter before, the young lady in whom we are interested had, on the spot, deeply, yet almost tacitly, appealed to her, dropped into her mind the shy conceit of some assistance, some devotion to render. Mrs. Stringham's little life had often been visited by shy conceits—secret dreams that had fluttered their hour between its narrow walls without, for any great part, so much as mustering courage to look out of its rather dim windows. But this imagination—the fancy of a possible link with the remarkable young thing from New York—*had* mustered courage: had perched, on the instant, at the clearest look-out it could find, and might be said to have remained there till, only a few months later, it had caught, in surprise and joy, the unmistakable flash of a signal.

Milly Theale had Boston friends, such as they were, and of recent making; and it was understood that her visit to them—a visit that was not to be meagre—had been undertaken, after a series of bereavements, in the interest of the particular peace that New York could not give. It was recognised, liberally enough, that there were many things—perhaps even too many—New York *could* give; but this was felt to make no difference in the constant fact that what you had most to do, under the discipline of life, or of death, was really to feel your situation as grave. Boston could help you to that as nothing else could, and it had extended to Milly, by every presumption, some such measure of assistance. Mrs. Stringham was never to forget—for the moment had not faded, nor the infinitely fine vibration it set up in any degree ceased—her own first sight of the striking apparition, then unheralded and unexplained: the slim, constantly pale, delicately haggard, anomalously, agreeably angular young person, of not more than two-and-twenty in spite of her marks, whose hair was some how exceptionally red even for the real thing, which it innocently confessed to being, and whose clothes were remarkably black even for robes of mourning, which was the meaning they expressed. It was New York mourning, it was New York hair, it was a New York history, confused as yet, but multitudinous, of the loss of parents, brothers, sisters, almost every human appendage, all on a scale and with a sweep that had required the greater stage; it was a New York legend of affecting, of romantic isolation, and, beyond everything, it was by most accounts, in respect to the mass of money so piled on the girl's back, a set of New York possibilities. She was alone, she was stricken, she was rich, and, in particular, she was strange—a combination in itself of a nature to engage Mrs. Stringham's attention. But it was the strangeness that most determined our good lady's sympathy, convinced as she was that it was much greater than any one else—any one but the sole Susan Stringham—supposed. Susan privately settled it that Boston was not in the least seeing her, was only occupied with her seeing Boston, and that any assumed affinity between the two characters was delusive and vain. She was seeing her, and she had quite the deepest moment of her life in now obeying the instinct to conceal the vision. She couldn't explain it—no one would understand. They would say clever Boston things—Mrs. Stringham was from Burlington, Vermont, which she boldly upheld as the real heart of New England, Boston being "too far south"—but they would only darken counsel.

There could be no better proof, than this quick intellectual split, of the impression made on our friend, who shone, herself, she was well aware, with but the reflected light of the admirable city. She too had had her discipline, but it had not made her striking; it had been prosaically usual, though doubtless a decent dose; and had only made her usual to match it—usual, that is, as Boston went. She had lost first her husband, and then her mother, with whom, on her husband's death, she had lived again; so that now, childless, she was but more sharply single than before. But she sat rather coldly light, having, as she called it, enough to live on—so far, that is, as she lived by bread alone: how little indeed she was regularly content with that diet appeared from the name she had made—Susan Shepherd Stringham—as a contributor to the best magazines. She wrote short stories, and she fondly believed she had her "note," the art of showing New England without showing it wholly in the kitchen. She had not herself been brought up in the kitchen; she knew others who had not; and to speak for them had thus become with her a literary mission. To *be* in truth literary had ever been her dearest thought, the thought that kept her bright little nippers perpetually in position. There were masters, models, celebrities, mainly foreign, whom she finely accounted so and in whose light she ingeniously laboured; there were others whom, however chattered about, she ranked with the inane, for she was full of discrimination; but all categories failed her—they ceased at least to signify—as soon as she found herself in presence of the real thing, the romantic life itself. That was what she saw in Mildred—what positively made her hand a while tremble too much for the pen. She had had, it seemed to her, a revelation—such as even New England refined and grammatical couldn't give; and, all made up as she was of small neat memories and ingenuities, little industries and ambitions, mixed with something moral, personal, that was still more intensely responsive, she felt her new friend would have done her an ill turn if their friendship shouldn't develop, and yet that nothing would be left of anything else if it should. It was for the surrender of everything else that she was, however, quite prepared, and while she went about her usual Boston business with her usual Boston probity she was really all the while holding herself. She wore her "handsome" felt hat, so Tyrolese, yet some how, though feathered from the eagle's wing, so truly domestic, with the same straightness and security; she attached her fur boa with the same honest precautions; she preserved her balance on the ice-slopes with the same practised skill; she opened, each evening, her "Transcript" with the same interfusion of suspense and resignation; she attended her almost daily concert with the same expenditure of patience and the same economy of passion; she flitted in and out of the Public Library with the air of conscientiously returning or bravely carrying off in her pocket the key of knowledge itself; and finally—it was what she most did—she watched the thin trickle of a fictive "love-interest" through that somewhat serpentine channel, in the magazines, which she mainly managed to keep clear for it. But the real thing, all the while, was elsewhere; the real thing had gone back to New York, leaving behind it the two unsolved questions, quite distinct, of why it *was* real, and whether she should ever be so near it again.

309

For the figure to which these questions attached themselves she had found a convenient description—she thought of it for herself, always, as that of a girl with a background. The great reality was in the fact that, very soon, after but two or three meetings, the girl with the background, the girl with the crown of old gold and the mourning that was not as the mourning of Boston, but at once more rebellious in its gloom and more frivolous in its frills, had told her she had never seen any one like her. They had met thus as opposed curiosities, and that simple remark of Milly's—if simple it was—became the most important thing that had ever happened to her; it deprived the love-interest, for the time, of actuality and even of pertinence; it moved her first, in short, in a high degree, to gratitude, and then to no small compassion. Yet in respect to this relation at least it was what did prove the key of knowledge; it lighted up as nothing else could do the poor young woman's history. That the potential heiress of all the ages should never have seen any one like a mere typical subscriber, after all, to the "Transcript" was a truth that—in especial as announced with modesty, with humility, with regret—described a situation. It laid upon the elder woman, as to the void to be filled, a weight of responsibility; but in particular it led her to ask whom poor Mildred *had* then seen, and what range of contacts it had taken to produce such queer surprises. That was really the inquiry that had ended by clearing the air: the key of knowledge was felt to click in the lock from the moment it flashed upon Mrs. Stringham that her friend had been starved for culture. Culture was what she herself represented for her, and it was living up to that principle that would surely prove the great business. She knew, the clever lady, what the principle itself represented, and the limits of her own store; and a certain alarm would have grown upon her if something else hadn't grown faster.

This was, fortunately for her—and we give it in her own words—the sense of a harrowing pathos. That, primarily, was what appealed to her, what seemed to open the door of romance for her still wider than any, than a still more reckless, connection with the "picture-papers." For such was essentially the point: it was rich, romantic, abysmal, to have, as was evident, thousands and thousands a year, to have youth and intelligence and if not beauty, at least, in equal measure, a high, dim, charming, ambiguous oddity, which was even better, and then on top of all to enjoy boundless freedom, the freedom of the wind in the desert—it was unspeakably touching to be so equipped and yet to have been reduced by fortune to little humble-minded mistakes.

It brought our friend's imagination back again to New York, where aberrations were so possible in the intellectual sphere, and it in fact caused a visit she presently paid there to overflow with interest. As Milly had beautifully invited her, so she would hold out if she could against the strain of so much confidence in her mind; and the remarkable thing was that even at the end of three weeks she *had* held out. But by this time her mind had grown comparatively bold and free; it was dealing with new quantities, a different proportion altogether—and that had made for refreshment: she had accordingly gone home in convenient possession of her subject. New York was vast, New York was startling, with strange histories, with wild cosmopolite backward generations that accounted for anything; and to have got nearer the luxuriant tribe of which the rare creature was the final flower, the immense, extravagant, unregulated cluster, with free-living ancestors, handsome dead cousins, lurid uncles, beautiful vanished aunts, persons all busts and curls, preserved, though so exposed, in the marble of famous French chisels—all this, to say nothing of the effect of closer growths of the stem, was to have had one's small world-space both crowded and enlarged. Our couple had at all events effected an exchange; the elder friend had been as consciously intellectual as possible, and the younger, abounding in personal revelation, had been as unconsciously distinguished. This was poetry—it was also history—Mrs. Stringham thought, to a finer tune even than Maeterlink and Pater, than Marbot and Gregorovius. She appointed occasions for the reading of these authors with her hostess, rather perhaps than actually achieved great spans; but what they managed and what they missed speedily sank for her into the dim depths of the merely relative, so quickly, so strongly had she clutched her central clue. All her scruples and hesitations, all her anxious enthusiasms, had reduced themselves to a single alarm—the fear that she really might act on her companion clumsily and coarsely. She was positively afraid of what she might do to her, and to avoid that, to avoid it with piety and passion, to do, rather, nothing at all, to leave her untouched because no touch one could apply, however light, however just, however earnest and anxious, would be half good enough, would be anything but an ugly smutch upon perfection—this now imposed itself as a consistent, an inspiring thought.

Less than a month after the event that had so determined Mrs. Stringham's attitude—close upon the heels, that is, of her return from New York—she was reached by a proposal that brought up for her the kind of question her delicacy might have to contend with. Would she start for Europe with her young friend at the earliest possible date, and should she be willing to do so without making conditions? The inquiry was launched by wire; explanations, in sufficiency, were promised; extreme urgency was suggested, and a general surrender invited. It was to the honour of her sincerity that she made the surrender on the spot, though it was not perhaps altogether to that of her logic. She had wanted, very consciously, from the first, to give something up for her new acquaintance, but she had now no doubt that she was practically giving up all. What settled this was the fulness of a particular impression, the impression that had throughout more and more supported her and which she would have uttered so far as she might by saying that the charm of the creature was positively in the creature's greatness. She would have been content so to leave it; unless indeed she had said, more familiarly, that Mildred was the biggest impression of her life. That was at all events the biggest account of her, and none but a big, clearly, would do. Her situation, as such things were called, was on the grand scale; but it still was not that. It was her nature, once for all—a nature that reminded Mrs. Stringham of the term always used in the newspapers about the great new steamers, the inordinate number of "feet of water" they drew; so that if, in your little boat, you had chosen to hover and approach, you had but yourself to thank, when once motion was started, for the way the draught pulled you. Milly drew the feet of water, and odd though it might seem that a lonely girl, who was not robust and who hated sound and show, should stir the stream like a leviathan, her companion floated off with the sense of rocking violently at her side. More than prepared, however, for that excitement, Mrs. Stringham mainly failed of ease in respect to her own consistency. To attach herself for an indefinite time seemed a roundabout way of holding her hands off. If she wished to be sure of neither touching nor smutching, the straighter plan would doubtless have been not to keep her friend within reach. This in fact she fully recognised, and with it the degree to which she desired that the girl should lead her life, a life certain to be so much finer than that of anybody else. The difficulty, however, by good fortune, cleared away as soon as she had further recognised, as she was speedily able to do, that she, Susan Shepherd—the name with which Milly for the most part amused herself—was *not* anybody else. She had renounced that character; she had now no life to lead; and she honestly believed that she was thus supremely equipped for leading Milly's own. No other person whatever, she was sure, had to an equal degree this qualification, and it was really to assert it that she fondly embarked.

Many things, though not in many weeks, had come and gone since then, and one of the best of them, doubtless, had been the voyage itself, by the happy southern course, to the succession of Mediterranean ports, with the dazzled wind-up at Naples. Two or three others had preceded this; incidents, indeed rather lively marks, of their last fortnight at home, and one of which had determined on Mrs. Stringham's part a rush to New York, forty-eight breathless hours there, previous to her final rally. But the great sustained sea-light had drunk up the rest of the picture, so that for many days other questions and other possibilities sounded with as little effect as a trio of penny whistles might sound in a Wagner overture. It was the Wagner overture that practically prevailed, up through Italy, where Milly had already been, still further up and across the Alps, which were also partly known to Mrs. Stringham; only perhaps "taken" to a time not wholly congruous, hurried in fact on account of the girl's high restlessness. She had been expected, she had frankly promised, to be restless—that was partly why she was "great"—or was a consequence, at any rate, if not a cause; yet she had not perhaps altogether announced herself as straining so hard at the cord. It was familiar, it was beautiful to Mrs. Stringham that she had arrears to make up, the chances that had lapsed for her through the wanton ways of forefathers fond of Paris, but not of its higher sides, and fond almost of nothing else; but the vagueness, the openness, the eagerness without point and the interest without pause—all a part of the charm of her oddity as at first presented—had become more striking in proportion as they triumphed over movement and change. She had arts and idiosyncrasies of which no great account could have been given, but which were a daily grace if you lived with them; such as the art of being almost tragically impatient and yet making it as light as air; of being inexplicably sad and yet making it as clear as noon; of being unmistakably gay, and yet making it as soft as dusk. Mrs. Stringham by this time understood everything, was more than ever confirmed in wonder and admiration, in her view that it was life enough simply to feel her companion's feelings; but there were special keys she had not yet added to her bunch, impressions that, of a sudden, were apt to affect her as new.

This particular day on the great Swiss road had been, for some reason, full of them, and they referred themselves, provisionally, to some deeper depth than she had touched—though into two or three such depths, it must be added, she had peeped long enough to find herself suddenly draw back. It was not Milly's unpacified state, in short, that now troubled her—though certainly, as Europe was the great American sedative, the failure was to some extent to be noted: it was the suspected presence of something behind it— which, however, could scarcely have taken its place there since their departure. What any fresh motive of unrest could suddenly have sprung from was, in short, not to be divined. It was but half an explanation to say that excitement, for each of them, had naturally dropped, and that what they had left behind, or tried to—the great serious facts of life, as Mrs. Stringham liked to call them—was once more coming into sight as objects loom through smoke when smoke begins to clear; for these were general appearances from which the girl's own aspect, her really larger vagueness, seemed rather to disconnect itself. The nearest approach to a personal anxiety indulged in as yet by the elder lady was on her taking occasion to wonder if what she had more than anything else got hold of mightn't be one of the finer, one of the finest, one of the rarest—as she called it so that she might call it nothing worse—cases of American intensity. She had just had a moment of alarm—asked herself if her young friend were merely going to treat her to some complicated drama of nerves. At the end of a week, however, with their further progress, her young friend had effectively answered the question and given her the impression, indistinct indeed as yet, of something that had a reality compared with which the nervous explanation would have been coarse. Mrs. Stringham found herself from that hour, in other words, in presence of an explanation that remained a muffled and intangible form, but that, assuredly, should it take on sharpness, would explain everything and more than everything, would become instantly the light in which Milly was to be read.

Such a matter as this may at all events speak of the style in which our young woman could affect those who were near her, may testify to the sort of interest she could inspire. She worked—and seemingly quite without design—upon the sympathy, the curiosity, the fancy of her associates, and we shall really ourselves scarce otherwise come closer to her than by feeling their impression and sharing, if need be, their confusion. She reduced them, Mrs. Stringham would have said, reduced them to a consenting bewilderment; which was precisely, for that good lady, on a last analysis, what was most in harmony with her greatness. She exceeded, escaped measure, was surprising only because *they* were so far from great. Thus it was that on this wondrous day on the Brünig the spell of watching her had grown more than ever irresistible; a proof of what—or of a part of what—Mrs. Stringham had, with all the rest, been reduced to. She had almost the sense of tracking her young friend as if at a given moment to pounce. She knew she shouldn't pounce, she hadn't come out to pounce; yet she felt her attention secretive, all the same, and her observation scientific. She struck herself as hovering like a spy, applying tests, laying traps, concealing signs. This would last, however, only till she should fairly know what was the matter; and to watch was, after all, meanwhile, a way of clinging to the girl, not less than an occupation, a satisfaction in itself. The pleasure of watching, moreover, if a reason were needed, came from a sense of her beauty. Her beauty hadn't at all originally seemed a part of the situation, and Mrs. Stringham had, even in the first flush of friendship, not named it, grossly, to any one; having seen early that, for stupid people—and who, she sometimes secretly asked herself, wasn't stupid?—it would take a great deal of explaining. She had learned not to mention it till it was mentioned first—which occasionally happened, but not too often; and then she was there in force. Then she both warmed to the perception that met her own perception, and disputed it, suspiciously, as to special items; while, in general, she had learned to refine even to the point of herself employing the word that most people employed. She employed it to pretend that she was also stupid and so have done with the matter; spoke of her friend as plain, as ugly even, in a case of especially dense insistence; but as, in appearance, so "awfully full of things." This was her own way of describing a face that, thanks, doubtless, to rather too much forehead, too much nose and too much mouth, together with too little mere conventional colour and conventional line, was expressive, irregular, exquisite, both for speech and for silence. When Milly smiled it was a public event—when she didn't it was a chapter of history. They had stopped, on the Brünig, for luncheon, and there had come up for them under the charm of the place the question of a longer stay.

Mrs. Stringham was now on the ground of thrilled recognitions, small sharp echoes of a past which she kept in a well-thumbed case, but which, on pressure of a spring and exposure to the air, still showed itself ticking as hard as an honest old watch. The embalmed "Europe" of her younger time had partly stood for three years of Switzerland, a term of continuous school at Vevey, with rewards of merit in the form of silver medals tied by blue ribbons and mild mountain-passes attacked with alpenstocks. It was the good girls who, in the holidays, were taken highest, and our friend could now judge, from what she supposed her familiarity with the minor peaks, that she had been one of the best. These reminiscences, sacred to-day because prepared in the hushed chambers of the past, had been part of the general train laid for the pair of sisters, daughters early fatherless, by their brave Vermont mother, who struck her at present as having apparently, almost like Columbus, worked out, all unassisted, a conception of the other side of the globe. She had focussed Vevey, by the light of nature, and with extraordinary completeness, at Burlington; after which she had embarked, sailed, landed, explored and, above all, made good her presence. She had given her daughters the five years in Switzerland and Germany that were to leave them ever afterwards a standard of comparison for all cycles of Cathay, and to stamp the younger in especial—Susan was the younger—with a character that, as Mrs. Stringham had often had occasion, through life, to say to herself, made all the difference. It made all the difference for Mrs. Stringham, over and over again and in the most remote connections, that, thanks to her parent's lonely, thrifty, hardy faith, she was a woman of the world. There were plenty of women who were all sorts of things that she wasn't, but who, on the other hand, were not that, and who didn't know *she* was (which she liked—it relegated them still further) and didn't know, either, how it enabled her to judge them. She had never seen herself so much in this light as during the actual phase of her associated, if slightly undirected, pilgrimage; and the consciousness gave perhaps to her plea for a pause more intensity than she knew. The irrecoverable days had come back to her from far off; they were part of the sense of the cool upper air and of everything else that hung like an indestructible scent to the torn garment of youth—the taste of honey and the luxury of milk, the sound of cattle-bells and the rush of streams, the fragrance of trodden balms and the dizziness of deep gorges.

Milly clearly felt these things too, but they affected her companion at moments—that was quite the way Mrs. Stringham would have expressed it—as the princess in a conventional tragedy might have affected the confidant if a personal emotion had ever been permitted to the latter. That a princess could only be a princess was a truth with which, essentially, a confidant, however responsive, had to live. Mrs. Stringham was a woman of the world, but Milly Theale was a princess, the only one she had yet had to deal with, and this in its way, too, made all the difference. It was a perfectly definite doom for the wearer—it was for every one else a perfectly palpable quality. It might have been, possibly, with its involved loneliness and other mysteries, the weight under which she fancied her companion's admirable head occasionally, and ever so submissively, bowed. Milly had quite assented at luncheon to their staying over, and had left her to look at rooms, settle questions, arrange about their keeping on their carriage and horses; cares that had now moreover fallen to Mrs. Stringham as a matter of course and that yet for some reason, on this occasion particularly, brought home to her—all agreeably, richly, almost grandly—what it was to live with the great. Her young friend had, in a sublime degree, a sense closed to the general question of difficulty, which she got rid of, furthermore, not in the least as one had seen many charming persons do, by merely passing it on to others. She kept it completely at a distance: it never entered the circle; the most plaintive confidant couldn't have dragged it in; and to tread the path of a confidant was accordingly to live exempt. Service was in other words so easy to render that the whole thing was like court life without the hardships. It came back of course to the question of money, and our observant lady had by this time repeatedly reflected that if one were talking of the "difference," it was just this, this incomparably and nothing else, that when all was said and done most made it. A less vulgarly, a less obviously purchasing or parading person she couldn't have imagined; but it was, all the same, the truth of truths that the girl couldn't get away from her wealth. She might leave her conscientious companion as freely alone with it as possible and never ask a question, scarce even tolerate a reference; but it was in the fine folds of the helplessly expensive little black frock that she drew over the grass as she now strolled vaguely off; it was in the curious and splendid coils of hair, "done" with no eye whatever to the *mode du jour,* that peeped from under the corresponding indifference of her hat, the merely personal tradition that suggested a sort of noble inelegance; it lurked between the leaves of the uncut but antiquated Tauchnitz volume of which, before going out, she had mechanically possessed herself. She couldn't dress it away, nor walk it away, nor read it away, nor think it away; she could neither smile it away in any dreamy absence nor blow it away in any softened sigh. She couldn't have lost it if she had tried—that was what it was to be really rich. It had to be *the* thing you were. When at the end of an hour she had not returned to the house Mrs. Stringham, though the bright afternoon was yet young, took, with precautions, the same direction, went to join her in case of her caring for a walk. But the purpose of joining her was in truth less distinct than that of a due regard for a possibly preferred detachment: so that, once more, the good lady proceeded with a quietness that made her slightly "underhand" even in her own eyes. She couldn't help that, however, and she didn't care, sure as she was that what she really wanted was not to overstep, but to stop in time. It was to be able to stop in time that she went softly, but she had on this occasion further to go than ever yet, for she followed in vain, and at last with some anxiety, the footpath she believed Milly to have taken. It wound up a hillside and into the higher Alpine meadows in which, all these last days, they had so often wanted, as they passed above or below, to stray; and then it obscured itself in a wood, but always going up, up, and with a small cluster of brown old high-perched chalets evidently for its goal. Mrs. Stringham reached in due course the chalets, and there received from a bewildered old woman, a very fearful person to behold, an indication that sufficiently guided her. The young lady had been seen not long before passing further on, over a crest and to a place where the way would drop again, as our unappeased inquirer found it, in fact, a quarter of an hour later, markedly and almost alarmingly to do. It led somewhere, yet apparently quite into space, for the great side of the mountain appeared, from where she pulled up, to fall away altogether, though probably but to some issue below and out of sight. Her uncertainty moreover was brief, for she next became aware of the presence on a fragment of rock, twenty yards off, of the Tauchnitz volume that the girl had brought out, and that therefore pointed to her shortly previous passage. She had rid herself of the book, which was an encumbrance, and meant of course to pick it up on her return; but as she hadn't yet picked it up what on earth had become of her? Mrs. Stringham, I hasten to add, was within a few moments to see; but it was quite an accident that she had not, before they were over, betrayed by her deeper agitation the fact of her own nearness.

The whole place, with the descent of the path and as a sequel to a sharp turn that was masked by rocks and shrubs, appeared to fall precipitously and to become a "view" pure and simple, a view of great extent and beauty, but thrown forward and vertiginous. Milly, with the promise of it from just above, had gone straight down to it, not stopping till it was all before her; and here, on what struck her friend as the dizzy edge of it, she was seated at her ease. The path somehow took care of itself and its final business, but the girl's seat was a slab of rock at the end of a short promontory or excrescence that merely pointed off to the right into gulfs of air and that was so placed by good fortune, if not by the worst, as to be at last completely visible. For Mrs. Stringham stifled a cry on taking in what she believed to be the danger of such a perch for a mere maiden; her liability to slip, to slide, to leap, to be precipitated by a single false movement, by a turn of the head—how could one tell? into whatever was beneath. A thousand thoughts, for the minute, roared in the poor lady's ears, but without reaching, as happened, Milly's. It was a commotion that left our observer intensely still and holding her breath. What had first been offered her was the possibility of a latent intention—however wild the idea—in such a posture; of some betrayed accordance of Milly's caprice with a horrible hidden obsession. But since Mrs. Stringham stood as motionless as if a sound, a syllable, must have produced the start that would be fatal, so even the lapse of a few seconds had a partly reassuring effect. It gave her time to receive the impression which, when she some minutes later softly retraced her steps, was to be the sharpest she carried away. This was the impression that if the girl was deeply and recklessly meditating there, she was not meditating a jump; she was on the contrary, as she sat, much more in a state of uplifted and unlimited possession that had nothing to gain from violence. She was looking down on the kingdoms of the earth, and though indeed that of itself might well go to the brain, it wouldn't be with a view of renouncing them. Was she choosing among them, or did she want them all? This question, before Mrs. Stringham had decided what to do, made others vain; in accordance with which she saw, or believed she did, that if it might be dangerous to call out, to sound in any way a surprise, it would probably be safe enough to withdraw as she had come. She watched a while longer, she held her breath, and she never knew afterwards what time had elapsed.

Not many minutes probably, yet they had not seemed few, and they had given her so much to think of, not only while creeping home, but while waiting afterwards at the inn, that she was still busy with them when, late in the afternoon, Milly reappeared. She had stopped at the point of the path where the Tauchnitz lay, had taken it up and, with the pencil attached to her watch-guard, had scrawled a word—*à bientôt!*—across the cover; then, even under the girl's continued delay, had measured time without a return of alarm. For she now saw that the great thing she had brought away was precisely a conviction that the future was not to exist for her princess in the form of any sharp or simple release from the human predicament. It wouldn't be for her a question of a flying leap and thereby of a quick escape. It would be a question of taking full in the face the whole assault of life, to the general muster of which indeed her face might have been directly presented as she sat there on her rock. Mrs. Stringham was thus able to say to herself, even after another interval of some length, that if her young friend still continued absent it wouldn't be because—whatever the opportunity—she had cut short the thread. She wouldn't have committed suicide; she knew herself unmistakably reserved for some more complicated passage; this was the very vision in which she had, with no little awe, been discovered. The image that thus remained with the elder lady kept the character of revelation. During the breathless minutes of her watch she had seen her companion afresh; the latter's type, aspect, marks, her history, her state, her beauty, her mystery, all unconsciously betrayed themselves to the Alpine air, and all had been gathered in again to feed Mrs. Stringham's flame. They are things that will more distinctly appear for us, and they are meanwhile briefly represented by the enthusiasm that was stronger on our friend's part than any doubt. It was a consciousness she was scarce yet used to carrying, but she had as beneath her feet a mine of something precious. She seemed to herself to stand near the mouth, not yet quite cleared. The mine but needed working and would certainly yield a treasure. She was not thinking, either, of Milly's gold.

VI

The girl said nothing, when they met, about the words scrawled on the Tauchnitz, and Mrs. Stringham then noticed that she had not the book with her. She had left it lying and probably would never remember it at all. Her comrade's decision was therefore quickly made not to speak of having followed her; and within five minutes of her return, wonderfully enough, the preoccupation denoted by her forgetfulness further declared itself. "Should you think me quite abominable if I were to say that after all——?"

Mrs. Stringham had already thought, with the first sound of the question, everything she was capable of thinking, and had immediately made such a sign that Milly's words gave place to visible relief at her assent. "You don't care for our stop here—you'd rather go straight on? We'll start then with the peep of to-morrow's dawn—or as early as you like; it's only rather late now to take the road again." And she smiled to show how she meant it for a joke that an instant onward rush was what the girl would have wished. "I bullied you into stopping," she added; "so it serves me right."

Milly made in general the most of her good friend's jokes; but she humoured this one a little absently. "Oh yes, you do bully me." And it was thus arranged between them, with no discussion at all, that they would resume their journey in the morning. The younger tourist's interest in the detail of the matter—in spite of a declaration from the elder that she would consent to be dragged anywhere—appeared almost immediately afterwards quite to lose itself; she promised, however, to think till supper of where, with the world all before them, they might go—supper having been ordered for such time as permitted of lighted candles. It had been agreed between them that lighted candles at wayside inns, in strange countries, amid mountain scenery, gave the evening meal a peculiar poetry—such being the mild adventures, the refinements of impression, that they, as they would have said, went in for. It was now as if, before this repast, Milly had designed to "lie down"; but at the end of three minutes more she was not lying down, she was saying instead, abruptly, with a transition that was like a jump of four thousand miles: "What was it that, in New York, on the ninth, when you saw him alone, Dr. Finch said to you?"

It was not till later that Mrs. Stringham fully knew why the question had startled her still more than its suddenness explained; though the effect of it even at the moment was almost to frighten her into a false answer. She had to think, to remember the occasion, the "ninth," in New York, the time she had seen Dr. Finch alone, and to recall what he had then said to her; and when everything had come back it was quite, at first, for a moment, as if he had said something that immensely mattered. He hadn't, however, in fact; it was only as if he might perhaps after all have been going to. It was on the sixth—within ten days of their sailing—that she had hurried from Boston under the alarm, a small but a sufficient shock, of hearing that Mildred had suddenly been taken ill, had had, from some obscure cause, such an upset as threatened to stay their journey. The bearing of the accident had happily soon announced itself as slight, and there had been, in the event, but a few hours of anxiety; the journey had been pronounced again not only possible, but, as representing "change," highly advisable; and if the zealous guest had had five minutes by herself with the doctor, that was, clearly, no more at his instance than at her own. Almost nothing had passed between them but an easy exchange of enthusiasms in respect to the remedial properties of "Europe"; and this assurance, as the facts came back to her, she was now able to give. "Nothing whatever, on my word of honour, that you mayn't know or mightn't then have known. I've no secret with him about you. What makes you suspect it? I don't quite make out how you know I did see him alone."

"No—you never told me," said Milly. "And I don't mean," she went on, "during the twenty-four hours while I was bad, when your putting your heads together was natural enough. I mean after I was better—the last thing before you went home."

Mrs. Stringham continued to wonder. "Who told you I saw him then?"

"*He* didn't himself—nor did you write me it afterwards. We speak of it now for the first time. That's exactly why!" Milly declared—with something in her face and voice that, the next moment, betrayed for her companion that she had really known nothing, had only conjectured and, chancing her charge, made a hit. Yet why had her mind been busy with the question? "But if you're not, as you now assure me, in his confidence," she smiled, "it's no matter."

"I'm not in his confidence, and he had nothing to confide. But are you feeling unwell?"

The elder woman was earnest for the truth, though the possibility she named was not at all the one that seemed to fit—witness the long climb Milly had just indulged in. The girl showed her constant white face, but that her friends had all learned to discount, and it was often brightest when superficially not bravest. She continued for a little mysteriously to smile. "I don't know—haven't really the least idea. But it might be well to find out."

Mrs. Stringham, at this, flared into sympathy. "Are you in trouble—in pain?"

"Not the least little bit. But I sometimes wonder——!"

"Yes"—she pressed: "wonder what?"

"Well, if I shall have much of it."

Mrs. Stringham stared. "Much of what? Not of pain?"

"Of everything. Of everything I have."

Anxiously again, tenderly, our friend cast about. "You 'have' everything; so that when you say 'much' of it——"

"I only mean," the girl broke in, "shall I have it for long? That is if I *have* got it."

She had at present the effect, a little, of confounding, or at least of perplexing her comrade, who was touched, who was always touched, by something helpless in her grace and abrupt in her turns, and yet actually half made out in her a sort of mocking light. "If you've got an ailment?"

"If I've got everything," Milly laughed.

"Ah, *that*—like almost nobody else."

"Then for how long?"

Mrs. Stringham's eyes entreated her; she had gone close to her, half enclosed her with urgent arms. "Do you want to see some one?" And then as the girl only met it with a slow headshake, though looking perhaps a shade more conscious: "We'll go straight to the best near doctor." This too, however, produced but a gaze of qualified assent and a silence, sweet and vague, that left everything open. Our friend decidedly lost herself. "Tell me, for God's sake, if you're in distress."

"I don't think I've really *everything,*" Milly said as if to explain—and as if also to put it pleasantly.

"But what on earth can I do for you?" The girl hesitated, then seemed on the point of being able to say; but suddenly changed and expressed herself otherwise. "Dear, dear thing—I'm only too happy!"

It brought them closer, but it rather confirmed Mrs. Stringham's doubt. "Then what's the matter?"

"That's the matter—that I can scarcely bear it."

"But what is it you think you haven't got?"

Milly waited another moment; then she found it, and found for it a dim show of joy. "The power to resist the bliss of what I *have!*"

Mrs. Stringham took it in—her sense of being "put off" with it, the possible, probable irony of it—and her tenderness renewed itself in the positive grimness of a long murmur. "Whom will you see?"—for it was as if they looked down from their height at a continent of doctors. "Where will you first go?"

Milly had for the third time her air of consideration; but she came back with it to her plea of some minutes before. "I'll tell you at supper—good-bye till then." And she left the room with a lightness that testified for her companion to something that again particularly pleased her in the renewed promise of motion. The odd passage just concluded, Mrs. Stringham mused as she once more sat alone with a hooked needle and a ball of silk, the "fine" work with which she was always provided—this mystifying mood had simply been precipitated, no doubt, by their prolonged halt, with which the girl hadn't really been in sympathy. One had only to admit that her complaint was in fact but the excess of the joy of life, and everything *did* then fit. She couldn't stop for the joy, but she could go on for it, and with the sense of going on she floated again, was restored to her great spaces. There was no evasion of any truth—so at least Susan Shepherd hoped—in one's sitting there while the twilight deepened and feeling still more finely that the position of this young lady was magnificent. The evening at that height had naturally turned to cold, and the travellers had bespoken a fire with their meal; the great Alpine road asserted its brave presence through the small panes of the low, clean windows, with incidents at the inn-door, the yellow *diligence,* the great waggons, the hurrying, hooded, private conveyances, reminders, for our fanciful friend, of old stories, old pictures, historic flights, escapes, pursuits, things that had happened, things indeed that by a sort of strange congruity helped her to read the meanings of the greatest interest into the relation in which she was now so deeply involved. It was natural that this record of the magnificence of her companion's position should strike her as, after all, the best meaning she could extract; for she herself was seated in the magnificence as in a court-carriage—she came back to that, and such a method of progression, such a view from crimson cushions, would evidently have a great deal more to give. By the time the candles were lighted for supper and the short, white curtains were drawn, Milly had reappeared, and the little scenic room had then all its romance. That charm moreover was far from broken by the words in which she, without further loss of time, satisfied her patient mate. "I want to go straight to London."

It was unexpected, corresponding with no view positively taken at their departure; when England had appeared, on the contrary, rather relegated and postponed—seen for the moment, as who should say, at the end of an avenue of preparations and introductions. London, in short, might have been supposed to be the crown, and to be achieved like a siege by gradual approaches. Milly's actual fine stride was therefore the more exciting, as any simplification almost always was to Mrs. Stringham; who, besides, was afterwards to recall as the very beginning of a drama the terms in which, between their smoky candles, the girl had put her preference and in which still other things had come up, come while the clank of waggon-chains in the sharp air reached their ears, with the stamp of hoofs, the rattle of buckets and the foreign questions, foreign answers, that were all alike a part of the cheery converse of the road. The girl brought it out in truth as she might have brought a huge confession, something she admitted herself shy about and that would seem to show her as frivolous; it had rolled over her that what she wanted of Europe was "people," so far as they were to be had, and that if her friend really wished to know, the vision of this same equivocal quantity was what had haunted her during their previous days, in museums and churches, and what was again spoiling for her the pure taste of scenery. She was all for scenery—yes; but she wanted it human and personal, and all she could say was that there would be in London—wouldn't there? more of that kind than anywhere else. She came back to her idea that if it wasn't for long—if nothing should happen to be so for *her*—why, the particular thing she spoke of would probably have most to give her in the time, would probably be less than anything else a waste of her remainder. She produced this last consideration indeed with such gaiety that Mrs. Stringham was not again disconcerted by it, was in fact quite ready—if talk of early dying was in order—to match it from her own future. Good, then; they would, eat and drink because of what might happen to-morrow; and they would direct their course from that moment with a view to such eating and drinking. They ate and drank that night, in truth, as if in the spirit of this decision; whereby the air, before they separated, felt itself the clearer.

It had cleared perhaps to a view only too extensive—extensive, that is, in proportion to the signs of life presented. The idea of "people" was not so entertained on Milly's part as to connect itself with particular persons, and the fact remained for each of the ladies that they would, completely unknown, disembark at Dover amid the completely unknowing. They had no relation already formed; this plea Mrs. Stringham put forward to see what it would produce. It produced nothing at first but the observation on the girl's side that what she had in mind was no thought of society nor of scraping acquaintance; nothing was further from her than to desire the opportunities represented for the compatriot in general by a trunkful of "letters." It wasn't a question, in short, of the people the compatriot was after; it was the human, the English picture itself, as they might see it in their own way—the world imagined always in what one had read and dreamed. Mrs. Stringham did every justice to this world, but when later on an occasion chanced to present itself, she made a point of not omitting to remark that it might be a comfort to know in advance even an individual. This still, however, failed in vulgar parlance, to "fetch" Milly, so that she had presently to go all the way. "Haven't I understood from you, for that matter, that you gave Mr. Densher something of a promise?"

There was a moment, on this, when Milly's look had to be taken as representing one of two things—either that she was completely vague about the promise or that Mr. Densher's name itself started no train. But she really couldn't be so vague about the promise, her interlocutress quickly saw, without attaching it to something; it had to be a promise to somebody in particular to be so repudiated. In the event, accordingly, she acknowledged Mr. Merton Densher, the so unusually clever young Englishman who had made his appearance in New York on some special literary business—wasn't it?—shortly before their departure, and who had been three or four times in her house during the brief period between her visit to Boston and her companion's subsequent stay with her; but she required much reminding before it came back to her that she had mentioned to this companion just afterwards the confidence expressed by the personage in question in her never doing so dire a thing as to come to London without, as the phrase was, looking a fellow up. She had left him the enjoyment of his confidence, the form of which might have appeared a trifle free—that she now reasserted; she had done nothing either to impair or to enhance it; but she had also left Mrs. Stringham, in the connection and at the time, rather sorry to have missed Mr. Densher. She had thought of him again after that, the elder woman; she had likewise gone so far as to notice that Milly appeared not to have done so—which the girl might easily have betrayed; and, interested as she was in everything that concerned her, she had made out for herself, for herself only and rather idly, that, but for interruptions, the young Englishman might have become a better acquaintance. His being an acquaintance at all was one of the signs that in the first days had helped to place Milly, as a young person with the world before her, for sympathy and wonder. Isolated, unmothered, unguarded, but with her other strong marks, her big house, her big fortune, her big freedom, she had lately begun to "receive," for all her few years, as an older woman might have done—as was done, precisely, by princesses who had public considerations to observe and who came of age very early. If it was thus distinct to Mrs. Stringham then that Mr. Densher had gone off somewhere else in connection with his errand before her visit to New York, it had been also not undiscoverable that he had come back for a day or two later on, that is after her own second excursion—that he had in fine reappeared on a single occasion on his way to the West: his way from Washington as she believed, though he was out of sight at the time of her joining her friend for their departure. It had not occurred to her before to exaggerate—it had not occurred to her that she could; but she seemed to become aware to-night that there had been just enough in this relation to meet, to provoke, the free conception of a little more.

She presently put it that, at any rate, promise or no promise, Milly would, at a pinch, be able, in London, to act on his permission to make him a sign; to which Milly replied with readiness that her ability, though evident, would be none the less quite wasted, inasmuch as the gentleman would, to a certainty, be still in America. He had a great deal to do there—which he would scarce have begun; and in fact she might very well not have thought of London at all if she hadn't been sure he wasn't yet near coming back. It was perceptible to her companion that the moment our young woman had so far committed herself she had a sense of having overstepped; which was not quite patched up by her saying the next minute, possibly with a certain failure of presence of mind, that the last thing she desired was the air of running after him. Mrs. Stringham wondered privately what question there could be of any such appearance—the danger of which thus suddenly came up; but she said, for the time, nothing of it—she only said other things: one of which was, for instance, that if Mr. Densher was away he was away, and that this was the end of it; also that of course they must be discreet at any price. But what was the measure of discretion, and how was one to be sure? So it was that, as they sat there, she produced her own case: *she* had a possible tie with London, which she desired as little to disown as she might wish to risk presuming on it. She treated her companion, in short, for their evening's end, to the story of Maud Manningham, the odd but interesting English girl who had formed her special affinity in the old days at the Vevey school; whom she had written to, after their separation, with a regularity that had at first faltered and then altogether failed, yet that had been for the time quite a fine case of crude constancy; so that it had in fact flickered up again of itself on the occasion of the marriage of each. They had then once more fondly, scrupulously written—Mrs. Lowder first; and even another letter or two had afterwards passed. This, however, had been the end—though with no rupture, only a gentle drop: Maud Manningham had made, she believed, a great marriage, while she herself had made a small; on top of which, moreover, distance, difference, diminished community and impossible reunion had done the rest of the work. It was but after all these years that reunion had begun to show as possible—if the other party to it, that is, should be still in existence. That was exactly what it now struck our friend as interesting to ascertain, as, with one aid and another, she believed she might. It was an experiment she would at all events now make if Milly didn't object.

Milly in general objected to nothing, and, though she asked a question or two, she raised no present plea. Her questions—or at least her own answers to them—kindled, on Mrs. Stringham's part, a backward train: she hadn't known till tonight how much she remembered, or how fine it might be to see what had become of large, high-coloured Maud, florid, exotic and alien—which had been just the spell—even to the perceptions of youth. There was the danger—she frankly touched it—that such a temperament mightn't have matured, with the years, all in the sense of fineness; it was the sort of danger that, in renewing relations after long breaks, one had always to look in the face. To gather in strayed threads was to take a risk—for which, however, she was prepared if Milly was. The possible "fun," she confessed, was by itself rather tempting; and she fairly sounded, with this—wound up a little as she was—the note of fun as the harmless final right of fifty years of mere New England virtue. Among the things she was afterwards to recall was the indescribable look dropped on her, at this, by her companion; she was still seated there between the candles and before the finished supper, while Milly moved about, and the look was long to figure for her as an inscrutable comment on *her* notion of freedom. Challenged, at any rate, as for the last wise word, Milly showed perhaps, musingly, charmingly, that, though her attention had been mainly soundless, her friend's story—produced as a resource unsuspected, a card from up the sleeve—half surprised, half beguiled her. Since the matter, such as it was, depended on that, she brought out, before she went to bed, an easy, a light "Risk everything!"

This quality in it seemed possibly a little to deny weight to Maud Lowder's evoked presence—as Susan Stringham, still sitting up, became, in excited reflection, a trifle more conscious. Something determinant, when the girl had left her, took place in her—nameless but, as soon as she had given way, coercive. It was as if she knew again, in this fulness of time, that she had been, after Maud's marriage, just sensibly outlived or, as people nowadays said, shunted. Mrs. Lowder had left her behind, and on the occasion, subsequently, of the corresponding date in her own life—not the second, the sad one, with its dignity of sadness, but the first, with the meagreness of its supposed felicity—she had been, in the same spirit, almost patronisingly pitied. If that suspicion, even when it had ceased to matter, had never quite died out for her, there was doubtless some oddity in its now offering itself as a link, rather than as another break, in the chain; and indeed there might well have been for her a mood in which the notion of the development of patronage in her quondam schoolmate would have settled her question in another sense. It was actually settled—if the case be worth our analysis—by the happy consummation, the poetic justice, the generous revenge, of her having at last something to show. Maud, on their parting company, had appeared to have so much, and would now—for wasn't it also, in general, quite the rich law of English life?—have, with accretions, promotions, expansions, ever so much more. Very good; such things might be; she rose to the sense of being ready for them. Whatever Mrs. Lowder might have to show—and one hoped one did the presumptions all justice—she would have nothing like Milly Theale, who constituted the trophy producible by poor Susan. Poor Susan lingered late—till the candles were low, and as soon as the table was cleared she opened her neat portfolio. She had not lost the old clue; there were connections she remembered, addresses she could try; so the thing was to begin. She wrote on the spot.

BOOK FOURTH

VII

It had all gone so fast after this that Milly uttered but the truth nearest to hand in saying to the gentleman on her right—who was, by the same token, the gentleman on her hostess's left—that she scarce even then knew where she was: the words marking her first full sense of a situation really romantic. They were already dining, she and her friend, at Lancaster Gate, and surrounded, as it seemed to her, with every English accessory; though her consciousness of Mrs. Lowder's existence, and still more of her remarkable identity, had been of so recent and so sudden a birth. Susie, as she was apt to call her companion for a lighter change, had only had to wave a neat little wand for the fairy-tale to begin at once; in consequence of which Susie now glittered—for, with Mrs. Stringham's new sense of success, it came to that—in the character of a fairy godmother. Milly had almost insisted on dressing her, for the present occasion, as one; and it was no fault of the girl's if the good lady had not now appeared in a peaked hat, a short petticoat and diamond shoe-buckles, brandishing the magic crutch. The good lady, in truth, bore herself not less contentedly than if these insignia had marked her work; and Milly's observation to Lord Mark had just been, doubtless, the result of such a light exchange of looks with her as even the great length of the table had not baffled. There were twenty persons between them, but this sustained passage was the sharpest sequel yet to that other comparison of views during the pause on the Swiss pass. It almost appeared to Milly that their fortune had been unduly precipitated—as if, properly, they were in the position of having ventured on a small joke and found the answer out of proportion grave. She could not at this moment, for instance, have said whether, with her quickened perceptions, she were more enlivened or oppressed; and the case might in fact have been serious had she not, by good fortune, from the moment the picture loomed, quickly made up her mind that what finally most concerned her was neither to seek nor to shirk, was not even to wonder too much, but was to let things come as they would, since there was little enough doubt of how they would go.

Lord Mark had been brought to her before dinner—not by Mrs. Lowder, but by the handsome girl, that lady's niece, who was now at the other end and on the same side as Susie; he had taken her in, and she meant presently to ask him about Miss Croy, the handsome girl, actually offered to her sight— though now in a splendid way—but for the second time. The first time had been the occasion—only three days before—of her calling at their hotel with her aunt and then making, for our other two heroines, a great impression of beauty and eminence. This impression had remained so with Milly that, at present, and although her attention was aware at the same time of everything else, her eyes were mainly engaged with Kate Croy when not engaged with Susie. That wonderful creature's eyes moreover readily met them—she ranked now as a wonderful creature; and it seemed a part of the swift prosperity of the American visitors that, so little in the original reckoning, she should yet appear conscious, charmingly, frankly conscious, of possibilities of friendship for them. Milly had easily and, as a guest, gracefully generalised: English girls had a special, strong beauty, and it particularly showed in evening dress— above all when, as was strikingly the case with this one, the dress itself was what it should be. That observation she had all ready for Lord Mark when they should, after a little, get round to it. She seemed even now to see that there might be a good deal they would get round to; the indication being that, taken up once for all with her other neighbour, their hostess would leave them much to themselves. Mrs. Lowder's other neighbour was the Bishop of Murrum—a real bishop, such as Milly had never seen, with a complicated costume, a voice like an old-fashioned wind instrument, and a face all the portrait of a prelate; while the gentleman on our young lady's left, a gentleman thick-necked, large and literal, who looked straight before him and as if he were not to be diverted by vain words from that pursuit, clearly counted as an offset to the possession of Lord Mark. As Milly made out these things— with a shade of exhilaration at the way she already fell in—she saw how she was justified of her plea for people and her love of life. It wasn't then, as the prospect seemed to show, so difficult to get into the current, or to stand, at any rate, on the bank. It was easy to get near—if they *were* near; and yet the elements were different enough from any of her old elements, and positively rich and strange.

She asked herself if her right-hand neighbour would understand what she meant by such a description of them, should she throw it off; but another of the things to which, precisely, her sense was awakened was that no, decidedly, he wouldn't. It was nevertheless by this time open to her that his line would be to be clever; and indeed, evidently, no little of the interest was going to be in the fresh reference and fresh effect both of people's cleverness and of their simplicity. She thrilled, she consciously flushed, and turned pale with the certitude—it had never been so present—that she should find herself completely involved: the very air of the place, the pitch of the occasion, had for her so positive a taste and so deep an undertone. The smallest things, the faces, the hands, the jewels of the women, the sound of words, especially of names, across the table, the shape of the forks, the arrangement of the flowers, the attitude of the servants, the walls of the room, were all touches in a picture and denotements in a play; and they marked for her, moreover, her alertness of vision. She had never, she might well believe, been in such a state of vibration; her sensibility was almost too sharp for her comfort: there were, for example, more indications than she could reduce to order in the manner of the friendly niece, who struck her as distinguished and interesting, as in fact surprisingly genial. This young woman's type had, visibly, other possibilities; yet here, of its own free movement, it had already sketched a relation. Were they, Miss Croy and she, to take up the tale where their two elders had left it off so many years before?—were they to find they liked each other and to try for themselves if a scheme of constancy on more modern lines could be worked? She had doubted, as they came to England, of Maud Manningham, had believed her a broken reed and a vague resource, had seen their dependence on her as a state of mind that would have been shamefully silly—so far as it *was* dependence—had they wished to do any thing so inane as "get into society." To have made their pilgrimage all for the sake of such society as

Mrs. Lowder might have in reserve for them—that didn't bear thinking of at all, and she herself had quite chosen her course for curiosity about other matters. She would have described this curiosity as a desire to see the places she had read about, and *that* description of her motive she was prepared to give her neighbour—even though, as a consequence of it, he should find how little she had read. It was almost at present as if her poor prevision had been rebuked by the majesty—she could scarcely call it less—of the event, or at all events by the commanding character of the two figures—she could scarcely call *that* less either—mainly presented. Mrs. Lowder and her niece, however dissimilar, had at least in common that each was a great reality. That was true, primarily, of the aunt—so true that Milly wondered how her own companion had arrived, in other days, at so odd an alliance; yet she none the less felt Mrs. Lowder as a person of whom the mind might in two or three days roughly make the circuit. She would sit there massive, at least, while one attempted it; whereas Miss Croy, the handsome girl, would indulge in incalculable movements that might interfere with one's tour. She was real, none the less, and everything and everybody were real; and it served them right, no doubt, the pair of them, for having rushed into their adventure.

Lord Mark's intelligence meanwhile, however, had met her own quite sufficiently to enable him to tell her how little he could clear up her situation. He explained, for that matter—or at least he hinted—that there was no such thing, to-day in London, as saying where any one was. Every one was everywhere—nobody was anywhere. He should be put to it—yes, frankly— to give a name of any sort or kind to their hostess's "set." *Was* it a set at all, or wasn't it, and were there not really no such things as sets, in the place, any more?—was there any thing but the senseless shifting tumble, like that of some great greasy sea in mid-Channel, of an overwhelming melted mixture? He threw out the question, which seemed large; Milly felt that at the end of five minutes he had thrown out a great many, though he followed none more than a step or two; perhaps he would prove suggestive, but he helped her as yet to no discriminations: he spoke as if he had given them up from too much knowledge. He was thus at the opposite extreme from herself, but, as a consequence of it, also wandering and lost; and he was furthermore, for all his temporary incoherence, to which she guessed there would be some key, as great a reality as either Mrs. Lowder or Kate. The only light in which he placed the former of these ladies was that of an extraordinary woman—a most extraordinary woman, and "the more extraordinary the more one knows her," while of the latter he said nothing, for the moment, but that she was tremendously, yes, quite tremendously, good-looking. It was some time, she thought, before his talk showed his cleverness, and yet each minute she believed in it more, quite apart from what her hostess had told her on first naming him. Perhaps he was one of the cases she had heard of at home— those characteristic cases of people in England who concealed their play of mind so much more than they showed it. Even Mr. Densher a little did that. And what made Lord Mark, at any rate, so real either, when this was a thing he so definitely insisted on? His type some how, as by a life, a need, an intention of its own, insisted *for* him; but that was all. It was difficult to guess his age—whether he were a young man who looked old or an old man who looked young; it seemed to prove nothing, as against other things, that he was bald and, as might have been said, slightly stale, or, more delicately perhaps, dry: there was such a fine little fidget of preoccupied life in him, and his eyes, at moments—though it was an appearance they could suddenly lose—were as candid and clear as those of a pleasant boy. Very neat, very light, and so fair that there was little other indication of his moustache than his constantly feeling it—which was again boyish—he would have affected her as the most intellectual person present if he had not affected her as the most frivolous. The latter quality was rather in his look than in anything else, though he constantly wore his double eyeglass, which was, much more, Bostonian and thoughtful.

The idea of his frivolity had, no doubt, to do with his personal designation, which represented—as yet, for our young woman, a little confusedly—a connection with an historic patriciate, a class that, in turn, also confusedly, represented an affinity with a social element that she had never heard otherwise described than as "fashion." The supreme social element in New York had never known itself but as reduced to that category, and though Milly was aware that, as applied to a territorial and political aristocracy, the label was probably too simple, she had for the time none other at hand. She presently, it is true, enriched her idea with the perception that her interlocutor was indifferent; yet this, indifferent as aristocracies notoriously were, saw her but little further, inasmuch as she felt that, in the first place, he would much rather get on with her than not, and in the second was only thinking of too many matters of his own. If he kept her in view on the one hand and kept so much else on the other—the way he crumbed up his bread was a proof—why did he hover before her as a potentially insolent noble? She couldn't have answered the question, and it was precisely one of those that swarmed. They were complicated, she might fairly have said, by his visibly knowing, having known from afar off, that she was a stranger and an American, and by his none the less making no more of it than if she and her like were the chief of his diet. He took her, kindly enough, but imperturbably, irreclaimably, for granted, and it wouldn't in the least help that she herself knew him, as quickly, for having been in her country and threshed it out. There would be nothing for her to explain or attenuate or brag about; she could neither escape nor prevail by her strangeness; he would have, for that matter, on such a subject, more to tell her than to learn from her. She might learn from *him* why she was so different from the handsome girl—which she didn't know, being merely able to feel it; or at any rate might learn from him why the handsome girl was so different from her.

On these lines, however, they would move later; the lines immediately laid down were, in spite of his vagueness for his own convenience, definite enough. She was already, he observed to her, thinking what she should say on her other side—which was what Americans were always doing. She needn't in conscience say anything at all; but Americans never knew that, nor ever, poor creatures, yes (*she* had interposed the "poor creatures!") what not to do. The burdens they took on—the things, positively, they made an affair of! This easy and, after all, friendly jibe at her race was really for her, on her new friend's part, the note of personal recognition so far as she required it; and she gave him a prompt and conscious example of morbid anxiety by insisting that her desire to be, herself, "lovely" all round was justly founded on the lovely way Mrs. Lowder had met her. He was directly interested in that, and it was not till afterwards that she fully knew how much more information about their friend he had taken than given. Here again, for instance, was a pertinent note for her: she had, on the spot, with her first plunge into the obscure depths of a society constituted from far back, encountered the interesting phenomenon of complicated, of possibly sinister motive. However, Maud Manningham (her name, even in her presence, somehow still fed the fancy) *had,* all the same, been lovely, and one was going to meet her now quite as far on as one had one's self been met. She had been with them at their hotel—they were a pair—before even they had supposed she could have got their letter. Of course indeed they had written in advance, but they had followed that up very fast. She had thus engaged them to dine but two days later, and on the morrow again, without waiting for a return visit, waiting for anything, she had called with her niece. It was as if she really cared for them, and it was magnificent fidelity—fidelity to Mrs. Stringham, her own companion and Mrs. Lowder's former schoolmate, the lady with the charming face and the rather high dress down there at the end.

Lord Mark took in through his nippers these balanced attributes of Susie. "But isn't Mrs. Stringham's fidelity then equally magnificent?"

"Well, it's a beautiful sentiment; but it isn't as if she had anything to *give.*"

"Hasn't she got you?" Lord Mark presently asked.

"Me—to give Mrs. Lowder?" Milly had clearly not yet seen herself in the light of such an offering. "Oh, I'm rather a poor present; and I don't feel as if, even at that, I've as yet quite been given."

"You've been shown, and if our friend has jumped at you it comes to the same thing." He made his jokes, Lord Mark, without amusement for himself; yet it wasn't that he was grim. "To be seen you must recognise, *is,* for you, to be jumped at; and, if it's a question of being shown, here you are again. Only it has now been taken out of your friend's hands; it's Mrs. Lowder, already, who's getting the benefit. Look round the table and you'll make out, I think, that you're being, from top to bottom, jumped at."

"Well, then," said Milly, "I seem also to feel that I like it better than being made fun of."

It was one of the things she afterwards saw—Milly was for ever seeing things afterwards—that her companion had here had some way of his own, quite unlike any one's else, of assuring her of his consideration. She wondered how he had done it, for he had neither apologised nor protested. She said to herself, at any rate, that he had led her on; and what was most odd was the question by which he had done so. "Does she know much about you?"

"No, she just likes us."

Even for this his travelled lordship, seasoned and saturated, had no laugh. "I mean *you* particularly. Has that lady with the charming face, which *is* charming, told her?"

Milly hesitated. "Told her what?"

"Everything."

This, with the way he dropped it, again considerably moved her—made her feel for a moment that, as a matter of course, she was a subject for disclosures. But she quickly found her answer. "Oh, as for that, you must ask *her.*"

"Your clever companion?"

"Mrs. Lowder."

He replied to this that their hostess was a person with whom there were certain liberties one never took, but that he was none the less fairly upheld, inasmuch as she was for the most part kind to him and as, should he be very good for a while, she would probably herself tell him. "And I shall have, at any rate, in the meantime, the interest of seeing what she does with you. That will teach me more or less, you see, how much she knows."

Milly followed this—it was lucid; but it suggested something apart. "How much does she know about *you?*"

"Nothing," said Lord Mark serenely. "But that doesn't matter—for what she does with me." And then, as to anticipate Milly's question about the nature of such doing: "This, for instance—turning me straight on for *you.*"

The girl thought. "And you mean she wouldn't if she did know——?"

He met it as if it were really a point. "No. I believe, to do her justice, she still would. So you can be easy."

Milly had the next instant, then, acted on the permission. "Because you're even at the worst the best thing she has?"

With this he was at last amused. "I was till you came. You're the best now."

It was strange his words should have given her the sense of his knowing, but it was positive that they did so, and to the extent of making her believe them, though still with wonder. That, really, from this first of their meetings, was what was most to abide with her: she accepted almost helplessly, she surrendered to the inevitability of being the sort of thing, as he might have said, that he at least thoroughly believed he had, in going about, seen here enough of for all practical purposes. Her submission was naturally, moreover, not to be impaired by her learning later on that he had paid at short intervals, though at a time apparently just previous to her own emergence from the obscurity of extreme youth, three separate visits to New York, where his nameable friends and his contrasted contacts had been numerous. His impression, his recollection of the whole mixed quantity, was still visibly rich. It had helped him to place her, and she was more and more sharply conscious of having—as with the door sharply slammed upon her and the guard's hand raised in signal to the train—been popped into the compartment in which she was to travel for him. It was a use of her that many a girl would have been doubtless quick to resent; and the kind of mind that thus, in our young lady, made all for mere seeing and taking is precisely one of the charms of our subject. Milly had practically just learned from him, had made out, as it were, from her rumbling compartment, that he gave her the highest place among their friend's actual properties. She was a success, that was what it came to, he presently assured her, and that was what it was to be a success: it always happened before one could know it. One's ignorance was in fact often the greatest part of it. "You haven't had time yet," he said; "this is nothing. But you'll see. You'll see everything. You can, you know—everything you dream of."

He made her more and more wonder; she almost felt as if he were showing her visions while he spoke; and strangely enough, though it was visions that had drawn her on, she hadn't seen them in connection—that is in such preliminary and necessary connection—with such a face as Lord Mark's, such eyes and such a voice, such a tone and such a manner. He had for an instant the effect of making her ask herself if she were after all going to be afraid; so distinct was it for fifty seconds that a fear passed over her. There they were again—yes, certainly: Susie's overture to Mrs. Lowder had been their joke, but they had pressed in that gaiety an electric bell that continued to sound. Positively, while she sat there, she had the loud rattle in her ears, and she wondered, during these moments, why the others didn't hear it. They didn't stare, they didn't smile, and the fear in her that I speak of was but her own desire to stop it. That dropped, however, as if the alarm itself had ceased; she seemed to have seen in a quick, though tempered glare that there were two courses for her, one to leave London again the first thing in the morning, the other to do nothing at all. Well, she would do nothing at all; she was already doing it; more than that, she had already done it, and her chance was gone. She gave herself up—she had the strangest sense, on the spot, of so deciding; for she had turned a corner before she went on again with Lord Mark. Inexpressive, but intensely significant, he met as no one else could have done the very question she had suddenly put to Mrs. Stringham on the Brünig. Should she have it, whatever she did have, that question had been, for long? "Ah, so possibly not," her neighbour appeared to reply; "therefore, don't you see? *I'm* the way." It was vivid that he might be, in spite of his absence of flourish; the way being doubtless just *in* that absence. The handsome girl, whom she didn't lose sight of and who, she felt, kept her also in view—Mrs. Lowder's striking niece would, perhaps, be the way as well, for in her too was the absence of flourish, though she had little else, so far as one could tell, in common with Lord Mark. Yet how indeed *could* one tell, what did one understand, and of what was one, for that matter, provisionally conscious but of their being somehow together in what they represented? Kate Croy, fine but friendly, looked over at her as really with a guess at Lord Mark's effect on her. If she could guess this effect what then did she know about it and in what degree had she felt it herself? Did that represent, as between them, anything particular, and should she have to count with them as duplicating, as intensifying by a mutual intelligence, the relation into which she was sinking? Nothing was so odd as that she should have to recognise so quickly in each of these glimpses of an instant the various signs of a relation; and this anomaly itself, had she had more time to give to it, might well, might almost terribly have suggested to her that her doom was to live fast. It was queerly a question of the short run and the consciousness proportionately crowded.

These were immense excursions for the spirit of a young person at Mrs. Lowder's mere dinner-party; but what was so significant and so admonitory as the fact of their being possible? What could they have been but just a part, already, of the crowded consciousness? And it was just a part, likewise, that while plates were changed and dishes presented and periods in the banquet marked; while appearances insisted and phenomena multiplied and words reached her from here and there like plashes of a slow, thick tide; while Mrs. Lowder grew somehow more stout and more instituted and Susie, at her distance and in comparison, more thinly improvised and more different— different, that is, from every one and everything: it was just a part that while this process went forward our young lady alighted, came back, taking up her destiny again as if she had been able by a wave or two of her wings to place herself briefly in sight of an alternative to it. Whatever it was it had showed in this brief interval as better than the alternative; and it now presented itself altogether in the image and in the place in which she had left it. The image was that of her being, as Lord Mark had declared, a success. This depended more or less of course on his idea of the thing—into which at present, however, she wouldn't go. But, renewing soon, she had asked him what he meant then that Mrs. Lowder would do with her, and he had replied that this might safely be left. "She'll get back," he pleasantly said, "her money." He could say it too—which was singular—without affecting her either as vulgar or as "nasty "; and he had soon explained himself by adding: "Nobody here, you know, does anything for nothing."

"Ah, if you mean that we shall reward her as hard as ever we can, nothing is more certain. But she's an idealist," Milly continued, "and idealists, in the long run, I think, *don't* feel that they lose."

Lord Mark seemed, within the limits of his enthusiasm, to find this charming. "Ah, she strikes you as an idealist?"

"She idealises *us,* my friend and me, absolutely. She sees us in a light," said Milly. "That's all I've got to hold on by. So don't deprive me of it."

"I wouldn't for the world. But do you think," he continued as if it were suddenly important for him—"do you think she sees *me* in a light?"

She neglected his question for a little, partly because her attention attached itself more and more to the handsome girl, partly because, placed so near their hostess, she wished not to show as discussing her too freely. Mrs. Lowder, it was true, steering in the other quarter a course in which she called at subjects as if they were islets in an archipelago, continued to allow them their ease, and Kate Croy, at the same time, steadily revealed herself as interesting. Milly in fact found, of a sudden, her ease—found it all—as she bethought herself that what Mrs. Lowder was really arranging for was a report on her quality and, as perhaps might be said, her value from Lord Mark. She wished him, the wonderful lady, to have no pretext for not knowing what he thought of Miss Theale. Why his judgment so mattered remained to be seen; but it was this divination, in any case, that now determined Milly's rejoinder. "No. She knows you. She has probably reason to. And you all, here, know each other—I see that—so far as you know anything. You know what you're used to, and it's your being used to it—that, and that only—that makes you. But there are things you don't know."

He took it in as if it might fairly, to do him justice, be a point. "Things that *I* don't—with all the pains I take and the way I've run about the world to leave nothing unlearned?"

Milly thought, and it was perhaps the very truth of his claim—its not being negligible—that sharpened her impatience and thereby her wit. "You're *blasé*, but you're not enlightened. You're familiar with everything, but conscious, really of nothing. What I mean is that you've no imagination."

Lord Mark, at this, threw back his head, ranging with his eyes the opposite side of the room and showing himself at last so much more completely as diverted that it fairly attracted their hostess's notice. Mrs. Lowder, however, only smiled on Milly for a sign that something racy was what she had expected, and resumed, with a splash of her screw, her cruise among the islands. "Oh, I've heard that," the young man replied, "before!"

"There it is then. You've heard everything before. You've heard *me* of course before, in my country, often enough."

"Oh, never too often," he protested; "I'm sure I hope I shall still hear you again and again."

"But what good then has it done you?" the girl went on as if now frankly to amuse him.

"Oh, you'll see when you know me."

"But, most assuredly, I shall never know you."

"Then that will be exactly," he laughed, "the good!"

If it established thus that they couldn't, or Wouldn't, mix, why, none the less, did Milly feel, through it, a perverse quickening of the relation to which she had been, in spite of herself, appointed?

What queerer consequence of their not mixing than their talking—for it was what they had arrived at—almost intimately? She wished to get away from him, or indeed, much rather, away from herself so far as she was present to him. She saw already—wonderful creature, after all, herself too—that there would be a good deal more of him to come for her, and that the special sign of their intercourse would be to keep herself out of the question. Everything else might come in—only never that; and with such an arrangement they might even go far. This in fact might quite have begun, on the spot, with her returning again to the topic of the handsome girl. If she was to keep herself out she could naturally best do so by putting in somebody else. She accordingly put in Kate Croy, being ready to that extent—as she was not at all afraid for her—to sacrifice her if necessary. Lord Mark himself, for that matter, had made it easy by saying a little while before that no one among them did anything for nothing. "What then"—she was aware of being abrupt—"does Miss Croy, if she's so interested, do it for? What has she to gain by *her* lovely welcome? Look at her *now!*" Milly broke out with characteristic freedom of praise, though pulling herself up also with a compunctious "Oh!" as the direction thus given to their eyes happened to coincide with a turn of Kate's face to them. All she had meant to do was to insist that this face was fine; but what she had in fact done was to renew again her effect of showing herself to its possessor as conjoined with Lord Mark for some interested view of it. He had, however, promptly met her question.

"To gain? Why, your acquaintance."

"Well, what's my acquaintance to her? She can care for me—she must feel that—only by being sorry for me; and that's why she's lovely: to be already willing to take the trouble to be. It's the height of the disinterested."

There were more things in this than one that Lord Mark might have taken up; but in a minute he had made his choice. "Ah then, I'm nowhere, for I'm afraid *I'm* not sorry for you in the least. What do you make then," he asked, "of your success?"

"Why, just the great reason of all. It's just because our friend there sees it that she pities me. She understands," Milly said; "she's better than any of you. She's beautiful."

He appeared struck with this at last—with the point the girl made of it; to which she came back even after a diversion created by a dish presented between them. "Beautiful in character, I see. *Is* she so? You must tell me about her."

Milly wondered. "But haven't you known her longer than I? Haven't you seen her for yourself?"

"No—I've failed with her. It's no use. I don't make her out. And I assure you I really should like to." His assurance had in fact for his companion a positive suggestion of sincerity; he affected her as now saying something that he felt; and she was the more struck with it as she was still conscious of the failure even of curiosity he had just shown in respect to herself. She had meant something—though indeed for herself almost only—in speaking of their friend's natural pity; it had been a note, doubtless, of questionable taste, but it had quavered out in spite of her; and he had not so much as cared to inquire "Why 'natural'?" Not that it wasn't really much better for her that he shouldn't: explanations would in truth have taken her much too far. Only she now perceived that, in comparison, her word about this other person really "drew" him; and there were things in that, probably, many things, as to which she would learn more and which glimmered there already as part and parcel of that larger "real" with which, in her new situation, she was to be beguiled. It was in fact at the very moment, this element, not absent from what Lord Mark was further saying. "So you're wrong, you see, as to our knowing all about each other. There are cases where we break down. I at any rate give *her* up—up, that is, to you. You must do her for me—tell me, I mean, when you know more. You'll notice," he pleasantly wound up, "that I've confidence in you."

"Why shouldn't you have?" Milly asked, observing in this, as she thought, a fine, though, for such a man, a surprisingly artless, fatuity. It was as if there might have been a question of her falsifying for the sake of her own show— that is of her honesty not being proof against her desire to keep well with him herself. She didn't, none the less, otherwise protest against his remark; there was something else she was occupied in seeing. It was the handsome girl alone, one of his own species and his own society, who had made him feel uncertain; of his certainties about a mere little American, a cheap exotic, imported almost wholesale, and whose habitat, with its conditions of climate, growth, and cultivation, its immense profusion, but its few varieties and thin development, he was perfectly satisfied. The marvel was, too, that Milly understood his satisfaction—feeling that she expressed the truth in presently saying: "Of course; I make out that she must be difficult; just as I see that I myself must be easy." And that was what, for all the rest of this occasion, remained with her—as the most interesting thing that could remain. She was more and more content herself to be easy; she would have been resigned, even had it been brought straighter home to her, to passing for a cheap exotic. Provisionally, at any rate, that protected her wish to keep herself, with Lord Mark, in abeyance. They *had* all affected her as inevitably knowing each other, and if the handsome girl's place among them was something even their initiation couldn't deal with—why, then, she would indeed be a quantity.

VIII

That sense of quantities, separate or mixed, was indeed doubtless what most prevailed at first for our slightly gasping American pair; it found utterance for them in their frequent remark to each other that they had no one but themselves to thank. It dropped from Milly more than once that if she had ever known it was so easy—! though her exclamation mostly ended without completing her idea. This, however, was a trifle to Mrs. Stringham, who cared little whether she meant that in this case she would have come sooner. She couldn't have come sooner, and she perhaps, on the contrary, meant—for it would have been like her—that she wouldn't have come at all; why it was so easy being at any rate a matter as to which her companion had begun quickly to pick up views. Susie kept some of these lights for the present to herself, since, freely communicated, they might have been a little disturbing; with which, moreover, the quantities that we speak of as surrounding the two ladies were, in many cases, quantities of things—and of other things—to talk about. Their immediate lesson, accordingly, was that they just had been caught up by the incalculable strength of a wave that was actually holding them aloft and that would naturally dash them wherever it liked. They meanwhile, we hasten to add, make the best of their precarious position, and if Milly had had no other help for it she would have found not a little in the sight of Susan Shepherd's state. The girl had had nothing to say to her, for three days, about the "success" announced by Lord Mark—which they saw, besides, otherwise established; she was too taken up, too touched, by Susie's own exaltation. Susie glowed in the light of her justified faith; everything had happened that she had been acute enough to think least probable; she had appealed to a possible delicacy in Maud Manningham—a delicacy, mind you, but *barely* possible—and her appeal had been met in a way that was an honour to human nature. This proved sensibility of the lady of Lancaster Gate performed verily, for both our friends, during these first days, the office of a fine floating gold-dust, something that threw over the prospect a harmonising blur. The forms, the colours behind it were strong and deep—we have seen how they already stood out for Milly; but nothing, comparatively, had had so much of the dignity of truth as the fact of Maud's fidelity to a sentiment. That was what Susie was proud of, much more than of her great place in the world, which she was moreover conscious of not as yet wholly measuring. That was what was more vivid even than her being—in senses more worldly and in fact almost in the degree of a revelation—English and distinct and positive, with almost no inward, but with the finest outward resonance.

Susan Shepherd's word for her, again and again, was that she was "large"; yet it was not exactly a case, as to the soul, of echoing chambers: she might have been likened rather to a capacious receptacle, originally perhaps loose, but now drawn as tightly as possible over its accumulated contents—a packed mass, for her American admirer, of curious detail. When the latter good lady, at home, had handsomely figured her friends as not small—which was the way she mostly figured them—there was a certain implication that they were spacious because they were empty. Mrs. Lowder, by a different law, was spacious because she was full, because she had something in common, even in repose, with a projectile, of great size, loaded and ready for use. That indeed, to Susie's romantic mind, announced itself as half the charm of their renewal—a charm as of sitting in springtime, during a long peace, on the daisied, grassy bank of some great slumbering fortress. True to her psychological instincts, certainly, Mrs. Stringham had noted that the "sentiment" she rejoiced in on her old schoolmate's part was all a matter of action and movement, was not, save for the interweaving of a more frequent plump "dearest" than she would herself perhaps have used, a matter of much other embroidery. She brooded, with interest, on this further remark of race, feeling in her own spirit a different economy. The joy, for her, was to know *why* she acted—the reason was half the business; whereas with Mrs. Lowder there might have been no reason: "why" was the trivial seasoning-substance, the vanilla or the nutmeg, omittable from the nutritive pudding without spoiling it. Mrs. Lowder's desire was clearly sharp that their young companions should also prosper together; and Mrs. Stringham's account of it all to Milly, during the first days, was that when, at Lancaster Gate, she was not occupied in telling, as it were, about her, she was occupied in hearing much of the history of her hostess's brilliant niece.

They had plenty, on these lines, the two elder women, to give and to take, and it was even not quite clear to the pilgrim from Boston that what she should mainly have arranged for in London was not a series of thrills for herself. She had a bad conscience, indeed almost a sense of immorality, in having to recognise that she was, as she said, carried away. She laughed to Milly when she also said that she didn't know where it would end; and the principal of her uneasiness was that Mrs. Lowder's life bristled for her with elements that she was really having to look at for the first time. They represented, she believed, the world, the world that, as a consequence of the cold shoulder turned to it by the Pilgrim Fathers, had never yet boldly crossed to Boston— it would surely have sunk the stoutest Cunarder—and she couldn't pretend that she faced the prospect simply because Milly had had a caprice. She was in the act herself of having one, directed precisely to their present spectacle. She could but seek strength in the thought that she had never had one—or had never yielded to one, which came to the same thing—before. The sustaining sense of it all, moreover, as literary material—that quite dropped from her. She must wait, at any rate, she should see: it struck her, so far as she had got, as vast, obscure, lurid. She reflected in the watches of the night that she was probably just going to love it for itself—that is for itself and Milly. The odd thing was that she could think of Milly's loving it without dread—or with dread, at least not on the score of conscience, only on the score of peace. It was a mercy, at all events, for the hour, that their fancies jumped together.

While, for this first week that followed their dinner, she drank deep at Lancaster Gate, her companion was no less happily, appeared to be indeed on the whole quite as romantically, provided for. The handsome English girl from the heavy English house had been as a figure in a picture stepping by magic out of its frame: it was a case, in truth, for which Mrs. Stringham presently found the perfect image. She had lost none of her grasp, but quite the contrary, of that other conceit in virtue of which Milly was the wandering princess: so what could be more in harmony now than to see the princess waited upon at the city gate by the worthiest maiden, the chosen daughter of the burgesses? It was the real again, evidently, the amusement of the meeting for the princess too; princesses living for the most part, in such an appeased way, on the plane of mere elegant representation. That was why they pounced, at city gates, on deputed flower-strewing damsels; that was why, after effigies, processions, and other stately games, frank human company was pleasant to them. Kate Croy really presented herself to Milly—the latter abounded for Mrs. Stringham in accounts of it—as the wondrous London girl in person, by what she had conceived, from far back, of the London girl; conceived from the tales of travellers and the anecdotes of New York, from old porings over *Punch* and a liberal acquaintance with the fiction of the day. The only thing was that she was nicer, for the creature in question had rather been, to our young woman, an image of dread. She had thought of her, at her best, as handsome just as Kate was, with turns of head and tones of voice, felicities of stature and attitude, things "put on" and, for that matter, put off, all the marks of the product of a packed society who should be at the same time the heroine of a strong story. She placed this striking young person from the first in a story, saw her, by a necessity of the imagination, for a heroine, felt it the only character in which she wouldn't be wasted; and this in spite of the heroine's pleasant abruptness, her forbearance from gush, her umbrellas and jackets and shoes—as these things sketched themselves to Milly—and something rather of a breezy boy in the carriage of her arms and the occasional freedom of her slang.

When Milly had settled that the extent of her goodwill itself made her shy, she had found for the moment quite a sufficient key, and they were by that time thoroughly afloat together. This might well have been the happiest hour they were to know, attacking in friendly independence their great London— the London of shops and streets and suburbs oddly interesting to Milly, as well as of museums, monuments, "sights" oddly unfamiliar to Kate, while their elders pursued a separate course, both rejoicing in their intimacy and each thinking the other's young woman a great acquisition for her own. Milly expressed to Susan Shepherd more than once that Kate had some secret, some smothered trouble, besides all the rest of her history; and that if she had so good-naturedly helped Mrs. Lowder to meet them this was exactly to create a diversion, to give herself something else to think about. But on the case thus postulated our young American had as yet had no light: she only felt that when the light should come it would greatly deepen the colour; and she liked to think she was prepared for anything. What she already knew, moreover, was full to her vision, of English, of eccentric, of Thackerayan character, Kate Croy having gradually become not a little explicit on the subject of her situation, her past, her present, her general predicament, her small success, up to the present hour, in contenting at the same time her father, her sister, her aunt and herself. It was Milly's subtle guess, imparted to her Susie, that the girl had somebody else as well, as yet unnamed, to content, it being manifest that such a creature couldn't help having; a creature not perhaps, if one would, exactly formed to inspire passions, since that always implied a certain silliness, but essentially seen, by the admiring eye of friendship, under the clear shadow of some probably eminent male interest. The clear shadow, from whatever source projected, hung, at any rate, over Milly's companion the whole week, and Kate Croy's handsome face smiled out of it, under bland skylights, in the presence alike of old masters passive in their glory and of thoroughly new ones, the newest, who bristled restlessly with pins and brandished snipping shears.

It was meanwhile a pretty part of the intercourse of these young ladies that each thought the other more remarkable than herself—that each thought herself, or assured the other she did, a comparatively dusty object and the other a favourite of nature and of fortune. Kate was amused, amazed at the way her friend insisted on "taking" her, and Milly wondered if Kate were sincere in finding her the most extraordinary—quite apart from her being the most charming—person she had come across. They had talked, in long drives, and quantities of history had not been wanting—in the light of which Mrs. Lowder's niece might superficially seem to have had the best of the argument. Her visitor's American references, with their bewildering immensities, their confounding moneyed New York, their excitements of high pressure, their opportunities of wild freedom, their record of used-up relatives, parents, clever, eager, fair, slim brothers—these the most loved—all engaged, as well as successive superseded guardians, in a high extravagance of speculation and dissipation that had left this exquisite being her black dress, her white face and her vivid hair as the mere last broken link: such a picture quite threw into the shade the brief biography, however sketchily amplified, of a mere middle-class nobody in Bayswater. And though that indeed might be but a Bayswater way of putting it, in addition to which Milly was in the stage of interest in Bayswater ways, this critic so far prevailed that, like Mrs. Stringham herself, she fairly got her companion to accept from her that she was quite the nearest approach to a practical princess Bayswater could hope ever to know. It was a fact—it became one at the end of three days—that Milly actually began to borrow from the handsome girl a sort of view of her state; the handsome girl's impression of it was clearly so sincere. This impression was a tribute, a tribute positively to power, power the source of which was the last thing Kate treated as a mystery. There were passages, under all their skylights, the succession of their shops being large, in which the latter's easy, yet the least bit dry manner sufficiently gave out that if she had had so deep a pocket——!

It was not moreover by any means with not having the imagination of expenditure that she appeared to charge her friend, but with not having the imagination of terror, of thrift, the imagination or in any degree the habit of a conscious dependence on others. Such moments, when all Wigmore Street, for instance, seemed to rustle about and the pale girl herself to be facing the different rustlers, usually so undiscriminated, as individual Britons too, Britons personal, parties to a relation and perhaps even intrinsically remarkable—such moments in especial determined in Kate a perception of the high happiness of her companion's liberty. Milly's range was thus immense; she had to ask nobody for anything, to refer nothing to any one; her freedom, her fortune and her fancy were her law; an obsequious world surrounded her, she could sniff up at every step its fumes. And Kate, in these days, was altogether in the phase of forgiving her so much bliss; in the phase moreover of believing that, should they continue to go on together, she would abide in that generosity. She had, at such a point as this, no suspicion of a rift within the lute—by which we mean not only none of anything's coming between them, but none of any definite flaw in so much clearness of quality. Yet, all the same, if Milly, at Mrs. Lowder's banquet, had described herself to Lord Mark as kindly used by the young woman on the other side because of some faintly-felt special propriety in it, so there really did match with this, privately, on the young woman's part, a feeling not analysed but divided, a latent impression that Mildred Theale was not, after all, a person to change places, to change even chances with. Kate, verily, would perhaps not quite have known what she meant by this reservation, and she came near naming it only when she said to herself that, rich as Milly was, one probably wouldn't—which was singular—ever hate her for it. The handsome girl had, with herself, these felicities and crudities: it wasn't obscure to her that, without some very particular reason to help, it might have proved a test of one's philosophy not to be irritated by a mistress of millions, or whatever they were, who, as a girl, so easily might have been, like herself, only vague and fatally female. She was by no means sure of liking Aunt Maud as much as she deserved, and Aunt Maud's command of funds was obviously inferior to Milly's. There was thus clearly, as pleading for the latter, some influence that would later on become distinct; and meanwhile, decidedly, it was enough that she was as charming as she was queer and as queer as she was charming—all of which was a rare amusement; as well, for that matter, as further sufficient that there were objects of value she had already pressed on Kate's acceptance. A week of her society in these conditions—conditions that Milly chose to sum up as ministering immensely, for a blind, vague pilgrim, to aid and comfort—announced itself from an early hour as likely to become a week of presents, acknowledgments, mementos, pledges of gratitude and admiration that were all on one side. Kate as promptly embraced the propriety of making it clear that she must forswear shops till she should receive some guarantee that the contents of each one she entered as a humble companion should not be placed at her feet; yet that was in truth not before she had found herself in possession, under whatever protests, of several precious ornaments and other minor conveniences.

Great was the absurdity, too, that there should have come a day, by the end of the week, when it appeared that all Milly would have asked in definite "return," as might be said, was to be told a little about Lord Mark and to be promised the privilege of a visit to Mrs. Condrip. Far other amusements had been offered her, but her eagerness was shamelessly human, and she seemed really to count more on the revelation of the anxious lady of Chelsea than on the best nights of the opera. Kate admired, and showed it, such an absence of fear: to the fear of being bored, in such a connection, she would have been so obviously entitled. Milly's answer to this was the plea of her curiosities— which left her friend wondering as to their odd direction. Some among them, no doubt, were rather more intelligible, and Kate had heard without wonder that she was blank about Lord Mark. This young lady's account of him, at the same time, professed itself as frankly imperfect; for what they best knew him by at Lancaster Gate was a thing difficult to explain. One knew people in general by something they had to show, something that, either for them or against, could be touched or named or proved; and she could think of no other case of a value taken as so great and yet flourishing untested. His value was his future, which had somehow got itself as accepted by Aunt Maud as if it had been his good cook or his steam-launch. She, Kate, didn't mean she thought him a humbug; he might do great things—but they were all, as yet, so to speak, he had done. On the other hand it was of course something of an achievement, and not open to every one, to have got one's self taken so seriously by Aunt Maud. The best thing about him, doubtless, on the whole, was that Aunt Maud believed in him. She was often fantastic, but she knew a humbug, and—no, Lord Mark wasn't that. He had been a short time in the House, on the Tory side, but had lost his seat on the first opportunity, and this was all he had to point to. However, he pointed to nothing; which was very possibly just a sign of his real cleverness, one of those that the really clever had in common with the really void. Even Aunt Maud frequently admitted that there was a good deal, for her view of him, to come up in the rear. And he wasn't meanwhile himself indifferent—indifferent to himself—for he was working Lancaster Gate for all it was worth: just as it was, no doubt, working *him,* and just as the working and the worked were in London, as one might explain, the parties to every relation.

Kate did explain, for her listening friend: every one who had anything to give—it was true they were the fewest—made the sharpest possible bargain for it, got at least its value in return. The strangest thing, furthermore, was that this might be, in cases, a happy understanding. The worker in one connection was the worked in another; it was as broad as it was long—with the wheels of the system, as might be seen, wonderfully oiled. People could quite like each other in the midst of it, as Aunt Maud, by every appearance, quite liked Lord Mark, and as Lord Mark, it was to be hoped, liked Mrs. Lowder, since if he didn't he was a greater brute than one could believe. She, Kate, had not yet, it was true, made out what he was doing for her—besides which the dear woman needed him, even at the most he could do, much less than she imagined; so far as all of which went, moreover, there were plenty of things on every side she had not yet made out. She believed, on the whole, in any one Aunt Maud took up; and she gave it to Milly as worth thinking of that, whatever wonderful people this young lady might meet in the land, she would meet no more extraordinary woman. There were greater celebrities by the million, and of course greater swells, but a bigger *person,* by Kate's view, and a larger natural handful every way, would really be far to seek. When Milly inquired with interest if Kate's belief in *her* was primarily on the lines of what Mrs. Lowder "took up," her interlocutress could handsomely say yes, since by the same principle she believed in herself. Whom but Aunt Maud's niece, pre-eminently, had Aunt Maud taken up, and who was thus more in the current, with her, of working and of being worked? "You may ask," Kate said, "what in the world I have to give; and that indeed is just what I'm trying to learn. There must be something, for her to think she can get it out of me. She *will* get it—trust her; and then I shall see what it is; which I beg you to believe I should never have found out for myself." She declined to treat any question of Milly's own "paying" power as discussable; that Milly would pay a hundred per cent.—and even to the end, doubtless, through the nose—was just the beautiful basis on which they found themselves.

These were fine facilities, pleasantries, ironies, all these luxuries of gossip and philosophies of London and of life, and they became quickly, between the pair, the common form of talk, Milly professing herself delighted to know that something was to be done with her. If the most remarkable woman in England was to do it, so much the better, and if the most remarkable woman in England had them both in hand together, why, what could be jollier for each? When she reflected indeed a little on the oddity of her wanting two at once, Kate had the natural reply that it was exactly what showed her sincerity. She invariably gave way to feeling, and feeling had distinctly popped up in her on the advent of her girlhood's friend. The way the cat would jump was always, in presence of anything that moved her, interesting to see; visibly enough, moreover, for a long time, it hadn't jumped anything like so far. This, in fact, as we already know, remained the marvel for Milly Theale, who, on sight of Mrs. Lowder, found fifty links in respect to Susie absent from the chain of association. She knew so herself what she thought of Susie that she would have expected the lady of Lancaster Gate to think something quite different; the failure of which endlessly mystified her. But her mystification was the cause for her of another fine impression, inasmuch as when she went so far as to observe to Kate that Susan Shepherd—and especially Susan Shepherd emerging so uninvited from an irrelevant past—ought, by all the proprieties, simply to have bored Aunt Maud, her confidant agreed with her without a protest and abounded in the sense of her wonder. Susan Shepherd at least bored the niece—that was plain; this young woman saw nothing in her—nothing to account for anything, not even for Milly's own indulgence: which little fact became in turn to the latter's mind a fact of significance. It was a light on the handsome girl—representing more than merely showed— that poor Susie was simply as nought to her. This was, in a manner too, a general admonition to poor Susie's companion, who seemed to see marked by it the direction in which she had best most look out.

It just faintly rankled in her that a person who was good enough and to spare for Milly Theale shouldn't be good enough for another girl; though, oddly enough, she could easily have forgiven Mrs. Lowder herself the impatience. Mrs. Lowder didn't feel it, and Kate Croy felt it with ease; yet in the end, be it added, she grasped the reason, and the reason enriched her mind. Wasn't it sufficiently the reason that the handsome girl was, with twenty other splendid qualities, the least bit brutal too, and didn't she suggest, as no one yet had ever done for her new friend, that there might be a wild beauty in that, and even a strange grace? Kate wasn't brutally brutal—which Milly had hitherto benightedly supposed the only way; she wasn't even aggressively so, but rather indifferently, defensively and, as might be said, by the habit of anticipation. She simplified in advance, was beforehand with her doubts, and knew with singular quickness what she wasn't, as they said in New York, going to like. In that way at least people were clearly quicker in England than at home; and Milly could quite see, after a little, how such instincts might become usual in a world in which dangers abounded. There were more dangers, clearly, round about Lancaster Gate than one suspected in New York or could dream of in Boston. At all events, with more sense of them, there were more precautions, and it was a remarkable world altogether in which there could be precautions, on whatever ground, against Susie.

IX

She certainly made up with Susie directly, however, for any allowance she might have had privately to extend to tepid appreciation; since the late and long talks of these two embraced not only everything offered and suggested by the hours they spent apart, but a good deal more besides. She might be as detached as the occasion required at four o'clock in the afternoon, but she used no such freedom to any one about anything as she habitually used about everything to Susan Shepherd at midnight. All the same, it should with much less delay than this have been mentioned, she had not yet—had not, that is, at the end of six days—produced any news for her comrade to compare with an announcement made her by the latter as a result of a drive with Mrs. Lowder, for a change, in the remarkable Battersea Park. The elder friends had sociably revolved there while the younger ones followed bolder fancies in the admirable equipage appointed to Milly at the hotel—a heavier, more emblazoned, more amusing chariot than she had ever, with "stables" notoriously mismanaged, known at home; whereby, in the course of the circuit, more than once repeated, it had "come out," as Mrs. Stringham said, that the couple at Lancaster Gate were, of all people, acquainted with Mildred's other English friend—the gentleman, the one connected with the English newspaper (Susie hung fire a little over his name) who had been with her in New York so shortly previous to present adventures. He had been named of course in Battersea Park—else he couldn't have been identified; and Susie had naturally, before she could produce her own share in the matter as a kind of confession, to make it plain that her allusion was to Mr. Merton Densher. This was because Milly had at first a little air of not knowing whom she meant; and the girl really kept, as well, a certain control of herself while she remarked that the case was surprising, the chance one in a thousand. They knew him, both Maud and Miss Croy knew him, she gathered too, rather well, though indeed it was not on any show of intimacy that he had happened to be mentioned. It had not been—Susie made the point—she herself who brought him in: he had in fact not been brought in at all, but only referred to as a young journalist known to Mrs. Lowder and who had lately gone to their wonderful country—Mrs. Lowder always said "your wonderful country"— on behalf of his journal. But Mrs. Stringham had taken it up—with the tips of her fingers indeed; and that was the confession: she had, without meaning any harm, recognised Mr. Densher as an acquaintance of Milly's, though she had also pulled herself up before getting in too far. Mrs. Lowder had been struck, clearly—it wasn't too much to say; then she also, it had rather seemed, had pulled herself up; and there had been a little moment during which each might have been keeping something from the other. "Only," said Milly's mate, "I luckily remembered in time that I had nothing whatever to keep—which was much simpler and nicer. I don't know what Maud has, but there it is. She was interested, distinctly, in your knowing him—in his having met you over there with so little loss of time. But I ventured to tell her it hadn't been so long as to make you as yet great friends. I don't know if I was right."

Whatever time this explanation might have taken, there had been moments enough in the matter now—before the elder woman's conscience had done itself justice—to enable Milly to reply that although the fact in question doubtless had its importance she imagined they wouldn't find the importance overwhelming. It *was* odd that their one Englishman should so instantly fit; it wasn't, however, miraculous—they surely all had often seen that, as every one said, the world was extraordinarily "small." Undoubtedly, too, Susie had done just the plain thing in not letting his name pass. Why in the world should there be a mystery?—and what an immense one they would appear to have made if he should come back and find they had concealed their knowledge of him! "I don't know, Susie dear," the girl observed, "what you think I have to conceal."

"It doesn't matter, at a given moment," Mrs. Stringham returned, "what you know or don't know as to what I think; for you always find out the very next moment, and when you do find out, dearest, you never *really* care. Only," she presently asked, "have you heard of him from Miss Croy?"

"Heard of Mr. Densher? Never a word. We haven't mentioned him. Why should we?"

"That *you* haven't, I understand; but that she hasn't," Susie opined, "may mean something."

"May mean what?"

"Well," Mrs. Stringham presently brought out, "I tell you all when I tell you that Maud asks me to suggest to you that it may perhaps be better for the present not to speak of him: not to speak of him to her niece, that is, unless she herself speaks to you first. But Maud thinks she won't."

Milly was ready to engage for anything; but in respect to the facts—as they so far possessed them—it all sounded a little complicated. "Is it because there's anything between them?"

"No—I gather not; but Maud's state of mind is precautionary. She's afraid of something. Or perhaps it would be more correct to say she's afraid of everything."

"She's afraid, you mean," Milly asked, "of their—a—liking each other?"

Susie had an intense thought and then an effusion. "My dear child, we move in a labyrinth."

"Of course we do. That's just the fun of it!" said Milly with a strange gaiety. Then she added: "Don't tell me that—in this for instance—there are not abysses. I want abysses."

Her friend looked at her—it was not unfrequently the case—a little harder than the surface of the occasion seemed to require; and another person present at such times might have wondered to what inner thought of her own the good lady was trying to fit the speech. It was too much her disposition, no doubt, to treat her young companion's words as symptoms of an imputed malady. It was none the less, however, her highest law to be light when the girl was light. She knew how to be quaint with the new quaintness—the great Boston gift; it had been, happily, her note in the magazines; and Maud Lowder, to whom it was new indeed and who had never heard anything remotely like it, quite cherished her, as a social resource, for it. It should not therefore fail her now; with it in fact one might face most things. "Ah, then let us hope we shall sound the depths—I'm prepared for the worst—of sorrow and sin! But she would like her niece—we're not ignorant of that, are we?—to marry Lord Mark. Hasn't she told you so?"

"Hasn't Mrs. Lowder told me?"

"No; hasn't Kate? It isn't, you know, that she doesn't know it."

Milly had, under her comrade's eyes, a minute of mute detachment. She had lived with Kate Croy for several days in a state of intimacy as deep as it had been sudden, and they had clearly, in talk, in many directions, proceeded to various extremities. Yet it now came over her as in a clear cold way that there was a possible account of their relations in which the quantity her new friend had told her might have figured as small, as smallest, beside the quantity she hadn't. She couldn't say, at any rate, whether or no she had made the point that her aunt designed her for Lord Mark: it had only sufficiently come out—which had been, moreover, eminently guessable—that she was involved in her aunt's designs. Somehow, for Milly, brush it over nervously as she might and with whatever simplifying hand, this abrupt extrusion of Mr. Densher altered all proportions, had an effect on all values. It was fantastic of her to let it make a difference that she couldn't in the least have defined—and she was at least, even during these instants, rather proud of being able to hide, on the spot, the difference it did make. Yet, all the same, the effect for her was, almost violently, of Mr. Densher's having been there—having been where she had stood till now in her simplicity—before her. It would have taken but another free moment to make her see abysses—since abysses were what she wanted—in the mere circumstance of his own silence, in New York, about his English friends. There had really been in New York little time for anything; but, had she liked, Milly could have made it out for herself that he had avoided the subject of Miss Croy, and that Miss Croy was yet a subject it could never be natural to avoid. It was to be added at the same time that even if his silence had been labyrinthe—which was absurd in view of all the other things too he couldn't possibly have spoken of—this was exactly what must suit her, since it fell under the head of the plea she had just uttered to Susie. These things, however, came and went, and it set itself up between the companions, for the occasion, in the oddest way, both that their happening all to know Mr. Densher—except indeed that Susie didn't, but probably would,—was a fact belonging, in a world of rushing about, to one of the common orders of chance; and yet further that it was amusing—oh, awfully amusing!—to be able fondly to hope that there was "something in" its having been left to crop up with such suddenness. There seemed somehow a possibility that the ground or, as it were, the air might, in a manner, have undergone some pleasing preparation; though the question of this possibility would probably, after all, have taken some threshing out. The truth, moreover—and there they were, already, our pair, talking about it, the "truth!"—had not in fact quite cropped out. This, obviously, in view of Mrs. Lowder's request to her old friend.

It was accordingly on Mrs. Lowder's recommendation that nothing should be said to Kate—it was on this rich attitude of Aunt Maud's that the idea of an interesting complication might best hope to perch; and when, in fact, after the colloquy we have reported Milly saw Kate again without mentioning any name, her silence succeeded in passing muster with her as the beginning of a new sort of fun. The sort was all the newer by reason of its containing a small element of anxiety: when she had gone in for fun before it had been with her hands a little more free. Yet it *was,* none the less, rather exciting to be conscious of a still sharper reason for interest in the handsome girl, as Kate continued, even now, pre-eminently to remain for her; and a reason—this was the great point—of which the young woman herself could have no suspicion. Twice over, thus, for two or three hours together, Milly found herself seeing Kate, quite fixing her in the light of the knowledge that it was a face on which Mr. Densher's eyes had more or less familiarly rested and which, by the same token, had looked, rather *more* beautifully than less, into his own. She pulled herself up indeed with the thought that it had inevitably looked, as beautifully as one would, into thousands of faces in which one might one's self never trace it; but just the odd result of the thought was to intensify for the girl that side of her friend which she had doubtless already been more prepared than she quite knew to think of as the "other," the not wholly calculable. It was fantastic, and Milly was aware of this; but the other side was what had, of a sudden, been turned straight towards her by the show of Mr. Densher's propinquity. She hadn't the excuse of knowing it for Kate's own, since nothing whatever as yet proved it particularly to be such. Never mind; it was with this other side now fully presented that Kate came and went, kissed her for greeting and for parting, talked, as usual, of everything but—as it had so abruptly become for Milly—*the* thing. Our young woman, it is true, would doubtless not have tasted so sharply a difference in this pair of occasions had she not been tasting so peculiarly her own possible betrayals. What happened was that afterwards, on separation, she wondered if the matter had not mainly been that she herself was so "other," so taken up with the unspoken; the strangest thing of all being, still subsequently, that when she asked herself how Kate could have failed to feel it she became conscious of being here on the edge of a great darkness. She should never know how Kate truly felt about anything such a one as Milly Theale should give her to feel. Kate would never—and not from ill-will, nor from duplicity, but from a sort of failure of common terms—reduce it to such a one's comprehension or put it within her convenience.

It was as such a one, therefore, that, for three or four days more, Milly watched Kate as just such another; and it was presently as such a one that she threw herself into their promised visit, at last achieved, to Chelsea, the quarter of the famous Carlyle, the field of exercise of his ghost, his votaries, and the residence of "poor Marian," so often referred to and actually a somewhat incongruous spirit there. With our young woman's first view of poor Marian everything gave way but the sense of how, in England, apparently, the social situation of sisters could be opposed, how common ground, for a place in the world, could quite fail them: a state of things sagely perceived to be involved in an hierarchical, an aristocratic order. Just whereabouts in the order Mrs. Lowder had established her niece was a question not wholly void, as yet, no doubt, of ambiguity—though Milly was withal sure Lord Mark could exactly have fixed the point if he would, fixing it at the same time for Aunt Maud herself; but it was clear that Mrs. Condrip was, as might have been said, in quite another geography. She would not, in short, have been to be found on the same social map, and it was as if her visitors had turned over page after page together before the final relief of their benevolent "Here!" The interval was bridged, of course, but the bridge, verily, was needed, and the impression left Milly to wonder whether, in the general connection, it were of bridges or of intervals that the spirit not locally disciplined would find itself most conscious. It was as if at home, by contrast, there were neither—neither the difference itself, from position to position, nor, on either side, and particularly on one, the awfully good manner, the conscious sinking of a consciousness, that made up for it. The conscious sinking, at all events, and the awfully good manner, the difference, the bridge, the interval, the skipped leaves of the social atlas—these, it was to be confessed, had a little, for our young lady, in default of stouter stuff, to work themselves into the light literary legend—a mixed, wandering echo of Trollope, of Thackeray, perhaps mostly of Dickens—under favour of which her pilgrimage had so much appealed. She could relate to Susie later on, late the same evening, that the legend, before she had done with it, had run clear, that the adored author of *The Newcomes*, in fine, had been on the whole the note: the picture lacking thus more than she had hoped, or rather perhaps showing less than she had feared, a certain possibility of Pickwickian outline. She explained how she meant by this that Mrs. Condrip had not altogether proved another Mrs. Nickleby, nor even—for she might have proved almost anything, from the way poor worried Kate had spoken—a widowed and aggravated Mrs. Micawber.

Mrs. Stringham, in the midnight conference, intimated rather yearningly that, however the event might have turned, the side of English life such experiences opened to Milly were just those she herself seemed "booked"—as they were all, roundabout her now, always saying—to miss: she had begun to have a little, for her fellow-observer, these moments of fanciful reaction—reaction in which she was once more all Susan Shepherd—against the high sphere of colder conventions into which her overwhelming connection with Maud Manningham had rapt her. Milly never lost sight, for long, of the Susan Shepherd side of her, and was always there to meet it when it came up and vaguely, tenderly, impatiently to pat it, abounding in the assurance that they would still provide for it. They had, however, to-night, another matter in hand; which proved to be presently, on the girl's part, in respect to her hour of Chelsea, the revelation that Mrs. Condrip, taking a few minutes when Kate was away with one of the children, in bed upstairs for some small complaint, had suddenly, without its being in the least "led up to," broken ground on the subject of Mr. Densher, mentioned him with impatience as a person in love with her sister. "She wished me, if I cared for Kate, to know," Milly said—"for it would be quite too dreadful, and one might do something."

Susie wondered. "Prevent anything coming of it? That's easily said. Do what?"

Milly had a dim smile. "I think that what she would like is that I should come a good deal to see her about it."

"And doesn't she suppose you've anything else to do?"

The girl had by this time clearly made it out. "Nothing but to admire and make much of her sister—whom she doesn't, however, herself in the least understand—and give up one's time, and everything else, to it." It struck the elder friend that she spoke with an almost unprecedented approach to sharpness; as if Mrs. Condrip had been rather specially disconcerting. Never yet so much as just of late had Mrs. Stringham seen her companion as exalted, and by the very play of something within, into a vague golden air that left irritation below. That was the great thing with Milly—it was her characteristic poetry; or at least it was Susan Shepherd's. "But she made a point," the former continued, "of my keeping what she says from Kate. I'm not to mention that she has spoken."

"And why," Mrs. Stringham presently asked, "is Mr. Densher so dreadful?"

Milly had, she thought, an hesitation—something that suggested a fuller talk with Mrs. Condrip than she inclined perhaps to report. "It isn't so much he himself." Then the girl spoke a little as for the romance of it; one could never tell, with her, where romance would come in. "It's the state of his fortunes."

"And is that very bad?"

"He has no 'private means,' and no prospect of any. He has no income, and no ability, according to Mrs. Condrip, to make one. He's as poor, she calls it, as 'poverty,' and she says she knows what that is."

Again Mrs. Stringham considered, and it presently produced something. "But isn't he brilliantly clever?"

Milly had also then an instant that was not quite fruitless. "I haven't the least idea."

To which, for the time, Susie only answered "Oh!"—though by the end of a minute she had followed it with a slightly musing "I see"; and that in turn with: "It's quite what Maud Lowder thinks."

"That he'll never do anything?"

"No—quite the contrary: that he's exceptionally able."

"Oh yes; I know"—Milly had again, in reference to what her friend had already told her of this, her little tone of a moment before. "But Mrs. Condrip's own great point is that Aunt Maud herself won't hear of any such person. Mr. Densher, she holds that's the way, at any rate, it was explained to me—won't ever be either a public man or a rich man. If he were public she'd be willing, as I understand, to help him; if he were rich—without being anything else—she'd do her best to swallow him. As it is, she taboos him."

"In short," said Mrs. Stringham as with a private purpose, "she told you, the sister, all about it. But Mrs. Lowder likes him," she added.

"Mrs. Condrip didn't tell me that."

"Well, she does, all the same, my dear, extremely."

"Then there it is!" On which, with a drop and one of those sudden, slightly sighing surrenders to a vague reflux and a general fatigue that had recently more than once marked themselves for her companion, Milly turned away. Yet the matter was not left so, that night, between them, albeit neither perhaps could afterwards have said which had first come back to it. Milly's own nearest approach, at least, for a little, to doing so, was to remark that they appeared all—every one they saw—to think tremendously of money. This prompted in Susie a laugh, not untender, the innocent meaning of which was that it came, as a subject for indifference, money did, easier to some people than to others: she made the point in fairness, however, that you couldn't have told, by any too crude transparency of air, what place it held for Maud Manningham. She did her worldliness with grand proper silences—if it mightn't better be put perhaps that she did her detachment with grand occasional pushes. However Susie put it, in truth, she was really, in justice to herself, thinking of the difference, as favourites of fortune, between her old friend and her new. Aunt Maud sat somehow in the midst of her money, founded on it and surrounded by it, even if with a clever high manner about it, her manner of looking, hard and bright, as if it weren't there. Milly, about hers, had no manner at all—which was possibly, from a point of view, a fault: she was at any rate far away on the edge of it, and you hadn't, as might be said, in order to get at her nature, to traverse, by whatever avenue, any piece of her property. It was clear, on the other hand, that Mrs. Lowder was keeping her wealth as for purposes, imaginations, ambitions, that would figure as large, as honourably unselfish, on the day they should take effect. She would impose her will, but her will would be only that a person or two shouldn't lose a benefit by not submitting if they could be made to submit. To Milly, as so much younger, such far views couldn't be imputed: there was nobody she was supposable as interested for. It was too soon, since she wasn't interested for herself. Even the richest woman, at her age, lacked motive, and Milly's motive doubtless had plenty of time to arrive. She was meanwhile beautiful, simple, sublime without it—whether missing it and vaguely reaching out for it or not; and with it, for that matter, in the event, would really be these things just as much. Only then she might very well have, like Aunt Maud, a manner. Such were the connections, at all events, in which the colloquy of our two ladies freshly flickered up—in which it came round that the elder asked the younger if she had herself, in the afternoon, named Mr. Densher as an acquaintance.

"Oh no—I said nothing of having seen him. I remembered," the girl explained, "Mrs. Lowder's wish."

"But that," her friend observed after a moment, "was for silence to Kate."

"Yes—but Mrs. Condrip would immediately have told Kate."

"Why so?—since she must dislike to talk about him."

"Mrs. Condrip must?" Milly thought. "What she would like most is that her sister should be brought to think ill of him; and if anything she can tell her will help that—" But Milly dropped suddenly here, as if her companion would see.

Her companion's interest, however, was all for what she herself saw. "You mean she'll immediately speak?" Mrs. Stringham gathered that this was what Milly meant, but it left still a question. "How will it be against him that you know him?"

"Oh, I don't know. It won't be so much one's knowing him as one's having kept it out of sight."

"Ah," said Mrs. Stringham, as if for comfort, "*you* haven't kept it out of sight. Isn't it much rather Miss Croy herself who has?"

"It isn't my acquaintance with him," Milly smiled, "that she has dissimulated."

"She has dissimulated only her own? Well then, the responsibility's hers."

"Ah but," said the girl, not perhaps with marked consequence, "she has a right to do as she likes."

"Then so, my dear, have you!" smiled Susan Shepherd.

Milly looked at her as if she were almost venerably simple, but also as if this were what one loved her for. "We're not quarrelling about it, Kate and I, *yet.*"

"I only meant," Mrs. Stringham explained, "that I don't see what Mrs. Condrip would gain."

"By her being able to tell Kate?" Milly thought. "I only meant that I don't see what I myself should gain."

"But it will have to come out—that he knows you both—some time."

Milly scarce assented. "Do you mean when he comes back?"

"He'll find you both here, and he can hardly be looked to, I take it, to 'cut' either of you for the sake of the other."

This placed the question at last on a basis more distinctly cheerful. "I might get at him somehow beforehand," the girl suggested; "I might give him what they call here the tip—that he's not to know me when we meet. Or, better still, I mightn't be here at all."

"Do you want to run away from him?"

It was, oddly enough, an idea Milly seemed half to accept. "I don't know *what* I want to run away from!"

It dispelled, on the spot—something, to the elder woman's ear, in the sad, sweet sound of it—any ghost of any need of explaining. The sense was constant for her that their relation was as if afloat, like some island of the south, in a great warm sea that made, for every conceivable chance, a margin, an outer sphere of general emotion; and the effect of the occurrence of anything in particular was to make the sea submerge the island, the margin flood the text. The great wave now for a moment swept over. "I'll go anywhere else in the world you like."

But Milly came up through it. "Dear old Susie—how I do work you!"

"Oh, this is nothing yet."

"No indeed—to what it will be."

"You're not—and it's vain to pretend," said dear old Susie, who had been taking her in, "as sound and strong as I insist on having you."

"Insist, insist—the more the better. But the day I *look* as sound and strong as that, you know," Milly went on—"on that day I shall be just sound and strong enough to take leave of you sweetly for ever. That's where one is," she continued thus agreeably to embroider, "when even one's *most* 'beaux moments' aren't such as to qualify, so far as appearance goes, for anything gayer than a handsome cemetery. Since I've lived all these years as if I were dead, I shall die, no doubt, as if I were alive—which will happen to be as you want me. So, you see," she wound up, "you'll never really know where I am. Except indeed when I'm gone; and then you'll only know where I'm not."

"I'd die *for* you," said Susan Shepherd after a moment.

"'Thanks awfully'! Then stay here for me."

"But we can't be in London for August, nor for many of all these next weeks."

"Then we'll go back."

Susie blenched. "Back to America?"

"No, abroad—to Switzerland, Italy, anywhere. I mean by your staying here for me," Milly pursued, "your staying with me wherever I may be, even though we may neither of us know at the time where it is. No," she insisted,

"I *don't* know where I am, and you never will, and it doesn't matter—and I dare say it's quite true," she broke off, "that everything will have to come out." Her friend would have felt of her that she joked about it now, had not her scale from grave to gay been a thing of such unnamable shades that her contrasts were never sharp. She made up for failures of gravity by failures of mirth; if she hadn't, that is, been at times as earnest as might have been liked, so she was certain not to be at other times as easy as she would like herself. "I must face the music. It isn't, at any rate, its 'coming out,'" she added; "it's that Mrs. Condrip would put the fact before her to his injury."

Her companion wondered. "But how to *his?*"

"Why, if he pretends to love her——!"

"And does he only 'pretend'?"

"I mean if, trusted by her in strange countries, he forgets her so far as to make up to other people."

The amendment, however, brought Susie in, as if with gaiety, for a comfortable end. "Did he make up, the false creature, to *you?*"

"No—but the question isn't of that. It's of what Kate might be made to believe."

"That, given the fact that he evidently more or less followed up his acquaintance with you, to say nothing of your obvious weird charm, he must have been all ready if you had at all led him on?"

Milly neither accepted nor qualified this; she only said, after a moment, as with a conscious excess of the pensive: "No, I don't think she'd quite wish to suggest that I made up to *him;* for that I should have had to do so would only bring out his constancy. All I mean is," she added—and now at last, as with a supreme impatience "that her being able to make him out a little a person who could give cause for jealousy would evidently help her, since she's afraid of him, to do him in her sister's mind a useful ill turn."

Susan Shepherd perceived in this explanation such signs of an appetite for motive as would have sat gracefully even on one of her own New England heroines. It was seeing round several corners; but that was what New England heroines did, and it was moreover interesting for the moment to make out how many really her young friend had undertaken to see round. Finally, too, weren't they braving the deeps? They got their amusement where they could. "Isn't it only," she asked, "rather probable she'd see that Kate's knowing him as (what's the pretty old word?) *volage*——?"

"Well?" She hadn't filled out her idea, but neither, it seemed, could Milly.

"Well, might but do what that often does—by all *our* blessed little laws and arrangements at least; excite Kate's own sentiment instead of depressing it."

The idea was bright, yet the girl but beautifully stared. "Kate's own sentiment? Oh, she didn't speak of that. I don't think," she added as if she had been unconsciously giving a wrong impression, "I don't think Mrs. Condrip imagines *she's* in love."

It made Mrs. Stringham stare in turn. "Then what's her fear?"

"Well, only the fact of Mr. Densher's possibly himself keeping it up—the fear of some final result from *that*."

"Oh," said Susie, intellectually a little disconcerted—"she looks far ahead!"

At this, however, Milly threw off another of her sudden vague "sports." "No—it's only we who do."

"Well, don't let us be more interested for them than they are for themselves!"

"Certainly not"—the girl promptly assented. A certain interest nevertheless remained; she appeared to wish to be clear. "It wasn't of anything on Kate's own part she spoke."

"You mean she thinks her sister does *not* care for him?"

It was still as if, for an instant, Milly had to be sure of what she meant; but there it presently was. "If she did care Mrs. Condrip would have told me."

What Susan Shepherd seemed hereupon for a little to wonder was why then they had been talking so. "But did you ask her?"

"Ah, no!"

"Oh!" said Susan Shepherd.

Milly, however, easily explained that she wouldn't have asked her for the world.

BOOK FIFTH

X

Lord Mark looked at her to-day in particular as if to wring from her a confession that she had originally done him injustice; and he was entitled to whatever there might be in it of advantage or merit that his intention really in a manner took effect: he cared about something, that is, after all, sufficiently to make her feel absurdly as if she *were* confessing—all the while it was quite the case that neither justice nor injustice was what had been in question between them. He had presented himself at the hotel, had found her and had found Susan Shepherd at home, had been "civil" to Susan—it was just that shade, and Susan's fancy had fondly caught it; and then had come again and missed them, and then had come and found them once more: besides letting them easily see that if it hadn't by this time been the end of everything—which they could feel in the exhausted air, that of the season at its last gasp—the places they might have liked to go to were such as they would have had only to mention. Their feeling was—or at any rate their modest general plea—that there was no place they would have liked to go to; there was only the sense of finding they liked, wherever they were, the place to which they had been brought. Such was highly the case as to their current consciousness—which could be indeed, in an equally eminent degree, but a matter of course; impressions this afternoon having by a happy turn of their wheel been gathered for them into a splendid cluster, an offering like an armful of the rarest flowers. They were in presence of the offering—they had been led up to it; and if it had been still their habit to look at each other across distances for increase of unanimity his hand would have been silently named between them as the hand applied to the wheel. He had administered the touch that, under light analysis, made the difference—the difference of their not having lost, as Susie on the spot and at the hour phrased it again and again, both for herself and for such others as the question might concern, so beautiful and interesting an experience; the difference also, in fact, of Mrs. Lowder's not having lost it either, though it was with Mrs. Lowder, superficially, they had come, and though it was further with that lady that our young woman was directly engaged during the half-hour or so of her most agreeably inward response to the scene.

The great historic house had, for Milly, beyond terrace and garden, as the centre of an almost extravagantly grand Watteau-composition, a tone as of old gold kept "down" by the quality of the air, summer full-flushed, but attuned to the general perfect taste. Much, by her measure, for the previous hour, appeared, in connection with this revelation of it, to have happened to her—a quantity expressed in introductions of charming new people, in walks through halls of armour, of pictures, of cabinets, of tapestry, of tea-tables, in an assault of reminders that this largeness of style was the sign of *appointed* felicity. The largeness of style was the great containing vessel, while everything else, the pleasant personal affluence, the easy, murmurous welcome, the honoured age of illustrious host and hostess, all at once so distinguished and so plain, so public and so shy, became but this or that element of the infusion. The elements melted together and seasoned the draught, the essence of which might have struck the girl as distilled into the small cup of iced coffee she had vaguely accepted from somebody, while a fuller flood, somehow, kept bearing her up—all the freshness of response of her young life the freshness of the first and only prime. What had perhaps brought on just now a kind of climax was the fact of her appearing to make out, through Aunt Maud, what was really the matter. It couldn't be less than a climax for a poor shaky maiden to find it put to her of a sudden that she herself was the matter—for that was positively what, on Mrs. Lowder's part, it came to. Everything was great, of course, in great pictures, and it was doubtless precisely a part of the brilliant life—since the brilliant life, as one had faintly figured it, clearly *was* humanly led—that all impressions within its area partook of its brilliancy; still, letting that pass, it fairly stamped an hour as with the official seal for one to be able to take in so comfortably one's companion's broad blandness. "You must stay among us—you must stay;

anything else is impossible and ridiculous; you don't know yet, no doubt—you can't; but you will soon enough: you can stay in *any* position." It had been as the murmurous consecration to follow the murmurous welcome; and even if it were but part of Aunt Maud's own spiritual ebriety—for the dear woman, one could see, was spiritually "keeping" the day—it served to Milly, then and afterwards, as a high-water mark of the imagination.

It was to be the end of the short parenthesis which had begun but the other day at Lancaster Gate with Lord Mark's informing her that she was a "success"—the key thus again struck; and though no distinct, no numbered revelations had crowded in, there had, as we have seen, been plenty of incident for the space and the time. There had been thrice as much, and all gratuitous and genial—if, in portions, not exactly hitherto *the* revelation—as three unprepared weeks could have been expected to produce. Mrs. Lowder had improvised a "rush" for them, but out of elements, as Milly was now a little more freely aware, somewhat roughly combined. Therefore if at this very instant she had her reasons for thinking of the parenthesis as about to close—reasons completely personal—she had on behalf of her companion a divination almost as deep. The parenthesis would close with this admirable picture, but the admirable picture still would show Aunt Maud as not absolutely sure either if she herself were destined to remain in it. What she was doing, Milly might even not have escaped seeming to see, was to talk herself into a sublimer serenity while she ostensibly talked Milly. It was fine, the girl fully felt, the way she did talk *her*, little as, at bottom, our young woman needed it or found other persuasions at fault. It was in particular during the minutes of her grateful absorption of iced coffee—qualified by a sharp doubt of her wisdom—that she most had in view Lord Mark's relation to her being there, or at least to the question of her being amused at it. It wouldn't have taken much by the end of five minutes quite to make her feel that this relation was charming. It might, once more, simply have been that everything, anything, was charming when one was so justly and completely charmed; but, frankly, she had not supposed anything so serenely sociable could define itself between them as the friendly understanding that was at present somehow in the air. They were, many of them together, near the marquee that had been erected on a stretch of sward as a temple of refreshment and that happened to have the property—which was all to the good of making Milly think of a "durbar"; her iced coffee had been a consequence of this connection, in which, further, the bright company scattered about fell thoroughly into place. Certain of its members might have represented the contingent of "native princes"—familiar, but scarce the less grandly gregarious term!—and Lord Mark would have done for one of these even though for choice he but presented himself as a supervisory friend of the family. The Lancaster Gate family, he clearly intended, in which he included its American recruits, and included above all Kate Croy—a young person blessedly easy to take care of. She knew people, and people knew her, and she was the handsomest thing there—this last a declaration made by Milly, in a sort of soft mid-summer madness, a straight skylark-flight of charity, to Aunt Maud.

Kate had, for her new friend's eyes, the extraordinary and attaching property of appearing at a given moment to show as a beautiful stranger, to cut her connections and lose her identity, letting the imagination for the time make what it would of them—make her merely a person striking from afar, more and more pleasing as one watched, but who was above all a subject for curiosity. Nothing could have given her, as a party to a relation, a greater freshness than this sense—which sprang up at its own hours—of being as curious about her as if one hadn't known her. It had sprung up, we have gathered, as soon as Milly had seen her after hearing from Mrs. Stringham of her knowledge of Merton Densher; she had *looked* then other and, as Milly knew the real critical mind would call it, more objective; and our young woman had foreseen it of her, on the spot, that she would often look so again. It was exactly what she was doing this afternoon; and Milly, who had amusements of thought that were like the secrecies of a little girl playing with dolls when conventionally "too big," could almost settle to the game of what one would suppose her, how one would place her, if one didn't know her. She became thus, intermittently, a figure conditioned only by the great facts of aspect, a figure to be waited for, named and fitted. This was doubtless but a way of feeling that it was of her essence to be peculiarly what the occasion, whatever it might be, demanded when its demand was highest.

There were probably ways enough, on these lines, for such a consciousness; another of them would be, for instance, to say that she was made for great social uses. Milly was not wholly sure that she herself knew what great social uses might be—unless, as a good example, exerting just that sort of glamour in just that sort of frame were one of them: she would have fallen back on knowing sufficiently that they existed at all events for her friend. It imputed a primness, all round, to be reduced but to saying, by way of a translation of one's amusement, that she was always so *right*—since that, too often, was what the *insupportables* themselves were; yet it was, in overflow to Aunt Maud, what she had to content herself withal—save for the lame enhancement of saying she was lovely. It served, all the same, the purpose, strengthened the bond that for the time held the two ladies together, distilled in short its drop of rose-colour for Mrs. Lowder's own view. That was really the view Milly had, for most of the rest of the occasion, to give herself to immediately taking in; but it didn't prevent the continued play of those swift cross-lights, odd beguilements of the mind, at which we have already glanced.

Mrs. Lowder herself found it enough simply to reply, in respect to Kate, that she was indeed a luxury to take about the world: she expressed no more surprise than that at her "rightness" to-day. Wasn't it by this time sufficiently manifest that it was precisely as the very luxury she was proving that she had, from far back, been appraised and waited for? Crude elation, however, might be kept at bay, and the circumstance none the less demonstrated that they were all swimming together in the blue. It came back to Lord Mark again, as he seemed slowly to pass and repass and conveniently to linger before them; he was personally the note of the blue—like a suspended skein of silk within reach of the broiderer's hand. Aunt Maud's free-moving shuttle took a length of him at rhythmic intervals; and one of the intermixed truths that flickered across to Milly was that he ever so consentingly knew he was being worked in. This was almost like an understanding with her at Mrs. Lowder's expense, which she would have none of; she wouldn't for the world have had him make any such point as that he wouldn't have launched them at Matcham—or whatever it was he *had* done—only for Aunt Maud's *beaux yeux*. What he had done, it would have been guessable, was something he had for some time been desired in vain to do; and what they were all now profiting by was a change comparatively sudden, the cessation of hope delayed. What had caused the cessation easily showed itself as none of Milly's business; and she was luckily, for that matter, in no real danger of hearing from him directly that her individual weight had been felt in the scale. Why then indeed was it an effect of his diffused but subdued participation that he might absolutely have been saying to her "Yes, let the dear woman take her own tone? Since she's here she may stay," he might have been adding—"for whatever she can make of it. But you and I are different." Milly knew *she* was different in truth—his own difference was his own affair; but also she knew that, after all, even at their distinctest, Lord Mark's "tips" in this line would be tacit. He practically placed her—it came round again to that—under no obligation whatever. It was a matter of equal ease, moreover, her letting Mrs. Lowder take a tone. She might have taken twenty—they would have spoiled nothing.

"You must stay on with us; you *can,* you know, in any position you like; any, any, *any,* my dear child"—and her emphasis went deep. "You must make your home with us; and it's really open to you to make the most beautiful one in the world. You mustn't be under a mistake—under any of any sort; and you must let us all think for you a little, take care of you and watch over you. Above all you must help me with Kate, and you must stay a little *for* her; nothing for a long time has happened to me so good as that you and she should have become friends. It's beautiful; it's great; it's everything. What makes it perfect is that it should have come about through our dear delightful Susie, restored to me, after so many years, by such a miracle. No—that's more charming to me than even your hitting it off with Kate. God has been good to one—positively; for I couldn't, at my age, have made a new friend— undertaken, I mean, out of whole cloth, the real thing. It's like changing one's bankers—after fifty: one doesn't do that. That's why Susie has been kept for me, as you seem to keep people in your wonderful country, in lavender and pink paper—coming back at last as straight as out of a fairy-tale and with you as an attendant fairy." Milly hereupon replied appreciatively that such a description of herself made her feel as if pink paper were her dress and lavender its trimming; but Aunt Maud was not to be deterred by a weak joke from keeping it up. Her interlocutress could feel besides that she kept it up in perfect sincerity. She was somehow at this hour a very happy woman, and a part of her happiness might precisely have been that her affections and her views were moving as never before in concert. Unquestionably she loved Susie; but she also loved Kate and loved Lord Mark, loved their funny old host and hostess, loved every one within range, down to the very servant who came to receive Milly's empty iceplate—down, for that matter, to Milly herself, who was, while she talked, really conscious of the enveloping flap of a protective mantle, a shelter with the weight of an eastern carpet. An eastern carpet, for wishing-purposes of one's own, was a thing to be on rather than under; still, however, if the girl should fail of breath it wouldn't be, she could feel, by Mrs. Lowder's fault. One of the last things she was afterwards to recall of this was Aunt Maud's going on to say that she and Kate must stand together because together they could do anything. It was for Kate of course she was essentially planning; but the plan, enlarged and uplifted now, somehow required Milly's prosperity too for its full operation, just as Milly's prosperity at the same time involved Kate's. It was nebulous yet, it was slightly confused, but it was unmistakably free and genial, and it made our young woman understand things Kate had said of her aunt's possibilities as well as characterisations that had fallen from Susan Shepherd. One of the most frequent on the lips of the latter had been that dear Maud was a natural force.

XI

A prime reason, we must add, why sundry impressions were not to be fully present to the girl till later on was that they yielded at this stage, with an effect of sharp supersession, to a detached quarter of an hour—her only one—with Lord Mark. "Have you seen the picture in the house, the beautiful one that's so like you?"—he was asking that as he stood before her; having come up at last with his smooth intimation that any wire he had pulled and yet wanted not to remind her of wasn't quite a reason for his having no joy at all.

"I've been through rooms and I've seen pictures. But if I'm 'like' anything so beautiful as most of them seemed to me———!" It needed in short for Milly some evidence, which he only wanted to supply. She was the image of the wonderful Bronzino, which she must have a look at on every ground. He had thus called her off and led her away; the more easily that the house within was above all what had already drawn round her its mystic circle. Their progress, meanwhile, was not of the straightest; it was an advance, without haste, through innumerable natural pauses and soft concussions, determined for the most part by the appearance before them of ladies and gentlemen, singly, in couples, in groups, who brought them to a stand with an inveterate "I say, Mark." What they said she never quite made out; it was their all so domestically knowing him, and his knowing them, that mainly struck her, while her impression, for the rest, was but of fellow-strollers more vaguely afloat than themselves, supernumeraries mostly a little battered, whether as jaunty males or as ostensibly elegant women. They might have been moving a good deal by a momentum that had begun far back, but they were still brave and personable, still warranted for continuance as long again, and they gave her, in especial collectively, a sense of pleasant voices, pleasanter than those of actors, of friendly, empty words and kind, lingering eyes. The lingering eyes looked her over, the lingering eyes were what went, in almost confessed simplicity, with the pointless "I say, Mark "; and what was really most sensible of all was that, as a pleasant matter of course, if she didn't mind, he seemed to suggest their letting people, poor dear things, have the benefit of her.

The odd part was that he made her herself believe, for amusement, in the benefit, measured by him in mere manner—for wonderful, of a truth, was, as a means of expression, his slightness of emphasis—that her present good-nature conferred. It was, as she could easily see, a mild common carnival of good-nature—a mass of London people together, of sorts and sorts, but who mainly knew each other and who, in their way, did, no doubt, confess to curiosity. It had gone round that she was there; questions about her would be passing; the easiest thing was to run the gauntlet with *him*—just as the easiest thing was in fact to trust him generally. Couldn't she know for herself, passively, how little harm they meant her?—to that extent that it made no difference whether or not he introduced them. The strangest thing of all for Milly was perhaps the uplifted assurance and indifference with which she could simply give back the particular bland stare that appeared in such cases to mark civilisation at its highest. It was so little her fault, this oddity of what had "gone round" about her, that to accept it without question might be as good a way as another of feeling life. It was inevitable to supply the probable description—that of the awfully rich young American who was so queer to behold, but nice, by all accounts, to know; and she had really but one instant of speculation as to fables or fantasies perchance originally launched. She asked herself once only if Susie could, inconceivably, have been blatant about her; for the question, on the spot, was really blown away for ever. She knew in fact on the spot and with sharpness just why she had "elected" Susan Shepherd: she had had from the first hour the conviction of her being precisely the person in the world least possibly a trumpeter. So it wasn't their fault, it wasn't their fault, and anything might happen that would, and everything now again melted together, and kind eyes were always kind eyes—if it were never to be worse than that! She got with her companion into the house; they brushed, beneficently, past all their accidents. The Bronzino was, it appeared, deep within, and the long afternoon light lingered for them on patches of old colour and waylaid them, as they went, in nooks and opening vistas.

It was all the while for Milly as if Lord Mark had really had something other than this spoken pretext in view; as if there were something he wanted to say to her and were only—consciously yet not awkwardly, just delicately—hanging fire. At the same time it was as if the thing had practically been said by the moment they came in sight of the picture; since what it appeared to amount to was "Do let a fellow who isn't a fool take care of you a little." The thing somehow, with the aid of the Bronzino, was done; it hadn't seemed to matter to her before if he were a fool or no; but now, just where they were, she liked his not being; and it was all moreover none the worse for coming back to something of the same sound as Mrs. Lowder's so recent reminder. She too wished to take care of her—and wasn't it, *à peu près,* what all the people with the kind eyes were wishing? Once more things melted together—the beauty and the history and the facility and the splendid midsummer glow: it was a sort of magnificent maximum, the pink dawn of an apotheosis, coming so curiously soon. What in fact befell was that, as she afterwards made out, it was Lord Mark who said nothing in particular—it was she herself who said all. She couldn't help that—it came; and the reason it came was that she found herself, for the first moment, looking at the mysterious portrait through tears. Perhaps it was her tears that made it just then so strange and fair—as wonderful as he had said: the face of a young woman, all magnificently drawn, down to the hands, and magnificently dressed; a face almost livid in hue, yet handsome in sadness and crowned with a mass of hair rolled back and high, that must, before fading with time, have had a family resemblance to her own. The lady in question, at all events, with her slightly Michaelangelesque squareness, her eyes of other days, her full lips, her long neck, her recorded jewels, her brocaded and wasted reds, was a very great personage—only unaccompanied by a joy. And she was dead, dead, dead. Milly recognised her exactly in words that had nothing to do with her. "I shall never be better than this."

He smiled for her at the portrait. "Than she? You'd scarce need to be better, for surely that's well enough. But you *are*, one feels, as it happens, better; because, splendid as she is, one doubts if she was good."

He hadn't understood. She was before the picture, but she had turned to him, and she didn't care if, for the minute, he noticed her tears. It was probably as good a moment as she should ever have with him. It was perhaps as good a moment as she should have with any one, or have in any connection whatever. "I mean that everything this afternoon has been too beautiful, and that perhaps everything together will never be so right again. I'm very glad therefore you've been a part of it."

Though he still didn't understand her he was as nice as if he had; he didn't ask for insistence, and that was just a part of his looking after her. He simply protected her now from herself, and there was a world of practice in it. "Oh, we must talk about these things!"

Ah, they had already done that, she knew, as much as she ever would; and she was shaking her head at her pale sister the next moment with a world, on her side, of slowness. "I wish I could see the resemblance. Of course her complexion's green," she laughed; "but mine's several shades greener."

"It's down to the very hands," said Lord Mark.

"Her hands are large," Milly went on, "but mine are larger. Mine are huge."

"Oh, you go her, all round, 'one better'—which is just what I said. But you're a pair. You must surely catch it," he added as if it were important to his character as a serious man not to appear to have invented his plea.

"I don't know one never knows one's self. It's a funny fancy, and I don't imagine it would have occurred——"

"I see it *has* occurred"—he has already taken her up. She had her back, as she faced the picture, to one of the doors of the room, which was open, and on her turning, as he spoke, she saw that they were in the presence of three other persons, also, as appeared, interested inquirers. Kate Croy was one of these; Lord Mark had just become aware of her, and she, all arrested, had immediately seen, and made the best of it, that she was far from being first in the field. She had brought a lady and a gentleman to whom she wished to show what Lord Mark was showing Milly, and he took her straightway as a reinforcement. Kate herself had spoken, however, before he had had time to tell her so.

"*You* had noticed too?"—she smiled at him without looking at Milly. "Then I'm not original—which one always hopes one has been. But the likeness is so great." And now she looked at Milly—for whom again it was, all round indeed, kind, kind eyes. "Yes, there you are, my dear, if you want to know. And you're superb." She took now but a glance at the picture, though it was enough to make her question to her friends not too straight. "Isn't she superb?"

"I brought Miss Theale," Lord Mark explained to the latter, "quite off my own bat."

"I wanted Lady Aldershaw," Kate continued to Milly, "to see for herself."

"Les grands esprits se rencontrent!" laughed her attendant gentleman, a high, but slightly stooping, shambling and wavering person, who represented urbanity by the liberal aid of certain prominent front teeth and whom Milly vaguely took for some sort of great man.

Lady Aldershaw meanwhile looked at Milly quite as if Milly had been the Bronzino and the Bronzino only Milly. "Superb, superb. Of course I had noticed you. It is wonderful," she went on with her back to the picture, but with some other eagerness which Milly felt gathering, directing her motions now. It was enough—they were introduced, and she was saying "I wonder if you could give us the pleasure of coming——" She was not fresh, for she was not young, even though she denied at every pore that she was old; but she was vivid and much bejewelled for the midsummer daylight; and she was all in the palest pinks and blues. She didn't think, at this pass, that she could "come" anywhere—Milly didn't; and she already knew that somehow Lord Mark was saving her from the question. He had interposed, taking the words out of the lady's mouth and not caring at all if the lady minded. That was clearly the right way to treat her—at least for him; as she had only dropped, smiling, and then turned away with him. She had been dealt with—it would have done an enemy good. The gentleman still stood, a little helpless, addressing himself to the intention of urbanity as if it were a large loud whistle; he had been signing sympathy, in his way, while the lady made her overture; and Milly had, in this light, soon arrived at their identity. They were Lord and Lady Aldershaw, and the wife was the clever one. A minute or two later the situation had changed, and she knew it afterwards to have been by the subtle operation of Kate. She was herself saying that she was afraid she must go now if Susie could be found; but she was sitting down on the nearest seat to say it. The prospect, through opened doors, stretched before her into other rooms, down the vista of which Lord Mark was strolling with Lady Aldershaw, who, close to him and much intent, seemed to show from behind as peculiarly expert. Lord Aldershaw, for his part, had been left in the middle of the room, while Kate, with her back to him, was standing before her with much sweetness of manner. The sweetness was all for *her;* she had the sense of the poor gentleman's having somehow been handled as Lord Mark had handled his wife. He dangled there, he shambled a little; then he bethought himself of the Bronzino, before which, with his eyeglass, he hovered. It drew from him an odd, vague sound, not wholly distinct from a grunt, and a "Humph—most remarkable!" which lighted Kate's face with amusement. The next moment he had creaked away, over polished floors, after the others, and Milly was feeling as if *she* had been rude. But Lord Aldershaw was in every way a detail, and Kate was saying to her that she hoped she wasn't ill.

Thus it was that, aloft there in the great gilded historic chamber and the presence of the pale personage on the wall, whose eyes all the while seemed engaged with her own, she found herself suddenly sunk in something quite intimate and humble and to which these grandeurs were strange enough witnesses. It had come up, in the form in which she had had to accept it, all suddenly, and nothing about it, at the same time, was more marked than that she had in a manner plunged into it to escape from something else. Something else, from her first vision of her friend's appearance three minutes before, had been present to her even through the call made by the others on her attention; something that was perversely *there,* she was more and more uncomfortably finding, at least for the first moments and by some spring of its own, with every renewal of their meeting. "Is it the way she looks to *him?"* she asked herself—the perversity being that she kept in remembrance that Kate was known to him. It wasn't a fault in Kate—nor in him assuredly; and she had a horror, being generous and tender, of treating either of them as if it had been. To Densher himself she couldn't make it up—he was too far away; but her secondary impulse was to make it up to Kate. She did so now with a strange soft energy—the impulse immediately acting. "Will you render me to-morrow a great service?"

"Any service, dear child, in the world."

"But it's a secret one—nobody must know. I must be wicked and false about it."

"Then I'm your woman," Kate smiled, "for that's the kind of thing I love. *Do* let us do something bad. You're impossibly without sin, you know."

385

Milly's eyes, on this, remained a little with their companion's. "Ah, I shan't perhaps come up to your idea. It's only to deceive Susan Shepherd."

"Oh!" said Kate as if this were indeed mild.

"But thoroughly—as thoroughly as I can."

"And for cheating," Kate asked, "my powers will contribute? Well, I'll do my best for you." In accordance with which it was presently settled between them that Milly should have the aid and comfort of her presence for a visit to Sir Luke Strett. Kate had needed a minute for enlightenment, and it was quite grand for her comrade that this name should have said nothing to her. To Milly herself it had for some days been secretly saying much. The personage in question was, as she explained, the greatest of medical lights if she had got hold, as she believed (and she had used to this end the wisdom of the serpent) of the right, the special man. She had written to him three days before, and he had named her an hour, eleven-twenty; only it had come to her, on the eve, that she couldn't go alone. Her maid, on the other hand, wasn't good enough, and Susie was too good. Kate had listened, above all, with high indulgence. "And I'm betwixt and between, happy thought! Too good for what?"

Milly thought. "Why, to be worried if it's nothing. And to be still more worried—I mean before she need be—if it isn't."

Kate fixed her with deep eyes. "What in the world is the matter with you?" It had inevitably a sound of impatience, as if it had been a challenge really to produce something; so that Milly felt her for the moment only as a much older person, standing above her a little, doubting the imagined ailments, suspecting the easy complaints, of ignorant youth. It somewhat checked her, further, that the matter with her was what exactly as yet she wanted knowledge about; and she immediately declared, for conciliation, that if she were merely fanciful Kate would see her put to shame. Kate vividly uttered, in return, the hope that, since she could come out and be so charming, could so universally dazzle and interest, she wasn't all the while in distress or in anxiety—didn't believe herself, in short, to be in any degree seriously menaced. "Well, I want to make out—to make out!" was all that this consistently produced. To which Kate made clear answer: "Ah then, let us by all means!"

"I thought," Milly said, "you would like to help me. But I must ask you, please, for the promise of absolute silence."

"And how, if you *are* ill, can your friends remain in ignorance?"

"Well, if I am, it must of course finally come out. But I can go for a long time." Milly spoke with her eyes again on her painted sister's—almost as if under their suggestion. She still sat there before Kate, yet not without a light in her face. "That will be one of my advantages. I think I could die without its being noticed."

"You're an extraordinary young woman," her friend, visibly held by her, declared at last. "What a remarkable time to talk of such things!"

"Well, we won't talk, precisely"—Milly got herself together again. "I only wanted to make sure of you."

"Here in the midst of——!" But Kate could only sigh for wonder—almost visibly too for pity.

It made a moment during which her companion waited on her word; partly as if from a yearning, shy but deep, to have her case put to her just as Kate was struck by it; partly as if the hint of pity were already giving a sense to her whimsical "shot," with Lord Mark, at Mrs. Lowder's first dinner. Exactly this—the handsome girl's compassionate manner, her friendly descent from her own strength—was what she had then foretold. She took Kate up as if positively for the deeper taste of it. "Here in the midst of what?"

"Of everything. There's nothing you can't have. There's nothing you can't do."

"So Mrs. Lowder tells me."

It just kept Kate's eyes fixed as possibly for more of that; then, however, without waiting, she went on. "We all adore you."

"You're wonderful—you dear things!" Milly laughed.

"No, it's *you.*" And Kate seemed struck with the real interest of it. "In three weeks!"

Milly kept it up. "Never were people on such terms! All the more reason," she added, "that I shouldn't needlessly torment you."

"But me? what becomes of *me?*" said Kate.

"Well, you—" Milly thought—"if there's anything to bear, you'll bear it."

"But I *won't* bear it!" said Kate Croy.

"Oh yes, you will: all the same! You'll pity me awfully, but you'll help me very much. And I absolutely trust you. So there we are." There they were, then, since Kate had so to take it; but there, Milly felt, she herself in particular was; for it was just the point at which she had wished to arrive. She had wanted to prove to herself that she didn't horribly blame her friend for any reserve; and what better proof could there be than this quite special confidence? If she desired to show Kate that she really believed the latter liked her, how could she show it more than by asking her for help?

XII

What it really came to, on the morrow, this first time—the time Kate went with her—was that the great man had, a little, to excuse himself; had, by a rare accident—for he kept his consulting-hours in general rigorously free—but ten minutes to give her; ten mere minutes which he yet placed at her service in a manner that she admired even more than she could meet it: so crystal-clean the great empty cup of attention that he set between them on the table. He was presently to jump into his carriage, but he promptly made the point that he must see her again, see her within a day or two; and he named for her at once another hour—easing her off beautifully too even then in respect to her possibly failing of justice to her errand. The minutes affected her in fact as ebbing more swiftly than her little army of items could muster, and they would probably have gone without her doing much more than secure another hearing, had it not been for her sense, at the last, that she had gained above all an impression. The impression—all the sharp growth of the final few moments—was neither more nor less than that she might make, of a sudden, in quite another world, another straight friend, and a friend who would moreover be, wonderfully, the most appointed, the most thoroughly adjusted of the whole collection, inasmuch as he would somehow wear the character scientifically, ponderably, proveably—not just loosely and sociably. Literally, furthermore, it wouldn't really depend on herself, Sir Luke Strett's friendship, in the least; perhaps what made her most stammer and pant was its thus queerly coming over her that she might find she had interested him even beyond her intention, find she was in fact launched in some current that would lose itself in the sea of science. At the same time that she struggled, however, she also surrendered; there was a moment at which she almost dropped the form of stating, of explaining, and threw herself, without violence, only with a supreme pointless quaver that had turned, the next instant, to an intensity of interrogative stillness, upon his general goodwill. His large, settled face, though firm, was not, as she had thought at first, hard; he looked, in the oddest manner, to her fancy, half like a general and half like a bishop, and she was soon sure that, within some such handsome range, what it would show her would be what was good, what was best for her. She had established, in other words, in this time-saving way, a relation with it; and the relation was the special trophy that, for the hour, she bore off. It was like an absolute possession, a new resource altogether, something done up in the softest silk and tucked away under the arm of memory. She hadn't had it when she went in, and she had it when she came out; she had it there under her cloak, but dissimulated, invisibly carried, when smiling, smiling, she again faced Kate Croy. That young lady had of course awaited her in another room, where, as the great man was to absent himself, no one else was in attendance; and she rose for her with such a face of sympathy as might have graced the vestibule of a dentist. "Is it out?" she seemed to ask as if it had been a question of a tooth; and Milly indeed kept her in no suspense at all.

"He's a dear. I'm to come again."

"But what does he say?"

Milly was almost gay. "That I'm not to worry about anything in the world, and that if I'll be a good girl and do exactly what he tells me, he'll take care of me for ever and ever."

Kate wondered as if things scarce fitted. "But does he allow then that you're ill?"

"I don't know what he allows, and I don't care. I shall know, and whatever it is it will be enough. He knows all about me, and I like it. I don't hate it a bit."

Still, however, Kate stared. "But could he, in so few minutes, ask you enough——?"

"He asked me scarcely anything—he doesn't need to do anything so stupid," Milly said. "He can tell. He knows," she repeated; "and when I go back—for he'll have thought me over a little—it will be all right."

Kate, after a moment, made the best of this. "Then when are we to come?"

It just pulled her friend up, for even while they talked—at least it was one of the reasons—she stood there suddenly, irrelevantly, in the light of her *other* identity, the identity she would have for Mr. Densher. This was always, from one instant to another, an incalculable light, which, though it might go off faster than it came on, necessarily disturbed. It sprang, with a perversity all its own, from the fact that, with the lapse of hours and days, the chances themselves that made for his being named continued so oddly to fail. There were twenty, there were fifty, but none of them turned up. This, in particular, was of course not a juncture at which the least of them would naturally be present; but it would make, none the less, Milly saw, another day practically all stamped with avoidance. She saw in a quick glimmer, and with it all Kate's unconsciousness; and then she shook off the obsession. But it had lasted long enough to qualify her response. No, she had shown Kate how she trusted her; and that, for loyalty, would somehow do. "Oh, dear thing, now that the ice is broken I shan't trouble *you* again."

"You'll come alone?"

"Without a scruple. Only I shall ask you, please, for your absolute discretion still."

Outside, before the door, on the wide pavement of the great square, they had to wait again while their carriage, which Milly had kept, completed a further turn of exercise, engaged in by the coachman for reasons of his own. The footman was there, and had indicated that he was making the circuit; so Kate went on while they stood. "But don't you ask a good deal, darling, in proportion to what you give?"

This pulled Milly up still shorter—so short in fact that she yielded as soon as she had taken it in. But she continued to smile. "I see. Then you *can* tell."

"I don't want to 'tell,'" said Kate. "I'll be as silent as the tomb if I can only have the truth from you. All I want is that you shouldn't keep from me how you find out that you really are."

"Well then, I won't, ever. But you see for yourself," Milly went on, "how I really am. I'm satisfied. I'm happy."

Kate looked at her long. "I believe you like it. The way things turn out for you———!"

Milly met her look now without a thought of anything but the spoken. She had ceased to be Mr. Densher's image; she was all her own memento and she was none the less fine. Still, still, what had passed was a fair bargain, and it would do. "Of course I like it. I feel—I can't otherwise describe it—as if I had been, on my knees, to the priest. I've confessed and I've been absolved. It has been lifted off."

Kate's eyes never quitted her. "He must have liked *you.*"

"Oh—doctors!" Milly said. "But I hope," she added, "he didn't like me too much." Then as if to escape a little from her friend's deeper sounding, or as impatient for the carriage, not yet in sight, her eyes, turning away, took in the great stale square. As its staleness, however, was but that of London fairly fatigued, the late hot London with its dance all danced and its story all told, the air seemed a thing of blurred pictures and mixed echoes, and an impression met the sense—an impression that broke, the next moment, through the girl's tightened lips. "Oh, it's a beautiful big world, and everyone, yes, everyone——!" It presently brought her back to Kate, and she hoped she didn't actually look as much as if she were crying as she must have looked to Lord Mark among the portraits at Matcham.

Kate at all events understood. "Everyone wants to be so nice?"

"So nice," said the grateful Milly.

"Oh," Kate laughed, "we'll pull you through! And won't you now bring Mrs. Stringham?"

But Milly after an instant was again clear about that. "Not till I've seen him once more."

She was to have found this preference, two days later, abundantly justified; and yet when, in prompt accordance with what had passed between them, she reappeared before her distinguished friend—that character having, for him, in the interval, built itself up still higher—the first thing he asked her was whether she had been accompanied. She told him, on this, straightway, everything; completely free at present from her first embarrassment, disposed even—as she felt she might become—to undue volubility, and conscious moreover of no alarm from his thus perhaps wishing that she had not come alone. It was exactly as if, in the forty-eight hours that had passed, her acquaintance with him had somehow increased, and his own knowledge in particular received mysterious additions. They had been together, before, scarce ten minutes; but the relation, the one the ten minutes had so beautifully created, was there to take straight up: and this not, on his own part, from mere professional heartiness, mere bedside manner, which she would have disliked—much rather from a quiet, pleasant air in him of having positively asked about her, asked here and there and found out. Of course he couldn't in the least have asked, or have wanted to; there was no source of information to his hand, and he had really needed none: he had found out simply by his genius—and found out, she meant, literally everything. Now she knew not only that she didn't dislike this—the state of being found out about; but that, on the contrary, it was truly what she had come for, and that, for the time at least, it would give her something firm to stand on. She struck herself as aware, aware as she had never been, of really not having had from the beginning anything firm. It would be strange for the firmness to come, after all, from her learning in these agreeable conditions that she was in some way doomed; but above all it would prove how little she had hitherto had to hold her up. If she was now to be held up by the mere process—since that was perhaps on the cards—of being let down, this would only testify in turn to her queer little history. *That* sense of loosely rattling had been no process at all; and it was ridiculously true that her thus sitting there to see her life put into the scales represented her first approach to the taste of orderly living. Such was Milly's romantic version—that her life, especially by the fact of this second interview, *was* put into the scales; and just the best part of the relation established might have been, for that matter, that the great grave charming man knew, had known at once, that it was romantic, and in that measure allowed for it. Her only doubt, her only fear, was whether he perhaps wouldn't even take advantage of her being a little romantic to treat her as romantic altogether. This doubtless was her danger with him; but she should see, and dangers in general meanwhile dropped and dropped.

The very place, at the end of a few minutes, the commodious, "handsome" room, far back in the fine old house, soundless from position, somewhat sallow with years of celebrity, somewhat sombre even at midsummer—the very place put on for her a look of custom and use, squared itself solidly round her as with promises and certainties. She had come forth to see the world, and this then was to be the world's light, the rich dusk of a London "back," these the world's walls, those the world's curtains and carpet. She should be intimate with the great bronze clock and mantel-ornaments, conspicuously presented in gratitude and long ago; she should be as one of the circle of eminent contemporaries, photographed, engraved, signatured, and in particular framed and glazed, who made up the rest of the decoration, and made up as well so much of the human comfort; and while she thought of all the clean truths, unfringed, unfingered, that the listening stillness, strained into pauses and waits, would again and again, for years, have kept distinct, she also wondered what she would eventually decide upon to present in gratitude. She would give something better at least than the brawny Victorian bronzes. This was precisely an instance of what she felt he knew of her before he had done with her: that she was secretly romancing at that rate, in the midst of so much else that was more urgent, all over the place. So much for her secrets with him, none of which really required to be phrased. It would have been, for example, a secret for her from any one else that without a dear lady she had picked up just before coming over she wouldn't have a decently near connection, of any sort, for such an appeal as she was making, to put forward: no one in the least, as it were, to produce for respectability. But *his* seeing it she didn't mind a scrap, and not a scrap either his knowing how she had left the dear lady in the dark. She had come alone, putting her friend off with a fraud: giving a pretext of shops, of a whim, of she didn't know what—the amusement of being for once in the streets by herself. The streets by herself were new to her—she had always had in them a companion, or a maid; and he was never to believe, moreover, that she couldn't take full in the face anything he might have to say. He was softly amused at her account of her courage; though he yet showed it somehow without soothing her too grossly. Still, he did want to know whom she had. Hadn't there been a lady with her on Wednesday?

"Yes—a different one. Not the one who's travelling with me. I've told *her.*"

Distinctly he was amused, and it added to his air—the greatest charm of all—of giving her lots of time. "You've told her what?"

"Well," said Milly, "that I visit you in secret."

"And how many persons will she tell?"

"Oh, she's devoted. Not one."

"Well, if she's devoted doesn't that make another friend for you?"

It didn't take much computation, but she nevertheless had to think a moment, conscious as she was that he distinctly *would* want to fill out his notion of her—even a little, as it were, to warm the air for her. That, however—and better early than late—he must accept as of no use; and she herself felt for an instant quite a competent certainty on the subject of any such warming. The air, for Milly Theale, was, from the very nature of the case, destined never to rid itself of a considerable chill. This she could tell him with authority, if she could tell him nothing else; and she seemed to see now, in short, that it would importantly simplify. "Yes, it makes another; but they all together wouldn't make—well, I don't know what to call it but the difference. I mean when one is—really alone. I've never seen anything like the kindness." She pulled up a minute while he waited—waited again as if with his reasons for letting her, for almost making her, talk. What she herself wanted was not, for the third time, to cry, as it were, in public. She *had* never seen anything like the kindness, and she wished to do it justice; but she knew what she was about, and justice was not wronged by her being able presently to stick to her point. "Only one's situation is what it is. It's me it concerns. The rest is delightful and useless. Nobody can really help. That's why I'm by myself to-day. I *want* to be—in spite of Miss Croy, who came with me last. If you can help, so much the better and also of course if one can, a little, one's self. Except for that—you and me doing our best—I like you to see me just as I am. Yes, I like it—and I don't exaggerate. Shouldn't one, at the start, show the worst—so that anything after that may be better? It wouldn't make any real difference— it *won't* make any, anything that may happen won't—to any one. Therefore I feel myself, this way, with you, just as I am; and—if you do in the least care to know—it quite positively bears me up." She put it as to his caring to know, because his manner seemed to give her all her chance, and the impression was there for her to take. It was strange and deep for her, this impression, and she did, accordingly, take it straight home. It showed him—showed him in spite of himself—as allowing, somewhere far within, things comparatively remote, things in fact quite, as she would have said, outside, delicately to weigh with him; showed him as interested, on her behalf, in other questions beside the question of what was the matter with her. She accepted such an interest as regular in the highest type of scientific mind—his *being* the even highest, magnificently because otherwise, obviously, it wouldn't be there; but she could at the same time take it as a direct source of light upon herself, even though that might present her a little as pretending to equal him. Wanting to know more about a patient than how a patient was constructed or deranged couldn't be, even on the part of the greatest of doctors, anything but some form or other of the desire to let the patient down easily. When that was the case the reason, in turn, could only be, too manifestly, pity; and when pity held up its tell-tale face like a head on a pike, in a French revolution, bobbing before a window, what was the inference but that the patient was bad? He might say what he would now—she would always have seen the head at the window; and in fact from this moment she only wanted him to say what he would. He might say it too with the greater ease to himself as there wasn't one of her divinations that—as her own—he would in any way put himself out for. Finally, if he was making her talk she *was* talking; and what it could, at any rate, come to for him was that she wasn't afraid. If he wanted to do the dearest thing in the world for her he would show her he believed she wasn't; which undertaking of hers—not to have misled him—was what she counted at the moment as her presumptuous little hint to him that she was as good as himself. It put forward the bold idea that he could really *be* misled; and there actually passed between them for some seconds a sign, a sign of the eyes only, that they knew together where they were. This made, in their brown old temple of truth, its momentary flicker; then what followed it was that he had her, all the same, in his pocket; and the whole thing wound up, for that consummation, with its kind dim smile. Such kindness was wonderful with such dimness; but brightness—that even of sharp steel—was of course for the other side of the business, and it would all come in for her in one way or another. "Do you mean," he asked, "that you've no relations at all?—not a parent, not a sister, not even a cousin nor an aunt?"

She shook her head as with the easy habit of an interviewed heroine or a freak of nature at a show. "Nobody whatever." But the last thing she had come for was to be dreary about it. "I'm a survivor—a survivor of a general wreck. You see," she added, "how that's to be taken into account—that everyone else *has* gone. When I was ten years old there were, with my father and my mother, six of us. I'm all that's left. But they died," she went on, to be fair all round, "of different things. Still, there it is. And, as I told you before, I'm American. Not that I mean that makes me worse. However, you'll probably know what it makes me."

"Yes," he discreetly indulged her; "I know perfectly what it makes you. It makes you, to begin with, a capital case."

She sighed, though gratefully, as if again before the social scene. "Ah, there you are!"

"Oh, no; there 'we' aren't at all. There I am only—but as much as you like. I've no end of American friends: there *they* are, if you please, and it's a fact that you couldn't very well be in a better place than in their company. It puts you with plenty of others—and that isn't pure solitude." Then he pursued: "I'm sure you've an excellent spirit; but don't try to bear more things than you need." Which after an instant he further explained. "Hard things have come to you in youth, but you mustn't think life will be for you all hard things. You've the right to be happy. You must make up your mind to it. You must accept any form in which happiness may come."

"Oh, I'll accept any whatever!" she almost gaily returned. "And it seems to me, for that matter, that I'm accepting a new one every day. Now *this!*" she smiled.

"This is very well so far as it goes. You can depend on me," the great man said, "for unlimited interest. But I'm only, after all, one element in fifty. We must gather in plenty of others. Don't mind who knows. Knows, I mean, that you and I are friends."

"Ah, you do want to see some one!" she broke out. "You want to get at some one who cares for me." With which, however, as he simply met this spontaneity in a manner to show that he had often had it from young persons of her race, and that he was familiar even with the possibilities of their familiarity, she felt her freedom rendered vain by his silence, and she immediately tried to think of the most reasonable thing she could say. This would be, precisely, on the subject of that freedom, which she now quickly spoke of as complete. "That's of course by itself a great boon; so please don't think I don't know it. I can do exactly what I like—anything in all the wide world. I haven't a creature to ask—there's not a finger to stop me. I can shake about till I'm black and blue. That perhaps isn't *all* joy; but lots of people, I know, would like to try it." He had appeared about to put a question, but then had let her go on, which she promptly did, for she understood him the next moment as having thus taken it from her that her means were as great as might be. She had simply given it to him so, and this was all that would ever pass between them on the odious head. Yet she couldn't help also knowing that an important effect, for his judgment, or at least for his amusement— which was his feeling, since, marvellously, he did have feeling—was produced by it. All her little pieces had now then fallen together for him like the morsels of coloured glass that used to make combinations, under the hand, in the depths of one of the polygonal peepshows of childhood. "So that if it's a question of my doing anything under the sun that will help——!"

"You'll *do* anything under the sun? Good." He took that beautifully, ever so pleasantly, for what it was worth; but time was needed—ten minutes or so were needed on the spot—to deal even provisionally, with the substantive question. It was convenient, in its degree, that there was nothing she wouldn't do; but it seemed also highly and agreeably vague that she should have to do anything. They thus appeared to be taking her, together, for the moment, and almost for sociability, as prepared to proceed to gratuitous extremities; the upshot of which was in turn, that after much interrogation, auscultation, exploration, much noting of his own sequences and neglecting of hers, had duly kept up the vagueness, they might have struck themselves, or may at least strike us, as coming back from an undeterred but useless voyage to the north pole. Milly was ready, under orders, for the north pole; which fact was doubtless what made a blinding anticlimax of her friend's actual abstention from orders. "No," she heard him again distinctly repeat it, "I don't want you for the present to do anything at all; anything, that is, but obey a small prescription or two that will be made clear to you, and let me within a few days come to see you at home."

It was at first heavenly. "Then you'll see Mrs. Stringham." But she didn't mind a bit now.

"Well, I shan't be afraid of Mrs. Stringham." And he said it once more as she asked once more: "Absolutely not; I 'send' you nowhere. England's all right—anywhere that's pleasant, convenient, decent, will be all right. You say you can do exactly as you like. Oblige me therefore by being so good as to do it. There's only one thing: you ought of course, now, as soon as I've seen you again, to get out of London."

Milly thought. "May I then go back to the continent?"

"By all means back to the continent. Do go back to the continent."

"Then how will you keep seeing me? But perhaps," she quickly added, "you won't want to keep seeing me."

He had it all ready; he had really everything all ready. "I shall follow you up; though if you mean that I don't want you to keep seeing *me*——"

"Well?" she asked.

It was only just here that he struck her the least bit as stumbling. "Well, see all you can. That's what it comes to. Worry about nothing. You *have* at least no worries. It's a great, rare chance."

She had got up, for she had had from him both that he would send her something and would advise her promptly of the date of his coming to her, by which she was virtually dismissed. Yet, for herself, one or two things kept her. "May I come back to England too?"

"Rather! Whenever you like. But always, when you do come, immediately let me know."

"Ah," said Milly, "it won't be a great going to and fro."

"Then if you'll stay with us, so much the better."

It touched her, the way he controlled his impatience of her; and the fact itself affected her as so precious that she yielded to the wish to get more from it. "So you don't think I'm out of my mind?"

"Perhaps that *is*," he smiled, "all that's the matter."

She looked at him longer. "No, that's too good. Shall I, at any rate, suffer?"

"Not a bit."

"And yet then live?"

"My dear young lady," said her distinguished friend, "isn't to 'live' exactly what I'm trying to persuade you to take the trouble to do?"

XIII

She had gone out with these last words so in her ears that when once she was well away—back this time in the great square alone—it was as if some instant application of them had opened out there before her. It was positively, this effect, an excitement that carried her on; she went forward into space under the sense of an impulse received—an impulse simple and direct, easy above all to act upon. She was borne up for the hour, and now she knew why she had wanted to come by herself. No one in the world could have sufficiently entered into her state; no tie would have been close enough to enable a companion to walk beside her without some disparity. She literally felt, in this first flush, that her only company must be the human race at large, present all round her, but inspiringly impersonal, and that her only field must be, then and there, the grey immensity of London. Grey immensity had somehow of a sudden become her element; grey immensity was what her distinguished friend had, for the moment, furnished her world with and what the question of "living," as he put it to her, living by option, by volition, inevitably took on for its immediate face. She went straight before her, without weakness, altogether with strength; and still as she went she was more glad to be alone, for nobody—not Kate Croy, not Susan Shepherd either—would have wished to rush with her as she rushed. She had asked him at the last whether, being on foot, she might go home so, or elsewhere, and he had replied as if almost amused again at her extravagance: "You're active, luckily, by nature—it's beautiful: therefore rejoice in it. *Be* active, without folly—for you're not foolish: be as active as you can and as you like." That had been in fact the final push, as well as the touch that most made a mixture of her consciousness—a strange mixture that tasted at one and the same time of what she had lost and what had been given her. It was wonderful to her, while she took her random course, that these quantities felt so equal: she had been treated—hadn't she?—as if it were in her power to live; and yet one wasn't treated so—was one?—unless it came up, quite as much, that one might die. The beauty of the bloom had gone from the small old sense of safety—that was distinct: she had left it behind her there forever. But the beauty of the idea of a great adventure, a big dim experiment or struggle in which she might, more responsibly than ever before, take a hand, had been offered her instead. It was as if she had had to pluck off her breast, to throw away, some friendly ornament, a familiar flower, a little old jewel, that was part of her daily dress; and to take up and shoulder as a substitute some queer defensive weapon, a musket, a spear, a battle-axe conducive possibly in a higher degree to a striking appearance, but demanding all the effort of the military posture. She felt this instrument, for that matter, already on her back, so that she proceeded now in very truth as a soldier on a march—proceeded as if, for her initiation, the first charge had been sounded. She passed along unknown streets, over dusty littery ways, between long rows of fronts not enhanced by the August light; she felt good for miles and only wanted to get lost; there were moments at corners, where she stopped and chose her direction, in which she quite lived up to his injunction to rejoice that she was active. It was like a new pleasure to have so new a reason; she would affirm, without delay, her option, her volition; taking this personal possession of what surrounded her was a fair affirmation to start with; and she really didn't care if she made it at the cost of alarms for Susie. Susie would wonder in due course "whatever," as they said at the hotel, had become of her; yet this would be nothing either, probably, to wonderments still in store. Wonderments in truth, Milly felt, even now attended her steps: it was quite as if she saw in people's eyes the reflection of her appearance and pace. She found herself moving at times in regions visibly not haunted by odd-looking girls from New York, duskily draped, sable-plumed, all but incongruously shod and gazing about them with extravagance; she might, from the curiosity she clearly excited in byways, in side-streets peopled with grimy children and costermongers carts, which she hoped were slums, literally have had her musket on her shoulder, have announced herself as freshly on the warpath. But for the fear of overdoing this character she would here and there have begun conversation, have asked her way; in spite of the fact that, as that would help the requirements of adventure, her way was exactly what she wanted not to know. The difficulty was that she at last accidentally found it; she had come out, she presently saw, at the Regent's Park, round which, on two or three occasions with Kate Croy, her public chariot had solemnly rolled. But she went into it further now; this was the real thing; the real thing was to be quite away from the pompous roads, well within the centre and on the stretches of shabby grass. Here were benches and smutty sheep; here were idle lads at games of ball, with their cries mild in the thick air; here were wanderers, anxious and tired like herself; here doubtless were hundreds of others just in the same box. Their box, their great common anxiety, what was it, in this grim breathing-space, but the practical question of life? They could live if they would; that is, like herself, they had been told so; she saw them all about her, on seats, digesting the information, feeling it altered, assimilated, recognising it again as something, in a slightly different shape, familiar enough, the blessed old truth that they would live if they could. All she thus shared with them made her wish to sit in their company; which she so far did that she looked for a bench that was empty, eschewing a still emptier chair that she saw hard by and for which she would have paid, with superiority, a fee.

The last scrap of superiority had soon enough left her, if only because she before long knew herself for more tired than she had proposed. This and the charm, after a fashion, of the situation in itself made her linger and rest; there was a sort of spell in the sense that nobody in the world knew where she was. It was the first time in her life that this had happened; somebody, everybody appeared to have known before, at every instant of it, where she was; so that she was now suddenly able to put it to herself that that hadn't been a life. This present kind of thing therefore might be—which was where precisely her distinguished friend seemed to be wishing her to come out. He wished her also, it was true, not to make, as she was perhaps doing now, too much of her isolation; at the same time however as he clearly desired to deny her no decent source of interest. He was interested—she arrived at that—in her appealing to as many sources as possible; and it fairly filtered into her, as she sat and sat, that he was essentially propping her up. Had she been doing it herself she would have called it bolstering—the bolstering that was simply for the weak; and she thought and thought as she put together the proofs that it was as one of the weak he was treating her. It was of course as one of the weak that she had gone to him—but, oh, with how sneaking a hope that he might pronounce her, as to all indispensables, a veritable young lioness! What indeed she was really confronted with was the consciousness that he had not, after all, pronounced her anything: she nursed herself into the sense that he had beautifully got out of it. Did he think, however, she wondered, that he could keep out of it to the end?—though, as she weighed the question, she yet felt it a little unjust. Milly weighed, in this extraordinary hour, questions numerous and strange; but she had, happily, before she moved, worked round to a simplification. Stranger than anything, for instance, was the effect of its rolling over her that, when one considered it, he might perhaps have "got out" by one door but to come in with a beautiful, beneficent dishonesty by another. It kept her more intensely motionless there that what he might fundamentally be "up to" was some disguised intention of standing by her as a friend. Wasn't that what women always said they wanted to do when they deprecated the addresses of gentlemen they couldn't more intimately go on with? It was what they, no doubt, sincerely fancied they could make of men of whom they couldn't make husbands. And she didn't even reason that it was, by a similar law, the expedient of doctors in general for the invalids of whom they couldn't make patients: she was somehow so sufficiently aware that *her* doctor was—however fatuous it might sound—exceptionally moved. This was the damning little fact—if she could talk of damnation: that she could believe herself to have caught him in the act of irrelevantly liking her. She hadn't gone to him to be liked, she had gone to him to be judged; and he was quite a great enough man to be in the habit, as a rule, of observing the difference. She could like *him,* as she distinctly did—that was another matter; all the more that her doing so was now, so obviously for herself, compatible with judgment. Yet it would have been all portentously mixed had not, as we say, a final, merciful wave, chilling rather, but washing clear, come to her assistance.

It came, of a sudden, when all other thought was spent. She had been asking herself why, if her case was grave—and she knew what she meant by that—he should have talked to her at all about what she might with futility "do"; or why on the other hand, if it were light, he should attach an importance to the office of friendship. She had him, with her little lonely acuteness—as acuteness went during the dog-days in the Regent's Park—in a cleft stick: she either mattered, and then she was ill; or she didn't matter, and then she was well enough. Now he was "acting," as they said at home, as if she did matter—until he should prove the contrary. It was too evident that a person at his high pressure must keep his inconsistencies, which were probably his highest amusements, only for the very greatest occasions. Her prevision, in fine, of just where she should catch him furnished the light of that judgment in which we describe her as daring to indulge. And the judgment it was that made her sensation simple. He *had* distinguished her—that was the chill. He hadn't known—how could he?—that she was devilishly subtle, subtle exactly in the manner of the suspected, the suspicious, the condemned. He in fact confessed to it, in his way, as to an interest in her combinations, her funny race, her funny losses, her funny gains, her funny freedom, and, no doubt, above all, her funny manners—funny, like those of Americans at their best, without being vulgar, legitimating amiability and helping to pass it off. In his appreciation of these redundancies he dressed out for her the compassion he so signally permitted himself to waste; but its operation for herself was as directly divesting, denuding, exposing. It reduced her to her ultimate state, which was that of a poor girl with her rent to pay for example—staring before her in a great city. Milly had her rent to pay, her rent for her future; everything else but how to meet it fell away from her in pieces, in tatters. This was the sensation the great man had doubtless not purposed. Well, she must go home, like the poor girl, and see. There might after all be ways; the poor girl too would be thinking. It came back for that matter perhaps to views already presented. She looked about her again, on her feet, at her scattered, melancholy comrades—some of them so melancholy as to be down on their stomachs in the grass, turned away, ignoring, burrowing; she saw once more, with them, those two faces of the question between which there was so little to choose for inspiration. It was perhaps superficially more striking that one could live if one would; but it was more appealing, insinuating, irresistible, in short, that one would live if one could.

She found after this, for the day or two, more amusement than she had ventured to count on in the fact, if it were not a mere fancy, of deceiving Susie; and she presently felt that what made the difference was the mere fancy—as this *was* one—of a countermove to her great man. His taking on himself—should he do so—to get at her companion made her suddenly, she held, irresponsible, made any notion of her own all right for her; though indeed at the very moment she invited herself to enjoy this impunity she became aware of new matter for surprise, or at least for speculation. Her idea would rather have been that Mrs. Stringham would have looked at her hard—her sketch of the grounds of her long, independent excursion showing, she could feel, as almost cynically superficial. Yet the dear woman so failed, in the event, to avail herself of any right of criticism that it was sensibly tempting, for an hour, to wonder if Kate Croy had been playing perfectly fair. Hadn't she possibly, from motives of the highest benevolence, promptings of the finest anxiety, just given poor Susie what she would have called the straight tip? It must immediately be mentioned, however, that, quite apart from a remembrance of the distinctness of Kate's promise, Milly, the next thing, found her explanation in a truth that had the merit of being general. If Susie, at this crisis, suspiciously spared her, it was really that Susie was always suspiciously sparing her—yet occasionally, too, with portentous and exceptional mercies. The girl was conscious of how she dropped at times into inscrutable, impenetrable deferences—attitudes that, though without at all intending it, made a difference for familiarity, for the ease of intimacy. It was as if she recalled herself to manners, to the law of court-etiquette—which last note above all helped our young woman to a just appreciation. It was definite for her, even if not quite solid, that to treat her as a princess was a positive need of her companion's mind; wherefore she couldn't help it if this lady had her transcendent view of the way the class in question were treated. Susan had read history, had read Gibbon and Froude and Saint-Simon; she had high-lights as to the special allowances made for the class, and, since she saw them, when young, as effete and overtutored, inevitably ironic and infinitely refined, one must take it for amusing if she inclined to an indulgence verily Byzantine. If one *could* only be Byzantine!—wasn't *that* what she insidiously led one on to sigh? Milly tried to oblige her—for it really placed Susan herself so handsomely to be Byzantine now. The great ladies of that race—it would be somewhere in Gibbon—weren't, apparently, questioned about their mysteries. But oh, poor Milly and hers! Susan at all events proved scarce more inquisitive than if she had been a mosaic at Ravenna. Susan was a porcelain monument to the odd moral that consideration might, like cynicism, have abysses. Besides, the Puritan finally disencumbered——! What starved generations wasn't Mrs. Stringham, in fancy, going to make up for?

Kate Croy came straight to the hotel—came that evening shortly before dinner; specifically and publicly moreover, in a hansom that, driven apparently very fast, pulled up beneath their windows almost with the clatter of an accident, a "smash." Milly, alone, as happened, in the great garnished void of their sitting-room, where, a little, really, like a caged Byzantine, she had been pacing through the queer, long-drawn, almost sinister delay of night, an effect she yet liked—Milly, at the sound, one of the French windows standing open, passed out to the balcony that overhung, with pretensions, the general entrance, and so was in time for the look that Kate, alighting, paying her cabman, happened to send up to the front. The visitor moreover had a shilling back to wait for, during which Milly, from the balcony, looked down at her, and a mute exchange, but with smiles and nods, took place between them on what had occurred in the morning. It was what Kate had called for, and the tone was thus, almost by accident, determined for Milly before her friend came up. What was also, however, determined for her was, again, yet irrepressibly again, that the image presented to her, the splendid young woman who looked so particularly handsome in impatience, with the fine freedom of her signal, was the peculiar property of somebody else's vision, that this fine freedom in short was the fine freedom she showed Mr. Densher.

Just so was how she looked to him, and just so was how Milly was held by her—held as by the strange sense of seeing through that distant person's eyes. It lasted, as usual, the strange sense, but fifty seconds; yet in so lasting it produced an effect. It produced in fact more than one, and we take them in their order. The first was that it struck our young woman as absurd to say that a girl's looking so to a man could possibly be without connections; and the second was that by the time Kate had got into the room Milly was in mental possession of the main connection it must have for herself.

She produced this commodity on the spot—produced it, that is, in straight response to Kate's frank "Well, what?" The inquiry bore of course, with Kate's eagerness, on the issue of the morning's scene, the great man's latest wisdom, and it doubtless affected Milly a little as the cheerful demand for news is apt to affect troubled spirits when news is not, in one of the neater forms, prepared for delivery. She couldn't have said what it was exactly that, on the instant, determined her; the nearest description of it would perhaps have been as the more vivid impression of all her friend took for granted. The contrast between this free quantity and the maze of possibilities through which, for hours, she had herself been picking her way, put on, in short, for the moment, a grossness that even friendly forms scarce lightened: it helped forward in fact the revelation to herself that she absolutely had nothing to tell. Besides which, certainly, there was something else—an influence, at the particular juncture, still more obscure. Kate had lost, on the way upstairs, the look—*the* look—that made her young hostess so subtly think and one of the signs of which was that she never kept it for many moments at once; yet she stood there, none the less, so in her bloom and in her strength, so completely again the "handsome girl" beyond all others, the "handsome girl" for whom Milly had at first gratefully taken her, that to meet her now with the note of the plaintive would amount somehow to a surrender, to a confession. *She* would never in her life be ill; the greatest doctor would keep her, at the worst, the fewest minutes; and it was as if she had asked just *with* all this practical impeccability for all that was most mortal in her friend. These things, for Milly, inwardly danced their dance; but the vibration produced and the dust kicked up had lasted less than our account of them. Almost before she knew it she was answering, and answering, beautifully, with no consciousness of fraud, only as with a sudden flare of the famous "will-power" she had heard about, read about, and which was what her medical adviser had mainly thrown her back on. "Oh, it's all right. He's lovely."

Kate was splendid, and it would have been clear for Milly now, had the further presumption been needed, that she had said no word to Mrs. Stringham. "You mean you've been absurd?"

"Absurd." It was a simple word to say, but the consequence of it, for our young woman, was that she felt it, as soon as spoken, to have done something for her safety.

And Kate really hung on her lips. "There's nothing at all the matter?"

"Nothing to worry about. I shall take a little watching, but I shan't have to do anything dreadful, or even, in the least, inconvenient. I can do in fact as I like." It was wonderful for Milly how just to put it so made all its pieces fall at present quite properly into places.

Yet even before the full effect came Kate had seized, kissed, blessed her. "My love, you're too sweet! It's too dear! But it's as I was sure." Then she grasped the full beauty. "You can do as you like?"

"Quite. Isn't it charming?"

"Ah, but catch you," Kate triumphed with gaiety, *"not* doing——! And what *shall* you do?"

"For the moment simply enjoy it. Enjoy"—Milly was completely luminous—"having got out of my scrape."

"Learning, you mean, so easily, that you *are* well."

It was as if Kate had but too conveniently put the words into her mouth. "Learning, I mean, so easily, that I *am* well."

"Only, no one's of course well enough to stay in London now. He can't," Kate went on, "want this of you."

"Mercy, no—I'm to knock about. I'm to go to places."

"But not beastly 'climates'—Engadines, Rivieras, boredoms?"

"No; just, as I say, where I prefer. I'm to go in for pleasure."

"Oh, the duck!"—Kate, with her own shades of familiarity, abounded. "But what kind of pleasure?"

"The highest," Milly smiled.

Her friend met it as nobly. "Which is the highest?"

"Well, it's just our chance to find out. You must help me."

"What have I wanted to do but help you," Kate asked, "from the moment I first laid eyes on you?" Yet with this too Kate had her wonder. "I like your talking, though, about that. What help, with your luck all round, do you want?"

XIV

Milly indeed at last couldn't say; so that she had really for the time brought it along to the point so oddly marked for her by her visitor's arrival, the truth that she was enviably strong. She carried this out, from that evening, for each hour still left her, and the more easily perhaps that the hours were now narrowly numbered. All she actually waited for was Sir Luke Strett's promised visit; as to her proceeding on which, however, her mind was quite made up. Since he wanted to get at Susie he should have the freest access, and then perhaps he would see how he liked it. What was between *them* they might settle as between them, and any pressure it should lift from her own spirit they were at liberty to convert to their use. If the dear man wished to fire Susan Shepherd with a still higher ideal, he would only after all, at the worst, have Susan on his hands. If devotion, in a word, was what it would come up for the interested pair to organise, she was herself ready to consume it as the dressed and served dish. He had talked to her of her "appetite" her account of which, she felt, must have been vague. But for devotion, she could now see, this appetite would be of the best. Gross, greedy, ravenous—these were doubtless the proper names for her: she was at all events resigned in advance to the machinations of sympathy. The day that followed her lonely excursion was to be the last but two or three of their stay in London; and the evening of that day practically ranked for them as, in the matter of outside relations, the last of all. People were by this time quite scattered, and many of those who had so liberally manifested in calls, in cards, in evident sincerity about visits, later on, over the land, had positively passed in music out of sight; whether as members, these latter, more especially, of Mrs. Lowder's immediate circle or as members of Lord Mark's—our friends being by this time able to make the distinction. The general pitch had thus, decidedly, dropped, and the occasions still to be dealt with were special and few. One of these, for Milly, announced itself as the doctor's call already mentioned, as to which she had now had a note from him: the single other, of importance, was their appointed leave-taking—for the shortest separation—in respect to Mrs. Lowder and Kate. The aunt and the niece were to dine with them alone, intimately and easily—as easily as should be consistent with the question of their afterwards going on together to some absurdly belated party, at which they had had it from Aunt Maud that they would do well to show. Sir Luke was to make his appearance on the morrow of this, and in respect to that complication Milly had already her plan.

The night was, at all events, hot and stale, and it was late enough by the time the four ladies had been gathered in, for their small session, at the hotel, where the windows were still open to the high balconies and the flames of the candles, behind the pink shades—disposed as for the vigil of watchers—were motionless in the air in which the season lay dead. What was presently settled among them was that Milly, who betrayed on this occasion a preference more marked than usual, should not hold herself obliged to climb that evening the social stair, however it might stretch to meet her, and that, Mrs. Lowder and Mrs. Stringham facing the ordeal together, Kate Croy should remain with her and await their return. It was a pleasure to Milly, ever, to send Susan Shepherd forth; she saw her go with complacency, liked, as it were, to put people off with her, and noted with satisfaction, when she so moved to the carriage, the further denudation—a markedly ebbing tide—of her little benevolent back. If it wasn't quite Aunt Maud's ideal, moreover, to take out the new American girl's funny friend instead of the new American girl herself, nothing could better indicate the range of that lady's merit than the spirit in which—as at the present hour for instance—she made the best of the minor advantage. And she did this with a broad, cheerful absence of illusion; she did it—confessing even as much to poor Susie—because, frankly, she *was* good-natured. When Mrs. Stringham observed that her own light was too abjectly borrowed and that it was as a link alone, fortunately not missing, that she was valued, Aunt Maud concurred to the extent of the remark: "Well, my dear, you're better than nothing." To-night, furthermore, it came up for Milly that Aunt Maud had something particular in mind. Mrs. Stringham, before adjourning with her, had gone off for some shawl or other accessory, and Kate, as if a little impatient for their withdrawal, had wandered out to the balcony, where she hovered, for the time, unseen, though with scarce more to look at than the dim London stars and the cruder glow, up the street, on a corner, of a small public-house, in front of which a fagged cab-horse was thrown into relief. Mrs. Lowder made use of the moment: Milly felt as soon as she had spoken that what she was doing was somehow for use.

"Dear Susan tells me that you saw, in America, Mr. Densher—whom I've never till now, as you may have noticed, asked you about. But do you mind at last, in connection with him, doing something for me?" She had lowered her fine voice to a depth, though speaking with all her rich glibness; and Milly, after a small sharpness of surprise, was already guessing the sense of her appeal. "Will you name him, in any way you like, to *her*"—and Aunt Maud gave a nod at the window; "so that you may perhaps find out whether he's back?"

Ever so many things, for Milly, fell into line at this; it was a wonder, she afterwards thought, that she could be conscious of so many at once. She smiled hard, however, for them all. "But I don't know that it's important to me to 'find out.'" The array of things was further swollen, however, even as she said this, by its striking her as too much to say. She therefore tried as quickly to say less. "Except you mean, of course, that it's important to *you.*" She fancied Aunt Maud was looking at her almost as hard as she was herself smiling, and that gave her another impulse. "You know I never *have* yet named him to her; so that if I should break out now——"

"Well?"—Mrs. Lowder waited.

"Why, she may wonder what I've been making a mystery of. She hasn't mentioned him, you know," Milly went on, "herself."

"No"—her friend a little heavily weighed it—"she wouldn't. So it's she, you see then, who has made the mystery."

Yes, Milly but wanted to see; only there was so much. "There has been of course no particular reason." Yet that indeed was neither here nor there. "Do you think," she asked, "he is back?"

"It will be about his time, I gather, and rather a comfort to me definitely to know."

"Then can't you ask her yourself?"

"Ah, we never speak of him!"

It helped Milly for the moment to the convenience of a puzzled pause. "Do you mean he's an acquaintance of whom you disapprove for her?"

Aunt Maud, as well, just hung fire. "I disapprove of *her* for the poor young man. She doesn't care for him."

"And *he* cares so much——?"

"Too much, too much. And my fear is," said Mrs. Lowder, "that he privately besets her. She keeps it to herself, but I don't want her worried. Neither, in truth," she both generously and confidentially concluded, "do I want *him.* "

Milly showed all her own effort to meet the case. "But what can *I* do?"

"You can find out where they are. If I myself try," Mrs. Lowder explained, "I shall appear to treat them as if I supposed them deceiving me."

"And you don't. You don't," Milly mused for her, "suppose them deceiving you."

"Well," said Aunt Maud, whose fine onyx eyes failed to blink, even though Milly's questions might have been taken as drawing her rather further than she had originally meant to go—"well, Kate is thoroughly aware of my views for her, and that I take her being with me, at present, in the way she is with me, if you know what I mean, as a loyal assent to them. Therefore as my views don't happen to provide a place, at all, for Mr. Densher, much, in a manner, as I like him"—therefore, therefore in short she had been prompted to this step, though she completed her sense, but sketchily, with the rattle of her large fan.

It assisted them perhaps, however, for the moment, that Milly was able to pick out of her sense what might serve as the clearest part of it. "You do like him then?"

"Oh dear, yes. Don't you?"

Milly hesitated, for the question was somehow as the sudden point of something sharp on a nerve that winced. She just caught her breath, but she had ground for joy afterwards, she felt, in not really having failed to choose with quickness sufficient, out of fifteen possible answers, the one that would best serve her. She was then almost proud, as well, that she had cheerfully smiled. "I did—three times—in New York." So came and went for her, in these simple words, the speech that was to figure for her, later on, that night, as the one she had ever uttered that cost her most. She was to lie awake, at all events, half the night, for the gladness of not having taken any line so really inferior as the denial of a happy impression.

For Mrs. Lowder also, moreover, her simple words were the right ones; they were at any rate, that lady's laugh showed, in the natural note of the racy. "You dear American thing! But people may be very good, and yet not good for what one wants."

413

"Yes," the girl assented, "even I suppose when what one wants is something very good."

"Oh, my child, it would take too long just now to tell you all *I* want! I want everything at once and together—and ever so much for you too, you know. But you've seen us," Aunt Maud continued; "you'll have made out."

"Ah," said Milly, "I *don't* make out"; for again—it came that way in rushes—she felt an obscurity in things. "Why, if our friend here doesn't like him——"

"Should I conceive her interested in keeping things from me?" Mrs. Lowder did justice to the question. "My dear, how can you ask? Put yourself in her place. She meets me, but on *her* terms. Proud young women are proud young women. And proud old ones are—well, what *I* am. Fond of you as we both are, you can help us."

Milly tried to be inspired. "Does it come back then to my asking her straight?"

At this, however, finally, Aunt Maud threw her up. "Oh, if you've so many reasons not——!"

"I've not so many," Milly smiled "but I've one. If I break out so suddenly as knowing him, what will she make of my not having spoken before?"

Mrs. Lowder looked blank at it. "Why should you care what she makes? You may have only been decently discreet."

"Ah, I *have* been," the girl made haste to say.

"Besides," her friend went on, "I suggested to you, through Susan, your line."

"Yes, that reason's a reason for *me.*"

"And for *me,*" Mrs. Lowder insisted. "She's not therefore so stupid as not to do justice to grounds so marked. You can tell her perfectly that I had asked you to say nothing."

"And may I tell her that you've asked me now to speak?"

Mrs. Lowder might well have thought, yet, oddly, this pulled her up. "You can't do it without——?"

Milly was almost ashamed to be raising so many difficulties. "I'll do what I can if you'll kindly tell me one thing more." She faltered a little—it was so prying; but she brought it out. "Will he have been writing to her?"

"It's exactly, my dear, what I should like to know." Mrs. Lowder was at last impatient. "Push in for yourself, and I dare say she'll tell you."

Even now, all the same, Milly had not quite fallen back. "It will be pushing in," she continued to smile, "for *you*" She allowed her companion, however, no time to take this up. "The point will be that if he *has* been writing she may have answered."

"But what point, you subtle thing, is that?"

"It isn't subtle, it seems to me, but quite simple," Milly said, "that if she has answered she has very possibly spoken of me."

"Very certainly indeed. But what difference will it make?"

The girl had a moment, at this, of thinking it natural that her interlocutress herself should so fail of subtlety. "It will make the difference that he will have written to her in answer that he knows me. And that, in turn," our young woman explained, "will give an oddity to my own silence."

"How so, if she's perfectly aware of having given you no opening? The only oddity," Aunt Maud lucidly professed, "is for yourself. It's in *her* not having spoken."

"Ah, there we are!" said Milly.

And she had uttered it, evidently, in a tone that struck her friend. "Then it *has* troubled you?"

But ah, the inquiry had only to be made to bring the rare colour with fine inconsequence, to her face. "Not, really, the least little bit!" And, quickly feeling the need to abound in this sense, she was on the point, to cut short, of declaring that she cared, after all, no scrap how much she obliged. Only she felt at this instant too the intervention of still other things. Mrs. Lowder was, in the first place, already beforehand, already affected as by the sudden vision of her having herself pushed too far. Milly could never judge from her face of her uppermost motive—it was so little, in its hard, smooth sheen, that kind of human countenance. She looked hard when she spoke fair; the only thing was that when she spoke hard she likewise didn't look soft. Something, none the less, had arisen in her now—a full appreciable tide, entering by the rupture of some bar. She announced that if what she had asked was to prove in the least a bore her young friend was not to dream of it; making her young friend at the same time, by the change in her tone, dream on the spot more profusely. She spoke with a belated light, Milly could apprehend—she could always apprehend—from pity; and the result of that perception, for the girl, was singular: it proved to her as quickly that Kate, keeping her secret, had been straight with her. From Kate distinctly then, as to why she was to be pitied, Aunt Maud knew nothing, and was thereby simply putting in evidence the fine side of her own character. This fine side was that she could almost at any hour, by a kindled preference or a diverted energy, glow for another interest than her own. She exclaimed as well, at this moment, that Milly must have been thinking, round the case, much more than she had supposed; and this remark could, at once, affect the girl as sharply as any other form of the charge of weakness. It was what everyone, if she didn't look out, would soon be saying—"There's something the matter with you!" What one was therefore one's self concerned immediately to establish was that there was nothing at all. "I shall like to help you; I shall like, so far as that goes, to help Kate herself," she made such haste as she could to declare; her eyes wandering meanwhile across the width of the room to that dusk of the balcony in which their companion perhaps a little unaccountably lingered. She suggested hereby her impatience to begin; she almost overtly wondered at the length of the opportunity this friend was giving them—referring it, however, so far as words went, to the other friend, breaking off with an amused: "How tremendously Susie must be beautifying!"

It only marked Aunt Maud, none the less, as too preoccupied for her allusion. The onyx eyes were fixed upon her with a polished pressure that must signify some enriched benevolence. "Let it go, my dear. We shall, after all, soon enough see."

"If he *has* come back we shall certainly see," Milly after a moment replied; "for he'll probably feel that he can't quite civilly not come to see me. Then *there,*" she remarked, "we shall be. It wouldn't then, you see, come through Kate at all—it would come through him. Except," she wound up with a smile, "that he won't find me."

She had the most extraordinary sense of interesting her interlocutress, in spite of herself, more than she wanted; it was as if her doom so floated her on that she couldn't stop—by very much the same trick it had played her with her doctor. "Shall you run away from him?"

She neglected the question, wanting only now to get off. "Then," she went on, "you'll deal with Kate directly."

"Shall you run away from *her?*" Mrs. Lowder profoundly inquired, while they became aware of Susie's return through the room, opening out behind them, in which they had dined.

This affected Milly as giving her but an instant; and suddenly, with it, everything she felt in the connection rose to her lips in a question that, even as she put it, she knew she was failing to keep colourless. "Is it your own belief that he *is* with her?"

Aunt Maud took it in—took in, that is, everything of the tone that she just wanted her not to; and the result for some seconds, was but to make their eyes meet in silence. Mrs. Stringham had rejoined them and was asking if Kate had gone—an inquiry at once answered by this young lady's reappearance. They saw her again in the open window, where, looking at them, she had paused—producing thus, on Aunt Maud's part, almost too impressive a "Hush!" Mrs. Lowder indeed, without loss of time, smothered any danger in a sweeping retreat with Susie; but Milly's words to her, just uttered, about dealing with her niece directly, struck our young woman as already recoiling on herself. Directness, however evaded, would be, fully, for *her;* nothing in fact would ever have been for her so direct as the evasion. Kate had remained in the window, very handsome and upright, the outer dark framing in a highly favourable way her summery simplicities and lightnesses of dress. Milly had, given the relation of space, no real fear she had heard their talk; only she hovered there as with conscious eyes and some added advantage. Then indeed, with small delay, her friend sufficiently saw. The conscious eyes, the added advantage were but those she had now always at command—those proper to the person Milly knew as known to Merton Densher. It was for several seconds again as if the *total* of her identity had been that of the person known to him—a determination having for result another sharpness of its own. Kate had positively but to be there just as she was to tell her he had come back. It seemed to pass between them, in fine, without a word, that he was in London, that he was perhaps only round the corner; and surely therefore no dealing of Milly's with her would yet have been so direct.

XV

It was doubtless because this queer form of directness had in itself, for the hour, seemed so sufficient that Milly was afterwards aware of having really, all the while—during the strange, indescribable session before the return of their companions—done nothing to intensify it. If she was most aware only afterwards, under the long, discurtained ordeal of the morrow's dawn, that was because she had really, till their evening's end came, ceased, after a little, to miss anything from their ostensible comfort. What was behind showed but in gleams and glimpses; what was in front never at all confessed to not holding the stage. Three minutes had not passed before Milly quite knew she should have done nothing Aunt Maud had just asked her. She knew it moreover by much the same light that had acted for her with that lady and with Sir Luke Strett. It pressed upon her then and there that she was still in a current determined, through her indifference, timidity, bravery, generosity— she scarce could say which—by others; that not she but the current acted, and that somebody else, always, was the keeper of the lock or the dam. Kate for example had but to open the flood-gate: the current moved in its mass—the current, as it had been, of her doing as Kate wanted. What, somehow, in the most extraordinary way in the world, *had* Kate wanted but to be, of a sudden, more interesting than she had ever been? Milly, for their evening then, quite held her breath with the appreciation of it. If she hadn't been sure her companion would have had nothing, from her moments with Mrs. Lowder, to go by, she would almost have seen the admirable creature "cutting in" to anticipate a danger. This fantasy indeed, while they sat together, dropped after a little; even if only because other fantasies multiplied and clustered, making fairly, for our young woman, the buoyant medium in which her friend talked and moved. They sat together, I say, but Kate moved as much as she talked; she figured there, restless and charming, just perhaps a shade perfunctory, repeatedly quitting her place, taking slowly, to and fro, in the trailing folds of her light dress, the length of the room, and almost avowedly performing for the pleasure of her hostess.

Mrs. Lowder had said to Milly at Matcham that she and her niece, as allies, could practically conquer the world; but though it was a speech about which there had even then been a vague, grand glamour, the girl read into it at present more of an approach to a meaning. Kate, for that matter, by herself, could conquer anything, and *she,* Milly Theale, was probably concerned with the "world" only as the small scrap of it that most impinged on her and that was therefore first to be dealt with. On this basis of being dealt with she would doubtless herself do her share of the conquering: she would have something to supply, Kate something to take—each of them thus, to that tune, something for squaring with Aunt Maud's ideal. This in short was what it came to now—that the occasion, in the quiet late lamplight, had the quality of a rough rehearsal of the possible big drama. Milly knew herself dealt with—handsomely, completely: she surrendered to the knowledge, for so it was, she felt, that she supplied her helpful force. And what Kate had to take Kate took as freely and, to all appearance, as gratefully; accepting afresh, with each of her long, slow walks, the relation between them so established and consecrating her companion's surrender simply by the interest she gave it. The interest to Milly herself we naturally mean; the interest to Kate Milly felt as probably inferior. It easily and largely came for their present talk, for the quick flight of the hour before the breach of the spell—it all came, when considered, from the circumstance, not in the least abnormal, that the handsome girl was in extraordinary "form." Milly remembered her having said that she was at her best late at night; remembered it by its having, with its fine assurance, made her wonder when *she* was at her best and how happy people must be who had such a fixed time. She had no time at all; she was never at her best—unless indeed it were exactly, as now, in listening, watching, admiring, collapsing. If Kate moreover, quite mercilessly, had never been so good, the beauty and the marvel of it was that she had never really been so frank; being a person of such a calibre, as Milly would have said, that, even while "dealing" with you and thereby, as it were, picking her steps, she could let herself go, could, in irony, in confidence, in extravagance, tell you things she had never told before. That was the impression—that she was telling things, and quite conceivably for her own relief as well; almost as if the errors of vision, the mistakes of proportion, the residuary innocence of spirit still to be remedied on the part of her auditor had their moments of proving too much for her nerves. She went at them just now, these sources of irritation, with an amused energy that it would have been open to Milly to regard as cynical and that was nevertheless called for—as to this the other was distinct—by the way that in certain connections the American mind broke down. It seemed at least—the American mind as sitting there thrilled and dazzled in Milly—not to understand English society without a separate confrontation with *all* the cases. It couldn't proceed by—there was some technical term she lacked until Milly suggested both analogy and induction, and then, differently, instinct, none of which were right: it had to be led up and introduced to each aspect of the monster, enabled to walk all round it, whether for the consequent exaggerated ecstasy or for the still more as appeared to this critic disproportionate shock. It might, the monster, Kate conceded, loom large for those born amid forms less developed and therefore no doubt less amusing; it might on some sides be a strange and dreadful monster, calculated to devour the unwary, to abase the proud, to scandalize the good; but if one had to live with it one must, not to be for ever sitting up, learn how: which was virtually in short to-night what the handsome girl showed herself as teaching.

She gave away publicly, in this process, Lancaster Gate and everything it contained; she gave away, hand over hand, Milly's thrill continued to note, Aunt Maud and Aunt Maud's glories and Aunt Maud's complacencies; she gave herself away most of all, and it was naturally what most contributed to her candour. She didn't speak to her friend once more, in Aunt Maud's strain, of how they could scale the skies; she spoke, by her bright, perverse preference on this occasion, of the need, in the first place, of being neither stupid nor vulgar. It might have been a lesson, for our young American, in the art of seeing things as they were—a lesson so various and so sustained that the pupil had, as we have shown, but receptively to gape. The odd thing furthermore was that it could serve its purpose while explicitly disavowing every personal bias. It wasn't that she disliked Aunt Maud, who was everything she had on other occasions declared; but the dear woman, ineffaceably stamped by inscrutable nature and a dreadful art, wasn't—how *could* she be?—what she wasn't. She wasn't any one. She wasn't anything. She wasn't anywhere. Milly mustn't think it—one couldn't, as a good friend, let her. Those hours at Matcham were *inespérées,* were pure manna from heaven; or if not wholly that perhaps, with humbugging old Lord Mark as a backer, were vain as a ground for hopes and calculations. Lord Mark was very well, but he wasn't *the* cleverest creature in England, and even if he had been he still wouldn't have been the most obliging. He weighed it out in ounces, and indeed each of the pair was really waiting for what the other would put down.

"She has put down *you.*" said Milly, attached to the subject still; "and I think what you mean is that, on the counter, she still keeps hold of you."

"Lest"—Kate took it up—"he should suddenly grab me and run? Oh, as he isn't ready to run, he's much less ready, naturally, to grab. I *am*—you're so far right as that—on the counter, when I'm not in the shop-window; in and out of which I'm thus conveniently, commercially whisked: the essence, all of it, of my position, and the price, as properly, of my aunt's protection." Lord Mark was substantially what she had begun with as soon as they were alone; the impression was even yet with Milly of her having sounded his name, having imposed it, as a topic, in direct opposition to the other name that Mrs. Lowder had left in the air and that all her own look, as we have seen, kept there at first for her companion. The immediate strange effect had been that of her consciously needing, as it were, an alibi—which, successfully, she so found. She had worked it to the end, ridden it to and fro across the course marked for Milly by Aunt Maud, and now she had quite, so to speak, broken it in. "The bore is that if she wants him so much—wants him, heaven forgive her! for *me*—he has put us all out, since your arrival, by wanting somebody else. I don't mean somebody else than you."

Milly threw off the charm sufficiently to shake her head. "Then I haven't made out who it is. If I'm any part of his alternative he had better stop where he is."

"Truly, truly?—always, always?"

Milly tried to insist with an equal gaiety. "Would you like me to swear?"

Kate appeared for a moment—though that was doubtless but gaiety too—to think. "Haven't we been swearing enough?"

"You have perhaps, but I haven't, and I ought to give you the equivalent. At any rate there it is. Truly, truly as you say—'always, always.' So I'm not in the way."

"Thanks," said Kate—"but that doesn't help me."

"Oh, it's as simplifying for *him* that I speak of it."

"The difficulty really is that he's a person with so many ideas that it's particularly hard to simplify for him. That's exactly of course what Aunt Maud has been trying. He won't," Kate firmly continued, "make up his mind about me."

"Well," Milly smiled, "give him time."

Her friend met it in perfection. "One is *doing* that—one *is*. But one remains, all the same, but one of his ideas."

"There's no harm in that," Milly returned, "if you come out in the end as the best of them. What's a man," she pursued, "especially an ambitious one, without a variety of ideas?"

"No doubt. The more the merrier." And Kate looked at her grandly. "One can but hope to come out, and do nothing to prevent it."

All of which made for the impression, fantastic or not, of the *alibi*. The splendour, the grandeur were, for Milly, the bold ironic spirit behind it, so interesting too in itself. What, moreover, was not less interesting was the fact, as our young woman noted it, that Kate confined her point to the difficulties, so far as *she* was concerned, raised only by Lord Mark. She referred now to none that her own taste might present; which circumstance again played its little part. She was doing what she liked in respect to another person, but she was in no way committed to the other person, and her furthermore talking of Lord Mark as not young and not true were only the signs of her clear self-consciousness, were all in the line of her slightly hard, but scarce the less graceful extravagance. She didn't wish to show too much her consent to be arranged for, but that was a different thing from not wishing sufficiently to give it. There was something moreover, on it all, that Milly still found occasion to say, "If your aunt has been, as you tell me, put out by me, I feel that she has remained remarkably kind."

"Oh, but she has—whatever might have happened in that respect—plenty of use for you! You put her in, my dear, more than you put her out. You don't half see it, but she has clutched your petticoat. You can do anything—you can do, I mean, lots that *we* can't. You're an outsider, independent and standing by yourself; you're not hideously relative to tiers and tiers of others." And Kate, facing in that direction, went further and further; wound up, while Milly gaped, with extraordinary words. "We're of no use to you—it's decent to tell you. You'd be of use to us, but that's a different matter. My honest advice to you would be—" she went indeed all lengths—"to drop us while you can. It would be funny if you didn't soon see how awfully better you can do. We've not really done for you the least thing worth speaking of—nothing you mightn't easily have had in some other way. Therefore you're under no obligation. You won't want us next year; we shall only continue to want *you*. But that's no reason for you, and you mustn't pay too dreadfully for poor Mrs. Stringham's having let you in. She has the best conscience in the world; she's enchanted with what she has done; but you shouldn't take your people from *her*. It has been quite awful to see you do it."

423

Milly tried to be amused, so as not—it was too absurd—to be fairly frightened. Strange enough indeed—if not natural enough—that, late at night thus, in a mere mercenary house, with Susie away, a want of confidence should possess her. She recalled, with all the rest of it, the next day, piecing things together in the dawn, that she had felt herself alone with a creature who paced like a panther. That was a violent image, but it made her a little less ashamed of having been scared. For all her scare, none the less, she had now the sense to find words. "And yet without Susie I shouldn't have had you."

It had been at this point, however, that Kate flickered highest. "Oh, you may very well loathe me yet!"

Really at last, thus, it had been too much; as, with her own least feeble flare, after a wondering watch, Milly had shown. She hadn't cared; she had too much wanted to know; and, though a small solemnity of reproach, a sombre strain, had broken into her tone, it was to figure as her nearest approach to serving Mrs. Lowder. "Why do you say such things to me?"

This unexpectedly had acted, by a sudden turn of Kate's attitude, as a happy speech. She had risen as she spoke, and Kate had stopped before her, shining at her instantly with a softer brightness. Poor Milly hereby enjoyed one of her views of how people, wincing oddly, were often touched by her. "Because you're a dove." With which she felt herself ever so delicately, so considerately, embraced; not with familiarity or as a liberty taken, but almost ceremonially and in the manner of an accolade; partly as if, though a dove who could perch on a finger, one were also a princess with whom forms were to be observed. It even came to her, through the touch of her companion's lips, that this form, this cool pressure, fairly sealed the sense of what Kate had just said. It was moreover, for the girl, like an inspiration: she found herself accepting as the right one, while she caught her breath with relief, the name so given her. She met it on the instant as she would have met the revealed truth; it lighted up the strange dusk in which she lately had walked. *That* was what was the matter with her. She was a dove. Oh, *wasn't* she?—it echoed within her as she became aware of the sound, outside, of the return of their friends. There was, the next thing, little enough doubt about it after Aunt Maud had been two minutes in the room. She had come up, Mrs. Lowder, with Susan—which she needn't have done, at that hour, instead of letting Kate come down to her; so that Milly could be quite sure it was to catch hold, in some way, of the loose end they had left. Well, the way she did catch was simply to make the point that it didn't now in the least matter. She had mounted the stairs for this, and she had her moment again with her younger hostess while Kate, on the spot, as the latter at the time noted, gave Susan Shepherd unwonted opportunities. Kate was in other words, as Aunt Maud engaged her friend, listening with the handsomest response to Mrs. Stringham's impression of the scene they had just quitted. It was in the tone of the fondest indulgence—almost, really, that of dove cooing to dove—that Mrs. Lowder expressed to Milly the hope that it had all gone beautifully. Her "all" had an ample benevolence; it soothed and simplified; she spoke as if it were the two young women, not she and her comrade, who had been facing the town together. But Milly's answer had prepared itself while Aunt Maud was on the stair; she had felt in a rush all the reasons that would make it the most dovelike; and she gave it, while she was about it, as earnest, as candid. "I don't *think,* dear lady, he's here."

It gave her straightway the measure of the success she could have as a dove: that was recorded in the long look of deep criticism, a look without a word, that Mrs. Lowder poured forth. And the word, presently, bettered it still. "Oh, you exquisite thing!" The luscious innuendo of it, almost startling, lingered in the room, after the visitors had gone, like an oversweet fragrance. But left alone with Mrs. Stringham Milly continued to breathe it: she studied again the dovelike and so set her companion to mere rich reporting that she averted all inquiry into her own case.

That, with the new day, was once more her law—though she saw before her, of course, as something of a complication, her need, each time, to decide. She should have to be clear as to how a dove *would* act. She settled it, she thought, well enough this morning by quite readopting her plan in respect to Sir Luke Strett. That, she was pleased to reflect, had originally been pitched in the key of a merely iridescent drab; and although Mrs. Stringham, after breakfast, began by staring at it as if it had been a priceless Persian carpet suddenly unrolled at her feet, she had no scruple, at the end of five minutes, in leaving her to make the best of it. "Sir Luke Strett comes, by appointment, to see me at eleven, but I'm going out on purpose. He's to be told, please, deceptively, that I'm at home, and, you, as my representative, when he comes up, are to see him instead. He will like that, this time, better. So do be nice to him." It had taken, naturally, more explanation, and the mention, above all, of the fact that the visitor was the greatest of doctors; yet when once the key had been offered Susie slipped it on her bunch, and her young friend could again feel her lovely imagination operate. It operated in truth very much as Mrs. Lowder's, at the last, had done the night before: it made the air heavy once more with the extravagance of assent. It might, afresh, almost have frightened our young woman to see how people rushed to meet her: *had* she then so little time to live that the road must always be spared her? It was as if they were helping her to take it out on the spot. Susie—she couldn't deny, and didn't pretend to—might, of a truth, on *her* side, have treated such news as a flash merely lurid; as to which, to do Susie justice, the pain of it was all there. But, none the less, the margin always allowed her young friend was all there as well; and the proposal now made her what was it in short but Byzantine? The vision of Milly's perception of the propriety of the matter had, at any rate, quickly engulfed, so far as her attitude was concerned, any surprise and any shock; so that she only desired, the next thing, perfectly to possess the facts. Milly could easily speak, on this, as if there were only one: she made nothing of such another as that she had felt herself menaced. The great fact, in fine, was that she *knew* him to desire just now, more than anything else, to meet, quite apart, some one interested in her. Who therefore so interested as her faithful Susan? The only other circumstance that, by the time she had quitted her friend, she had treated as worth mentioning was the circumstance of her having at first intended to keep quiet. She had originally best seen herself as sweetly secretive. As to that she had changed, and her present request was the result. She didn't say why she had changed, but she trusted her faithful Susan. Their visitor would trust her not less, and she herself would adore their visitor. Moreover he wouldn't—the girl felt sure—tell her anything dreadful. The worst would be that he was in love and that he needed a confidant to work it. And now she was going to the National Gallery.

XVI

The idea of the National Gallery had been with her from the moment of her hearing from Sir Luke Strett about his hour of coming. It had been in her mind as a place so meagrely visited, as one of the places that had seemed at home one of the attractions of Europe and one of its highest aids to culture, but that—the old story—the typical frivolous always ended by sacrificing to vulgar pleasures. She had had perfectly, at those whimsical moments on the Brünig, the half-shamed sense of turning her back on such opportunities for real improvement as had figured to her, from of old, in connection with the continental tour, under the general head of "pictures and things"; and now she knew for what she had done so. The plea had been explicit—she had done so for life, as opposed to learning; the upshot of which had been that life was now beautifully provided for. In spite of those few dips and dashes into the many-coloured stream of history for which of late Kate Croy had helped her to find time, there were possible great chances she had neglected, possible great moments she should, save for to-day, have all but missed. She might still, she had felt, overtake one or two of them among the Titians and the Turners; she had been honestly nursing the hour, and, once she was in the benignant halls, her faith knew itself justified. It was the air she wanted and the world she would now exclusively choose; the quiet chambers, nobly overwhelming, rich but slightly veiled, opened out round her and made her presently say "If I could lose myself *here!*" There were people, people in plenty, but, admirably, no personal question. It was immense, outside, the personal question; but she had blissfully left it outside, and the nearest it came, for a quarter of an hour, to glimmering again into sight was when she watched for a little one of the more earnest of the lady-copyists. Two or three in particular, spectacled, aproned, absorbed, engaged her sympathy to an absurd extent, seemed to show her for the time the right way to live. She should have been a lady copyist—it met so the case. The case was the case of escape, of living under water, of being at once impersonal and firm. There it was before one— one had only to stick and stick.

Milly yielded to this charm till she was almost ashamed; she watched the lady-copyists till she found herself wondering what would be thought by others of a young woman, of adequate aspect, who should appear to regard them as the pride of the place. She would have liked to talk to them, to get, as it figured to her, into their lives, and was deterred but by the fact that she didn't quite see herself as purchasing imitations and yet feared she might excite the expectation of purchase. She really knew before long that what held her was the mere refuge, that something within her was after all too weak for the Turners and Titians. They joined hands about her in a circle too vast, though a circle that a year before she would only have desired to trace. They were truly for the larger, not for the smaller life, the life of which the actual pitch, for example, was an interest, the interest of compassion, in misguided efforts. She marked absurdly her little stations, blinking, in her shrinkage of curiosity, at the glorious walls, yet keeping an eye on vistas and approaches, so that she shouldn't be flagrantly caught. The vistas and approaches drew her in this way from room to room, and she had been through many parts of the show, as she supposed, when she sat down to rest. There were chairs in scant clusters, places from which one could gaze. Milly indeed at present fixed her eyes more than elsewhere on the appearance, first, that she couldn't quite, after all, have accounted to an examiner for the order of her "schools," and then on that of her being more tired than she had meant, in spite of her having been so much less intelligent. They found, her eyes, it should be added, other occupation as well, which she let them freely follow: they rested largely, in her vagueness, on the vagueness of other visitors; they attached themselves in especial, with mixed results, to the surprising stream of her compatriots. She was struck with the circumstance that the great museum, early in August, was haunted with these pilgrims, as also with that of her knowing them from afar, marking them easily, each and all, and recognising not less promptly that they had ever new lights for her—new lights on their own darkness. She gave herself up at last, and it was a consummation like another: what she should have come to the National Gallery for to-day would be to watch the copyists and reckon the Baedekers. That perhaps was the moral of a menaced state of health—that one would sit in public places and count the Americans. It passed the time in a manner; but it seemed already the second line of defence, and this notwithstanding the pattern, so unmistakable, of her country-folk. They were cut out as by scissors, coloured, labelled, mounted; but their relation to her failed to act—they somehow did nothing for her. Partly, no doubt, they didn't so much as notice or know her, didn't even recognise their community of collapse with her, the sign on her, as she sat there, that for her too Europe was "tough." It came to her idly thus— for her humour could still play—that she didn't seem then the same success with them as with the inhabitants of London, who had taken her up on scarce more of an acquaintance. She could wonder if they would be different should she go back with that glamour attached; and she could also wonder, if it came to that, whether she should ever go back. Her friends straggled past, at any rate, in all the vividness of their absent criticism, and she had even at last the sense of taking a mean advantage. There was a finer instant, however, at which three ladies, clearly a mother and daughters, had paused before her under compulsion of a comment apparently just uttered by one of them and referring to some object on the other side of the room. Milly had her back to the object, but her face very much to her young compatriot, the one who had spoken and in whose look she perceived a certain gloom of recognition. Recognition, for that matter, sat confessedly in her own eyes: she *knew* the three, generically, as easily as a schoolboy with a crib in his lap would know the answer in class; she felt, like the schoolboy, guilty enough—questioned, as honour went, as to her right so to possess, to dispossess, people who hadn't consciously provoked her. She would have been able to say where they lived, and how, had the place and the way been but amenable to the positive; she bent tenderly, in imagination, over marital, paternal Mr. Whatever-he-was, at home, eternally named, with all the honours and placidities, but eternally unseen and existing only as some one who could be financially heard from. The mother, the puffed and composed whiteness of whose hair had no relation to her apparent age, showed a countenance almost chemically clean and dry; her companions wore an air of vague resentment humanised by fatigue; and the three were equally adorned with short cloaks of coloured cloth surmounted by little tartan hoods. The tartans were doubtless conceivable as different, but the cloaks, curiously, only thinkable as one. "Handsome? Well, if you choose to say so." It was the mother who had spoken, who herself added, after a pause during which Milly took the reference as to a picture: "In the English style." The three pair of eyes had converged, and their possessors had for an instant rested, with the effect of a drop of the subject, on this last characterisation—with that, too, of a gloom not less mute in one of the daughters than murmured in the other. Milly's heart went out to them while they turned their backs; she said to herself that they ought to have known her, that there was something between them they might have beautifully put together. But she had lost *them* also—they were cold; they left her in her weak wonder as to what they had been looking at. The "handsome" disposed her to turn—all the more that the "English style" would be the English school, which she liked; only she saw, before moving, by the array on the side facing her, that she was in fact among small Dutch pictures. The action of this was again appreciable—the dim surmise that it wouldn't then be by a picture that the spring in the three ladies had been pressed. It was at all events time she should go, and she turned as she got on her feet. She had had behind her one of the entrances and various visitors who had come in while she sat, visitors single and in pairs—by one of the former of whom she felt her eyes suddenly held.

This was a gentleman in the middle of the place, a gentleman who had removed his hat and was for a moment, while he glanced, absently, as she could see, at the top tier of the collection, tapping his forehead with his pocket-handkerchief. The occupation held him long enough to give Milly time to take for granted—and a few seconds sufficed—that his face was the object just observed by her friends. This could only have been because she concurred in their tribute, even qualified, and indeed "the English style" of the gentleman—perhaps by instant contrast to the American—was what had had the arresting power. This arresting power, at the same time—and that was the marvel—had already sharpened almost to pain, for in the very act of judging the bared head with detachment she felt herself shaken by a knowledge of it. It was Merton Densher's own, and he was standing there, standing long enough unconscious for her to fix him and then hesitate. These successions were swift, so that she could still ask herself in freedom if she had best let him see her. She could still reply to that that she shouldn't like him to catch her in the effort to prevent this; and she might further have decided that he was too preoccupied to see anything had not a perception intervened that surpassed the first in violence. She was unable to think afterwards how long she had looked at him before knowing herself as otherwise looked at; all she was coherently to put together was that she had had a second recognition without his having noticed her. The source of this latter shock was nobody less than Kate Croy— Kate Croy who was suddenly also in the line of vision and whose eyes met her eyes at their next movement. Kate was but two yards off—Mr. Densher wasn't alone. Kate's face specifically said so, for after a stare as blank at first as Milly's it broke into a far smile. That was what, wonderfully—in addition to the marvel of their meeting—passed from her for Milly; the instant reduction to easy terms of the fact of their being there, the two young women, together. It was perhaps only afterwards that the girl fully felt the connection between this touch and her already established conviction that Kate was a prodigious person; yet on the spot she none the less, in a degree, knew herself handled and again, as she had been the night before, dealt with—absolutely even dealt with for her greater pleasure. A minute in fine hadn't elapsed before Kate had somehow made her provisionally take everything as natural. The provisional was just the charm—acquiring that character from one moment to the other; it represented happily so much that Kate would explain on the very first chance. This left moreover—and that was the greatest wonder—all due margin for amusement at the way things happened, the monstrous oddity of their turning up in such a place on the very heels of their having separated without allusion to it. The handsome girl was thus literally in control of the scene by the time Merton Densher was ready to exclaim with a high flush, or a vivid blush—one didn't distinguish the embarrassment from the joy— "Why, Miss Theale: fancy!" and "Why, Miss Theale: what luck!"

Miss Theale had meanwhile the sense that for him too, on Kate's part, something wonderful and unspoken was determinant; and this although, distinctly, his companion had no more looked at him with a hint than he had looked at her with a question. He had looked and he was looking only at Milly herself, ever so pleasantly and considerately—she scarce knew what to call it; but without prejudice to her consciousness, all the same, that women

431

got out of predicaments better than men. The predicament of course wasn't definite or phraseable—and the way they let all phrasing pass was presently to recur to our young woman as a characteristic triumph of the civilised state; but she took it for granted, insistently, with a small private flare of passion, because the one thing she could think of to do for him was to show him how she eased him off. She would really, tired and nervous, have been much disconcerted, were it not that the opportunity in question had saved her. It was what had saved her most, what had made her, after the first few seconds, almost as brave for Kate as Kate was for her, had made her only ask herself what their friend would like of her. That he was at the end of three minutes, without the least complicated reference, so smoothly "their" friend was just the effect of their all being sublimely civilised. The flash in which he saw this was, for Milly, fairly inspiring—to that degree in fact that she was even now, on such a plane, yearning to be supreme. It took, no doubt, a big dose of inspiration to treat as not funny—or at least as not unpleasant—the anomaly, for Kate, that *she* knew their gentleman, and for herself, that Kate was spending the morning with him; but everything continued to make for this after Milly had tasted of her draught. She was to wonder in subsequent reflection what in the world they had actually said, since they had made such a success of what they didn't say; the sweetness of the draught for the time, at any rate, was to feel success assured. What depended on this for Mr. Densher was all obscurity to her, and she perhaps but invented the image of his need as a short cut to service. Whatever were the facts, their perfect manners, all round, saw them through. The finest part of Milly's own inspiration, it may further be mentioned, was the quick perception that what would be of most service was, so to speak, her own native wood-note. She had long been conscious with shame for her thin blood, or at least for her poor economy, of her unused margin as an American girl—closely indeed as, in English air, the text might appear to cover the page. She still had reserves of spontaneity, if not of comicality; so that all this cash in hand could now find employment. She became as spontaneous as possible and as American as it might conveniently appeal to Mr. Densher, after his travels, to find her. She said things in the air, and yet flattered herself that she struck him as saying them not in the tone of agitation but in the tone of New York. In the tone of New York agitation was beautifully discounted, and she had now a sufficient view of how much it might accordingly help her.

The help was fairly rendered before they left the place; when her friends presently accepted her invitation to adjourn with her to luncheon at her hotel, it was in the Fifth Avenue that the meal might have waited. Kate had never been there so straight, but Milly was at present taking her; and if Mr. Densher had been he had at least never had to come so fast. She proposed it as the natural thing—proposed it as the American girl; and she saw herself quickly justified by the pace at which she was followed. The beauty of the case was that to do it all she had only to appear to take Kate's hint. This had said, in its fine first smile, "Oh yes, our look is queer—but give me time;" and the American girl could give time as nobody else could. What Milly thus gave she therefore made them take—even if, as they might surmise, it was rather more than they wanted. In the porch of the museum she expressed her preference for a four-wheeler; they would take their course in that guise precisely to multiply the minutes. She was more than ever justified by the positive charm that her spirit imparted even to their use of this conveyance; and she touched her highest point—that is, certainly, for herself—as she ushered her companions into the presence of Susie. Susie was there with luncheon, with her return, in prospect; and nothing could now have filled her own consciousness more to the brim than to see this good friend take in how little she was abjectly anxious. The cup itself actually offered to this good friend might in truth well be startling, for it was composed beyond question of ingredients oddly mixed. She caught Susie fairly looking at her as if to know whether she had brought in guests to hear Sir Luke Strett's report. Well, it was better her companion should have too much than too little to wonder about; she had come out "anyway," as they said at home, for the interest of the thing; and interest truly sat in her eyes. Milly was none the less, at the sharpest crisis, a little sorry for her; she could of necessity extract from the odd scene so comparatively little of a soothing secret. She saw Mr. Densher suddenly popping up, but she saw nothing else that had happened. She saw in the same way her young friend indifferent to her young friend's doom, and she lacked what would explain it. The only thing to keep her in patience was the way, after luncheon, Kate almost, as might be said, made up to her. This was actually perhaps as well what most kept Milly herself in patience. It had in fact for our young woman a positive beauty—was so marked as a deviation from the handsome girl's previous courses. Susie had been a bore to the handsome girl, and the change was now suggestive. The two sat together, after they had risen from table, in the apartment in which they had lunched, making it thus easy for the other guest and his entertainer to sit in the room adjacent. This, for the latter personage, was the beauty; it was almost, on Kate's part, like a prayer to be relieved. If she honestly liked better to be "thrown with" Susan Shepherd than with their other friend, why that said practically everything. It didn't perhaps altogether say why she had gone out with him for the morning, but it said, as one thought, about as much as she could say to his face.

Little by little indeed, under the vividness of Kate's behaviour, the probabilities fell back into their order. Merton Densher was in love, and Kate couldn't help it—could only be sorry and kind: wouldn't that, without wild flurries, cover everything? Milly at all events tried it as a cover, tried it hard, for the time; pulled it over her, in the front, the larger room, drew it up to her chin with energy. If it didn't, so treated, do everything for her, it did so much that she could herself supply the rest. She made that up by the interest of her great question, the question of whether, seeing him once more, with all that, as she called it to herself, had come and gone, her impression of him would be different from the impression received in New York. That had held her from the moment of their leaving the museum; it kept her company through their drive and during luncheon; and now that she was a quarter of an hour alone with him it became acute. She was to feel at this crisis that no clear, no common answer, no direct satisfaction on this point, was to reach her; she was to see her question itself simply go to pieces. She couldn't tell if he were different or not, and she didn't know nor care if *she* were: these things had ceased to matter in the light of the only thing she did know. This was that she liked him, as she put it to herself, as much as ever; and if that were to amount to liking a new person the amusement would be but the greater. She had thought him at first very quiet, in spite of recovery from his original confusion; though even the shade of bewilderment, she yet perceived, had not been due to such vagueness on the subject of her reintensified identity as the probable sight, over there, of many thousands of her kind would sufficiently have justified. No, he was quiet, inevitably, for the first half of the time, because Milly's own lively line—the line of spontaneity—made everything else relative; and because too, so far as Kate was spontaneous, it was ever so finely in the air among them that the normal pitch must be kept. Afterwards, when they had got a little more used, as it were, to each other's separate felicity, he had begun to talk more, clearly bethought himself, at a given moment, of what *his* natural lively line would be. It would be to take for granted she must wish to hear of the States, and to give her, in its order, everything he had seen and done there. He abounded, of a sudden he almost insisted; he returned, after breaks, to the charge; and the effect was perhaps the more odd as he gave no clue whatever to what he had admired, as he went, or to what he hadn't. He simply drenched her with his sociable story—especially during the time they were away from the others. She had stopped then being American—all to let him be English; a permission of which he took, she could feel, both immense and unconscious advantage. She had really never cared less for the "States" than at this moment; but that had nothing to do with the matter. It would have been the occasion of her life to learn about them, for nothing could put him off, and he ventured on no reference to what had happened for herself. It might have been almost as if he had known that the greatest of all these adventures was her doing just what she did then.

It was at this point that she saw the smash of her great question as complete, saw that all she had to do with was the sense of being there with him. And there was no chill for this in what she also presently saw—that, however he had begun, he was now acting from a particular desire, determined either by new facts or new fancies, to be like everyone else, simplifyingly "kind" to her. He had caught on already as to manner—fallen into line with everyone else; and if his spirits verily *had* gone up it might well be that he had thus felt himself lighting on the remedy for all awkwardness. Whatever he did or he didn't, Milly knew she should still like him—there was no alternative to that; but her heart could none the less sink a little on feeling how much his view of her was destined to have in common with—as she now sighed over it—*the* view. She could have dreamed of his not having *the* view, of his having something or other, if need be quite viewless, of his own; but he might have what he could with least trouble, and *the* view wouldn't be, after all, a positive bar to her seeing him. The defect of it in general—if she might so ungraciously criticise—was that, by its sweet universality, it made relations rather prosaically a matter of course. It anticipated and superseded the—likewise sweet—operation of real affinities. It was this that was doubtless marked in her power to keep him now—this and her glassy lustre of attention to his pleasantness about the scenery in the Rockies. She was in truth a little measuring her success in detaining him by Kate's success in "standing" Susan. It would not be, if she could help it, Mr. Densher who should first break down. Such at least was one of the forms of the girl's inward tension; but beneath even this deep reason was a motive still finer. What she had left at home on going out to give it a chance was meanwhile still, was more sharply and actively, there. What had been at the top of her mind about it and then been violently pushed down—this quantity was again working up. As soon as their friends should go Susie would break out, and what she would break out upon wouldn't be—interested in that gentleman as she had more than once shown herself—the personal fact of Mr. Densher. Milly had found in her face at luncheon a feverish glitter, and it told what she was full of. She didn't care now for Mr. Densher's personal fact. Mr. Densher had risen before her only to find his proper place in her imagination already, of a sudden, occupied. His personal fact failed, so far as she was concerned, to be personal, and her companion noted the failure. This could only mean that she was full to the brim, of Sir Luke Strett, and of what she had had from him. What *had* she had from him? It was indeed now working upward again that Milly would do well to know, though knowledge looked stiff in the light of Susie's glitter. It was therefore, on the whole, because Densher's young hostess was divided from it by so thin a partition that she continued to cling to the Rockies.

VOL. II

BOOK SIXTH

I

"I say, you know, Kate—you *did* stay!" had been Merton Densher's punctual remark on their adventure after they had, as it were, got out of it; an observation which she not less promptly, on her side, let him see that she forgave in him only because he was a man. She had to recognise, with whatever disappointment, that it was doubtless the most helpful he could make in this character. The fact of the adventure was flagrant between them; they had looked at each other, on gaining the street, as people look who have just rounded together a dangerous corner, and there was therefore already enough unanimity sketched out to have lighted, for her companion, anything equivocal in her action. But the amount of light men *did* need!—Kate could have been eloquent at this moment about that. What, however, on his seeing more, struck him as most distinct in her was her sense that, reunited after his absence and having been now half the morning together, it behooved them to face without delay the question of handling their immediate future. That it would require some handling, that they should still have to deal, deal in a crafty manner, with difficulties and delays, was the great matter he had come back to, greater than any but the refreshed consciousness of their personal need of each other. This need had had twenty minutes, the afternoon before, to find out where it stood, and the time was fully accounted for by the charm of the demonstration. He had arrived at Euston at five, having wired her from Liverpool the moment he landed, and she had quickly decided to meet him at the station, whatever publicity might attend such an act. When he had praised her for it on alighting from his train she had answered frankly enough that such things should be taken at a jump. She didn't care to-day who saw her, and she profited by it for her joy. To-morrow, inevitably, she should have time to think and then, as inevitably, would become a baser creature, a creature of alarms and precautions. It was none the less for to-morrow at an early hour that she had appointed their next meeting, keeping in mind for the present a particular obligation to show at Lancaster Gate by six o'clock. She had given, with imprecations, her reason—people to tea, eternally, and a promise to Aunt Maud; but she had been liberal enough on the spot and had suggested the National Gallery for the morning quite as with an idea that had ripened in expectancy. They might be seen there too, but nobody would know them; just as, for that matter, now, in the refreshment-room to which they had adjourned, they would incur the notice but, at the worst, of the unacquainted. They would "have something" there for the facility it would give. Thus had it already come up for them again that they had no place of convenience.

He found himself on English soil with all sorts of feelings, but he hadn't quite faced having to reckon with a certain ruefulness in regard to that subject as one of the strongest. He was aware later on that there were questions his impatience had shirked; whereby it actually rather smote him, for want of preparation and assurance, that he had nowhere to "take" his love. He had taken it thus, at Euston—and on Kate's own suggestion—into the place where people had beer and buns, and had ordered tea at a small table in the corner; which, no doubt, as they were lost in the crowd, did well enough for a stop-gap. It perhaps did as well as her simply driving with him to the door of his lodging, which had had to figure as the sole device of his own wit. That wit, the truth was, had broken down a little at the sharp prevision that once at his door they would have to hang back. She would have to stop there, wouldn't come in with him, couldn't possibly; and he shouldn't be able to ask her, would feel he couldn't without betraying a deficiency of what would be called, even at their advanced stage, respect for her: that again was all that was clear except the further fact that it was maddening. Compressed and concentrated, confined to a single sharp pang or two, but none the less in wait for him there on the Euston platform and lifting its head as that of a snake in the garden, was the disconcerting sense that "respect," in their game, seemed somehow—he scarce knew what to call it—a fifth wheel to the coach. It was properly an inside thing, not an outside, a thing to make love greater, not to make happiness less. They had met again for happiness, and he distinctly felt, during his most lucid moment or two, how he must keep watch on anything that really menaced that boon. If Kate had consented to drive away with him and alight at his house there would probably enough have occurred for them, at the foot of his steps, one of those strange instants between man and woman that blow upon the red spark, the spark of conflict, ever latent in the depths of passion. She would have shaken her head—oh sadly, divinely—on the question of coming in; and he, though doing all justice to her refusal, would have yet felt his eyes reach further into her own than a possible word at such a time could reach. This would have meant the suspicion, the dread of the shadow, of an adverse will. Lucky therefore in the actual case that the scant minutes took another turn and that by the half-hour she did in spite of everything contrive to spend with him Kate showed so well how she could deal with things that maddened. She seemed to ask him, to beseech him, and all for his better comfort, to leave her, now and henceforth, to treat them in her own way.

She had still met it in naming so promptly, for their early convenience, one of the great museums; and indeed with such happy art that his fully seeing where she had placed him hadn't been till after he left her. His absence from her for so many weeks had had such an effect upon him that his demands, his desires had grown; and only the night before, as his ship steamed, beneath summer stars, in sight of the Irish coast, he had felt all the force of his particular necessity. He hadn't in other words at any point doubted he was on his way to say to her that really their mistake must end. Their mistake was to have believed that they *could hold out*—hold out, that is, not against Aunt Maud, but against an impatience that, prolonged and exasperated, made a man ill. He had known more than ever, on their separating in the court of the station, how ill a man, and even a woman, could feel from such a cause; but he struck himself as also knowing that he had already suffered Kate to begin finely to apply antidotes and remedies and subtle sedatives. It had a vulgar sound—as throughout, in love, the names of things, the verbal terms of intercourse, were, compared with love itself, horribly vulgar; but it was as if, after all, he might have come back to find himself "put off," though it would take him of course a day or two to see. His letters from the States had pleased whom it concerned, though not so much as he had meant they should; and he should be paid according to agreement and would now take up his money. It wasn't in truth very much to take up, so that he hadn't in the least come back flourishing a cheque-book; that new motive for bringing his mistress to terms he couldn't therefore pretend to produce. The ideal certainty would have been to be able to present a change of prospect as a warrant for the change of philosophy, and without it he should have to make shift but with the pretext of the lapse of time. The lapse of time—not so many weeks after all, she might always of course say—couldn't at any rate have failed to do something for him; and that consideration it was that had just now tided him over, all the more that he had his vision of what it had done personally for Kate. This had come out for him with a splendour that almost scared him even in their small corner of the room at Euston—almost scared him because it just seemed to blaze at him that waiting was the game of dupes. Not yet had she been so the creature he had originally seen; not yet had he felt so soundly safely sure. It was all there for him, playing on his pride of possession as a hidden master in a great dim church might play on the grandest organ. His final sense was that a woman couldn't be like that and then ask of one the impossible.

She had been like that afresh on the morrow; and so for the hour they had been able to float in the mere joy of contact—such contact as their situation in pictured public halls permitted. This poor makeshift for closeness confessed itself in truth, by twenty small signs of unrest even on Kate's part, inadequate; so little could a decent interest in the interesting place presume to remind them of its claims. They had met there in order not to meet in the streets and not again, with an equal want of invention and of style, at a railway-station; not again, either, in Kensington Gardens, which, they could easily and tacitly agree, would have had too much of the taste of their old frustrations. The present taste, the taste that morning in the pictured halls, had been a variation; yet Densher had at the end of a quarter of an hour fully known what to conclude from it. This fairly consoled him for their awkwardness, as if he had been watching it affect her. She might be as nobly charming as she liked, and he had seen nothing to touch her in the States; she couldn't pretend that in such conditions as those she herself *believed* it enough to appease him. She couldn't pretend she believed he would believe it enough to render her a like service. It wasn't enough for that purpose—she as good as showed him it wasn't. That was what he could be glad, by demonstration, to have brought her to. He would have said to her had he put it crudely and on the spot: "*Now* am I to understand you that you consider this sort of thing can go on?" It would have been open to her, no doubt, to reply that to have him with her again, to have him all kept and treasured, so still, under her grasping hand, as she had held him in their yearning interval, was a sort of thing that he must allow her to have no quarrel about; but that would be a mere gesture of her grace, a mere sport of her subtlety. She knew as well as he what they wanted; in spite of which indeed he scarce could have said how beautifully he mightn't once more have named it and urged it if she hadn't, at a given moment, blurred, as it were, the accord. They had soon seated themselves for better talk, and so they had remained a while, intimate and superficial. The immediate things to say had been many, for they hadn't exhausted them at Euston. They drew upon them freely now, and Kate appeared quite to forget—which was prodigiously becoming to her—to look about for surprises. He was to try afterwards, and try in vain, to remember what speech or what silence of his own, what natural sign of the eyes or accidental touch of the hand, had precipitated for her, in the midst of this, a sudden different impulse. She had got up, with inconsequence, as if to break the charm, though he wasn't aware of what he had done at the moment to make the charm a danger. She had patched it up agreeably enough the next minute by some odd remark about some picture, to which he hadn't so much as replied; it being quite independently of this that he had himself exclaimed on the dreadful closeness of the rooms. He had observed that they must go out again to breathe; and it was as if their common consciousness, while they passed into another part, was that of persons who, infinitely engaged together, had been startled and were trying to look natural. It was probably while they were so occupied—as the young man subsequently reconceived—that they had stumbled upon his little New York friend. He thought of her for some reason as little, though she was of about Kate's height, to which, any more than to any other felicity in his mistress, he had never applied the diminutive.

What was to be in the retrospect more distinct to him was the process by which he had become aware that Kate's acquaintance with her was greater than he had gathered. She had written of it in due course as a new and amusing one, and he had written back that he had met over there, and that he much liked, the young person; whereupon she had answered that he must find out about her at home. Kate, in the event, however, had not returned to that, and he had of course, with so many things to find out about, been otherwise taken up. Little Miss Theale's individual history was not stuff for his newspaper; besides which, moreover, he was seeing but too many little Miss Theales. They even went so far as to impose themselves as one of the groups of social phenomena that fell into the scheme of his public letters. For this group in especial perhaps—the irrepressible, the supereminent young persons—his best pen was ready. Thus it was that there could come back to him in London, an hour or two after their luncheon with the American pair, the sense of a situation for which Kate hadn't wholly prepared him. Possibly indeed as marked as this was his recovered perception that preparations, of more than one kind, had been exactly what, both yesterday and to-day, he felt her as having in hand. That appearance in fact, if he dwelt on it, so ministered to apprehension as to require some brushing away. He shook off the suspicion to some extent, on their separating first from their hostesses and then from each other, by the aid of a long and rather aimless walk. He was to go to the office later, but he had the next two or three hours, and he gave himself as a pretext that he had eaten much too much. After Kate had asked him to put her into a cab—which, as an announced, a resumed policy on her part, he found himself deprecating—he stood a while by a corner and looked vaguely forth at his London. There was always doubtless a moment for the absentee recaptured—*the* moment, that of the reflux of the first emotion—at which it was beyond disproof that one was back. His full parenthesis was closed, and he was once more but a sentence, of a sort, in the general text, the text that, from his momentary street-corner, showed as a great grey page of print that somehow managed to be crowded without being "fine." The grey, however, was more or less the blur of a point of view not yet quite seized again; and there would be colour enough to come out. He was back, flatly enough, but back to possibilities and prospects, and the ground he now somewhat sightlessly covered was the act of renewed possession.

He walked northward without a plan, without suspicion, quite in the direction his little New York friend, in her restless ramble, had taken a day or two before. He reached, like Milly, the Regent's Park; and though he moved further and faster he finally sat down, like Milly, from the force of thought. For him too in this position, be it added—and he might positively have occupied the same bench—various troubled fancies folded their wings. He had no more yet said what he really wanted than Kate herself had found time. She should hear enough of that in a couple of days. He had practically not pressed her as to what most concerned them; it had seemed so to concern them during these first hours but to hold each other, spiritually speaking, close. This at any rate was palpable, that there were at present more things rather than fewer between them. The explanation about the two ladies would be part of the lot, yet could wait with all the rest. They were not meanwhile certainly what most made him roam—the missing explanations weren't. That was what she had so often said before, and always with the effect of suddenly breaking off: "Now please call me a good cab." Their previous encounters, the times when they had reached in their stroll the south side of the park, had had a way of winding up with this special irrelevance. It was effectively what most divided them, for he would generally, but for her reasons, have been able to jump in with her. What did she think he wished to do to her?—it was a question he had had occasion to put. A small matter, however, doubtless—since, when it came to that, they didn't depend on cabs good or bad for the sense of union: its importance was less from the particular loss than as a kind of irritating mark of her expertness. This expertness, under providence, had been great from the first, so far as joining him was concerned; and he was critical only because it had been still greater, even from the first too, in respect to leaving him. He had put the question to her again that afternoon, on the repetition of her appeal—had asked her once more what she supposed he wished to do. He recalled, on his bench in the Regent's Park, the freedom of fancy, funny and pretty, with which she had answered; recalled the moment itself, while the usual hansom charged them, during which he felt himself, disappointed as he was, grimacing back at the superiority of her very "humour," in its added grace of gaiety, to the celebrated solemn American. Their fresh appointment had been at all events by that time made, and he should see what her choice in respect to it—a surprise as well as a relief—would do toward really simplifying. It meant either new help or new hindrance, though it took them at least out of the streets. And her naming this privilege had naturally made him ask if Mrs. Lowder knew of his return.

"Not from me," Kate had replied. "But I shall speak to her now." And she had argued, as with rather a quick fresh view, that it would now be quite easy. "We've behaved for months so properly that I've margin surely for my mention of you. You'll come to see *her*, and she'll leave you with me; she'll show her good nature, and her lack of betrayed fear, in that. With her, you know, you've never broken, quite the contrary, and she likes you as much as ever. We're leaving town; it will be the end; just now therefore it's nothing to ask. I'll ask to-night," Kate had wound up, "and if you'll leave it to me—my cleverness, I assure you, has grown infernal—I'll make it all right."

He had of course thus left it to her and he was wondering more about it now than he had wondered there in Brook Street. He repeated to himself that if it wasn't in the line of triumph it was in the line of muddle. This indeed, no doubt, was as a part of his wonder for still other questions. Kate had really got off without meeting his little challenge about the terms of their intercourse with her dear Milly. Her dear Milly, it was sensible, *was* somehow in the picture. Her dear Milly, popping up in his absence, occupied—he couldn't have said quite why he felt it—more of the foreground than one would have expected her in advance to find clear. She took up room, and it was almost as if room had been made for her. Kate had appeared to take for granted he would know why it had been made; but that was just the point. It was a foreground in which he himself, in which his connexion with Kate, scarce enjoyed a space to turn round. But Miss Theale was perhaps at the present juncture a possibility of the same sort as the softened, if not the squared, Aunt Maud. It might be true of her also that if she weren't a bore she'd be a convenience. It rolled over him of a sudden, after he had resumed his walk, that this might easily be what Kate had meant. The charming girl adored her—Densher had for himself made out that—and would protect, would lend a hand, to their interviews. These might take place, in other words, on her premises, which would remove them still better from the streets. *That* was an explanation which did hang together. It was impaired a little, of a truth, by this fact that their next encounter was rather markedly not to depend upon her. Yet this fact in turn would be accounted for by the need of more preliminaries. One of the things he conceivably should gain on Thursday at Lancaster Gate would be a further view of that propriety.

II

It was extraordinary enough that he should actually be finding himself, when Thursday arrived, none so wide of the mark. Kate hadn't come all the way to this for him, but she had come to a good deal by the end of a quarter of an hour. What she had begun with was her surprise at her appearing to have left him on Tuesday anything more to understand. The parts, as he now saw, under her hand, did fall more or less together, and it wasn't even as if she had spent the interval in twisting and fitting them. She was bright and handsome, not fagged and worn, with the general clearness; for it certainly stuck out enough that if the American ladies themselves weren't to be squared, which was absurd, they fairly imposed the necessity of trying Aunt Maud again. One couldn't say to them, kind as she had been to them: "We'll meet, please, whenever you'll let us, at your house; but we count on you to help us to keep it secret." They must in other terms inevitably speak to Aunt Maud—it would be of the last awkwardness to ask them not to: Kate had embraced all this in her choice of speaking first. What Kate embraced altogether was indeed wonderful to-day for Densher, though he perhaps struck himself rather as getting it out of her piece by piece than as receiving it in a steady light. He had always felt, however, that the more he asked of her the more he found her prepared, as he imaged it, to hand out. He had said to her more than once even before his absence: "You keep the key of the cupboard, and I foresee that when we're married you'll dole me out my sugar by lumps." She had replied that she rejoiced in his assumption that sugar would be his diet, and the domestic arrangement so prefigured might have seemed already to prevail. The supply from the cupboard at this hour was doubtless, of a truth, not altogether cloyingly sweet; but it met in a manner his immediate requirements. If her explanations at any rate prompted questions the questions no more exhausted them than they exhausted her patience. And they were naturally, of the series, the simpler; as for instance in his taking it from her that Miss Theale then could do nothing for them. He frankly brought out what he had ventured to think possible. "If we can't meet here and we've really exhausted the charms of the open air and the crowd, some such little raft in the wreck, some occasional opportunity like that of Tuesday, has been present to me these two days as better than nothing. But if our friends are so accountable to this house of course there's no more to be said. And it's one more nail, thank God, in the coffin of our odious delay." He was but too glad without more ado to point the moral. "Now I hope you see we can't work it anyhow."

If she laughed for this—and her spirits seemed really high—it was because of the opportunity that, at the hotel, he had most shown himself as enjoying. "Your idea's beautiful when one remembers that you hadn't a word except for Milly." But she was as beautifully good-humoured. "You might of course get used to her—you *will*. You're quite right—so long as they're with us or near us." And she put it, lucidly, that the dear things couldn't *help*, simply as charming friends, giving them a lift. "They'll speak to Aunt Maud, but they won't shut their doors to us: that would be another matter. A friend always helps—and she's a friend." She had left Mrs. Stringham by this time out of the question; she had reduced it to Milly. "Besides, she particularly likes us. She particularly likes *you*. I say, old boy, make something of that." He felt her dodging the ultimatum he had just made sharp, his definite reminder of how little, at the best, they could work it; but there were certain of his remarks—those mostly of the sharper penetration—that it had been quite her practice from the first not formally, not reverently to notice. She showed the effect of them in ways less trite. This was what happened now: he didn't think in truth that she wasn't really minding. She took him up, none the less, on a minor question. "You say we can't meet here, but you see it's just what we do. What could be more lovely than this?"

It wasn't to torment him—that again he didn't believe; but he had to come to the house in some discomfort, so that he frowned a little at her calling it thus a luxury. Wasn't there an element in it of coming back into bondage? The bondage might be veiled and varnished, but he knew in his bones how little the very highest privileges of Lancaster Gate could ever be a sign of their freedom. They were upstairs, in one of the smaller apartments of state, a room arranged as a boudoir, but visibly unused—it defied familiarity—and furnished in the ugliest of blues. He had immediately looked with interest at the closed doors, and Kate had met his interest with the assurance that it was all right, that Aunt Maud did them justice—so far, that was, as this particular time was concerned; that they should be alone and have nothing to fear. But the fresh allusion to this that he had drawn from her acted on him now more directly, brought him closer still to the question. They *were* alone—it *was* all right: he took in anew the shut doors and the permitted privacy, the solid stillness of the great house. They connected themselves on the spot with something made doubly vivid in him by the whole present play of her charming strong will. What it amounted to was that he couldn't have her—hanged if he could!—evasive. He couldn't and he wouldn't—wouldn't have her inconvenient and elusive. He didn't want her deeper than himself, fine as it might be as wit or as character; he wanted to keep her where their communications would be straight and easy and their intercourse independent. The effect of this was to make him say in a moment: "Will you take me just as I am?"

She turned a little pale for the tone of truth in it—which qualified to his sense delightfully the strength of her will; and the pleasure he found in this was not the less for her breaking out after an instant into a strain that stirred him more than any she had ever used with him. "Ah do let me try myself! I assure you I see my way—so don't spoil it: wait for me and give me time. Dear man," Kate said, "only believe in me, and it will be beautiful."

He hadn't come back to hear her talk of his believing in her as if he didn't; but he had come back—and it all was upon him now—to seize her with a sudden intensity that her manner of pleading with him had made, as happily appeared, irresistible. He laid strong hands upon her to say, almost in anger, "Do you love me, love me, love me?" and she closed her eyes as with the sense that he might strike her but that she could gratefully take it. Her surrender was her response, her response her surrender; and, though scarce hearing what she said, he so profited by these things that it could for the time be ever so intimately appreciable to him that he was keeping her. The long embrace in which they held each other was the rout of evasion, and he took from it the certitude that what she had from him was real to her. It was stronger than an uttered vow, and the name he was to give it in afterthought was that she had been sublimely sincere. *That* was all he asked—sincerity making a basis that would bear almost anything. This settled so much, and settled it so thoroughly, that there was nothing left to ask her to swear to. Oaths and vows apart, now they could talk. It seemed in fact only now that their questions were put on the table. He had taken up more expressly at the end of five minutes her plea for her own plan, and it was marked that the difference made by the passage just enacted was a difference in favour of her choice of means. Means had somehow suddenly become a detail— her province and her care; it had grown more consistently vivid that her intelligence was one with her passion. "I certainly don't want," he said—and he could say it with a smile of indulgence—"to be all the while bringing it up that I don't trust you."

"I should hope not! What do you think I want to do?"

He had really at this to make out a little what he thought, and the first thing that put itself in evidence was of course the oddity, after all, of their game, to which he could but frankly allude. "We're doing, at the best, in trying to temporise in so special a way, a thing most people would call us fools for." But his visit passed, all the same, without his again attempting to make "just as he was" serve. He had no more money just as he was than he had had just as he had been, or than he should have, probably, when it came to that, just as he always would be; whereas she, on her side, in comparison with her state of some months before, had measureably more to relinquish. He easily saw how their meeting at Lancaster Gate gave more of an accent to that quantity than their meeting at stations or in parks; and yet on the other hand he couldn't urge this against it. If Mrs. Lowder was indifferent her indifference added in a manner to what Kate's taking him as he was would call on her to sacrifice. Such in fine was her art with him that she seemed to put the question of their still waiting into quite other terms than the terms of ugly blue, of florid Sèvres, of complicated brass, in which their boudoir expressed it. She said almost all in fact by saying, on this article of Aunt Maud, after he had once more pressed her, that when he should see her, as must inevitably soon happen, he would understand. "Do you mean," he asked at this, "that there's any *definite* sign of her coming round? I'm not talking," he explained, "of mere hypocrisies in her, or mere brave duplicities. Remember, after all, that supremely clever as we are, and as strong a team, I admit, as there is going—remember that she can play with us quite as much as we play with her."

"She doesn't want to play with *me*, my dear," Kate lucidly replied; "she doesn't want to make me suffer a bit more than she need. She cares for me too much, and everything she does or doesn't do has a value. *This* has a value—her being as she has been about us to-day. I believe she's in her room, where she's keeping strictly to herself while you're here with me. But that isn't 'playing'— not a bit."

"What is it then," the young man returned—"from the moment it isn't her blessing and a cheque?"

Kate was complete. "It's simply her absence of smallness. There is something in her above trifles. She *generally* trusts us; she doesn't propose to hunt us into corners; and if we frankly ask for a thing—why," said Kate, "she shrugs, but she lets it go. She has really but one fault—she's indifferent, on such ground as she has taken about us, to details. However," the girl cheerfully went on, "it isn't in detail we fight her."

"It seems to me," Densher brought out after a moment's thought of this, "that it's in detail we deceive her"—a speech that, as soon as he had uttered it, applied itself for him, as also visibly for his companion, to the afterglow of their recent embrace.

Any confusion attaching to this adventure, however, dropped from Kate, whom, as he could see with sacred joy, it must take more than that to make compunctious. "I don't say we can do it again. I mean," she explained, "meet here."

Densher indeed had been wondering where they could do it again. If Lancaster Gate was so limited that issue reappeared. "I mayn't come back at all?"

"Certainly—to see her. It's she, really," his companion smiled, "who's in love with you."

But it made him—a trifle more grave—look at her a moment. "Don't make out, you know, that every one's in love with me."

She hesitated. "I don't say every one."

"You said just now Miss Theale."

"I said she liked you—yes."

"Well, it comes to the same thing." With which, however, he pursued: "Of course I ought to thank Mrs. Lowder in person. I mean for *this*—as from myself."

"Ah but, you know, not too much!" She had an ironic gaiety for the implications of his "this," besides wishing to insist on a general prudence. "She'll wonder what you're thanking her for!"

Densher did justice to both considerations. "Yes, I can't very well tell her all."

It was perhaps because he said it so gravely that Kate was again in a manner amused. Yet she gave out light. "You can't very well 'tell' her anything, and that doesn't matter. Only be nice to her. Please her; make her see how clever you are—only without letting her see that you're trying. If you're charming to her you've nothing else to do."

But she oversimplified too. "I can be 'charming' to her, so far as I see, only by letting her suppose I give you up—which I'll be hanged if I do! It *is*," he said with feeling, "a game."

"Of course it's a game. But she'll never suppose you give me up—or I give *you*—if you keep reminding her how you enjoy our interviews."

"Then if she has to see us as obstinate and constant," Densher asked, "what good does it do?"

Kate was for a moment checked. "What good does what—?"

"Does my pleasing her—does anything. I *can't*," he impatiently declared, "please her."

Kate looked at him hard again, disappointed at his want of consistency; but it appeared to determine in her something better than a mere complaint. "Then *I* can! Leave it to me." With which she came to him under the compulsion, again, that had united them shortly before, and took hold of him in her urgency to the same tender purpose. It was her form of entreaty renewed and repeated, which made after all, as he met it, their great fact clear. And it somehow clarified *all* things so to possess each other. The effect of it was that, once more, on these terms, he could only be generous. He had so on the spot then left everything to her that she reverted in the course of a few moments to one of her previous—and as positively seemed—her most precious ideas. "You accused me just now of saying that Milly's in love with you. Well, if you come to that, I do say it. So there you are. That's the good she'll do us. It makes a basis for her seeing you—so that she'll help us to go on."

Densher stared—she was wondrous all round. "And what sort of a basis does it make for my seeing *her?*"

"Oh I don't mind!" Kate smiled.

"Don't mind my leading her on?"

She put it differently. "Don't mind her leading *you*."

"Well, she won't—so it's nothing not to mind. But how can that 'help,'" he pursued, "with what she knows?"

"What she knows? That needn't prevent."

He wondered. "Prevent her loving us?"

"Prevent her helping you. She's *like* that," Kate Croy explained.

It took indeed some understanding. "Making nothing of the fact that I love another?"

"Making everything," said Kate. "To console you."

"But for what?"

"For not getting your other."

He continued to stare. "But how does she know—?"

"That you *won't* get her? She doesn't; but on the other hand she doesn't know you will. Meanwhile she sees you baffled, for she knows of Aunt Maud's stand. *That*"—Kate was lucid—"gives her the chance to be nice to you."

"And what does it give *me*," the young man none the less rationally asked, "the chance to be? A brute of a humbug to her?"

Kate so possessed her facts, as it were, that she smiled at his violence. "You'll extraordinarily like her. She's exquisite. And there are reasons. I mean others."

"What others?"

"Well, I'll tell you another time. Those I give you," the girl added, "are enough to go on with."

"To go on to what?"

"Why, to seeing her again—say as soon as you can: which, moreover, on all grounds, is no more than decent of you."

He of course took in her reference, and he had fully in mind what had passed between them in New York. It had been no great quantity, but it had made distinctly at the time for his pleasure; so that anything in the nature of an appeal in the name of it could have a slight kindling consequence. "Oh I shall naturally call again without delay. Yes," said Densher, "her being in love with me is nonsense; but I must, quite independently of that, make every acknowledgement of favours received."

It appeared practically all Kate asked. "Then you see. I shall meet you there."

"I don't quite see," he presently returned, "why she should wish to receive you for it."

"She receives me for myself—that is for *her* self. She thinks no end of me. That I should have to drum it into you!"

Yet still he didn't take it. "Then I confess she's beyond me."

Well, Kate could but leave it as she saw it. "She regards me as already—in these few weeks—her dearest friend. It's quite separate. We're in, she and I, ever so deep." And it was to confirm this that, as if it had flashed upon her that he was somewhere at sea, she threw out at last her own real light. "She doesn't of course know I care for *you*. She thinks I care so little that it's not worth speaking of." That he had been somewhere at sea these remarks made quickly clear, and Kate hailed the effect with surprise. "Have you been supposing that she does know—?"

"About our situation? Certainly, if you're such friends as you show me—and if you haven't otherwise represented it to her." She uttered at this such a sound of impatience that he stood artlessly vague. "You *have* denied it to her?"

She threw up her arms at his being so backward. "'Denied it'? My dear man, we've never spoken of you."

"Never, never?"

"Strange as it may appear to your glory—never."

He couldn't piece it together. "But won't Mrs. Lowder have spoken?"

"Very probably. But of *you*. Not of me."

This struck him as obscure. "How does she know me but as part and parcel of you?"

"How?" Kate triumphantly asked. "Why exactly to make nothing of it, to have nothing to do with it, to stick consistently to her line about it. Aunt Maud's line is to keep all reality out of our relation—that is out of my being in danger from you—by not having so much as suspected or heard of it. She'll get rid of it, as she believes, by ignoring it and sinking it—if she only does so hard enough. Therefore *she*, in her manner, 'denies' it if you will. That's how she knows you otherwise than as part and parcel of me. She won't for a moment have allowed either to Mrs. Stringham or to Milly that I've in any way, as they say, distinguished you."

"And you don't suppose," said Densher, "that they must have made it out for themselves?"

"No, my dear, I don't; not even," Kate declared, "after Milly's so funnily bumping against us on Tuesday."

"She doesn't see from *that*—?"

"That you're, so to speak, mad about me. Yes, she sees, no doubt, that you regard me with a complacent eye—for you show it, I think, always too much and too crudely. But nothing beyond that. I don't show it too much; I don't perhaps—to please you completely where others are concerned—show it enough."

"Can you show it or not as you like?" Densher demanded.

It pulled her up a little, but she came out resplendent. "Not where *you* are concerned. Beyond seeing that you're rather gone," she went on, "Milly only sees that I'm decently good to you."

"Very good indeed she must think it!"

"Very good indeed then. She easily sees me," Kate smiled, "as very good indeed."

The young man brooded. "But in a sense to take some explaining."

"Then I explain." She was really fine; it came back to her essential plea for her freedom of action and his beauty of trust. "I mean," she added, "I *will* explain."

"And what will I do?"

"Recognise the difference it must make if she thinks." But here in truth Kate faltered. It was his silence alone that, for the moment, took up her apparent meaning; and before he again spoke she had returned to remembrance and prudence. They were now not to forget that, Aunt Maud's liberality having put them on their honour, they mustn't spoil their case by abusing it. He must leave her in time; they should probably find it would help them. But she came back to Milly too. "Mind you go to see her."

Densher still, however, took up nothing of this. "Then I may come again?"

"For Aunt Maud—as much as you like. But we can't again," said Kate, "play her *this trick*. I can't see you here alone."

"Then where?"

"Go to see Milly," she for all satisfaction repeated.

"And what good will that do me?"

"Try it and you'll see."

"You mean you'll manage to be there?" Densher asked. "Say you are, how will that give us privacy?"

"Try it—you'll see," the girl once more returned. "We must manage as we can."

"That's precisely what *I* feel. It strikes me we might manage better." His idea of this was a thing that made him an instant hesitate; yet he brought it out with conviction. "Why won't you come to *me?*"

It was a question her troubled eyes seemed to tell him he was scarce generous in expecting her definitely to answer, and by looking to him to wait at least she appealed to something that she presently made him feel as his pity. It was on that special shade of tenderness that he thus found himself thrown back; and while he asked of his spirit and of his flesh just what concession they could arrange she pressed him yet again on the subject of her singular remedy for their embarrassment. It might have been irritating had she ever struck him as having in her mind a stupid corner. "You'll see," she said, "the difference it will make."

Well, since she wasn't stupid she was intelligent; it was he who was stupid—the proof of which was that he would do what she liked. But he made a last effort to understand, her allusion to the "difference" bringing him round to it. He indeed caught at something subtle but strong even as he spoke. "Is what you meant a moment ago that the difference will be in her being made to believe you hate me?"

Kate, however, had simply, for this gross way of putting it, one of her more marked shows of impatience; with which in fact she sharply closed their discussion. He opened the door on a sign from her, and she accompanied him to the top of the stairs with an air of having so put their possibilities before him that questions were idle and doubts perverse. "I verily believe I *shall* hate you if you spoil for me the beauty of what I see!"

III

He was really, notwithstanding, to hear more from her of what she saw; and the very next occasion had for him still other surprises than that. He received from Mrs. Lowder on the morning after his visit to Kate the telegraphic expression of a hope that he might be free to dine with them that evening; and his freedom affected him as fortunate even though in some degree qualified by her missive. "Expecting American friends whom I'm so glad to find you know!" His knowledge of American friends was clearly an accident of which he was to taste the fruit to the last bitterness. This apprehension, however, we hasten to add, enjoyed for him, in the immediate event, a certain merciful shrinkage; the immediate event being that, at Lancaster Gate, five minutes after his due arrival, prescribed him for eight-thirty, Mrs. Stringham came in alone. The long daylight, the postponed lamps, the habit of the hour, made dinners late and guests still later; so that, punctual as he was, he had found Mrs. Lowder alone, with Kate herself not yet in the field. He had thus had with her several bewildering moments—bewildering by reason, fairly, of their tacit invitation to him to be supernaturally simple. This was exactly, goodness knew, what he wanted to be; but he had never had it so largely and freely—*so* supernaturally simply, for that matter—imputed to him as of easy achievement. It was a particular in which Aunt Maud appeared to offer herself as an example, appeared to say quite agreeably: "What I want of you, don't you see? is to be just exactly as *I* am." The quantity of the article required was what might especially have caused him to stagger—he liked so, in general, the quantities in which Mrs. Lowder dealt. He would have liked as well to ask her how feasible she supposed it for a poor young man to resemble her at any point; but he had after all soon enough perceived that he was doing as she wished by letting his wonder show just a little as silly. He was conscious moreover of a small strange dread of the results of discussion with her— strange, truly, because it was her good nature, not her asperity, that he feared. Asperity might have made him angry—in which there was always a comfort; good nature, in his conditions, had a tendency to make him ashamed— which Aunt Maud indeed, wonderfully, liking him for himself, quite struck him as having guessed. To spare him therefore she also avoided discussion; she kept him down by refusing to quarrel with him. This was what she now proposed to him to enjoy, and his secret discomfort was his sense that on the whole it was what would best suit him. Being kept down was a bore, but his great dread, verily, was of being ashamed, which was a thing distinct; and it mattered but little that he was ashamed of that too. It was of the essence of his position that in such a house as this the tables could always be turned on him. "What do you offer, what do you offer?"—the place, however muffled in convenience and decorum, constantly hummed for him with that thick irony. The irony was a renewed reference to obvious bribes, and he had already seen how little aid came to him from denouncing the bribes as ugly in form. That was what the precious metals—they alone—could afford to be; it was vain enough for him accordingly to try to impart a gloss to his own comparative brummagem. The humiliation of this impotence was precisely what Aunt Maud sought to mitigate for him by keeping him down; and as her effort to that end had doubtless never yet been so visible he had probably never felt so definitely placed in the world as while he waited with her for her half-dozen other guests. She welcomed him genially back from the States, as to his view of which her few questions, though not coherent, were comprehensive, and he had the amusement of seeing in her, as through a clear glass, the outbreak of a plan and the sudden consciousness of a curiosity. She became aware of America, under his eyes, as a possible scene for social operations; the idea of a visit to the wonderful country had clearly but just occurred to her, yet she was talking of it, at the end of a minute, as her favourite dream. He didn't believe in it, but he pretended to; this helped her as well as anything else to treat him as harmless and blameless. She was so engaged, with the further aid of a complete absence of allusions, when the highest effect was given her method by the beautiful entrance of Kate. The method therefore received support all round, for no young man could have been less formidable than the person to the relief of whose shyness her niece ostensibly came. The ostensible, in Kate, struck him altogether, on this occasion, as prodigious; while scarcely less prodigious, for that matter, was his own reading, on the spot, of the relation between his companions—a relation lighted for him by the straight look, not exactly loving nor lingering, yet searching and soft, that, on the part of their hostess, the girl had to reckon with as she advanced. It took her in from head to foot, and in doing so it told a story that made poor Densher again the least bit sick: it marked so something with which Kate habitually and consummately reckoned.

That was the story—that she was always, for her beneficent dragon, under arms; living up, every hour, but especially at festal hours, to the "value"

Mrs. Lowder had attached to her. High and fixed, this estimate ruled on each occasion at Lancaster Gate the social scene; so that he now recognised in it something like the artistic idea, the plastic substance, imposed by tradition, by genius, by criticism, in respect to a given character, on a distinguished actress. As such a person was to dress the part, to walk, to look, to speak, in every way to express, the part, so all this was what Kate was to do for the character she had undertaken, under her aunt's roof, to represent. It was made up, the character, of definite elements and touches—things all perfectly ponderable to criticism; and the way for her to meet criticism was evidently at the start to be sure her make-up had had the last touch and that she looked at least no worse than usual. Aunt Maud's appreciation of that to-night was indeed managerial, and the performer's own contribution fairly that of the faultless soldier on parade. Densher saw himself for the moment as in his purchased stall at the play; the watchful manager was in the depths of a box and the poor actress in the glare of the footlights. But she *passed*, the poor performer—he could see how she always passed; her wig, her paint, her jewels, every mark of her expression impeccable, and her entrance accordingly greeted with the proper round of applause. Such impressions as we thus note for Densher come and go, it must be granted, in very much less time than notation demands; but we may none the less make the point that there was, still further, time among them for him to feel almost too scared to take part in the ovation. He struck himself as having lost, for the minute, his presence of mind—so that in any case he only stared in silence at the older woman's technical challenge and at the younger one's disciplined face. It was as if the drama—it thus came to him, for the fact of a drama there was no blinking—was between *them*, them quite preponderantly; with Merton Densher relegated to mere spectatorship, a paying place in front, and one of the most expensive. This was why his appreciation had turned for the instant to fear—had just turned, as we have said, to sickness; and in spite of the fact that the disciplined face did offer him over the footlights, as he believed, the small gleam, fine faint but exquisite, of a special intelligence. So might a practised performer, even when raked by double-barrelled glasses, seem to be all in her part and yet convey a sign to the person in the house she loved best.

The drama, at all events, as Densher saw it, meanwhile went on—amplified soon enough by the advent of two other guests, stray gentlemen both, stragglers in the rout of the season, who visibly presented themselves to Kate during the next moments as subjects for a like impersonal treatment and sharers in a like usual mercy. At opposite ends of the social course, they displayed, in respect to the "figure" that each, in his way, made, one the expansive, the other the contractile effect of the perfect white waistcoat. A scratch company of two innocuous youths and a pacified veteran was therefore what now offered itself to Mrs. Stringham, who rustled in a little breathless and full of the compunction of having had to come alone. Her companion, at the last moment, had been indisposed—positively not well enough, and so had packed her off, insistently, with excuses, with wild regrets. This circumstance of their charming friend's illness was the first thing Kate took up with Densher on their being able after dinner, without bravado, to have ten minutes "naturally," as she called it—which wasn't what *he* did—together; but it was already as if the young man had, by an odd impression, throughout the meal, not been wholly deprived of Miss Theale's participation. Mrs. Lowder had made dear Milly the topic, and it proved, on the spot, a topic as familiar to the enthusiastic younger as to the sagacious older man. Any knowledge they might lack Mrs. Lowder's niece was moreover alert to supply, while Densher himself was freely appealed to as the most privileged, after all, of the group. Wasn't it he who had in a manner invented the wonderful creature—through having seen her first, caught her in her native jungle? Hadn't he more or less paved the way for her by his prompt recognition of her rarity, by preceding her, in a friendly spirit—as he had the "ear" of society—with a sharp flashlight or two?

He met, poor Densher, these enquiries as he could, listening with interest, yet with discomfort; wincing in particular, dry journalist as he was, to find it seemingly supposed of him that he had put his pen—oh his "pen!"—at the service of private distinction. The ear of society?—they were talking, or almost, as if he had publicly paragraphed a modest young lady. They dreamt dreams, in truth, he appeared to perceive, that fairly waked *him* up, and he settled himself in his place both to resist his embarrassment and to catch the full revelation. His embarrassment came naturally from the fact that if he could claim no credit for Miss Theale's success, so neither could he gracefully insist on his not having been concerned with her. What touched him most nearly was that the occasion took on somehow the air of a commemorative banquet, a feast to celebrate a brilliant if brief career. There was of course more said about the heroine than if she hadn't been absent, and he found himself rather stupefied at the range of Milly's triumph. Mrs. Lowder had wonders to tell of it; the two wearers of the waistcoat, either with sincerity or with hypocrisy, professed in the matter an equal expertness; and Densher at last seemed to know himself in presence of a social "case." It was Mrs. Stringham, obviously, whose testimony would have been most invoked hadn't she been, as her friend's representative, rather confined to the function of inhaling the incense; so that Kate, who treated her beautifully, smiling at her, cheering and consoling her across the table, appeared benevolently both to speak and to interpret for her. Kate spoke as if she wouldn't perhaps understand *their* way of appreciating Milly, but would let them none the less, in justice to their good will, express it in their coarser fashion. Densher himself wasn't unconscious in respect to this of a certain broad brotherhood with Mrs. Stringham; wondering indeed, while he followed the talk, how it might move American nerves. He had only heard of them before, but in his recent tour he had caught them in the remarkable fact, and there was now a moment or two when it came to him that he had perhaps—and not in the way of an escape—taken a lesson from them. They quivered, clearly, they hummed and drummed, they leaped and bounded in Mrs. Stringham's typical organism—this lady striking him as before all things excited, as, in the native phrase, keyed-up to a perception of more elements in the occasion than he was himself able to count. She was accessible to sides of it, he imagined, that were as yet obscure to him; for, though she unmistakeably rejoiced and soared, he none the less saw her at moments as even more agitated than pleasure required. It was a state of emotion in her that could scarce represent simply an impatience to report at home. Her little dry New England brightness—he had "sampled" all the shades of the American complexity, if complexity it were—had its actual reasons for finding relief most in silence; so that before the subject was changed he perceived (with surprise at the others) that they had given her enough of it. He had quite had enough of it himself by the time he was asked if it were true that their friend had really not made in her own country the mark she had chalked so large in London. It was Mrs. Lowder herself who addressed him that enquiry; while he scarce knew if he were the more impressed with her launching it under Mrs. Stringham's nose or with her hope that he would allow to London the honour of discovery. The less expansive of the white waistcoats propounded the theory that they saw in London—for all that was said—much further than in the States: it wouldn't be the first time, he urged, that they had taught the Americans to appreciate (especially when it was funny) some native product. He didn't mean that Miss Theale was funny—though she was weird, and this was precisely her magic; but it might very well be that New York, in having her to show, hadn't been aware of its luck. There *were* plenty of people who were nothing over there and yet were awfully taken up in England; just as—to make the balance right, thank goodness—they sometimes sent out beauties and celebrities who left the Briton cold. The Briton's temperature in truth wasn't to be calculated—a formulation of the matter that was not reached, however, without producing in Mrs. Stringham a final feverish sally. She announced that if the point of view for a proper admiration of her young friend *had* seemed to fail a little in New York, there was no manner of doubt of her having carried Boston by storm. It pointed the moral that Boston, for the finer taste, left New York nowhere; and the good lady, as the exponent of this doctrine—which she set forth at a certain length—made, obviously, to Densher's mind, her nearest approach to supplying the weirdness in which Milly's absence had left them deficient. She made it indeed effective for him by suddenly addressing him. "You know nothing, sir—but not the least little bit—about my friend."

He hadn't pretended he did, but there was a purity of reproach in Mrs. Stringham's face and tone, a purity charged apparently with solemn meanings; so that for a little, small as had been his claim, he couldn't but feel that she exaggerated. He wondered what she did mean, but while doing so he defended himself. "I certainly don't know enormously much—beyond her having been most kind to me, in New York, as a poor bewildered and newly landed alien, and my having tremendously appreciated it." To which he added, he scarce knew why, what had an immediate success. "Remember, Mrs. Stringham, that you weren't then present."

"Ah there you are!" said Kate with much gay expression, though what it expressed he failed at the time to make out.

"You weren't present *then*, dearest," Mrs. Lowder richly concurred. "You don't know," she continued with mellow gaiety, "how far things may have gone."

It made the little woman, he could see, really lose her head. She had more things in that head than any of them in any other; unless perhaps it were Kate, whom he felt as indirectly watching him during this foolish passage, though it pleased him—and because of the foolishness—not to meet her eyes. He met Mrs. Stringham's, which affected him: with her he could on occasion clear it up—a sense produced by the mute communion between them and really the beginning, as the event was to show, of something extraordinary. It was even already a little the effect of this communion that Mrs. Stringham perceptibly faltered in her retort to Mrs. Lowder's joke. "Oh it's precisely my point that Mr. Densher *can't* have had vast opportunities." And then she smiled at him. "I wasn't away, you know, long."

It made everything, in the oddest way in the world, immediately right for him. "And I wasn't *there* long, either." He positively saw with it that nothing for him, so far as she was concerned, would again be wrong. "She's beautiful, but I don't say she's easy to know."

"Ah she's a thousand and one things!" replied the good lady, as if now to keep well with him.

He asked nothing better. "She was off with you to these parts before I knew it. I myself was off too—away off to wonderful parts, where I had endlessly more to see."

"But you didn't forget her!" Aunt Maud interposed with almost menacing archness.

"No, of course I didn't forget her. One doesn't forget such charming impressions. But I never," he lucidly maintained, "chattered to others about her."

"She'll thank you for that, sir," said Mrs. Stringham with a flushed firmness.

"Yet doesn't silence in such a case," Aunt Maud blandly enquired, "very often quite prove the depth of the impression?"

He would have been amused, hadn't he been slightly displeased, at all they seemed desirous to fasten on him. "Well, the impression was as deep as you like. But I really want Miss Theale to know," he pursued for Mrs. Stringham, "that I don't figure by any consent of my own as an authority about her."

Kate came to his assistance—if assistance it was—before their friend had had time to meet this charge. "You're right about her not being easy to know. One *sees* her with intensity—sees her more than one sees almost any one; but then one discovers that that isn't knowing her and that one may know better a person whom one doesn't 'see,' as I say, half so much."

The discrimination was interesting, but it brought them back to the fact of her success; and it was at that comparatively gross circumstance, now so fully placed before them, that Milly's anxious companion sat and looked—looked very much as some spectator in an old-time circus might have watched the oddity of a Christian maiden, in the arena, mildly, caressingly, martyred. It was the nosing and fumbling not of lions and tigers but of domestic animals let loose as for the joke. Even the joke made Mrs. Stringham uneasy, and her mute communion with Densher, to which we have alluded, was more and more determined by it. He wondered afterwards if Kate had made this out; though it was not indeed till much later on that he found himself, in thought, dividing the things she might have been conscious of from the things she must have missed. If she actually missed, at any rate, Mrs. Stringham's discomfort, that but showed how her own idea held her. Her own idea was, by insisting on the fact of the girl's prominence as a feature of the season's end, to keep

Densher in relation, for the rest of them, both to present and to past. "It's everything that has happened *since* that makes you naturally a little shy about her. You don't know what has happened since, but we do; we've seen it and followed it; we've a little been *of* it." The great thing for him, at this, as Kate gave it, *was* in fact quite irresistibly that the case was a real one—the kind of thing that, when one's patience was shorter than one's curiosity, one had vaguely taken for possible in London, but in which one had never been even to this small extent concerned. The little American's sudden social adventure, her happy and, no doubt, harmless flourish, had probably been favoured by several accidents, but it had been favoured above all by the simple spring-board of the scene, by one of those common caprices of the numberless foolish flock, gregarious movements as inscrutable as ocean-currents. The huddled herd had drifted to her blindly—it might as blindly have drifted away. There had been of course a signal, but the great reason was probably the absence at the moment of a larger lion. The bigger beast would come and the smaller would then incontinently vanish. It was at all events characteristic, and what was of the essence of it was grist to his scribbling mill, matter for his journalising hand. That hand already, in intention, played over it, the "motive," as a sign of the season, a feature of the time, of the purely expeditious and rough-and-tumble nature of the social boom. The boom as in *itself* required—that would be the note; the subject of the process a comparatively minor question. Anything was boomable enough when nothing else was more so: the author of the "rotten" book, the beauty who was no beauty, the heiress who was only that, the stranger who was for the most part saved from being inconveniently strange but by being inconveniently familiar, the American whose Americanism had been long desperately discounted, the creature in fine as to whom spangles or spots of any sufficiently marked and exhibited sort could be loudly enough predicated.

So he judged at least, within his limits, and the idea that what he had thus caught in the fact was the trick of fashion and the tone of society went so far as to make him take up again his sense of independence. He had supposed himself civilised; but if this was civilisation—! One could smoke one's pipe outside when twaddle was within. He had rather avoided, as we have remarked, Kate's eyes, but there came a moment when he would fairly have liked to put it, across the table, to her: "I say, light of my life, is *this* the great world?" There came another, it must be added—and doubtless as a result of something that, over the cloth, did hang between them—when she struck him as having quite answered: "Dear no—for what do you take me? Not the least little bit: only a poor silly, though quite harmless, imitation." What she might have passed for saying, however, was practically merged in what she did say, for she came overtly to his aid, very much as if guessing some of his thoughts. She enunciated, to relieve his bewilderment, the obvious truth that you couldn't leave London for three months at that time of the year and come back to find your friends just where they were. As they had *of course* been jigging away they might well be so red in the face that you wouldn't know them. She reconciled in fine his disclaimer about Milly with that honour of having discovered her which it was vain for him modestly to shirk. He *had* unearthed her, but it was they, all of them together, who had developed her. She was always a charmer, one of the greatest ever seen, but she wasn't the person he had "backed."

Densher was to feel sure afterwards that Kate had had in these pleasantries no conscious, above all no insolent purpose of making light of poor Susan Shepherd's property in their young friend—which property, by such remarks, was very much pushed to the wall; but he was also to know that Mrs. Stringham had secretly resented them, Mrs. Stringham holding the opinion, of which he was ultimately to have a glimpse, that all the Kate Croys in Christendom were but dust for the feet of her Milly. That, it was true, would be what she must reveal only when driven to her last entrenchments and well cornered in her passion—the rare passion of friendship, the sole passion of her little life save the one other, more imperturbably cerebral, that she entertained for the art of Guy de Maupassant. She slipped in the observation that her Milly was incapable of change, was just exactly, on the contrary, the same Milly; but this made little difference in the drift of Kate's contention. She was perfectly kind to Susie: it was as if she positively knew her as handicapped for any disagreement by feeling that she, Kate, had "type," and by being committed to admiration of type. Kate had occasion subsequently—she found it somehow—to mention to our young man Milly's having spoken to her of this view on the good lady's part. She would like—Milly had had it from her—to put Kate Croy in a book and see what she could so do with her. "Chop me up fine or serve me whole"—it was a way of being got at that Kate professed she dreaded. It would be Mrs. Stringham's, however, she understood, because Mrs. Stringham, oddly, felt that with such stuff as the strange English girl was made of, stuff that (in spite of Maud Manningham, who was full of sentiment) she had never known, there was none other to be employed. These things were of later evidence, yet Densher might even then have felt them in the air. They were practically in it already when Kate, waiving the question of her friend's chemical change, wound up with the comparatively unobjectionable proposition that he must now, having missed so much, take them all up, on trust, further on. He met it peacefully, a little perhaps as an example to Mrs. Stringham—"Oh as far on as you like!" This even had its effect: Mrs. Stringham appropriated as much of it as might be meant for herself. The nice thing about her was that she could measure how much; so that by the time dinner was over they had really covered ground.

IV

The younger of the other men, it afterwards appeared, was most in his element at the piano; so that they had coffee and comic songs upstairs—the gentlemen, temporarily relinquished, submitting easily in this interest to Mrs. Lowder's parting injunction not to sit too tight. Our especial young man sat tighter when restored to the drawing-room; he made it out perfectly with Kate that they might, off and on, foregather without offence. He had perhaps stronger needs in this general respect than she; but she had better names for the scant risks to which she consented. It was the blessing of a big house that intervals were large and, of an August night, that windows were open; whereby, at a given moment, on the wide balcony, with the songs sufficiently sung, Aunt Maud could hold her little court more freshly. Densher and Kate, during these moments, occupied side by side a small sofa—a luxury formulated by the latter as the proof, under criticism, of their remarkably good conscience. "To seem not to know each other—once you're here—would be," the girl said, "to overdo it"; and she arranged it charmingly that they *must* have some passage to put Aunt Maud off the scent. She would be wondering otherwise what in the world they found their account in. For Densher, none the less, the profit of snatched moments, snatched contacts, was partial and poor; there were in particular at present more things in his mind than he could bring out while watching the windows. It was true, on the other hand, that she suddenly met most of them—and more than he could see on the spot—by coming out for him with a reference to Milly that was not in the key of those made at dinner. "She's not a bit right, you know. I mean in health. Just see her to-night. I mean it looks grave. For you she would have come, you know, if it had been at all possible."

He took this in such patience as he could muster. "What in the world's the matter with her?"

But Kate continued without saying. "Unless indeed your being here has been just a reason for her funking it."

"What in the world's the matter with her?" Densher asked again.

"Why just what I've told you—that she likes you so much."

"Then why should she deny herself the joy of meeting me?"

Kate cast about—it would take so long to explain. "And perhaps it's true that she *is* bad. She easily may be."

"Quite easily, I should say, judging by Mrs. Stringham, who's visibly preoccupied and worried."

"Visibly enough. Yet it mayn't," said Kate, "be only for that."

"For what then?"

But this question too, on thinking, she neglected. "Why, if it's anything real, doesn't that poor lady go home? She'd be anxious, and she has done all she need to be civil."

"I think," Densher remarked, "she has been quite beautifully civil."

It made Kate, he fancied, look at him the least bit harder; but she was already, in a manner, explaining. "Her preoccupation is probably on two different heads. One of them would make her hurry back, but the other makes her stay. She's commissioned to tell Milly all about you."

"Well then," said the young man between a laugh and a sigh, "I'm glad I felt, downstairs, a kind of 'drawing' to her. Wasn't I rather decent to her?"

"Awfully nice. You've instincts, you fiend. It's all," Kate declared, "as it should be."

"Except perhaps," he after a moment cynically suggested, "that she isn't getting much good of me now. Will she report to Milly on *this?*" And then as Kate seemed to wonder what "this" might be: "On our present disregard for appearances."

"Ah leave appearances to me!" She spoke in her high way. "I'll make them all right. Aunt Maud, moreover," she added, "has her so engaged that she won't notice." Densher felt, with this, that his companion had indeed perceptive flights he couldn't hope to match—had for instance another when she still subjoined: "And Mrs. Stringham's appearing to respond just in order to make that impression."

"Well," Densher dropped with some humour, "life's very interesting! I hope it's really as much so for you as you make it for others; I mean judging by what you make it for me. You seem to me to represent it as thrilling for *ces dames*, and in a different way for each: Aunt Maud, Susan Shepherd, Milly. But what *is*," he wound up, "the matter? Do you mean she's as ill as she looks?"

Kate's face struck him as replying at first that his derisive speech deserved no satisfaction; then she appeared to yield to a need of her own—the need to make the point that "as ill as she looked" was what Milly scarce could be. If she had been as ill as she looked she could scarce be a question with them, for her end would in that case be near. She believed herself nevertheless—and Kate couldn't help believing her too—seriously menaced. There was always the fact that they had been on the point of leaving town, the two ladies, and had suddenly been pulled up. "We bade them good-bye—or all but—Aunt Maud and I, the night before Milly, popping so very oddly into the National Gallery for a farewell look, found you and me together. They were then to get off a day or two later. But they've not got off—they're not getting off. When I see them—and I saw them this morning—they have showy reasons. They do mean to go, but they've postponed it." With which the girl brought out: "They've postponed it for *you*." He protested so far as a man might without fatuity, since a protest was itself credulous; but Kate, as ever, understood herself. "You've made Milly change her mind. She wants not to miss you—though she wants also not to show she wants you; which is why, as I hinted a moment ago, she may consciously have hung back to-night. She doesn't know when she may see you again—she doesn't know she ever may. She doesn't see the future. It has opened out before her in these last weeks as a dark confused thing."

Densher wondered. "After the tremendous time you've all been telling me she has had?"

"That's it. There's a shadow across it."

"The shadow, you consider, of some physical break-up?"

"Some physical break-down. Nothing less. She's scared. She has so much to lose. And she wants more."

"Ah well," said Densher with a sudden strange sense of discomfort, "couldn't one say to her that she can't have everything?"

"No—for one wouldn't want to. She really," Kate went on, "has been somebody here. Ask Aunt Maud—you may think me prejudiced," the girl oddly smiled. "Aunt Maud will tell you—the world's before her. It has all come since you saw her, and it's a pity you've missed it, for it certainly would have amused you. She has really been a perfect success—I mean of course so far as possible in the scrap of time—and she has taken it like a perfect angel. If you can imagine an angel with a thumping bank-account you'll have the simplest expression of the kind of thing. Her fortune's absolutely huge; Aunt

Maud has had all the facts, or enough of them, in the last confidence, from 'Susie,' and Susie speaks by book. Take them then, in the last confidence, from *me*. There she is." Kate expressed above all what it most came to. "It's open to her to make, you see, the very greatest marriage. I assure you we're not vulgar about her. Her possibilities are quite plain."

Densher showed he neither disbelieved nor grudged them. "But what good then on earth can I do her?"

Well, she had it ready. "You can console her."

"And for what?"

"For all that, if she's stricken, she must see swept away. I shouldn't care for her if she hadn't so much," Kate very simply said. And then as it made him laugh not quite happily: "I shouldn't trouble about her if there were one thing she did have." The girl spoke indeed with a noble compassion. "She has nothing."

"Not all the young dukes?"

"Well we must see—see if anything can come of them. She at any rate does love life. To have met a person like you," Kate further explained, "is to have felt you become, with all the other fine things, a part of life. Oh she has you arranged!"

"*You* have, it strikes me, my dear"—and he looked both detached and rueful. "Pray what am I to do with the dukes?"

"Oh the dukes will be disappointed!"

"Then why shan't I be?"

"You'll have expected less," Kate wonderfully smiled. "Besides, you *will* be. You'll have expected enough for that."

"Yet it's what you want to let me in for?"

"I want," said the girl, "to make things pleasant for her. I use, for the purpose, what I have. You're what I have of most precious, and you're therefore what I use most."

He looked at her long. "I wish I could use *you* a little more." After which, as she continued to smile at him, "Is it a bad case of lungs?" he asked.

Kate showed for a little as if she wished it might be. "Not lungs, I think. Isn't consumption, taken in time, now curable?"

"People are, no doubt, patched up." But he wondered. "Do you mean she has something that's past patching?" And before she could answer: "It's really as if her appearance put her outside of such things—being, in spite of her youth, that of a person who has been through all it's conceivable she should be exposed to. She affects one, I should say, as a creature saved from a shipwreck. Such a creature may surely, in these days, on the doctrine of chances, go to sea again with confidence. She has *had* her wreck—she has met her adventure."

"Oh I grant you her wreck!"—Kate was all response so far. "But do let her have still her adventure. There are wrecks that are not adventures."

"Well—if there be also adventures that are not wrecks!" Densher in short was willing, but he came back to his point. "What I mean is that she has none of the effect—on one's nerves or whatever—of an invalid."

Kate on her side did this justice. "No—that's the beauty of her."

"The beauty—?"

"Yes, she's so wonderful. She won't show for that, any more than your watch, when it's about to stop for want of being wound up, gives you convenient notice or shows as different from usual. She won't die, she won't live, by inches. She won't smell, as it were, of drugs. She won't taste, as it were, of medicine. No one will know."

"Then what," he demanded, frankly mystified now, "are we talking about? In what extraordinary state *is* she?"

Kate went on as if, at this, making it out in a fashion for herself. "I believe that if she's ill at all she's very ill. I believe that if she's bad she's not a *little* bad. I can't tell you why, but that's how I see her. She'll really live or she'll really not. She'll have it all or she'll miss it all. Now I don't think she'll have it all."

Densher had followed this with his eyes upon her, her own having thoughtfully wandered, and as if it were more impressive than lucid. "You 'think' and you 'don't think,' and yet you remain all the while without an inkling of her complaint?"

"No, not without an inkling; but it's a matter in which I don't want knowledge. She moreover herself doesn't want one to want it: she has, as to what may be preying upon her, a kind of ferocity of modesty, a kind of—I don't know what to call it—intensity of pride. And then and then—" But with this she faltered.

"And then what?"

"I'm a brute about illness. I hate it. It's well for you, my dear," Kate continued, "that you're as sound as a bell."

"Thank you!" Densher laughed. "It's rather good then for yourself too that you're as strong as the sea."

She looked at him now a moment as for the selfish gladness of their young immunities. It was all they had together, but they had it at least without a flaw—each had the beauty, the physical felicity, the personal virtue, love and desire of the other. Yet it was as if that very consciousness threw them back the next moment into pity for the poor girl who had everything else in the world, the great genial good they, alas, didn't have, but failed on the other hand of this. "How we're talking about her!" Kate compunctiously sighed. But there were the facts. "From illness I keep away."

"But you don't—since here you are, in spite of all you say, in the midst of it."

"Ah I'm only watching—!"

"And putting me forward in your place? Thank you!"

"Oh," said Kate, "I'm breaking you in. Let it give you the measure of what I shall expect of you. One can't begin too soon."

She drew away, as from the impression of a stir on the balcony, the hand of which he had a minute before possessed himself; and the warning brought him back to attention. "You haven't even an idea if it's a case for surgery?"

"I dare say it may be; that is that if it comes to anything it may come to that. Of course she's in the highest hands."

"The doctors are after her then?"

"She's after *them*—it's the same thing. I think I'm free to say it now—she sees Sir Luke Strett."

It made him quickly wince. "Ah fifty thousand knives!" Then after an instant: "One seems to guess."

Yes, but she waved it away. "Don't guess. Only do as I tell you."

For a moment now, in silence, he took it all in, might have had it before him. "What you want of me then is to make up to a sick girl."

"Ah but you admit yourself that she doesn't affect you as sick. You understand moreover just how much—and just how little."

"It's amazing," he presently answered, "what you think I understand."

"Well, if you've brought me to it, my dear," she returned, "that has been your way of breaking *me* in. Besides which, so far as making up to her goes, plenty of others will."

Densher for a little, under this suggestion, might have been seeing their young friend on a pile of cushions and in a perpetual tea-gown, amid flowers and with drawn blinds, surrounded by the higher nobility. "Others can follow their tastes. Besides, others are free."

"But so are you, my dear!"

She had spoken with impatience, and her suddenly quitting him had sharpened it; in spite of which he kept his place, only looking up at her. "You're prodigious!"

"Of course I'm prodigious!"—and, as immediately happened, she gave a further sign of it that he fairly sat watching. The door from the lobby had, as she spoke, been thrown open for a gentleman who, immediately finding her within his view, advanced to greet her before the announcement of his name could reach her companion. Densher none the less felt himself brought quickly into relation; Kate's welcome to the visitor became almost precipitately an appeal to her friend, who slowly rose to meet it. "I don't know whether you know Lord Mark." And then for the other party: "Mr. Merton Densher—who has just come back from America."

"Oh!" said the other party while Densher said nothing—occupied as he mainly was on the spot with weighing the sound in question. He recognised it in a moment as less imponderable than it might have appeared, as having indeed positive claims. It wasn't, that is, he knew, the "Oh!" of the idiot, however great the superficial resemblance: it was that of the clever, the accomplished man; it was the very specialty of the speaker, and a deal of expensive training and experience had gone to producing it. Densher felt somehow that, as a thing of value accidentally picked up, it would retain an interest of curiosity. The three stood for a little together in an awkwardness to which he was conscious of contributing his share; Kate failing to ask Lord Mark to be seated, but letting him know that he would find Mrs. Lowder, with some others, on the balcony.

"Oh and Miss Theale I suppose?—as I seemed to hear outside, from below, Mrs. Stringham's unmistakeable voice."

"Yes, but Mrs. Stringham's alone. Milly's unwell," the girl explained, "and was compelled to disappoint us."

"Ah 'disappoint'—rather!" And, lingering a little, he kept his eyes on Densher. "She isn't really bad, I trust?"

Densher, after all he had heard, easily supposed him interested in Milly; but he could imagine him also interested in the young man with whom he had found Kate engaged and whom he yet considered without visible intelligence. That young man concluded in a moment that he was doing what he wanted, satisfying himself as to each. To this he was aided by Kate, who produced a prompt: "Oh dear no; I think not. I've just been reassuring Mr. Densher," she added—"who's as concerned as the rest of us. I've been calming his fears."

"Oh!" said Lord Mark again—and again it was just as good. That was for Densher, the latter could see, or think he saw. And then for the others: "*My* fears would want calming. We must take great care of her. This way?"

She went with him a few steps, and while Densher, hanging about, gave them frank attention, presently paused again for some further colloquy. What passed between them their observer lost, but she was presently with him again, Lord Mark joining the rest. Densher was by this time quite ready for her. "It's *he* who's your aunt's man?"

"Oh immensely."

"I mean for *you*."

"That's what I mean too," Kate smiled. "There he is. Now you can judge."

"Judge of what?"

"Judge of him."

"Why should I judge of him?" Densher asked. "I've nothing to do with him."

"Then why do you ask about him?"

"To judge of you—which is different."

Kate seemed for a little to look at the difference. "To take the measure, do you mean, of my danger?"

He hesitated; then he said: "I'm thinking, I dare say, of Miss Theale's. How does your aunt reconcile his interest in her—?"

"With his interest in me?"

"With her own interest in you," Densher said while she reflected. "If that interest—Mrs. Lowder's—takes the form of Lord Mark, hasn't he rather to look out for the forms *he* takes?"

Kate seemed interested in the question, but "Oh he takes them easily," she answered. "The beauty is that she doesn't trust him."

"That Milly doesn't?"

"Yes—Milly either. But I mean Aunt Maud. Not really."

Densher gave it his wonder. "Takes him to her heart and yet thinks he cheats?"

"Yes," said Kate—"that's the way people are. What they think of their enemies, goodness knows, is bad enough; but I'm still more struck with what they think of their friends. Milly's own state of mind, however," she went on, "is lucky. That's Aunt Maud's security, though she doesn't yet fully recognise it—besides being Milly's own."

"You conceive it a real escape then not to care for him?"

She shook her head in beautiful grave deprecation. "You oughtn't to make me say too much. But I'm glad I don't."

"Don't say too much?"

"Don't care for Lord Mark."

"Oh!" Densher answered with a sound like his lordship's own. To which he added: "You absolutely hold that that poor girl doesn't?"

"Ah you know what I hold about that poor girl!" It had made her again impatient.

Yet he stuck a minute to the subject. "You scarcely call him, I suppose, one of the dukes."

"Mercy, no—far from it. He's not, compared with other possibilities, 'in' it. Milly, it's true," she said, to be exact, "has no natural sense of social values, doesn't in the least understand our differences or know who's who or what's what."

"I see. That," Densher laughed, "is her reason for liking *me*."

"Precisely. She doesn't resemble me," said Kate, "who at least know what I lose."

Well, it had all risen for Densher to a considerable interest. "And Aunt Maud—why shouldn't *she* know? I mean that your friend there isn't really anything. Does she suppose him of ducal value?"

"Scarcely; save in the sense of being uncle to a duke. That's undeniably something. He's the best moreover we can get."

"Oh, oh!" said Densher; and his doubt was not all derisive.

"It isn't Lord Mark's grandeur," she went on without heeding this; "because perhaps in the line of that alone—as he has no money—more could be done. But she's not a bit sordid; she only counts with the sordidness of others. Besides, he's grand enough, with a duke in his family and at the other end of the string. *The* thing's his genius."

"And do you believe in that?"

"In Lord Mark's genius?" Kate, as if for a more final opinion than had yet been asked of her, took a moment to think. She balanced indeed so that one would scarce have known what to expect; but she came out in time with a very sufficient "Yes!"

"Political?"

"Universal. I don't know at least," she said, "what else to call it when a man's able to make himself without effort, without violence, without machinery of any sort, so intensely felt. He has somehow an effect without his being in any traceable way a cause."

"Ah but if the effect," said Densher with conscious superficiality, "isn't agreeable—?"

"Oh but it is!"

"Not surely for every one."

"If you mean not for you," Kate returned, "you may have reasons—and men don't count. Women don't know if it's agreeable or not."

"Then there you are!"

"Yes, precisely—that takes, on his part, genius."

Densher stood before her as if he wondered what everything she thus promptly, easily and above all amusingly met him with, would have been found, should it have come to an analysis, to "take." Something suddenly, as if under a last determinant touch, welled up in him and overflowed—the sense of his good fortune and her variety, of the future she promised, the interest she supplied. "All women but you are stupid. How can I look at another? You're different and different—and then you're different again. No marvel Aunt Maud builds on you—except that you're so much too good for what she builds *for*. Even 'society' won't know how good for it you are; it's too stupid, and you're beyond it. You'd have to pull it uphill—it's you yourself who are at the top. The women one meets—what are they but books one has already read? You're a whole library of the unknown, the uncut." He almost moaned, he ached, from the depth of his content. "Upon my word I've a subscription!"

She took it from him with her face again giving out all it had in answer, and they remained once more confronted and united in their essential wealth of life. "It's you who draw me out. I exist in you. Not in others."

It had been, however, as if the thrill of their association itself pressed in him, as great felicities do, the sharp spring of fear. "See here, you know: don't, *don't*—!"

"Don't what?"

"Don't fail me. It would kill me."

She looked at him a minute with no response but her eyes. "So you think you'll kill *me* in time to prevent it?" She smiled, but he saw her the next instant as smiling through tears; and the instant after this she had got, in respect to the particular point, quite off. She had come back to another, which was one of her own; her own were so closely connected that Densher's were at best but parenthetic. Still she had a distance to go. "You do then see your way?" She put it to him before they joined—as was high time—the others. And she made him understand she meant his way with Milly.

He had dropped a little in presence of the explanation; then she had brought him up to a sort of recognition. He could make out by this light something of what he saw, but a dimness also there was, undispelled since his return. "There's something you must definitely tell me. If our friend knows that all the while—?"

She came straight to his aid, formulating for him his anxiety, though quite to smooth it down. "All the while she and I here were growing intimate, you and I were in unmentioned relation? If she knows that, yes, she knows our relation must have involved your writing to me."

"Then how could she suppose you weren't answering?"

"She doesn't suppose it."

"How then can she imagine you never named her?"

"She doesn't. She knows now I did name her. I've told her everything. She's in possession of reasons that will perfectly do."

Still he just brooded. "She takes things from you exactly as I take them?"

"Exactly as you take them."

"She's just such another victim?"

"Just such another. You're a pair."

"Then if anything happens," said Densher, "we can console each other?"

"Ah something *may* indeed happen," she returned, "if you'll only go straight!"

He watched the others an instant through the window. "What do you mean by going straight?"

"Not worrying. Doing as you like. Try, as I've told you before, and you'll see. You'll have me perfectly, always, to refer to."

"Oh rather, I hope! But if she's going away?"

It pulled Kate up but a moment. "I'll bring her back. There you are. You won't be able to say I haven't made it smooth for you."

He faced it all, and certainly it was queer. But it wasn't the queerness that after another minute was uppermost. He was in a wondrous silken web, and it was amusing. "You spoil me!"

He wasn't sure if Mrs. Lowder, who at this juncture reappeared, had caught his word as it dropped from him; probably not, he thought, her attention being given to Mrs. Stringham, with whom she came through and who was now, none too soon, taking leave of her. They were followed by Lord Mark and by the other men, but two or three things happened before any dispersal of the company began. One of these was that Kate found time to say to him with furtive emphasis: "You must go now!" Another was that she next addressed herself in all frankness to Lord Mark, drew near to him with an almost reproachful "Come and talk to *me!*"—a challenge resulting after a minute for Densher in a consciousness of their installation together in an out-of-the-way corner, though not the same he himself had just occupied with her. Still another was that Mrs. Stringham, in the random intensity of her farewells, affected him as looking at him with a small grave intimation, something into which he afterwards read the meaning that if he had happened to desire a few words with her after dinner he would have found her ready. This impression was naturally light, but it just left him with the sense of something by his own act overlooked, unappreciated. It gathered perhaps a slightly sharper shade from the mild formality of her "Good-night, sir!" as she passed him; a matter as to which there was now nothing more to be done, thanks to the alertness of the young man he by this time had appraised as even more harmless than himself. This personage had forestalled him in opening the door for her and was evidently—with a view, Densher might have judged, to ulterior designs on Milly—proposing to attend her to her carriage. What further occurred was that Aunt Maud, having released her, immediately had a word for himself. It was an imperative "Wait a minute," by which she both detained and dismissed him; she was particular about her minute, but he hadn't yet given her, as happened, a sign of withdrawal.

"Return to our little friend. You'll find her really interesting."

"If you mean Miss Theale," he said, "I shall certainly not forget her. But you must remember that, so far as her 'interest' is concerned, I myself discovered, I—as was said at dinner—invented her."

"Well, one seemed rather to gather that you hadn't taken out the patent. Don't, I only mean, in the press of other things, too much neglect her."

Affected, surprised by the coincidence of her appeal with Kate's, he asked himself quickly if it mightn't help him with her. He at any rate could but try. "You're all looking after my manners. That's exactly, you know, what Miss Croy has been saying to me. *She* keeps me up—she has had so much to say about them."

He found pleasure in being able to give his hostess an account of his passage with Kate that, while quite veracious, might be reassuring to herself. But Aunt Maud, wonderfully and facing him straight, took it as if her confidence were supplied with other props. If she saw his intention in it she yet blinked neither with doubt nor with acceptance; she only said imperturbably: "Yes, she'll herself do anything for her friend; so that she but preaches what she practises."

Densher really quite wondered if Aunt Maud knew how far Kate's devotion went. He was moreover a little puzzled by this special harmony; in face of which he quickly asked himself if Mrs. Lowder had bethought herself of the American girl as a distraction for him, and if Kate's mastery of the subject were therefore but an appearance addressed to her aunt. What might really *become* in all this of the American girl was therefore a question that, on the latter contingency, would lose none of its sharpness. However, questions could wait, and it was easy, so far as he understood, to meet Mrs. Lowder. "It isn't a bit, all the same, you know, that I resist. I find Miss Theale charming."

Well, it was all she wanted. "Then don't miss a chance."

"The only thing is," he went on, "that she's—naturally now—leaving town and, as I take it, going abroad."

Aunt Maud looked indeed an instant as if she herself had been dealing with this difficulty. "She won't go," she smiled in spite of it, "till she has seen you. Moreover, when she does go—" She paused, leaving him uncertain. But the next minute he was still more at sea. "We shall go too."

He gave a smile that he himself took for slightly strange. "And what good will that do *me?*"

"We shall be near them somewhere, and you'll come out to us."

"Oh!" he said a little awkwardly.

"I'll see that you do. I mean I'll write to you."

"Ah thank you, thank you!" Merton Densher laughed. She was indeed putting him on his honour, and his honour winced a little at the use he rather helplessly saw himself suffering her to believe she could make of it. "There are all sorts of things," he vaguely remarked, "to consider."

"No doubt. But there's above all the great thing."

"And pray what's that?"

"Why the importance of your not losing the occasion of your life. I'm treating you handsomely, I'm looking after it for you. I *can*—I can smooth your path. She's charming, she's clever and she's good. And her fortune's a real fortune."

Ah there she was, Aunt Maud! The pieces fell together for him as he felt her thus buying him off, and buying him—it would have been funny if it hadn't been so grave—with Miss Theale's money. He ventured, derisive, fairly to treat it as extravagant. "I'm much obliged to you for the handsome offer—"

"Of what doesn't belong to me?" She wasn't abashed. "I don't say it does—but there's no reason it shouldn't to *you*. Mind you, moreover"—she kept it up—"I'm not one who talks in the air. And you owe me something—if you want to know why."

Distinct he felt her pressure; he felt, given her basis, her consistency; he even felt, to a degree that was immediately to receive an odd confirmation, her truth. Her truth, for that matter, was that she believed him bribeable: a belief that for his own mind as well, while they stood there, lighted up the impossible. What then in this light did Kate believe him? But that wasn't what he asked aloud. "Of course I know I owe you thanks for a deal of kind treatment. Your inviting me for instance to-night—!"

"Yes, my inviting you to-night's a part of it. But you don't know," she added, "how far I've gone for you."

He felt himself red and as if his honour were colouring up; but he laughed again as he could. "I see how far you're going."

"I'm the most honest woman in the world, but I've nevertheless done for you what was necessary." And then as her now quite sombre gravity only made him stare: "To start you it *was* necessary. From *me* it has the weight." He but continued to stare, and she met his blankness with surprise. "Don't you understand me? I've told the proper lie for you." Still he only showed her his flushed strained smile; in spite of which, speaking with force and as if he must with a minute's reflexion see what she meant, she turned away from him. "I depend upon you now to make me right!"

The minute's reflexion he was of course more free to take after he had left the house. He walked up the Bayswater Road, but he stopped short, under the murky stars, before the modern church, in the middle of the square that, going eastward, opened out on his left. He had had his brief stupidity, but now he understood. She had guaranteed to Milly Theale through Mrs.

Stringham that Kate didn't care for him. She had affirmed through the same source that the attachment was only his. He made it out, he made it out, and he could see what she meant by its starting him. She had described Kate as merely compassionate, so that Milly might be compassionate too. "Proper" indeed it was, her lie—the very properest possible and the most deeply, richly diplomatic. So Milly was successfully deceived.

V

To see her alone, the poor girl, he none the less promptly felt, was to see her after all very much on the old basis, the basis of his three visits in New York; the new element, when once he was again face to face with her, not really amounting to much more than a recognition, with a little surprise, of the positive extent of the old basis. Everything but that, everything embarrassing fell away after he had been present five minutes: it was in fact wonderful that their excellent, their pleasant, their permitted and proper and harmless American relation—the legitimacy of which he could thus scarce express in names enough—should seem so unperturbed by other matters. They had both since then had great adventures—such an adventure for him was his mental annexation of her country; and it was now, for the moment, as if the greatest of them all were this acquired consciousness of reasons other than those that had already served. Densher had asked for her, at her hotel, the day after Aunt Maud's dinner, with a rich, that is with a highly troubled, preconception of the part likely to be played for him at present, in any contact with her, by Kate's and Mrs. Lowder's so oddly conjoined and so really superfluous attempts to make her interesting. She had been interesting enough without them—that appeared to-day to come back to him; and, admirable and beautiful as was the charitable zeal of the two ladies, it might easily have nipped in the bud the germs of a friendship inevitably limited but still perfectly open to him. What had happily averted the need of his breaking off, what would as happily continue to avert it, was his own good sense and good humour, a certain spring of mind in him which ministered, imagination aiding, to understandings and allowances and which he had positively never felt such ground as just now to rejoice in the possession of. Many men—he practically made the reflexion—wouldn't have taken the matter that way, would have lost patience, finding the appeal in question irrational, exorbitant; and, thereby making short work with it, would have let it render any further acquaintance with Miss Theale impossible. He had talked with Kate of this young woman's being "sacrificed," and that would have been one way, so far as he was concerned, to sacrifice her. Such, however, had not been the tune to which his at first bewildered view had, since the night before, cleared itself up. It wasn't so much that he failed of being the kind of man who "chucked," for he knew himself as the kind of man wise enough to mark the case in which chucking might be the minor evil and the least cruelty. It was that he liked too much every one concerned willingly to show himself merely impracticable. He liked Kate, goodness knew, and he also clearly enough liked Mrs. Lowder. He liked in particular Milly herself; and hadn't it come up for him the evening before that he quite liked even Susan Shepherd? He had never known himself so generally merciful. It was a footing, at all events, whatever accounted for it, on which he should surely be rather a muff not to manage by one turn or another to escape disobliging. Should he find he couldn't work it there would still be time enough. The idea of working it crystallised before him in such guise as not only to promise much interest—fairly, in case of success, much enthusiasm; but positively to impart to failure an appearance of barbarity.

Arriving thus in Brook Street both with the best intentions and with a margin consciously left for some primary awkwardness, he found his burden, to his great relief, unexpectedly light. The awkwardness involved in the responsibility so newly and so ingeniously traced for him turned round on the spot to present him another face. This was simply the face of his old impression, which he now fully recovered—the impression that American girls, when, rare case, they had the attraction of Milly, were clearly the easiest people in the world. Had what had happened been that this specimen of the class was from the first so committed to ease that nothing subsequent *could* ever make her difficult? That affected him now as still more probable than on the occasion of the hour or two lately passed with her in Kate's society. Milly Theale had recognised no complication, to Densher's view, while bringing him, with his companion, from the National Gallery and entertaining them at luncheon; it was therefore scarce supposable that complications had become so soon too much for her. His pretext for presenting himself was fortunately of the best and simplest; the least he could decently do, given their happy acquaintance, was to call with an enquiry after learning that she had been prevented by illness from meeting him at dinner. And then there was the beautiful accident of her other demonstration; he must at any rate have given a sign as a sequel to the hospitality he had shared with Kate. Well, he was giving one now—such as it was; he was finding her, to begin with, accessible, and very naturally and prettily glad to see him. He had come, after luncheon, early, though not so early but that she might already be out if she were well enough; and she was well enough and yet was still at home. He had an inner glimpse, with this, of the comment Kate would have made on it; it wasn't absent from his thought that Milly would have been at home by *her* account because expecting, after a talk with Mrs. Stringham, that a certain person might turn up. He even—so pleasantly did things go— enjoyed freedom of mind to welcome, on that supposition, a fresh sign of the beautiful hypocrisy of women. He went so far as to enjoy believing the girl *might* have stayed in for him; it helped him to enjoy her behaving as if she hadn't. She expressed, that is, exactly the right degree of surprise; she didn't a bit overdo it: the lesson of which was, perceptibly, that, so far as his late lights had opened the door to any want of the natural in their meetings, he might trust her to take care of it for him as well as for herself. She had begun this, admirably, on his entrance, with her turning away from the table at which she had apparently been engaged in letter-writing; it was the very possibility of his betraying a concern for her as one of the afflicted that she had within the first minute conjured away. She was never, never—did he understand?— to be one of the afflicted for him; and the manner in which he understood it, something of the answering pleasure that he couldn't help knowing he showed, constituted, he was very soon after to acknowledge, something like a start for intimacy. When things like that could pass people had in truth to be equally conscious of a relation. It soon made one, at all events, when it didn't find one made. She had let him ask—there had been time for that, his allusion to her friend's explanatory arrival at Lancaster Gate without her being inevitable; but she had blown away, and quite as much with the look in her eyes as with the smile on her lips, every ground for anxiety and every chance for insistence. How was she?—why she was as he thus saw her and as she had reasons of her own, nobody else's business, for desiring to appear. Kate's account of her as too proud for pity, as fiercely shy about so personal a secret, came back to him; so that he rejoiced he could take a hint, especially when he wanted to. The question the girl had quickly disposed of—"Oh it was nothing: I'm all right, thank you!"—was one he was glad enough to be able to banish. It wasn't at all, in spite of the appeal Kate had made to him on it, his affair; for his interest had been invoked in the name of compassion, and the name of compassion was exactly what he felt himself at the end of two minutes forbidden so much as to whisper. He had been sent to see her in order to be sorry for her, and how sorry he might be, quite privately, he was yet to make out. Didn't that signify, however, almost not at all?—inasmuch as, whatever his upshot, he was never to give her a glimpse of it. Thus the ground was unexpectedly cleared; though it was not till a slightly longer time had passed that he read clear, at first with amusement and then with a strange shade of respect, what had most operated. Extraordinarily, quite amazingly, he began to see that if his pity hadn't had to yield to still other things it would have had to yield quite definitely to her own. That was the way the case had turned round: he had made his visit to be sorry for her, but he would repeat it—if he did repeat it—in order that she might be sorry for him. His situation made him, she judged—when once one liked him—a subject for that degree of tenderness: he felt this judgement in her, and felt it as something he should really, in decency, in dignity, in common honesty, have very soon to reckon with.

Odd enough was it certainly that the question originally before him, the question placed there by Kate, should so of a sudden find itself quite dislodged by another. This other, it was easy to see, came straight up with the fact of her beautiful delusion and her wasted charity; the whole thing preparing for him as pretty a case of conscience as he could have desired, and one at the prospect of which he was already wincing. If he was interesting it was because he was unhappy; and if he was unhappy it was because his passion for Kate had spent itself in vain; and if Kate was indifferent, inexorable, it was because she had left Milly in no doubt of it. That above all was what came up for him—how clear an impression of this attitude, how definite an account of his own failure, Kate must have given her friend. His immediate quarter of an hour there with the girl lighted up for him almost luridly such an inference; it was almost as if the other party to their remarkable understanding had been with them as they talked, had been hovering about, had dropped in to look after her work. The value of the work affected him as different from the moment he saw it so expressed in poor Milly. Since it was false that he wasn't loved, so his right was quite quenched to figure on that ground as important; and if he didn't look out he should find himself appreciating in a way quite at odds with straightness the good faith of Milly's benevolence. *There* was the place for scruples; there the need absolutely to mind what he was about. If it wasn't proper for him to enjoy consideration on a perfectly false footing, where was the guarantee that, if he kept on, he mightn't soon himself pretend to the grievance in order not to miss the sweet? Consideration— from a charming girl—was soothing on whatever theory; and it didn't take him far to remember that he had himself as yet done nothing deceptive. It was Kate's description of him, his defeated state, it was none of his own; his responsibility would begin, as he might say, only with acting it out. The sharp point was, however, in the difference between acting and not acting: this difference in fact it was that made the case of conscience. He saw it with a certain alarm rise before him that everything was acting that was not speaking the particular word. "If you like me because you think *she* doesn't, it isn't a bit true: she *does* like me awfully!"—that would have been the particular word; which there were at the same time but too palpably such difficulties about his uttering. Wouldn't it be virtually as indelicate to challenge her as to leave her deluded?—and this quite apart from the exposure, so to speak, of Kate, as to whom it would constitute a kind of betrayal. Kate's design was something so extraordinarily special to Kate that he felt himself shrink from the complications involved in judging it. Not to give away the woman one loved, but to back her up in her mistakes—once they had gone a certain length—that was perhaps chief among the inevitabilities of the abjection of love. Loyalty was of course supremely prescribed in presence of any design on her part, however roundabout, to do one nothing but good.

Densher had quite to steady himself not to be awestruck at the immensity of the good his own friend must on all this evidence have wanted to do him. Of one thing indeed meanwhile he was sure: Milly Theale wouldn't herself precipitate his necessity of intervention. She would absolutely never say to him: "*Is* it so impossible she shall ever care for you seriously?"—without which nothing could well be less delicate than for him aggressively to set her right. Kate would be free to do that if Kate, in some prudence, some contrition, for some better reason in fine, should revise her plan; but he asked himself what, failing this, *he* could do that wouldn't be after all more gross than doing nothing. This brought him round again to the acceptance of the fact that the poor girl liked him. She put it, for reasons of her own, on a simple, a beautiful ground, a ground that already supplied her with the pretext she required. The ground was there, that is, in the impression she had received, retained, cherished; the pretext, over and above it, was the pretext for acting on it. That she now believed as she did made her sure at last that she might act; so that what Densher therefore would have struck at would be the root, in her soul, of a pure pleasure. It positively lifted its head and flowered, this pure pleasure, while the young man now sat with her, and there were things she seemed to say that took the words out of his mouth. These were not all the things she did say; they were rather what such things meant in the light of what he knew. Her warning him for instance off the question of how she was, the quick brave little art with which she did that, represented to his fancy a truth she didn't utter. "I'm well for *you*—that's all you have to do with or need trouble about: I shall never be anything so horrid as ill for you. So there you are; worry about me, spare me, please, as little as you can. Don't be afraid, in short, to ignore my 'interesting' side. It isn't, you see, even now while you sit here, that there aren't lots of others. Only do *them* justice and we shall get on beautifully." This was what was folded finely up in her talk—all quite ostensibly about her impressions and her intentions. She tried to put Densher again on his American doings, but he wouldn't have that to-day. As he thought of the way in which, the other afternoon, before Kate, he had sat complacently "jawing," he accused himself of excess, of having overdone it, having made—at least apparently—more of a "set" at their entertainer than he was at all events then intending. He turned the tables, drawing her out about London, about her vision of life there, and only too glad to treat her as a person with whom he could easily have other topics than her aches and pains. He spoke to her above all of the evidence offered him at Lancaster Gate that she had come but to conquer; and when she had met this with full and gay assent—"How could I help being the feature of the season, the what-do-you-call-it, the theme of every tongue?"—they fraternised freely over all that had come and gone for each since their interrupted encounter in New York.

At the same time, while many things in quick succession came up for them, came up in particular for Densher, nothing perhaps was just so sharp as the odd influence of their present conditions on their view of their past ones. It was as if they hadn't known how "thick" they had originally become, as if, in a manner, they had really fallen to remembrance of more passages of intimacy than there had in fact at the time quite been room for. They were in a relation now so complicated, whether by what they said or by what they didn't say, that it might have been seeking to justify its speedy growth by reaching back to one of those fabulous periods in which prosperous states place their beginnings. He recalled what had been said at Mrs. Lowder's about the steps and stages, in people's careers, that absence caused one to miss, and about the resulting frequent sense of meeting them further on; which, with some other matters also recalled, he took occasion to communicate to Milly. The matters he couldn't mention mingled themselves with those he did; so that it would doubtless have been hard to say which of the two groups now played most of a part. He was kept face to face with this young lady by a force absolutely resident in their situation and operating, for his nerves, with the swiftness of the forces commonly regarded by sensitive persons as beyond their control. The current thus determined had positively become for him, by the time he had been ten minutes in the room, something that, but for the absurdity of comparing the very small with the very great, he would freely have likened to the rapids of Niagara. An uncriticised acquaintance between a clever young man and a responsive young woman could do nothing more, at the most, than go, and his actual experiment went and went and went. Nothing probably so conduced to make it go as the marked circumstance that they had spoken all the while not a word about Kate; and this in spite of the fact that, if it were a question for them of what had occurred in the past weeks, nothing had occurred comparable to Kate's predominance. Densher had but the night before appealed to her for instruction as to what he must do about her, but he fairly winced to find how little this came to. She had foretold him of course how little; but it was a truth that looked different when shown him by Milly. It proved to him that the latter had in fact been dealt with, but it produced in him the thought that Kate might perhaps again conveniently be questioned. He would have liked to speak to her before going further—to make sure she really meant him to succeed quite so much. With all the difference that, as we say, came up for him, it came up afresh, naturally, that he might make his visit brief and never renew it; yet the strangest thing of all was that the argument against that issue would have sprung precisely from the beautiful little eloquence involved in Milly's avoidances.

Precipitate these well might be, since they emphasised the fact that she was proceeding in the sense of the assurances she had taken. Over the latter she had visibly not hesitated, for hadn't they had the merit of giving her a chance? Densher quite saw her, felt her take it; the chance, neither more nor less, of help rendered him according to her freedom. It was what Kate had left her with: "Listen to him, *I?* Never! So do as you like." What Milly "liked" was to do, it thus appeared, as she was doing: our young man's glimpse of which was just what would have been for him not less a glimpse of the peculiar brutality of shaking her off. The choice exhaled its shy fragrance of heroism, for it was not aided by any question of parting with Kate. She would be charming to Kate as well as to Kate's adorer; she would incur whatever pain could dwell for her in the sight—should she continue to be exposed to the sight—of the adorer thrown with the adored. It wouldn't really have taken much more to make him wonder if he hadn't before him one of those rare cases of exaltation—food for fiction, food for poetry—in which a man's fortune with the woman who doesn't care for him is positively promoted by the woman who does. It was as if Milly had said to herself: "Well, he can at least meet her in my society, if that's anything to him; so that my line can only be to make my society attractive." She certainly couldn't have made a different impression if she *had* so reasoned. All of which, none the less, didn't prevent his soon enough saying to her, quite as if she were to be whirled into space: "And now, then, what becomes of you? Do you begin to rush about on visits to country-houses?"

She disowned the idea with a headshake that, put on what face she would, couldn't help betraying to him something of her suppressed view of the possibility—ever, ever perhaps—of any such proceedings. They weren't at any rate for her now. "Dear no. We go abroad for a few weeks somewhere of high air. That has been before us for many days; we've only been kept on by last necessities here. However, everything's done and the wind's in our sails."

"May you scud then happily before it! But when," he asked, "do you come back?"

She looked ever so vague; then as if to correct it: "Oh when the wind turns. And what do you do with your summer?"

"Ah I spend it in sordid toil. I drench it with mercenary ink. My work in your country counts for play as well. You see what's thought of the pleasure your country can give. My holiday's over."

"I'm sorry you had to take it," said Milly, "at such a different time from ours. If you could but have worked while we've been working—"

"I might be playing while you play? Oh the distinction isn't so great with me. There's a little of each for me, of work and of play, in either. But you and Mrs. Stringham, with Miss Croy and Mrs. Lowder—you all," he went on, "have been given up, like navvies or niggers, to real physical toil. Your rest is something you've earned and you need. My labour's comparatively light."

"Very true," she smiled; "but all the same I like mine."

"It doesn't leave you 'done'?"

"Not a bit. I don't get tired when I'm interested. Oh I could go far."

He bethought himself. "Then why don't you?—since you've got here, as I learn, the whole place in your pocket."

493

"Well, it's a kind of economy—I'm saving things up. I've enjoyed so what you speak of—though your account of it's fantastic—that I'm watching over its future, that I can't help being anxious and careful. I want—in the interest itself of what I've had and may still have—not to make stupid mistakes. The way not to make them is to get off again to a distance and see the situation from there. I shall keep it fresh," she wound up as if herself rather pleased with the ingenuity of her statement—"I shall keep it fresh, by that prudence, for my return."

"Ah then you *will* return? Can you promise one that?"

Her face fairly lighted at his asking for a promise; but she made as if bargaining a little. "Isn't London rather awful in winter?"

He had been going to ask her if she meant for the invalid; but he checked the infelicity of this and took the enquiry as referring to social life. "No—I like it, with one thing and another; it's less of a mob than later on; and it would have for *us* the merit—should you come here then—that we should probably see more of you. So do reappear for us—if it isn't a question of climate."

She looked at that a little graver. "If what isn't a question—?"

"Why the determination of your movements. You spoke just now of going somewhere for that."

"For better air?"—she remembered. "Oh yes, one certainly wants to get out of London in August."

"Rather, of course!"—he fully understood. "Though I'm glad you've hung on long enough for me to catch you. Try us at any rate," he continued, "once more."

"Whom do you mean by 'us'?" she presently asked.

It pulled him up an instant—representing, as he saw it might have seemed, an allusion to himself as conjoined with Kate, whom he was proposing not to mention any more than his hostess did. But the issue was easy. "I mean all of us together, every one you'll find ready to surround you with sympathy."

It made her, none the less, in her odd charming way, challenge him afresh. "Why do you say sympathy?"

"Well, it's doubtless a pale word. What we *shall* feel for you will be much nearer worship."

"As near then as you like!" With which at last Kate's name was sounded. "The people I'd most come back for are the people you know. I'd do it for Mrs. Lowder, who has been beautifully kind to me."

"So she has to *me*," said Densher. "I feel," he added as she at first answered nothing, "that, quite contrary to anything I originally expected, I've made a good friend of her."

"I didn't expect it either—its turning out as it has. But I did," said Milly, "with Kate. I shall come back for her too. I'd do anything"—she kept it up—"for Kate."

Looking at him as with conscious clearness while she spoke, she might for the moment have effectively laid a trap for whatever remains of the ideal straightness in him were still able to pull themselves together and operate. He was afterwards to say to himself that something had at that moment hung for him by a hair. "Oh I know what one would do for Kate!"—it had hung for him by a hair to break out with that, which he felt he had really been kept from by an element in his consciousness stronger still. The proof of the truth in question was precisely in his silence; resisting the impulse to break out was what he was doing for Kate. This at the time moreover came and went quickly enough; he was trying the next minute but to make Milly's allusion easy for herself. "Of course I know what friends you are—and of course I understand," he permitted himself to add, "any amount of devotion to a person so charming. That's the good turn then she'll do us all—I mean her working for your return."

"Oh you don't know," said Milly, "how much I'm really on her hands."

He could but accept the appearance of wondering how much he might show he knew. "Ah she's very masterful."

"She's great. Yet I don't say she bullies me."

"No—that's not the way. At any rate it isn't hers," he smiled. He remembered, however, then that an undue acquaintance with Kate's ways was just what he mustn't show; and he pursued the subject no further than to remark with a good intention that had the further merit of representing a truth: "I don't feel as if I knew her—really to call know."

"Well, if you come to that, I don't either!" she laughed. The words gave him, as soon as they were uttered, a sense of responsibility for his own; though during a silence that ensued for a minute he had time to recognise that his own contained after all no element of falsity. Strange enough therefore was it that he could go too far—if it *was* too far—without being false. His observation was one he would perfectly have made to Kate herself. And before he again spoke, and before Milly did, he took time for more still—for feeling how just here it was that he must break short off if his mind was really made up not to go further. It was as if he had been at a corner—and fairly put there by his last speech; so that it depended on him whether or no to turn it. The silence, if prolonged but an instant, might even have given him a sense of her waiting to see what he would do. It was filled for them the next thing by the sound, rather voluminous for the August afternoon, of the approach, in the street below them, of heavy carriage-wheels and of horses trained to "step." A rumble, a great shake, a considerable effective clatter, had been apparently succeeded by a pause at the door of the hotel, which was in turn accompanied by a due display of diminished prancing and stamping. "You've a visitor," Densher laughed, "and it must be at least an ambassador."

"It's only my own carriage; it does that—isn't it wonderful?—every day. But we find it, Mrs. Stringham and I, in the innocence of our hearts, very amusing." She had got up, as she spoke, to assure herself of what she said; and at the end of a few steps they were together on the balcony and looking down at her waiting chariot, which made indeed a brave show. "Is it very awful?"

It was to Densher's eyes—save for its absurd heaviness—only pleasantly pompous. "It seems to me delightfully rococo. But how do I know? You're mistress of these things, in contact with the highest wisdom. You occupy a position, moreover, thanks to which your carriage—well, by this time, in the eye of London, also occupies one." But she was going out, and he mustn't stand in her way. What had happened the next minute was first that she had denied she was going out, so that he might prolong his stay; and second that she had said she would go out with pleasure if he would like to drive—that in fact there were always things to do, that there had been a question for her to-day of several in particular, and that this in short was why the carriage had been ordered so early. They perceived, as she said these things, that an enquirer had presented himself, and, coming back, they found Milly's servant announcing the carriage and prepared to accompany her. This appeared to have for her the effect of settling the matter—on the basis, that is, of Densher's happy response. Densher's happy response, however, had as yet hung fire, the process we have described in him operating by this time with extreme intensity. The system of not pulling up, not breaking off, had already brought him headlong, he seemed to feel, to where they actually stood; and just now it was, with a vengeance, that he must do either one thing or the other. He had been waiting for some moments, which probably seemed to him longer than they were; this was because he was anxiously watching himself wait. He couldn't keep that up for ever; and since one thing or the other was what he must do, it was for the other that he presently became conscious of having decided. If he had been drifting it settled itself in the manner of a bump, of considerable violence, against a firm object in the stream. "Oh yes; I'll go with you with pleasure. It's a charming idea."

She gave no look to thank him—she rather looked away; she only said at once to her servant, "In ten minutes"; and then to her visitor, as the man went out, "We'll go somewhere—I shall like that. But I must ask of you time—as little as possible—to get ready." She looked over the room to provide for him, keep him there. "There are books and things—plenty; and I dress very quickly." He caught her eyes only as she went, on which he thought them pretty and touching.

Why especially touching at that instant he could certainly scarce have said; it was involved, it was lost in the sense of her wishing to oblige him. Clearly what had occurred was her having wished it so that she had made him simply wish, in civil acknowledgement, to oblige *her;* which he had now fully done by turning his corner. He was quite round it, his corner, by the time the door had closed upon her and he stood there alone. Alone he remained for three minutes more—remained with several very living little matters to think about. One of these was the phenomenon—typical, highly American, he would have said—of Milly's extreme spontaneity. It was perhaps rather as if he had sought refuge—refuge from another question—in the almost exclusive contemplation of this. Yet this, in its way, led him nowhere; not even to a sound generalisation about American girls. It was spontaneous for his young friend to have asked him to drive with her alone—since she hadn't mentioned her companion; but she struck him after all as no more advanced in doing it than Kate, for instance, who wasn't an American girl, might have struck him in not doing it. Besides, Kate *would* have done it, though Kate wasn't at all, in the same sense as Milly, spontaneous. And then in addition Kate *had* done it—or things very like it. Furthermore he was engaged to Kate—even if his ostensibly not being put her public freedom on other grounds. On all grounds, at any rate, the relation between Kate and freedom, between freedom and Kate, was a different one from any he could associate or cultivate, as to anything, with the girl who had just left him to prepare to give herself up to him. It had never struck him before, and he moved about the room while he thought of it, touching none of the books placed at his disposal. Milly was forward, as might be said, but not advanced; whereas Kate was backward—backward still, comparatively, as an English girl—and yet advanced in a high degree. However—though this didn't straighten it out—Kate was of course two or three years older; which at their time of life considerably counted.

Thus ingeniously discriminating, Densher continued slowly to wander; yet without keeping at bay for long the sense of having rounded his corner. He had so rounded it that he felt himself lose even the option of taking advantage of Milly's absence to retrace his steps. If he might have turned tail, vulgarly speaking, five minutes before, he couldn't turn tail now; he must simply wait there with his consciousness charged to the brim. Quickly enough moreover that issue was closed from without; in the course of three minutes more Miss Theale's servant had returned. He preceded a visitor whom he had met, obviously, at the foot of the stairs and whom, throwing open the door, he loudly announced as Miss Croy. Kate, on following him in, stopped short at sight of Densher—only, after an instant, as the young man saw with free amusement, not from surprise and still less from discomfiture. Densher immediately gave his explanation—Miss Theale had gone to prepare to drive—on receipt of which the servant effaced himself.

"And you're going with her?" Kate asked.

"Yes—with your approval; which I've taken, as you see, for granted."

"Oh," she laughed, "my approval's complete!" She was thoroughly consistent and handsome about it.

"What I mean is of course," he went on—for he was sensibly affected by her gaiety—"at your so lively instigation."

She had looked about the room—she might have been vaguely looking for signs of the duration, of the character of his visit, a momentary aid in taking a decision. "Well, instigation then, as much as you like." She treated it as pleasant, the success of her plea with him; she made a fresh joke of this direct impression of it. "So much so as that? Do you know I think I won't wait?"

"Not to see her—after coming?"

"Well, with you in the field—! I came for news of her, but she must be all right. If she *is*—"

But he took her straight up. "Ah how do I know?" He was moved to say more. "It's not I who am responsible for her, my dear. It seems to me it's you." She struck him as making light of a matter that had been costing him sundry qualms; so that they couldn't both be quite just. Either she was too easy or he had been too anxious. He didn't want at all events to feel a fool for that. "I'm doing nothing—and shall not, I assure you, do anything but what I'm told."

Their eyes met with some intensity over the emphasis he had given his words; and he had taken it from her the next moment that he really needn't get into a state. What in the world was the matter? She asked it, with interest, for all answer. "Isn't she better—if she's able to see you?"

"She assures me she's in perfect health."

Kate's interest grew. "I knew she would." On which she added: "It won't have been really for illness that she stayed away last night."

"For what then?"

"Well—for nervousness."

"Nervousness about what?"

"Oh you know!" She spoke with a hint of impatience, smiling however the next moment. "I've told you that."

He looked at her to recover in her face what she had told him; then it was as if what he saw there prompted him to say: "What have you told *her?*"

She gave him her controlled smile, and it was all as if they remembered where they were, liable to surprise, talking with softened voices, even stretching their opportunity, by such talk, beyond a quite right feeling. Milly's room would be close at hand, and yet they were saying things—! For a moment, none the less, they kept it up. "Ask *her*, if you like; you're free—she'll tell you. Act as you think best; don't trouble about what you think I may or mayn't have told. I'm all right with her," said Kate. "So there you are."

"If you mean *here* I am," he answered, "it's unmistakeable. If you also mean that her believing in you is all I have to do with you're so far right as that she certainly does believe in you."

"Well then take example by her."

"She's really doing it for you," Densher continued. "She's driving me out for you."

"In that case," said Kate with her soft tranquillity, "you can do it a little for *her*. I'm not afraid," she smiled.

He stood before her a moment, taking in again the face she put on it and affected again, as he had already so often been, by more things in this face and in her whole person and presence than he was, to his relief, obliged to find words for. It wasn't, under such impressions, a question of words. "I do nothing for any one in the world but you. But for you I'll do anything."

"Good, good," said Kate. "That's how I like you."

He waited again an instant. "Then you swear to it?"

"To 'it'? To what?"

"Why that you do 'like' me. Since it's all for that, you know, that I'm letting you do—well, God knows what with me."

She gave at this, with a stare, a disheartened gesture—the sense of which she immediately further expressed. "If you don't believe in me then, after all, hadn't you better break off before you've gone further?"

"Break off with you?"

"Break off with Milly. You might go now," she said, "and I'll stay and explain to her why it is."

He wondered—as if it struck him. "What would you say?"

"Why that you find you can't stand her, and that there's nothing for me but to bear with you as I best may."

He considered of this. "How much do you abuse me to her?"

"Exactly enough. As much as you see by her attitude."

Again he thought. "It doesn't seem to me I ought to mind her attitude."

"Well then, just as you like. I'll stay and do my best for you."

He saw she was sincere, was really giving him a chance; and that of itself made things clearer. The feeling of how far he had gone came back to him not in repentance, but in this very vision of an escape; and it Was not of what he had done, but of what Kate offered, that he now weighed the consequence. "Won't it make her—her not finding me here—be rather more sure there's something between us?"

Kate thought. "Oh I don't know. It will of course greatly upset her. But you needn't trouble about that. She won't die of it."

"Do you mean she *will?*" Densher presently asked.

"Don't put me questions when you don't believe what I say. You make too many conditions."

She spoke now with a shade of rational weariness that made the want of pliancy, the failure to oblige her, look poor and ugly; so that what it suddenly came back to for him was his deficiency in the things a man of any taste, so engaged, so enlisted, would have liked to make sure of being able to show— imagination, tact, positively even humour. The circumstance is doubtless odd, but the truth is none the less that the speculation uppermost with him at this juncture was: "What if I should begin to bore this creature?" And that, within a few seconds, had translated itself. "If you'll swear again you love me—!"

She looked about, at door and window, as if he were asking for more than he said. "Here? There's nothing between us here," Kate smiled.

"Oh *isn't* there?" Her smile itself, with this, had so settled something for him that he had come to her pleadingly and holding out his hands, which she immediately seized with her own as if both to check him and to keep him. It was by keeping him thus for a minute that she did check him; she held him long enough, while, with their eyes deeply meeting, they waited in silence for him to recover himself and renew his discretion. He coloured as with a return of the sense of where they were, and that gave her precisely one of her usual victories, which immediately took further form. By the time he had dropped her hands he had again taken hold, as it were, of Milly's. It was not at any rate with Milly he had broken. "I'll do all you wish," he declared as if to acknowledge the acceptance of his condition that he had practically, after all, drawn from her—a declaration on which she then, recurring to her first idea, promptly acted.

"If you *are* as good as that I go. You'll tell her that, finding you with her, I wouldn't wait. Say that, you know, from yourself. She'll understand."

She had reached the door with it—she was full of decision; but he had before she left him one more doubt. "I don't see how she can understand enough, you know, without understanding too much."

"You don't need to see."

He required then a last injunction. "I must simply go it blind?"

"You must simply be kind to her."

"And leave the rest to you?"

"Leave the rest to *her*," said Kate disappearing.

It came back then afresh to that, as it had come before. Milly, three minutes after Kate had gone, returned in her array—her big black hat, so little superstitiously in the fashion, her fine black garments throughout, the swathing of her throat, which Densher vaguely took for an infinite number of yards of priceless lace, and which, its folded fabric kept in place by heavy rows of pearls, hung down to her feet like the stole of a priestess. He spoke to her at once of their friend's visit and flight. "She hadn't known she'd find me," he said—and said at present without difficulty. He had so rounded his corner that it wasn't a question of a word more or less.

She took this account of the matter as quite sufficient; she glossed over whatever might be awkward. "I'm sorry—but I of course often see *her*." He felt the discrimination in his favour and how it justified Kate. This was Milly's tone when the matter was left to her. Well, it should now be wholly left.

BOOK SEVENTH

I

When Kate and Densher abandoned her to Mrs. Stringham on the day of her meeting them together and bringing them to luncheon, Milly, face to face with that companion, had had one of those moments in which the warned, the anxious fighter of the battle of life, as if once again feeling for the sword at his side, carries his hand straight to the quarter of his courage. She laid hers firmly on her heart, and the two women stood there showing each other a strange front. Susan Shepherd had received their great doctor's visit, which had been clearly no small affair for her; but Milly had since then, with insistence, kept in place, against communication and betrayal, as she now practically confessed, the barrier of their invited guests. "You've been too dear. With what I see you're full of you treated them beautifully. *Isn't* Kate charming when she wants to be?"

Poor Susie's expression, contending at first, as in a high fine spasm, with different dangers, had now quite let itself go. She had to make an effort to reach a point in space already so remote. "Miss Croy? Oh she was pleasant and clever. She knew," Mrs. Stringham added. "She knew."

Milly braced herself—but conscious above all, at the moment, of a high compassion for her mate. She made her out as struggling—struggling in all her nature against the betrayal of pity, which in itself, given her nature, could only be a torment. Milly gathered from the struggle how much there was of the pity, and how therefore it was both in her tenderness and in her conscience that Mrs. Stringham suffered. Wonderful and beautiful it was that this impression instantly steadied the girl. Ruefully asking herself on what basis of ease, with the drop of their barrier, they were to find themselves together, she felt the question met with a relief that was almost joy. The basis, the inevitable basis, was that she was going to be sorry for Susie, who, to all appearance, had been condemned in so much more uncomfortable a manner to be sorry for *her*. Mrs. Stringham's sorrow would hurt Mrs. Stringham, but how could her own ever hurt? She had, the poor girl, at all events, on the spot, five minutes of exaltation in which she turned the tables on her friend with a pass of the hand, a gesture of an energy that made a wind in the air. "Kate knew," she asked, "that you were full of Sir Luke Strett?"

"She spoke of nothing, but she was gentle and nice; she seemed to want to help me through." Which the good lady had no sooner said, however, than she almost tragically gasped at herself. She glared at Milly with a pretended pluck. "What I mean is that she saw one had been taken up with something. When I say she knows I should say she's a person who guesses." And her grimace was also, on its side, heroic. "But *she* doesn't matter, Milly."

The girl felt she by this time could face anything. "Nobody matters, Susie. Nobody." Which her next words, however, rather contradicted. "Did he take it ill that I wasn't here to see him? Wasn't it really just what he wanted—to have it out, so much more simply, with *you*?"

"We didn't have anything 'out,' Milly," Mrs. Stringham delicately quavered.

"Didn't he awfully like you," Milly went on, "and didn't he think you the most charming person I could possibly have referred him to for an account of me? Didn't you hit it off tremendously together and in fact fall quite in love, so that it will really be a great advantage for you to have me as a common ground? You're going to make, I can see, no end of a good thing of me."

"My own child, my own child!" Mrs. Stringham pleadingly murmured; yet showing as she did so that she feared the effect even of deprecation.

"Isn't he beautiful and good too himself?—altogether, whatever he may say, a lovely acquaintance to have made? You're just the right people for me—I see it now; and do you know what, between you, you must do?" Then as Susie still but stared, wonderstruck and holding herself: "You must simply see me through. Any way you choose. Make it out together. I, on my side, will be beautiful too, and we'll be—the three of us, with whatever others, oh as many as the case requires, any one you like!—a sight for the gods. I'll be as easy for you as carrying a feather." Susie took it for a moment in such silence that her young friend almost saw her—and scarcely withheld the observation—as taking it for "a part of the disease." This accordingly helped Milly to be, as she judged, definite and wise. "He's at any rate awfully interesting, isn't he?—which is so much to the good. We haven't at least—as we might have, with the way we tumbled into it—got hold of one of the dreary."

"Interesting, dearest?"—Mrs. Stringham felt her feet firmer. "I don't know if he's interesting or not; but I do know, my own," she continued to quaver, "that he's just as much interested as you could possibly desire."

"Certainly—that's it. Like all the world."

"No, my precious, not like all the world. Very much more deeply and intelligently."

"Ah there you are!" Milly laughed. "That's the way, Susie, I want you. So 'buck' up, my dear. We'll have beautiful times with him. Don't worry."

"I'm not worrying, Milly." And poor Susie's face registered the sublimity of her lie.

It was at this that, too sharply penetrated, her companion went to her, met by her with an embrace in which things were said that exceeded speech. Each held and clasped the other as if to console her for this unnamed woe, the woe for Mrs. Stringham of learning the torment of helplessness, the woe for Milly of having *her*, at such a time, to think of. Milly's assumption was immense, and the difficulty for her friend was that of not being able to gainsay it without bringing it more to the proof than tenderness and vagueness could permit. Nothing in fact came to the proof between them but that they could thus cling together—except indeed that, as we have indicated, the pledge of protection and support was all the younger woman's own. "I don't ask you," she presently said, "what he told you for yourself, nor what he told you to tell me, nor how he took it, really, that I had left him to you, nor what passed between you about me in any way. It wasn't to get that out of you that I took my means to make sure of your meeting freely—for there are things I don't want to know. I shall see him again and again and shall know more than enough. All I do want is that you shall see me through on *his* basis, whatever it is; which it's enough—for the purpose—that you yourself should know: that is with him to show you how. I'll make it charming for you—that's what I mean; I'll keep you up to it in such a way that half the time you won't know you're doing it. And for that you're to rest upon me. There. It's understood. We keep each other going, and you may absolutely feel of me that I shan't break down. So, with the way you haven't so much as a dig of the elbow to fear, how could you be safer?"

"He told me I *can* help you—of course he told me that," Susie, on her side, eagerly contended. "Why shouldn't he, and for what else have I come out with you? But he told me nothing dreadful—nothing, nothing, nothing," the poor lady passionately protested. "Only that you must do as you like and as he tells you—which *is* just simply to do as you like."

"I must keep in sight of him. I must from time to time go to him. But that's of course doing as I like. It's lucky," Milly smiled, "that I like going to him."

Mrs. Stringham was here in agreement; she gave a clutch at the account of their situation that most showed it as workable. "That's what *will* be charming for me, and what I'm sure he really wants of me—to help you to do as you like."

"And also a little, won't it be," Milly laughed, "to save me from the consequences? Of course," she added, "there must first *be* things I like."

"Oh I think you'll find some," Mrs. Stringham more bravely said. "I think there *are* some—as for instance just this one. I mean," she explained, "really having us so."

Milly thought. "Just as if I wanted you comfortable about *him*, and him the same about you? Yes—I shall get the good of it."

Susan Shepherd appeared to wander from this into a slight confusion. "Which of them are you talking of?"

Milly wondered an instant—then had a light. "I'm not talking of Mr. Densher." With which moreover she showed amusement. "Though if you can be comfortable about Mr. Densher too so much the better."

"Oh you meant Sir Luke Strett? Certainly he's a fine type. Do you know," Susie continued, "whom he reminds me of? Of *our* great man—Dr. Buttrick of Boston."

Milly recognised Dr. Buttrick of Boston, but she dropped him after a tributary pause. "What do you think, now that you've seen him, of Mr. Densher?"

It was not till after consideration, with her eyes fixed on her friend's, that Susie produced her answer. "I think he's very handsome."

Milly remained smiling at her, though putting on a little the manner of a teacher with a pupil. "Well, that will do for the first time. I *have* done," she went on, "what I wanted."

"Then that's all *we* want. You see there are plenty of things."

Milly shook her head for the "plenty." "The best is not to know—that includes them all. I don't—I don't know. Nothing about anything—except that you're *with* me. Remember that, please. There won't be anything that, on my side, for you, I shall forget. So it's all right."

The effect of it by this time was fairly, as intended, to sustain Susie, who dropped in spite of herself into the reassuring. "Most certainly it's all right. I think you ought to understand that he sees no reason—"

"Why I shouldn't have a grand long life?" Milly had taken it straight up, as to understand it and for a moment consider it. But she disposed of it otherwise. "Oh of course I know *that*." She spoke as if her friend's point were small.

Mrs. Stringham tried to enlarge it. "Well, what I mean is that he didn't say to me anything that he hasn't said to yourself."

"Really?—I would in his place!" She might have been disappointed, but she had her good humour. "He tells me to *live*"—and she oddly limited the word.

It left Susie a little at sea. "Then what do you want more?"

"My dear," the girl presently said, "I don't 'want,' as I assure you, anything. Still," she added, "I *am* living. Oh yes, I'm living."

It put them again face to face, but it had wound Mrs. Stringham up. "So am I then, you'll see!"—she spoke with the note of her recovery. Yet it was her wisdom now—meaning by it as much as she did—not to say more than that. She had risen by Milly's aid to a certain command of what was before them; the ten minutes of their talk had in fact made her more distinctly aware of the presence in her mind of a new idea. It was really perhaps an old idea with a new value; it had at all events begun during the last hour, though at first but feebly, to shine with a special light. That was because in the morning darkness had so suddenly descended—a sufficient shade of night to bring out the power of a star. The dusk might be thick yet, but the sky had comparatively cleared; and Susan Shepherd's star from this time on continued to twinkle for her. It was for the moment, after her passage with Milly, the one spark left in the heavens. She recognised, as she continued to watch it, that it had really been set there by Sir Luke Strett's visit and that the impressions immediately following had done no more than fix it. Milly's reappearance with Mr. Densher at her heels—or, so oddly perhaps, at Miss Croy's heels, Miss Croy being at Milly's—had contributed to this effect, though it was only with the lapse of the greater obscurity that Susie made that out. The obscurity had reigned during the hour of their friends' visit, faintly clearing indeed while, in one of the rooms, Kate Croy's remarkable advance to her intensified the fact that Milly and the young man were conjoined in the other. If it hadn't acquired on the spot all the intensity of which it was capable, this was because the poor lady still sat in her primary gloom, the gloom the great benignant doctor had practically left behind him.

The intensity the circumstance in question *might* wear to the informed imagination would have been sufficiently revealed for us, no doubt—and with other things to our purpose—in two or three of those confidential passages with Mrs. Lowder that she now permitted herself. She hadn't yet been so glad that she believed in her old friend; for if she hadn't had, at such a pass, somebody or other to believe in she should certainly have stumbled by the way. Discretion had ceased to consist of silence; silence was gross and thick, whereas wisdom should taper, however tremulously, to a point. She betook herself to Lancaster Gate the morning after the colloquy just noted; and there, in Maud Manningham's own sanctum, she gradually found relief in giving an account of herself. An account of herself was one of the things that she had long been in the habit of expecting herself regularly to give—the regularity depending of course much on such tests of merit as might, by laws beyond her control, rise in her path. She never spared herself in short a proper sharpness of conception of how she had behaved, and it was a statement that she for the most part found herself able to make. What had happened at present was that nothing, as she felt, was left of her to report to; she was all too sunk in the inevitable and the abysmal. To give an account of herself she must give it to somebody else, and her first instalment of it to her hostess was that she must please let her cry. She couldn't cry, with Milly in observation, at the hotel, which she had accordingly left for that purpose; and the power happily came to her with the good opportunity. She cried and cried at first—she confined herself to that; it was for the time the best statement of her business. Mrs. Lowder moreover intelligently took it as such, though knocking off a note or two more, as she said, while Susie sat near her table. She could resist the contagion of tears, but her patience did justice to her visitor's most vivid plea for it. "I shall never be able, you know, to cry again—at least not ever with *her;* so I must take it out when I can. Even if she does herself it won't be for me to give away; for what would that be but a confession of despair? I'm not with her for that—I'm with her to be regularly sublime. Besides, Milly won't cry herself."

"I'm sure I hope," said Mrs. Lowder, "that she won't have occasion to."

"She won't even if she does have occasion. She won't shed a tear. There's something that will prevent her."

"Oh!" said Mrs. Lowder.

"Yes, her pride," Mrs. Stringham explained in spite of her friend's doubt, and it was with this that her communication took consistent form. It had never been pride, Maud Manningham had hinted, that kept *her* from crying when other things made for it; it had only been that these same things, at such times, made still more for business, arrangements, correspondence, the ringing of bells, the marshalling of servants, the taking of decisions. "I might be crying now," she said, "if I weren't writing letters"—and this quite without harshness for her anxious companion, to whom she allowed just the administrative margin for difference. She had interrupted her no more than she would have interrupted the piano-tuner. It gave poor Susie time; and when Mrs. Lowder, to save appearances and catch the post, had, with her addressed and stamped notes, met at the door of the room the footman summoned by the pressure of a knob, the facts of the case were sufficiently ready for her. It took but two or three, however, given their importance, to lay the ground for the great one—Mrs. Stringham's interview of the day before with Sir Luke, who had wished to see her about Milly.

"He had wished it himself?"

"I think he was glad of it. Clearly indeed he was. He stayed a quarter of an hour. I could see that for *him* it was long. He's interested," said Mrs. Stringham.

"Do you mean in her case?"

"He says it *isn't* a case."

"What then is it?"

"It isn't, at least," Mrs. Stringham explained, "the case she believed it to be—thought it at any rate *might* be—when, without my knowledge, she went to see him. She went because there was something she was afraid of, and he examined her thoroughly—he has made sure. She's wrong—she hasn't what she thought."

"And what did she think?" Mrs. Lowder demanded.

"He didn't tell me."

"And you didn't ask?"

"I asked nothing," said poor Susie—"I only took what he gave me. He gave me no more than he had to—he was beautiful," she went on. "He *is*, thank God, interested."

"He must have been interested in *you*, dear," Maud Manningham observed with kindness.

Her visitor met it with candour. "Yes, love, I think he *is*. I mean that he sees what he can do with me."

Mrs. Lowder took it rightly. "For *her*."

"For her. Anything in the world he will or he must. He can use me to the last bone, and he likes at least that. He says the great thing for her is to be happy."

"It's surely the great thing for every one. Why, therefore," Mrs. Lowder handsomely asked, "should we cry so hard about it?"

"Only," poor Susie wailed, "that it's so strange, so beyond us. I mean if she can't be."

"She must be." Mrs. Lowder knew no impossibles. "She *shall* be."

"Well—if you'll help. He thinks, you know, we *can* help."

Mrs. Lowder faced a moment, in her massive way, what Sir Luke Strett thought. She sat back there, her knees apart, not unlike a picturesque ear-ringed matron at a market-stall; while her friend, before her, dropped their items, tossed the separate truths of the matter one by one, into her capacious apron. "But is that all he came to you for—to tell you she must be happy?"

"That she must be *made* so—that's the point. It seemed enough, as he told me," Mrs. Stringham went on; "he makes it somehow such a grand possible affair."

"Ah well, if he makes it possible!"

"I mean especially he makes it grand. He gave it to me, that is, as *my* part. The rest's his own."

"And what's the rest?" Mrs. Lowder asked.

"I don't know. *His* business. He means to keep hold of her."

"Then why do you say it isn't a 'case'? It must be very much of one."

Everything in Mrs. Stringham confessed to the extent of it. "It's only that it isn't *the* case she herself supposed."

"It's another?"

"It's another."

"Examining her for what she supposed he finds something else?"

"Something else."

"And what does he find?"

"Ah," Mrs. Stringham cried, "God keep me from knowing!"

"He didn't tell you that?"

But poor Susie had recovered herself. "What I mean is that if it's there I shall know in time. He's considering, but I can trust him for it—because he does, I feel, trust me. He's considering," she repeated.

"He's in other words not sure?"

"Well, he's watching. I think that's what he means. She's to get away now, but to come back to him in three months."

"Then I think," said Maud Lowder, "that he oughtn't meanwhile to scare us."

It roused Susie a little, Susie being already enrolled in the great doctor's cause. This came out at least in her glimmer of reproach. "Does it scare us to enlist us for her happiness?"

513

Mrs. Lowder was rather stiff for it. "Yes; it scares *me*. I'm always scared—I may call it so—till I understand. What happiness is he talking about?"

Mrs. Stringham at this came straight. "Oh you know!"

She had really said it so that her friend had to take it; which the latter in fact after a moment showed herself as having done. A strange light humour in the matter even perhaps suddenly aiding, she met it with a certain accommodation. "Well, say one seems to see. The point is—!" But, fairly too full now of her question, she dropped.

"The point is will it *cure?*"

"Precisely. Is it absolutely a remedy—the specific?"

"Well, I should think we might know!" Mrs. Stringham delicately declared.

"Ah but we haven't the complaint."

"Have you never, dearest, been in love?" Susan Shepherd enquired.

"Yes, my child; but not by the doctor's direction."

Maud Manningham had spoken perforce with a break into momentary mirth, which operated—and happily too—as a challenge to her visitor's spirit. "Oh of course we don't ask his leave to fall. But it's something to know he thinks it good for us."

"My dear woman," Mrs. Lowder cried, "it strikes me we know it without him. So that when *that's* all he has to tell us—!"

"Ah," Mrs. Stringham interposed, "it isn't 'all.' I feel Sir Luke will have more; he won't have put me off with anything inadequate. I'm to see him again; he as good as told me that he'll wish it. So it won't be for nothing."

"Then what will it be for? Do you mean he has somebody of his own to propose? Do you mean you told him nothing?"

Mrs. Stringham dealt with these questions. "I showed him I understood him. That was all I could do. I didn't feel at liberty to be explicit; but I felt, even though his visit so upset me, the comfort of what I had from you night before last."

"What I spoke to you of in the carriage when we had left her with Kate?"

"You had *seen*, apparently, in three minutes. And now that he's here, now that I've met him and had my impression of him, I feel," said Mrs. Stringham, "that you've been magnificent."

"Of course I've been magnificent. When," asked Maud Manningham, "was I anything else? But Milly won't be, you know, if she marries Merton Densher."

"Oh it's always magnificent to marry the man one loves. But we're going fast!" Mrs. Stringham woefully smiled.

"The thing *is* to go fast if I see the case right. What had I after all but my instinct of that on coming back with you, night before last, to pick up Kate? I felt what I felt—I knew in my bones the man had returned."

"That's just where, as I say, you're magnificent. But wait," said Mrs. Stringham, "till you've seen him."

"I shall see him immediately"—Mrs. Lowder took it up with decision. "What is then," she asked, "your impression?"

Mrs. Stringham's impression seemed lost in her doubts. "How can he ever care for her?"

Her companion, in her companion's heavy manner, sat on it. "By being put in the way of it."

"For God's sake then," Mrs. Stringham wailed, "*put* him in the way! You have him, one feels, in your hand."

Maud Lowder's eyes at this rested on her friend's. "Is that your impression of him?"

"It's my impression, dearest, of you. You handle every one."

Mrs. Lowder's eyes still rested, and Susan Shepherd now felt, for a wonder, not less sincere by seeing that she pleased her. But there was a great limitation. "I don't handle Kate."

It suggested something that her visitor hadn't yet had from her—something the sense of which made Mrs. Stringham gasp. "Do you mean Kate cares for *him*?"

That fact the lady of Lancaster Gate had up to this moment, as we know, enshrouded, and her friend's quick question had produced a change in her face. She blinked—then looked at the question hard; after which, whether she had inadvertently betrayed herself or had only reached a decision and then been affected by the quality of Mrs. Stringham's surprise, she accepted all results. What took place in her for Susan Shepherd was not simply that she made the best of them, but that she suddenly saw more in them to her purpose than she could have imagined. A certain impatience in fact marked in her this transition: she had been keeping back, very hard, an important truth, and wouldn't have liked to hear that she hadn't concealed it cleverly. Susie nevertheless felt herself pass as not a little of a fool with her for not having thought of it. What Susie indeed, however, most thought of at present, in the quick, new light of it, was the wonder of Kate's dissimulation. She had time for that view while she waited for an answer to her cry. "Kate thinks she cares. But she's mistaken. And no one knows it." These things, distinct and responsible, were Mrs. Lowder's retort. Yet they weren't all of it. "*You* don't know it—that must be your line. Or rather your line must be that you deny it utterly."

"Deny that she cares for him?"

"Deny that she so much as thinks that she does. Positively and absolutely. Deny that you've so much as heard of it."

Susie faced this new duty. "To Milly, you mean—if she asks?"

"To Milly, naturally. No one else *will* ask."

"Well," said Mrs. Stringham after a moment, "Milly won't."

Mrs. Lowder wondered. "Are you sure?"

"Yes, the more I think of it. And luckily for *me*. I lie badly."

"*I* lie well, thank God," Mrs. Lowder almost snorted, "when, as sometimes will happen, there's nothing else so good. One must always do the best. But without lies then," she went on, "perhaps we can work it out." Her interest had risen; her friend saw her, as within some minutes, more enrolled and inflamed—presently felt in her what had made the difference. Mrs. Stringham, it was true, descried this at the time but dimly; she only made out at first that Maud had found a reason for helping her. The reason was that, strangely, she might help Maud too, for which she now desired to profess herself ready even to lying. What really perhaps most came out for her was that her hostess was a little disappointed at her doubt of the social solidity of this appliance; and that in turn was to become a steadier light. The truth about Kate's delusion, as her aunt presented it, the delusion about the state of her affections, which might be removed—this was apparently the ground on which they now might more intimately meet. Mrs. Stringham saw herself recruited for the removal of Kate's delusion—by arts, however, in truth, that she as yet quite failed to compass. Or was it perhaps to be only for the removal of Mr. Densher's?—success in which indeed might entail other successes. Before that job, unfortunately, her heart had already failed. She felt that she believed in her bones what Milly believed, and what would now make working for Milly such a dreadful upward tug. All this within her was confusedly present—a cloud of questions out of which Maud Manningham's large seated self loomed, however, as a mass more and more definite, taking in fact for the consultative relation something of the form of an oracle. From the oracle the sound did come—or at any rate the sense did, a sense all accordant with the insufflation she had just seen working. "Yes," the sense was, "I'll help you for Milly, because if that comes off I shall be helped, by its doing so, for Kate"—a view into which Mrs. Stringham could now sufficiently enter. She found herself of a sudden, strange to say, quite willing to operate to Kate's harm, or at least to Kate's good as Mrs. Lowder with a noble anxiety measured it. She found herself in short not caring what became of Kate—only convinced at bottom of the predominance of Kate's star. Kate wasn't in danger, Kate wasn't pathetic; Kate Croy, whatever happened, would take care of Kate Croy. She saw moreover by this time that her friend was travelling even beyond her own speed. Mrs. Lowder had already, in mind, drafted a rough plan of action, a plan vividly enough thrown off as she said: "You must stay on a few days, and you must immediately, both of you, meet him at dinner." In addition to which Maud claimed the merit of having by an instinct of pity, of prescient wisdom, done much, two nights before, to prepare that ground. "The poor child, when I was with her there while you were getting your shawl, quite gave herself away to me."

"Oh I remember how you afterwards put it to me. Though it was nothing more," Susie did herself the justice to observe, "than what I too had quite felt."

But Mrs. Lowder fronted her so on this that she wondered what she had said. "I suppose I ought to be edified at what you can so beautifully give up."

"Give up?" Mrs. Stringham echoed. "Why, I give up nothing—I cling."

Her hostess showed impatience, turning again with some stiffness to her great brass-bound cylinder-desk and giving a push to an object or two disposed there. "I give up then. You know how little such a person as Mr. Densher was to be my idea for her. You know what I've been thinking perfectly possible."

"Oh you've been great"—Susie was perfectly fair. "A duke, a duchess, a princess, a palace: you've made me believe in them too. But where we break down is that *she* doesn't believe in them. Luckily for her—as it seems to be turning out—she doesn't want them. So what's one to do? I assure you I've had many dreams. But I've only one dream now."

Mrs. Stringham's tone in these last words gave so fully her meaning that Mrs. Lowder could but show herself as taking it in. They sat a moment longer confronted on it. "Her having what she does want?"

"If it *will* do anything for her."

Mrs. Lowder seemed to think what it might do; but she spoke for the instant of something else. "It does provoke me a bit, you know—for of course I'm a brute. And I had thought of all sorts of things. Yet it doesn't prevent the fact that we must be decent."

"We must take her"—Mrs. Stringham carried that out—"as she is."

"And we must take Mr. Densher as *he* is." With which Mrs. Lowder gave a sombre laugh. "It's a pity he isn't better!"

"Well, if he were better," her friend rejoined, "you'd have liked him for your niece; and in that case Milly would interfere. I mean," Susie added, "interfere with *you*."

"She interferes with me as it is—not that it matters now. But I saw Kate and her—really as soon as you came to me—set up side by side. I saw your girl—I don't mind telling—you helping my girl; and when I say that," Mrs. Lowder continued, "you'll probably put in for yourself that it was part of the reason of my welcome to you. So you see what I give up. I do give it up. But when I take that line," she further set forth, "I take it handsomely. So good-bye to it all. Good-day to Mrs. Densher! Heavens!" she growled.

Susie held herself a minute. "Even as Mrs. Densher my girl will be somebody."

"Yes, she won't be nobody. Besides," said Mrs. Lowder, "we're talking in the air."

Her companion sadly assented. "We're leaving everything out."

"It's nevertheless interesting." And Mrs. Lowder had another thought. "*He's* not quite nobody either." It brought her back to the question she had already put and which her friend hadn't at the time dealt with. "What in fact do you make of him?"

Susan Shepherd, at this, for reasons not clear even to herself, was moved a little to caution. So she remained general. "He's charming."

She had met Mrs. Lowder's eyes with that extreme pointedness in her own to which people resort when they are not quite candid—a circumstance that had its effect. "Yes; he's charming."

The effect of the words, however, was equally marked; they almost determined in Mrs. Stringham a return of amusement. "I thought you didn't like him!"

"I don't like him for Kate."

"But you don't like him for Milly either."

Mrs. Stringham rose as she spoke, and her friend also got up. "I like him, my dear, for myself."

"Then that's the best way of all."

"Well, it's one way. He's not good enough for my niece, and he's not good enough for you. One's an aunt, one's a wretch and one's a fool."

"Oh *I'm* not—not either," Susie declared.

But her companion kept on. "One lives for others. *You* do that. If I were living for myself I shouldn't at all mind him."

But Mrs. Stringham was sturdier. "Ah if I find him charming it's however I'm living."

Well, it broke Mrs. Lowder down. She hung fire but an instant, giving herself away with a laugh. "Of course he's all right in himself."

"That's all I contend," Susie said with more reserve; and the note in question—what Merton Densher was "in himself"—closed practically, with some inconsequence, this first of their councils.

II

It had at least made the difference for them, they could feel, of an informed state in respect to the great doctor, whom they were now to take as watching, waiting, studying, or at any rate as proposing to himself some such process before he should make up his mind. Mrs. Stringham understood him as considering the matter meanwhile in a spirit that, on this same occasion, at Lancaster Gate, she had come back to a rough notation of before retiring. She followed the course of his reckoning. If what they had talked of *could* happen—if Milly, that is, could have her thoughts taken off herself—it wouldn't do any harm and might conceivably do much good. If it couldn't happen—if, anxiously, though tactfully working, they themselves, conjoined, could do nothing to contribute to it—they would be in no worse a box than before. Only in this latter case the girl would have had her free range for the summer, for the autumn; she would have done her best in the sense enjoined on her, and, coming back at the end to her eminent man, would—besides having more to show him—find him more ready to go on with her. It was visible further to Susan Shepherd—as well as being ground for a second report to her old friend—that Milly did her part for a working view of the general case, inasmuch as she mentioned frankly and promptly that she meant to go and say good-bye to Sir Luke Strett and thank him. She even specified what she was to thank him for, his having been so easy about her behaviour.

"You see I didn't know that—for the liberty I took—I shouldn't afterwards get a stiff note from him."

So much Milly had said to her, and it had made her a trifle rash. "Oh you'll never get a stiff note from him in your life."

She felt her rashness, the next moment, at her young friend's question. "Why not, as well as any one else who has played him a trick?"

"Well, because he doesn't regard it as a trick. He could understand your action. It's all right, you see."

"Yes—I do see. It *is* all right. He's easier with me than with any one else, because that's the way to let me down. He's only making believe, and I'm not worth hauling up."

Rueful at having provoked again this ominous flare, poor Susie grasped at her only advantage. "Do you really accuse a man like Sir Luke Strett of trifling with you?"

She couldn't blind herself to the look her companion gave her—a strange half-amused perception of what she made of it. "Well, so far as it's trifling with me to pity me so much."

"He doesn't pity you," Susie earnestly reasoned. "He just—the same as any one else—likes you."

"He has no business then to like me. He's not the same as any one else."

"Why not, if he wants to work for you?"

Milly gave her another look, but this time a wonderful smile. "Ah there you are!" Mrs. Stringham coloured, for there indeed she was again. But Milly let her off. "Work for me, all the same—work for me! It's of course what I want." Then as usual she embraced her friend. "I'm not going to be as nasty as this to *him*."

"I'm sure I hope not!"—and Mrs. Stringham laughed for the kiss. "I've no doubt, however, he'd take it from you! It's *you*, my dear, who are not the same as any one else."

Milly's assent to which, after an instant, gave her the last word. "No, so that people can take anything from me." And what Mrs. Stringham did indeed resignedly take after this was the absence on her part of any account of the visit then paid. It was the beginning in fact between them of an odd independence—an independence positively of action and custom—on the subject of Milly's future. They went their separate ways with the girl's intense assent; this being really nothing but what she had so wonderfully put in her plea for after Mrs. Stringham's first encounter with Sir Luke. She fairly favoured the idea that Susie had or was to have other encounters—private pointed personal; she favoured every idea, but most of all the idea that she herself was to go on as if nothing were the matter. Since she was to be worked for that would be her way; and though her companions learned from herself nothing of it this was in the event her way with her medical adviser. She put her visit to him on the simplest ground; she had come just to tell him how touched she had been by his good nature. That required little explaining, for, as Mrs. Stringham had said, he quite understood he could but reply that it was all right.

"I had a charming quarter of an hour with that clever lady. You've got good friends."

"So each one of them thinks of all the others. But so I also think," Milly went on, "of all of them together. You're excellent for each other. And it's in that way, I dare say, that you're best for me."

There came to her on this occasion one of the strangest of her impressions, which was at the same time one of the finest of her alarms—the glimmer of a vision that if she should go, as it were, too far, she might perhaps deprive their relation of facility if not of value. Going too far was failing to try at least to remain simple. He would be quite ready to hate her if she did, by heading him off at every point, embarrass his exercise of a kindness that, no doubt, rather constituted for him a high method. Susie wouldn't hate her, since Susie positively wanted to suffer for her; Susie had a noble idea that she might somehow so do her good. Such, however, was not the way in which the greatest of London doctors was to be expected to wish to do it. He wouldn't have time even should he wish; whereby, in a word, Milly felt herself intimately warned. Face to face there with her smooth strong director, she enjoyed at a given moment quite such another lift of feeling as she had known in her crucial talk with Susie. It came round to the same thing; him too she would help to help her if that could possibly be; but if it couldn't possibly be she would assist also to make this right.

It wouldn't have taken many minutes more, on the basis in question, almost to reverse for her their characters of patient and physician. What *was* he in fact but patient, what was she but physician, from the moment she embraced once for all the necessity, adopted once for all the policy, of saving him alarms about her subtlety? She would leave the subtlety to him: he would enjoy his use of it, and she herself, no doubt, would in time enjoy his enjoyment. She went so far as to imagine that the inward success of these reflexions flushed her for the minute, to his eyes, with a certain bloom, a comparative appearance of health; and what verily next occurred was that he gave colour to the presumption. "Every little helps, no doubt!"—he noticed good-humouredly her harmless sally. "But, help or no help, you're looking, you know, remarkably well."

"Oh I thought I was," she answered; and it was as if already she saw his line. Only she wondered what he would have guessed. If he had guessed anything at all it would be rather remarkable of him. As for what there *was* to guess, he couldn't—if this was present to him—have arrived at it save by his own acuteness. That acuteness was therefore immense; and if it supplied the subtlety she thought of leaving him to, his portion would be none so bad. Neither, for that matter, would hers be—which she was even actually enjoying. She wondered if really then there mightn't be something for her. She hadn't been sure in coming to him that she was "better," and he hadn't used, he would be awfully careful not to use, that compromising term about her; in spite of all of which she would have been ready to say, for the amiable sympathy of it, "Yes, I *must* be," for he had this unaided sense of something that had happened to her. It was a sense unaided, because who could have told him of anything? Susie, she was certain, hadn't yet seen him again, and there were things it was impossible she could have told him the first time. Since such was his penetration, therefore, why shouldn't she gracefully, in recognition of it, accept the new circumstance, the one he was clearly wanting to congratulate her on, as a sufficient cause? If one nursed a cause tenderly enough it might produce an effect; and this, to begin with, would be a way of nursing. "You gave me the other day," she went on, "plenty to think over, and I've been doing that—thinking it over—quite as you'll have probably wished me. I think I must be pretty easy to treat," she smiled, "since you've already done me so much good."

The only obstacle to reciprocity with him was that he looked in advance so closely related to all one's possibilities that one missed the pleasure of really improving it. "Oh no, you're extremely difficult to treat. I've need with you, I assure you, of all my wit."

"Well, I mean I do come up." She hadn't meanwhile a bit believed in his answer, convinced as she was that if she *had* been difficult it would be the last thing he would have told her. "I'm doing," she said, "as I like."

"Then it's as *I* like. But you must really, though we're having such a decent month, get straight away." In pursuance of which, when she had replied with promptitude that her departure—for the Tyrol and then for Venice—was quite fixed for the fourteenth, he took her up with alacrity. "For Venice? That's perfect, for we shall meet there. I've a dream of it for October, when I'm hoping for three weeks off; three weeks during which, if I can get them clear, my niece, a young person who has quite the whip hand of me, is to take me where she prefers. I heard from her only yesterday that she expects to prefer Venice."

"That's lovely then. I shall expect you there. And anything that, in advance or in any way, I can do for you—!"

"Oh thank you. My niece, I seem to feel, does for me. But it will be capital to find you there."

"I think it ought to make you feel," she said after a moment, "that I *am* easy to treat."

But he shook his head again; he wouldn't have it. "You've not come to that *yet*."

"One has to be so bad for it?"

"Well, I don't think I've ever come to it—to 'ease' of treatment. I doubt if it's possible. I've not, if it is, found any one bad enough. The ease, you see, is for *you*."

"I see—I see."

They had an odd friendly, but perhaps the least bit awkward pause on it; after which Sir Luke asked: "And that clever lady—she goes with you?"

"Mrs. Stringham? Oh dear, yes. She'll stay with me, I hope, to the end."

He had a cheerful blankness. "To the end of what?"

"Well—of everything."

"Ah then," he laughed, "you're in luck. The end of everything is far off. This, you know, I'm hoping," said Sir Luke, "is only the beginning." And the next question he risked might have been a part of his hope. "Just you and she together?"

"No, two other friends; two ladies of whom we've seen more here than of any one and who are just the right people for us."

He thought a moment. "You'll be four women together then?"

"Ah," said Milly, "we're widows and orphans. But I think," she added as if to say what she saw would reassure him, "that we shall not be unattractive, as we move, to gentlemen. When you talk of 'life' I suppose you mean mainly gentlemen."

"When I talk of 'life,'" he made answer after a moment during which he might have been appreciating her raciness—"when I talk of life I think I mean more than anything else the beautiful show of it, in its freshness, made by young persons of your age. So go on as you are. I see more and more *how* you are. You can't," he went so far as to say for pleasantness, "better it."

She took it from him with a great show of peace. "One of our companions will be Miss Croy, who came with me here first. It's in *her* that life is splendid; and a part of that is even that she's devoted to me. But she's above all magnificent in herself. So that if you'd like," she freely threw out, "to see *her*—"

"Oh I shall like to see any one who's devoted to you, for clearly it will be jolly to be 'in' it. So that if she's to be at Venice I *shall* see her?"

"We must arrange it—I shan't fail. She moreover has a friend who may also be there"—Milly found herself going on to this. "He's likely to come, I believe, for he always follows her."

Sir Luke wondered. "You mean they're lovers?"

"*He* is," Milly smiled; "but not she. She doesn't care for him."

Sir Luke took an interest. "What's the matter with him?"

"Nothing but that she doesn't like him."

Sir Luke kept it up. "Is he all right?"

"Oh he's very nice. Indeed he's remarkably so."

"And he's to be in Venice?"

"So she tells me she fears. For if he is there he'll be constantly about with her."

"And she'll be constantly about with you?"

"As we're great friends—yes."

"Well then," said Sir Luke, "you won't be four women alone."

"Oh no; I quite recognise the chance of gentlemen. But he won't," Milly pursued in the same wondrous way, "have come, you see, for me."

"No—I see. But can't you help him?"

"Can't *you?*" Milly after a moment quaintly asked. Then for the joke of it she explained. "I'm putting you, you see, in relation with my entourage."

It might have been for the joke of it too, by this time, that her eminent friend fell in. "But if this gentleman *isn't* of your 'entourage '? I mean if he's of—what do you call her?—Miss Croy's. Unless indeed you also take an interest in him."

"Oh certainly I take an interest in him!"

"You think there may be then some chance for him?"

"I like him," said Milly, "enough to hope so."

"Then that's all right. But what, pray," Sir Luke next asked, "have I to do with him?"

"Nothing," said Milly, "except that if you're to be there, so may he be. And also that we shan't in that case be simply four dreary women."

He considered her as if at this point she a little tried his patience. "*You're* the least 'dreary' woman I've ever, ever seen. Ever, do you know? There's no reason why you shouldn't have a really splendid life."

"So every one tells me," she promptly returned.

"The conviction—strong already when I had seen you once—is strengthened in me by having seen your friend. There's no doubt about it. The world's before you."

"What did my friend tell you?" Milly asked.

"Nothing that wouldn't have given you pleasure. We talked about you—and freely. I don't deny that. But it shows me I don't require of you the impossible."

She was now on her feet. "I think I know what you require of me."

"Nothing, for you," he went on, "*is* impossible. So go on." He repeated it again—wanting her so to feel that to-day he saw it. "You're all right."

"Well," she smiled—"keep me so."

"Oh you'll get away from me."

"Keep me, keep me," she simply continued with her gentle eyes on him.

She had given him her hand for good-bye, and he thus for a moment did keep her. Something then, while he seemed to think if there were anything more, came back to him; though something of which there wasn't too much to be made. "Of course if there's anything I *can* do for your friend: I mean the gentleman you speak of—?" He gave out in short that he was ready.

"Oh Mr. Densher?" It was as if she had forgotten.

"Mr. Densher—is that his name?"

"Yes—but his case isn't so dreadful." She had within a minute got away from that.

"No doubt—if *you* take an interest." She had got away, but it was as if he made out in her eyes—though they also had rather got away—a reason for calling her back. "Still, if there's anything one can do—?"

She looked at him while she thought, while she smiled. "I'm afraid there's really nothing one can do."

III

Not yet so much as this morning had she felt herself sink into possession; gratefully glad that the warmth of the Southern summer was still in the high florid rooms, palatial chambers where hard cool pavements took reflexions in their lifelong polish, and where the sun on the stirred sea-water, flickering up through open windows, played over the painted "subjects" in the splendid ceilings—medallions of purple and brown, of brave old melancholy colour, medals as of old reddened gold, embossed and beribboned, all toned with time and all flourished and scolloped and gilded about, set in their great moulded and figured concavity (a nest of white cherubs, friendly creatures of the air) and appreciated by the aid of that second tier of smaller lights, straight openings to the front, which did everything, even with the Baedekers and photographs of Milly's party dreadfully meeting the eye, to make of the place an apartment of state. This at last only, though she had enjoyed the palace for three weeks, seemed to count as effective occupation; perhaps because it was the first time she had been alone—really to call alone—since she had left London, it ministered to her first full and unembarrassed sense of what the great Eugenio had done for her. The great Eugenio, recommended by grand-dukes and Americans, had entered her service during the last hours of all—had crossed from Paris, after multiplied *pourparlers* with Mrs. Stringham, to whom she had allowed more than ever a free hand, on purpose to escort her to the Continent and encompass her there, and had dedicated to her, from the moment of their meeting, all the treasures of his experience. She had judged him in advance—polyglot and universal, very dear and very deep—as probably but a swindler finished to the finger-tips; for he was forever carrying one well-kept Italian hand to his heart and plunging the other straight into her pocket, which, as she had instantly observed him to recognise, fitted it like a glove. The remarkable thing was that these elements of their common consciousness had rapidly gathered into an indestructible link, formed the ground of a happy relation; being by this time, strangely, grotesquely, delightfully, what most kept up confidence between them and what most expressed it.

She had seen quickly enough what was happening—the usual thing again, yet once again. Eugenio had, in an interview of five minutes, understood her, had got hold, like all the world, of the idea not so much of the care with which she must be taken up as of the care with which she must be let down. All the world understood her, all the world had got hold; but for nobody yet, she felt, would the idea have been so close a tie or won from herself so patient a surrender. Gracefully, respectfully, consummately enough—always with hands in position and the look, in his thick neat white hair, smooth fat face and black professional, almost theatrical eyes, as of some famous tenor grown too old to make love, but with an art still to make money—did he on occasion convey to her that she was, of all the clients of his glorious career, the one in whom his interest was most personal and paternal. The others had come in the way of business, but for her his sentiment was special. Confidence rested thus on her completely believing that: there was nothing of which she felt more sure. It passed between them every time they conversed; he was abysmal, but this intimacy lived on the surface. He had taken his place already for her among those who were to see her through, and meditation ranked him, in the constant perspective, for the final function, side by side with poor Susie—whom she was now pitying more than ever for having to be herself so sorry and to say so little about it. Eugenio had the general tact of a residuary legatee—which was a character that could be definitely worn; whereas she could see Susie, in the event of her death, in no character at all, Susie being insistently, exclusively concerned in her mere makeshift duration. This principle, for that matter, Milly at present, with a renewed flare of fancy, felt she should herself have liked to believe in. Eugenio had really done for her more than he probably knew—he didn't after all know everything—in having, for the wind-up of the autumn, on a weak word from her, so admirably, so perfectly established her. Her weak word, as a general hint, had been: "At Venice, please, if possible, no dreadful, no vulgar hotel; but, if it can be at all managed—you know what I mean—some fine old rooms, wholly independent, for a series of months. Plenty of them too, and the more interesting the better: part of a palace, historic and picturesque, but strictly inodorous, where we shall be to ourselves, with a cook, don't you know?—with servants, frescoes, tapestries, antiquities, the thorough make-believe of a settlement."

The proof of how he better and better understood her was in all the place; as to his masterly acquisition of which she had from the first asked no questions. She had shown him enough what she thought of it, and her forbearance pleased him; with the part of the transaction that mainly concerned her she would soon enough become acquainted, and his connexion with such values as she would then find noted could scarce help growing, as it were, still more residuary. Charming people, conscious Venice-lovers, evidently, had given up their house to her, and had fled to a distance, to other countries, to hide their blushes alike over what they had, however briefly, alienated, and over what they had, however durably, gained. They had preserved and consecrated, and she now—her part of it was shameless—appropriated and enjoyed. Palazzo Leporelli held its history still in its great lap, even like a painted idol, a solemn puppet hung about with decorations. Hung about with pictures and relics, the rich Venetian past, the ineffaceable character, was here the presence revered and served: which brings us back to our truth of a moment ago—the fact that, more than ever, this October morning, awkward novice though she might be, Milly moved slowly to and fro as the priestess of the worship. Certainly it came from the sweet taste of solitude, caught again and cherished for the hour; always a need of her nature, moreover, when things spoke to her with penetration. It was mostly in stillness they spoke to her best; amid voices she lost the sense. Voices had surrounded her for weeks, and she had tried to listen, had cultivated them and had answered back; these had been weeks in which there were other things they might well prevent her from hearing. More than the prospect had at first promised or threatened she had felt herself going on in a crowd and with a multiplied escort; the four ladies pictured by her to Sir Luke Strett as a phalanx comparatively closed and detached had in fact proved a rolling snowball, condemned from day to day to cover more ground. Susan Shepherd had compared this portion of the girl's excursion to the Empress Catherine's famous progress across the steppes of Russia; improvised settlements appeared at each turn of the road, villagers waiting with addresses drawn up in the language of London. Old friends in fine were in ambush, Mrs. Lowder's, Kate Croy's, her own; when the addresses weren't in the language of London they were in the more insistent idioms of American centres. The current was swollen even by Susie's social connexions; so that there were days, at hotels, at Dolomite picnics, on lake steamers, when she could almost repay to Aunt Maud and Kate with interest the debt contracted by the London "success" to which they had opened the door.

Mrs. Lowder's success and Kate's, amid the shock of Milly's and Mrs. Stringham's compatriots, failed but little, really, of the concert-pitch; it had gone almost as fast as the boom, over the sea, of the last great native novel. Those ladies were "so different"—different, observably enough, from the ladies so appraising them; it being throughout a case mainly of ladies, of a dozen at once sometimes, in Milly's apartment, pointing, also at once, that moral and many others. Milly's companions were acclaimed not only as perfectly fascinating in themselves, the nicest people yet known to the acclaimers, but as obvious helping hands, socially speaking, for the eccentric young woman, evident initiators and smoothers of her path, possible subduers of her eccentricity. Short intervals, to her own sense, stood now for great differences, and this renewed inhalation of her native air had somehow left her to feel that she already, that she mainly, struck the compatriot as queer and dissociated. She moved such a critic, it would appear, as to rather an odd suspicion, a benevolence induced by a want of complete trust: all of which showed her in the light of a person too plain and too ill-clothed for a thorough good time, and yet too rich and too befriended—an intuitive cunning within her managing this last—for a thorough bad one. The compatriots, in short, by what she made out, approved her friends for their expert wisdom with her; in spite of which judicial sagacity it was the compatriots who recorded themselves as the innocent parties. She saw things in these days that she had never seen before, and she couldn't have said why save on a principle too terrible to name; whereby she saw that neither Lancaster Gate was what New York took it for, nor New York what Lancaster Gate fondly fancied it in coquetting with the plan of a series of American visits. The plan might have been, humorously, on Mrs. Lowder's part, for the improvement of her social position—and it had verily in that direction lights that were perhaps but half a century too prompt; at all of which Kate Croy assisted with the cool controlled facility that went so well, as the others said, with her particular kind of good looks, the kind that led you to expect the person enjoying them *would* dispose of disputations, speculations, aspirations, in a few very neatly and brightly uttered words, so simplified in sense, however, that they sounded, even when guiltless, like rather aggravated slang. It wasn't that Kate hadn't pretended too that *she* should like to go to America; it was only that with this young woman Milly had constantly proceeded, and more than ever of late, on the theory of intimate confessions, private frank ironies that made up for their public grimaces and amid which, face to face, they wearily put off the mask.

These puttings-off of the mask had finally quite become the form taken by their moments together, moments indeed not increasingly frequent and not prolonged, thanks to the consciousness of fatigue on Milly's side whenever, as she herself expressed it, she got out of harness. They flourished their masks, the independent pair, as they might have flourished Spanish fans; they smiled and sighed on removing them; but the gesture, the smiles, the sighs, strangely enough, might have been suspected the greatest reality in the business. Strangely enough, we say, for the volume of effusion in general would have been found by either on measurement to be scarce proportional to the paraphernalia of relief. It was when they called each other's attention to their ceasing to pretend, it was then that what they were keeping back was most in the air. There was a difference, no doubt, and mainly to Kate's advantage: Milly didn't quite see what her friend could keep back, was possessed of, in fine, that would be so subject to retention; whereas it was comparatively plain sailing for Kate that poor Milly had a treasure to hide. This was not the treasure of a shy, an abject affection—concealment, on that head, belonging to quite another phase of such states; it was much rather a principle of pride relatively bold and hard, a principle that played up like a fine steel spring at the lightest pressure of too near a footfall. Thus insuperably guarded was the truth about the girl's own conception of her validity; thus was a wondering pitying sister condemned wistfully to look at her from the far side of the moat she had dug round her tower. Certain aspects of the connexion of these young women show for us, such is the twilight that gathers about them, in the likeness of some dim scene in a Maeterlinck play; we have positively the image, in the delicate dusk, of the figures so associated and yet so opposed, so mutually watchful: that of the angular pale princess, ostrich-plumed, black-robed, hung about with amulets, reminders, relics, mainly seated, mainly still, and that of the upright restless slow-circling lady of her court who exchanges with her, across the black water streaked with evening gleams, fitful questions and answers. The upright lady, with thick dark braids down her back, drawing over the grass a more embroidered train, makes the whole circuit, and makes it again, and the broken talk, brief and sparingly allusive, seems more to cover than to free their sense. This is because, when it fairly comes to not having others to consider, they meet in an air that appears rather anxiously to wait for their words. Such an impression as that was in fact grave, and might be tragic; so that, plainly enough, systematically at last, they settled to a care of what they said.

There could be no gross phrasing to Milly, in particular, of the probability that if she wasn't so proud she might be pitied with more comfort—more to the person pitying; there could be no spoken proof, no sharper demonstration than the consistently considerate attitude, that this marvellous mixture of her weakness and of her strength, her peril, if such it were, and her option, made her, kept her, irresistibly interesting. Kate's predicament in the matter was, after all, very much Mrs. Stringham's own, and Susan Shepherd herself indeed, in our Maeterlinck picture, might well have hovered in the gloaming by the moat. It may be declared for Kate, at all events, that her sincerity about her friend, through this time, was deep, her compassionate imagination strong; and that these things gave her a virtue, a good conscience, a credibility for herself, so to speak, that were later to be precious to her. She grasped with her keen intelligence the logic of their common duplicity, went unassisted through the same ordeal as Milly's other hushed follower, easily saw that for the girl to be explicit was to betray divinations, gratitudes, glimpses of the felt contrast between her fortune and her fear—all of which would have contradicted her systematic bravado. That was it, Kate wonderingly saw: to recognise was to bring down the avalanche—the avalanche Milly lived so in watch for and that might be started by the lightest of breaths; though less possibly the breath of her own stifled plaint than that of the vain sympathy, the mere helpless gaping inference of others. With so many suppressions as these, therefore, between them, their withdrawal together to unmask had to fall back, as we have hinted, on a nominal motive—which was decently represented by a joy at the drop of chatter. Chatter had in truth all along attended their steps, but they took the despairing view of it on purpose to have ready, when face to face, some view or other of something. The relief of getting out of harness—that was the moral of their meetings; but the moral of this, in turn, was that they couldn't so much as ask each other why harness need be worn. Milly wore it as a general armour.

She was out of it at present, for some reason, as she hadn't been for weeks; she was always out of it, that is, when alone, and her companions had never yet so much as just now affected her as dispersed and suppressed. It was as if still again, still more tacitly and wonderfully, Eugenio had understood her, taking it from her without a word and just bravely and brilliantly in the name, for instance, of the beautiful day: "Yes, get me an hour alone; take them off—I don't care where; absorb, amuse, detain them; drown them, kill them if you will: so that I may just a little, all by myself, see where I am." She was conscious of the dire impatience of it, for she gave up Susie as well as the others to him—Susie who would have drowned her very self for her; gave her up to a mercenary monster through whom she thus purchased respites. Strange were the turns of life and the moods of weakness; strange the flickers of fancy and the cheats of hope; yet lawful, all the same—weren't they?—

those experiments tried with the truth that consisted, at the worst, but in practising on one's self. She was now playing with the thought that Eugenio might *inclusively* assist her: he had brought home to her, and always by remarks that were really quite soundless, the conception, hitherto ungrasped, of some complete use of her wealth itself, some use of it as a counter-move to fate. It had passed between them as preposterous that with so much money she should just stupidly and awkwardly *want*—any more want a life, a career, a consciousness, than want a house, a carriage or a cook. It was as if she had had from him a kind of expert professional measure of what he was in a position, at a stretch, to undertake for her; the thoroughness of which, for that matter, she could closely compare with a looseness on Sir Luke Strett's part that—at least in Palazzo Leporelli when mornings were fine—showed as almost amateurish. Sir Luke hadn't said to her "Pay enough money and leave the rest to *me*"—which was distinctly what Eugenio did say. Sir Luke had appeared indeed to speak of purchase and payment, but in reference to a different sort of cash. Those were amounts not to be named nor reckoned, and such moreover as she wasn't sure of having at her command. Eugenio—this was the difference—could name, could reckon, and prices of *his* kind were things she had never suffered to scare her. She had been willing, goodness knew, to pay enough for anything, for everything, and here was simply a new view of the sufficient quantity. She amused herself—for it came to that, since Eugenio was there to sign the receipt—with possibilities of meeting the bill. She was more prepared than ever to pay enough, and quite as much as ever to pay too much. What else—if such were points at which your most trusted servant failed—was the use of being, as the dear Susies of earth called you, a princess in a palace?

She made now, alone, the full circuit of the place, noble and peaceful while the summer sea, stirring here and there a curtain or an outer blind, breathed into its veiled spaces. She had a vision of clinging to it; that perhaps Eugenio could manage. She was *in* it, as in the ark of her deluge, and filled with such a tenderness for it that why shouldn't this, in common mercy, be warrant enough? She would never, never leave it—she would engage to that; would ask nothing more than to sit tight in it and float on and on. The beauty and intensity, the real momentary relief of this conceit, reached their climax in the positive purpose to put the question to Eugenio on his return as she had not yet put it; though the design, it must be added, dropped a little when, coming back to the great saloon from which she had started on her pensive progress, she found Lord Mark, of whose arrival in Venice she had been unaware, and who had now—while a servant was following her through empty rooms—been asked, in her absence, to wait. He had waited then, Lord Mark, he was waiting—oh unmistakeably; never before had he so much struck her as the man to do that on occasion with patience, to do it indeed almost as with gratitude for the chance, though at the same time with a sort of notifying firmness. The odd thing, as she was afterwards to recall, was that her wonder for what had brought him was not immediate, but had come at the end of five minutes; and also, quite incoherently, that she felt almost as glad to see him, and almost as forgiving of his interruption of her solitude, as if he had already been in her thought or acting at her suggestion. He was some-how, at the best, the end of a respite; one might like him very much and yet feel that his presence tempered precious solitude more than any other known to one: in spite of all of which, as he was neither dear Susie, nor dear Kate, nor dear Aunt Maud, nor even, for the least, dear Eugenio in person, the sight of him did no damage to her sense of the dispersal of her friends. She hadn't been so thoroughly alone with him since those moments of his showing her the great portrait at Matcham, the moments that had exactly made the high-water-mark of her security, the moments during which her tears themselves, those she had been ashamed of, were the sign of her consciously rounding her protective promontory, quitting the blue gulf of comparative ignorance and reaching her view of the troubled sea. His presence now referred itself to his presence then, reminding her how kind he had been, altogether, at Matcham, and telling her, unexpectedly, at a time when she could particularly feel it, that, for such kindness and for the beauty of what they remembered together, she hadn't lost him—quite the contrary. To receive him handsomely, to receive him there, to see him interested and charmed, as well, clearly, as delighted to have found her without some other person to spoil it—these things were so pleasant for the first minutes that they might have represented on her part some happy foreknowledge. She gave an account of her companions while he on his side failed to press her about them, even though describing his appearance, so unheralded, as the result of an impulse obeyed on the spot. He had been shivering at Carlsbad, belated there and blue, when taken by it; so that, knowing where they all were, he had simply caught the first train. He explained how he had known where they were; he had heard—what more natural?—from their friends, Milly's and his. He mentioned this betimes, but it was with his mention, singularly, that the girl became conscious of her inner question about his reason. She noticed his plural, which added to Mrs. Lowder or added to Kate; but she presently noticed also that it didn't affect her as explaining. Aunt Maud had written to him, Kate apparently—and this was interesting—had written to him; but their design presumably hadn't been that he should come and sit there as if rather relieved, so far as *they* were concerned, at postponements. He only said "Oh!" and again "Oh!" when she sketched their probable morning for him, under Eugenio's care and Mrs. Stringham's—sounding it quite as if any suggestion that he should overtake them at the Rialto or the Bridge of Sighs would leave him temporarily cold. This precisely it was that, after a little, operated for Milly as an obscure but still fairly direct check to confidence. He had known where they all were from the others, but it was not for the others that, in his actual dispositions, he had come. That, strange to say, was a pity; for, stranger still to say, she could have shown him more confidence if he himself had had less intention. His intention so chilled her, from the moment she found herself divining it, that, just for the pleasure of going on with him fairly, just for the pleasure of their remembrance together of Matcham and the Bronzino, the climax of her fortune, she could have fallen to pleading with him and to reasoning, to undeceiving him in time. There had been, for ten minutes, with the directness of her welcome to him and the way this clearly pleased him, something of the grace of amends made, even though he couldn't know it—amends for her not having been originally sure, for instance at that first dinner of Aunt Maud's, that he was adequately human. That first dinner of Aunt Maud's added itself to the hour at Matcham, added itself to other things, to consolidate, for her present benevolence, the ease of their relation, making it suddenly delightful that he had thus turned up. He exclaimed, as he looked about, on the charm of the place: "What a temple to taste and an expression of the pride of life, yet, with all that, what a jolly *home!*"—so that, for his entertainment, she could offer to walk him about though she mentioned that she had just been, for her own purposes, in a general prowl, taking everything in more susceptibly than before. He embraced her offer without a scruple and seemed to rejoice that he was to find her susceptible.

IV

She couldn't have said what it was, in the conditions, that renewed the whole solemnity, but by the end of twenty minutes a kind of wistful hush had fallen upon them, as before something poignant in which her visitor also participated. That was nothing verily but the perfection of the charm—or nothing rather but their excluded disinherited state in the presence of it. The charm turned on them a face that was cold in its beauty, that was full of a poetry never to be theirs, that spoke with an ironic smile of a possible but forbidden life. It all rolled afresh over Milly: "Oh the impossible romance—!" The romance for her, yet once more, would be to sit there for ever, through all her time, as in a fortress; and the idea became an image of never going down, of remaining aloft in the divine dustless air, where she would hear but the plash of the water against stone. The great floor on which they moved was at an altitude, and this prompted the rueful fancy. "Ah not to go down—never, never to go down!" she strangely sighed to her friend.

"But why shouldn't you," he asked, "with that tremendous old staircase in your court? There ought of course always to be people at top and bottom, in Veronese costumes, to watch you do it."

She shook her head both lightly and mournfully enough at his not understanding. "Not even for people in Veronese costumes. I mean that the positive beauty is that one needn't go down. I don't move in fact," she added—"now. I've not been out, you know. I stay up. That's how you happily found me."

539

Lord Mark wondered—he was, oh yes, adequately human. "You don't go about?"

She looked over the place, the storey above the apartments in which she had received him, the sala corresponding to the sala below and fronting the great canal with its gothic arches. The casements between the arches were open, the ledge of the balcony broad, the sweep of the canal, so overhung, admirable, and the flutter toward them of the loose white curtain an invitation to she scarce could have said what. But there was no mystery after a moment; she had never felt so invited to anything as to make that, and that only, just where she was, her adventure. It would be—to this it kept coming back—the adventure of not stirring. "I go about just here."

"Do you mean," Lord Mark presently asked, "that you're really not well?"

They were at the window, pausing, lingering, with the fine old faded palaces opposite and the slow Adriatic tide beneath; but after a minute, and before she answered, she had closed her eyes to what she saw and unresistingly dropped her face into her arms, which rested on the coping. She had fallen to her knees on the cushion of the window-place, and she leaned there, in a long silence, with her forehead down. She knew that her silence was itself too straight an answer, but it was beyond her now to say that she saw her way. She would have made the question itself impossible to others—impossible for example to such a man as Merton Densher; and she could wonder even on the spot what it was a sign of in her feeling for Lord Mark that from his lips it almost tempted her to break down. This was doubtless really because she cared for him so little; to let herself go with him thus, suffer his touch to make her cup overflow, would be the relief—since it was actually, for her nerves, a question of relief—that would cost her least. If he had come to her moreover with the intention she believed, or even if this intention had but been determined in him by the spell of their situation, he mustn't be mistaken about her value—for what value did she now have? It throbbed within her as she knelt there that she had none at all; though, holding herself, not yet speaking, she tried, even in the act, to recover what might be possible of it. With that there came to her a light: wouldn't her value, for the man who should marry her, be precisely in the ravage of her disease? *She* mightn't last, but her money would. For a man in whom the vision of her money should be intense, in whom it should be most of the ground for "making up" to her, any prospective failure on her part to be long for this world might easily count as a positive attraction. Such a man, proposing to please, persuade, secure her, appropriate her for such a time, shorter or longer, as nature and the doctors should allow, would make the best of her, ill, damaged, disagreeable though she might be, for the sake of eventual benefits: she being clearly a person of the sort esteemed likely to do the handsome thing by a stricken and sorrowing husband.

She had said to herself betimes, in a general way, that whatever habits her youth might form, that of seeing an interested suitor in every bush should certainly never grow to be one of them—an attitude she had early judged as ignoble, as poisonous. She had had accordingly in fact as little to do with it as possible and she scarce knew why at the present moment she should have had to catch herself in the act of imputing an ugly motive. It didn't sit, the ugly motive, in Lord Mark's cool English eyes; the darker side of it at any rate showed, to her imagination, but briefly. Suspicion moreover, with this, simplified itself: there was a beautiful reason—indeed there were two—why her companion's motive shouldn't matter. One was that even should he desire her without a penny she wouldn't marry him for the world; the other was that she felt him, after all, perceptively, kindly, very pleasantly and humanly, concerned for her. They were also two things, his wishing to be well, to be very well, with her, and his beginning to feel her as threatened, haunted, blighted; but they were melting together for him, making him, by their combination, only the more sure that, as he probably called it to himself, he liked her. That was presently what remained with her—his really doing it; and with the natural and proper incident of being conciliated by her weakness. Would she really have had him—she could ask herself that—disconcerted or disgusted by it? If he could only be touched enough to do what she preferred, not to raise, not to press any question, he might render her a much better service than by merely enabling her to refuse him. Again, again it was strange, but he figured to her for the moment as the one safe sympathiser. It would have made her worse to talk to others, but she wasn't afraid with him of how he might wince and look pale. She would keep him, that is, her one easy relation—in the sense of easy for himself. Their actual outlook had meanwhile such charm, what surrounded them within and without did so much toward making appreciative stillness as natural as at the opera, that she could consider she hadn't made him hang on her lips when at last, instead of saying if she were well or ill, she repeated: "I go about here. I don't get tired of it. I never should—it suits me so. I adore the place," she went on, "and I don't want in the least to give it up."

"Neither should I if I had your luck. Still, with that luck, for one's *all*—! Should you positively like to live here?"

"I think I should like," said poor Milly after an instant, "to die here."

Which made him, precisely, laugh. That was what she wanted—when a person did care: it was the pleasant human way, without depths of darkness. "Oh it's not good enough for *that!* That requires picking. But can't you keep it? It is, you know, the sort of place to see you in; you carry out the note, fill it, people it, quite by yourself, and you might do much worse—I mean for your friends—than show yourself here a while, three or four months, every year. But it's not my notion for the rest of the time. One has quite other uses for you."

"What sort of a use for me is it," she smilingly enquired, "to kill me?"

"Do you mean we should kill you in England?"

"Well, I've seen you and I'm afraid. You're too much for me—too many. England bristles with questions. This is more, as you say there, my form."

"Oho, oho!"—he laughed again as if to humour her. "Can't you then buy it—for a price? Depend upon it they'll treat for money. That is for money enough."

"I've exactly," she said, "been wondering if they won't. I think I shall try. But if I get it I shall cling to it." They were talking sincerely. "It will be my life—paid for as that. It will become my great gilded shell; so that those who wish to find me must come and hunt me up."

"Ah then you *will* be alive," said Lord Mark.

"Well, not quite extinct perhaps, but shrunken, wasted, wizened; rattling about here like the dried kernel of a nut."

"Oh," Lord Mark returned, "we, much as you mistrust us, can do better for you than that."

"In the sense that you'll feel it better for me really to have it over?"

He let her see now that she worried him, and after a look at her, of some duration, without his glasses—which always altered the expression of his eyes—he re-settled the nippers on his nose and went back to the view. But the view, in turn, soon enough released him. "Do you remember something I said to you that day at Matcham—or at least fully meant to?"

"Oh yes, I remember everything at Matcham. It's another life."

"Certainly it will be—I mean the kind of thing: what I then wanted it to represent for you. Matcham, you know," he continued, "is symbolic. I think I tried to rub that into you a little."

She met him with the full memory of what he had tried—not an inch, not an ounce of which was lost to her. "What I meant is that it seems a hundred years ago."

"Oh for me it comes in better. Perhaps a part of what makes me remember it," he pursued, "is that I was quite aware of what might have been said about what I was doing. I wanted you to take it from me that I should perhaps be able to look after you—well, rather better. Rather better, of course, than certain other persons in particular."

"Precisely—than Mrs. Lowder, than Miss Croy, even than Mrs. Stringham."

"Oh Mrs. Stringham's all right!" Lord Mark promptly amended.

It amused her even with what she had else to think of; and she could show him at all events how little, in spite of the hundred years, she had lost what he alluded to. The way he was with her at this moment made in fact the other moment so vivid as almost to start again the tears it had started at the time. "You could do so much for me, yes. I perfectly understood you."

"I wanted, you see," he despite this explained, "to *fix* your confidence. I mean, you know, in the right place."

"Well, Lord Mark, you did—it's just exactly now, my confidence, where you put it then. The only difference," said Milly, "is that I seem now to have no use for it. Besides," she then went on, "I do seem to feel you disposed to act in a way that would undermine it a little."

He took no more notice of these last words than if she hadn't said them, only watching her at present as with a gradual new light. "Are you *really* in any trouble?"

To this, on her side, she gave no heed. Making out his light was a little a light for herself. "Don't say, don't try to say, anything that's impossible. There are much better things you can do."

He looked straight at it and then straight over it. "It's too monstrous that one can't ask you as a friend what one wants so to know."

"What is it you want to know?" She spoke, as by a sudden turn, with a slight hardness. "Do you want to know if I'm badly ill?"

The sound of it in truth, though from no raising of her voice, invested the idea with a kind of terror, but a terror all for others. Lord Mark winced and flushed—clearly couldn't help it; but he kept his attitude together and spoke even with unwonted vivacity. "Do you imagine I can see you suffer and not say a word?"

"You won't see me suffer—don't be afraid. I shan't be a public nuisance. That's why I should have liked *this*: it's so beautiful in itself and yet it's out of the gangway. You won't know anything about anything," she added; and then as if to make with decision an end: "And you *don't!* No, not even you." He faced her through it with the remains of his expression, and she saw him as clearly—for *him*—bewildered; which made her wish to be sure not to have been unkind. She would be kind once for all; that would be the end. "I'm very badly ill."

"And you don't do anything?"

"I do everything. Everything's *this*," she smiled. "I'm doing it now. One can't do more than live."

"Ah than live in the right way, no. But is that what you do? Why haven't you advice?"

He had looked about at the rococo elegance as if there were fifty things it didn't give her, so that he suggested with urgency the most absent. But she met his remedy with a smile. "I've the best advice in the world. I'm acting under it now. I act upon it in receiving you, in talking with you thus. One can't, as I tell you, do more than live."

"Oh live!" Lord Mark ejaculated.

"Well, it's immense for *me*." She finally spoke as if for amusement; now that she had uttered her truth, that he had learnt it from herself as no one had yet done, her emotion had, by the fact, dried up. There she was; but it was as if she would never speak again. "I shan't," she added, "have missed everything."

"Why should you have missed *anything?*" She felt, as he sounded this, to what, within the minute, he had made up his mind. "You're the person in the world for whom that's least necessary; for whom one would call it in fact most impossible; for whom 'missing' at all will surely require an extraordinary amount of misplaced good will. Since you believe in advice, for God's sake take *mine*. I know what you want."

Oh she knew he would know it. But she had brought it on herself—or almost. Yet she spoke with kindness. "I think I want not to be too much worried."

"You want to be adored." It came at last straight. "Nothing would worry you less. I mean as I shall do it. It *is* so"—he firmly kept it up. "You're not loved enough."

"Enough for what, Lord Mark?"

"Why to get the full good of it."

Well, she didn't after all mock at him. "I see what you mean. That full good of it which consists in finding one's self forced to love in return." She had grasped it, but she hesitated. "Your idea is that I might find myself forced to love *you?*"

"Oh 'forced'—!" He was so fine and so expert, so awake to anything the least ridiculous, and of a type with which the preaching of passion somehow so ill consorted—he was so much all these things that he had absolutely to take account of them himself. And he did so, in a single intonation, beautifully. Milly liked him again, liked him for such shades as that, liked him so that it was woeful to see him spoiling it, and still more woeful to have to rank him among those minor charms of existence that she gasped at moments to remember she must give up. "Is it inconceivable to you that you might try?"

"To be so favourably affected by you—?"

"To believe in me. To believe in me," Lord Mark repeated.

Again she hesitated. "To 'try' in return for your trying?"

"Oh I shouldn't have to!" he quickly declared. The prompt neat accent, however, his manner of disposing of her question, failed of real expression, as he himself the next moment intelligently, helplessly, almost comically saw—a failure pointed moreover by the laugh into which Milly was immediately startled. As a suggestion to her of a healing and uplifting passion it *was* in truth deficient; it wouldn't do as the communication of a force that should sweep them both away. And the beauty of him was that he too, even in the act of persuasion, of self-persuasion, could understand that, and could thereby show but the better as fitting into the pleasant commerce of prosperity. The way she let him see that she looked at him was a thing to shut him out, of itself, from services of danger, a thing that made a discrimination against him never yet made—made at least to any consciousness of his own. Born to float in a sustaining air, this would be his first encounter with a judgement formed in the sinister light of tragedy. The gathering dusk of *her* personal world presented itself to him, in her eyes, as an element in which it was vain for him to pretend he could find himself at home, since it was charged with depressions and with dooms, with the chill of the losing game. Almost without her needing to speak, and simply by the fact that there could be, in such a case, no decent substitute for a felt intensity, he had to take it from her that practically he was afraid—whether afraid to protest falsely enough, or only afraid of what might be eventually disagreeable in a compromised alliance, being a minor question. She believed she made out besides, wonderful girl, that he had never quite expected to have to protest about anything beyond his natural convenience—more, in fine, than his disposition and habits, his education as well, his personal *moyens*, in short, permitted. His predicament was therefore one he couldn't like, and also one she willingly would have spared him hadn't he brought it on himself. No man, she was quite aware, could enjoy thus having it from her that he wasn't good for what she would have called her reality. It wouldn't have taken much more to enable her positively to make out in him that he was virtually capable of hinting— had his innermost feeling spoken—at the propriety rather, in his interest, of some cutting down, some dressing up, of the offensive real. He would meet that halfway, but the real must also meet *him*. Milly's sense of it for herself, which was so conspicuously, so financially supported, couldn't, or wouldn't, so accommodate him, and the perception of that fairly showed in his face after a moment like the smart of a blow. It had marked the one minute during which he could again be touching to her. By the time he had tried once more, after all, to insist, he had quite ceased to be so.

By this time she had turned from their window to make a diversion, had walked him through other rooms, appealing again to the inner charm of the place, going even so far for that purpose as to point afresh her independent moral, to repeat that if one only had such a house for one's own and loved it and cherished it enough, it would pay one back in kind, would close one in from harm. He quite grasped for the quarter of an hour the perch she held out to him—grasped it with one hand, that is, while she felt him attached to his own clue with the other; he was by no means either so sore or so stupid, to do him all justice, as not to be able to behave more or less as if nothing had happened. It was one of his merits, to which she did justice too, that both his native and his acquired notion of behaviour rested on the general assumption that nothing—nothing to make a deadly difference for him—ever *could* happen. It was, socially, a working view like another, and it saw them easily enough through the greater part of the rest of their adventure. Downstairs again, however, with the limit of his stay in sight, the sign of his smarting, when all was said, reappeared for her—breaking out moreover, with an effect of strangeness, in another quite possibly sincere allusion to her state of health. He might for that matter have been seeing what he could do in the way of making it a grievance that she should snub him for a charity, on his own part, exquisitely roused. "It's true, you know, all the same, and I don't care a straw for your trying to freeze one up." He seemed to show her, poor man, bravely, how little he cared. "Everybody knows affection often makes things out when indifference doesn't notice. And that's why I know that *I* notice."

"Are you sure you've got it right?" the girl smiled. "I thought rather that affection was supposed to be blind."

"Blind to faults, not to beauties," Lord Mark promptly returned.

"And are my extremely private worries, my entirely domestic complications, which I'm ashamed to have given you a glimpse of—are they beauties?"

"Yes, for those who care for you—as every one does. Everything about you is a beauty. Besides which I don't believe," he declared, "in the seriousness of what you tell me. It's too absurd you should have *any* trouble about which something can't be done. If you can't get the right thing, who can, in all the world, I should like to know? You're the first young woman of your time. I mean what I say." He looked, to do him justice, quite as if he did; not ardent, but clear—simply so competent, in such a position, to compare, that his quiet assertion had the force not so much perhaps of a tribute as of a warrant. "We're all in love with you. I'll put it that way, dropping any claim of my own, if you can bear it better. I speak as one of the lot. You weren't born simply to torment us—you were born to make us happy. Therefore you must listen to us."

She shook her head with her slowness, but this time with all her mildness. "No, I mustn't listen to you—that's just what I mustn't do. The reason is, please, that it simply kills me. I must be as attached to you as you will, since you give that lovely account of yourselves. I give you in return the fullest possible belief of what it would be—" And she pulled up a little. "I give and give and give—there you are; stick to me as close as you like and see if I don't. Only I can't listen or receive or accept—I can't *agree*. I can't make a bargain. I can't really. You must believe that from me. It's all I've wanted to say to you, and why should it spoil anything?"

He let her question fall—though clearly, it might have seemed, because, for reasons or for none, there was so much that *was* spoiled. "You want somebody of your own." He came back, whether in good faith or in bad, to that; and it made her repeat her headshake. He kept it up as if his faith were of the best. "You want somebody, you want somebody."

She was to wonder afterwards if she hadn't been at this juncture on the point of saying something emphatic and vulgar—"Well, I don't at all events want *you!*" What somehow happened, nevertheless, the pity of it being greater than the irritation—the sadness, to her vivid sense, of his being so painfully astray, wandering in a desert in which there was nothing to nourish him—was that his error amounted to positive wrongdoing. She was moreover so acquainted with quite another sphere of usefulness for him that her having suffered him to insist almost convicted her of indelicacy. Why hadn't she stopped him off with her first impression of his purpose? She could do so now only by the allusion she had been wishing not to make. "Do you know I don't think you're doing very right?—and as a thing quite apart, I mean, from my listening to you. That's not right either—except that I'm *not* listening. You oughtn't to have come to Venice to see *me*—and in fact you've not come, and you mustn't behave as if you had. You've much older friends than I, and ever so much better. Really, if you've come at all, you can only have come—properly, and if I may say so honourably—for the best friend, as I believe her to be, that you have in the world."

549

When once she had said it he took it, oddly enough, as if he had been more or less expecting it. Still, he looked at her very hard, and they had a moment of this during which neither pronounced a name, each apparently determined that the other should. It was Milly's fine coercion, in the event, that was the stronger. "Miss Croy?" Lord Mark asked.

It might have been difficult to make out that she smiled. "Mrs. Lowder." He did make out something, and then fairly coloured for its attestation of his comparative simplicity. "I call *her* on the whole the best. I can't imagine a man's having a better."

Still with his eyes on her he turned it over. "Do you want me to marry Mrs. Lowder?"

At which it seemed to her that it was he who was almost vulgar! But she wouldn't in any way have that. "You know, Lord Mark, what I mean. One isn't in the least turning you out into the cold world. There's no cold world for you at all, I think," she went on; "nothing but a very warm and watchful and expectant world that's waiting for you at any moment you choose to take it up."

He never budged, but they were standing on the polished concrete and he had within a few minutes possessed himself again of his hat. "Do you want me to marry Kate Croy?"

"Mrs. Lowder wants it—I do no wrong, I think, in saying that; and she understands moreover that you know she does."

Well, he showed how beautifully he could take it; and it wasn't obscure to her, on her side, that it was a comfort to deal with a gentleman. "It's ever so kind of you to see such opportunities for me. But what's the use of my tackling Miss Croy?"

Milly rejoiced on the spot to be so able to point out. "Because she's the handsomest and cleverest and most charming creature I ever saw, and because if I were a man I should simply adore her. In fact I do as it is." It was a luxury of response.

"Oh, my dear lady, plenty of people adore her. But that can't further the case of *all.*"

"Ah," she went on, "I know about 'people.' If the case of one's bad, the case of another's good. I don't see what you have to fear from any one else," she said, "save through your being foolish, this way, about *me.*"

So she said, but she was aware the next moment of what he was making of what she didn't see. "Is it your idea—since we're talking of these things in these ways—that the young lady you describe in such superlative terms is to be had for the asking?"

"Well, Lord Mark, try. She is a great person. But don't be humble." She was almost gay.

It was this apparently, at last, that was too much for him. "But don't you really *know?*"

As a challenge, practically, to the commonest intelligence she could pretend to, it made her of course wish to be fair. "I 'know' yes, that a particular person's very much in love with her."

"Then you must know by the same token that she's very much in love with a particular person."

"Ah I beg your pardon!"—and Milly quite flushed at having so crude a blunder imputed to her. "You're wholly mistaken."

"It's not true?"

"It's not true."

His stare became a smile. "Are you very, very sure?"

"As sure as one can be"—and Milly's manner could match it—"when one has every assurance. I speak on the best authority."

He hesitated. "Mrs. Lowder's?"

"No. I don't call Mrs. Lowder's the best."

"Oh I thought you were just now saying," he laughed, "that everything about her's so good."

"Good for you"—she was perfectly clear. "For you," she went on, "let her authority be the best. She doesn't believe what you mention, and you must know yourself how little she makes of it. So you can take it from her. *I* take it—" But Milly, with the positive tremor of her emphasis, pulled up.

"You take it from Kate?"

"From Kate herself."

"That she's thinking of no one at all?"

"Of no one at all." Then, with her intensity, she went on. "She has given me her word for it."

"Oh!" said Lord Mark. To which he next added: "And what do you call her word?"

It made Milly, on her side, stare—though perhaps partly but with the instinct of gaining time for the consciousness that she was already a little further "in" than she had designed. "Why, Lord Mark, what should *you* call her word?"

"Ah I'm not obliged to say. I've not asked her. You apparently have."

Well, it threw her on her defence—a defence that she felt, however, especially as of Kate. "We're very intimate," she said in a moment; "so that, without prying into each other's affairs, she naturally tells me things."

Lord Mark smiled as at a lame conclusion. "You mean then she made you of her own movement the declaration you quote?"

Milly thought again, though with hindrance rather than help in her sense of the way their eyes now met—met as for their each seeing in the other more than either said. What she most felt that she herself saw was the strange disposition on her companion's part to disparage Kate's veracity. She could be only concerned to "stand up" for that.

"I mean what I say: that when she spoke of her having no private interest—"

"She took her oath to you?" Lord Mark interrupted.

Milly didn't quite see why he should so catechise her; but she met it again for Kate. "She left me in no doubt whatever of her being free."

At this Lord Mark did look at her, though he continued to smile. "And thereby in no doubt of *your* being too?" It was as if as soon as he had said it, however, he felt it as something of a mistake, and she couldn't herself have told by what queer glare at him she had instantly signified that. He at any rate gave her glare no time to act further; he fell back on the spot, and with a light enough movement, within his rights. "That's all very well, but why in the world, dear lady, should she be swearing to you?"

She had to take this "dear lady" as applying to herself; which disconcerted her when he might now so gracefully have used it for the aspersed Kate. Once more it came to her that she must claim her own part of the aspersion. "Because, as I've told you, we're such tremendous friends."

"Oh," said Lord Mark, who for the moment looked as if that might have stood rather for an absence of such rigours. He was going, however, as if he had in a manner, at the last, got more or less what he wanted. Milly felt, while he addressed his next few words to leave-taking, that she had given rather more than she intended or than she should be able, when once more getting herself into hand, theoretically to defend. Strange enough in fact that he had had from her, about herself—and, under the searching spell of the place, infinitely straight—what no one else had had: neither Kate, nor Aunt Maud, nor Merton Densher, nor Susan Shepherd. He had made her within a minute, in particular, she was aware, lose her presence of mind, and she now wished he would take himself off, so that she might either recover it or bear the loss better in solitude. If he paused, however, she almost at the same time saw, it was because of his watching the approach, from the end of the sala, of one of the gondoliers, who, whatever excursions were appointed for the party with the attendance of the others, always, as the most decorative, most sashed and starched, remained at the palace on the theory that she might whimsically want him—which she never, in her caged freedom, had yet done. Brown Pasquale, slipping in white shoes over the marble and suggesting to her perpetually charmed vision she could scarce say what, either a mild Hindoo, too noiseless almost for her nerves, or simply a barefooted seaman on the deck of a ship—Pasquale offered to sight a small salver, which he obsequiously held out to her with its burden of a visiting-card. Lord Mark—and as if also for admiration of him—delayed his departure to let her receive it; on which she read it with the instant effect of another blow to her presence of mind. This precarious quantity was indeed now so gone that even for dealing with Pasquale she had to do her best to conceal its disappearance. The effort was made, none the less, by the time she had asked if the gentleman were below and had taken in the fact that he had come up. He had followed the gondolier and was waiting at the top of the staircase.

"I'll see him with pleasure." To which she added for her companion, while Pasquale went off: "Mr. Merton Densher."

"Oh!" said Lord Mark—in a manner that, making it resound through the great cool hall, might have carried it even to Densher's ear as a judgement of his identity heard and noted once before

BOOK EIGHTH

I

Densher became aware, afresh, that he disliked his hotel—and all the more promptly that he had had occasion of old to make the same discrimination. The establishment, choked at that season with the polyglot herd, cockneys of all climes, mainly German, mainly American, mainly English, it appeared as the corresponding sensitive nerve was touched, sounded loud and not sweet, sounded anything and everything but Italian, but Venetian. The Venetian was all a dialect, he knew; yet it was pure Attic beside some of the dialects at the bustling inn. It made, "abroad," both for his pleasure and his pain that he had to feel at almost any point how he had been through every thing before. He had been three or four times, in Venice, during other visits, through this pleasant irritation of paddling away—away from the concert of false notes in the vulgarised hall, away from the amiable American families and overfed German porters. He had in each case made terms for a lodging more private and not more costly, and he recalled with tenderness these shabby but friendly asylums, the windows of which he should easily know again in passing on canal or through campo. The shabbiest now failed of an appeal to him, but he found himself at the end of forty-eight hours forming views in respect to a small independent *quartiere*, far down the Grand Canal, which he had once occupied for a month with a sense of pomp and circumstance and yet also with a growth of initiation into the homelier Venetian mysteries. The humour of those days came back to him for an hour, and what further befell in this interval, to be brief, was that, emerging on a traghetto in sight of the recognised house, he made out on the green shutters of his old, of his young windows the strips of white pasted paper that figure in Venice as an invitation to tenants. This was in the course of his very first walk apart, a walk replete with impressions to which he responded with force. He had been almost without cessation, since his arrival, at Palazzo Leporelli, where, as happened, a turn of bad weather on the second day had kept the whole party continuously at home. The episode had passed for him like a series of hours in a museum, though without the fatigue of that; and it had also resembled something that he was still, with a stirred imagination, to find a name for. He might have been looking for the name while he gave himself up, subsequently, to the ramble—he saw that even after years he couldn't lose his way—crowned with his stare across the water at the little white papers.

He was to dine at the palace in an hour or two, and he had lunched there, at an early luncheon, that morning. He had then been out with the three ladies, the three being Mrs. Lowder, Mrs. Stringham and Kate, and had kept afloat with them, under a sufficient Venetian spell, until Aunt Maud had directed him to leave them and return to Miss Theale. Of two circumstances connected with this disposition of his person he was even now not unmindful; the first being that the lady of Lancaster Gate had addressed him with high publicity and as if expressing equally the sense of her companions, who had not spoken, but who might have been taken—yes, Susan Shepherd quite equally with Kate—for inscrutable parties to her plan. What he could as little contrive to forget was that he had, before the two others, as it struck him—that was to say especially before Kate—done exactly as he was bidden; gathered himself up without a protest and retraced his way to the palace. Present with him still was the question of whether he looked a fool for it, of whether the awkwardness he felt as the gondola rocked with the business of his leaving it—they could but make, in submission, for a landing-place that was none of the best—had furnished his friends with such entertainment as was to cause them, behind his back, to exchange intelligent smiles. He had found Milly Theale twenty minutes later alone, and he had sat with her till the others returned to tea. The strange part of this was that it had been very easy, extraordinarily easy. He knew it for strange only when he was away from her, because when he was away from her he was in contact with particular things that made it so. At the time, in her presence, it was as simple as sitting with his sister might have been, and not, if the point were urged, very much more thrilling. He continued to see her as he had first seen her—that remained ineffaceably behind. Mrs. Lowder, Susan Shepherd, his own Kate, might, each in proportion, see her as a princess, as an angel, as a star, but for himself, luckily, she hadn't as yet complications to any point of discomfort: the princess, the angel, the star, were muffled over, ever so lightly and brightly, with the little American girl who had been kind to him in New York and to whom certainly—though without making too much of it for either of them—he was perfectly willing to be kind in return. She appreciated his coming in on purpose, but there was nothing in that—from the moment she was always at home—that they couldn't easily keep up. The only note the least bit high that had even yet sounded between them was this admission on her part that she found it best to remain within. She wouldn't let him call it keeping quiet, for she insisted that her palace—with all its romance and art and history—had set up round her a whirlwind of suggestion that never dropped for an hour. It wasn't therefore, within such walls, confinement, it was the freedom of all the centuries: in respect to which Densher granted good-humouredly that they were then blown together, she and he, as much as she liked, through space.

Kate had found on the present occasion a moment to say to him that he suggested a clever cousin calling on a cousin afflicted, and bored for his pains; and though he denied on the spot the "bored" he could so far see it as an impression he might make that he wondered if the same image wouldn't have occurred to Milly. As soon as Kate appeared again the difference came up—the oddity, as he then instantly felt it, of his having sunk so deep. It was sinking because it was all doing what Kate had conceived for him; it wasn't in the least doing—and that had been his notion of his life—anything he himself had conceived. The difference, accordingly, renewed, sharp, sore, was the irritant under which he had quitted the palace and under which he was to make the best of the business of again dining there. He said to himself that he must make the best of everything; that was in his mind, at the traghetto, even while, with his preoccupation about changing quarters, he studied, across the canal, the look of his former abode. It had done for the past, would it do for the present? would it play in any manner into the general necessity of which he was conscious? That necessity of making the best was the instinct—as he indeed himself knew—of a man somehow aware that if he let go at one place he should let go everywhere. If he took off his hand, the hand that at least helped to hold it together, the whole queer fabric that built him in would fall away in a minute and admit the light. It was really a matter of nerves; it was exactly because he was nervous that he *could* go straight; yet if that condition should increase he must surely go wild. He was walking in short on a high ridge, steep down on either side, where the proprieties—once he could face at all remaining there—reduced themselves to his keeping his head. It was Kate who had so perched him, and there came up for him at moments, as he found himself planting one foot exactly before another, a sensible sharpness of irony as to her management of him. It wasn't that she had put him in danger—to be in real danger with her would have had another quality. There glowed for him in fact a kind of rage at what he wasn't having; an exasperation, a resentment, begotten truly by the very impatience of desire, in respect to his postponed and relegated, his so extremely manipulated state. It was beautifully done of her, but what was the real meaning of it unless that he was perpetually bent to her will? His idea from the first, from the very first of his knowing her, had been to be, as the French called it, *bon prince* with her, mindful of the good humour and generosity, the contempt, in the matter of confidence, for small outlays and small savings, that belonged to the man who wasn't generally afraid. There were things enough, goodness knew—for it was the moral of his plight—that he couldn't afford; but what had had a charm for him if not the notion of living handsomely, to make up for it, in another way? of not at all events reading the romance of his existence in a cheap edition. All he had originally felt in her came back to him, was indeed actually as present as ever—how he had admired and envied what he called to himself her pure talent for life, as distinguished from his own, a poor weak thing of the occasion, amateurishly patched up; only it irritated him the more that this was exactly what was now, ever so characteristically, standing out in her.

It was thanks to her pure talent for life, verily, that he was just where he was and that he was above all just *how* he was. The proof of a decent reaction in him against so much passivity was, with no great richness, that he at least knew—knew, that is, how he was, and how little he liked it as a thing accepted in mere helplessness. He was, for the moment, wistful—that above all described it; that was so large a part of the force that, as the autumn afternoon closed in, kept him, on his traghetto, positively throbbing with his question. His question connected itself, even while he stood, with his special smothered soreness, his sense almost of shame; and the soreness and the shame were less as he let himself, with the help of the conditions about him, regard it as serious. It was born, for that matter, partly of the conditions, those conditions that Kate had so almost insolently braved, had been willing, without a pang, to see him ridiculously—ridiculously so far as just complacently—exposed to. How little it *could* be complacently he was to feel with the last thoroughness before he had moved from his point of vantage. His question, as we have called it, was the interesting question of whether he had really no will left. How could he know—that was the point—without putting the matter to the test? It had been right to be *bon prince,* and the joy, something of the pride, of having lived, in spirit, handsomely, was even now compatible with the impulse to look into their account; but he held his breath a little as it came home to him with supreme sharpness that, whereas he had done absolutely everything that Kate had wanted, she had done nothing whatever that he had. So it was in fine that his idea of the test by which he must try that possibility kept referring itself, in the warm early dusk, the approach of the Southern night—"conditions" these, such as we just spoke of—to the glimmer, more and more ghostly as the light failed, of the little white papers on his old green shutters. By the time he looked at his watch he had been for a quarter of an hour at this post of observation and reflexion; but by the time he walked away again he had found his answer to the idea that had grown so importunate. Since a proof of his will was wanted it was indeed very exactly in wait for him—it lurked there on the other side of the Canal. A ferryman at the little pier had from time to time accosted him; but it was a part of the play of his nervousness to turn his back on that facility. He would go over, but he walked, very quickly, round and round, crossing finally by the Rialto. The rooms, in the event, were unoccupied; the ancient padrona was there with her smile all a radiance but her recognition all a fable; the ancient rickety objects too, refined in their shabbiness, amiable in their decay, as to which, on his side, demonstrations were tenderly veracious; so that before he took his way again he had arranged to come in on the morrow.

559

He was amusing about it that evening at dinner—in spite of an odd first impulse, which at the palace quite melted away, to treat it merely as matter for his own satisfaction. This need, this propriety, he had taken for granted even up to the moment of suddenly perceiving, in the course of talk, that the incident would minister to innocent gaiety. Such was quite its effect, with the aid of his picture—an evocation of the quaint, of the humblest rococo, of a Venetian interior in the true old note. He made the point for his hostess that her own high chambers, though they were a thousand grand things, weren't really this; made it in fact with such success that she presently declared it his plain duty to invite her on some near day to tea. She had expressed as yet—he could feel it as felt among them all—no such clear wish to go anywhere, not even to make an effort for a parish feast, or an autumn sunset, nor to descend her staircase for Titian or Gianbellini. It was constantly Densher's view that, as between himself and Kate, things were understood without saying, so that he could catch in her, as she but too freely could in him, innumerable signs of it, the whole soft breath of consciousness meeting and promoting consciousness. This view was so far justified to-night as that Milly's offer to him of her company was to his sense taken up by Kate in spite of her doing nothing to show it. It fell in so perfectly with what she had desired and foretold that she was—and this was what most struck him—sufficiently gratified and blinded by it not to know, from the false quality of his response, from his tone and his very look, which for an instant instinctively sought her own, that he had answered inevitably, almost shamelessly, in a mere time-gaining sense. It gave him on the spot, her failure of perception, almost a beginning of the advantage he had been planning for—that is at least if she too were not darkly dishonest. She might, he was not unaware, have made out, from some deep part of her, the bearing, in respect to herself, of the little fact he had announced; for she was after all capable of that, capable of guessing and yet of simultaneously hiding her guess. It wound him up a turn or two further, none the less, to impute to her now a weakness of vision by which he could himself feel the stronger. Whatever apprehension of his motive in shifting his abode might have brushed her with its wings, she at all events certainly didn't guess that he was giving their friend a hollow promise. That was what she had herself imposed on him; there had been in the prospect from the first a definite particular point at which hollowness, to call it by its least compromising name, would have to begin. Therefore its hour had now charmingly sounded. Whatever in life he had recovered his old rooms for, he had not recovered them to receive Milly Theale: which made no more difference in his expression of happy readiness than if he had been—just what he was trying not to be—fully hardened and fully base. So rapid in fact was the rhythm of his inward drama that the quick vision of impossibility produced in him by his hostess's direct and unexpected appeal had the effect, slightly sinister, of positively scaring him. It gave him a measure of the intensity, the reality of his now mature motive. It prompted in him certainly no quarrel with these things, but it made them as vivid as if they already flushed with success. It was before the flush of success that his heart beat almost to dread. The dread was but the dread of the happiness to be compassed; only that was in itself a symptom. That a visit from Milly should, in this projection of necessities, strike him as of the last incongruity, quite as a hateful idea, and above all as spoiling, should one put it grossly, his game—the adoption of such a view might of course have an identity with one of those numerous ways of being a fool that seemed so to abound for him. It would remain none the less the way to which he should be in advance most reconciled. His mature motive, as to which he allowed himself no grain of illusion, had thus in an hour taken imaginative possession of the place: that precisely was how he saw it seated there, already unpacked and settled, for Milly's innocence, for Milly's beauty, no matter how short a time, to be housed with. There were things she would never recognise, never feel, never catch in the air; but this made no difference in the fact that her brushing against them would do nobody any good. The discrimination and the scruple were for *him*. So he felt all the parts of the case together, while Kate showed admirably as feeling none of them. Of course, however—when hadn't it to be his last word?—Kate was always sublime.

That came up in all connexions during the rest of these first days; came up in especial under pressure of the fact that each time our plighted pair snatched, in its passage, at the good fortune of half an hour together, they were doomed—though Densher felt it as all by *his* act—to spend a part of the rare occasion in wonder at their luck and in study of its queer character. This was the case after he might be supposed to have got, in a manner, used to it; it was the case after the girl—ready always, as we say, with the last word—had given him the benefit of her righting of every wrong appearance, a support familiar to him now in reference to other phases. It was still the case after he possibly might, with a little imagination, as she freely insisted, have made out, by the visible working of the crisis, what idea on Mrs. Lowder's part had determined it. Such as the idea was—and that it suited Kate's own book she openly professed—he had only to see how things were turning out to feel it strikingly justified. Densher's reply to all this vividness was that of course Aunt Maud's intervention hadn't been occult, even for *his* vividness, from the moment she had written him, with characteristic concentration, that if he should see his way to come to Venice for a fortnight she should engage he would find it no blunder. It took Aunt Maud really to do such things in such ways; just as it took him, he was ready to confess, to do such others as he must now strike them all—didn't he?—as committed to. Mrs. Lowder's admonition had been of course a direct reference to what she had said to him at Lancaster Gate before his departure the night Milly had failed them through illness; only it had at least matched that remarkable outbreak in respect to the quantity of good nature it attributed to him. The young man's discussions of his situation—which were confined to Kate; he had none with Aunt Maud herself—suffered a little, it may be divined, by the sense that he couldn't put everything off, as he privately expressed it, on other people. His ears, in solitude, were apt to burn with the reflexion that Mrs. Lowder had simply tested him, seen him as he was and made out what could be done with him. She had had but to whistle for him and he had come. If she had taken for granted his good nature she was as justified as Kate declared. This awkwardness of his conscience, both in respect to his general plasticity, the fruit of his feeling plasticity, within limits, to be a mode of life like another— certainly better than some, and particularly in respect to such confusion as might reign about what he had really come for—this inward ache was not wholly dispelled by the style, charming as that was, of Kate's poetic versions. Even the high wonder and delight of Kate couldn't set him right with himself when there was something quite distinct from these things that kept him wrong.

In default of being right with himself he had meanwhile, for one thing, the interest of seeing—and quite for the first time in his life—whether, on a given occasion, that might be quite so necessary to happiness as was commonly assumed and as he had up to this moment never doubted. He was engaged distinctly in an adventure—he who had never thought himself cut out for them, and it fairly helped him that he was able at moments to say to himself that he mustn't fall below it. At his hotel, alone, by night, or in the course of the few late strolls he was finding time to take through dusky labyrinthine alleys and empty *campi*, overhung with mouldering palaces, where he paused in disgust at his want of ease and where the sound of a rare footstep on the enclosed pavement was like that of a retarded dancer in a banquet-hall deserted—during these interludes he entertained cold views, even to the point, at moments, on the principle that the shortest follies are the best, of thinking of immediate departure as not only possible but as indicated. He had however only to cross again the threshold of Palazzo Leporelli to see all the elements of the business compose, as painters called it, differently. It began to strike him then that departure wouldn't curtail, but would signally coarsen his folly, and that above all, as he hadn't really "begun" anything, had only submitted, consented, but too generously indulged and condoned the beginnings of others, he had no call to treat himself with superstitious rigour. The single thing that was clear in complications was that, whatever happened, one was to behave as a gentleman—to which was added indeed the perhaps slightly less shining truth that complications might sometimes have their tedium beguiled by a study of the question of how a gentleman would behave. This question, I hasten to add, was not in the last resort Densher's greatest worry. Three women were looking to him at once, and, though such a predicament could never be, from the point of view of facility, quite the ideal, it yet had, thank goodness, its immediate workable law. The law was not to be a brute—in return for amiabilities. He hadn't come all the way out from England to be a brute. He hadn't thought of what it might give him to have a fortnight, however handicapped, with Kate in Venice, to be a brute. He hadn't treated Mrs. Lowder as if in responding to her suggestion he had understood her—he hadn't done that either to be a brute. And what he had prepared least of all for such an anti-climax was the prompt and inevitable, the achieved surrender—*as* a gentleman, oh that indubitably!—to the unexpected impression made by poor pale exquisite Milly as the mistress of a grand old palace and the dispenser of an hospitality more irresistible, thanks to all the conditions, than any ever known to him.

This spectacle had for him an eloquence, an authority, a felicity—he scarce knew by what strange name to call it—for which he said to himself that he had not consciously bargained. Her welcome, her frankness, sweetness, sadness, brightness, her disconcerting poetry, as he made shift at moments to call it, helped as it was by the beauty of her whole setting and by the perception at the same time, on the observer's part, that this element gained from her, in a manner, for effect and harmony, as much as it gave—her whole attitude had, to his imagination, meanings that hung about it, waiting upon her, hovering, dropping and quavering forth again, like vague faint snatches, mere ghosts of sound, of old-fashioned melancholy music. It was positively well for him, he had his times of reflecting, that he couldn't put it off on Kate and Mrs. Lowder, as a gentleman so conspicuously wouldn't, that—well, that he had been rather taken in by not having known in advance! There had been now five days of it all without his risking even to Kate alone any hint of what he ought to have known and of what in particular therefore had taken him in. The truth was doubtless that really, when it came to any free handling and naming of things, they were living together, the five of them, in an air in which an ugly effect of "blurting out" might easily be produced. He came back with his friend on each occasion to the blest miracle of renewed propinquity, which had a double virtue in that favouring air. He breathed on it as if he could scarcely believe it, yet the time had passed, in spite of this privilege, without his quite committing himself, for her ear, to any such comment on Milly's high style and state as would have corresponded with the amount of recognition it had produced in him. Behind everything for him was his renewed remembrance, which had fairly become a habit, that he had been the first to know her. This was what they had all insisted on, in her absence, that day at Mrs. Lowder's; and this was in especial what had made him feel its influence on his immediately paying her a second visit. Its influence had been all there, been in the high-hung, rumbling carriage with them, from the moment she took him to drive, covering them in together as if it had been a rug of softest silk. It had worked as a clear connexion with something lodged in the past, something already their own. He had more than once recalled how he had said to himself even at that moment, at some point in the drive, that he was not *there*, not just as he was in so doing it, through Kate and Kate's idea, but through Milly and Milly's own, and through himself and *his* own, unmistakeably—as well as through the little facts, whatever they had amounted to, of his time in New York.

II

There was at last, with everything that made for it, an occasion when he got from Kate, on what she now spoke of as his eternal refrain, an answer of which he was to measure afterwards the precipitating effect. His eternal refrain was the way he came back to the riddle of Mrs. Lowder's view of her profit—a view so hard to reconcile with the chances she gave them to meet. Impatiently, at this, the girl denied the chances, wanting to know from him, with a fine irony that smote him rather straight, whether he felt their opportunities as anything so grand. He looked at her deep in the eyes when she had sounded this note; it was the least he could let her off with for having made him visibly flush. For some reason then, with it, the sharpness dropped out of her tone, which became sweet and sincere. "'Meet,' my dear man," she expressively echoed; "does it strike you that we get, after all, so very much out of our meetings?"

"On the contrary—they're starvation diet. All I mean is—and it's all I've meant from the day I came—that we at least get more than Aunt Maud."

"Ah but you see," Kate replied, "you don't understand what Aunt Maud gets."

"Exactly so—and it's what I don't understand that keeps me so fascinated with the question. *She* gives me no light; she's prodigious. She takes everything as of a natural—!"

"She takes it as 'of a natural' that at this rate I shall be making my reflexions about you. There's every appearance for her," Kate went on, "that what she had made her mind up to as possible is possible; that what she had thought more likely than not to happen is happening. The very essence of her, as you surely by this time have made out for yourself, is that when she adopts a view she—well, to her own sense, really brings the thing about, fairly terrorizes with her view any other, any opposite view, and those, not less, who represent that. I've often thought success comes to her"—Kate continued to study the phenomenon—"by the spirit in her that dares and defies her idea not to prove the right one. One has seen it so again and again, in the face of everything, become the right one."

Densher had for this, as he listened, a smile of the largest response. "Ah my dear child, if you can explain I of course needn't not 'understand.' I'm condemned to that," he on his side presently explained, "only when understanding fails." He took a moment; then he pursued: "Does she think she terrorises *us?*" To which he added while, without immediate speech, Kate but looked over the place: "Does she believe anything so stiff as that you've really changed about me?" He knew now that he was probing the girl deep—something told him so; but that was a reason the more. "Has she got it into her head that you dislike me?"

To this, of a sudden, Kate's answer was strong. "You could yourself easily put it there!"

He wondered. "By telling her so?"

"No," said Kate as with amusement at his simplicity; "I don't ask that of you."

"Oh my dear," Densher laughed, "when you ask, you know, so little—!"

There was a full irony in this, on his own part, that he saw her resist the impulse to take up. "I'm perfectly justified in what I've asked," she quietly returned. "It's doing beautifully for you." Their eyes again intimately met, and the effect was to make her proceed. "You're not a bit unhappy."

"Oh ain't I?" he brought out very roundly.

"It doesn't practically show—which is enough for Aunt Maud. You're wonderful, you're beautiful," Kate said; "and if you really want to know whether I believe you're doing it you may take from me perfectly that I see it coming." With which, by a quick transition, as if she had settled the case, she asked him the hour.

"Oh only twelve-ten"—he had looked at his watch. "We've taken but thirteen minutes; we've time yet."

"Then we must walk. We must go toward them."

Densher, from where they had been standing, measured the long reach of the Square. "They're still in their shop. They're safe for half an hour."

"That shows then, that shows!" said Kate.

This colloquy had taken place in the middle of Piazza San Marco, always, as a great social saloon, a smooth-floored, blue-roofed chamber of amenity, favourable to talk; or rather, to be exact, not in the middle, but at the point where our pair had paused by a common impulse after leaving the great mosque-like church. It rose now, domed and pinnacled, but a little way behind them, and they had in front the vast empty space, enclosed by its arcades, to which at that hour movement and traffic were mostly confined. Venice was at breakfast, the Venice of the visitor and the possible acquaintance, and, except for the parties of importunate pigeons picking up the crumbs of perpetual feasts, their prospect was clear and they could see their companions hadn't yet been, and weren't for a while longer likely to be, disgorged by the lace-shop, in one of the *loggie*, where, shortly before, they had left them for a look-in—the expression was artfully Densher's—at Saint Mark's. Their morning had happened to take such a turn as brought this chance to the surface; yet his allusion, just made to Kate, hadn't been an overstatement of their general opportunity. The worst that could be said of their general opportunity was that it was essentially in presence—in presence of every one; every one consisting at this juncture, in a peopled world, of Susan Shepherd, Aunt Maud and Milly. But the proof how, even in presence, the opportunity could become special was furnished precisely by this view of the compatibility of their comfort with a certain amount of lingering. The others had assented to their not waiting in the shop; it was of course the least the others could do. What had really helped them this morning was the fact that, on his turning up, as he always called it, at the palace, Milly had not, as before, been able to present herself. Custom and use had hitherto seemed fairly established; on his coming round, day after day—eight days had been now so conveniently marked—their friends, Milly's and his, conveniently dispersed and left him to sit with her till luncheon. Such was the perfect operation of the scheme on which he had been, as he phrased it to himself, had out; so that certainly there was that amount of justification for Kate's vision of success. He *had*, for Mrs. Lowder—he couldn't help it while sitting there—the air, which was the thing to be desired, of no absorption in Kate sufficiently deep to be alarming. He had failed their young hostess each morning as little as she had failed him; it was only to-day that she hadn't been well enough to see him.

That had made a mark, all round; the mark was in the way in which, gathered in the room of state, with the place, from the right time, all bright and cool and beflowered, as always, to receive her descent, they—the rest of them—simply looked at each other. It was lurid—lurid, in all probability, for each of them privately—that they had uttered no common regrets. It was strange for our young man above all that, if the poor girl was indisposed to *that* degree, the hush of gravity, of apprehension, of significance of some sort, should be the most the case—that of the guests—could permit itself. The hush, for that matter, continued after the party of four had gone down to the gondola and taken their places in it. Milly had sent them word that she hoped they would go out and enjoy themselves, and this indeed had produced a second remarkable look, a look as of their knowing, one quite as well as the other, what such a message meant as provision for the alternative beguilement of Densher. She wished not to have spoiled his morning, and he had therefore, in civility, to take it as pleasantly patched up. Mrs. Stringham had helped the affair out, Mrs. Stringham who, when it came to that, knew their friend better than any of them. She knew her so well that she knew herself as acting in exquisite compliance with conditions comparatively obscure, approximately awful to them, by not thinking it necessary to stay at home. She had corrected that element of the perfunctory which was the slight fault, for all of them, of the occasion; she had invented a preference for Mrs. Lowder and herself; she had remembered the fond dreams of the visitation of lace that had hitherto always been brushed away by accidents, and it had come up as well for her that Kate had, the day before, spoken of the part played by fatality in her own failure of real acquaintance with the inside of Saint Mark's. Densher's sense of Susan Shepherd's conscious intervention had by this time a corner of his mind all to itself; something that had begun for them at Lancaster Gate was now a sentiment clothed in a shape; her action, ineffably discreet, had at all events a way of affecting him as for the most part subtly, even when not superficially, in his own interest. They were not, as a pair, as a "team," really united; there were too many persons, at least three, and too many things, between them; but meanwhile something was preparing that would draw them closer. He scarce knew what: probably nothing but his finding, at some hour when it would be a service to do so, that she had all the while understood him. He even had a presentiment of a juncture at which the understanding of every one else would fail and this deep little person's alone survive.

Such was to-day, in its freshness, the moral air, as we may say, that hung about our young friends; these had been the small accidents and quiet forces to which they owed the advantage we have seen them in some sort enjoying. It seemed in fact fairly to deepen for them as they stayed their course again; the splendid Square, which had so notoriously, in all the years, witnessed more of the joy of life than any equal area in Europe, furnished them, in their remoteness from earshot, with solitude and security. It was as if, being in possession, they could say what they liked; and it was also as if, in consequence of that, each had an apprehension of what the other wanted to say. It was most of all for them, moreover, as if this very quantity, seated on their lips in the bright historic air, where the only sign for their ears was the flutter of the doves, begot in the heart of each a fear. There might have been a betrayal of that in the way Densher broke the silence resting on her last words. "What did you mean just now that I can do to make Mrs. Lowder believe? For myself, stupidly, if you will, I don't see, from the moment I can't lie to her, what else there is but lying."

Well, she could tell him. "You can say something both handsome and sincere to her about Milly—whom you honestly like so much. That wouldn't be lying; and, coming from you, it would have an effect. You don't, you know, say much about her."

And Kate put before him the fruit of observation. "You don't, you know, speak of her at all."

"And has Aunt Maud," Densher asked, "told you so?" Then as the girl, for answer, only seemed to bethink herself, "You must have extraordinary conversations!" he exclaimed.

Yes, she had bethought herself. "We have extraordinary conversations."

His look, while their eyes met, marked him as disposed to hear more about them; but there was something in her own, apparently, that defeated the opportunity. He questioned her in a moment on a different matter, which had been in his mind a week, yet in respect to which he had had no chance so good as this. "Do you happen to know then, as such wonderful things pass between you, what she makes of the incident, the other day, of Lord Mark's so very superficial visit?—his having spent here, as I gather, but the two or three hours necessary for seeing our friend and yet taken no time at all, since he went off by the same night's train, for seeing any one else. What can she make of his not having waited to see *you*, or to see herself—with all he owes her?"

"Oh of course," said Kate, "she understands. He came to make Milly his offer of marriage—he came for nothing but that. As Milly wholly declined it his business was for the time at an end. He couldn't quite on the spot turn round to make up to *us*."

Kate had looked surprised that, as a matter of taste on such an adventurer's part, Densher shouldn't see it. But Densher was lost in another thought. "Do you mean that when, turning up myself, I found him leaving her, that was what had been taking place between them?"

"Didn't you make it out, my dear?" Kate enquired.

"What sort of a blundering weathercock then *is* he?" the young man went on in his wonder.

"Oh don't make too little of him!" Kate smiled. "Do you pretend that Milly didn't tell you?"

"How great an ass he had made of himself?"

Kate continued to smile. "You *are* in love with her, you know."

He gave her another long look. "Why, since she has refused him, should my opinion of Lord Mark show it? I'm not obliged, however, to think well of him for such treatment of the other persons I've mentioned, and I feel I don't understand from you why Mrs. Lowder should."

"She doesn't—but she doesn't care," Kate explained. "You know perfectly the terms on which lots of London people live together even when they're supposed to live very well. He's not committed to us—he was having his try. Mayn't an unsatisfied man," she asked, "always have his try?"

"And come back afterwards, with confidence in a welcome, to the victim of his inconstancy?"

Kate consented, as for argument, to be thought of as a victim. "Oh but he has *had* his try at *me.* So it's all right."

"Through your also having, you mean, refused him?"

She balanced an instant during which Densher might have just wondered if pure historic truth were to suffer a slight strain. But she dropped on the right side. "I haven't let it come to that. I've been too discouraging. Aunt Maud," she went on—now as lucid as ever—"considers, no doubt, that she has a pledge from him in respect to me; a pledge that would have been broken if Milly had accepted him. As the case stands that makes no difference."

Densher laughed out. "It isn't *his* merit that he has failed."

"It's still his merit, my dear, that he's Lord Mark. He's just what he was, and what he knew he was. It's not for me either to reflect on him after I've so treated him."

"Oh," said Densher impatiently, "you've treated him beautifully."

"I'm glad," she smiled, "that you can still be jealous." But before he could take it up she had more to say. "I don't see why it need puzzle you that Milly's so marked line gratifies Aunt Maud more than anything else can displease her. What does she see but that Milly herself recognises her situation with you as too precious to be spoiled? Such a recognition as that can't but seem to her to involve in some degree your own recognition. Out of which she therefore gets it that the more you have for Milly the less you have for me."

There were moments again—we know that from the first they had been numerous—when he felt with a strange mixed passion the mastery of her mere way of putting things. There was something in it that bent him at once to conviction and to reaction. And this effect, however it be named, now broke into his tone. "Oh if she began to know what I have for you—!"

It wasn't ambiguous, but Kate stood up to it. "Luckily for us we may really consider she doesn't. So successful have we been."

"Well," he presently said, "I take from you what you give me, and I suppose that, to be consistent—to stand on my feet where I do stand at all—I ought to thank you. Only, you know, what you give me seems to me, more than anything else, the larger and larger size of my job. It seems to me more than anything else what you expect of me. It never seems to me somehow what I may expect of *you*. There's so much you *don't* give me."

She appeared to wonder. "And pray what is it I don't—?"

"I give you proof," said Densher. "You give me none."

"What then do you call proof?" she after a moment ventured to ask.

"Your doing something for me."

She considered with surprise. "Am I not doing *this* for you? Do you call this nothing?"

"Nothing at all."

"Ah I risk, my dear, everything for it."

They had strolled slowly further, but he was brought up short. "I thought you exactly contend that, with your aunt so bamboozled, you risk nothing!"

It was the first time since the launching of her wonderful idea that he had seen her at a loss. He judged the next instant moreover that she didn't like it—either the being so or the being seen, for she soon spoke with an impatience that showed her as wounded; an appearance that produced in himself, he no less quickly felt, a sharp pang of indulgence. "What then do you wish me to risk?"

The appeal from danger touched him, but all to make him, as he would have said, worse. "What I wish is to be loved. How can I feel at this rate that I *am*?" Oh she understood him, for all she might so bravely disguise it, and that made him feel straighter than if she hadn't. Deep, always, was his sense of life with her—deep as it had been from the moment of those signs of life that in the dusky London of two winters ago they had originally exchanged. He had never taken her for unguarded, ignorant, weak; and if he put to her a claim for some intenser faith between them this was because he believed it could reach her and she could meet it. "I can go on perhaps," he said, "with help. But I can't go on without."

She looked away from him now, and it showed him how she understood. "We ought to be there—I mean when they come out."

"They *won't* come out—not yet. And I don't care if they do." To which he straightway added, as if to deal with the charge of selfishness that his words, sounding for himself, struck him as enabling her to make: "Why not have done with it all and face the music as we are?" It broke from him in perfect sincerity. "Good God, if you'd only *take* me!"

It brought her eyes round to him again, and he could see how, after all, somewhere deep within, she felt his rebellion more sweet than bitter. Its effect on her spirit and her sense was visibly to hold her an instant. "We've gone too far," she none the less pulled herself together to reply. "Do you want to kill her?"

He had an hesitation that wasn't all candid. "Kill, you mean, Aunt Maud?"

"You know whom I mean. We've told too many lies."

Oh at this his head went up. "I, my dear, have told none!"

He had brought it out with a sharpness that did him good, but he had naturally, none the less, to take the look it made her give him. "Thank you very much."

Her expression, however, failed to check the words that had already risen to his lips. "Rather than lay myself open to the least appearance of it I'll go this very night."

"Then go," said Kate Croy.

He knew after a little, while they walked on again together, that what was in the air for him, and disconcertingly, was not the violence, but much rather the cold quietness, of the way this had come from her. They walked on together, and it was for a minute as if their difference had become of a sudden, in all truth, a split—as if the basis of his departure had been settled. Then, incoherently and still more suddenly, recklessly moreover, since they now might easily, from under the arcades, be observed, he passed his hand into her arm with a force that produced for them another pause. "I'll tell any lie you want, any your idea requires, if you'll only come to me."

"Come to you?"

"Come to me."

"How? Where?"

She spoke low, but there was somehow, for his uncertainty, a wonder in her being so equal to him. "To my rooms, which are perfectly possible, and in taking which, the other day, I had you, as you must have felt, in view. We can arrange it—with two grains of courage. People in our case always arrange it." She listened as for the good information, and there was support for him—since it was a question of his going step by step—in the way she took no refuge in showing herself shocked. He had in truth not expected of her that particular vulgarity, but the absence of it only added the thrill of a deeper reason to his sense of possibilities. For the knowledge of what she was he had absolutely to *see* her now, incapable of refuge, stand there for him in all the light of the day and of his admirable merciless meaning. Her mere listening in fact made him even understand himself as he hadn't yet done. Idea for idea, his own was thus already, and in the germ, beautiful. "There's nothing for me possible but to feel that I'm not a fool. It's all I have to say, but you must know what it means. *With* you I can do it—I'll go as far as you demand or as you will yourself. Without you—I'll be hanged! And I must be sure."

She listened so well that she was really listening after he had ceased to speak. He had kept his grasp of her, drawing her close, and though they had again, for the time, stopped walking, his talk—for others at a distance—might have been, in the matchless place, that of any impressed tourist to any slightly more detached companion. On possessing himself of her arm he had made her turn, so that they faced afresh to Saint Mark's, over the great presence of which his eyes moved while she twiddled her parasol. She now, however, made a motion that confronted them finally with the opposite end. Then only she spoke—"Please take your hand out of my arm." He understood at once: she had made out in the shade of the gallery the issue of the others from their place of purchase. So they went to them side by side, and it was all right. The others had seen them as well and waited for them, complacent enough, under one of the arches. They themselves too—he argued that Kate would argue—looked perfectly ready, decently patient, properly accommodating. They themselves suggested nothing worse—always by Kate's system—than a pair of the children of a supercivilised age making the best of an awkwardness. They didn't nevertheless hurry—that would overdo it; so he had time to feel, as it were, what he felt. He felt, ever so distinctly—it was with this he faced Mrs. Lowder—that he was already in a sense possessed of what he wanted. There was more to come—everything; he had by no means, with his companion, had it all out. Yet what he was possessed of was real—the fact that she hadn't thrown over his lucidity the horrid shadow of cheap reprobation. Of this he had had so sore a fear that its being dispelled was in itself of the nature of bliss. The danger had dropped—it was behind him there in the great sunny space. So far she was good for what he wanted.

III

She was good enough, as it proved, for him to put to her that evening, and with further ground for it, the next sharpest question that had been on his lips in the morning—which his other preoccupation had then, to his consciousness, crowded out. His opportunity was again made, as befell, by his learning from Mrs. Stringham, on arriving, as usual, with the close of day, at the palace, that Milly must fail them again at dinner, but would to all appearance be able to come down later. He had found Susan Shepherd alone in the great saloon, where even more candles than their friend's large common allowance—she grew daily more splendid; they were all struck with it and chaffed her about it—lighted up the pervasive mystery of Style. He had thus five minutes with the good lady before Mrs. Lowder and Kate appeared—minutes illumined indeed to a longer reach than by the number of Milly's candles.

"*May* she come down—ought she if she isn't really up to it?"

He had asked that in the wonderment always stirred in him by glimpses—rare as were these—of the inner truth about the girl. There was of course a question of health—it was in the air, it was in the ground he trod, in the food he tasted, in the sounds he heard, it was everywhere. But it was everywhere with the effect of a request to him—to his very delicacy, to the common discretion of others as well as his own—that no allusion to it should be made. There had practically been none, that morning, on her explained non-appearance—the absence of it, as we know, quite monstrous and awkward; and this passage with Mrs. Stringham offered him his first licence to open his eyes. He had gladly enough held them closed; all the more that his doing so performed for his own spirit a useful function. If he positively wanted not to be brought up with his nose against Milly's facts, what better proof could he have that his conduct was marked by straightness? It was perhaps pathetic for her, and for himself was perhaps even ridiculous; but he hadn't even the amount of curiosity that he would have had about an ordinary friend. He might have shaken himself at moments to try, for a sort of dry decency, to have it; but that too, it appeared, wouldn't come. In what therefore was the duplicity? He was at least sure about his feelings—it being so established that he had none at all. They were all for Kate, without a feather's weight to spare. He was acting for Kate—not, by the deviation of an inch, for her friend. He was accordingly not interested, for had he been interested he would have cared, and had he cared he would have wanted to know. Had he wanted to know he wouldn't have been purely passive, and it was his pure passivity that had to represent his dignity and his honour. His dignity and his honour, at the same time, let us add, fortunately fell short to-night of spoiling his little talk with Susan Shepherd. One glimpse—it was as if she had wished to give him that; and it was as if, for himself, on current terms, he could oblige her by accepting it. She not only permitted, she fairly invited him to open his eyes. "I'm so glad you're here." It was no answer to his question, but it had for the moment to serve. And the rest was fully to come.

He smiled at her and presently found himself, as a kind of consequence of communion with her, talking her own language. "It's a very wonderful experience."

"Well"—and her raised face shone up at him—"that's all I want you to feel about it. If I weren't afraid," she added, "there are things I should like to say to you."

"And what are you afraid of, please?" he encouragingly asked.

"Of other things that I may possibly spoil. Besides, I don't, you know, seem to have the chance. You're always, you know, *with* her."

He was strangely supported, it struck him, in his fixed smile; which was the more fixed as he felt in these last words an exact description of his course. It was an odd thing to have come to, but he was always with her. "Ah," he none the less smiled, "I'm not with her now."

"No—and I'm so glad, since I get this from it. She's ever so much better."

"Better? Then she *has* been worse?"

Mrs. Stringham waited. "She has been marvellous—that's what she has been. She *is* marvellous. But she's really better."

"Oh then if she's really better—!" But he checked himself, wanting only to be easy about it and above all not to appear engaged to the point of mystification. "We shall miss her the more at dinner."

Susan Shepherd, however, was all there for him. "She's keeping herself. You'll see. You'll not really need to miss anything. There's to be a little party."

"Ah I do see—by this aggravated grandeur."

"Well, it *is* lovely, isn't it? I want the whole thing. She's lodged for the first time as she ought, from her type, to be; and doing it—I mean bringing out all the glory of the place—makes her really happy. It's a Veronese picture, as near as can be—with me as the inevitable dwarf, the small blackamoor, put into a corner of the foreground for effect. If I only had a hawk or a hound or something of that sort I should do the scene more honour. The old housekeeper, the woman in charge here, has a big red cockatoo that I might borrow and perch on my thumb for the evening." These explanations and sundry others Mrs. Stringham gave, though not all with the result of making him feel that the picture closed him in. What part was there for *him*, with his attitude that lacked the highest style, in a composition in which everything else would have it? "They won't, however, be at dinner, the few people she expects—they come round afterwards from their respective hotels; and Sir Luke Strett and his niece, the principal ones, will have arrived from London but an hour or two ago. It's for *him* she has wanted to do something—to let it begin at once. We shall see more of him, because she likes him; and I'm so glad—she'll be glad too—that *you're* to see him." The good lady, in connexion with it, was urgent, was almost unnaturally bright. "So I greatly hope—!" But her hope fairly lost itself in the wide light of her cheer.

He considered a little this appearance, while she let him, he thought, into still more knowledge than she uttered. "What is it you hope?"

"Well, that you'll stay on."

"Do you mean after dinner?" She meant, he seemed to feel, so much that he could scarce tell where it ended or began.

"Oh that, of course. Why we're to have music—beautiful instruments and songs; and not Tasso declaimed as in the guide-books either. She has arranged it—or at least I have. That is Eugenio has. Besides, you're in the picture."

"Oh—I!" said Densher almost with the gravity of a real protest.

"You'll be the grand young man who surpasses the others and holds up his head and the wine-cup. What we hope," Mrs. Stringham pursued, "is that you'll be faithful to us—that you've not come for a mere foolish few days."

Densher's more private and particular shabby realities turned, without comfort, he was conscious, at this touch, in the artificial repose he had in his anxiety about them but half-managed to induce. The way smooth ladies, travelling for their pleasure and housed in Veronese pictures, talked to plain embarrassed working-men, engaged in an unprecedented sacrifice of time and of the opportunity for modest acquisition! The things they took for granted and the general misery of explaining! He couldn't tell them how he had tried to work, how it was partly what he had moved into rooms for, only to find himself, almost for the first time in his life, stricken and sterile; because that would give them a false view of the source of his restlessness, if not of the degree of it. It would operate, indirectly perhaps, but infallibly, to add to that weight as of expected performance which these very moments with Mrs. Stringham caused more and more to settle on his heart. He had incurred it, the expectation of performance; the thing was done, and there was no use talking; again, again the cold breath of it was in the air. So there he was. And at best he floundered. "I'm afraid you won't understand when I say I've very tiresome things to consider. Botherations, necessities at home. The pinch, the pressure in London."

But she understood in perfection; she rose to the pinch and the pressure and showed how they had been her own very element. "Oh the daily task and the daily wage, the golden guerdon or reward? No one knows better than I how they haunt one in the flight of the precious deceiving days. Aren't they just what I myself have given up? I've given up all to follow *her*. I wish you could feel as I do. And can't you," she asked, "write about Venice?"

He very nearly wished, for the minute, that he could feel as she did; and he smiled for her kindly. "Do *you* write about Venice?"

"No; but I would—oh wouldn't I?—if I hadn't so completely given up. She's, you know, my princess, and to one's princess—"

"One makes the whole sacrifice?"

"Precisely. There you are!"

It pressed on him with this that never had a man been in so many places at once. "I quite understand that she's yours. Only you see she's not mine." He felt he could somehow, for honesty, risk that, as he had the moral certainty she wouldn't repeat it and least of all to Mrs. Lowder, who would find in it a disturbing implication. This was part of what he liked in the good lady, that she didn't repeat, and also that she gave him a delicate sense of her shyly wishing him to know it. That was in itself a hint of possibilities between them, of a relation, beneficent and elastic for him, which wouldn't engage him further than he could see. Yet even as he afresh made this out he felt how strange it all was. She wanted, Susan Shepherd then, as appeared, the same thing Kate wanted, only wanted it, as still further appeared, in so different a way and from a motive so different, even though scarce less deep. Then Mrs. Lowder wanted, by so odd an evolution of her exuberance, exactly what each of the others did; and he was between them all, he was in the midst. Such perceptions made occasions—well, occasions for fairly wondering if it mightn't be best just to consent, luxuriously, to *be* the ass the whole thing involved. Trying not to be and yet keeping in it was of the two things the more asinine. He was glad there was no male witness; it was a circle of petticoats; he shouldn't have liked a man to see him. He only had for a moment a sharp thought of Sir Luke Strett, the great master of the knife whom Kate in London had spoken of Milly as in commerce with, and whose renewed intervention at such a distance, just announced to him, required some accounting for. He had a vision of great London surgeons—if this one was a surgeon—as incisive all round; so that he should perhaps after all not wholly escape the ironic attention of his own sex. The most he might be able to do was not to care; while he was trying not to he could take that in. It was a train, however, that brought up the vision of Lord Mark as well. Lord Mark had caught him twice in the fact—the fact of his absurd posture; and that made a second male. But it was comparatively easy not to mind Lord Mark.

His companion had before this taken him up, and in a tone to confirm her discretion, on the matter of Milly's not being his princess. "Of course she's not. You must do something first."

Densher gave it his thought. "Wouldn't it be rather *she* who must?"

It had more than he intended the effect of bringing her to a stand. "I see. No doubt, if one takes it so." Her cheer was for the time in eclipse, and she looked over the place, avoiding his eyes, as in the wonder of what Milly could do. "And yet she has wanted to be kind."

It made him on the spot feel a brute. "Of course she has. No one could be more charming. She has treated me as if *I* were somebody. Call her my hostess as I've never had nor imagined a hostess, and I'm with you altogether. Of course," he added in the right spirit for her, "I do see that it's quite court life."

She promptly showed how this was almost all she wanted of him. "That's all I mean, if you understand it of such a court as never was: one of the courts of heaven, the court of a reigning seraph, a sort of a vice-queen of an angel. That will do perfectly."

"Oh well then I grant it. Only court life as a general thing, you know," he observed, "isn't supposed to pay."

"Yes, one has read; but this is beyond any book. That's just the beauty here; it's why she's the great and only princess. With her, at her court," said Mrs. Stringham, "it does pay." Then as if she had quite settled it for him: "You'll see for yourself."

He waited a moment, but said nothing to discourage her. "I think you were right just now. One must do something first."

"Well, you've done something."

"No—I don't see that. I can do more."

Oh well, she seemed to say, if he would have it so! "You can do everything, you know."

"Everything" was rather too much for him to take up gravely, and he modestly let it alone, speaking the next moment, to avert fatuity, of a different but a related matter. "Why has she sent for Sir Luke Strett if, as you tell me, she's so much better?"

"She hasn't sent. He has come of himself," Mrs. Stringham explained. "He has wanted to come."

"Isn't that rather worse then—if it means he mayn't be easy?"

"He was coming, from the first, for his holiday. She has known that these several weeks." After which Mrs. Stringham added: "You can *make* him easy."

"*I* can?" he candidly wondered. It was truly the circle of petticoats. "What have I to do with it for a man like that?"

"How do you know," said his friend, "what he's like? He's not like any one you've ever seen. He's a great beneficent being."

"Ah then he can do without me. I've no call, as an outsider, to meddle."

"Tell him, all the same," Mrs. Stringham urged, "what you think."

"What I think of Miss Theale?" Densher stared. It was, as they said, a large order. But he found the right note. "It's none of his business."

It did seem a moment for Mrs. Stringham too the right note. She fixed him at least with an expression still bright, but searching, that showed almost to excess what she saw in it; though what this might be he was not to make out till afterwards. "Say *that* to him then. Anything will do for him as a means of getting at you."

"And why should he get at me?"

"Give him a chance to. Let him talk to you. Then you'll see."

All of which, on Mrs. Stringham's part, sharpened his sense of immersion in an element rather more strangely than agreeably warm—a sense that was moreover, during the next two or three hours, to be fed to satiety by several other impressions. Milly came down after dinner, half a dozen friends—objects of interest mainly, it appeared, to the ladies of Lancaster Gate—having by that time arrived; and with this call on her attention, the further call of her musicians ushered by Eugenio, but personally and separately welcomed, and the supreme opportunity offered in the arrival of the great doctor, who came last of all, he felt her diffuse in wide warm waves the spell of a general, a beatific mildness. There was a deeper depth of it, doubtless, for some than for others; what he in particular knew of it was that he seemed to stand in it up to his neck. He moved about in it and it made no plash; he floated, he noiselessly swam in it, and they were all together, for that matter, like fishes in a crystal pool. The effect of the place, the beauty of the scene, had probably much to do with it; the golden grace of the high rooms, chambers of art in themselves, took care, as an influence, of the general manner, and made people bland without making them solemn. They were only people, as Mrs. Stringham had said, staying for the week or two at the inns, people who during the day had fingered their Baedekers, gaped at their frescoes and differed, over fractions of francs, with their gondoliers. But Milly, let loose among them in a wonderful white dress, brought them somehow into relation with something that made them more finely genial; so that if the Veronese picture of which he had talked with Mrs. Stringham was not quite constituted, the comparative prose of the previous hours, the traces of insensibility qualified by "beating down," were at last almost nobly disowned. There was perhaps something for him in the accident of his seeing her for the first time in white, but she hadn't yet had occasion—circulating with a clearness intensified—to strike him as so happily pervasive. She was different, younger, fairer, with the colour of her braided hair more than ever a not altogether lucky challenge to attention; yet he was loth wholly to explain it by her having quitted this once, for some obscure yet doubtless charming reason, her almost monastic, her hitherto inveterate black. Much as the change did for the value of her presence, she had never yet, when all was said, made it for *him*; and he was not to fail of the further amusement of judging her determined in the matter by Sir Luke Strett's visit. If he could in this connexion have felt jealous of Sir Luke Strett, whose strong face and type, less assimilated by the scene perhaps than any others, he was anon to study from the other side of the saloon, that would doubtless have been most amusing of all. But he couldn't be invidious, even to profit by so high a tide; he felt himself too much "in" it, as he might have said: a moment's reflexion put him more in than any one. The way Milly neglected him for other cares while Kate and Mrs. Lowder, without so much as the attenuation of a joke, introduced him to English ladies—that was itself a proof; for nothing really of so close a communion had up to this time passed between them as the single bright look and the three gay words (all ostensibly of the last lightness) with which her confessed consciousness brushed by him.

She was acquitting herself to-night as hostess, he could see, under some supreme idea, an inspiration which was half her nerves and half an inevitable harmony; but what he especially recognised was the character that had already several times broken out in her and that she so oddly appeared able, by choice or by instinctive affinity, to keep down or to display. She was the American girl as he had originally found her—found her at certain moments, it was true, in New York, more than at certain others; she was the American girl as, still more than then, he had seen her on the day of her meeting him in London and in Kate's company. It affected him as a large though queer social resource in her—such as a man, for instance, to his diminution, would never in the world be able to command; and he wouldn't have known whether to see it in an extension or a contraction of "personality," taking it as he did most directly for a confounding extension of surface. Clearly too it was the right thing this evening all round: that came out for him in a word from Kate as she approached him to wreak on him a second introduction. He had under cover of the music melted away from the lady toward whom she had first pushed him; and there was something in her to affect him as telling evasively a tale of their talk in the Piazza. To what did she want to coerce him as a form of penalty for what he had done to her there? It was thus in contact uppermost for him that he had done something; not only caused her perfect intelligence to act in his interest, but left her unable to get away, by any mere private effort, from his inattackable logic. With him thus in presence, and near him—and it had been as unmistakeable through dinner—there was no getting away for her at all, there was less of it than ever: so she could only either deal with the question straight, either frankly yield or ineffectually struggle or insincerely argue, or else merely express herself by following up the advantage she did possess. It was part of that advantage for the hour—a brief fallacious makeweight to his pressure—that there were plenty of things left in which he must feel her will. They only told him, these indications, how much she was, in such close quarters, feeling his; and it was enough for him again that her very aspect, as great a variation in its way as Milly's own, gave him back the sense of his action. It had never yet in life been granted him to know, almost materially to taste, as he could do in these minutes, the state of what was vulgarly called conquest. He had lived long enough to have been on occasion "liked," but it had never begun to be allowed him to be liked to any such tune in any such quarter. It was a liking greater than Milly's—or it would be: he felt it in him to answer for that. So at all events he read the case while he noted that Kate was somehow—for Kate—wanting in lustre. As a striking young presence she was practically superseded; of the mildness that Milly diffused she had assimilated all her share; she might fairly have been dressed to-night in the little black frock, superficially indistinguishable, that Milly had laid aside. This represented, he perceived, the opposite pole from such an effect as that of her wonderful entrance, under her aunt's eyes—he had never forgotten it—the day of their younger friend's failure at Lancaster Gate. She was, in her accepted effacement—it was actually her acceptance that made the beauty and repaired the damage—under her aunt's eyes now; but whose eyes were not effectually preoccupied? It struck him none the less certainly that almost the first thing she said to him showed an exquisite attempt to appear if not unconvinced at least self-possessed.

"Don't you think her good enough *now?*" Almost heedless of the danger of overt freedoms, she eyed Milly from where they stood, noted her in renewed talk, over her further wishes, with the members of her little orchestra, who had approached her with demonstrations of deference enlivened by native humours—things quite in the line of old Venetian comedy. The girl's idea of music had been happy—a real solvent of shyness, yet not drastic; thanks to the intermissions, discretions, a general habit of mercy to gathered barbarians, that reflected the good manners of its interpreters, representatives though these might be but of the order in which taste was natural and melody rank. It was easy at all events to answer Kate. "Ah my dear, you know how good I think her!"

"But she's *too* nice," Kate returned with appreciation. "Everything suits her so—especially her pearls. They go so with her old lace. I'll trouble you really to look at them." Densher, though aware he had seen them before, had perhaps not "really" looked at them, and had thus not done justice to the embodied poetry—his mind, for Milly's aspects, kept coming back to that— which owed them part of its style. Kate's face, as she considered them, struck him: the long, priceless chain, wound twice round the neck, hung, heavy and pure, down the front of the wearer's breast—so far down that Milly's trick, evidently unconscious, of holding and vaguely fingering and entwining a part of it, conduced presumably to convenience. "She's a dove," Kate went on, "and one somehow doesn't think of doves as bejewelled. Yet they suit her down to the ground."

"Yes—down to the ground is the word." Densher saw now how they suited her, but was perhaps still more aware of something intense in his companion's feeling about them. Milly was indeed a dove; this was the figure, though it most applied to her spirit. Yet he knew in a moment that Kate was just now, for reasons hidden from him, exceptionally under the impression of that element of wealth in her which was a power, which was a great power, and which was dove-like only so far as one remembered that doves have wings and wondrous flights, have them as well as tender tints and soft sounds. It even came to him dimly that such wings could in a given case—*had*, truly, in the case with which he was concerned—spread themselves for protection. Hadn't they, for that matter, lately taken an inordinate reach, and weren't Kate and Mrs. Lowder, weren't Susan Shepherd and he, wasn't he in particular, nestling under them to a great increase of immediate ease? All this was a brighter blur in the general light, out of which he heard Kate presently going on.

"Pearls have such a magic that they suit every one."

"They would uncommonly suit you," he frankly returned.

"Oh yes, I see myself!"

As she saw herself, suddenly, he saw her—she would have been splendid; and with it he felt more what she was thinking of. Milly's royal ornament had—under pressure now not wholly occult—taken on the character of a symbol of differences, differences of which the vision was actually in Kate's face. It might have been in her face too that, well as she certainly would look in pearls, pearls were exactly what Merton Densher would never be able to give her. Wasn't *that* the great difference that Milly to-night symbolised? She unconsciously represented to Kate, and Kate took it in at every pore, that there was nobody with whom she had less in common than a remarkably handsome girl married to a man unable to make her on any such lines as that the least little present. Of these absurdities, however, it was not till afterwards that Densher thought. He could think now, to any purpose, only of what Mrs. Stringham had said to him before dinner. He could but come back to his friend's question of a minute ago. "She's certainly good enough, as you call it, in the sense that I'm assured she's better. Mrs. Stringham, an hour or two since, was in great feather to me about it. She evidently believes her better."

"Well, if they choose to call it so—!"

"And what do *you* call it—as against them?"

"I don't call it anything to any one but you. I'm not 'against' them!" Kate added as with just a fresh breath of impatience for all he had to be taught.

"That's what I'm talking about," he said. "What do you call it to me?"

It made her wait a little. "She isn't better. She's worse. But that has nothing to do with it."

"Nothing to do?" He wondered.

But she was clear. "Nothing to do with us. Except of course that we're doing our best for her. We're making her want to live." And Kate again watched her. "To-night she does want to live." She spoke with a kindness that had the strange property of striking him as inconsequent—so much, and doubtless so unjustly, had all her clearness been an implication of the hard. "It's wonderful. It's beautiful."

"It's beautiful indeed."

He hated somehow the helplessness of his own note; but she had given it no heed. "She's doing it for *him*"—and she nodded in the direction of Milly's medical visitor. "She wants to be for him at her best. But she can't deceive him."

Densher had been looking too; which made him say in a moment: "And do you think *you* can? I mean, if he's to be with us here, about your sentiments. If Aunt Maud's so thick with him—!"

Aunt Maud now occupied in fact a place at his side and was visibly doing her best to entertain him, though this failed to prevent such a direction of his own eyes—determined, in the way such things happen, precisely by the attention of the others—as Densher became aware of and as Kate promptly marked. "He's looking at *you*. He wants to speak to you."

"So Mrs. Stringham," the young man laughed, "advised me he would."

"Then let him. Be right with him. I don't need," Kate went on in answer to the previous question, "to deceive him. Aunt Maud, if it's necessary, will do that. I mean that, knowing nothing about me, he can see me only as she sees me. She sees me now so well. He has nothing to do with me."

"Except to reprobate you," Densher suggested.

"For not caring for *you?* Perfectly. As a brilliant young man driven by it into your relation with Milly—as all *that* I leave you to him."

"Well," said Densher sincerely enough, "I think I can thank you for leaving me to some one easier perhaps with me than yourself."

She had been looking about again meanwhile, the lady having changed her place, for the friend of Mrs. Lowder's to whom she had spoken of introducing him. "All the more reason why I should commit you then to Lady Wells."

"Oh but wait." It was not only that he distinguished Lady Wells from afar, that she inspired him with no eagerness, and that, somewhere at the back of his head, he was fairly aware of the question, in germ, of whether this was the kind of person he should be involved with when they were married. It was furthermore that the consciousness of something he had not got from Kate in the morning, and that logically much concerned him, had been made more keen by these very moments—to say nothing of the consciousness that, with their general smallness of opportunity, he must squeeze each stray instant hard. If Aunt Maud, over there with Sir Luke, noted him as a little "attentive," that might pass for a futile demonstration on the part of a gentleman who had to confess to having, not very gracefully, changed his mind. Besides, just now, he didn't care for Aunt Maud except in so far as he was immediately to show. "How can Mrs. Lowder think me disposed of with any finality, if I'm disposed of only to a girl who's dying? If you're right about that, about the state of the case, you're wrong about Mrs. Lowder's being squared. If Milly, as you say," he lucidly pursued, "can't deceive a great surgeon, or whatever, the great surgeon won't deceive other people—not those, that is, who are closely concerned. He won't at any rate deceive Mrs. Stringham, who's Milly's greatest friend; and it will be very odd if Mrs. Stringham deceives Aunt Maud, who's her own."

Kate showed him at this the cold glow of an idea that really was worth his having kept her for. "Why will it be odd? I marvel at your seeing your way so little."

Mere curiosity even, about his companion, had now for him its quick, its slightly quaking intensities. He had compared her once, we know, to a "new book," an uncut volume of the highest, the rarest quality; and his emotion (to justify that) was again and again like the thrill of turning the page. "Well, you know how deeply I marvel at the way *you* see it!"

"It doesn't in the least follow," Kate went on, "that anything in the nature of what you call deception on Mrs. Stringham's part will be what you call odd. Why shouldn't she hide the truth?"

"From Mrs. Lowder?" Densher stared. "Why should she?"

"To please you."

"And how in the world can it please me?"

Kate turned her head away as if really at last almost tired of his density. But she looked at him again as she spoke. "Well then to please Milly." And before he could question: "Don't you feel by this time that there's nothing Susan Shepherd won't do for you?"

He had verily after an instant to take it in, so sharply it corresponded with the good lady's recent reception of him. It was queerer than anything again, the way they all came together round him. But that was an old story, and Kate's multiplied lights led him on and on. It was with a reserve, however, that he confessed this. "She's ever so kind. Only her view of the right thing may not be the same as yours."

"How can it be anything different if it's the view of serving you?"

Densher for an instant, but only for an instant, hung fire. "Oh the difficulty is that I don't, upon my honour, even yet quite make out how yours does serve me."

"It helps you—put it then," said Kate very simply—"to serve *me*. It gains you time."

"Time for what?"

"For everything!" She spoke at first, once more, with impatience; then as usual she qualified. "For anything that may happen."

Densher had a smile, but he felt it himself as strained. "You're cryptic, love!"

It made her keep her eyes on him, and he could thus see that, by one of those incalculable motions in her without which she wouldn't have been a quarter so interesting, they half-filled with tears from some source he had too roughly touched. "I'm taking a trouble for you I never dreamed I should take for any human creature."

Oh it went home, making him flush for it; yet he soon enough felt his reply on his lips. "Well, isn't my whole insistence to you now that I can conjure trouble away?" And he let it, his insistence, come out again; it had so constantly had, all the week, but its step or two to make. "There *need* be none whatever between us. There need be nothing but our sense of each other."

It had only the effect at first that her eyes grew dry while she took up again one of the so numerous links in her close chain. "You can tell her anything you like, anything whatever."

"Mrs. Stringham? I *have* nothing to tell her."

"You can tell her about *us*. I mean," she wonderfully pursued, "that you do still like me."

It was indeed so wonderful that it amused him. "Only not that you still like me."

She let his amusement pass. "I'm absolutely certain she wouldn't repeat it."

"I see. To Aunt Maud."

"You don't quite see. Neither to Aunt Maud nor to any one else." Kate then, he saw, was always seeing Milly much more, after all, than he was; and she showed it again as she went on. "*There*, accordingly, is your time."

She did at last make him think, and it was fairly as if light broke, though not quite all at once. "You must let me say I *do* see. Time for something in particular that I understand you regard as possible. Time too that, I further understand, is time for you as well."

"Time indeed for me as well." And encouraged visibly by his glow of concentration, she looked at him as through the air she had painfully made clear. Yet she was still on her guard. "Don't think, however, I'll do all the work for you. If you want things named you must name them."

He had quite, within the minute, been turning names over; and there was only one, which at last stared at him there dreadful, that properly fitted. "Since she's to die I'm to marry her?"

It struck him even at the moment as fine in her that she met it with no wincing nor mincing. She might for the grace of silence, for favour to their conditions, have only answered him with her eyes. But her lips bravely moved. "To marry her."

"So that when her death has taken place I shall in the natural course have money?"

It was before him enough now, and he had nothing more to ask; he had only to turn, on the spot, considerably cold with the thought that all along—to his stupidity, his timidity—it had been, it had been only, what she meant. Now that he was in possession moreover she couldn't forbear, strangely enough, to pronounce the words she hadn't pronounced: they broke through her controlled and colourless voice as if she should be ashamed, to the very end, to have flinched. "You'll in the natural course have money. We shall in the natural course be free."

"Oh, oh, oh!" Densher softly murmured.

"Yes, yes, yes." But she broke off. "Come to Lady Wells."

He never budged—there was too much else. "I'm to propose it then—marriage—on the spot?"

There was no ironic sound he needed to give it; the more simply he spoke the more he seemed ironic. But she remained consummately proof. "Oh I can't go into that with you, and from the moment you don't wash your hands of me I don't think you ought to ask me. You must act as you like and as you can."

He thought again. "I'm far—as I sufficiently showed you this morning—from washing my hands of you."

"Then," said Kate, "it's all right."

"All right?" His eagerness flamed. "You'll come?"

But he had had to see in a moment that it wasn't what she meant. "You'll have a free hand, a clear field, a chance—well, quite ideal."

"Your descriptions"—her "ideal" was such a touch!—"are prodigious. And what I don't make out is how, caring for me, you can like it."

"I don't like it, but I'm a person, thank goodness, who can do what I don't like."

It wasn't till afterwards that, going back to it, he was to read into this speech a kind of heroic ring, a note of character that belittled his own incapacity for action. Yet he saw indeed even at the time the greatness of knowing so well what one wanted. At the time too, moreover, he next reflected that he after all knew what *he* did. But something else on his lips was uppermost. "What I don't make out then is how you can even bear it."

"Well, when you know me better you'll find out how much I can bear." And she went on before he could take up, as it were, her too many implications. That it was left to him to know her, spiritually, "better" after his long sacrifice to knowledge—this for instance was a truth he hadn't been ready to receive so full in the face. She had mystified him enough, heaven knew, but that was rather by his own generosity than by hers. And what, with it, did she seem to suggest she might incur at his hands? In spite of these questions she was carrying him on. "All you'll have to do will be to stay."

"And proceed to my business under your eyes?"

"Oh dear no—we shall go."

"'Go?'" he wondered. "Go when, go where?"

"In a day or two—straight home. Aunt Maud wishes it now."

It gave him all he could take in to think of. "Then what becomes of Miss Theale?"

"What I tell you. She stays on, and you stay with her."

He stared. "All alone?"

She had a smile that was apparently for his tone. "You're old enough—with plenty of Mrs. Stringham."

Nothing might have been so odd for him now, could he have measured it, as his being able to feel, quite while he drew from her these successive cues, that he was essentially "seeing what she would say"—an instinct compatible for him therefore with that absence of a need to know her better to which she had a moment before done injustice. If it hadn't been appearing to him in gleams that she would somewhere break down, he probably couldn't have gone on. Still, as she wasn't breaking down there was nothing for him but to continue. "Is your going Mrs. Lowder's idea?"

"Very much indeed. Of course again you see what it does for us. And I don't," she added, "refer only to our going, but to Aunt Maud's view of the general propriety of it."

"I see again, as you say," Densher said after a moment. "It makes everything fit."

"Everything."

The word, for a little, held the air, and he might have seemed the while to be looking, by no means dimly now, at all it stood for. But he had in fact been looking at something else. "You leave her here then to die?"

"Ah she believes she won't die. Not if you stay. I mean," Kate explained, "Aunt Maud believes."

"And that's all that's necessary?"

Still indeed she didn't break down. "Didn't we long ago agree that what she believes is the principal thing for us?"

He recalled it, under her eyes, but it came as from long ago. "Oh yes. I can't deny it." Then he added: "So that if I stay—"

"It won't"—she was prompt—"be our fault."

"If Mrs. Lowder still, you mean, suspects us?"

"If she still suspects us. But she won't."

Kate gave it an emphasis that might have appeared to leave him nothing more; and he might in fact well have found nothing if he hadn't presently found: "But what if she doesn't accept me?"

It produced in her a look of weariness that made the patience of her tone the next moment touch him. "You can but try."

"Naturally I can but try. Only, you see, one has to try a little hard to propose to a dying girl."

"She isn't for you as if she's dying." It had determined in Kate the flash of *justesse* he could perhaps most, on consideration, have admired, since her retort touched the truth. There before him was the fact of how Milly to-night impressed him, and his companion, with her eyes in his own and pursuing his impression to the depths of them, literally now perched on the fact in triumph. She turned her head to where their friend was again in range, and it made him turn his, so that they watched a minute in concert. Milly, from the other side, happened at the moment to notice them, and she sent across toward them in response all the candour of her smile, the lustre of her pearls, the value of her life, the essence of her wealth. It brought them together again with faces made fairly grave by the reality she put into their plan. Kate herself grew a little pale for it, and they had for a time only a silence. The music, however, gay and vociferous, had broken out afresh and protected more than interrupted them. When Densher at last spoke it was under cover.

"I might stay, you know, without trying."

"Oh to stay *is* to try."

"To have for herself, you mean, the appearance of it?"

"I don't see how you can have the appearance more."

Densher waited. "You think it then possible she may *offer* marriage?"

"I can't think—if you really want to know—what she may *not* offer!"

"In the manner of princesses, who do such things?"

"In any manner you like. So be prepared."

Well, he looked as if he almost were. "It will be for me then to accept. But that's the way it must come."

Kate's silence, so far, let it pass; but she presently said: "You'll, on your honour, stay then?"

His answer made her wait, but when it came it was distinct. "Without you, you mean?"

"Without us."

"And you yourselves go at latest—?"

"Not later than Thursday."

It made three days. "Well," he said, "I'll stay, on my honour, if you'll come to me. On your honour."

Again, as before, this made her momentarily rigid, with a rigour out of which, at a loss, she vaguely cast about her. Her rigour was more to him, nevertheless, than all her readiness; for her readiness was the woman herself, and this other thing a mask, a stop-gap and a "dodge." She cast about, however, as happened, and not for the instant in vain. Her eyes, turned over the room, caught at a pretext. "Lady Wells is tired of waiting: she's coming—see—to *us*."

Densher saw in fact, but there was a distance for their visitor to cross, and he still had time. "If you decline to understand me I wholly decline to understand you. I'll do nothing."

"Nothing?" It was as if she tried for the minute to plead.

"I'll do nothing. I'll go off before you. I'll go to-morrow."

He was to have afterwards the sense of her having then, as the phrase was—and for vulgar triumphs too—seen he meant it. She looked again at Lady Wells, who was nearer, but she quickly came back. "And if I do understand?"

"I'll do everything."

She found anew a pretext in her approaching friend: he was fairly playing with her pride. He had never, he then knew, tasted, in all his relation with her, of anything so sharp—too sharp for mere sweetness—as the vividness with which he saw himself master in the conflict. "Well, I understand."

"On your honour?"

"On my honour."

"You'll come?"

"I'll come."

BOOK NINTH

I

It was after they had gone that he truly felt the difference, which was most to be felt moreover in his faded old rooms. He had recovered from the first a part of his attachment to this scene of contemplation, within sight, as it was, of the Rialto bridge, on the hither side of that arch of associations and the left going up the Canal; he had seen it in a particular light, to which, more and more, his mind and his hands adjusted it; but the interest the place now wore for him had risen at a bound, becoming a force that, on the spot, completely engaged and absorbed him, and relief from which—if relief was the name—he could find only by getting away and out of reach. What had come to pass within his walls lingered there as an obsession importunate to all his senses; it lived again, as a cluster of pleasant memories, at every hour and in every object; it made everything but itself irrelevant and tasteless. It remained, in a word, a conscious watchful presence, active on its own side, for ever to be reckoned with, in face of which the effort at detachment was scarcely less futile than frivolous. Kate had come to him; it was only once— and this not from any failure of their need, but from such impossibilities, for bravery alike and for subtlety, as there was at the last no blinking; yet she had come, that once, to stay, as people called it; and what survived of her, what reminded and insisted, was something he couldn't have banished if he had wished. Luckily he didn't wish, even though there might be for a man almost a shade of the awful in so unqualified a consequence of his act. It had simply *worked*, his idea, the idea he had made her accept; and all erect before him, really covering the ground as far as he could see, was the fact of the gained success that this represented. It was, otherwise, but the fact of the idea as directly applied, as converted from a luminous conception into an historic truth. He had known it before but as desired and urged, as convincingly insisted on for the help it would render; so that at present, *with* the help rendered, it seemed to acknowledge its office and to set up, for memory and faith, an insistence of its own. He had in fine judged his friend's pledge in advance as an inestimable value, and what he must now know his case for was that of a possession of the value to the full. Wasn't it perhaps even rather the value that possessed *him*, kept him thinking of it and waiting on it, turning round and round it and making sure of it again from this side and that?

It played for him—certainly in this prime afterglow—the part of a treasure kept at home in safety and sanctity, something he was sure of finding in its place when, with each return, he worked his heavy old key in the lock. The door had but to open for him to be with it again and for it to be all there; so intensely there that, as we say, no other act was possible to him than the renewed act, almost the hallucination, of intimacy. Wherever he looked or sat or stood, to whatever aspect he gave for the instant the advantage, it was in view as nothing of the moment, nothing begotten of time or of chance could be, or ever would; it was in view as, when the curtain has risen, the play on the stage is in view, night after night, for the fiddlers. He remained thus, in his own theatre, in his single person, perpetual orchestra to the ordered drama, the confirmed "run"; playing low and slow, moreover, in the regular way, for the situations of most importance. No other visitor was to come to him; he met, he bumped occasionally, in the Piazza or in his walks, against claimants to acquaintance, remembered or forgotten, at present mostly effusive, sometimes even inquisitive; but he gave no address and encouraged no approach; he couldn't for his life, he felt, have opened his door to a third person. Such a person would have interrupted him, would have profaned his secret or perhaps have guessed it; would at any rate have broken the spell of what he conceived himself—in the absence of anything "to show"—to be inwardly doing. He was giving himself up—that was quite enough—to the general feeling of his renewed engagement to fidelity. The force of the engagement, the quantity of the article to be supplied, the special solidity of the contract, the way, above all, as a service for which the price named by him had been magnificently paid, his equivalent office was to take effect— such items might well fill his consciousness when there was nothing from outside to interfere. Never was a consciousness more rounded and fastened down over what filled it; which is precisely what we have spoken of as, in its degree, the oppression of success, the somewhat chilled state—tending to the solitary—of supreme recognition. If it was slightly awful to feel so justified, this was by the loss of the warmth of the element of mystery. The lucid reigned instead of it, and it was into the lucid that he sat and stared. He shook himself out of it a dozen times a day, tried to break by his own act his constant still communion. It wasn't still communion she had meant to bequeath him; it was the very different business of that kind of fidelity of which the other name was careful action.

Nothing, he perfectly knew, was less like careful action than the immersion he enjoyed at home. The actual grand queerness was that to be faithful to Kate he had positively to take his eyes, his arms, his lips straight off her—he had to let her alone. He had to remember it was time to go to the palace—which in truth was a mercy, since the check was not less effectual than imperative. What it came to, fortunately, as yet, was that when he closed the door behind him for an absence he always shut her in. Shut her out—it came to that rather, when once he had got a little away; and before he reached the palace, much more after hearing at his heels the bang of the greater *portone*, he felt free enough not to know his position as oppressively false. As Kate was *all* in his poor rooms, and not a ghost of her left for the grander, it was only on reflexion that the falseness came out; so long as he left it to the mercy of beneficent chance it offered him no face and made of him no claim that he couldn't meet without aggravation of his inward sense. This aggravation had been his original horror; yet what—in Milly's presence, each day—was horror doing with him but virtually letting him off? He shouldn't perhaps get off to the end; there was time enough still for the possibility of shame to pounce. Still, however, he did constantly a little more what he liked best, and that kept him for the time more safe. What he liked best was, in any case, to know why things were as he felt them; and he knew it pretty well, in this case, ten days after the retreat of his other friends. He then fairly perceived that—even putting their purity of motive at its highest—it was neither Kate nor he who made his strange relation to Milly, who made her own, so far as it might be, innocent; it was neither of them who practically purged it—if practically purged it was. Milly herself did everything—so far at least as he was concerned—Milly herself, and Milly's house, and Milly's hospitality, and Milly's manner, and Milly's character, and, perhaps still more than anything else, Milly's imagination, Mrs. Stringham and Sir Luke indeed a little aiding: whereby he knew the blessing of a fair pretext to ask himself what more he had to do. Something incalculable wrought for them—for him and Kate; something outside, beyond, above themselves, and doubtless ever so much better than they: which wasn't a reason, however—its being so much better—for them not to profit by it. Not to profit by it, so far as profit could be reckoned, would have been to go directly against it; and the spirit of generosity at present engendered in Densher could have felt no greater pang than by his having to go directly against Milly.

To go *with* her was the thing, so far as she could herself go; which, from the moment her tenure of her loved palace stretched on, was possible but by his remaining near her. This remaining was of course on the face of it the most "marked" of demonstrations—which was exactly why Kate had required it; it was so marked that on the very evening of the day it had taken effect Milly herself hadn't been able not to reach out to him, with an exquisite awkwardness, for some account of it. It was as if she had wanted from him some name that, now they were to be almost alone together, they could, for their further ease, know it and call it by—it being, after all, almost rudimentary that his presence, of which the absence of the others made quite a different thing, couldn't but have for himself some definite basis. She only wondered about the basis it would have for himself, and how he would describe it; that would quite do for her—it even would have done for her, he could see, had he produced some reason merely trivial, had he said he was waiting for money or clothes, for letters or for orders from Fleet Street, without which, as she might have heard, newspaper men never took a step. He hadn't in the event quite sunk to that; but he had none the less had there with her, that night, on Mrs. Stringham's leaving them alone—Mrs. Stringham proved really prodigious—his acquaintance with a shade of awkwardness darker than any Milly could know. He had supposed himself beforehand, on the question of what he was doing or pretending, in possession of some tone that would serve; but there were three minutes of his feeling incapable of promptness quite in the same degree in which a gentleman whose pocket has been picked feels incapable of purchase. It even didn't help him, oddly, that he was sure Kate would in some way have spoken for him—or rather not so much in some way as in one very particular way. He hadn't asked her, at the last, what she might, in the connexion, have said; nothing would have induced him to put such a question after she had been to see him: his lips were so sealed by that passage, his spirit in fact so hushed, in respect to any charge upon her freedom. There was something he could only therefore read back into the probabilities, and when he left the palace an hour afterwards it was with a sense of having breathed there, in the very air, the truth he had been guessing.

Just this perception it was, however, that had made him for the time ugly to himself in his awkwardness. It was horrible, with this creature, to *be* awkward; it was odious to be seeking excuses for the relation that involved it. Any relation that involved it was by the very fact as much discredited as a dish would be at dinner if one had to take medicine as a sauce. What Kate would have said in one of the young women's last talks was that—if Milly absolutely must have the truth about it—Mr. Densher was staying because she had really seen no way but to require it of him. If he stayed he didn't follow her—or didn't appear to her aunt to be doing so; and when she kept him from following her Mrs. Lowder couldn't pretend, in scenes, the renewal of which at this time of day was painful, that she after all didn't snub him as she might. She did nothing in fact *but* snub him—wouldn't that have been part of the story?—only Aunt Maud's suspicions were of the sort that had repeatedly to be dealt with. He had been, by the same token, reasonable enough—as he now, for that matter, well might; he had consented to oblige them, aunt and niece, by giving the plainest sign possible that he could exist away from London. To exist away from London was to exist away from Kate Croy—which was a gain, much appreciated, to the latter's comfort. There was a minute, at this hour, out of Densher's three, during which he knew the terror of Milly's uttering some such allusion to their friend's explanation as he must meet with words that wouldn't destroy it. To destroy it was to destroy everything, to destroy probably Kate herself, to destroy in particular by a breach of faith still uglier than anything else the beauty of their own last passage. He had given her his word of honour that if she would come to him he would act absolutely in her sense, and he had done so with a full enough vision of what her sense implied. What it implied for one thing was that to-night in the great saloon, noble in its half-lighted beauty, and straight in the white face of his young hostess, divine in her trust, or at any rate inscrutable in her mercy—what it implied was that he should lie with his lips. The single thing, of all things, that could save him from it would be Milly's letting him off after having thus scared him. What made her mercy inscrutable was that if she had already more than once saved him it was yet apparently without knowing how nearly he was lost.

These were transcendent motions, not the less blest for being obscure; whereby yet once more he was to feel the pressure lighten. He was kept on his feet in short by the felicity of her not presenting him with Kate's version as aversion to adopt. He couldn't stand up to lie—he felt as if he should have to go down on his knees. As it was he just sat there shaking a little for nervousness the leg he had crossed over the other. She was sorry for his suffered snub, but he had nothing more to subscribe to, to perjure himself about, than the three or four inanities he had, on his own side, feebly prepared for the crisis. He scrambled a little higher than the reference to money and clothes, letters and directions from his manager; but he brought out the beauty of the chance for him—there before him like a temptress painted by Titian—to do a little quiet writing. He was vivid for a moment on the difficulty of writing quietly in London; and he was precipitate, almost explosive, on his idea, long cherished, of a book.

The explosion lighted her face. "You'll do your book here?"

"I hope to begin it."

"It's something you haven't begun?"

"Well, only just."

"And since you came?"

She was so full of interest that he shouldn't perhaps after all be too easily let off. "I tried to think a few days ago that I had broken ground."

Scarcely anything, it was indeed clear, could have let him in deeper. "I'm afraid we've made an awful mess of your time."

"Of course you have. But what I'm hanging on for now is precisely to repair that ravage."

"Then you mustn't mind me, you know."

"You'll see," he tried to say with ease, "how little I shall mind anything."

"You'll want"—Milly had thrown herself into it—"the best part of your days."

He thought a moment: he did what he could to wreathe it in smiles. "Oh I shall make shift with the worst part. The best will be for *you*." And he wished Kate could hear him. It didn't help him moreover that he visibly, even pathetically, imaged to her by such touches his quest for comfort against discipline. He was to bury Kate's so signal snub, and also the hard law she had now laid on him, under a high intellectual effort. This at least was his crucifixion—that Milly was so interested. She was so interested that she presently asked him if he found his rooms propitious, while he felt that in just decently answering her he put on a brazen mask. He should need it quite particularly were she to express again her imagination of coming to tea with him—an extremity that he saw he was not to be spared. "We depend on you, Susie and I, you know, not to forget we're coming"—the extremity was but to face that remainder, yet it demanded all his tact. Facing their visit itself—to that, no matter what he might have to do, he would never consent, as we know, to be pushed; and this even though it might be exactly such a demonstration as would figure for him at the top of Kate's list of his proprieties. He could wonder freely enough, deep within, if Kate's view of that especial propriety had not been modified by a subsequent occurrence; but his deciding that it was quite likely not to have been had no effect on his own preference for tact. It pleased him to think of "tact" as his present prop in doubt; that glossed his predicament over, for it was of application among the sensitive and the kind. He wasn't inhuman, in fine, so long as it would serve. It had to serve now, accordingly, to help him not to sweeten Milly's hopes. He didn't want to be rude to them, but he still less wanted them to flower again in the particular connexion; so that, casting about him in his anxiety for a middle way to meet her, he put his foot, with unhappy effect, just in the wrong place. "Will it be safe for you to break into your custom of not leaving the house?"

"'Safe'—?" She had for twenty seconds an exquisite pale glare. Oh but he didn't need it, by that time, to wince; he had winced for himself as soon as he had made his mistake. He had done what, so unforgettably, she had asked him in London not to do; he had touched, all alone with her here, the supersensitive nerve of which she had warned him. He had not, since the occasion in London, touched it again till now; but he saw himself freshly warned that it was able to bear still less. So for the moment he knew as little what to do as he had ever known it in his life. He couldn't emphasise that he thought of her as dying, yet he couldn't pretend he thought of her as indifferent to precautions. Meanwhile too she had narrowed his choice. "You suppose me so awfully bad?"

He turned, in his pain, within himself; but by the time the colour had mounted to the roots of his hair he had found what he wanted. "I'll believe whatever you tell me."

"Well then, I'm splendid."

"Oh I don't need you to tell me that."

"I mean I'm capable of life."

"I've never doubted it."

"I mean," she went on, "that I want so to live—!"

"Well?" he asked while she paused with the intensity of it.

"Well, that I know I *can*."

"Whatever you do?" He shrank from solemnity about it.

"Whatever I do. If I want to."

"If you want to do it?"

"If I want to live. I *can*," Milly repeated.

He had clumsily brought it on himself, but he hesitated with all the pity of it. "Ah then that I believe."

"I will, I will," she declared; yet with the weight of it somehow turned for him to mere light and sound.

He felt himself smiling through a mist. "You simply must!"

It brought her straight again to the fact. "Well then, if you say it, why mayn't we pay you our visit?"

"Will it help you to live?"

"Every little helps," she laughed; "and it's very little for me, in general, to stay at home. Only I shan't want to miss it—!"

"Yes?"—she had dropped again.

"Well, on the day you give us a chance."

It was amazing what so brief an exchange had at this point done with him. His great scruple suddenly broke, giving way to something inordinately strange, something of a nature to become clear to him only when he had left her. "You can come," he said, "when you like."

What had taken place for him, however—the drop, almost with violence, of everything but a sense of her own reality—apparently showed in his face or his manner, and even so vividly that she could take it for something else. "I see how you feel—that I'm an awful bore about it and that, sooner than have any such upset, you'll go. So it's no matter."

"No matter? Oh!"—he quite protested now.

"If it drives you away to escape us. We want you not to go."

It was beautiful how she spoke for Mrs. Stringham. Whatever it was, at any rate, he shook his head. "I won't go."

"Then I won't go!" she brightly declared.

"You mean you won't come to me?"

"No—never now. It's over. But it's all right. I mean, apart from that," she went on, "that I won't do anything I oughtn't or that I'm not forced to."

"Oh who can ever force you?" he asked with his hand-to-mouth way, at all times, of speaking for her encouragement. "You're the least coercible of creatures."

"Because, you think, I'm so free?"

"The freest person probably now in the world. You've got everything."

"Well," she smiled, "call it so. I don't complain."

On which again, in spite of himself, it let him in. "No I know you don't complain."

As soon as he had said it he had himself heard the pity in it. His telling her she had "everything" was extravagant kind humour, whereas his knowing so tenderly that she didn't complain was terrible kind gravity. Milly felt, he could see, the difference; he might as well have praised her outright for looking death in the face. This was the way she just looked *him* again, and it was of no attenuation that she took him up more gently than ever. "It isn't a merit—when one sees one's way."

"To peace and plenty? Well, I dare say not."

"I mean to keeping what one has."

"Oh that's success. If what one has is good," Densher said at random, "it's enough to try for."

"Well, it's my limit. I'm not trying for more." To which then she added with a change: "And now about your book."

607

"My book—?" He had got in a moment so far from it.

"The one you're now to understand that nothing will induce either Susie or me to run the risk of spoiling."

He cast about, but he made up his mind. "I'm not doing a book."

"Not what you said?" she asked in a wonder. "You're not writing?"

He already felt relieved. "I don't know, upon my honour, what I'm doing."

It made her visibly grave; so that, disconcerted in another way, he was afraid of what she would see in it. She saw in fact exactly what he feared, but again his honour, as he called it, was saved even while she didn't know she had threatened it. Taking his words for a betrayal of the sense that he, on his side, *might* complain, what she clearly wanted was to urge on him some such patience as he should be perhaps able to arrive at with her indirect help. Still more clearly, however, she wanted to be sure of how far she might venture; and he could see her make out in a moment that she had a sort of test.

"Then if it's not for your book—?"

"What *am* I staying for?"

"I mean with your London work—with all you have to do. Isn't it rather empty for you?"

"Empty for me?" He remembered how Kate had held that she might propose marriage, and he wondered if this were the way she would naturally begin it. It would leave him, such an incident, he already felt, at a loss, and the note of his finest anxiety might have been in the vagueness of his reply. "Oh well—!"

"I ask too many questions?" She settled it for herself before he could protest. "You stay because you've got to."

He grasped at it. "I stay because I've got to." And he couldn't have said when he had uttered it if it were loyal to Kate or disloyal. It gave her, in a manner, away; it showed the tip of the ear of her plan. Yet Milly took it, he perceived, but as a plain statement of his truth. He was waiting for what Kate would have told her of—the permission from Lancaster Gate to come any nearer. To remain friends with either niece or aunt he mustn't stir without it. All this Densher read in the girl's sense of the spirit of his reply; so that it made him feel he was lying, and he had to think of something to correct that. What he thought of was, in an instant, "Isn't it enough, whatever may be one's other complications, to stay after all for *you?*"

"Oh you must judge."

He was by this time on his feet to take leave, and was also at last too restless. The speech in question at least wasn't disloyal to Kate; that was the very tone of their bargain. So was it, by being loyal, another kind of lie, the lie of the uncandid profession of a motive. He was staying so little "for" Milly that he was staying positively against her. He didn't, none the less, know, and at last, thank goodness, didn't care. The only thing he could say might make it either better or worse. "Well then, so long as I don't go, you must think of me all *as* judging!"

II

He didn't go home, on leaving her—he didn't want to; he walked instead, through his narrow ways and his *campi* with gothic arches, to a small and comparatively sequestered café where he had already more than once found refreshment and comparative repose, together with solutions that consisted mainly and pleasantly of further indecisions. It was a literal fact that those awaiting him there to-night, while he leaned back on his velvet bench with his head against a florid mirror and his eyes not looking further than the fumes of his tobacco, might have been regarded by him as a little less limp than usual. This wasn't because, before getting to his feet again, there was a step he had seen his way to; it was simply because the acceptance of his position took sharper effect from his sense of what he had just had to deal with. When half an hour before, at the palace, he had turned about to Milly on the question of the impossibility so inwardly felt, turned about on the spot and under her eyes, he had acted, by the sudden force of his seeing much further, seeing how little, how not at all, impossibilities mattered. It wasn't a case for pedantry; when people were at *her* pass everything was allowed. And her pass was now, as by the sharp click of a spring, just completely his own—to the extent, as he felt, of her deep dependence on him. Anything he should do or shouldn't would have close reference to her life, which was thus absolutely in his hands—and ought never to have reference to anything else. It was on the cards for him that he might kill her—that was the way he read the cards as he sat in his customary corner. The fear in this thought made him let everything go, kept him there actually, all motionless, for three hours on end. He renewed his consumption and smoked more cigarettes than he had ever done in the time. What had come out for him had come out, with this first intensity, as a terror; so that action itself, of any sort, the right as well as the wrong—if the difference even survived—had heard in it a vivid "Hush!" the injunction to keep from that moment intensely still. He thought in fact while his vigil lasted of several different ways for his doing so, and the hour might have served him as a lesson in going on tiptoe.

What he finally took home, when he ventured to leave the place, was the perceived truth that he might on any other system go straight to destruction. Destruction was represented for him by the idea of his really bringing to a point, on Milly's side, anything whatever. Nothing so "brought," he easily argued, but *must* be in one way or another a catastrophe. He was mixed up in her fate, or her fate, if that should be better, was mixed up in *him*, so that a single false motion might either way snap the coil. They helped him, it was true, these considerations, to a degree of eventual peace, for what they luminously amounted to was that he was to do nothing, and that fell in after all with the burden laid on him by Kate. He was only not to budge without the girl's leave—not, oddly enough at the last, to move without it, whether further or nearer, any more than without Kate's. It was to this his wisdom reduced itself—to the need again simply to be kind. That was the same as being still—as studying to create the minimum of vibration. He felt himself as he smoked shut up to a room on the wall of which something precious was

Henry James

too precariously hung. A false step would bring it down, and it must hang as long as possible. He was aware when he walked away again that even Fleet Street wouldn't at this juncture successfully touch him. His manager might wire that he was wanted, but he could easily be deaf to his manager. His money for the idle life might be none too much; happily, however, Venice was cheap, and it was moreover the queer fact that Milly in a manner supported him. The greatest of his expenses really was to walk to the palace to dinner. He didn't want, in short, to give that up, and he should probably be able, he felt, to stay his breath and his hand. He should be able to be still enough through everything.

He tried that for three weeks, with the sense after a little of not having failed. There had to be a delicate art in it, for he wasn't trying—quite the contrary—to be either distant or dull. That would not have been being "nice," which in its own form was the real law. That too might just have produced the vibration he desired to avert; so that he best kept everything in place by not hesitating or fearing, as it were, to let himself go—go in the direction, that is to say, of staying. It depended on where he went; which was what he meant by taking care. When one went on tiptoe one could turn off for retreat without betraying the manoeuvre. Perfect tact—the necessity for which he had from the first, as we know, happily recognised—was to keep all intercourse in the key of the absolutely settled. It was settled thus for instance that they were indissoluble good friends, and settled as well that her being the American girl was, just in time and for the relation they found themselves concerned in, a boon inappreciable. If, at least, as the days went on, she was to fall short of her prerogative of the great national, the great maidenly ease, if she didn't diviningly and responsively desire and labour to record herself as possessed of it, this wouldn't have been for want of Densher's keeping her, with his idea, well up to it—wouldn't have been in fine for want of his encouragement and reminder. He didn't perhaps in so many words speak to her of the quantity itself as of the thing she was least to intermit; but he talked of it, freely, in what he flattered himself was an impersonal way, and this held it there before her—since he was careful also to talk pleasantly. It was at once their idea, when all was said, and the most marked of their conveniences. The

611

type was so elastic that it could be stretched to almost anything; and yet, not stretched, it kept down, remained normal, remained properly within bounds. And he *had* meanwhile, thank goodness, without being too much disconcerted, the sense, for the girl's part of the business, of the queerest conscious compliance, of her doing very much what he wanted, even though without her quite seeing why. She fairly touched this once in saying: "Oh yes, you like us to be as we are because it's a kind of facilitation to you that we don't quite measure: I think one would have to be English to measure it!"—and that too, strangely enough, without prejudice to her good nature. She might have been conceived as doing—that is of being—what he liked in order perhaps only to judge where it would take them. They really as it went on *saw* each other at the game; she knowing he tried to keep her in tune with his conception, and he knowing she thus knew it. Add that he again knew she knew, and yet that nothing was spoiled by it, and we get a fair impression of the line they found most completely workable. The strangest fact of all for us must be that the success he himself thus promoted was precisely what figured to his gratitude as the something above and beyond him, above and beyond Kate, that made for daily decency. There would scarce have been felicity—certainly too little of the right lubricant—had not the national character so invoked been, not less inscrutably than entirely, in Milly's chords. It made up her unity and was the one thing he could unlimitedly take for granted.

He did so then, daily, for twenty days, without deepened fear of the undue vibration that was keeping him watchful. He knew in his nervousness that he was living at best from day to day and from hand to mouth; yet he had succeeded, he believed, in avoiding a mistake. All women had alternatives, and Milly's would doubtless be shaky too; but the national character was firm in her, whether as all of her, practically, by this time, or but as a part; the national character that, in a woman still so young, made of the air breathed a virtual non-conductor. It wasn't till a certain occasion when the twenty days had passed that, going to the palace at tea-time, he was met by the information that the signorina padrona was not "receiving." The announcement met him, in the court, on the lips of one of the gondoliers, met him, he thought, with such a conscious eye as the knowledge of his freedoms of access, hitherto conspicuously shown, could scarce fail to beget. Densher had not been at Palazzo Leporelli among the mere receivable, but had taken his place once for all among the involved and included, so that on being so flagrantly braved he recognised after a moment the propriety of a further appeal. Neither of the two ladies, it appeared, received, and yet Pasquale was not prepared to say that either was *poco bene*. He was yet not prepared to say that either was anything, and he would have been blank, Densher mentally noted, if the term could ever apply to members of a race in whom vacancy was but a nest of darknesses—not a vain surface, but a place of withdrawal in which something obscure, something always ominous, indistinguishably lived. He felt afresh indeed at this hour the force of the veto laid within the palace on any mention, any cognition, of the liabilities of its mistress. The state of her health was never confessed to there as a reason. How much it might deeply be taken for one was another matter; of which he grew fully aware on carrying his question further. This appeal was to his friend Eugenio, whom he immediately sent for, with whom, for three rich minutes, protected from the weather, he was confronted in the gallery that led from the water-steps to the court, and whom he always called, in meditation, his friend; seeing it was so elegantly presumable he would have put an end to him if he could. That produced a relation which required a name of its own, an intimacy of consciousness in truth for each—an intimacy of eye, of ear, of general sensibility, of everything but tongue. It had been, in other words, for the five weeks, far from occult to our young man that Eugenio took a view of him not less finely formal than essentially vulgar, but which at the same time he couldn't himself raise an eyebrow to prevent. It was all in the air now again; it was as much between them as ever while Eugenio waited on him in the court.

The weather, from early morning, had turned to storm, the first sea-storm of the autumn, and Densher had almost invidiously brought him down the outer staircase—the massive ascent, the great feature of the court, to Milly's *piano nobile*. This was to pay him—it was the one chance—for all imputations; the imputation in particular that, clever, *tanto bello* and not rich, the young man from London was—by the obvious way—pressing Miss Theale's fortune hard. It was to pay him for the further ineffable intimation that a gentleman must take the young lady's most devoted servant (interested scarcely less in the high attraction) for a strangely casual appendage if he counted in such a connexion on impunity and prosperity. These interpretations were odious to Densher for the simple reason that they might have been so true of the attitude of an inferior man, and three things alone, accordingly, had kept him from righting himself. One of these was that his critic sought expression only in an impersonality, a positive inhumanity, of politeness; the second was that refinements of expression in a friend's servant were not a thing a visitor could take action on; and the third was the fact that the particular attribution of motive did him after all no wrong. It was his own fault if the vulgar view, the view that might have been taken of an inferior man, happened so incorrigibly to fit him. He apparently wasn't so different from inferior men as that came to. If therefore, in fine, Eugenio figured to him as "my friend" because he was conscious of his seeing so much of him, what he made him see on the same lines in the course of their present interview was ever so much more. Densher felt that he marked himself, no doubt, as insisting, by dissatisfaction with the gondolier's answer, on the pursuit taken for granted in him; and yet felt it only in the augmented, the exalted distance that was by this time established between them. Eugenio had of course reflected that a word to Miss Theale from such a pair of lips would cost him his place; but he could also bethink himself that, so long as the word never came—and it was, on the basis he had arranged, impossible—he enjoyed the imagination of mounting guard. He had never so mounted guard, Densher could see, as during these minutes in the damp *loggia* where the storm-gusts were strong; and there came in fact for our young man, as a result of his presence, a sudden sharp sense that everything had turned to the dismal. Something had happened—he didn't know what; and it wasn't Eugenio who would tell him. What Eugenio told him was that he thought the ladies—as if their liability had been equal—were a "leetle" fatigued, just a "leetle leetle," and without any cause named for it. It was one of the signs of what Densher felt in him that, by a profundity, a true deviltry of resource, he always met the latter's Italian with English and his English with Italian. He now, as usual, slightly smiled at him in the process— but ever so slightly this time, his manner also being attuned, our young man made out, to the thing, whatever it was, that constituted the rupture of peace.

This manner, while they stood a long minute facing each other over all they didn't say, played a part as well in the sudden jar to Densher's protected state. It was a Venice all of evil that had broken out for them alike, so that they were together in their anxiety, if they really could have met on it; a Venice of cold lashing rain from a low black sky, of wicked wind raging through narrow passes, of general arrest and interruption, with the people engaged in all the water-life huddled, stranded and wageless, bored and cynical, under archways and bridges. Our young man's mute exchange with his friend contained meanwhile such a depth of reference that, had the pressure been but slightly prolonged, they might have reached a point at which they were equally weak. Each had verily something in mind that would have made a hash of mutual suspicion and in presence of which, as a possibility, they were more united than disjoined. But it was to have been a moment for Densher that nothing could ease off—not even the formal propriety with which his interlocutor finally attended him to the *portone* and bowed upon his retreat. Nothing had passed about his coming back, and the air had made itself felt as a non-conductor of messages. Densher knew of course, as he took his way again, that Eugenio's invitation to return was not what he missed; yet he knew at the same time that what had happened to him was part of his punishment. Out in the square beyond the *fondamenta* that gave access to the land-gate of the palace, out where the wind was higher, he fairly, with the thought of it, pulled his umbrella closer down. It couldn't be, his consciousness, unseen enough by others—the base predicament of having, by a concatenation, just to *take* such things: such things as the fact that one very acute person in the world, whom he couldn't dispose of as an interested scoundrel, enjoyed an opinion of him that there was no attacking, no disproving, no (what was worst of all) even noticing. One had come to a queer pass when a servant's opinion so mattered. Eugenio's would have mattered even if, as founded on a low vision of appearances, it had been quite wrong. It was the more disagreeable accordingly that the vision of appearances was quite right, and yet was scarcely less low.

Such as it was, at any rate, Densher shook it off with the more impatience that he was independently restless. He had to walk in spite of weather, and he took his course, through crooked ways, to the Piazza, where he should have the shelter of the galleries. Here, in the high arcade, half Venice was crowded close, while, on the Molo, at the limit of the expanse, the old columns of the Saint Theodore and of the Lion were the frame of a door wide open to the storm. It was odd for him, as he moved, that it should have made such a difference—if the difference wasn't only that the palace had for the first time failed of a welcome. There was more, but it came from that; that gave the harsh note and broke the spell. The wet and the cold were now to reckon with, and it was to Densher precisely as if he had seen the obliteration, at a stroke, of the margin on a faith in which they were all living. The margin had been his name for it—for the thing that, though it had held out, could bear no shock. The shock, in some form, had come, and he wondered about it while, threading his way among loungers as vague as himself, he dropped his eyes sightlessly on the rubbish in shops. There were stretches of the gallery paved with squares of red marble, greasy now with the salt spray; and the whole place, in its huge elegance, the grace of its conception and the beauty of its detail, was more than ever like a great drawing-room, the drawing-room of Europe, profaned and bewildered by some reverse of fortune. He brushed shoulders with brown men whose hats askew, and the loose sleeves of whose pendent jackets, made them resemble melancholy maskers. The tables and chairs that overflowed from the cafés were gathered, still with a pretence of service, into the arcade, and here and there a spectacled German, with his coat-collar up, partook publicly of food and philosophy. These were impressions for Densher too, but he had made the whole circuit thrice before he stopped short, in front of Florian's, with the force of his sharpest. His eye had caught a face within the café—he had spotted an acquaintance behind the glass. The person he had thus paused long enough to look at twice was seated, well within range, at a small table on which a tumbler, half-emptied and evidently neglected, still remained; and though he had on his knee, as he leaned back, a copy of a French newspaper—the heading of the *Figaro* was visible—he stared straight before him at the little opposite rococo wall. Densher had him for a minute in profile, had him for a time during which his identity produced, however quickly, all the effect of establishing connexions—connexions startling and direct; and then, as if it were the one thing more needed, seized the look, determined by a turn of the head, that might have been a prompt result of the sense of being noticed. This wider view showed him *all* Lord Mark—Lord Mark as encountered, several weeks before, the day of the first visit of each to Palazzo Leporelli. For it had been all Lord Mark that was going out, on that occasion, as he came in—he had felt it, in the hall, at the time; and he was accordingly the less at a loss to recognise in a few seconds, as renewed meeting brought it to the surface, the same potential quantity.

It was a matter, the whole passage—it could only be—but of a few seconds; for as he might neither stand there to stare nor on the other hand make any advance from it, he had presently resumed his walk, this time to another pace. It had been for all the world, during his pause, as if he had caught his answer to the riddle of the day. Lord Mark had simply faced him—as he had faced *him*, not placed by him, not at first—as one of the damp shuffling crowd. Recognition, though hanging fire, had then clearly come; yet no light of salutation had been struck from these certainties. Acquaintance between them was scant enough for neither to take it up. That neither had done so was not, however, what now mattered, but that the gentleman at Florian's should be in the place at all. He couldn't have been in it long; Densher, as inevitably a haunter of the great meeting-ground, would in that case have seen him before. He paid short visits; he was on the wing; the question for him even as he sat there was of his train or of his boat. He had come back for something—as a sequel to his earlier visit; and whatever he had come back for it had had time to be done. He might have arrived but last night or that morning; he had already made the difference. It was a great thing for Densher to get this answer. He held it close, he hugged it, quite leaned on it as he continued to circulate. It kept him going and going—it made him no less restless. But it explained—and that was much, for with explanations he might somehow deal. The vice in the air, otherwise, was too much like the breath of fate. The weather had changed, the rain was ugly, the wind wicked, the sea impossible, *because* of Lord Mark. It was because of him, *a fortiori*, that the palace was closed. Densher went round again twice; he found the visitor each time as he had found him first. Once, that is, he was staring before him; the next time he was looking over his *Figaro*, which he had opened out. Densher didn't again stop, but left him apparently unconscious of his passage—on another repetition of which Lord Mark had disappeared. He had spent but the day; he would be off that night; he had now gone to his hotel for arrangements. These things were as plain to Densher as if he had had them in words. The obscure had cleared for him—if cleared it was; there was something he didn't see, the great thing; but he saw so round it and so close to it that this was almost as good. He had been looking at a man who had done what he had come for, and for whom, as done, it temporarily sufficed. The man had come again to see Milly, and Milly had received him. His visit would have taken place just before or just after luncheon, and it was the reason why he himself had found her door shut.

He said to himself that evening, he still said even on the morrow, that he only wanted a reason, and that with this perception of one he could now mind, as he called it, his business. His business, he had settled, as we know, was to keep thoroughly still; and he asked himself why it should prevent this that he could feel, in connexion with the crisis, so remarkably blameless. He gave the appearances before him all the benefit of being critical, so that if blame were to accrue he shouldn't feel he had dodged it. But it wasn't a bit he who, that day, had touched her, and if she was upset it wasn't a bit his act. The ability so to think about it amounted for Densher during several hours to a kind of exhilaration. The exhilaration was heightened fairly, besides, by the visible conditions—sharp, striking, ugly to him—of Lord Mark's return. His constant view of it, for all the next hours, of which there were many, was as a demonstration on the face of it sinister even to his own actual ignorance. He didn't need, for seeing it as evil, seeing it as, to a certainty, in a high degree "nasty," to know more about it than he had so easily and so wonderfully picked up. You couldn't drop on the poor girl that way without, by the fact, being brutal. Such a visit was a descent, an invasion, an aggression, constituting precisely one or other of the stupid shocks he himself had so decently sought to spare her. Densher had indeed drifted by the next morning to the reflexion—which he positively, with occasion, might have brought straight out—that the only delicate and honourable way of treating a person in such a state was to treat her as *he*, Merton Densher, did. With time, actually—for the impression but deepened—this sense of the contrast, to the advantage of Merton Densher, became a sense of relief, and that in turn a sense of escape. It was for all the world—and he drew a long breath on it—as if a special danger for him had passed. Lord Mark had, without in the least intending such a service, got it straight out of the way. It was *he*, the brute, who had stumbled into just the wrong inspiration and who had therefore produced, for the very person he had wished to hurt, an impunity that was comparative innocence, that was almost like purification. The person he had wished to hurt could only be the person so unaccountably hanging about. To keep still meanwhile was, for this person, more comprehensively, to keep it all up; and to keep it all up was, if that seemed on consideration best, not, for the day or two, to go back to the palace.

The day or two passed—stretched to three days; and with the effect, extraordinarily, that Densher felt himself in the course of them washed but the more clean. Some sign would come if his return should have the better effect; and he was at all events, in absence, without the particular scruple. It wouldn't have been meant for him by either of the women that he was to come back but to face Eugenio. That was impossible—the being again denied; for it made him practically answerable, and answerable was what he wasn't. There was no neglect either in absence, inasmuch as, from the moment he didn't get in, the one message he could send up would be some hope on the score of health. Since accordingly that sort of expression was definitely forbidden him he had only to wait—which he was actually helped to do by his feeling with the lapse of each day more and more wound up to it. The days in themselves were anything but sweet; the wind and the weather lasted, the fireless cold hinted at worse; the broken charm of the world about was broken into smaller pieces. He walked up and down his rooms and listened to the wind—listened also to tinkles of bells and watched for some servant of the palace. He might get a note, but the note never came; there were hours when he stayed at home not to miss it. When he wasn't at home he was in circulation again as he had been at the hour of his seeing Lord Mark. He strolled about the Square with the herd of refugees; he raked the approaches and the cafés on the chance the brute, as he now regularly imaged him, *might* be still there. He could only be there, he knew, to be received afresh; and that—one had but to think of it—would be indeed stiff. He had gone, however—it was proved; though Densher's care for the question either way only added to what was most acrid in the taste of his present ordeal. It all came round to what he was doing for Milly—spending days that neither relief nor escape could purge of a smack of the abject. What was it but abject for a man of his parts to be reduced to such pastimes? What was it but sordid for him, shuffling about in the rain, to have to peep into shops and to consider possible meetings? What was it but odious to find himself wondering what, as between him and another man, a possible meeting would produce? There recurred moments when in spite of everything he felt no straighter than another man. And yet even on the third day, when still nothing had come, he more than ever knew that he wouldn't have budged for the world.

He thought of the two women, in their silence, at last—he at all events thought of Milly—as probably, for her reasons, now intensely wishing him to go. The cold breath of her reasons was, with everything else, in the air; but he didn't care for them any more than for her wish itself, and he would stay in spite of her, stay in spite of odium, stay in spite perhaps of some final experience that would be, for the pain of it, all but unbearable. That would be his one way, purified though he was, to mark his virtue beyond any mistake. It would be accepting the disagreeable, and the disagreeable would be a proof; a proof of his not having stayed for the thing—the agreeable, as it were—that Kate had named. The thing Kate had named was not to have been the odium of staying in spite of hints. It was part of the odium as actual too that Kate was, for her comfort, just now well aloof. These were the first hours since her flight in which his sense of what she had done for him on the eve of that event was to incur a qualification. It was strange, it was perhaps base, to be thinking such things so soon; but one of the intimations of his solitude was that she had provided for herself. She was out of it all, by her act, as much as he was in it; and this difference grew, positively, as his own intensity increased. She had said in their last sharp snatch of talk—sharp though thickly muffled, and with every word in it final and deep, unlike even the deepest words they had ever yet spoken: "Letters? Never—*now*. Think of it. Impossible." So that as he had sufficiently caught her sense—into which he read, all the same, a strange inconsequence—they had practically wrapped their understanding in the breach of their correspondence. He had moreover, on losing her, done justice to her law of silence; for there was doubtless a finer delicacy in his not writing to her than in his writing as he must have written had he spoken of themselves. That would have been a turbid strain, and her idea had been to be noble; which, in a degree, was a manner. Only it left her, for the pinch, comparatively at ease. And it left *him*, in the conditions, peculiarly alone. He was alone, that is, till, on the afternoon of his third day, in gathering dusk and renewed rain, with his shabby rooms looking doubtless, in their confirmed dreariness, for the mere eyes of others, at their worst, the grinning padrona threw open the door and introduced Mrs. Stringham. That made at a bound a difference, especially when he saw that his visitor was weighted. It appeared part of her weight that she was in a wet waterproof, that she allowed her umbrella to be taken from her by the good woman without consciousness or care, and that her face, under her veil, richly rosy with the driving wind, was—and the veil too—as splashed as if the rain were her tears.

III

They came to it almost immediately; he was to wonder afterwards at the fewness of their steps. "She has turned her face to the wall."

"You mean she's worse?"

The poor lady stood there as she had stopped; Densher had, in the instant flare of his eagerness, his curiosity, all responsive at sight of her, waved away, on the spot, the padrona, who had offered to relieve her of her mackintosh. She looked vaguely about through her wet veil, intensely alive now to the step she had taken and wishing it not to have been in the dark, but clearly, as yet, seeing nothing. "I don't know *how* she is—and it's why I've come to you."

"I'm glad enough you've come," he said, "and it's quite—you make me feel—as if I had been wretchedly waiting for you."

She showed him again her blurred eyes—she had caught at his word. "Have you been wretched?"

Now, however, on his lips, the word expired. It would have sounded for him like a complaint, and before something he already made out in his visitor he knew his own trouble as small. Hers, under her damp draperies, which shamed his lack of a fire, was great, and he felt she had brought it all with her. He answered that he had been patient and above all that he had been still. "As still as a mouse—you'll have seen it for yourself. Stiller, for three days together, than I've ever been in my life. It has seemed to me the only thing."

This qualification of it as a policy or a remedy was straightway for his friend, he saw, a light that her own light could answer. "It has been best. I've wondered for you. But it has been best," she said again.

"Yet it has done no good?"

"I don't know. I've been afraid you were gone." Then as he gave a headshake which, though slow, was deeply mature: "You *won't* go?"

"Is to 'go,'" he asked, "to be still?"

"Oh I mean if you'll stay for me."

"I'll do anything for you. Isn't it for you alone now I can?"

She thought of it, and he could see even more of the relief she was taking from him. His presence, his face, his voice, the old rooms themselves, so meagre yet so charged, where Kate had admirably been to him—these things counted for her, now she had them, as the help she had been wanting: so that she still only stood there taking them all in. With it however popped up characteristically a throb of her conscience. What she thus tasted was almost a personal joy. It told Densher of the three days she on her side had spent. "Well, anything you do for me—*is* for her too. Only, only—!"

"Only nothing now matters?"

She looked at him a minute as if he were the fact itself that he expressed. "Then you know?"

"Is she dying?" he asked for all answer.

Mrs. Stringham waited—her face seemed to sound him. Then her own reply was strange. "She hasn't so much as named you. We haven't spoken."

"Not for three days?"

"No more," she simply went on, "than if it were all over. Not even by the faintest allusion."

"Oh," said Densher with more light, "you mean you haven't spoken about *me?*"

"About what else? No more than if you were dead."

"Well," he answered after a moment, "I *am* dead."

"Then I am," said Susan Shepherd with a drop of her arms on her waterproof.

It was a tone that, for the minute, imposed itself in its dry despair; it represented, in the bleak place, which had no life of its own, none but the life Kate had left—the sense of which, for that matter, by mystic channels, might fairly be reaching the visitor—the very impotence of their extinction. And Densher had nothing to oppose it withal, nothing but again: "Is she dying?"

It made her, however, as if these were crudities, almost material pangs, only say as before: "Then you know?"

"Yes," he at last returned, "I know. But the marvel to me is that *you* do. I've no right in fact to imagine or to assume that you do."

"You may," said Susan Shepherd, "all the same. I know."

"Everything?"

Her eyes, through her veil, kept pressing him. "No—not everything. That's why I've come."

"That I shall really tell you?" With which, as she hesitated and it affected him, he brought out in a groan a doubting "Oh, oh!" It turned him from her to the place itself, which was a part of what was in him, was the abode, the worn shrine more than ever, of the fact in possession, the fact, now a thick association, for which he had hired it. *That* was not for telling, but Susan Shepherd was, none the less, so decidedly wonderful that the sense of it might really have begun, by an effect already operating, to be a part of her knowledge. He saw, and it stirred him, that she hadn't come to judge him; had come rather, so far as she might dare, to pity. This showed him her own abasement—that, at any rate, of grief; and made him feel with a rush of friendliness that he liked to be with her. The rush had quickened when she met his groan with an attenuation.

"We shall at all events—if that's anything—be together."

It was his own good impulse in herself. "It's what I've ventured to feel. It's much." She replied in effect, silently, that it was whatever he liked; on which, so far as he had been afraid for anything, he knew his fear had dropped. The comfort was huge, for it gave back to him something precious, over which, in the effort of recovery, his own hand had too imperfectly closed. Kate, he remembered, had said to him, with her sole and single boldness—and also on grounds he hadn't then measured—that Mrs. Stringham was a person who *wouldn't*, at a pinch, in a stretch of confidence, wince. It was but another of the cases in which Kate was always showing. "You don't think then very horridly of me?"

And her answer was the more valuable that it came without nervous effusion—quite as if she understood what he might conceivably have believed. She turned over in fact what she thought, and that was what helped him. "Oh you've been extraordinary!"

It made him aware the next moment of how they had been planted there. She took off her cloak with his aid, though when she had also, accepting a seat, removed her veil, he recognised in her personal ravage that the words she had just uttered to him were the one flower she had to throw. They were all her consolation for him, and the consolation even still depended on the event. She sat with him at any rate in the grey clearance, as sad as a winter dawn, made by their meeting. The image she again evoked for him loomed in it but the larger. "She has turned her face to the wall."

He saw with the last vividness, and it was as if, in their silences, they were simply so leaving what he saw. "She doesn't speak at all? I don't mean not of me."

"Of nothing—of no one." And she went on, Susan Shepherd, giving it out as she had had to take it. "She doesn't *want* to die. Think of her age. Think of her goodness. Think of her beauty. Think of all she is. Think of all she *has*. She lies there stiffening herself and clinging to it all. So I thank God—!" the poor lady wound up with a wan inconsequence.

He wondered. "You thank God—?"

"That she's so quiet."

He continued to wonder. "*Is* she so quiet?"

"She's more than quiet. She's grim. It's what she has never been. So you see—all these days. I can't tell you—but it's better so. It would kill me if she *were* to tell me."

"To tell you?" He was still at a loss.

"How she feels. How she clings. How she doesn't want it."

"How she doesn't want to die? Of course she doesn't want it." He had a long pause, and they might have been thinking together of what they could even now do to prevent it. This, however, was not what he brought out. Milly's "grimness" and the great hushed palace were present to him; present with the little woman before him as she must have been waiting there and listening. "Only, what harm have *you* done her?"

Mrs. Stringham looked about in her darkness. "I don't know. I come and talk of her here with you."

It made him again hesitate. "Does she utterly hate me?"

"I don't know. How *can* I? No one ever will."

"She'll never tell?"

"She'll never tell."

Once more he thought. "She must be magnificent."

"She *is* magnificent."

His friend, after all, helped him, and he turned it, so far as he could, all over. "Would she see me again?"

It made his companion stare. "Should you like to see her?"

"You mean as you describe her?" He felt her surprise, and it took him some time. "No."

"Ah then!" Mrs. Stringham sighed.

"But if she could bear it I'd do anything."

She had for the moment her vision of this, but it collapsed. "I don't see what you can do."

"I don't either. But *she* might."

Mrs. Stringham continued to think. "It's too late."

"Too late for her to see—?"

"Too late."

The very decision of her despair—it was after all so lucid—kindled in him a heat. "But the doctor, all the while—?"

"Tacchini? Oh he's kind. He comes. He's proud of having been approved and coached by a great London man. He hardly in fact goes away; so that I scarce know what becomes of his other patients. He thinks her, justly enough, a great personage; he treats her like royalty; he's waiting on events. But she has barely consented to see him, and, though she has told him, generously—for she *thinks* of me, dear creature—that he may come, that he may stay, for my sake, he spends most of his time only hovering at her door, prowling through the rooms, trying to entertain me, in that ghastly saloon, with the gossip of Venice, and meeting me, in doorways, in the sala, on the staircase, with an agreeable intolerable smile. We don't," said Susan Shepherd, "talk of her."

"By her request?"

"Absolutely. I don't do what she doesn't wish. We talk of the price of provisions."

"By her request too?"

"Absolutely. She named it to me as a subject when she said, the first time, that if it would be any comfort to me he might stay as much as we liked."

Densher took it all in. "But he isn't any comfort to you!"

"None whatever. That, however," she added, "isn't his fault. Nothing's any comfort."

"Certainly," Densher observed, "as I but too horribly feel, *I'm* not."

"No. But I didn't come for that."

"You came for *me*."

"Well then call it that." But she looked at him a moment with eyes filled full, and something came up in her the next instant from deeper still. "I came at bottom of course—"

"You came at bottom of course for our friend herself. But if it's, as you say, too late for me to do anything?"

She continued to look at him, and with an irritation, which he saw grow in her, from the truth itself. "So I did say. But, with you here"—and she turned her vision again strangely about her—"with you here, and with everything, I feel we mustn't abandon her."

"God forbid we should abandon her."

"Then you *won't?*" His tone had made her flush again.

"How do you mean I 'won't,' if she abandons *me?* What can I do if she won't see me?"

627

"But you said just now you wouldn't like it."

"I said I shouldn't like it in the light of what you tell me. I shouldn't like it only to see her as you make me. I should like it if I could help her. But even then," Densher pursued without faith, "she would have to want it first herself. And there," he continued to make out, "is the devil of it. She *won't* want it herself. She *can't!*"

He had got up in his impatience of it, and she watched him while he helplessly moved. "There's one thing you can do. There's only that, and even for that there are difficulties. But there *is* that." He stood before her with his hands in his pockets, and he had soon enough, from her eyes, seen what was coming. She paused as if waiting for his leave to utter it, and as he only let her wait they heard in the silence, on the Canal, the renewed downpour of rain. She had at last to speak, but, as if still with her fear, she only half-spoke. "I think you really know yourself what it is."

He did know what it was, and with it even, as she said—rather!—there were difficulties. He turned away on them, on everything, for a moment; he moved to the other window and looked at the sheeted channel, wider, like a river, where the houses opposite, blurred and belittled, stood at twice their distance. Mrs. Stringham said nothing, was as mute in fact, for the minute, as if she had "had" him, and he was the first again to speak. When he did so, however, it was not in straight answer to her last remark—he only started from that. He said, as he came back to her, "Let me, you know, *see*—one must understand," almost as if he had for the time accepted it. And what he wished to understand was where, on the essence of the question, was the voice of Sir Luke Strett. If they talked of not giving her up shouldn't *he* be the one least of all to do it? "Aren't we, at the worst, in the dark without him?"

"Oh," said Mrs. Stringham, "it's he who has kept me going. I wired the first night, and he answered like an angel. He'll come like one. Only he can't arrive, at the nearest, till Thursday afternoon."

"Well then that's something."

She considered. "Something—yes. She likes him."

"Rather! I can see it still, the face with which, when he was here in October—that night when she was in white, when she had people there and those musicians—she committed him to my care. It was beautiful for both of us—she put us in relation. She asked me, for the time, to take him about; I did so, and we quite hit it off. That proved," Densher said with a quick sad smile, "that she liked him."

"He liked *you*," Susan Shepherd presently risked.

"Ah I know nothing about that."

"You ought to then. He went with you to galleries and churches; you saved his time for him, showed him the choicest things, and you perhaps will remember telling me myself that if he hadn't been a great surgeon he might really have been a great judge. I mean of the beautiful."

"Well," the young man admitted, "that's what he is—in having judged *her*. He hasn't," he went on, "judged her for nothing. His interest in her—which we must make the most of—can only be supremely beneficent."

He still roamed, while he spoke, with his hands in his pockets, and she saw him, on this, as her eyes sufficiently betrayed, trying to keep his distance from the recognition he had a few moments before partly confessed to. "I'm glad," she dropped, "you like him!"

There was something for him in the sound of it. "Well, I do no more, dear lady, than you do yourself. Surely *you* like him. Surely, when he was here, we all liked him."

"Yes, but I seem to feel I know what he thinks. And I should think, with all the time you spent with him, you'd know it," she said, "yourself."

Densher stopped short, though at first without a word. "We never spoke of her. Neither of us mentioned her, even to sound her name, and nothing whatever in connexion with her passed between us."

Mrs. Stringham stared up at him, surprised at this picture. But she had plainly an idea that after an instant resisted it. "That was his professional propriety."

"Precisely. But it was also my sense of that virtue in him, and it was something more besides." And he spoke with sudden intensity. "I couldn't *talk* to him about her!"

"Oh!" said Susan Shepherd.

"I can't talk to any one about her."

"Except to *me*," his friend continued.

"Except to you." The ghost of her smile, a gleam of significance, had waited on her words, and it kept him, for honesty, looking at her. For honesty too—that is for his own words—he had quickly coloured: he was sinking so, at a stroke, the burden of his discourse with Kate. His visitor, for the minute, while their eyes met, might have been watching him hold it down. And he *had* to hold it down—the effort of which, precisely, made him red. He couldn't let it come up; at least not yet. She might make what she would of it. He attempted to repeat his statement, but he really modified it. "Sir Luke, at all events, had nothing to tell me, and I had nothing to tell him. Make-believe talk was impossible for us, and—"

"And *real*"—she had taken him right up with a huge emphasis—"was more impossible still." No doubt—he didn't deny it; and she had straightway drawn her conclusion. "Then that proves what I say—that there were immensities between you. Otherwise you'd have chattered."

"I dare say," Densher granted, "we were both thinking of her."

"You were neither of you thinking of any one else. That's why you kept together."

Well, that too, if she desired, he took from her; but he came straight back to what he had originally said. "I haven't a notion, all the same, of what he thinks." She faced him, visibly, with the question into which he had already observed that her special shade of earnestness was perpetually flowering, right and left—"Are you *very* sure?"—and he could only note her apparent difference from himself. "You, I judge, believe that he thinks she's gone."

She took it, but she bore up. "It doesn't matter what I believe."

"Well, we shall see"—and he felt almost basely superficial. More and more, for the last five minutes, had he known she had brought something with her, and never in respect to anything had he had such a wish to postpone. He would have liked to put everything off till Thursday; he was sorry it was now Tuesday; he wondered if he were afraid. Yet it wasn't of Sir Luke, who was coming; nor of Milly, who was dying; nor of Mrs. Stringham, who was sitting there. It wasn't, strange to say, of Kate either, for Kate's presence affected him suddenly as having swooned or trembled away. Susan Shepherd's, thus prolonged, had cast on it some influence under which it had ceased to act. She was as absent to his sensibility as she had constantly been, since her departure, absent, as an echo or a reference, from the palace; and it was the first time, among the objects now surrounding him, that his sensibility so noted her. He knew soon enough that it was of himself he was afraid, and that even, if he didn't take care, he should infallibly be more so. "Meanwhile," he added for his companion, "it has been everything for me to see you." She slowly rose at the words, which might almost have conveyed to her the hint of his taking care. She stood there as if she had in fact seen him abruptly moved to dismiss her. But the abruptness would have been in this case so marked as fairly to offer ground for insistence to her imagination of his state. It would take her moreover, she clearly showed him she was thinking, but a minute or two to insist. Besides, she had already said it. "Will you do it if *he* asks you? I mean if Sir Luke himself puts it to you. And will you give him"—oh she was earnest now!—"the opportunity to put it to you?"

"The opportunity to put what?"

"That if you deny it to her, that may still do something."

Densher felt himself—as had already once befallen him in the quarter of an hour—turn red to the top of his forehead. Turning red had, however, for him, as a sign of shame, been, so to speak, discounted: his consciousness of it at the present moment was rather as a sign of his fear. It showed him sharply enough of what he was afraid. "If I deny what to her?"

Hesitation, on the demand, revived in her, for hadn't he all along been letting her see that he knew? "Why, what Lord Mark told her."

"And what did Lord Mark tell her?"

Mrs. Stringham had a look of bewilderment—of seeing him as suddenly perverse. "I've been judging that you yourself know." And it was she who now blushed deep.

It quickened his pity for her, but he was beset too by other things. "Then *you* know—"

"Of his dreadful visit?" She stared. "Why it's what has done it."

"Yes—I understand that. But you also know—"

He had faltered again, but all she knew she now wanted to say. "I'm speaking," she said soothingly, "of what he told her. It's *that* that I've taken you as knowing."

"Oh!" he sounded in spite of himself.

It appeared to have for her, he saw the next moment, the quality of relief, as if he had supposed her thinking of something else. Thereupon, straightway, that lightened it. "Oh you thought I've known it for *true!*"

Her light had heightened her flush, and he saw that he had betrayed himself. Not, however, that it mattered, as he immediately saw still better. There it was now, all of it at last, and this at least there was no postponing. They were left with her idea—the one she was wishing to make him recognise. He had expressed ten minutes before his need to understand, and she was acting after all but on that. Only what he was to understand was no small matter; it might be larger even than as yet appeared.

He took again one of his turns, not meeting what she had last said; he mooned a minute, as he would have called it, at a window; and of course she could see that she had driven him to the wall. She did clearly, without delay, see it; on which her sense of having "caught" him became as promptly a scruple, which she spoke as if not to press. "What I mean is that he told her you've been all the while engaged to Miss Croy."

He gave a jerk round; it was almost—to hear it—the touch of a lash; and he said—idiotically, as he afterwards knew—the first thing that came into his head. "All *what* while?"

"Oh it's not I who say it." She spoke in gentleness. "I only repeat to you what he told her."

Densher, from whom an impatience had escaped, had already caught himself up. "Pardon my brutality. Of course I know what you're talking about. I saw him, toward the evening," he further explained, "in the Piazza; only just saw him—through the glass at Florian's—without any words. In fact I scarcely know him—there wouldn't have been occasion. It was but once, moreover—he must have gone that night. But I knew he wouldn't have come for nothing, and I turned it over—what he would have come for."

Oh so had Mrs. Stringham. "He came for exasperation."

Densher approved. "He came to let her know that he knows better than she for whom it was she had a couple of months before, in her fool's paradise, refused him."

"How you *do* know!"—and Mrs. Stringham almost smiled.

"I know that—but I don't know the good it does him."

"The good, he thinks, if he has patience—not too much—may be to come. He doesn't know what he has done to her. Only *we*, you see, do that."

He saw, but he wondered. "She kept from him—what she felt?"

"She was able—I'm sure of it—not to show anything. He dealt her his blow, and she took it without a sign." Mrs. Stringham, it was plain, spoke by book, and it brought into play again her appreciation of what she related. "She's magnificent."

Densher again gravely assented. "Magnificent!"

"And *he*," she went on, "is an idiot of idiots."

"An idiot of idiots." For a moment, on it all, on the stupid doom in it, they looked at each other. "Yet he's thought so awfully clever."

"So awfully—it's Maud Lowder's own view. And he was nice, in London," said Mrs. Stringham, "to *me*. One could almost pity him—he has had such a good conscience."

"That's exactly the inevitable ass."

"Yes, but it wasn't—I could see from the only few things she first told me—that he meant *her* the least harm. He intended none whatever."

"That's always the ass at his worst," Densher returned. "He only of course meant harm to me."

"And good to himself—he thought that would come. He had been unable to swallow," Mrs. Stringham pursued, "what had happened on his other visit. He had been then too sharply humiliated."

"Oh I saw that."

"Yes, and he also saw you. He saw you received, as it were, while he was turned away."

"Perfectly," Densher said—"I've filled it out. And also that he has known meanwhile for *what* I was then received. For a stay of all these weeks. He had had it to think of."

"Precisely—it was more than he could bear. But he has it," said Mrs. Stringham, "to think of still."

"Only, after all," asked Densher, who himself somehow, at this point, was having more to think of even than he had yet had—"only, after all, how has he happened to know? That is, to know enough."

"What do you call enough?" Mrs. Stringham enquired.

"He can only have acted—it would have been his sole safety—from full knowledge."

He had gone on without heeding her question; but, face to face as they were, something had none the less passed between them. It was this that, after an instant, made her again interrogative. "What do you mean by full knowledge?"

Densher met it indirectly. "Where has he been since October?"

"I think he has been back to England. He came in fact, I've reason to believe, straight from there."

"Straight to do this job? All the way for his half-hour?"

"Well, to try again—with the help perhaps of a new fact. To make himself possibly right with her—a different attempt from the other. He had at any rate something to tell her, and he didn't know his opportunity would reduce itself to half an hour. Or perhaps indeed half an hour would be just what was most effective. It *has* been!" said Susan Shepherd.

Her companion took it in, understanding but too well; yet as she lighted the matter for him more, really, than his own courage had quite dared—putting the absent dots on several i's—he saw new questions swarm. They had been till now in a bunch, entangled and confused; and they fell apart, each showing for itself. The first he put to her was at any rate abrupt. "Have you heard of late from Mrs. Lowder."

"Oh yes, two or three times. She depends naturally upon news of Milly."

He hesitated. "And does she depend, naturally, upon news of *me?*"

His friend matched for an instant his deliberation.

"I've given her none that hasn't been decently good. This will have been the first."

"'This'?" Densher was thinking.

"Lord Mark's having been here, and her being as she is."

He thought a moment longer. "What has Mrs. Lowder written about him? Has she written that he has been with them?"

635

"She has mentioned him but once—it was in her letter before the last. Then she said something."

"And what did she say?"

Mrs. Stringham produced it with an effort. "Well it was in reference to Miss Croy. That she thought Kate was thinking of him. Or perhaps I should say rather that he was thinking of *her*—only it seemed this time to have struck Maud that he was seeing the way more open to him."

Densher listened with his eyes on the ground, but he presently raised them to speak, and there was that in his face which proved him aware of a queerness in his question. "Does she mean he has been encouraged to *propose* to her niece?"

"I don't know what she means."

"Of course not"—he recovered himself; "and I oughtn't to seem to trouble you to piece together what I can't piece myself. Only I 'guess,'" he added, "I *can* piece it."

She spoke a little timidly, but she risked it. "I dare say I can piece it too."

It was one of the things in her—and his conscious face took it from her as such—that from the moment of her coming in had seemed to mark for him, as to what concerned him, the long jump of her perception. They had parted four days earlier with many things, between them, deep down. But these things were now on their troubled surface, and it wasn't he who had brought them so quickly up. Women were wonderful—at least this one was. But so, not less, was Milly, was Aunt Maud; so, most of all, was his very Kate. Well, he already knew what he had been feeling about the circle of petticoats. They were all *such* petticoats! It was just the fineness of his tangle. The sense of that, in its turn, for us too, might have been not unconnected with his putting to his visitor a question that quite passed over her remark. "Has Miss Croy meanwhile written to our friend?"

"Oh," Mrs. Stringham amended, "*her* friend also. But not a single word that I know of."

He had taken it for certain she hadn't—the thing being after all but a shade more strange than his having himself, with Milly, never for six weeks mentioned the young lady in question. It was for that matter but a shade more strange than Milly's not having mentioned her. In spite of which, and however inconsequently, he blushed anew for Kate's silence. He got away from it in fact as quickly as possible, and the furthest he could get was by reverting for a minute to the man they had been judging. "How did he manage to get *at* her? She had only—with what had passed between them before—to say she couldn't see him."

"Oh she was disposed to kindness. She was easier," the good lady explained with a slight embarrassment, "than at the other time."

"Easier?"

"She was off her guard. There was a difference."

"Yes. But exactly not *the* difference."

"Exactly not the difference of her having to be harsh. Perfectly. She could afford to be the opposite." With which, as he said nothing, she just impatiently completed her sense. "She had had *you* here for six weeks."

"Oh!" Densher softly groaned.

"Besides, I think he must have written her first—written I mean in a tone to smooth his way. That it would be a kindness to himself. Then on the spot—"

"On the spot," Densher broke in, "he unmasked? The horrid little beast!"

It made Susan Shepherd turn slightly pale, though quickening, as for hope, the intensity of her look at him. "Oh he went off without an alarm."

"And he must have gone off also without a hope."

"Ah that, certainly."

"Then it *was* mere base revenge. Hasn't he known her, into the bargain," the young man asked—"didn't he, weeks before, see her, judge her, feel her, as having for such a suit as his not more perhaps than a few months to live?"

Mrs. Stringham at first, for reply, but looked at him in silence; and it gave more force to what she then remarkably added. "He has doubtless been aware of what you speak of, just as you have yourself been aware."

"He has wanted her, you mean, just *because*—?"

"Just because," said Susan Shepherd.

"The hound!" Merton Densher brought out. He moved off, however, with a hot face, as soon as he had spoken, conscious again of an intention in his visitor's reserve. Dusk was now deeper, and after he had once more taken counsel of the dreariness without he turned to his companion. "Shall we have lights—a lamp or the candles?"

"Not for me."

"Nothing?"

"Not for me."

He waited at the window another moment and then faced his friend with a thought. "He *will* have proposed to Miss Croy. That's what has happened."

Her reserve continued. "It's you who must judge."

"Well, I do judge. Mrs. Lowder will have done so too—only *she*, poor lady, wrong. Miss Croy's refusal of him will have struck him"—Densher continued to make it out—"as a phenomenon requiring a reason."

"And you've been clear to him *as* the reason?"

"Not too clear—since I'm sticking here and since that has been a fact to make his descent on Miss Theale relevant. But clear enough. He has believed," said Densher bravely, "that I may have been a reason at Lancaster Gate, and yet at the same time have been up to something in Venice."

Mrs. Stringham took her courage from his own. "'Up to' something? Up to what?"

"God knows. To some 'game,' as they say. To some deviltry. To some duplicity."

"Which of course," Mrs. Stringham observed, "is a monstrous supposition." Her companion, after a stiff minute—sensibly long for each—fell away from her again, and then added to it another minute, which he spent once more looking out with his hands in his pockets. This was no answer, he perfectly knew, to what she had dropped, and it even seemed to state for his own ears that no answer was possible. She left him to himself, and he was glad she had declined, for their further colloquy, the advantage of lights. These would have been an advantage mainly to herself. Yet she got her benefit too even from the absence of them. It came out in her very tone when at last she addressed him—so differently, for confidence—in words she had already used. "If Sir Luke himself asks it of you as something you can do for *him*, will you deny to Milly herself what she has been made so dreadfully to believe?"

Oh how he knew he hung back! But at last he said: "You're absolutely certain then that she does believe it?"

"Certain?" She appealed to their whole situation. "Judge!"

He took his time again to judge. "Do *you* believe it?"

He was conscious that his own appeal pressed her hard; it eased him a little that her answer must be a pain to her discretion. She answered none the less, and he was truly the harder pressed. "What I believe will inevitably depend more or less on your action. You can perfectly settle it—if you care. I promise to believe you down to the ground if, to save her life, you consent to a denial."

"But a denial, when it comes to that—confound the whole thing, don't you see!—of exactly what?"

It was as if he were hoping she would narrow; but in fact she enlarged. "Of everything."

Everything had never even yet seemed to him so incalculably much. "Oh!" he simply moaned into the gloom.

IV

The near Thursday, coming nearer and bringing Sir Luke Strett, brought also blessedly an abatement of other rigours. The weather changed, the stubborn storm yielded, and the autumn sunshine, baffled for many days, but now hot and almost vindictive, came into its own again and, with an almost audible paean, a suffusion of bright sound that was one with the bright colour, took large possession. Venice glowed and plashed and called and chimed again; the air was like a clap of hands, and the scattered pinks, yellows, blues, sea-greens, were like a hanging-out of vivid stuffs, a laying-down of fine carpets. Densher rejoiced in this on the occasion of his going to the station to meet the great doctor. He went after consideration, which, as he was constantly aware, was at present his imposed, his only, way of doing anything. That was where the event had landed him—where no event in his life had landed him before. He had thought, no doubt, from the day he was born, much more than he had acted; except indeed that he remembered thoughts—a few of them—which at the moment of their coming to him had thrilled him almost like adventures. But anything like his actual state he had not, as to the prohibition of impulse, accident, range—the prohibition in other words of freedom—hitherto known. The great oddity was that if he had felt his arrival, so few weeks back, especially as an adventure, nothing could now less resemble one than the fact of his staying. It would be an adventure to break away, to depart, to go back, above all, to London, and tell Kate Croy he had done so; but there was something of the merely, the almost meanly, obliged and involved sort in his going on as he was. That was the effect in particular of Mrs. Stringham's visit, which had left him as with such a taste in his mouth of what he couldn't do. It had made this quantity clear to him, and yet had deprived him of the sense, the other sense, of what, for a refuge, he possibly *could*.

It was but a small make-believe of freedom, he knew, to go to the station for Sir Luke. Nothing equally free, at all events, had he yet turned over so long. What then was his odious position but that again and again he was afraid? He stiffened himself under this consciousness as if it had been a tax levied by a tyrant. He hadn't at any time proposed to himself to live long enough for fear to preponderate in his life. Such was simply the advantage it had actually got of him. He was afraid for instance that an advance to his distinguished friend might prove for him somehow a pledge or a committal. He was afraid of it as a current that would draw him too far; yet he thought with an equal aversion of being shabby, being poor, through fear. What finally prevailed with him was the reflexion that, whatever might happen, the great man had, after that occasion at the palace, their young woman's brief sacrifice to society—and the hour of Mrs. Stringham's appeal had brought it well to the surface—shown him marked benevolence. Mrs. Stringham's comments on the relation in which Milly had placed them made him—it was unmistakeable—feel things he perhaps hadn't felt. It was in the spirit of seeking a chance to feel again adequately whatever it was he had missed—it was, no doubt, in that spirit, so far as it went a stroke for freedom, that Densher, arriving betimes, paced the platform before the train came in. Only, after it had come and he had presented himself at the door of Sir Luke's compartment with everything that followed—only, as the situation developed, the sense of an anti-climax to so many intensities deprived his apprehensions and hesitations even of the scant dignity they might claim. He could scarce have said if the visitor's manner less showed the remembrance that might have suggested expectation, or made shorter work of surprise in presence of the fact.

Sir Luke had clean forgotten—so Densher read—the rather remarkable young man he had formerly gone about with, though he picked him up again, on the spot, with one large quiet look. The young man felt himself so picked, and the thing immediately affected him as the proof of a splendid economy. Opposed to all the waste with which he was now connected the exhibition was of a nature quite nobly to admonish him. The eminent pilgrim, in the train, all the way, had used the hours as he needed, thinking not a moment in advance of what finally awaited him. An exquisite case awaited him—of which, in this queer way, the remarkable young man was an outlying part; but the single motion of his face, the motion into which Densher, from the platform, lightly stirred its stillness, was his first renewed cognition. If, however, he had suppressed the matter by leaving Victoria he would at once suppress now, in turn, whatever else suited. The perception of this became as a symbol of the whole pitch, so far as one might one's self be concerned, of his visit. One saw, our friend further meditated, everything that, in contact, he appeared to accept—if only, for much, not to trouble to sink it: what one missed was the inward use he made of it. Densher began wondering, at the great water-steps outside, what use he would make of the anomaly of their having there to separate. Eugenio had been on the platform, in the respectful rear, and the gondola from the palace, under his direction, bestirred itself, with its attaching mixture of alacrity and dignity, on their coming out of the station together. Densher didn't at all mind now that, he himself of necessity refusing a seat on the deep black cushions beside the guest of the palace, he had Milly's three emissaries for spectators; and this susceptibility, he also knew, it was something to have left behind. All he did was to smile down vaguely from the steps—they could see him, the donkeys, as shut out as they would. "I don't," he said with a sad headshake, "go there now."

"Oh!" Sir Luke Strett returned, and made no more of it; so that the thing was splendid, Densher fairly thought, as an inscrutability quite inevitable and unconscious. His friend appeared not even to make of it that he supposed it might be for respect to the crisis. He didn't moreover afterwards make much more of anything—after the classic craft, that is, obeying in the main Pasquale's inimitable stroke from the poop, had performed the manoeuvre by which it presented, receding, a back, so to speak, rendered positively graceful by the high black hump of its *felze*. Densher watched the gondola out of sight—he heard Pasquale's cry, borne to him across the water, for the sharp firm swerve into a side-canal, a short cut to the palace. He had no gondola of his own; it was his habit never to take one; and he humbly—as in Venice it *is* humble—walked away, though not without having for some time longer stood as if fixed where the guest of the palace had left him. It was strange enough, but he found himself as never yet, and as he couldn't have reckoned, in presence of the truth that was the truest about Milly. He couldn't have reckoned on the force of the difference instantly made—for it was all in the air as he heard Pasquale's cry and saw the boat disappear—by the mere visibility, on the spot, of the personage summoned to her aid. He hadn't only never been near the facts of her condition—which counted so as a blessing for him; he hadn't only, with all the world, hovered outside an impenetrable ring fence, within which there reigned a kind of expensive vagueness made up of smiles and silences and beautiful fictions and priceless arrangements, all strained to breaking; but he had also, with every one else, as he now felt, actively fostered suppressions which were in the direct interest of every one's good manner, every one's pity, every one's really quite generous ideal. It was a conspiracy of silence, as the *cliché* went, to which no one had made an exception, the great smudge of mortality across the picture, the shadow of pain and horror, finding in no quarter a surface of spirit or of speech that consented to reflect it. "The mere aesthetic instinct of mankind—!" our young man had more than once, in the connexion, said to himself; letting the rest of the proposition drop, but touching again thus sufficiently on the outrage even to taste involved in one's having to *see*. So then it had been—a general conscious fool's paradise, from which the specified had been chased like a dangerous animal. What therefore had at present befallen was that the specified, standing all the while at the gate, had now crossed the threshold as in Sir Luke Strett's person and quite on such a scale as to fill out the whole precinct. Densher's nerves, absolutely his heart-beats too, had measured the change before he on this occasion moved away.

The facts of physical suffering, of incurable pain, of the chance grimly narrowed, had been made, at a stroke, intense, and this was to be the way he was now to feel them. The clearance of the air, in short, making vision not only possible but inevitable, the one thing left to be thankful for was the breadth of Sir Luke's shoulders, which, should one be able to keep in line with them, might in some degree interpose. It was, however, far from plain to Densher for the first day or two that he was again to see his distinguished friend at all. That he couldn't, on any basis actually serving, return to the palace—this was as solid to him, every whit, as the other feature of his case, the fact of the publicity attaching to his proscription through his not having taken himself off. He had been seen often enough in the Leporelli gondola. As, accordingly, he was not on any presumption destined to meet Sir Luke about the town, where the latter would have neither time nor taste to lounge, nothing more would occur between them unless the great man should surprisingly wait upon him. His doing that, Densher further reflected, wouldn't even simply depend on Mrs. Stringham's having decided to—as they might say—turn him on. It would depend as well—for there would be practically some difference to her—on her actually attempting it; and it would depend above all on what Sir Luke would make of such an overture. Densher had for that matter his own view of the amount, to say nothing of the particular sort, of response it might expect from him. He had his own view of the ability of such a personage even to understand such an appeal. To what extent could he be prepared, and what importance in fine could he attach? Densher asked himself these questions, in truth, to put his own position at the worst. He should miss the great man completely unless the great man should come to see him, and the great man could only come to see him for a purpose unsupposable. Therefore he wouldn't come at all, and consequently there was nothing to hope.

It wasn't in the least that Densher invoked this violence to all probability; but it pressed on him that there were few possible diversions he could afford now to miss. Nothing in his predicament was so odd as that, incontestably afraid of himself, he was not afraid of Sir Luke. He had an impression, which he clung to, based on a previous taste of the visitor's company, that *he* would somehow let him off. The truth about Milly perched on his shoulders and sounded in his tread, became by the fact of his presence the name and the form, for the time, of everything in the place; but it didn't, for the difference, sit in his face, the face so squarely and easily turned to Densher at the earlier season. His presence on the first occasion, not as the result of a summons, but as a friendly whim of his own, had had quite another value; and though our young man could scarce regard that value as recoverable he yet reached out in imagination to a renewal of the old contact. He didn't propose, as he privately and forcibly phrased the matter, to be a hog; but there was something he after all did want for himself. It was something—this stuck to him—that Sir Luke would have had for him if it hadn't been impossible. These were his worst days, the two or three; those on which even the sense of the tension at the palace didn't much help him not to feel that his destiny made but light of him. He had never been, as he judged it, so down. In mean conditions, without books, without society, almost without money, he had nothing to do but to wait. His main support really was his original idea, which didn't leave him, of waiting for the deepest depth his predicament could sink him to. Fate would invent, if he but gave it time, some refinement of the horrible. It was just inventing meanwhile this suppression of Sir Luke. When the third day came without a sign he knew what to think. He had given Mrs. Stringham during her call on him no such answer as would have armed her faith, and the ultimatum she had described as ready for him when *he* should be ready was therefore—if on no other ground than her want of this power to answer for him—not to be presented. The presentation, heaven knew, was not what he desired.

That was not, either, we hasten to declare—as Densher then soon enough saw—the idea with which Sir Luke finally stood before him again. For stand before him again he finally did; just when our friend had gloomily embraced the belief that the limit of his power to absent himself from London obligations would have been reached. Four or five days, exclusive of journeys, represented the largest supposable sacrifice—to a head not crowned—on the part of one of the highest medical lights in the world; so that really when the personage in question, following up a tinkle of the bell, solidly rose in the doorway, it was to impose on Densher a vision that for the instant cut like a knife. It spoke, the fact, and in a single dreadful word, of the magnitude—he shrank from calling it anything else—of Milly's case. The great man had not gone then, and an immense surrender to her immense need was so expressed in it that some effect, some help, some hope, were flagrantly part of the expression. It was for Densher, with his reaction from disappointment, as if he were conscious of ten things at once—the foremost being that just conceivably, since Sir Luke *was* still there, she had been saved. Close upon its heels, however, and quite as sharply, came the sense that the crisis—plainly even now to be prolonged for him—was to have none of that sound simplicity. Not only had his visitor not dropped in to gossip about Milly, he hadn't dropped in to mention her at all; he had dropped in fairly to show that during the brief remainder of his stay, the end of which was now in sight, as little as possible of that was to be looked for. The demonstration, such as it was, was in the key of their previous acquaintance, and it was their previous acquaintance that had made him come. He was not to stop longer than the Saturday next at hand, but there were things of interest he should like to see again meanwhile. It was for these things of interest, for Venice and the opportunity of Venice, for a prowl or two, as he called it, and a turn about, that he had looked his young man up—producing on the latter's part, as soon as the case had, with the lapse of a further twenty-four hours, so defined itself, the most incongruous, yet most beneficent revulsion. Nothing could in fact have been more monstrous on the surface—and Densher was well aware of it—than the relief he found during this short period in the tacit drop of all reference to the palace, in neither hearing news nor asking for it. That was what had come out for him, on his visitor's entrance, even in the very seconds of suspense that were connecting the fact also directly and intensely with Milly's state. He had come to say he had saved her—he had come, as from Mrs. Stringham, to say how she might *be* saved—he had come, in spite of Mrs. Stringham, to say she was lost: the distinct throbs of hope, of fear, simultaneous for all their distinctness, merged their identity in a bound of the heart just as immediate and which remained after they had passed. It simply did wonders for him—this was the truth—that Sir Luke was, as he would have said, quiet.

The result of it was the oddest consciousness as of a blest calm after a storm. He had been trying for weeks, as we know, to keep superlatively still, and trying it largely in solitude and silence; but he looked back on it now as on the heat of fever. The real, the right stillness was this particular form of society. They walked together and they talked, looked up pictures again and recovered impressions—Sir Luke knew just what he wanted; haunted a little the dealers in old wares; sat down at Florian's for rest and mild drinks; blessed above all the grand weather, a bath of warm air, a pageant of autumn light. Once or twice while they rested the great man closed his eyes—keeping them so for some minutes while his companion, the more easily watching his face for it, made private reflexions on the subject of lost sleep. He had been up at night with her—he in person, for hours; but this was all he showed of it and was apparently to remain his nearest approach to an allusion. The extraordinary thing was that Densher could take it in perfectly as evidence, could turn cold at the image looking out of it; and yet that he could at the same time not intermit a throb of his response to accepted liberation. The liberation was an experience that held its own, and he continued to know why, in spite of his deserts, in spite of his folly, in spite of everything, he had so fondly hoped for it. He had hoped for it, had sat in his room there waiting for it, because he had thus divined in it, should it come, some power to let him off. He was *being* let off; dealt with in the only way that didn't aggravate his responsibility. The beauty was also that this wasn't on system or on any basis of intimate knowledge; it was just by being a man of the world and by knowing life, by feeling the real, that Sir Luke did him good. There had been in all the case too many women. A man's sense of it, another man's, changed the air; and he wondered what man, had he chosen, would have been more to his purpose than this one. He was large and easy—that was the benediction; he knew what mattered and what didn't; he distinguished between the essence and the shell, the just grounds and the unjust for fussing. One was thus—if one were concerned with him or exposed to him at all—in his hands for whatever he should do, and not much less affected by his mercy than one might have been by his rigour. The grand thing—it did come to that—was the way he carried off, as one might fairly call it, the business of making odd things natural. Nothing, if they hadn't taken it so, could have exceeded the unexplained oddity, between them, of Densher's now complete detachment from the poor ladies at the palace; nothing could have exceeded the no less marked anomaly of the great man's own abstentions of speech. He made, as he had done when they met at the station, nothing whatever of anything; and the effect of it, Densher would have said, was a relation with him quite resembling that of doctor and patient. One took the cue from him as one might have taken a dose—except that the cue was pleasant in the taking.

That was why one could leave it to his tacit discretion, why for the three or four days Densher again and again did so leave it; merely wondering a little, at the most, on the eve of Saturday, the announced term of the episode. Waiting once more on this latter occasion, the Saturday morning, for Sir

Luke's reappearance at the station, our friend had to recognise the drop of his own borrowed ease, the result, naturally enough, of the prospect of losing a support. The difficulty was that, on such lines as had served them, the support was Sir Luke's personal presence. Would he go without leaving some substitute for that?—and without breaking, either, his silence in respect to his errand? Densher was in still deeper ignorance than at the hour of his call, and what was truly prodigious at so supreme a moment was that—as had immediately to appear—no gleam of light on what he had been living with for a week found its way out of him. What he had been doing was proof of a huge interest as well as of a huge fee; yet when the Leporelli gondola again, and somewhat tardily, approached, his companion, watching from the water-steps, studied his fine closed face as much as ever in vain. It was like a lesson, from the highest authority, on the subject of the relevant, so that its blankness affected Densher of a sudden almost as a cruelty, feeling it quite awfully compatible, as he did, with Milly's having ceased to exist. And the suspense continued after they had passed together, as time was short, directly into the station, where Eugenio, in the field early, was mounting guard over the compartment he had secured. The strain, though probably lasting, at the carriage-door, but a couple of minutes, prolonged itself so for our poor gentleman's nerves that he involuntarily directed a long look at Eugenio, who met it, however, as only Eugenio could. Sir Luke's attention was given for the time to the right bestowal of his numerous effects, about which he was particular, and Densher fairly found himself, so far as silence could go, questioning the representative of the palace. It didn't humiliate him now; it didn't humiliate him even to feel that that personage exactly knew how little he satisfied him. Eugenio resembled to that extent Sir Luke—to the extent of the extraordinary things with which his facial habit was compatible. By the time, however, that Densher had taken from it all its possessor intended Sir Luke was free and with a hand out for farewell. He offered the hand at first without speech; only on meeting his eyes could our young man see that they had never yet so completely looked at him. It was never, with Sir Luke, that they looked harder at one time than at another; but they looked longer, and this, even a shade of it, might mean on his part everything. It meant, Densher for ten seconds believed, that Milly Theale was dead; so that the word at last spoken made him start.

"I shall come back."

"Then she's better?"

"I shall come back within the month," Sir Luke repeated without heeding the question. He had dropped Densher's hand, but he held him otherwise still. "I bring you a message from Miss Theale," he said as if they hadn't spoken of her. "I'm commissioned to ask you from her to go and see her."

Densher's rebound from his supposition had a violence that his stare betrayed. "She asks me?"

Sir Luke had got into the carriage, the door of which the guard had closed; but he spoke again as he stood at the window, bending a little but not leaning out. "She told me she'd like it, and I promised that, as I expected to find you here, I'd let you know."

Densher, on the platform, took it from him, but what he took brought the blood into his face quite as what he had had to take from Mrs. Stringham. And he was also bewildered. "Then she can receive—?"

"She can receive you."

"And you're coming back—?"

"Oh because I must. She's not to move. She's to stay. I come to her."

"I see, I see," said Densher, who indeed did see—saw the sense of his friend's words and saw beyond it as well. What Mrs. Stringham had announced, and what he had yet expected not to have to face, *had* then come. Sir Luke had kept it for the last, but there it was, and the colourless compact form it was now taking—the tone of one man of the world to another, who, after what had happened, would understand—was but the characteristic manner of his appeal. Densher was to understand remarkably much; and the great thing certainly was to show that he did. "I'm particularly obliged, I'll go to-day." He brought that out, but in his pause, while they continued to look at each other, the train had slowly creaked into motion. There was time but for one more word, and the young man chose it, out of twenty, with intense concentration. "Then she's better?"

Sir Luke's face was wonderful. "Yes, she's better." And he kept it at the window while the train receded, holding him with it still. It was to be his nearest approach to the utter reference they had hitherto so successfully avoided. If it stood for everything; never had a face had to stand for more. So Densher, held after the train had gone, sharply reflected; so he reflected, asking himself into what abyss it pushed him, even while conscious of retreating under the maintained observation of Eugenio.

BOOK TENTH

I

"Then it has been—what do you say? a whole fortnight?—without your making a sign?"

Kate put that to him distinctly, in the December dusk of Lancaster Gate and on the matter of the time he had been back; but he saw with it straightway that she was as admirably true as ever to her instinct—which was a system as well—of not admitting the possibility between them of small resentments, of trifles to trip up their general trust. That by itself, the renewed beauty of it, would at this fresh sight of her have stirred him to his depths if something else, something no less vivid but quite separate, hadn't stirred him still more. It was in seeing her that he felt what their interruption had been, and that they met across it even as persons whose adventures, on either side, in time and space, of the nature of perils and exiles, had had a peculiar strangeness. He wondered if he were as different for her as she herself had immediately appeared: which was but his way indeed of taking in, with his thrill, that—even going by the mere first look—she had never been so handsome. That fact bloomed for him, in the firelight and lamplight that glowed their welcome through the London fog, as the flower of her difference; just as her difference itself—part of which was her striking him as older in a degree for which no mere couple of months could account—was the fruit of their intimate relation. If she was different it was because they had chosen together that she should be, and she might now, as a proof of their wisdom, their success, of the reality of what had happened—of what in fact, for the spirit of each, was still happening—been showing it to him for pride. His having returned and yet kept, for numbered days, so still, had been, he was quite aware, the first point he should have to tackle; with which consciousness indeed he had made a clean breast of it in finally addressing Mrs. Lowder a note that had led to his present visit. He had written to Aunt Maud as the finer way; and it would doubtless have been to be noted that he needed no effort not to write to Kate. Venice was three weeks behind him—he had come up slowly; but it was still as if even in London he must conform to her law. That was exactly how he was able, with his faith in her steadiness, to appeal to her feeling for the situation and explain his stretched delicacy. He had come to tell her everything, so far as occasion would serve them; and if nothing was more distinct than that his slow journey, his waits, his delay to reopen communication had kept pace with this resolve, so the inconsequence was doubtless at bottom but one of the elements of intensity. He was gathering everything up, everything he should tell her. That took time, and the proof was that, as he felt on the spot, he couldn't have brought it all with him before this afternoon. He *had* brought it, to the last syllable, and, out of the quantity it wouldn't be hard—as he in fact found—to produce, for Kate's understanding, his first reason.

"A fortnight, yes—it was a fortnight Friday; but I've only been keeping in, you see, with our wonderful system." He was so easily justified as that this of itself plainly enough prevented her saying she didn't see. Their wonderful system was accordingly still vivid for her; and such a gage of its equal vividness for himself was precisely what she must have asked. He hadn't even to dot his i's beyond the remark that on the very face of it, she would remember, their wonderful system attached no premium to rapidities of transition. "I couldn't quite—don't you know?—take my rebound with a rush; and I suppose I've been instinctively hanging off to minimise, for you as well as for myself, the appearances of rushing. There's a sort of fitness. But I knew you'd understand." It was presently as if she really understood so well that she almost appealed from his insistence—yet looking at him too, he was not unconscious, as if this mastery of fitnesses was a strong sign for her of what she had done to him. He might have struck her as expert for contingencies in the very degree of her having in Venice struck *him* as expert. He smiled over his plea for a renewal with stages and steps, a thing shaded, as they might say, and graduated; though—finely as she must respond—she met the smile but as she had met his entrance five minutes before. Her soft gravity at that moment—which was yet not solemnity, but the look of a consciousness charged with life to the brim and wishing not to overflow—had not qualified her welcome; what had done this being much more the presence in the room, for a couple of minutes, of the footman who had introduced him and who had been interrupted in preparing the tea-table.

Mrs. Lowder's reply to Densher's note had been to appoint the tea-hour, five o'clock on Sunday, for his seeing them. Kate had thereafter wired him, without a signature, "Come on Sunday *before* tea—about a quarter of an hour, which will help us"; and he had arrived therefore scrupulously at twenty minutes to five. Kate was alone in the room and hadn't delayed to tell him that Aunt Maud, as she had happily gathered, was to be, for the interval—not long but precious—engaged with an old servant, retired and pensioned, who had been paying her a visit and who was within the hour to depart again for the suburbs. They were to have the scrap of time, after the withdrawal of the footman, to themselves, and there was a moment when, in spite of their wonderful system, in spite of the proscription of rushes and the propriety of shades, it proclaimed itself indeed precious. And all without prejudice—that was what kept it noble—to Kate's high sobriety and her beautiful self-command. If he had his discretion she had her perfect manner, which was *her* decorum. Mrs. Stringham, he had, to finish with the question of his delay, furthermore observed, Mrs. Stringham would have written to Mrs. Lowder of his having quitted the place; so that it wasn't as if he were hoping to cheat them. They'd know he was no longer there.

"Yes, we've known it."

"And you continue to hear?"

"From Mrs. Stringham? Certainly. By which I mean Aunt Maud does."

"Then you've recent news?"

Her face showed a wonder. "Up to within a day or two I believe. But haven't *you?*"

"No—I've heard nothing." And it was now that he felt how much he had to tell her. "I don't get letters. But I've been sure Mrs. Lowder does." With which he added: "Then of course you know." He waited as if she would show what she knew; but she only showed in silence the dawn of a surprise that she couldn't control. There was nothing but for him to ask what he wanted. "Is Miss Theale alive?"

Kate's look at this was large. "Don't you *know?*"

"How should I, my dear—in the absence of everything?" And he himself stared as for light. "She's dead?" Then as with her eyes on him she slowly shook her head he uttered a strange "Not yet?"

It came out in Kate's face that there were several questions on her lips, but the one she presently put was: "Is it very terrible?"

"The manner of her so consciously and helplessly dying?" He had to think a moment. "Well, yes—since you ask me: very terrible to *me*—so far as, before I came away, I had any sight of it. But I don't think," he went on, "that—though I'll try—I *can* quite tell you what it was, what it is, for me. That's why I probably just sounded to you," he explained, "as if I hoped it might be over."

She gave him her quietest attention, but he by this time saw that, so far as telling her all was concerned, she would be divided between the wish and the reluctance to hear it; between the curiosity that, not unnaturally, would consume her and the opposing scruple of a respect for misfortune. The more she studied him too—and he had never so felt her closely attached to his face—the more the choice of an attitude would become impossible to her. There would simply be a feeling uppermost, and the feeling wouldn't be eagerness. This perception grew in him fast, and he even, with his imagination, had for a moment the quick forecast of her possibly breaking out at him, should he go too far, with a wonderful: "What horrors are you telling me?" It would have the sound—wouldn't it be open to him fairly to bring that out himself?—of a repudiation, for pity and almost for shame, of everything that in Venice had passed between them. Not that she would confess to any return upon herself; not that she would let compunction or horror give her away; but it was in the air for him—yes—that she wouldn't want details, that she positively wouldn't take them, and that, if he would generously understand it from her, she would prefer to keep him down. Nothing, however, was more definite for him than that at the same time he must remain down but so far as it suited him. Something rose strong within him against his not being free with her. She had been free enough about it all, three months before, with *him*. That was what she was at present only in the sense of treating him handsomely. "I can believe," she said with perfect consideration, "how dreadful for you much of it must have been."

He didn't however take this up; there were things about which he wished first to be clear. "There's no other possibility, by what you now know? I mean for her life." And he had just to insist—she would say as little as she could. "She *is* dying?"

"She's dying."

It was strange to him, in the matter of Milly, that Lancaster Gate could make him any surer; yet what in the world, in the matter of Milly, wasn't strange? Nothing was so much so as his own behaviour—his present as well as his past. He could but do as he must. "Has Sir Luke Strett," he asked, "gone back to her?"

"I believe he's there now."

"Then," said Densher, "it's the end."

She took it in silence for whatever he deemed it to be; but she spoke otherwise after a minute. "You won't know, unless you've perhaps seen him yourself, that Aunt Maud has been to him."

"Oh!" Densher exclaimed, with nothing to add to it.

"For real news," Kate herself after an instant added.

"She hasn't thought Mrs. Stringham's real?"

"It's perhaps only I who haven't. It was on Aunt Maud's trying again three days ago to see him that she heard at his house of his having gone. He had started I believe some days before."

"And won't then by this time be back?"

Kate shook her head. "She sent yesterday to know."

"He won't leave her then"—Densher had turned it over—"while she lives. He'll stay to the end. He's magnificent."

"I think *she* is," said Kate.

It had made them again look at each other long; and what it drew from him rather oddly was: "Oh you don't know!"

"Well, she's after all my friend."

It was somehow, with her handsome demur, the answer he had least expected of her; and it fanned with its breath, for a brief instant, his old sense of her variety. "I see. You would have been sure of it. You *were* sure of it."

"Of course I was sure of it."

And a pause again, with this, fell upon them; which Densher, however, presently broke. "If you don't think Mrs. Stringham's news 'real' what do you think of Lord Mark's?"

She didn't think anything. "Lord Mark's?"

"You haven't seen him?"

"Not since he saw her."

"You've known then of his seeing her?"

"Certainly. From Mrs. Stringham."

"And have you known," Densher went on, "the rest?"

Kate wondered. "What rest?"

"Why everything. It was his visit that she couldn't stand—it was what then took place that simply killed her."

"Oh!" Kate seriously breathed. But she had turned pale, and he saw that, whatever her degree of ignorance of these connexions, it wasn't put on. "Mrs. Stringham hasn't said *that*."

He observed none the less that she didn't ask what had then taken place; and he went on with his contribution to her knowledge. "The way it affected her was that it made her give up. She has given up beyond all power to care again, and that's why she's dying."

"Oh!" Kate once more slowly sighed, but with a vagueness that made him pursue.

"One can see now that she was living by will—which was very much what you originally told me of her."

"I remember. That was it."

"Well then her will, at a given moment, broke down, and the collapse was determined by that fellow's dastardly stroke. He told her, the scoundrel, that you and I are secretly engaged."

Kate gave a quick glare. "But he doesn't know it!"

"That doesn't matter. *She* did by the time he had left her. Besides," Densher added, "he does know it. When," he continued, "did you last see him?"

But she was lost now in the picture before her. "*That* was what made her worse?"

He watched her take it in—it so added to her sombre beauty. Then he spoke as Mrs. Stringham had spoken. "She turned her face to the wall."

"Poor Milly!" said Kate.

Slight as it was, her beauty somehow gave it style; so that he continued consistently: "She learned it, you see, too soon—since of course one's idea had been that she might never even learn it at all. And she *had* felt sure—through everything we had done—of there not being between us, so far at least as you were concerned, anything she need regard as a warning."

She took another moment for thought. "It wasn't through anything *you* did—whatever that may have been—that she gained her certainty. It was by the conviction she got from me."

"Oh it's very handsome," Densher said, "for you to take your share!"

"Do you suppose," Kate asked, "that I think of denying it?"

Her look and her tone made him for the instant regret his comment, which indeed had been the first that rose to his lips as an effect absolutely of what they would have called between them her straightness. Her straightness, visibly, was all his own loyalty could ask. Still, that was comparatively beside the mark. "Of course I don't suppose anything but that we're together in our recognitions, our responsibilities—whatever we choose to call them. It isn't a question for us of apportioning shares or distinguishing invidiously among such impressions as it was our idea to give."

"It wasn't *your* idea to give impressions," said Kate.

He met this with a smile that he himself felt, in its strained character, as queer. "Don't go into that!"

It was perhaps not as going into it that she had another idea—an idea born, she showed, of the vision he had just evoked. "Wouldn't it have been possible then to deny the truth of the information? I mean of Lord Mark's."

Densher wondered. "Possible for whom?"

"Why for you."

"To tell her he lied?"

"To tell her he's mistaken."

Densher stared—he was stupefied; the "possible" thus glanced at by Kate being exactly the alternative he had had to face in Venice and to put utterly away from him. Nothing was stranger than such a difference in their view of it. "And to lie myself, you mean, to do it? We *are*, my dear child," he said, "I suppose, still engaged."

"Of course we're still engaged. But to save her life—!"

He took in for a little the way she talked of it. Of course, it was to be remembered, she had always simplified, and it brought back his sense of the degree in which, to her energy as compared with his own, many things were easy; the very sense that so often before had moved him to admiration. "Well, if you must know—and I want you to be clear about it—I didn't even seriously think of a denial to her face. The question of it—*as* possibly saving her—was put to me definitely enough; but to turn it over was only to dismiss it. Besides," he added, "it wouldn't have done any good."

"You mean she would have had no faith in your correction?" She had spoken with a promptitude that affected him of a sudden as almost glib; but he himself paused with the overweight of all he meant, and she meanwhile went on. "Did you try?"

"I hadn't even a chance."

Kate maintained her wonderful manner, the manner of at once having it all before her and yet keeping it all at its distance. "She wouldn't see you?"

"Not after your friend had been with her."

She hesitated. "Couldn't you write?"

It made him also think, but with a difference. "She had turned her face to the wall."

This again for a moment hushed her, and they were both too grave now for parenthetic pity. But her interest came out for at least the minimum of light. "She refused even to let you speak to her?"

"My dear girl," Densher returned, "she was miserably, prohibitively ill."

"Well, that was what she had been before."

"And it didn't prevent? No," Densher admitted, "it didn't; and I don't pretend that she's not magnificent."

"She's prodigious," said Kate Croy.

He looked at her a moment. "So are you, my dear. But that's how it is," he wound up; "and there we are."

His idea had been in advance that she would perhaps sound him much more deeply, asking him above all two or three specific things. He had fairly fancied her even wanting to know and trying to find out how far, as the odious phrase was, he and Milly had gone, and how near, by the same token, they had come. He had asked himself if he were prepared to hear her do that, and had had to take for answer that he was prepared of course for everything. Wasn't he prepared for her ascertaining if her two or three prophecies had found time to be made true? He had fairly believed himself ready to say whether or no the overture on Milly's part promised according to the boldest of them had taken place. But what was in fact blessedly coming to him was that so far as such things were concerned his readiness wouldn't be taxed. Kate's pressure on the question of what had taken place remained so admirably general that even her present enquiry kept itself free of sharpness. "So then that after Lord Mark's interference you never again met?"

It was what he had been all the while coming to. "No; we met once—so far as it could be called a meeting. I had stayed—I didn't come away."

"That," said Kate, "was no more than decent."

"Precisely"—he felt himself wonderful; "and I wanted to be no less. She sent for me, I went to her, and that night I left Venice."

His companion waited. "Wouldn't *that* then have been your chance?"

"To refute Lord Mark's story? No, not even if before her there I had wanted to. What did it signify either? She was dying."

"Well," Kate in a manner persisted, "why not just *because* she was dying?" She had however all her discretion. "But of course I know that seeing her you could judge."

"Of course seeing her I could judge. And I did see her! If I had denied you moreover," Densher said with his eyes on her, "I'd have stuck to it."

She took for a moment the intention of his face. "You mean that to convince her you'd have insisted or somehow proved—?"

"I mean that to convince *you* I'd have insisted or somehow proved—!"

Kate looked for her moment at a loss. "To convince 'me'?"

"I wouldn't have made my denial, in such conditions, only to take it back afterwards."

With this quickly light came for her, and with it also her colour flamed. "Oh you'd have broken with me to make your denial a truth? You'd have 'chucked' me"—she embraced it perfectly—"to save your conscience?"

"I couldn't have done anything else," said Merton Densher. "So you see how right I was not to commit myself, and how little I could dream of it. If it ever again appears to you that I *might* have done so, remember what I say."

Kate again considered, but not with the effect at once to which he pointed. "You've fallen in love with her."

"Well then say so—with a dying woman. Why need you mind and what does it matter?"

It came from him, the question, straight out of the intensity of relation and the face-to-face necessity into which, from the first, from his entering the room, they had found themselves thrown; but it gave them their most extraordinary moment. "Wait till she is dead! Mrs. Stringham," Kate added, "is to telegraph." After which, in a tone still different, "For what then," she asked, "did Milly send for you?"

"It was what I tried to make out before I went. I must tell you moreover that I had no doubt of its really being to give me, as you say, a chance. She believed, I suppose, that I *might* deny; and what, to my own mind, was before me in going to her was the certainty that she'd put me to my test. She wanted from my own lips—so I saw it—the truth. But I was with her for twenty minutes, and she never asked me for it."

"She never wanted the truth"—Kate had a high headshake. "She wanted *you*. She would have taken from you what you could give her and been glad of it, even if she had known it false. You might have lied to her from pity, and she have seen you and felt you lie, and yet—since it was all for tenderness—she would have thanked you and blessed you and clung to you but the more. For that was your strength, my dear man—that she loves you with passion."

"Oh my 'strength'!" Densher coldly murmured.

"Otherwise, since she had sent for you, what was it to ask of you?" And then—quite without irony—as he waited a moment to say: "Was it just once more to look at you?"

"She had nothing to ask of me—nothing, that is, but not to stay any longer. She did to that extent want to see me. She had supposed at first— after he had been with her—that I had seen the propriety of taking myself off. Then since I hadn't—seeing my propriety as I did in another way—she found, days later, that I was still there. This," said Densher, "affected her."

"Of course it affected her."

Again she struck him, for all her dignity, as glib. "If it was somehow for *her* I was still staying, she wished that to end, she wished me to know how little there was need of it. And as a manner of farewell she wished herself to tell me so."

"And she did tell you so?"

"Face-to-face, yes. Personally, as she desired."

"And as *you* of course did."

"No, Kate," he returned with all their mutual consideration; "not as I did. I hadn't desired it in the least."

"You only went to oblige her?"

"To oblige her. And of course also to oblige you."

"Oh for myself certainly I'm glad."

"'Glad'?"—he echoed vaguely the way it rang out.

"I mean you did quite the right thing. You did it especially in having stayed. But that was all?" Kate went on. "That you mustn't wait?"

"That was really all—and in perfect kindness."

"Ah kindness naturally: from the moment she asked of you such a—well, such an effort. That you mustn't wait—that was the point," Kate added—"to see her die."

"That was the point, my dear," Densher said.

"And it took twenty minutes to make it?"

He thought a little. "I didn't time it to a second. I paid her the visit—just like another."

"Like another person?"

"Like another visit."

"Oh!" said Kate. Which had apparently the effect of slightly arresting his speech—an arrest she took advantage of to continue; making with it indeed her nearest approach to an enquiry of the kind against which he had braced himself. "Did she receive you—in her condition—in her room?"

"Not she," said Merton Densher. "She received me just as usual: in that glorious great *salone*, in the dress she always wears, from her inveterate corner of her sofa." And his face for the moment conveyed the scene, just as hers equally embraced it. "Do you remember what you originally said to me of her?"

"Ah I've said so many things."

"That she wouldn't smell of drugs, that she wouldn't taste of medicine. Well, she didn't."

"So that it was really almost happy?"

It took him a long time to answer, occupied as he partly was in feeling how nobody but Kate could have invested such a question with the tone that was perfectly right. She meanwhile, however, patiently waited. "I don't think I can attempt to say now what it was. Some day—perhaps. For it would be worth it for us."

"Some day—certainly." She seemed to record the promise. Yet she spoke again abruptly. "She'll recover."

"Well," said Densher, "you'll see."

She had the air an instant of trying to. "Did she show anything of her feeling? I mean," Kate explained, "of her feeling of having been misled."

She didn't press hard, surely; but he had just mentioned that he would have rather to glide. "She showed nothing but her beauty and her strength."

"Then," his companion asked, "what's the use of her strength?"

He seemed to look about for a use he could name; but he had soon given it up. "She must die, my dear, in her own extraordinary way."

"Naturally. But I don't see then what proof you have that she was ever alienated."

"I have the proof that she refused for days and days to see me."

"But she was ill."

"That hadn't prevented her—as you yourself a moment ago said—during the previous time. If it had been only illness it would have made no difference with her."

"She would still have received you?"

"She would still have received me."

"Oh well," said Kate, "if you know—!"

"Of course I know. I know moreover as well from Mrs. Stringham."

"And what does Mrs. Stringham know?"

"Everything."

She looked at him longer. "Everything?"

"Everything."

"Because you've told her?"

"Because she has seen for herself. I've told her nothing. She's a person who does see."

Kate thought. "That's by her liking you too. She as well is prodigious. You see what interest in a man does. It does it all round. So you needn't be afraid."

"I'm not afraid," said Densher.

Kate moved from her place then, looking at the clock, which marked five. She gave her attention to the tea-table, where Aunt Maud's huge silver kettle, which had been exposed to its lamp and which she had not soon enough noticed, was hissing too hard. "Well, it's all most wonderful!" she exclaimed as she rather too profusely—a sign her friend noticed—ladled tea into the pot. He watched her a moment at this occupation, coming nearer the table while she put in the steaming water. "You'll have some?"

He hesitated. "Hadn't we better wait—?"

"For Aunt Maud?" She saw what he meant—the deprecation, by their old law, of betrayals of the intimate note. "Oh you needn't mind now. We've done it!"

"Humbugged her?"

"Squared her. You've pleased her."

Densher mechanically accepted his tea. He was thinking of something else, and his thought in a moment came out. "What a brute then I must be!"

"A brute—?"

"To have pleased so many people."

"Ah," said Kate with a gleam of gaiety, "you've done it to please *me*." But she was already, with her gleam, reverting a little. "What I don't understand is—won't you have any sugar?"

"Yes, please."

"What I don't understand," she went on when she had helped him, "is what it was that had occurred to bring her round again. If she gave you up for days and days, what brought her back to you?"

She asked the question with her own cup in her hand, but it found him ready enough in spite of his sense of the ironic oddity of their going into it over the tea-table. "It was Sir Luke Strett who brought her back. His visit, his presence there did it."

"He brought her back then to life."

"Well, to what I saw."

"And by interceding for you?"

"I don't think he interceded. I don't indeed know what he did."

Kate wondered. "Didn't he tell you?"

"I didn't ask him. I met him again, but we practically didn't speak of her."

Kate stared. "Then how do you know?"

"I see. I feel. I was with him again as I had been before—"

"Oh and you pleased him too? That was it?"

"He understood," said Densher.

"But understood what?"

He waited a moment. "That I had meant awfully well."

"Ah, and made *her* understand? I see," she went on as he said nothing. "But how did he convince her?"

Densher put down his cup and turned away. "You must ask Sir Luke."

He stood looking at the fire and there was a time without sound. "The great thing," Kate then resumed, "is that she's satisfied. Which," she continued, looking across at him, "is what I've worked for."

"Satisfied to die in the flower of her youth?"

"Well, at peace with you."

"Oh 'peace'!" he murmured with his eyes on the fire.

"The peace of having loved."

He raised his eyes to her. "Is *that* peace?"

"Of having *been* loved," she went on. "That is. Of having," she wound up, "realised her passion. She wanted nothing more. She has had *all* she wanted."

Lucid and always grave, she gave this out with a beautiful authority that he could for the time meet with no words. He could only again look at her, though with the sense in so doing that he made her more than he intended take his silence for assent. Quite indeed as if she did so take it she quitted the table and came to the fire. "You may think it hideous that I should now, that I should *yet*"—she made a point of the word—"pretend to draw conclusions. But we've not failed."

"Oh!" he only again murmured.

She was once more close to him, close as she had been the day she came to him in Venice, the quickly returning memory of which intensified and enriched the fact. He could practically deny in such conditions nothing that she said, and what she said was, with it, visibly, a fruit of that knowledge. "We've succeeded." She spoke with her eyes deep in his own. "She won't have loved you for nothing." It made him wince, but she insisted. "And you won't have loved *me*."

II

He was to remain for several days under the deep impression of this inclusive passage, so luckily prolonged from moment to moment, but interrupted at its climax, as may be said, by the entrance of Aunt Maud, who found them standing together near the fire. The bearings of the colloquy, however, sharp as they were, were less sharp to his intelligence, strangely enough, than those of a talk with Mrs. Lowder alone for which she soon gave him—or for which perhaps rather Kate gave him—full occasion. What had happened on her at last joining them was to conduce, he could immediately see, to her desiring to have him to herself. Kate and he, no doubt, at the opening of the door, had fallen apart with a certain suddenness, so that she had turned her hard fine eyes from one to the other; but the effect of this lost itself, to his mind, the next minute, in the effect of his companion's rare alertness. She instantly spoke to her aunt of what had first been uppermost for herself, inviting her thereby intimately to join them, and doing it the more happily also, no doubt, because the fact she resentfully named gave her ample support. "Had you quite understood, my dear, that it's full three weeks—?" And she effaced herself as if to leave Mrs. Lowder to deal from her own point of view with this extravagance. Densher of course straightway noted that his cue for the protection of Kate was to make, no less, all of it he could; and their tracks, as he might have said, were fairly covered by the time their hostess had taken afresh, on his renewed admission, the measure of his scant eagerness. Kate had moved away as if no great showing were needed for her personal situation to be seen as delicate. She had been entertaining their visitor on her aunt's behalf—a visitor she had been at one time suspected of favouring too much and who had now come back to them as the stricken suitor of another person. It wasn't that the fate of the other person, her exquisite friend, didn't, in its tragic turn, also concern herself: it was only that her acceptance of Mr. Densher as a source of information could scarcely help having an awkwardness. She invented the awkwardness under Densher's eyes, and he marvelled on his side at the instant creation. It served her as the fine cloud that hangs about a goddess in an epic, and the young man was but vaguely to know at what point of the rest of his visit she had, for consideration, melted into it and out of sight.

He was taken up promptly with another matter—the truth of the remarkable difference, neither more nor less, that the events of Venice had introduced into his relation with Aunt Maud and that these weeks of their separation had caused quite richly to ripen for him. She had not sat down to her tea-table before he felt himself on terms with her that were absolutely new, nor could she press on him a second cup without her seeming herself, and quite wittingly, so to define and establish them. She regretted, but she quite understood, that what was taking place had obliged him to hang off; they had—after hearing of him from poor Susan as gone—been hoping for an early sight of him; they would have been interested, naturally, in his arriving straight from the scene. Yet she needed no reminder that the scene precisely—by which she meant the tragedy that had so detained and absorbed him, the memory, the shadow, the sorrow of it—was what marked him for unsociability. She thus presented him to himself, as it were, in the guise in which she had now adopted him, and it was the element of truth in the character that he found himself, for his own part, adopting. She treated him as blighted and ravaged, as frustrate and already bereft; and for him to feel that this opened for him a new chapter of frankness with her he scarce had also to perceive how it smoothed his approaches to Kate. It made the latter accessible as she hadn't yet begun to be; it set up for him at Lancaster Gate an association positively hostile to any other legend. It was quickly vivid to him that, were he minded, he could "work" this association: he had but to use the house freely for his prescribed attitude and he need hardly ever be out of it. Stranger than anything moreover was to be the way that by the end of a week he stood convicted to his own sense of a surrender to Mrs. Lowder's view. He had somehow met it at a point that had brought him on—brought him on a distance that he couldn't again retrace. He had private hours of wondering what had become of his sincerity; he had others of simply reflecting that he had it all in use. His only want of candour was Aunt Maud's wealth of sentiment. She was hugely sentimental, and the worst he did was to take it from her. He wasn't so himself—everything was too real; but it was none the less not false that he *had* been through a mill.

It was in particular not false for instance that when she had said to him, on the Sunday, almost cosily, from her sofa behind the tea, "I want you not to doubt, you poor dear, that I'm *with* you to the end!" his meeting her halfway had been the only course open to him. She was with him to the end—or she might be—in a way Kate wasn't; and even if it literally made her society meanwhile more soothing he must just brush away the question of why it shouldn't. Was he professing to her in any degree the possession of an aftersense that wasn't real? How in the world *could* he, when his aftersense, day by day, was his greatest reality? Such only was at bottom what there was between them, and two or three times over it made the hour pass. These were occasions—two and a scrap—on which he had come and gone without mention of Kate. Now that almost as never yet he had licence to ask for her, the queer turn of their affair made it a false note. It was another queer turn that when he talked with Aunt Maud about Milly nothing else seemed to come up. He called upon her almost avowedly for that purpose, and it was the queerest turn of all that the state of his nerves should require it. He liked her better; he was really behaving, he had occasion to say to himself, as if he liked her best. The thing was absolutely that she met *him* halfway. Nothing could have been broader than her vision, than her loquacity, than her sympathy. It appeared to gratify, to satisfy her to see him as he was; that too had its effect. It was all of course the last thing that could have seemed on the cards, a change by which he was completely *free* with this lady; and it wouldn't indeed have come about if—for another monstrosity—he hadn't ceased to be free with Kate. Thus it was that on the third time in especial of being alone with her he found himself uttering to the elder woman what had been impossible of utterance to the younger. Mrs. Lowder gave him in fact, on the ground of what he must keep from her, but one uneasy moment. That was when, on the first Sunday, after Kate had suppressed herself, she referred to her regret that he mightn't have stayed to the end. He found his reason difficult to give her, but she came after all to his help.

"You simply couldn't stand it?"

"I simply couldn't stand it. Besides you see—!" But he paused.

"Besides what?" He had been going to say more—then he saw dangers; luckily however she had again assisted him. "Besides—oh I know!—men haven't, in many relations, the courage of women."

"They haven't the courage of women."

"Kate or I would have stayed," she declared—"if we hadn't come away for the special reason that you so frankly appreciated."

Densher had said nothing about his appreciation: hadn't his behaviour since the hour itself sufficiently shown it? But he presently said—he couldn't help going so far: "I don't doubt, certainly, that Miss Croy would have stayed." And he saw again into the bargain what a marvel was Susan Shepherd. She did nothing but protect him—she had done nothing but keep it up. In copious communication with the friend of her youth she had yet, it was plain, favoured this lady with nothing that compromised him. Milly's act of renouncement she had described but as a change for the worse; she had mentioned Lord Mark's descent, as even without her it might be known, so that she mustn't appear to conceal it; but she had suppressed explanations and connexions, and indeed, for all he knew, blessed Puritan soul, had invented commendable fictions. Thus it was absolutely that he was at his ease. Thus it was that, shaking for ever, in the unrest that didn't drop, his crossed leg, he leaned back in deep yellow satin chairs and took such comfort as came. She asked, it was true, Aunt Maud, questions that Kate hadn't; but this was just the difference, that from her he positively liked them. He had taken with himself on leaving Venice the resolution to regard Milly as already dead to him—that being for his spirit the only thinkable way to pass the time of waiting. He had left her because it was what suited her, and it wasn't for him to go, as they said in America, behind this; which imposed on him but the sharper need to arrange himself with his interval. Suspense was the ugliest ache to him, and he would have nothing to do with it; the last thing he wished was to be unconscious of her—what he wished to ignore was her own consciousness, tortured, for all he knew, crucified by its pain. Knowingly to hang about in London while the pain went on—what would that do but make his days impossible? His scheme was accordingly to convince himself—and by some art about which he was vague—that the sense of waiting had passed. "What in fact," he restlessly reflected, "have I any further to do with it? Let me assume the thing actually over—as it at any moment may be—and I become good again for something at least to somebody. I'm good, as it is, for nothing to anybody, least of all to *her*." He consequently tried, so far as shutting his eyes and stalking grimly about was a trial; but his plan was carried out, it may well be guessed, neither with marked success nor with marked consistency. The days, whether lapsing or lingering, were a stiff reality; the suppression of anxiety was a thin idea; the taste of life itself was the taste of suspense. That he *was* waiting was in short at the bottom of everything; and it required no great sifting presently to feel that if he took so much more, as he called it, to Mrs. Lowder this was just for that reason.

She helped him to hold out, all the while that she was subtle enough—and he could see her divine it as what he wanted—not to insist on the actuality of their tension. His nearest approach to success was thus in being good for something to Aunt Maud, in default of any one better; her company eased his nerves even while they pretended together that they had seen their tragedy out. They spoke of the dying girl in the past tense; they said no worse of her than that she had *been* stupendous. On the other hand, however—and this was what wasn't for Densher pure peace—they insisted enough that stupendous was the word. It was the thing, this recognition, that kept him most quiet; he came to it with her repeatedly; talking about it against time and, in particular, we have noted, speaking of his supreme personal impression as he hadn't spoken to Kate. It was almost as if she herself enjoyed the perfection of the pathos; she sat there before the scene, as he couldn't help giving it out to her, very much as a stout citizen's wife might have sat, during a play that made people cry, in the pit or the family-circle. What most deeply stirred her was the way the poor girl must have wanted to live.

"Ah yes indeed—she did, she did: why in pity shouldn't she, with everything to fill her world? The mere *money* of her, the darling, if it isn't too disgusting at such a time to mention that—!"

Aunt Maud mentioned it—and Densher quite understood—but as fairly giving poetry to the life Milly clung to: a view of the "might have been" before which the good lady was hushed anew to tears. She had had her own vision of these possibilities, and her own social use for them, and since Milly's spirit had been after all so at one with her about them, what was the cruelty of the event but a cruelty, of a sort, to herself? That came out when he named, as *the* horrible thing to know, the fact of their young friend's unapproachable terror of the end, keep it down though she would; coming out therefore often, since in so naming it he found the strangest of reliefs. He allowed it all its vividness, as if on the principle of his not at least spiritually shirking. Milly had held with passion to her dream of a future, and she was separated from it, not shrieking indeed, but grimly, awfully silent, as one might imagine some noble young victim of the scaffold, in the French Revolution, separated at the prison-door from some object clutched for resistance. Densher, in a cold moment, so pictured the case for Mrs. Lowder, but no moment cold enough had yet come to make him so picture it to Kate. And it was the front so presented that had been, in Milly, heroic; presented with the highest heroism, Aunt Maud by this time knew, on the occasion of his taking leave of her. He had let her know, absolutely for the girl's glory, how he had been received on that occasion: with a positive effect—since she was indeed so perfectly the princess that Mrs. Stringham always called her—of princely state.

Before the fire in the great room that was all arabesques and cherubs, all gaiety and gilt, and that was warm at that hour too with a wealth of autumn sun, the state in question had been maintained and the situation—well, Densher said for the convenience of exquisite London gossip, sublime. The gossip—for it came to as much at Lancaster Gate—wasn't the less exquisite for his use of the silver veil, nor on the other hand was the veil, so touched, too much drawn aside. He himself for that matter took in the scene again at moments as from the page of a book. He saw a young man far off and in a relation inconceivable, saw him hushed, passive, staying his breath, but half understanding, yet dimly conscious of something immense and holding himself painfully together not to lose it. The young man at these moments so seen was too distant and too strange for the right identity; and yet, outside, afterwards, it was his own face Densher had known. He had known then at the same time what the young man had been conscious of, and he was to measure after that, day by day, how little he had lost. At present there with Mrs. Lowder he knew he had gathered all—that passed between them mutely as in the intervals of their associated gaze they exchanged looks of intelligence. This was as far as association could go, but it was far enough when she knew the essence. The essence was that something had happened to him too beautiful and too sacred to describe. He had been, to his recovered sense, forgiven, dedicated, blessed; but this he couldn't coherently express. It would have required an explanation—fatal to Mrs. Lowder's faith in him—of the nature of Milly's wrong. So, as to the wonderful scene, they just stood at the door. They had the sense of the presence within—they felt the charged stillness; after which, their association deepened by it, they turned together away.

That itself indeed, for our restless friend, became by the end of a week the very principle of reaction: so that he woke up one morning with such a sense of having played a part as he needed self-respect to gainsay. He hadn't in the least stated at Lancaster Gate that, as a haunted man—a man haunted with a memory—he was harmless; but the degree to which Mrs. Lowder accepted, admired and explained his new aspect laid upon him practically the weight of a declaration. What he hadn't in the least stated her own manner was perpetually stating; it was as haunted and harmless that she was constantly putting him down. There offered itself however to his purpose such an element as plain honesty, and he had embraced, by the time he dressed, his proper corrective. They were on the edge of Christmas, but Christmas this year was, as in the London of so many other years, disconcertingly mild; the still air was soft, the thick light was grey, the great town looked empty, and in the Park, where the grass was green, where the sheep browsed, where the birds multitudinously twittered, the straight walks lent themselves to slowness and the dim vistas to privacy. He held it fast this morning till he had got out, his sacrifice to honour, and then went with it to the nearest post-office and fixed it fast in a telegram; thinking of it moreover as a sacrifice only because he had, for reasons, felt it as an effort. Its character of effort it would owe to Kate's expected resistance, not less probable than on the occasion of past appeals; which was precisely why he—perhaps innocently—made his telegram persuasive. It had, as a recall of tender hours, to be, for the young woman at the counter, a trifle cryptic; but there was a good deal of it in one way and another, representing as it did a rich impulse and costing him a couple of shillings. There was also a moment later on, that day, when, in the Park, as he measured watchfully one of their old alleys, he might have been supposed by a cynical critic to be reckoning his chance of getting his money back. He was waiting—but he had waited of old; Lancaster Gate as a danger was practically at hand—but she had risked that danger before. Besides it was smaller now, with the queer turn of their affair; in spite of which indeed he was graver as he lingered and looked out.

Kate came at last by the way he had thought least likely, came as if she had started from the Marble Arch; but her advent was response—that was the great matter; response marked in her face and agreeable to him, even after Aunt Maud's responses, as nothing had been since his return to London. She had not, it was true, answered his wire, and he had begun to fear, as she was late, that with the instinct of what he might be again intending to press upon her she had decided—though not with ease—to deprive him of his chance. He would have of course, she knew, other chances, but she perhaps saw the present as offering her special danger. This, in fact, Densher could himself feel, was exactly why he had so prepared it, and he had rejoiced, even while he waited, in all that the conditions had to say to him of their simpler and better time. The shortest day of the year though it might be, it was, in the same place, by a whim of the weather, almost as much to their purpose as the days of sunny afternoons when they had taken their first trysts. This and that tree, within sight, on the grass, stretched bare boughs over the couple of chairs in which they had sat of old and in which—for they really could sit down again—they might recover the clearness of their prime. It was to all intents however this very reference that showed itself in Kate's face as, with her swift motion, she came toward him. It helped him, her swift motion, when it finally brought her nearer; helped him, for that matter, at first, if only by showing him afresh how terribly well she looked. It had been all along, he certainly remembered, a phenomenon of no rarity that he had felt her, at particular moments, handsomer than ever before; one of these for instance being still present to him as her entrance, under her aunt's eyes, at Lancaster Gate, the day of his dinner there after his return from America; and another her aspect on the same spot two Sundays ago—the light in which she struck the eyes he had brought back from Venice. In the course of a minute or two now he got, as he had got it the other times, his apprehension of the special stamp of the fortune of the moment.

Whatever it had been determined by as the different hours recurred to him, it took on at present a prompt connexion with an effect produced for him in truth more than once during the past week, only now much intensified. This effect he had already noted and named: it was that of the attitude assumed by his friend in the presence of the degree of response on his part to Mrs. Lowder's welcome which she couldn't possibly have failed to notice. She *had* noticed it, and she had beautifully shown him so; wearing in its honour the finest shade of studied serenity, a shade almost of gaiety over the workings of time. Everything of course was relative, with the shadow they were living under; but her condonation of the way in which he now, for confidence, distinguished Aunt Maud had almost the note of cheer. She had so by her own air consecrated the distinction, invidious in respect to herself though it might be; and nothing, really, more than this demonstration, could have given him had he still wanted it the measure of her superiority. It was doubtless for that matter this superiority alone that on the winter noon gave smooth decision to her step and charming courage to her eyes—a courage that deepened in them when he had presently got to what he did want. He had delayed after she had joined him not much more than long enough for him to say to her, drawing her hand into his arm and turning off where they had turned of old, that he wouldn't pretend he hadn't lately had moments of not quite believing he should ever again be so happy. She answered, passing over the reasons, whatever they had been, of his doubt, that her own belief was in high happiness for them if they would only have patience; though nothing at the same time could be dearer than his idea for their walk. It was only make-believe of course, with what had taken place for them, that they couldn't meet at home; she spoke of their opportunities as suffering at no point. He had at any rate soon let her know that he wished the present one to suffer at none, and in a quiet spot, beneath a great wintry tree, he let his entreaty come sharp.

"We've played our dreadful game and we've lost. We owe it to ourselves, we owe it to our feeling *for* ourselves and for each other, not to wait another day. Our marriage will—fundamentally, somehow, don't you see?—right everything that's wrong, and I can't express to you my impatience. We've only to announce it—and it takes off the weight."

"To 'announce' it?" Kate asked. She spoke as if not understanding, though she had listened to him without confusion.

"To accomplish it then—to-morrow if you will; *do* it and announce it as done. That's the least part of it—after it nothing will matter. We shall be so right," he said, "that we shall be strong; we shall only wonder at our past fear. It will seem an ugly madness. It will seem a bad dream."

She looked at him without flinching—with the look she had brought at his call; but he felt now the strange chill of her brightness. "My dear man, what has happened to you?"

"Well, that I can bear it no longer. *That's* simply what has happened. Something has snapped, has broken in me, and here I am. It's *as* I am that you must have me."

He saw her try for a time to appear to consider it; but he saw her also not consider it. Yet he saw her, felt her, further—he heard her, with her clear voice—try to be intensely kind with him. "I don't see, you know, what has changed." She had a large strange smile. "We've been going on together so well, and you suddenly desert me?"

It made him helplessly gaze. "You call it so 'well'? You've touches, upon my soul—!"

"I call it perfect—from my original point of view. I'm just where I was; and you must give me some better reason than you do, my dear, for *your* not being. It seems to me," she continued, "that we're only right as to what has been between us so long as we do wait. I don't think we wish to have behaved like fools." He took in while she talked her imperturbable consistency; which it was quietly, queerly hopeless to see her stand there and breathe into their mild remembering air. He had brought her there to be moved, and she was only immoveable—which was not moreover, either, because she didn't understand. She understood everything, and things he refused to; and she had reasons, deep down, the sense of which nearly sickened him. She had too again most of all her strange significant smile. "Of course if it's that you really *know* something—?" It was quite conceivable and possible to her, he could see, that he did. But he didn't even know what she meant, and he only looked at her in gloom. His gloom however didn't upset her. "You do, I believe, only you've a delicacy about saying it. Your delicacy to me, my dear, is a scruple too much. I should have no delicacy in hearing it, so that if you can *tell* me you know—"

"Well?" he asked as she still kept what depended on it.

"Why then I'll do what you want. We needn't, I grant you, in that case wait; and I can see what you mean by thinking it nicer of us not to. I don't even ask you," she continued, "for a proof. I'm content with your moral certainty."

By this time it had come over him—it had the force of a rush. The point she made was clear, as clear as that the blood, while he recognised it, mantled in his face. "I know nothing whatever."

"You've not an idea?"

"I've not an idea."

"I'd consent," she said—"I'd announce it to-morrow, to-day, I'd go home this moment and announce it to Aunt Maud, for an idea: I mean an idea straight *from* you, I mean as your own, given me in good faith. There, my dear!"—and she smiled again. "I call that really meeting you."

If it *was* then what she called it, it disposed of his appeal, and he could but stand there with his wasted passion—for it was in high passion that he had from the morning acted—in his face. She made it all out, bent upon her—the idea he didn't have, and the idea he had, and his failure of insistence when it brought up *that* challenge, and his sense of her personal presence, and his horror, almost, of her lucidity. They made in him a mixture that might have been rage, but that was turning quickly to mere cold thought, thought which led to something else and was like a new dim dawn. It affected her then, and she had one of the impulses, in all sincerity, that had before this, between them, saved their position. When she had come nearer to him, when, putting her hand upon him, she made him sink with her, as she leaned to him, into their old pair of chairs, she prevented irresistibly, she forestalled, the waste of his passion. She had an advantage with his passion now.

III

He had said to her in the Park when challenged on it that nothing had "happened" to him as a cause for the demand he there made of her— happened he meant since the account he had given, after his return, of his recent experience. But in the course of a few days—they had brought him to Christmas morning—he was conscious enough, in preparing again to seek her out, of a difference on that score. Something had in this case happened to him, and, after his taking the night to think of it he felt that what it most, if not absolutely first, involved was his immediately again putting himself in relation with her. The fact itself had met him there—in his own small quarters—on Christmas Eve, and had not then indeed at once affected him as implying that consequence. So far as he on the spot and for the next hours took its measure—a process that made his night mercilessly wakeful—the consequences possibly implied were numerous to distraction. His spirit dealt with them, in the darkness, as the slow hours passed; his intelligence and his imagination, his soul and his sense, had never on the whole been so intensely engaged. It was his difficulty for the moment that he was face to face with alternatives, and that it was scarce even a question of turning from one to the other. They were not in a perspective in which they might be compared and considered; they were, by a strange effect, as close as a pair of monsters of whom he might have felt on either cheek the hot breath and the huge eyes. He saw them at once and but by looking straight before him; he wouldn't for that matter, in his cold apprehension, have turned his head by an inch. So it was that his agitation was still—was not, for the slow hours a matter of restless motion. He lay long, after the event, on the sofa where, extinguishing at a touch the white light of convenience that he hated, he had thrown himself without undressing. He stared at the buried day and wore out the time; with the arrival of the Christmas dawn moreover, late and grey, he felt himself somehow determined. The common wisdom had had its say to him—that safety in doubt was *not* action; and perhaps what most helped him was this very commonness. In his case there was nothing of *that*—in no case in his life had there ever been less: which association, from one thing to another, now worked for him as a choice. He acted, after his bath and his breakfast, in the sense of that marked element of the rare which he felt to be the sign of his crisis. And that is why, dressed with more state than usual and quite as if for church, he went out into the soft Christmas day.

Action, for him, on coming to the point, it appeared, carried with it a certain complexity. We should have known, walking by his side, that his final prime decision hadn't been to call at the door of Sir Luke Strett, and yet that this step, though subordinate, was none the less urgent. His prime decision was for another matter, to which impatience, once he was on the way, had now added itself; but he remained sufficiently aware that he must compromise with the perhaps excessive earliness. This, and the ferment set up within him, were together a reason for not driving; to say nothing of the absence of cabs in the dusky festal desert. Sir Luke's great square was not near, but he walked the Distance without seeing a hansom. He had his interval thus to turn over his view—the view to which what had happened the night before had not sharply reduced itself; but the complexity just mentioned was to be offered within the next few minutes another item to assimilate. Before Sir Luke's house, when he reached it, a brougham was drawn up—at the sight of which his heart had a lift that brought him for the instant to a stand. This pause wasn't long, but it was long enough to flash upon him a revelation in the light of which he caught his breath. The carriage, so possibly at such an hour and on such a day Sir Luke's own, had struck him as a sign that the great doctor was back. This would prove something else, in turn, still more intensely, and it was in the act of the double apprehension that Densher felt himself turn pale. His mind rebounded for the moment like a projectile that has suddenly been met by another: he stared at the strange truth that what he wanted *more* than to see Kate Croy was to see the witness who had just arrived from Venice. He wanted positively to be in his presence and to hear his voice—which was the spasm of his consciousness that produced the flash. Fortunately for him, on the spot, there supervened something in which the flash went out. He became aware within this minute that the coachman on the box of the brougham had a face known to him, whereas he had never seen before, to his knowledge, the great doctor's carriage. The carriage, as he came nearer, was simply Mrs. Lowder's; the face on the box was just the face that, in coming and going at Lancaster Gate, he would vaguely have noticed, outside, in attendance. With this the rest came: the lady of Lancaster Gate had, on a prompting not wholly remote from his own, presented herself for news; and news, in the house, she was clearly getting, since her brougham had stayed. Sir Luke *was* then back—only Mrs. Lowder was with him.

It was under the influence of this last reflexion that Densher again delayed; and it was while he delayed that something else occurred to him. It was all round, visibly—given his own new contribution—a case of pressure; and in a case of pressure Kate, for quicker knowledge, might have come out with her aunt. The possibility that in this event she might be sitting in the carriage—the thing most likely—had had the effect, before he could check it, of bringing him within range of the window. It wasn't there he had wished to see her; yet if she *was* there he couldn't pretend not to. What he had however the next moment made out was that if some one was there it wasn't Kate Croy. It was, with a sensible shock for him, the person who had last offered him a conscious face from behind the clear plate of a café in Venice. The great glass at Florian's was a medium less obscure, even with the window down, than the air of the London Christmas; yet at present also, none the less, between the two men, an exchange of recognitions could occur. Densher felt his own look a gaping arrest—which, he disgustedly remembered, his back as quickly turned, appeared to repeat itself as his special privilege. He mounted the steps of the house and touched the bell with a keen consciousness of being habitually looked at by Kate's friend from positions of almost insolent vantage. He forgot for the time the moment when, in Venice, at the palace, the encouraged young man had in a manner assisted at the departure of the disconcerted, since Lord Mark was not looking disconcerted now any more than he had looked from his bench at his café. Densher was thinking that *he* seemed to show as vagrant while another was ensconced. He was thinking of the other as—in spite of the difference of situation—more ensconced than ever; he was thinking of him above all as the friend of the person with whom his recognition had, the minute previous, associated him. The man was seated in the very place in which, beside Mrs. Lowder's, he had looked to find Kate, and that was a sufficient identity. Meanwhile at any rate the door of the house had opened and Mrs. Lowder stood before him. It was something at least that *she* wasn't Kate. She was herself, on the spot, in all her affluence; with presence of mind both to decide at once that Lord Mark, in the brougham, didn't matter and to prevent Sir Luke's butler, by a firm word thrown over her shoulder, from standing there to listen to her passage with the gentleman who had rung. "*I'll* tell Mr. Densher; you needn't wait!" And the passage, promptly and richly, took place on the steps.

"He arrives, travelling straight, to-morrow early. I couldn't not come to learn."

"No more," said Densher simply, "could I. On my way," he added, "to Lancaster Gate."

"Sweet of you." She beamed on him dimly, and he saw her face was attuned. It made him, with what she had just before said, know all, and he took the thing in while he met the air of portentous, of almost functional, sympathy that had settled itself as her medium with him and that yet had now a fresh glow. "So you *have* had your message?"

He knew so well what she meant, and so equally with it what he "*had* had" no less than what he hadn't, that, with but the smallest hesitation, he strained the point. "Yes—my message."

"Our dear dove then, as Kate calls her, has folded her wonderful wings."

"Yes—folded them."

It rather racked him, but he tried to receive it as she intended, and she evidently took his formal assent for self-control. "Unless it's more true," she accordingly added, "that she has spread them the wider."

He again but formally assented, though, strangely enough, the words fitted a figure deep in his own imagination. "Rather, yes—spread them the wider."

"For a flight, I trust, to some happiness greater—!"

"Exactly. Greater," Densher broke in; but now with a look, he feared, that did a little warn her off.

"You were certainly," she went on with more reserve, "entitled to direct news. Ours came late last night: I'm not sure otherwise I shouldn't have gone to you. But you're coming," she asked, "to *me?*"

He had had a minute by this time to think further, and the window of the brougham was still within range. Her rich "me," reaching him moreover through the mild damp, had the effect of a thump on his chest. "Squared," Aunt Maud? She was indeed squared, and the extent of it just now perversely enough took away his breath. His look from where they stood embraced the aperture at which the person sitting in the carriage might have shown, and he saw his interlocutress, on her side, understand the question in it, which he moreover then uttered. "Shall you be alone?" It was, as an immediate instinctive parley with the image of his condition that now flourished in her, almost hypocritical. It sounded as if he wished to come and overflow to her, yet this was exactly what he didn't. The need to overflow had suddenly—since the night before—dried up in him, and he had never been aware of a deeper reserve.

But she had meanwhile largely responded. "Completely alone. I should otherwise never have dreamed; feeling, dear friend, but too much!" Failing on her lips what she felt came out for him in the offered hand with which she had the next moment condolingly pressed his own. "Dear friend, dear friend!"— she was deeply "with" him, and she wished to be still more so: which was what made her immediately continue. "Or wouldn't you this evening, for the sad Christmas it makes us, dine with me *tête-à-tête?*"

It put the thing off, the question of a talk with her—making the difference, to his relief, of several hours; but it also rather mystified him. This however didn't diminish his need of caution. "Shall you mind if I don't tell you at once?"

"Not in the least—leave it open: it shall be as you may feel, and you needn't even send me word. I only *will* mention that to-day, of all days, I shall otherwise sit there alone."

Now at least he could ask. "Without Miss Croy?"

"Without Miss Croy. Miss Croy," said Mrs. Lowder, "is spending her Christmas in the bosom of her more immediate family."

He was afraid, even while he spoke, of what his face might show. "You mean she has left you?"

Aunt Maud's own face for that matter met the enquiry with a consciousness in which he saw a reflexion of events. He was made sure by it, even at the moment and as he had never been before, that since he had known these two women no confessed nor commented tension, no crisis of the cruder sort would really have taken form between them: which was precisely a high proof of how Kate had steered her boat. The situation exposed in Mrs. Lowder's present expression lighted up by contrast that superficial smoothness; which afterwards, with his time to think of it, was to put before him again the art, the particular gift, in the girl, now so placed and classed, so intimately familiar for him, as her talent for life. The peace, within a day or two—since his seeing her last—had clearly been broken; differences, deep down, kept there by a diplomacy on Kate's part as deep, had been shaken

684

to the surface by some exceptional jar; with which, in addition, he felt Lord Mark's odd attendance at such an hour and season vaguely associated. The talent for life indeed, it at the same time struck him, would probably have shown equally in the breach, or whatever had occurred; Aunt Maud having suffered, he judged, a strain rather than a stroke. Of these quick thoughts, at all events, that lady was already abreast. "She went yesterday morning—and not with my approval, I don't mind telling you—to her sister: Mrs. Condrip, if you know who I mean, who lives somewhere in Chelsea. My other niece and her affairs—that I should have to say such things to-day!—are a constant worry; so that Kate, in consequence—well, of events!—has simply been called in. My own idea, I'm bound to say, was that with *such* events she need have, in her situation, next to nothing to do."

"But she differed with you?"

"She differed with me. And when Kate differs with you—!"

"Oh I can imagine." He had reached the point in the scale of hypocrisy at which he could ask himself why a little more or less should signify. Besides, with the intention he had had he *must* know. Kate's move, if he didn't know, might simply disconcert him; and of being disconcerted his horror was by this time fairly superstitious. "I hope you don't allude to events at all calamitous."

"No—only horrid and vulgar."

"Oh!" said Merton Densher.

Mrs. Lowder's soreness, it was still not obscure, had discovered in free speech to him a momentary balm. "They've the misfortune to have, I suppose you know, a dreadful horrible father."

"Oh!" said Densher again.

"He's too bad almost to name, but he has come upon Marian, and Marian has shrieked for help."

Densher wondered at this with intensity; and his curiosity compromised for an instant with his discretion. "Come upon her—for money?"

"Oh for that of course always. But, at *this* blessed season, for refuge, for safety: for God knows what. He's *there*, the brute. And Kate's with them. And that," Mrs. Lowder wound up, going down the steps, "is her Christmas."

She had stopped again at the bottom while he thought of an answer. "Yours then is after all rather better."

"It's at least more decent." And her hand once more came out. "But why do I talk of *our* troubles? Come if you can."

He showed a faint smile. "Thanks. If I can."

"And now—I dare say—you'll go to church?"

She had asked it, with her good intention, rather in the air and by way of sketching for him, in the line of support, something a little more to the purpose than what she had been giving him. He felt it as finishing off their intensities of expression that he found himself to all appearance receiving her hint as happy. "Why yes—I think I will": after which, as the door of the brougham, at her approach, had opened from within, he was free to turn his back. He heard the door, behind him, sharply close again and the vehicle move off in another direction than his own.

He had in fact for the time no direction; in spite of which indeed he was at the end of ten minutes aware of having walked straight to the south. That, he afterwards recognised, was, very sufficiently, because there had formed itself in his mind, even while Aunt Maud finally talked, an instant recognition of his necessary course. Nothing was open to him but to follow Kate, nor was anything more marked than the influence of the step she had taken on the emotion itself that possessed him. Her complications, which had fairly, with everything else, an awful sound—what were they, a thousand times over, but his own? His present business was to see that they didn't escape an hour longer taking their proper place in his life. He accordingly would have held his course hadn't it suddenly come over him that he had just lied to Mrs. Lowder—a term it perversely eased him to keep using—even more than was necessary. To what church was he going, to what church, in such a state of his nerves, *could* he go?—he pulled up short again, as he had pulled up in sight of Mrs. Lowder's carriage, to ask it. And yet the desire queerly stirred in him not to have wasted his word. He was just then however by a happy chance in the Brompton Road, and he bethought himself with a sudden light that the Oratory was at hand. He had but to turn the other way and he should find himself soon before it. At the door then, in a few minutes, his idea was really—as it struck him—consecrated: he was, pushing in, on the edge of a splendid service—the flocking crowd told of it—which glittered and resounded, from distant depths, in the blaze of altar-lights and the swell of organ and choir. It didn't match his own day, but it was much less of a discord than some other things actual and possible. The Oratory in short, to make him right, would do.

IV

The difference was thus that the dusk of afternoon—dusk thick from an early hour—had gathered when he knocked at Mrs. Condrip's door. He had gone from the church to his club, wishing not to present himself in Chelsea at luncheon-time and also remembering that he must attempt independently to make a meal. This, in the event, he but imperfectly achieved: he dropped into a chair in the great dim void of the club library, with nobody, up or down, to be seen, and there after a while, closing his eyes, recovered an hour of the sleep he had lost during the night. Before doing this indeed he had written—it was the first thing he did—a short note, which, in the Christmas desolation of the place, he had managed only with difficulty and doubt to commit to a messenger. He wished it carried by hand, and he was obliged, rather blindly, to trust the hand, as the messenger, for some reason, was unable to return with a gage of delivery. When at four o'clock he was face to face with Kate in Mrs. Condrip's small drawing-room he found to his relief that his notification had reached her. She was expectant and to that extent prepared; which simplified a little—if a little, at the present pass, counted. Her conditions were vaguely vivid to him from the moment of his coming in, and vivid partly by their difference, a difference sharp and suggestive, from those in which he had hitherto constantly seen her. He had seen her but in places comparatively great; in her aunt's pompous house, under the high trees of Kensington and the storied ceilings of Venice. He had seen her, in Venice, on a great occasion, as the centre itself of the splendid Piazza: he had seen her there, on a still greater one, in his own poor rooms, which yet had consorted with her, having state and ancientry even in their poorness; but Mrs. Condrip's interior, even by this best view of it and though not flagrantly mean, showed itself as a setting almost grotesquely inapt. Pale, grave and charming, she affected him at once as a distinguished stranger—a stranger to the little Chelsea street—who was making the best of a queer episode and a place of exile. The extraordinary thing was that at the end of three minutes he felt himself less appointedly a stranger in it than she.

A part of the queerness—this was to come to him in glimpses—sprang from the air as of a general large misfit imposed on the narrow room by the scale and mass of its furniture. The objects, the ornaments were, for the sisters, clearly relics and survivals of what would, in the case of Mrs. Condrip at least, have been called better days. The curtains that overdraped the windows, the sofas and tables that stayed circulation, the chimney-ornaments that reached to the ceiling and the florid chandelier that almost dropped to the floor, were so many mementoes of earlier homes and so many links with their unhappy mother. Whatever might have been in itself the quality of these elements Densher could feel the effect proceeding from them, as they lumpishly blocked out the decline of the dim day, to be ugly almost to the point of the sinister. They failed to accommodate or to compromise; they asserted their differences without tact and without taste. It was truly having a sense of Kate's own quality thus promptly to see them in reference to it. But that Densher had this sense was no new thing to him, nor did he in strictness need, for the hour, to be reminded of it. He only knew, by one of the tricks his imagination so constantly played him, that he was, so far as her present tension went, very specially sorry for her—which was not the view that had determined his start in the morning; yet also that he himself would have taken it all, as he might say, less hard. *He* could have lived in such a place; but it wasn't given to those of his complexion, so to speak, to be exiled anywhere. It was by their comparative grossness that they could somehow make shift. His natural, his inevitable, his ultimate home—left, that is, to itself—wasn't at all unlikely to be as queer and impossible as what was just round them, though doubtless in less ample masses. As he took in moreover how Kate wouldn't have been in the least the creature she was if what was just round them hadn't mismatched her, hadn't made for her a medium involving compunction in the spectator, so, by the same stroke, that became the very fact of her relation with her companions there, such a fact as filled him at once, oddly, both with assurance and with suspense. If he himself, on this brief vision, felt her as alien and as ever so unwittingly ironic, how must they not feel her and how above all must she not feel them?

Densher could ask himself that even after she had presently lighted the tall candles on the mantel-shelf. This was all their illumination but the fire, and she had proceeded to it with a quiet dryness that yet left play, visibly, to her implication between them, in their trouble and failing anything better, of the presumably genial Christmas hearth. So far as the genial went this had in strictness, given their conditions, to be all their geniality. He had told her in his note nothing but that he must promptly see her and that he hoped she might be able to make it possible; but he understood from the first look at her that his promptitude was already having for her its principal reference. "I was prevented this morning, in the few minutes," he explained, "asking Mrs. Lowder if she had let you know, though I rather gathered she had; and it's what I've been in fact since then assuming. It was because I was so struck at the moment with your having, as she did tell me, so suddenly come here."

"Yes, it was sudden enough." Very neat and fine in the contracted firelight, with her hands in her lap, Kate considered what he had said. He had spoken immediately of what had happened at Sir Luke Strett's door. "She has let me know nothing. But that doesn't matter—if it's what *you* mean."

"It's part of what I mean," Densher said; but what he went on with, after a pause during which she waited, was apparently not the rest of that. "She had had her telegram from Mrs. Stringham; late last night. But to me the poor lady hasn't wired. The event," he added, "will have taken place yesterday, and Sir Luke, starting immediately, one can see, and travelling straight, will get back to-morrow morning. So that Mrs. Stringham, I judge, is left to face in some solitude the situation bequeathed to her. But of course," he wound up, "Sir Luke couldn't stay."

Her look at him might have had in it a vague betrayal of the sense that he was gaining time. "Was your telegram from Sir Luke?"

"No—I've had no telegram."

She wondered. "But not a letter—?"

"Not from Mrs. Stringham—no." He failed again however to develop this—for which her forbearance from another question gave him occasion. From whom then had he heard? He might at last, confronted with her, really have been gaining time; and as if to show that she respected this impulse she made her enquiry different. "Should you like to go out to her—to Mrs. Stringham?"

About that at least he was clear. "Not at all. She's alone, but she's very capable and very courageous. Besides—!" He had been going on, but he dropped.

"Besides," she said, "there's Eugenio? Yes, of course one remembers Eugenio."

She had uttered the words as definitely to show them for not untender; and he showed equally every reason to assent. "One remembers him indeed, and with every ground for it. He'll be of the highest value to her—he's capable of anything. What I was going to say," he went on, "is that some of their people from America must quickly arrive."

On this, as happened, Kate was able at once to satisfy him. "Mr. Someone-or-other, the person principally in charge of Milly's affairs—her first trustee, I suppose—had just got there at Mrs. Stringham's last writing."

"Ah that then was after your aunt last spoke to me—I mean the last time before this morning. I'm relieved to hear it. So," he said, "they'll do."

"Oh they'll do." And it came from each still as if it wasn't what each was most thinking of. Kate presently got however a step nearer to that. "But if you had been wired to by nobody what then this morning had taken you to Sir Luke?"

"Oh something else—which I'll presently tell you. It's what made me instantly need to see you; it's what I've come to speak to you of. But in a minute. I feel too many things," he went on, "at seeing you in this place." He got up as he spoke; she herself remained perfectly still. His movement had been to the fire, and, leaning a little, with his back to it, to look down on her from where he stood, he confined himself to his point. "Is it anything very bad that has brought you?"

He had now in any case said enough to justify her wish for more; so that, passing this matter by, she pressed her own challenge. "Do you mean, if I may ask, that *she*, dying—?" Her face, wondering, pressed it more than her words.

"Certainly you may ask," he after a moment said. "What has come to me is what, as I say, I came expressly to tell you. I don't mind letting you know," he went on, "that my decision to do this took for me last night and this morning a great deal of thinking of. But here I am." And he indulged in a smile that couldn't, he was well aware, but strike her as mechanical.

She went straighter with him, she seemed to show, than he really went with her. "You didn't want to come?"

"It would have been simple, my dear"—and he continued to smile—"if it had been, one way or the other, only a question of 'wanting.' It took, I admit it, the idea of what I had best do, all sorts of difficult and portentous forms. It came up for me really—well, not at all for my happiness."

This word apparently puzzled her—she studied him in the light of it. "You look upset—you've certainly been tormented. You're not well."

"Oh—well enough!"

But she continued without heeding. "You hate what you're doing."

"My dear girl, you simplify"—and he was now serious enough. "It isn't so simple even as that."

She had the air of thinking what it then might be. "I of course can't, with no clue, know what it is." She remained none the less patient and still. "If at such a moment she could write you one's inevitably quite at sea. One doesn't, with the best will in the world, understand." And then as Densher had a pause which might have stood for all the involved explanation that, to his discouragement, loomed before him: "You *haven't* decided what to do."

She had said it very gently, almost sweetly, and he didn't instantly say otherwise. But he said so after a look at her. "Oh yes—I have. Only with this sight of you here and what I seem to see in it for you—!" And his eyes, as at suggestions that pressed, turned from one part of the room to another.

"Horrible place, isn't it?" said Kate.

It brought him straight back to his enquiry. "Is it for anything awful you've had to come?"

"Oh that will take as long to tell you as anything *you* may have. Don't mind," she continued, "the 'sight of me here,' nor whatever—which is more than I yet know myself—may be 'in it' for me. And kindly consider too that, after all, if you're in trouble I can a little wish to help you. Perhaps I can absolutely even do it."

"My dear child, it's just because of the sense of your wish—! I suppose I'm in trouble—I suppose that's it." He said this with so odd a suddenness of simplicity that she could only stare for it—which he as promptly saw. So he turned off as he could his vagueness. "And yet I oughtn't to be." Which sounded indeed vaguer still.

She waited a moment. "Is it, as you say for my own business, anything very awful?"

"Well," he slowly replied, "you'll tell me if you find it so. I mean if you find my idea—"

He was so slow that she took him up. "Awful?" A sound of impatience—the form of a laugh—at last escaped her. "I can't find it anything at all till I know what you're talking about."

It brought him then more to the point, though it did so at first but by making him, on the hearthrug before her, with his hands in his pockets, turn awhile to and fro. There rose in him even with this movement a recall of another time—the hour in Venice, the hour of gloom and storm, when Susan Shepherd had sat in his quarters there very much as Kate was sitting now, and he had wondered, in pain even as now, what he might say and mightn't. Yet the present occasion after all was somehow the easier. He tried at any rate to attach that feeling to it while he stopped before his companion. "The communication I speak of can't possibly belong—so far as its date is concerned—to these last days. The postmark, which is legible, does; but it isn't thinkable, for anything else, that she wrote—!" He dropped, looking at her as if she'd understand.

It was easy to understand. "On her deathbed?" But Kate took an instant's thought. "Aren't we agreed that there was never any one in the world like her?"

"Yes." And looking over her head he spoke clearly enough. "There was never any one in the world like her."

Kate, from her chair, always without a movement, raised her eyes to the unconscious reach of his own. Then when the latter again dropped to her she added a question. "And won't it further depend a little on what the communication is?"

"A little perhaps—but not much. It's a communication," said Densher.

"Do you mean a letter?"

"Yes, a letter. Addressed to me in her hand—in hers unmistakeably."

Kate thought. "Do you know her hand very well?"

"Oh perfectly."

It was as if his tone for this prompted—with a slight strangeness—her next demand. "Have you had many letters from her?"

"No. Only three notes." He spoke looking straight at her. "And very, very short ones."

"Ah," said Kate, "the number doesn't matter. Three lines would be enough if you're sure you remember."

"I'm sure I remember. Besides," Densher continued, "I've seen her hand in other ways. I seem to recall how you once, before she went to Venice, showed me one of her notes precisely *for* that. And then she once copied me something."

"Oh," said Kate almost with a smile, "I don't ask you for the detail of your reasons. One good one's enough." To which however she added as if precisely not to speak with impatience or with anything like irony: "And the writing has its usual look?"

Densher answered as if even to better that description of it. "It's beautiful."

"Yes—it *was* beautiful. Well," Kate, to defer to him still, further remarked, "it's not news to us now that she was stupendous. Anything's possible."

"Yes, anything's possible"—he appeared oddly to catch at it. "That's what I say to myself. It's what I've been believing you," he a trifle vaguely explained, "still more certain to feel."

She waited for him to say more, but he only, with his hands in his pockets, turned again away, going this time to the single window of the room, where in the absence of lamplight the blind hadn't been drawn. He looked out into the lamplit fog, lost himself in the small sordid London street—for sordid, with his other association, he felt it—as he had lost himself, with Mrs. Stringham's eyes on him, in the vista of the Grand Canal. It was present then to his recording consciousness that when he had last been driven to such an attitude the very depth of his resistance to the opportunity to give Kate away was what had so driven him. His waiting companion had on that occasion waited for him to say he *would*; and what he had meantime glowered forth at was the inanity of such a hope. Kate's attention, on her side, during these minutes, rested on the back and shoulders he thus familiarly presented—rested as with a view of their expression, a reference to things unimparted, links still missing and that she must ever miss, try to make them out as she would. The result of her tension was that she again took him up. "You received—what you spoke of—last night?"

It made him turn round. "Coming in from Fleet Street—earlier by an hour than usual—I found it with some other letters on my table. But my eyes went straight to it, in an extraordinary way, from the door. I recognised it, knew what it was, without touching it."

"One can understand." She listened with respect. His tone however was so singular that she presently added: "You speak as if all this while you *hadn't* touched it."

"Oh yes, I've touched it. I feel as if, ever since, I'd been touching nothing else. I quite firmly," he pursued as if to be plainer, "took hold of it."

"Then where is it?"

"Oh I have it here."

"And you've brought it to show me?"

"I've brought it to show you."

So he said with a distinctness that had, among his other oddities, almost a sound of cheer, yet making no movement that matched his words. She could accordingly but offer again her expectant face, while his own, to her impatience, seemed perversely to fill with another thought. "But now that you've done so you feel you don't want to."

"I want to immensely," he said. "Only you tell me nothing."

She smiled at him, with this, finally, as if he were an unreasonable child. "It seems to me I tell you quite as much as you tell me. You haven't yet even told me how it is that such explanations as you require don't come from your document itself." Then as he answered nothing she had a flash. "You mean you haven't read it?"

"I haven't read it."

She stared. "Then how am I to help you with it?"

Again leaving her while she never budged he paced five strides, and again he was before her. "By telling me *this*. It's something, you know, that you wouldn't tell me the other day."

She was vague. "The other day?"

"The first time after my return—the Sunday I came to you. What's he doing," Densher went on, "at that hour of the morning with her? What does his having been with her there mean?"

"Of whom are you talking?"

"Of that man—Lord Mark of course. What does it represent?"

"Oh with Aunt Maud?"

"Yes, my dear—and with you. It comes more or less to the same thing; and it's what you didn't tell me the other day when I put you the question."

Kate tried to remember the other day. "You asked me nothing about any hour."

"I asked you when it was you last saw him—previous, I mean, to his second descent at Venice. You wouldn't say, and as we were talking of a matter comparatively more important I let it pass. But the fact remains, you know, my dear, that you haven't told me."

Two things in this speech appeared to have reached Kate more distinctly than the others. "I 'wouldn't say'?—and you 'let it pass'?" She looked just coldly blank. "You really speak as if I were keeping something back."

"Well, you see," Densher persisted, "you're not even telling me now. All I want to know," he nevertheless explained, "is whether there was a connexion between that proceeding on his part, which was practically—oh beyond all doubt!—the shock precipitating for her what has now happened, and anything that had occurred with him previously for yourself. How in the world did he know we're engaged?"

V

Kate slowly rose; it was, since she had lighted the candles and sat down, the first movement she had made. "Are you trying to fix it on me that I must have told him?"

She spoke not so much in resentment as in pale dismay—which he showed he immediately took in. "My dear child, I'm not trying to 'fix' anything; but I'm extremely tormented and I seem not to understand. What has the brute to do with us anyway?"

"What has he indeed?" Kate asked.

She shook her head as if in recovery, within the minute, of some mild allowance for his unreason. There was in it—and for his reason really—one of those half-inconsequent sweetnesses by which she had often before made, over some point of difference, her own terms with him. Practically she was making them now, and essentially he was knowing it; yet inevitably, all the same, he was accepting it. She stood there close to him, with something in her patience that suggested her having supposed, when he spoke more appealingly, that he was going to kiss her. He hadn't been, it appeared; but his continued appeal was none the less the quieter. "What's he doing, from ten o'clock on Christmas morning, with Mrs. Lowder?"

Kate looked surprised. "Didn't she tell you he's staying there?"

"At Lancaster Gate?" Densher's surprise met it. "'Staying'?—since when?"

"Since day before yesterday. He was there before I came away." And then she explained—confessing it in fact anomalous. "It's an accident—like Aunt

Maud's having herself remained in town for Christmas, but it isn't after all so monstrous. *We* stayed—and, with my having come here, she's sorry now—because we neither of us, waiting from day to day for the news you brought, seemed to want to be with a lot of people."

"You stayed for thinking of—Venice?"

"Of course we did. For what else? And even a little," Kate wonderfully added—"it's true at least of Aunt Maud—for thinking of you."

He appreciated. "I see. Nice of you every way. But whom," he enquired, "has Lord Mark stayed for thinking of?"

"His being in London, I believe, is a very commonplace matter. He has some rooms which he has had suddenly some rather advantageous chance to let—such as, with his confessed, his decidedly proclaimed want of money, he hasn't had it in him, in spite of everything, not to jump at."

Densher's attention was entire. "In spite of everything? In spite of what?"

"Well, I don't know. In spite, say, of his being scarcely supposed to do that sort of thing."

"To try to get money?"

"To try at any rate in little thrifty ways. Apparently however he has had for some reason to do what he can. He turned at a couple of days' notice out of his place, making it over to his tenant; and Aunt Maud, who's deeply in his confidence about all such matters, said: 'Come then to Lancaster Gate—to sleep at least—till, like all the world, you go to the country.' He was to have gone to the country—I think to Matcham—yesterday afternoon: Aunt Maud, that is, told me he was."

Kate had been somehow, for her companion, through this statement, beautifully, quite soothingly, suggestive. "Told you, you mean, so that you needn't leave the house?"

"Yes—so far as she had taken it into her head that his being there was part of my reason."

"And *was* it part of your reason?"

"A little if you like. Yet there's plenty here—as I knew there would be—without it. So that," she said candidly, "doesn't matter. I'm glad I am here: even if for all the good I do—!" She implied however that that didn't matter either. "He didn't, as you tell me, get off then to Matcham; though he may possibly, if it is possible, be going this afternoon. But what strikes me as most probable—and it's really, I'm bound to say, quite amiable of him—is that he has declined to leave Aunt Maud, as I've been so ready to do, to spend her Christmas alone. If moreover he has given up Matcham for her it's a *procédé* that won't please her less. It's small wonder therefore that she insists, on a dull day, in driving him about. I don't pretend to know," she wound up, "what may happen between them; but that's all I see in it."

"You see in everything, and you always did," Densher returned, "something that, while I'm with you at least, I always take from you as the truth itself."

She looked at him as if consciously and even carefully extracting the sting of his reservation; then she spoke with a quiet gravity that seemed to show how fine she found it. "Thank you." It had for him, like everything else, its effect. They were still closely face to face, and, yielding to the impulse to which he hadn't yielded just before, he laid his hands on her shoulders, held her hard a minute and shook her a little, far from untenderly, as if in expression of more mingled things, all difficult, than he could speak. Then bending his head he applied his lips to her cheek. He fell, after this, away for an instant, resuming his unrest, while she kept the position in which, all passive and as a statue, she had taken his demonstration. It didn't prevent her, however, from offering him, as if what she had had was enough for the moment, a further indulgence. She made a quiet lucid connexion and as she made it sat down again. "I've been trying to place exactly, as to its date, something that did happen to me while you were in Venice. I mean a talk with him. He spoke to me—spoke out."

"Ah there you are!" said Densher who had wheeled round.

"Well, if I'm 'there,' as you so gracefully call it, by having refused to meet him as he wanted—as he pressed—I plead guilty to being so. Would you have liked me," she went on, "to give him an answer that would have kept him from going?"

It made him a little awkwardly think. "Did you know he was going?"

"Never for a moment; but I'm afraid that—even if it doesn't fit your strange suppositions—I should have given him just the same answer if I had known. If it's a matter I haven't, since your return, thrust upon you, that's simply because it's not a matter in the memory of which I find a particular joy. I hope that if I've satisfied you about it," she continued, "it's not too much to ask of you to let it rest."

"Certainly," said Densher kindly, "I'll let it rest." But the next moment he pursued: "He saw something. He guessed."

"If you mean," she presently returned, "that he was unfortunately the one person we hadn't deceived, I can't contradict you."

"No—of course not. But *why*," Densher still risked, "was he unfortunately the one person—? He's not really a bit intelligent."

"Intelligent enough apparently to have seen a mystery, a riddle, in anything so unnatural as—all things considered and when it came to the point—my attitude. So he gouged out his conviction, and on his conviction he acted."

Densher seemed for a little to look at Lord Mark's conviction as if it were a blot on the face of nature. "Do you mean because you had appeared to him to have encouraged him?"

"Of course I had been decent to him. Otherwise where *were* we?"

"'Where'—?"

"You and I. What I appeared to him, however, hadn't mattered. What mattered was how I appeared to Aunt Maud. Besides, you must remember that he has had all along his impression of *you*. You can't help it," she said, "but you're after all—well, yourself."

700

"As much myself as you please. But when I took myself to Venice and kept myself there—what," Densher asked, "did he make of that?"

"Your being in Venice and liking to be—which is never on any one's part a monstrosity—was explicable for him in other ways. He was quite capable moreover of seeing it as dissimulation."

"In spite of Mrs. Lowder?"

"No," said Kate, "not in spite of Mrs. Lowder now. Aunt Maud, before what you call his second descent, hadn't convinced him—all the more that my refusal of him didn't help. But he came back convinced." And then as her companion still showed a face at a loss: "I mean after he had seen Milly, spoken to her and left her. Milly convinced him."

"Milly?" Densher again but vaguely echoed.

"That you were sincere. That it was *her* you loved." It came to him from her in such a way that he instantly, once more, turned, found himself yet again at his window. "Aunt Maud, on his return here," she meanwhile continued, "had it from him. And that's why you're now so well with Aunt Maud."

He only for a minute looked out in silence—after which he came away. "And why *you* are." It was almost, in its extremely affirmative effect between them, the note of recrimination; or it would have been perhaps rather if it hadn't been so much more the note of truth. It was sharp because it was true, but its truth appeared to impose it as an argument so conclusive as to permit on neither side a sequel. That made, while they faced each other over it without speech, the gravity of everything. It was as if there were almost danger, which the wrong word might start. Densher accordingly at last acted to better purpose: he drew, standing there before her, a pocket-book from the breast of his waistcoat and he drew from the pocket-book a folded letter to which her eyes attached themselves. He restored then the receptacle to its place and, with a movement not the less odd for being visibly instinctive and unconscious, carried the hand containing his letter behind him. What he thus finally spoke of was a different matter. "Did I understand from Mrs. Lowder that your father's in the house?"

If it never had taken her long in such excursions to meet him it was not to take her so now. "In the house, yes. But we needn't fear his interruption"—she spoke as if he had thought of that. "He's in bed."

"Do you mean with illness?"

She sadly shook her head. "Father's never ill. He's a marvel. He's only—endless."

Densher thought. "Can I in any way help you with him?"

"Yes." She perfectly, wearily, almost serenely, had it all. "By our making your visit as little of an affair as possible for him—and for Marian too."

"I see. They hate so your seeing me. Yet I couldn't—could I?—not have come."

"No, you couldn't not have come."

"But I can only, on the other hand, go as soon as possible?"

Quickly it almost upset her. "Ah don't, to-day, put ugly words into my mouth. I've enough of my trouble without it."

"I know—I know!" He spoke in instant pleading. "It's all only that I'm as troubled *for* you. When did he come?"

"Three days ago—after he hadn't been near her for more than a year, after he had apparently, and not regrettably, ceased to remember her existence; and in a state which made it impossible not to take him in."

Densher hesitated. "Do you mean in such want—?"

"No, not of food, of necessary things—not even, so far as his appearance went, of money. He looked as wonderful as ever. But he was—well, in terror."

"In terror of what?"

"I don't know. Of somebody—of something. He wants, he says, to be quiet. But his quietness is awful."

She suffered, but he couldn't not question. "What does he do?"

It made Kate herself hesitate. "He cries."

Again for a moment he hung fire, but he risked it. "What *has* he done?"

It made her slowly rise, and they were once more fully face to face. Her eyes held his own and she was paler than she had been. "If you love me—now—don't ask me about father."

He waited again a moment. "I love you. It's because I love you that I'm here. It's because I love you that I've brought you this." And he drew from behind him the letter that had remained in his hand.

But her eyes only—though he held it out—met the offer. "Why you've not broken the seal!"

"If I had broken the seal—exactly—I should know what's within. It's for *you* to break the seal that I bring it."

She looked—still not touching the thing—inordinately grave. "To break the seal of something to you from *her?*"

"Ah precisely because it's from her. I'll abide by whatever you think of it."

"I don't understand," said Kate. "What do you yourself think?" And then as he didn't answer: "It seems to me *I* think you know. You have your instinct. You don't need to read. It's the proof."

Densher faced her words as if they had been an accusation, an accusation for which he was prepared and which there was but one way to face. "I have indeed my instinct. It came to me, while I worried it out, last night. It came to me as an effect of the hour." He held up his letter and seemed now to insist more than to confess. "This thing had been timed."

"For Christmas Eve?"

"For Christmas Eve."

Kate had suddenly a strange smile. "The season of gifts!" After which, as he said nothing, she went on: "And had been written, you mean, while she could write, and kept to *be* so timed?"

Only meeting her eyes while he thought, he again didn't reply. "What do *you* mean by the proof?"

"Why of the beauty with which you've been loved. But I won't," she said, "break your seal."

"You positively decline?"

"Positively. Never." To which she added oddly: "I know without."

He had another pause. "And what is it you know?"

"That she announces to you she has made you rich."

His pause this time was longer. "Left me her fortune?"

"Not all of it, no doubt, for it's immense. But money to a large amount. I don't care," Kate went on, "to know how much." And her strange smile recurred. "I trust her."

"Did she tell you?" Densher asked.

"Never!" Kate visibly flushed at the thought. "That wouldn't, on my part, have been playing fair with her. And I did," she added, "play fair."

Densher, who had believed her—he couldn't help it—continued, holding his letter, to face her. He was much quieter now, as if his torment had somehow passed. "You played fair with me, Kate; and that's why—since we talk of proofs—I want to give *you* one. I've wanted to let you see—and in preference even to myself—something I feel as sacred."

She frowned a little. "I don't understand."

"I've asked myself for a tribute, for a sacrifice by which I can peculiarly recognise—"

"Peculiarly recognise what?" she demanded as he dropped.

"The admirable nature of your own sacrifice. You were capable in Venice of an act of splendid generosity."

"And the privilege you offer me with that document is my reward?"

He made a movement. "It's all I can do as a symbol of my attitude."

She looked at him long. "Your attitude, my dear, is that you're afraid of yourself. You've had to take yourself in hand. You've had to do yourself violence."

"So it is then you meet me?"

She bent her eyes hard a moment to the letter, from which her hand still stayed itself. "You absolutely *desire* me to take it?"

"I absolutely desire you to take it."

"To do what I like with it?"

"Short of course of making known its terms. It must remain—pardon my making the point—between you and me."

She had a last hesitation, but she presently broke it. "Trust me." Taking from him the sacred script she held it a little while her eyes again rested on those fine characters of Milly's that they had shortly before discussed. "To hold it," she brought out, "is to know."

"Oh I *know!*" said Merton Densher.

"Well then if we both do—!" She had already turned to the fire, nearer to which she had moved, and with a quick gesture had jerked the thing into the flame. He started—but only half—as to undo her action: his arrest was as prompt as the latter had been decisive. He only watched, with her, the paper burn; after which their eyes again met. "You'll have it all," Kate said, "from New York."

It was after he had in fact, two months later, heard from New York that she paid him a visit one morning at his own quarters—coming not as she had come in Venice, under his extreme solicitation, but as a need recognised in

705

the first instance by herself, even though also as the prompt result of a missive delivered to her. This had consisted of a note from Densher accompanying a letter, "just to hand," addressed him by an eminent American legal firm, a firm of whose high character he had become conscious while in New York as of a thing in the air itself, and whose head and front, the principal executor of Milly Theale's copious will, had been duly identified at Lancaster Gate as the gentleman hurrying out, by the straight southern course, before the girl's death, to the support of Mrs. Stringham. Densher's act on receipt of the document in question—an act as to which and to the bearings of which his resolve had had time to mature—constituted in strictness, singularly enough, the first reference to Milly, or to what Milly might or might not have done, that had passed between our pair since they had stood together watching the destruction, in the little vulgar grate at Chelsea, of the undisclosed work of her hand. They had at the time, and in due deference now, on his part, to Kate's mention of her responsibility for his call, immediately separated, and when they met again the subject was made present to them—at all events till some flare of new light—only by the intensity with which it mutely expressed its absence. They were not moreover in these weeks to meet often, in spite of the fact that this had, during January and a part of February, actually become for them a comparatively easy matter. Kate's stay at Mrs. Condrip's prolonged itself under allowances from her aunt which would have been a mystery to Densher had he not been admitted, at Lancaster Gate, really in spite of himself, to the esoteric view of them. "It's her idea," Mrs. Lowder had there said to him as if she really despised ideas—which she didn't; "and I've taken up with my own, which is to give her her head till she has had enough of it. She *has* had enough of it, she had that soon enough; but as she's as proud as the deuce she'll come back when she has found some reason—having nothing in common with her disgust—of which she can make a show. She calls it her holiday, which she's spending in her own way—the holiday to which, once a year or so, as she says, the very maids in the scullery have a right. So we're taking it on that basis. But we shall not soon, I think, take another of the same sort. Besides, she's quite decent; she comes often—whenever I make her a sign; and she has been good, on the whole, this year or two, so that, to be decent myself, I don't complain. She has really been, poor dear, very much what one hoped; though I needn't, you know," Aunt Maud wound up, "tell *you*, after all, you clever creature, what that was."

It had been partly in truth to keep down the opportunity for this that Densher's appearances under the good lady's roof markedly, after Christmas, interspaced themselves. The phase of his situation that on his return from Venice had made them for a short time almost frequent was at present quite obscured, and with it the impulse that had then acted. Another phase had taken its place, which he would have been painfully at a loss as yet to name or otherwise set on its feet, but of which the steadily rising tide left Mrs. Lowder, for his desire, quite high and dry. There had been a moment when it seemed possible that Mrs. Stringham, returning to America under convoy, would pause in London on her way and be housed with her old friend; in which case he was prepared for some apparent zeal of attendance. But this danger passed—he had felt it a danger, and the person in the world whom he would just now have most valued seeing on his own terms sailed away westward from Genoa. He thereby only wrote to her, having broken, in this respect, after Milly's death, the silence as to the sense of which, before that event, their agreement had been so deep. She had answered him from Venice twice, and had had time to answer him twice again from New York. The last letter of her four had come by the same post as the document he sent on to Kate, but he hadn't gone into the question of also enclosing that. His correspondence with Milly's companion was somehow already presenting itself to him as a feature—as a factor, he would have said in his newspaper—of the time whatever it might be, long or short, in store for him; but one of his acutest current thoughts was apt to be devoted to his not having yet mentioned it to Kate. She had put him no question, no "Don't you ever hear?"—so that he hadn't been brought to the point. This he described to himself as a mercy, for he liked his secret. It was as a secret that, in the same personal privacy, he described his transatlantic commerce, scarce even wincing while he recognised it as the one connexion in which he wasn't straight. He had in fact for this connexion a vivid mental image—he saw it as a small emergent rock in the waste of waters, the bottomless grey expanse of straightness. The fact that he had on several recent occasions taken with Kate an out-of-the-way walk that was each time to define itself as more remarkable for what they didn't say than for what they did—this fact failed somehow to mitigate for him a strange consciousness of exposure. There was something deep within him that he had absolutely shown to no one—to the companion of these walks in particular not a bit more than he could help; but he was none the less haunted, under its shadow, with a dire apprehension of publicity. It was as if he had invoked that ugliness in some stupid good faith; and it was queer enough that on his emergent rock, clinging to it and to Susan Shepherd, he should figure himself as hidden from view. That represented no doubt his belief in her power, or in her delicate disposition to protect him. Only Kate at all events knew—what Kate did know, and she was also the last person interested to tell it; in spite of which it was as if his *act*, so deeply associated with her and never to be recalled nor recovered, was abroad on the winds of the world. His honesty, as he viewed it with Kate, was the very element of that menace: to the degree that he saw at moments, as to their final impulse or their final remedy, the need to bury in the dark blindness of each other's arms the knowledge of each other that they couldn't undo.

Save indeed that the sense in which it was in these days a question of arms was limited, this might have been the intimate expedient to which they were actually resorting. It had its value, in conditions that made everything count, that thrice over, in Battersea Park—where Mrs. Lowder now never drove—he had adopted the usual means, in sequestered alleys, of holding her close to his side. She could make absences, on her present footing, without having too inordinately to account for them at home—which was exactly what gave them for the first time an appreciable margin. He supposed she could always say in Chelsea—though he didn't press it—that she had been across the town, in decency, for a look at her aunt; whereas there had always been reasons at Lancaster Gate for her not being able to plead the look at her other relatives. It was therefore between them a freedom of a purity as yet untasted; which for that matter also they made in various ways no little show of cherishing as such. They made the show indeed in every way but the way of a large use—an inconsequence that they almost equally gave time to helping each other to regard as natural. He put it to his companion that the kind of favour he now enjoyed at Lancaster Gate, the wonderful warmth of his reception there, cut in a manner the ground from under their feet. He was too horribly trusted—they had succeeded too well. He couldn't in short make appointments with her without abusing Aunt Maud, and he couldn't on the other hand haunt that lady without tying his hands. Kate saw what he meant just as he saw what she did when she admitted that she was herself, to a degree scarce less embarrassing, in the enjoyment of Aunt Maud's confidence. It was special at present—she was handsomely used; she confessed accordingly to a scruple about misapplying her licence. Mrs. Lowder then finally had found—and all unconsciously now—the way to baffle them. It wasn't however that they didn't meet a little, none the less, in the southern quarter, to point for their common benefit the moral of their defeat. They crossed the river; they wandered in neighbourhoods sordid and safe; the winter was mild, so that, mounting to the top of trams, they could rumble together to Clapham or to Greenwich. If at the same time their minutes had never been so counted it struck Densher that by a singular law their tone—he scarce knew what to call it—had never been so bland. Not to talk of what they *might* have talked of drove them to other ground; it was as if they used a perverse insistence to make up what they ignored. They concealed their pursuit of the irrelevant by the charm of their manner; they took precautions for the courtesy they had formerly left to come of itself; often, when he had quitted her, he stopped short, walking off, with the aftersense of their change. He would have described their change—had he so far faced it as to describe it—by their being so damned civil. That had even, with the intimate, the familiar at the point to which they had brought them, a touch almost of the droll. What danger had there ever been of their becoming rude—after each had long since made the other so tremendously tender? Such were the things he asked himself when he wondered what in particular he most feared.

Yet all the while too the tension had its charm—such being the interest of a creature who could bring one back to her by such different roads. It was her talent for life again; which found in her a difference for the differing time. She didn't give their tradition up; she but made of it something new. Frankly moreover she had never been more agreeable nor in a way—to put it prosaically—better company: he felt almost as if he were knowing her on that defined basis—which he even hesitated whether to measure as reduced or as extended; as if at all events he were admiring her as she was probably admired by people she met "out." He hadn't in fine reckoned that she would still have something fresh for him; yet this was what she had—that on the top of a tram in the Borough he felt as if he were next her at dinner. What a person she would be if they *had* been rich—with what a genius for the so-called great life, what a presence for the so-called great house, what a grace for the so-called great positions! He might regret at once, while he was about it, that they weren't princes or billionaires. She had treated him on their Christmas to a softness that had struck him at the time as of the quality of fine velvet, meant to fold thick, but stretched a little thin; at present, however, she gave him the impression of a contact multitudinous as only the superficial can be. She had throughout never a word for what went on at home. She came out of that and she returned to it, but her nearest reference was the look with which, each time, she bade him good-bye. The look was her repeated prohibition: "It's what I *have* to see and to know—so don't touch it. That but wakes up the old evil, which I keep still, in my way, by sitting by it. I go now—leave me alone!—to sit by it again. The way to pity me—if that's what you want—is to believe in me. If we could really *do* anything it would be another matter."

He watched her, when she went her way, with the vision of what she thus a little stiffly carried. It was confused and obscure, but how, with her head high, it made her hold herself! He really in his own person might at these moments have been swaying a little aloft as one of the objects in her poised basket. It was doubtless thanks to some such consciousness as this that he felt the lapse of the weeks, before the day of Kate's mounting of his stair, almost swingingly rapid. They contained for him the contradiction that, whereas periods of waiting are supposed in general to keep the time slow, it was the wait, actually, that made the pace trouble him. The secret of that anomaly, to be plain, was that he was aware of how, while the days melted, something rare went with them. This something was only a thought, but a thought precisely of such freshness and such delicacy as made the precious, of whatever sort, most subject to the hunger of time. The thought was all his own, and his intimate companion was the last person he might have shared it with. He kept it back like a favourite pang; left it behind him, so to say, when he went out, but came home again the sooner for the certainty of finding it there. Then he took it out of its sacred corner and its soft wrappings; he undid them one by one, handling them, handling *it*, as a father, baffled and tender, might handle a maimed child. But so it was before him—in his dread of who else might see it. Then he took to himself at such hours, in other words, that he should never, never know what had been in Milly's letter. The intention announced in it he should but too probably know; only that would have been, but for the depths of his spirit, the least part of it. The part of it missed for ever was the turn she would have given her act. This turn had possibilities that, somehow, by wondering about them, his imagination had extraordinarily filled out and refined. It had made of them a revelation the loss of which was like the sight of a priceless pearl cast before his eyes—his pledge given not to save it—into the fathomless sea, or rather even it was like the sacrifice of something sentient and throbbing, something that, for the spiritual ear, might have been audible as a faint far wail. This was the sound he cherished when alone in the stillness of his rooms. He sought and guarded the stillness, so that it might prevail there till the inevitable sounds of life, once more, comparatively coarse and harsh, should smother and deaden it—doubtless by the same process with which they would officiously heal the ache in his soul that was somehow one with it. It moreover deepened the sacred hush that he couldn't complain. He had given poor Kate her freedom.

The great and obvious thing, as soon as she stood there on the occasion we have already named, was that she was now in high possession of it. This would have marked immediately the difference—had there been nothing else to do it—between their actual terms and their other terms, the character of their last encounter in Venice. That had been *his* idea, whereas her present step was her own; the few marks they had in common were, from the first moment, to his conscious vision, almost pathetically plain. She was as grave now as before; she looked around her, to hide it, as before; she pretended, as before, in an air in which her words at the moment itself fell flat, to an interest in the place and a curiosity about his "things"; there was a recall in the way in which, after she had failed a little to push up her veil symmetrically and he had said she had better take it off altogether, she had acceded to his suggestion before the glass. It was just these things that were vain; and what was real was that his fancy figured her after the first few minutes as literally now providing the element of reassurance which had previously been his care. It was she, supremely, who had the presence of mind. She made indeed for that matter very prompt use of it. "You see I've not hesitated this time to break your seal."

She had laid on the table from the moment of her coming in the long envelope, substantially filled, which he had sent her enclosed in another of still ampler make. He had however not looked at it—his belief being that he wished never again to do so; besides which it had happened to rest with its addressed side up. So he "saw" nothing, and it was only into her eyes that her remark made him look, declining any approach to the object indicated. "It's not 'my' seal, my dear; and my intention—which my note tried to express—was all to treat it to you as not mine."

"Do you mean that it's to that extent mine then?"

"Well, let us call it, if we like, theirs—that of the good people in New York, the authors of our communication. If the seal is broken well and good; but we *might*, you know," he presently added, "have sent it back to them intact and inviolate. Only accompanied," he smiled with his heart in his mouth, "by an absolutely kind letter."

Kate took it with the mere brave blink with which a patient of courage signifies to the exploring medical hand that the tender place is touched. He saw on the spot that she was prepared, and with this signal sign that she was too intelligent not to be, came a flicker of possibilities. She was—merely to put it at that—intelligent enough for anything. "Is it what you're proposing we *should* do?"

"Ah it's too late to do it—well, ideally. Now, with that sign that we *know*—!"

"But you don't know," she said very gently.

"I refer," he went on without noticing it, "to what would have been the handsome way. Its being dispatched again, with no cognisance taken but one's assurance of the highest consideration, and the proof of this in the state of the envelope—*that* would have been really satisfying."

She thought an instant. "The state of the envelope proving refusal, you mean, not to be based on the insufficiency of the sum?"

Densher smiled again as for the play, however whimsical, of her humour. "Well yes—something of that sort."

"So that if cognisance *has* been taken—so far as I'm concerned—it spoils the beauty?"

"It makes the difference that I'm disappointed in the hope—which I confess I entertained—that you'd bring the thing back to me as you had received it."

"You didn't express that hope in your letter."

"I didn't want to. I wanted to leave it to yourself. I wanted—oh yes, if that's what you wish to ask me—to see what you'd do."

"You wanted to measure the possibilities of my departure from delicacy?"

He continued steady now; a kind of ease—from the presence, as in the air, of something he couldn't yet have named—had come to him. "Well, I wanted—in so good a case—to test you."

She was struck—it showed in her face—by his expression. "It *is* a good case. I doubt whether a better," she said with her eyes on him, "has ever been known."

"The better the case then the better the test!"

"How do you know," she asked in reply to this, "what I'm capable of?"

"I don't, my *dear*! Only with the seal unbroken I should have known sooner."

"I see"—she took it in. "But I myself shouldn't have known at all. And you wouldn't have known, either, what I do know."

"Let me tell you at once," he returned, "that if you've been moved to correct my ignorance I very particularly request you not to."

She just hesitated. "Are you afraid of the effect of the corrections? Can you only do it by doing it blindly?"

He waited a moment. "What is it that you speak of my doing?"

"Why the only thing in the world that I take you as thinking of. Not accepting—what she has done. Isn't there some regular name in such cases? Not taking up the bequest."

"There's something you forget in it," he said after a moment. "My asking you to join with me in doing so."

Her wonder but made her softer, yet at the same time didn't make her less firm. "How can I 'join' in a matter with which I've nothing to do?"

"How? By a single word."

"And what word?"

"Your consent to my giving up."

"My consent has no meaning when I can't prevent you."

"You can perfectly prevent me. Understand that well," he said.

She seemed to face a threat in it. "You mean you won't give up if I *don't* consent?"

"Yes. I do nothing."

"That, as I understand, is accepting."

Densher paused. "I do nothing formal."

"You won't, I suppose you mean, touch the money."

"I won't touch the money."

It had a sound—though he had been coming to it—that made for gravity. "Who then in such an event *will?*"

"Any one who wants or who can."

Again a little she said nothing: she might say too much. But by the time she spoke he had covered ground. "How can I touch it but *through* you?"

"You can't. Any more," he added, "than I can renounce it except through you."

"Oh ever so much less! There's nothing," she explained, "in my power."

"I'm in your power," Merton Densher said.

"In what way?"

"In the way I show—and the way I've always shown. When have I shown," he asked as with a sudden cold impatience, "anything else? You surely must feel—so that you needn't wish to appear to spare me in it—how you 'have' me."

"It's very good of you, my dear," she nervously laughed, "to put me so thoroughly up to it!"

"I put you up to nothing. I didn't even put you up to the chance that, as I said a few moments ago, I saw for you in forwarding that thing. Your liberty is therefore in every way complete."

It had come to the point really that they showed each other pale faces, and that all the unspoken between them looked out of their eyes in a dim terror of their further conflict. Something even rose between them in one of their short silences—something that was like an appeal from each to the other not to be too true. Their necessity was somehow before them, but which of them must meet it first? "Thank you!" Kate said for his word about her freedom, but taking for the minute no further action on it. It was blest at least that all ironies failed them, and during another slow moment their very sense of it cleared the air.

There was an effect of this in the way he soon went on. "You must intensely feel that it's the thing for which we worked together."

She took up the remark, however, no more than if it were commonplace; she was already again occupied with a point of her own. "Is it absolutely true—for if it is, you know, it's tremendously interesting—that you haven't so much as a curiosity about what she has done for you?"

"Would you like," he asked, "my formal oath on it?"

"No—but I don't understand. It seems to me in your place—!"

"Ah," he couldn't help breaking in, "what do you know of my place? Pardon me," he at once added; "my preference is the one I express."

She had in an instant nevertheless a curious thought. "But won't the facts be published?"

"'Published'?"—he winced.

"I mean won't you see them in the papers?"

"Ah never! I shall know how to escape that."

It seemed to settle the subject, but she had the next minute another insistence. "Your desire is to escape everything?"

"Everything."

"And do you need no more definite sense of what it is you ask me to help you to renounce?"

"My sense is sufficient without being definite. I'm willing to believe that the amount of money's not small."

"Ah there you are!" she exclaimed.

"If she was to leave me a remembrance," he quietly pursued, "it would inevitably not be meagre."

716

Kate waited as for how to say it. "It's worthy of her. It's what she was herself—if you remember what we once said *that* was."

He hesitated—as if there had been many things. But he remembered one of them. "Stupendous?"

"Stupendous." A faint smile for it—ever so small—had flickered in her face, but had vanished before the omen of tears, a little less uncertain, had shown themselves in his own. His eyes filled—but that made her continue. She continued gently. "I think that what it really is must be that you're afraid. I mean," she explained, "that you're afraid of *all* the truth. If you're in love with her without it, what indeed can you be more? And you're afraid—it's wonderful!—to be in love with her."

"I never was in love with her," said Densher.

She took it, but after a little she met it. "I believe that now—for the time she lived. I believe it at least for the time you were there. But your change came—as it might well—the day you last saw her; she died for you then that you might understand her. From that hour you *did*." With which Kate slowly rose. "And I do now. She did it *for* us." Densher rose to face her, and she went on with her thought. "I used to call her, in my stupidity—for want of anything better—a dove. Well she stretched out her wings, and it was to *that* they reached. They cover us."

"They cover us," Densher said.

"That's what I give you," Kate gravely wound up. "That's what I've done for you."

His look at her had a slow strangeness that had dried, on the moment, his tears. "Do I understand then—?"

"That I do consent?" She gravely shook her head. "No—for I see. You'll marry me without the money; you won't marry me with it. If I don't consent *you* don't."

717

"You lose me?" He showed, though naming it frankly, a sort of awe of her high grasp. "Well, you lose nothing else. I make over to you every penny."

Prompt was his own clearness, but she had no smile this time to spare. "Precisely—so that I must choose."

"You must choose."

Strange it was for him then that she stood in his own rooms doing it, while, with an intensity now beyond any that had ever made his breath come slow, he waited for her act. "There's but one thing that can save you from my choice."

"From your choice of my surrender to you?"

"Yes"—and she gave a nod at the long envelope on the table—"your surrender of that."

"What is it then?"

"Your word of honour that you're not in love with her memory."

"Oh—her memory!"

"Ah"—she made a high gesture—"don't speak of it as if you couldn't be. I could in your place; and you're one for whom it will do. Her memory's your love. You *want* no other."

He heard her out in stillness, watching her face but not moving. Then he only said: "I'll marry you, mind you, in an hour."

"As we were?"

"As we were."

But she turned to the door, and her headshake was now the end. "We shall never be again as we were!"

THE END

About Author

Henry James OM (15 April 1843 – 28 February 1916) was an American-British author regarded as a key transitional figure between literary realism and literary modernism, and is considered by many to be among the greatest novelists in the English language. He was the son of Henry James Sr. and the brother of renowned philosopher and psychologist William James and diarist Alice James.

He is best known for a number of novels dealing with the social and marital interplay between émigré Americans, English people, and continental Europeans. Examples of such novels include The Portrait of a Lady, The Ambassadors, and The Wings of the Dove. His later works were increasingly experimental. In describing the internal states of mind and social dynamics of his characters, James often made use of a style in which ambiguous or contradictory motives and impressions were overlaid or juxtaposed in the discussion of a character's psyche. For their unique ambiguity, as well as for other aspects of their composition, his late works have been compared to impressionist painting.

His novella The Turn of the Screw has garnered a reputation as the most analysed and ambiguous ghost story in the English language and remains his most widely adapted work in other media. He also wrote a number of other highly regarded ghost stories and is considered one of the greatest masters of the field.

James published articles and books of criticism, travel, biography, autobiography, and plays. Born in the United States, James largely relocated to Europe as a young man and eventually settled in England, becoming a British subject in 1915, one year before his death. James was nominated for the Nobel Prize in Literature in 1911, 1912 and 1916.

Life

Early years, 1843–1883

James was born at 2 Washington Place in New York City on 15 April 1843. His parents were Mary Walsh and Henry James Sr. His father was intelligent and steadfastly congenial. He was a lecturer and philosopher who had inherited independent means from his father, an Albany banker and investor. Mary came from a wealthy family long settled in New York City. Her sister Katherine lived with her adult family for an extended period of time. Henry Jr. had three brothers, William, who was one year his senior, and younger brothers Wilkinson (Wilkie) and Robertson. His younger sister was Alice. Both of his parents were of Irish and Scottish descent.

The family first lived in Albany, at 70 N. Pearl St., and then moved to Fourteenth Street in New York City when James was still a young boy. His education was calculated by his father to expose him to many influences, primarily scientific and philosophical; it was described by Percy Lubbock, the editor of his selected letters, as "extraordinarily haphazard and promiscuous." James did not share the usual education in Latin and Greek classics. Between 1855 and 1860, the James' household traveled to London, Paris, Geneva, Boulogne-sur-Mer and Newport, Rhode Island, according to the father's current interests and publishing ventures, retreating to the United States when funds were low. Henry studied primarily with tutors and briefly attended schools while the family traveled in Europe. Their longest stays were in France, where Henry began to feel at home and became fluent in French. He was afflicted with a stutter, which seems to have manifested itself only when he spoke English; in French, he did not stutter.

In 1860 the family returned to Newport. There Henry became a friend of the painter John La Farge, who introduced him to French literature, and in particular, to Balzac. James later called Balzac his "greatest master," and said that he had learned more about the craft of fiction from him than from anyone else.

In the autumn of 1861 Henry received an injury, probably to his back, while fighting a fire. This injury, which resurfaced at times throughout his life, made him unfit for military service in the American Civil War.

In 1864 the James family moved to Boston, Massachusetts to be near William, who had enrolled first in the Lawrence Scientific School at Harvard and then in the medical school. In 1862 Henry attended Harvard Law School, but realised that he was not interested in studying law. He pursued his interest in literature and associated with authors and critics William Dean Howells and Charles Eliot Norton in Boston and Cambridge, formed lifelong friendships with Oliver Wendell Holmes Jr., the future Supreme Court Justice, and with James and Annie Fields, his first professional mentors.

His first published work was a review of a stage performance, "Miss Maggie Mitchell in Fanchon the Cricket," published in 1863. About a year later, A Tragedy of Error, his first short story, was published anonymously. James's first payment was for an appreciation of Sir Walter Scott's novels, written for the North American Review. He wrote fiction and non-fiction pieces for The Nation and Atlantic Monthly, where Fields was editor. In 1871 he published his first novel, Watch and Ward, in serial form in the Atlantic Monthly. The novel was later published in book form in 1878.

During a 14-month trip through Europe in 1869–70 he met Ruskin, Dickens, Matthew Arnold, William Morris, and George Eliot. Rome impressed him profoundly. "Here I am then in the Eternal City," he wrote to his brother William. "At last—for the first time—I live!" He attempted to support himself as a freelance writer in Rome, then secured a position as Paris correspondent for the New York Tribune, through the influence of its editor John Hay. When these efforts failed he returned to New York City. During 1874 and 1875 he published Transatlantic Sketches, A Passionate Pilgrim, and Roderick Hudson. During this early period in his career he was influenced by Nathaniel Hawthorne.

In 1869 he settled in London. There he established relationships with Macmillan and other publishers, who paid for serial installments that they would later publish in book form. The audience for these serialized novels was largely made up of middle-class women, and James struggled to fashion serious literary work within the strictures imposed by editors' and publishers' notions of what was suitable for young women to read. He lived in rented rooms but was able to join gentlemen's clubs that had libraries and where he could entertain male friends. He was introduced to English society by Henry Adams and Charles Milnes Gaskell, the latter introducing him to the Travellers' and the Reform Clubs.

In the fall of 1875 he moved to the Latin Quarter of Paris. Aside from two trips to America, he spent the next three decades—the rest of his life—in Europe. In Paris he met Zola, Alphonse Daudet, Maupassant, Turgenev, and others. He stayed in Paris only a year before moving to London.

In England he met the leading figures of politics and culture. He continued to be a prolific writer, producing The American (1877), The Europeans (1878), a revision of Watch and Ward (1878), French Poets and Novelists (1878), Hawthorne (1879), and several shorter works of fiction. In 1878 Daisy Miller established his fame on both sides of the Atlantic. It drew notice perhaps mostly because it depicted a woman whose behavior is outside the social norms of Europe. He also began his first masterpiece, The Portrait of a Lady, which would appear in 1881.

In 1877 he first visited Wenlock Abbey in Shropshire, home of his friend Charles Milnes Gaskell whom he had met through Henry Adams. He was much inspired by the darkly romantic Abbey and the surrounding countryside, which features in his essay Abbeys and Castles. In particular the gloomy monastic fishponds behind the Abbey are said to have inspired the lake in The Turn of the Screw.

While living in London, James continued to follow the careers of the "French realists", Émile Zola in particular. Their stylistic methods influenced his own work in the years to come. Hawthorne's influence on him faded during this period, replaced by George Eliot and Ivan Turgenev. 1879–1882 saw the publication of The Europeans, Washington Square, Confidence, and The Portrait of a Lady. He visited America in 1882–1883, then returned to London.

The period from 1881 to 1883 was marked by several losses. His mother died in 1881, followed by his father a few months later, and then by his brother Wilkie. Emerson, an old family friend, died in 1882. His friend Turgenev died in 1883.

Middle years, 1884–1897

In 1884 James made another visit to Paris. There he met again with Zola, Daudet, and Goncourt. He had been following the careers of the French "realist" or "naturalist" writers, and was increasingly influenced by them. In 1886, he published The Bostonians and The Princess Casamassima, both influenced by the French writers he'd studied assiduously. Critical reaction and sales were poor. He wrote to Howells that the books had hurt his career rather than helped because they had "reduced the desire, and demand, for my productions to zero". During this time he became friends with Robert Louis Stevenson, John Singer Sargent, Edmund Gosse, George du Maurier, Paul Bourget, and Constance Fenimore Woolson. His third novel from the 1880s was The Tragic Muse. Although he was following the precepts of Zola in his novels of the '80s, their tone and attitude are closer to the fiction of Alphonse Daudet. The lack of critical and financial success for his novels during this period led him to try writing for the theatre. (His dramatic works and his experiences with theatre are discussed below.)

In the last quarter of 1889, he started translating "for pure and copious lucre" Port Tarascon, the third volume of Alphonse Daudet adventures of Tartarin de Tarascon. Serialized in Harper's Monthly Magazine from June 1890, this translation praised as "clever" by The Spectator was published in January 1891 by Sampson Low, Marston, Searle & Rivington.

After the stage failure of Guy Domville in 1895, James was near despair and thoughts of death plagued him. The years spent on dramatic works were not entirely a loss. As he moved into the last phase of his career he found ways to adapt dramatic techniques into the novel form.

In the late 1880s and throughout the 1890s James made several trips through Europe. He spent a long stay in Italy in 1887. In that year the short novel The Aspern Papers and The Reverberator were published.

Late years, 1898–1916

In 1897–1898 he moved to Rye, Sussex, and wrote The Turn of the Screw. 1899–1900 saw the publication of The Awkward Age and The Sacred

Fount. During 1902–1904 he wrote The Ambassadors, The Wings of the Dove, and The Golden Bowl.

In 1904 he revisited America and lectured on Balzac. In 1906–1910 he published The American Scene and edited the "New York Edition", a 24-volume collection of his works. In 1910 his brother William died; Henry had just joined William from an unsuccessful search for relief in Europe on what then turned out to be his (Henry's) last visit to the United States (from summer 1910 to July 1911), and was near him, according to a letter he wrote, when he died.

In 1913 he wrote his autobiographies, A Small Boy and Others, and Notes of a Son and Brother. After the outbreak of the First World War in 1914 he did war work. In 1915 he became a British subject and was awarded the Order of Merit the following year. He died on 28 February 1916, in Chelsea, London. As he requested, his ashes were buried in Cambridge Cemetery in Massachusetts.

Biographers

James regularly rejected suggestions that he should marry, and after settling in London proclaimed himself "a bachelor". F. W. Dupee, in several volumes on the James family, originated the theory that he had been in love with his cousin Mary ("Minnie") Temple, but that a neurotic fear of sex kept him from admitting such affections: "James's invalidism ... was itself the symptom of some fear of or scruple against sexual love on his part." Dupee used an episode from James's memoir A Small Boy and Others, recounting a dream of a Napoleonic image in the Louvre, to exemplify James's romanticism about Europe, a Napoleonic fantasy into which he fled.

Dupee had not had access to the James family papers and worked principally from James's published memoir of his older brother, William, and the limited collection of letters edited by Percy Lubbock, heavily weighted toward James's last years. His account therefore moved directly from James's childhood, when he trailed after his older brother, to elderly invalidism. As more material became available to scholars, including the diaries of contemporaries and hundreds of affectionate and sometimes erotic letters written by James to younger men, the picture of neurotic celibacy gave way to a portrait of a closeted homosexual.

Between 1953 and 1972, Leon Edel authored a major five-volume biography of James, which accessed unpublished letters and documents after Edel gained the permission of James's family. Edel's portrayal of James included the suggestion he was celibate. It was a view first propounded by critic Saul Rosenzweig in 1943. In 1996 Sheldon M. Novick published Henry James: The Young Master, followed by Henry James: The Mature Master (2007). The first book "caused something of an uproar in Jamesian circles" as it challenged the previous received notion of celibacy, a once-familiar paradigm in biographies of homosexuals when direct evidence was non-existent. Novick also criticised Edel for following the discounted Freudian interpretation of homosexuality "as a kind of failure." The difference of opinion erupted in a series of exchanges between Edel and Novick which were published by the online magazine Slate, with the latter arguing that even the suggestion of celibacy went against James's own injunction "live!"—not "fantasize!"

A letter James wrote in old age to Hugh Walpole has been cited as an explicit statement of this. Walpole confessed to him of indulging in "high jinks", and James wrote a reply endorsing it: "We must know, as much as possible, in our beautiful art, yours & mine, what we are talking about — & the only way to know it is to have lived & loved & cursed & floundered & enjoyed & suffered — I don't think I regret a single 'excess' of my responsive youth".

The interpretation of James as living a less austere emotional life has been subsequently explored by other scholars. The often intense politics of Jamesian scholarship has also been the subject of studies. Author Colm Tóibín has said that Eve Kosofsky Sedgwick's Epistemology of the Closet made a landmark difference to Jamesian scholarship by arguing that he be read as a homosexual writer whose desire to keep his sexuality a secret shaped his layered style and dramatic artistry. According to Tóibín such a reading "removed James from the realm of dead white males who wrote about posh people. He became our contemporary."

James's letters to expatriate American sculptor Hendrik Christian Andersen have attracted particular attention. James met the 27-year-old Andersen in Rome in 1899, when James was 56, and wrote letters to Andersen that are intensely emotional: "I hold you, dearest boy, in my innermost love, & count on your feeling me—in every throb of your soul". In a letter of 6 May 1904, to his brother William, James referred to himself as "always your hopelessly celibate even though sexagenarian Henry". How accurate that description might have been is the subject of contention among James's biographers,   but the letters to Andersen were occasionally quasi-erotic: "I put, my dear boy, my arm around you, & feel the pulsation, thereby, as it were, of our excellent future & your admirable endowment." To his homosexual friend Howard Sturgis, James could write: "I repeat, almost to indiscretion, that I could live with you. Meanwhile I can only try to live without you."

His numerous letters to the many young gay men among his close male friends are more forthcoming. In a letter to Howard Sturgis, following a long visit, James refers jocularly to their "happy little congress of two" and in letters to Hugh Walpole he pursues convoluted jokes and puns about their relationship, referring to himself as an elephant who "paws you oh so benevolently" and winds about Walpole his "well meaning old trunk". His letters to Walter Berry printed by the Black Sun Press have long been celebrated for their lightly veiled eroticism.

He corresponded in almost equally extravagant language with his many female friends, writing, for example, to fellow novelist Lucy Clifford: "Dearest Lucy! What shall I say? when I love you so very, very much, and see you nine times for once that I see Others! Therefore I think that—if you want it made clear to the meanest intelligence—I love you more than I love Others." To his New York friend Mary Cadwalader Jones: "Dearest Mary Cadwalader. I yearn over you, but I yearn in vain; & your long silence really breaks my heart, mystifies, depresses, almost alarms me, to the point even of making me wonder if poor unconscious & doting old Célimare [Jones's pet name for James] has 'done' anything, in some dark somnambulism of the spirit, which has ... given you a bad moment, or a wrong impression, or a 'colourable pretext' ... However these things may be, he loves you as tenderly as ever;

nothing, to the end of time, will ever detach him from you, & he remembers those Eleventh St. matutinal intimes hours, those telephonic matinées, as the most romantic of his life ..." His long friendship with American novelist Constance Fenimore Woolson, in whose house he lived for a number of weeks in Italy in 1887, and his shock and grief over her suicide in 1894, are discussed in detail in Edel's biography and play a central role in a study by Lyndall Gordon. (Edel conjectured that Woolson was in love with James and killed herself in part because of his coldness, but Woolson's biographers have objected to Edel's account.)

Works

Style and themes

James is one of the major figures of trans-Atlantic literature. His works frequently juxtapose characters from the Old World (Europe), embodying a feudal civilisation that is beautiful, often corrupt, and alluring, and from the New World (United States), where people are often brash, open, and assertive and embody the virtues—freedom and a more highly evolved moral character—of the new American society. James explores this clash of personalities and cultures, in stories of personal relationships in which power is exercised well or badly. His protagonists were often young American women facing oppression or abuse, and as his secretary Theodora Bosanquet remarked in her monograph Henry James at Work:

> When he walked out of the refuge of his study and into the world and looked around him, he saw a place of torment, where creatures of prey perpetually thrust their claws into the quivering flesh of doomed, defenseless children of light ... His novels are a repeated exposure of this wickedness, a reiterated and passionate plea for the fullest freedom of development, unimperiled by reckless and barbarous stupidity.

Critics have jokingly described three phases in the development of James's prose: "James I, James II, and The Old Pretender." He wrote short stories and plays. Finally, in his third and last period he returned to the long, serialised novel. Beginning in the second period, but most noticeably in the third, he increasingly abandoned direct statement in favour of frequent double negatives, and complex descriptive imagery. Single paragraphs began to run for page after page, in which an initial noun would be succeeded by pronouns surrounded by clouds of adjectives and prepositional clauses, far from their original referents, and verbs would be deferred and then preceded by a series of adverbs. The overall effect could be a vivid evocation of a scene as perceived by a sensitive observer. It has been debated whether this change of style was engendered by James's shifting from writing to dictating to a typist, a change made during the composition of What Maisie Knew.

In its intense focus on the consciousness of his major characters, James's later work foreshadows extensive developments in 20th century fiction. Indeed, he might have influenced stream-of-consciousness writers such as Virginia Woolf, who not only read some of his novels but also wrote essays about them. Both contemporary and modern readers have found the late style difficult and unnecessary; his friend Edith Wharton, who admired him greatly, said that there were passages in his work that were all but incomprehensible. James was harshly portrayed by H. G. Wells as a hippopotamus laboriously attempting to pick up a pea that had got into a corner of its cage. The "late James" style was ably parodied by Max Beerbohm in "The Mote in the Middle Distance".

More important for his work overall may have been his position as an expatriate, and in other ways an outsider, living in Europe. While he came from middle-class and provincial beginnings (seen from the perspective of European polite society) he worked very hard to gain access to all levels of society, and the settings of his fiction range from working class to aristocratic, and often describe the efforts of middle-class Americans to make their way in European capitals. He confessed he got some of his best story ideas from gossip at the dinner table or at country house weekends. He worked for a living, however, and lacked the experiences of select schools, university, and army service, the common bonds of masculine society. He was furthermore a man whose tastes and interests were, according to the prevailing standards of Victorian era Anglo-American culture, rather feminine, and who was shadowed by the cloud of prejudice that then and later accompanied suspicions of his homosexuality. Edmund Wilson famously compared James's objectivity to Shakespeare's:

One would be in a position to appreciate James better if one compared him with the dramatists of the seventeenth century—Racine and Molière, whom he resembles in form as well as in point of view, and even Shakespeare, when allowances are made for the most extreme differences in subject and form. These poets are not, like Dickens and Hardy, writers of melodrama—either humorous or pessimistic, nor secretaries of society like Balzac, nor prophets like Tolstoy: they are occupied simply with the presentation of conflicts of moral character, which they do not concern themselves about softening or averting. They do not indict society for these situations: they regard them as universal and inevitable. They do not even blame God for allowing them: they accept them as the conditions of life.

It is also possible to see many of James's stories as psychological thought-experiments. In his preface to the New York edition of The American he describes the development of the story in his mind as exactly such: the "situation" of an American, "some robust but insidiously beguiled and betrayed, some cruelly wronged, compatriot..." with the focus of the story being on the response of this wronged man. The Portrait of a Lady may be an experiment to see what happens when an idealistic young woman suddenly becomes very rich. In many of his tales, characters seem to exemplify alternative futures and possibilities, as most markedly in "The Jolly Corner", in which the protagonist and a ghost-doppelganger live alternative American and European lives; and in others, like The Ambassadors, an older James seems fondly to regard his own younger self facing a crucial moment.

Major novels

The first period of James's fiction, usually considered to have culminated in The Portrait of a Lady, concentrated on the contrast between Europe and America. The style of these novels is generally straightforward and, though personally characteristic, well within the norms of 19th-century fiction. Roderick Hudson (1875) is a Künstlerroman that traces the development of the title character, an extremely talented sculptor. Although the book shows some signs of immaturity—this was James's first serious attempt at a full-length novel—it has attracted favourable comment due to the vivid realisation of the three major characters: Roderick Hudson, superbly gifted but unstable and unreliable; Rowland Mallet, Roderick's limited but much more mature friend and patron; and Christina Light, one of James's most enchanting and maddening femmes fatales. The pair of Hudson and Mallet has been seen as representing the two sides of James's own nature: the wildly imaginative artist and the brooding conscientious mentor.

In The Portrait of a Lady (1881) James concluded the first phase of his career with a novel that remains his most popular piece of long fiction. The story is of a spirited young American woman, Isabel Archer, who "affronts her destiny" and finds it overwhelming. She inherits a large amount of money and subsequently becomes the victim of Machiavellian scheming by two American expatriates. The narrative is set mainly in Europe, especially in England and Italy. Generally regarded as the masterpiece of his early phase, The Portrait of a Lady is described as a psychological novel, exploring the minds of his characters, and almost a work of social science, exploring the differences between Europeans and Americans, the old and the new worlds.

The second period of James's career, which extends from the publication of The Portrait of a Lady through the end of the nineteenth century, features less popular novels including The Princess Casamassima, published serially in The Atlantic Monthly in 1885–1886, and The Bostonians, published serially in The Century Magazine during the same period. This period also featured James's celebrated Gothic novella, The Turn of the Screw.

The third period of James's career reached its most significant achievement in three novels published just around the start of the 20th century: The Wings of the Dove (1902), The Ambassadors (1903), and The Golden Bowl (1904). Critic F. O. Matthiessen called this "trilogy" James's major phase, and these novels have certainly received intense critical study. It was the second-written of the books, The Wings of the Dove (1902) that was the first published because it attracted no serialization. This novel tells the story of Milly Theale, an American heiress stricken with a serious disease, and her impact on the people around her. Some of these people befriend Milly with honourable motives, while others are more self-interested. James stated in his autobiographical books that Milly was based on Minny Temple, his beloved cousin who died at an early age of tuberculosis. He said that he attempted in the novel to wrap her memory in the "beauty and dignity of art".

Shorter narratives

James was particularly interested in what he called the "beautiful and blest nouvelle", or the longer form of short narrative. Still, he produced a number of very short stories in which he achieved notable compression of sometimes complex subjects. The following narratives are representative of James's achievement in the shorter forms of fiction.

- "A Tragedy of Error" (1864), short story
- "The Story of a Year" (1865), short story
- A Passionate Pilgrim (1871), novella
- Madame de Mauves (1874), novella
- Daisy Miller (1878), novella
- The Aspern Papers (1888), novella
- The Lesson of the Master (1888), novella
- The Pupil (1891), short story
- "The Figure in the Carpet" (1896), short story
- The Beast in the Jungle (1903), novella
- An International Episode (1878)
- Picture and Text
- Four Meetings (1885)
- A London Life, and Other Tales (1889)
- The Spoils of Poynton (1896)

- Embarrassments (1896)

- The Two Magics: The Turn of the Screw, Covering End (1898)

- A Little Tour of France (1900)

- The Sacred Fount (1901)

- Views and Reviews (1908)

- The Wings of the Dove, Volume I (1902)

- The Wings of the Dove, Volume II (1909)

- The Finer Grain (1910)

- The Outcry (1911)

- Lady Barbarina: The Siege of London, An International Episode and Other Tales (1922)

- The Birthplace (1922)

Plays

At several points in his career James wrote plays, beginning with one-act plays written for periodicals in 1869 and 1871 and a dramatisation of his popular novella Daisy Miller in 1882. From 1890 to 1892, having received a bequest that freed him from magazine publication, he made a strenuous effort to succeed on the London stage, writing a half-dozen plays of which only one, a dramatisation of his novel The American, was produced. This play was performed for several years by a touring repertory company and had a respectable run in London, but did not earn very much money for James. His other plays written at this time were not produced.

In 1893, however, he responded to a request from actor-manager George Alexander for a serious play for the opening of his renovated St. James's Theatre, and wrote a long drama, Guy Domville, which Alexander produced. There was a noisy uproar on the opening night, 5 January 1895, with hissing from the gallery when James took his bow after the final curtain, and the author was upset. The play received moderately good reviews and had a modest run of four weeks before being taken off to make way for Oscar Wilde's The Importance of Being Earnest, which Alexander thought would have better prospects for the coming season.

After the stresses and disappointment of these efforts James insisted that he would write no more for the theatre, but within weeks had agreed to write a curtain-raiser for Ellen Terry. This became the one-act "Summersoft", which he later rewrote into a short story, "Covering End", and then expanded into a full-length play, The High Bid, which had a brief run in London in 1907, when James made another concerted effort to write for the stage. He wrote three new plays, two of which were in production when the death of Edward VII on 6 May 1910 plunged London into mourning and theatres closed. Discouraged by failing health and the stresses of theatrical work, James did not renew his efforts in the theatre, but recycled his plays as successful novels. The Outcry was a best-seller in the United States when it was published in 1911. During the years 1890–1893 when he was most engaged with the theatre, James wrote a good deal of theatrical criticism and assisted Elizabeth Robins and others in translating and producing Henrik Ibsen for the first time in London.

Leon Edel argued in his psychoanalytic biography that James was traumatised by the opening night uproar that greeted Guy Domville, and that it plunged him into a prolonged depression. The successful later novels, in Edel's view, were the result of a kind of self-analysis, expressed in fiction, which partly freed him from his fears. Other biographers and scholars have not accepted this account, however; the more common view being that of F.O. Matthiessen, who wrote: "Instead of being crushed by the collapse of his hopes [for the theatre]... he felt a resurgence of new energy."

Non-fiction

Beyond his fiction, James was one of the more important literary critics in the history of the novel. In his classic essay The Art of Fiction (1884), he argued against rigid prescriptions on the novelist's choice of subject and method of treatment. He maintained that the widest possible freedom in content and approach would help ensure narrative fiction's continued vitality.

James wrote many valuable critical articles on other novelists; typical is his book-length study of Nathaniel Hawthorne, which has been the subject of critical debate. Richard Brodhead has suggested that the study was emblematic of James's struggle with Hawthorne's influence, and constituted an effort to place the elder writer "at a disadvantage." Gordon Fraser, meanwhile, has suggested that the study was part of a more commercial effort by James to introduce himself to British readers as Hawthorne's natural successor.

When James assembled the New York Edition of his fiction in his final years, he wrote a series of prefaces that subjected his own work to searching, occasionally harsh criticism.

At 22 James wrote The Noble School of Fiction for The Nation's first issue in 1865. He would write, in all, over 200 essays and book, art, and theatre reviews for the magazine.

For most of his life James harboured ambitions for success as a playwright. He converted his novel The American into a play that enjoyed modest returns in the early 1890s. In all he wrote about a dozen plays, most of which went unproduced. His costume drama Guy Domville failed disastrously on its opening night in 1895. James then largely abandoned his efforts to conquer the stage and returned to his fiction. In his Notebooks he maintained that his theatrical experiment benefited his novels and tales by helping him dramatise his characters' thoughts and emotions. James produced a small but valuable amount of theatrical criticism, including perceptive appreciations of Henrik Ibsen.

With his wide-ranging artistic interests, James occasionally wrote on the visual arts. Perhaps his most valuable contribution was his favourable assessment of fellow expatriate John Singer Sargent, a painter whose critical status has improved markedly in recent decades. James also wrote sometimes charming, sometimes brooding articles about various places he visited and lived in. His most famous books of travel writing include Italian Hours (an example of the charming approach) and The American Scene (most definitely on the brooding side).

James was one of the great letter-writers of any era. More than ten thousand of his personal letters are extant, and over three thousand have been published in a large number of collections. A complete edition of James's letters began publication in 2006, edited by Pierre Walker and Greg Zacharias. As of 2014, eight volumes have been published, covering the period from 1855 to 1880. James's correspondents included celebrated contemporaries like Robert Louis Stevenson, Edith Wharton and Joseph Conrad, along with many others in his wide circle of friends and acquaintances. The letters range from the "mere twaddle of graciousness" to serious discussions of artistic, social and personal issues.

Very late in life James began a series of autobiographical works: A Small Boy and Others, Notes of a Son and Brother, and the unfinished The Middle Years. These books portray the development of a classic observer who was passionately interested in artistic creation but was somewhat reticent about participating fully in the life around him.

Reception

Criticism, biographies and fictional treatments

James's work has remained steadily popular with the limited audience of educated readers to whom he spoke during his lifetime, and has remained firmly in the canon, but, after his death, some American critics, such as Van Wyck Brooks, expressed hostility towards James for his long expatriation and eventual naturalisation as a British subject. Other critics such as E. M. Forster complained about what they saw as James's squeamishness in the treatment of sex and other possibly controversial material, or dismissed his late style as difficult and obscure, relying heavily on extremely long sentences and excessively latinate language. Similarly Oscar Wilde criticised him for writing "fiction as if it were a painful duty". Vernon Parrington, composing a canon of American literature, condemned James for having cut himself off from America. Jorge Luis Borges wrote about him, "Despite the scruples and delicate complexities of James, his work suffers from a major defect: the absence of life." And Virginia Woolf, writing to Lytton Strachey, asked, "Please tell me what you find in Henry James. ... we have his works here, and

I read, and I can't find anything but faintly tinged rose water, urbane and sleek, but vulgar and pale as Walter Lamb. Is there really any sense in it?" The novelist W. Somerset Maugham wrote, "He did not know the English as an Englishman instinctively knows them and so his English characters never to my mind quite ring true," and argued "The great novelists, even in seclusion, have lived life passionately. Henry James was content to observe it from a window." Maugham nevertheless wrote, "The fact remains that those last novels of his, notwithstanding their unreality, make all other novels, except the very best, unreadable." Colm Tóibín observed that James "never really wrote about the English very well. His English characters don't work for me."

Despite these criticisms, James is now valued for his psychological and moral realism, his masterful creation of character, his low-key but playful humour, and his assured command of the language. In his 1983 book, The Novels of Henry James, Edward Wagenknecht offers an assessment that echoes Theodora Bosanquet's:

> "To be completely great," Henry James wrote in an early review, "a work of art must lift up the heart," and his own novels do this to an outstanding degree ... More than sixty years after his death, the great novelist who sometimes professed to have no opinions stands foursquare in the great Christian humanistic and democratic tradition. The men and women who, at the height of World War II, raided the secondhand shops for his out-of-print books knew what they were about. For no writer ever raised a braver banner to which all who love freedom might adhere.

William Dean Howells saw James as a representative of a new realist school of literary art which broke with the English romantic tradition epitomised by the works of Charles Dickens and William Makepeace Thackeray. Howells wrote that realism found "its chief exemplar in Mr. James... A novelist he is not, after the old fashion, or after any fashion but his own." F.R. Leavis championed Henry James as a novelist of "established pre-eminence" in The Great Tradition (1948), asserting that The Portrait of a Lady and The Bostonians were "the two most brilliant novels in the language." James is now prized as a master of point of view who moved literary fiction forward by insisting in showing, not telling, his stories to the reader. (Source: Wikipedia)

NOTABLE WORKS

NOVELS

Watch and Ward (1871)

Roderick Hudson (1875)

The American (1877)

The Europeans (1878)

Confidence (1879)

Washington Square (1880)

The Portrait of a Lady (1881)

The Bostonians (1886)

The Princess Casamassima (1886)

The Reverberator (1888)

The Tragic Muse (1890)

The Other House (1896)

The Spoils of Poynton (1897)

What Maisie Knew (1897)

The Awkward Age (1899)

The Sacred Fount (1901)

The Wings of the Dove (1902)

The Ambassadors (1903)

The Golden Bowl (1904)

The Whole Family (collaborative novel with eleven other authors, 1908)

The Outcry (1911)

The Ivory Tower (unfinished, published posthumously 1917)

The Sense of the Past (unfinished, published posthumously 1917)

SHORT STORIES AND NOVELLAS

A Tragedy of Error (1864)

The Story of a Year (1865)

A Landscape Painter (1866)

A Day of Days (1866)

My Friend Bingham (1867)

Poor Richard (1867)

The Story of a Masterpiece (1868)

A Most Extraordinary Case (1868)

A Problem (1868)

De Grey: A Romance (1868)

Osborne's Revenge (1868)

The Romance of Certain Old Clothes (1868)

A Light Man (1869)

Gabrielle de Bergerac (1869)

Travelling Companions (1870)

A Passionate Pilgrim (1871)

At Isella (1871)

Master Eustace (1871)

Guest's Confession (1872)

The Madonna of the Future (1873)

The Sweetheart of M. Briseux (1873)

The Last of the Valerii (1874)

Madame de Mauves (1874)

Adina (1874)

Professor Fargo (1874)

Eugene Pickering (1874)

Benvolio (1875)

Crawford's Consistency (1876)

The Ghostly Rental (1876)

Four Meetings (1877)

Rose-Agathe (1878, as Théodolinde)

Daisy Miller (1878)

Longstaff's Marriage (1878)

An International Episode (1878)

The Pension Beaurepas (1879)

A Diary of a Man of Fifty (1879)

A Bundle of Letters (1879)

The Point of View (1882)

The Siege of London (1883)

Impressions of a Cousin (1883)

Lady Barberina (1884)

Pandora (1884)

The Author of Beltraffio (1884)

Georgina's Reasons (1884)

A New England Winter (1884)

The Path of Duty (1884)

Mrs. Temperly (1887)

Louisa Pallant (1888)

The Aspern Papers (1888)

The Liar (1888)

The Modern Warning (1888, originally published as The Two Countries)

A London Life (1888)

The Patagonia (1888)

The Lesson of the Master (1888)

The Solution (1888)

The Pupil (1891)

Brooksmith (1891)

The Marriages (1891)

The Chaperon (1891)

Sir Edmund Orme (1891)

Nona Vincent (1892)

The Real Thing (1892)

The Private Life (1892)

Lord Beaupré (1892)

The Visits (1892)

Sir Dominick Ferrand (1892)

Greville Fane (1892)

Collaboration (1892)

Owen Wingrave (1892)

The Wheel of Time (1892)

The Middle Years (1893)

The Death of the Lion (1894)

The Coxon Fund (1894)

The Next Time (1895)

Glasses (1896)

The Altar of the Dead (1895)

The Figure in the Carpet (1896)

The Way It Came (1896, also published as The Friends of the Friends)

The Turn of the Screw (1898)

Covering End (1898)

In the Cage (1898)

John Delavoy (1898)

The Given Case (1898)

Europe (1899)

The Great Condition (1899)

The Real Right Thing (1899)

Paste (1899)

The Great Good Place (1900)

Maud-Evelyn (1900)

Miss Gunton of Poughkeepsie (1900)

The Tree of Knowledge (1900)

The Abasement of the Northmores (1900)

The Third Person (1900)

The Special Type (1900)

The Tone of Time (1900)

Broken Wings (1900)

The Two Faces (1900)

Mrs. Medwin (1901)

The Beldonald Holbein (1901)

The Story in It (1902)

Flickerbridge (1902)

The Birthplace (1903)

The Beast in the Jungle (1903)

The Papers (1903)

Fordham Castle (1904)

Julia Bride (1908)

The Jolly Corner (1908)

The Velvet Glove (1909)

Mora Montravers (1909)

Crapy Cornelia (1909)

The Bench of Desolation (1909)

A Round of Visits (1910)

<u>OTHER</u>

Transatlantic Sketches (1875)

French Poets and Novelists (1878)

Hawthorne (1879)

Portraits of Places (1883)

A Little Tour in France (1884)

Partial Portraits (1888)

Essays in London and Elsewhere (1893)

Picture and Text (1893)

Terminations (1893)

Theatricals (1894)

Theatricals: Second Series (1895)

Guy Domville (1895)

The Soft Side (1900)

William Wetmore Story and His Friends (1903)

The Better Sort (1903)

English Hours (1905)

The Question of our Speech; The Lesson of Balzac. Two Lectures (1905)

The American Scene (1907)

Views and Reviews (1908)

Italian Hours (1909)

A Small Boy and Others (1913)

Notes on Novelists (1914)

Notes of a Son and Brother (1914)

Within the Rim (1918)

Travelling Companions (1919)

Notebooks (various, published posthumously)

The Middle Years (unfinished, published posthumously 1917)

A Most Unholy Trade (1925, published posthumously)

The Art of the Novel : Critical Prefaces (1934)

CPSIA information can be obtained
at www.ICGtesting.com
Printed in the USA
LVHW092117021120
670493LV00003B/145